A WINTER'S DAY: A RESTORATION TRAGEDY

Volume 1, Acts I–II

Bunny Paine-Clemes

Book Guild Publishing

Sussex, England

First published in Great Britain in 2012 by
The Book Guild Ltd
Pavilion View
19 New Road
Brighton, BN1 1UF

Typesetting in Baskerville by
YHT Ltd, London

Printed and bound in Great Britain by
CPI Group (UK) Ltd, Croydon, CR0 4YY

A catalogue record for this book is available from
The British Library.

ISBN 978 1 84624 720 0

A Restoration tragedy (written during the English Restoration era, 1660–1689, which corresponds to the last years of the direct Stuart reign in Great Britain) was a heroic play featuring conflicts between love and honour, passion and reason, and usually ending with unhappiness or death for two lovers. In a tragicomedy, however, there are two pairs of lovers who contrast with one another: a witty 'gay couple', such as Shakespeare's Beatrice and Benedick in *Much Ado About Nothing*, and a more serious couple cast as their foils.

Acknowledgements and Dedications

For my greatest supporters, my husband and father; my dear friends at Book Guild; and the old friends I knew back in Texas: I could not have published this book without you.

Portrait of the Earl of Rochester
Reproduced by courtesy of Sir Harry Malet

Nay then let's rave and eulogise together,
When Rosidor is now but common clay,
Whom every wiser Emmet bears away
And lays him up against a winter's day.
    —Nathaniel Lee, *The Princess of Cleves* (on the death of
        John Wilmot, Earl of Rochester)

An age in her embraces passed
Would seem a winter's day,
Where life and light with envious haste
Are torn and snatched away.
But oh, how slowly minutes roll
When absent from her eyes,
That feed my love, which is my soul:
It languishes and dies.
For then no more a soul, but shade,
It mournfully does move
And haunts my breast, by absence made
The living tomb of love.
You wiser men, despise me not
Whose lovesick fancy raves
On shades of souls, and heaven knows what:
Short ages live in graves.
Whene'er those wounding eyes, so full
Of sweetness you did see,
Had you not been profoundly dull,
You had gone mad like me.
Nor censure us, you who perceive
My best beloved and me
Sigh and lament, complain and grieve:
You think we disagree.
Alas! 'tis sacred jealousy,
Love raised to an extreme:
The only proof 'twixt her and me
We love and do not dream.
Fantastic fancies fondly move
And in frail joys believe,
Taking false pleasure for true love;
But pain can ne'er deceive.
Kind jealous doubts, tormenting fears,
And anxious cares, when past,
Prove our hearts' treasure fixed and dear,
And make us blest at last.

—John Wilmot, Earl of Rochester (1647–1680)

Portrait of Elizabeth Mallet
Reproduced by courtesy of Sir Harry Malet

Prologue: 'Eclipsing More Placid Affections'

A love story, eclipsing more placid affections, may have lain hidden between these two young, witty and unhappy people.
—Graham Greene, *Lord Rochester's Monkey*

He was the greatest wit, poet, and lover at the court of Charles II in England. She was the woman who loved him more than life itself. In his thirty-third year he was dead from alcoholism, syphilis, and despair. She died a year after from grief.

They left four children, whom they had adored and carefully nurtured. The son and heir, Charles, survived only a few months in his grandmother's hands.

Their love story is unknown to the general public, and it has never been told thoroughly, though biographers of the famous earl have followed its thread through his life. Usually the treatment of the earl's character in novels is superficial: he is part of the general background of any narrative about the Restoration, and he is usually portrayed as wasting his wife's money (which, counter to the custom of the times, he actually reserved for her own use), or as whoring and drinking about London. In no novel that I have read are his wit and charm captured, and in none is his devotion to his wife and family mentioned. The most outlandish deviations, however, appear in the movie *The Libertine*, the most arrant fiction I have ever observed, with no more truth than a bawd's promises. It aims to show one side of him but doesn't even get that right; most of the incidents are made up, and his wife serenely watches him die at Adderbury when, in truth, she was falling apart with him at Woodstock, in the presence of some of the children (nonexistent in the movie).

It is true that he was an alcoholic, driven by personal demons. Conflicted by the inherited tendencies of his judgmental Puritan mother and his hard-drinking Cavalier father, he was compulsively promiscuous but gnawed at by his guilty conscience and his hatred of the vices he felt compelled to indulge. Life at court both attracted him with its merry fellowship and repelled him with its tawdry vices.

xi

Obliged by necessity to earn money through court posts, he was trapped in London, in a life he both enjoyed and despised, and which he enlivened by various tricks of wit and buffoonery and nights of hard drinking and whoring. He balanced this with visits to the country, where his wife and family resided, and he always returned, penitent, to the bosom of his adoring wife, 'where love and peace and truth doth flow'. Lord Rochester was wracked by inner conflict and illness, attracted to the life he hated and driven by boredom from the country to London, where 'a devil entered into him.' As Jeremy Lamb says, the earl suffered from the same conflict as Catullus: *Odi et amo,* 'I hate and I love'.

Lady Rochester's story, in particular, has never been told. The various biographers guess at her motives, especially during the courtship; they contradict one another and, in my estimation, often go wildly off the mark by using logic instead of intuition to figure out, from their point of view, what she must have been thinking and feeling. I have worked by another method, inviting her mind into mine, and supplementing the results with copious research.

Central to my interpretation is that she immediately fell madly in love with Rochester and plotted to get him for almost two years thereafter; her motives never wavered, but the tricks she sometimes used have been misinterpreted by those who view her behaviour from a distance.

This volume, comprising Acts I and II of the tragedy, deals with that courtship and concludes with the marriage. A second volume, Acts III–V, will deal with the marriage and the couple's deaths.

Part I

'Kind Jealous Doubts, Tormenting Fears'

Betty Mallet

April-May 1665

Kind jealous doubts, tormenting fears,
And anxious cares, when past,
Prove our hearts' treasure fixed and dear,
And make us blest at last.
—John Wilmot, Earl of Rochester (1647–1680), 'An Age in Her
Embraces Passed would seem a Winter's Day'

1

'Something Extremely Engaging'
8 April, 1665

His person was graceful, tho' tall and slender, his mien and shape having something extremely engaging; and for his mind, it discover'd charms not to be withstood. His wit was strong, subtle, sublime, and sprightly; he was perfectly well-bred, and adorned with a natural modesty which extremely became him. He was master both of the ancient and modern authors, as well as all those of the modern French and Italian, to say nothing of the English, which were worthy the perusal of a man of fine sense. From all which he drew a conversation so engaging, that none could enjoy without admiration and delight, and few without love.

—St Evremond, Description of my Lord of Rochester at Seventeen after his presentation at Court, Christmas Day, 1664

In London at last! But for all the good it does me, I might squat i' th' pasture at Enmore and admire the latest cow chip: my occupations are just so base. For I am the sad country heiress: I sit on display, a tart in a shop: 'Come, who'll buy? Here's cherry and sweetness enow.'

Indeed it is unjust. For thirteen years I paid my tithes and indulgences: followed, a most fretful duckling, whither my witless mama led. I marched up the stairs to bed and down again to sit – followed the shadows that crept along the ceiling, one by one. And now, to be in Paradise at last, but to have no heavenly mansion, only the four dull walls of these lodgings! And then to endure a grumpy grandpa as Jehovah – and my mother such a close keeper, I may be in London the whole season and never see the Mall! The harps I hear in theatres, but the melodious clinks of moneybags, a tune warbled to delight Jehovah's ear; and the warblers, so many dull men-at-law, offering Such a Sum that I will to lay myself out to the son of Sir Whoozits Lucre.

But I've decided to lay myself out in love.

Anon an invitation comes, to a treat in the Holbein Gate, at the apartments of my Lady Castlemaine. My heart whispers, *Go!*

'Oh, Lord,' says my mother, holding the invitation 'twixt dainty

3

fingers as if 'twere meat with maggots and a smell. 'The apartments of the King's whore? At Whitehall Palace? Why, that's the very bowels of sin and infamy!'

A promising forecast.

'How now, Unton,' says Grandpa. 'Take her thither: I'll dispatch a note to Lady Sandwich, to further our business.'

My business, too, Grandpa.

As Mama and I alight from the coach, on the cobbles before the Great Banqueting House, I tingle from neck to spine.

Here sedan chairs deposit ladies who fling off 'safe-guards' of grey or black homespun, dust-covered, to reveal skirts of rich brocade or silk; or hold up skirts to dig in the embroidered pockets dangling beneath for fare, or pull off soft leather boots to disclose tiny shoes of pale satin or brocade. Here too sleek horses are tied up at posts; and coaches are drawn together in convivial knots, the drivers liveried, periwigged, lounging insolently and trading witticisms, the footmen calling to one another or eating oranges from the hollowed tops of their batons.

Mama clasps my hand to propel me toward the Holbein Gate, straddling King Street. Through the arch of its first storey the public road passes; its second is a long gallery; and the upper two, the public and private rooms of the Lady Castlemaine.

As Mama shows our invitation to the scarlet-coated Yeomen of the Guard, I stare up at the red-and-flint storeys topped by a crennellated parapet and flanked on either side by an octagonal turret. Suddenly I know, *He's there.*

His name and person I know not, but reaching out my thoughts for the essence of my True Love, I'd felt him at court, Christmas Eve last, when I wished for love upon the comet that curled its dull silver tail in the midnight sky above Great House, Enmore.

I tell Mama, often, 'I know things without knowing how': to which she always responds, 'Hmmph!'

Mama circles some chairs near the wall to construct a fortification again the corrupted company, lest someone interesting appear, and the dull early part of the afternoon crawls wormlike past, slow stump to belly.

On my right lounges an elegant rooster plumed, Sir Francis Popham, who believes it gallant to have discovered a *belle passion* for me and omits no occasion of commending my gloves, remarking my hair how 'tis dressed so fine, and making shift to leer down into my bosom. On my right sits Mama, like some engraving of Judgment, her gaunt body stiff as a pitchfork.

But the feather in the cap of dullness is the Lord Hinchingbrooke, son of the Lady Sandwich. The whole wretched afternoon, she has been full of wondering where this prodigy was and promising him to us: 'Dear me, I should have thought that by now – ' 'Why, wherever can he be?'

Wherever he can have been, he's here now: he can gratify his mama by making his bow to the West Country heiress.

The doting mama spies her hatchling. 'Oh, here's Hinch!'

A tall, stout body, chest thrust out and back straight like a poker, struts hither on stiff legs like a goose's. His mama flutters a hand at him. 'Hinch, dear!'

He goose-steps grandly to us, hook nose elevated as if above a bad smell, tiny eyes darting about. High-crowned hat on arm, he clicks his heels, bows straight from the waist toward his limp shoestring.

'Madam! I cannot say I've had the honour.'

'Hinch, dear,' cries his mama, whose curls are wired to stand out on two sides like a farthingale, 'come and sit with us. This is Lady Warre with her daughter, Elizabeth Mallet.'

At this intelligence the beams roll around in their sockets, searching – then alight on me and brighten to flames.

He clicks heels, bows stiffly. 'Your servant, madam.'

Then the world changes. No longer see I this goose, fluttering and posturing. My eyes go soft, a white veil descending, causing the outlines of objects to waver. A knowing prickles the back of my neck, and I turn my head.

There he is.

He does not see me yet. He listens to a short, pudgy man with long feathers in his hat and twin tails to a fantastic wig – a leprechaun of a fellow, who makes arcs with his hands as he speaks. Beside him stands a grinning gentleman, round of jowl and protuberant of eye; a skinny, dark man with fast movements like a bird's; and a well-looked lazy lounger in a fair periwig.

I drop my cup and saucer, clattering, to the floor and arise.

Mama hisses, 'Betty!'

Oh, how tall and slender he is: leg breeched in blue satin to the knee, upper breast covered in a tiny jackanapes coat of blue satin stretched only to the ribs, so's the sensual white shirt can billow beneath to the small waist, looped with ribbons in rows.

Then he shifts his weight to one hip and sweeps out an arm to rest his long, tapering fingers on the black enamel of his hanger hilt, the movement so lithe and sensual it makes my gut twang.

'Betty!' hisses Mama.

5

I gather up skirts for an exit.

The goose looks gravely displeased but apparently has not the sense to honk; for it but clicks heels again, knees stiff, then struts to a chair by wire-haired mama, where she pats the seat. As it sits, its chest collapses downward, past the little coat, to belly out into the shirt below.

Mama glares at me and shakes her head.

I whirl about and flounce off.

His face is oval, framed by brown locks to the shoulders. There's a devilish expression in the quirk of one black brow and the down-droop of an eyelid – in the pouting nether lip, the lazy smile with a laugh line on either side. There's a prettiness in his ivory skin and features: his lashes curved upward in a thick black screen, his nose pinched at the top, straight and long, delicate and flaring.

I creep up to his elbow. Above me's his dimpled chin; at my eye level, his cravat, with swirls of dainty white lace.

Jesus, but he's clean! No dirt even on his neck and fingernails. His white hose are spotless but for a line of blue diamonds embroidered up the inside above each ankle. Not a louse or a flea anywhere on him – no stain even on the hanging lace of his cuffs or armpits of his jacket – not a speck, even on his shoes or white gloves tucked in at the waist.

And he smells – not sweat, not tobacco, not sour beef-and-wine – but a faint and enticing odour of rose and sandalwood.

The arm nearest me's swung out to make an angle with the hanger hilt. The white silk sleeve puffs out from his elbow to his wrist, where hangs moonbeam-white lace. He inclines his hat to make a pretty tilt of the ostrich plume on his sky-blue broad-brimmed hat.

I'm glad of the daring scooped neck I fought Mama to wear – glad of the vexing hours spent in my maid's hands: the dressing of my head last night in oil of white herrbone mixed with a little gum Arabic; the sitting all morning still pinned up, then the crimping of the loose rivulets into waves and locks, to be gathered in a knot of blue ribbons. I'm glad of the new sky-coloured silk overskirt, the royal blue bodice with the white stomacher embroidered in azure like my shoes and fan; glad that my sleeves, midway to my elbow, expose the white puffed sleeves of my shift.

We're clad alike, in blue!

Now he glances down and spies a female head midway 'twixt his shoulder and elbow.

His eyes are like dark almonds, fringed with black lashes. His gaze is steady – without any flinching nor looking away nor the slightest uneasiness. He breaks into a conspiratorial grin and winks, his eyes projecting warmth and pleasure.

I feel a blush creep up my neck. I glance away. I dare not look at him again, for the confusion and heat in my face. But I feel his gaze on me – intense and elemental – like the stream that sings in the salmon's blood to call it to its early death.

I summon up my best pert-mouthed manner; and, still not daring to look at Him again, address the leprechaun brightly.

'You gentlemen look mighty merry.'

The little man makes a leg, sweeping off his great hat. Then, as he straightens, he replies, eyes twinkling, 'We try to be, madam,'

I pop open my fan. 'The group I am with, sir, is trying to be as well – but only proving to be tedious.'

'Tedium is de rigueur at these gatherings, madam. Did we not have it, we would not appreciate the bliss of our own company and that of our friends who provide it.'

I purr brightly, 'If your friends are so diverting, sir, perhaps you would present them to me.'

Now behold how beyond all shame my mission has made me: for I not only flounce over to a strange group of men, I even beg introductions of 'em. Am I not wicked?

But the little man is politeness itself. He smiles, his tiny black eyes plunked into a puffy face like a doughman's, his cravat spewing tiers of ruffles and lace.

'Madam, you justly reprehend my negilgence. I am Sir Charles Sedley; this, my companion,' he bows toward the pop-eyed man, 'Lord Buckhurst, heir to the Earl of Dorset; and this,' he indicates the tall, muscled lounger with the lazy grin, 'his companion from Westminster School, the Earl of Ashfield; and this' – he nods to the skinny birdlike man – 'Lord Buckhurst's steward and companion, Fleetwood Shepherd.'

Sedley and Buckhurst! I've just presented myself to the King's drinking companions – the wild leaders of those debauching, whoring, versifying tricksters known as 'the court wits'. My mama will have a falling-fit.

But I'm pleased with myself. This group is bound to be more thrilling than the one I've just given up.

I curtsey to my Lord of Buckhurst just as blandly as if I'd never heard how he and Sir Charles got drunk and stripped to their shirts and preached from the balcony of Oxford Kate's, Bow Street, and caused a disturbance and were sent before the magistrates. 'Sir.'

'Madam.' The pop-eyed man bows his puff-bellied form.

Then I curtsey to Mr Shepherd, dark and skinny and grinning; and to my Lord of Ashfield, who is well-looked, truly, with a strong jaw and cheekbones in a square face, and whose mischievous green eyes, muscular person, and long, fair periwig would have been worthy of note, had he not been standing near Adonis. With both I go through the silly bows and pleasantries.

'Sir.'

'Madam.'

'And this young rascal, who behaves no better than he should,' continues Sir Charles, 'is John Wilmot, Earl of Rochester.'

Now I *must* look at him or be impolite. I set myself to play the court coquette, inviting and beckoning: Mistress Minx, with her bold brown eyes and dancing honey curls, her rosebud lip, pouting and winsome.

First I curtsey low, my skirts spread out and eyes lowered above the open fan. 'Sir.'

Then I arise, snap my fan closed, and throw a pert look from 'neath my lashes.

He grins.

Sir Charles warns, 'I advise you to have a care with that one, madam. He may look a cherub, flitted from a wall-hanging, but he's a dangerous child.'

Conscious of my lord's eyes upon me, I pop open my fan, tilt my head at a demure angle, and sally brightly, 'And you, Sir Charles, are recommending yourself as a suitable substitute?'

The group laughs. I am well pleased with myself, to be witty for the wits.

Still my lord has said nothing particular to me. And I long that he do so.

I also see my mama with the fidgets in her chair. She keeps shooting me looks, and I know I'll not have long.

I turn to him and gaze up. 'I've heard naught of you, sir.'

There is a pause. Then he speaks.

I recall the biblical verse, 'the tongue of men and angels'. Now I know what the voice of angels is: a low murmur, rich and vibrant, honey-dripping, caressing, seducing, and recalling the melody strings of harps and viols.

'No wonder,' he says, with mischief in his eyes. 'I've been at court but these three months, madam, since the Holy Season.'

'Except that he's left behind him left behind him a trail of maidenheads,' guffaws Sir Charles.

I laugh; my lord, grinning, lowers his lashes and turns a charming pink.

Sir Charles laughs some more. 'I' faith, he's but a week beyond his eighteenth birthday, and he leads us all in wickedness.'

'Sedley,' says my lord in those melting tones, 'would you have the young lady flee me as if I were some malign fate?'

'Nay, I but say what would have her seek you out.'

But here comes Mama bearing down on me.

'Oh,' I cry, 'how tedious! Now 'tis back to the maternal clutches.'

Mama grasps me. Her mien is grim, and, without so much as a polite nod at such fine gentlemen, she marches me back over in her claws.

I glance a demure invitation over my shoulder.

They saunter after me.

'Mama!' I begin. 'I have been presenting myself to these gentlemen here.'

'And a fine state of affairs it is that you should be,' she grumbles.

Back we traipse to our melancholy circle of nobodies. The deadly scenery awaits to embrace me again: the circle of chairs, pulled tight against the wall, where Mama has judged it to be safer from court corruptions; the wood-panelled carvings of squares and leaves I've stared at these three hours; the treat-table below it, laid with a Turkey carpet, where at the anchovies, honey cakes, and china pot nobody ever gathers.

Our little party of dullards waits to swallow me up again: the eager mama, her hair on end as if with anticipation to present the marriageable spawn; the great goose himself, his beak elevated higher to see what a prize my voyage has secured.

Sir Francis even makes a stir to seduce my senses. Apprehending my approach, he has arisen to pose before the treat-table. Now he turns toward me with a pointed ogle, carefully posing his left leg before his figure to present a rounded calf in a green stocking, and seductively (as he thinks) running the periwig comb through his sausagey curls.

Mama thrusts me back into my dull chair.

'Madam,' says Sir Charles, 'permit me to present myself and my friends.'

She gives him a baleful look. 'I have heard of you, sir.'

Indeed, he is one of her favourite topics. How many times have I heard her sermon, her litany, read over four times in the year, like the Old Testament in the Church calendar!

'His Majesty winks at all they do,' she complains, 'whether they murder decent folk on the high road' – for so she would describe the mistake of my Lord Buckhurst in seeking to catch the highwayman – 'or show themselves naked on balconies, abusing the Scripture' – this for the drunken frolic on the balcony of Oxford Kate's, Bow Street. 'They can be charged with a riot, hauled before the bar, and what happens? A slap on the wrist.' This for the conclusion of the Bow

Street riot, where my Lord Buckhurst got off with a warning, and Sir Charles with a fine waived by His Majesty.

My mother grimly sweeps her dun-coloured skirts about her and installs her gaunt frame on the chair so one skinny back's before another.

My Lord Rochester, standing behind her chair like a page, says smoothly, 'Indeed, madam: he has been a disgrace to his own good name: an arch-heretic that would make even Thomas Hobbes ashamed.'

His long, slender hands on Mama's chair back, his voice earnest, with just a soft hint of indignation in't, the rascal turns to me behind her back and winks.

Sir Charles snickers behind my chair to hear my lord reprove the theory of self-interest and materialism all the wits follow. And with that wink, my lord tells me he is a Hobbist also, embracing self-interest by pleasing my mama.

I pop up my fan, the better to hide my smile, whilst shooting my temptor a conspiratorial look, to let him know I have the joke and will play along.

Then I say, 'Mama, pay no heed to my Lord of Rochester. He is one of those tedious young men who would impress us all with his virtue.'

My lord regards me with mock sobriety. 'Indeed, madam: virtue may be rare in this court, but not tedious.'

How I long to let out the laugh that my gut grips like furies from holding in.

Sir Francis perceives the inattentiveness of his audience. To make a stir of noise and movement, if not of sense, he struts, like an elegant rooster plumed, back to his chair on t'other side of Mama. He throws himself down into a lounging pose and sticks out a leg *en cavalier*, to reveal the grandeur of a yellow leather shoe with a pink butterfly bow, lace-trimmed.

'La, you say true, Lord Rochester: we're all of us deceivers, there's the truth on't!' He holds a snuffbox 'twixt two dainty fingers. 'La, Lady Warre, what villains, we!'

Mama turns about in her chair to regard the lovely, sober-faced young man behind her. 'My Lord, I'm amazed that a man of your complexion would abide in a court so depraved.'

'It is the centre of fashion, Lady Warre, and so we must thither, like rays to a sun, whether it suits our taste or no. Have you not found it so?'

'Yes, you speak true, Lord Rochester. For here I am, indeed. We have brought Betty to court that we may make freer contact with all the men suing for her hand.' Proud of her chicklet, my mama boasts, 'She's Elizabeth Mallet, the heiress.'

Without looking at me, but smiling well-bred at my mother, he says, in polite tones, 'Her greatest fortune's in her face.'

I feel a blush creep all up my neck. I dare not look at him, so I study my shoe, where a manikin fly rubs its hands in glee.

'Well.' My mother glows all over. 'How charming you are, Lord Rochester. But she has more than beauty to recommend her. She will be worth about twenty-five hundred a year at her marriage when her grandpa and I give consent.'

I'm both pleased and uneasy he should know of my fortune. Pleased, that it might arouse his interest. Uneasy, that it might be the only interest aroused.

My mother continues to puff me after the fashion of mothers, saying I am the only child of the late John Mallet and so have inherited all his vast holdings in Somerset and Wiltshire – or will do so at my wedding. So she and my grandpa, being my guardians, have the weighty charge of examining all my prospective suitors.

My lord replies in his melodious, caressing voice, 'You indeed have a heavy charge, madam. For to say truth, it would be no great amazement to me did every creature in breeches on this isle apply for her hand.'

My mama glows like a petted pup-dog.

'But to say truth,' he continues smoothly, 'in these wicked times, it must be no easy task to find a suitable candidate.'

This turn is clever. It launches her into her favourite sermon again, against the times.

'Well, 'tis beyond my understanding, the wicked taste, these days, that would prefer a lady of the streets to a lady of the court. All the young gentlemen here –' This with a polite nod to my Lords Ashfield and Buckhurst and to Sir Charles '– are led astray, and 'tis hard but they drink overmuch and get too much atheism.'

'Madam, you say true,' agrees my lord. 'And now, they all so conspire in leading one another astray, 'tis a conundrum who began the business.'

A general laugh goes up. Behind my fan I roll up my eyes at Sir Charles.

'Well,' says my mother, ''tis no conundrum to say who began it, but 'tis not proper to say it here.'

I know she means the King. Who else, being restored to the throne five years ago, brought with him the French fashion of keeping mistresses, together with the French refinements and vices? Who else brought, far more, his nature, which was frivolous, gay?

'Tis said, at His Majesty's entrance into London on his thirtieth birthday, the 29th day of May, 1660, the street conduits ran wine, and the whole city turned out to cheer his progress and light bonfires of welcome. 'Tis said he jested that everyone received him so cordially, he wondered why he'd stayed gone so long.

'Tis also said he spent that night not at Whitehall Palace but at the domicile of his mistress, Barbara Villers Palmer, now Lady Castlemaine. And so began the tenor of his reign; and soon after, the text of my mother's complaints.

She little knows I myself have small reason to trust him; for, being at Tunbridge last June, where the court took the waters and we took the court, he made a shift to get me in a dark corner for kissing and muzzling. But I got away – Lord! How I wish I could get that image out of my head – his long, dark, horsey face – that leer with the moustache above it, looming toward my mouth. I can smell his sour breath yet, feel his long, lean fingers on my arm.

But I managed to pass all off with a jest, shake off his grip, slide beneath his arm. Wicked old man – always after fresh meat – he's no more faithful to his mistress than he is to his wife.

'But the worst of it,' Mother is complaining to her new confidant milord, 'is that so many of the young men are atheists.'

'The Bible is laid aside for Hobbes,' he agrees sombrely. 'Knowledge, they say, enters only through the senses; and life is to gratify them.'

A strangled noise behind me hints that Sir Charles is as near to guffawing as I.

'Why, that is very true,' I cut in. 'Sir Charles was telling me of a young man newly arrived at court who leads all in wickedness – what was his name, Lord Rochester?'

'Forgive me, madam: I am new at court myself.'

I fan myself demurely. 'He is said to be a great seducer. What must he look and sound like, think you?'

All at once the goose opens its beak. 'Methinks 'tis idle to speculate.'

With a long, censorious look, it lets us know it has our game; and its disgust says plainly it is offended to be in company with a man so wicked as my lord; it is more offended yet at the frivolous trick we play, and most offended of all that my lord plays its character attractively.

Then Sir Charles must needs tease the joke higher: 'And the worst thing about this wicked fellow, madam, is his power of deceit. He can read any character; play any role, and, by the persuasiveness of his speech, coax his victim to believe what he will. He has the tongue of Lucifer; any woman seen in his company three times is considered already ruined.'

'Tee-hee!' Sir Francis waves his laced handkerchief. ''Tis true, is it not, my Lord Rochester? – We are arrant deceivers all.'

'Sir Francis,' says my lord, 'I fear you give us all away.'

Mama sets her lip and grasps my hand. 'Well, 'tis time we should be gone. Come, Betty.'

The Lady Sandwich so droops at this doleful news, her two panniers of curls sag.

'Lady Warre, may we not discuss the business of our two young people here?'

Mother shrugs. 'Send a note round to our lodgings. My father will attend to it.'

Mother Goose looks desperate, as indeed anyone must be, with such a honker on her hands. 'We are prepared to offer very high.'

'Good. Send a man to my father. He handles all the money business. Betty –'

She tugs my hand. Reluctantly I arise with her and cast into my lord's face a look of pure regret and longing.

He trains on me a speculative gaze. Then he turns to my mother.

'Lady Warre, I hope we'll see you again at one of our little divertissements.'

Mother shrugs. 'Well, 'tis likely. We plan to stay in town till we find Betty a husband.'

She clasps my hand hard and tilts her head at him. He responds with a genteel inclination of the head.

As she tugs me away, I cast one forlorn look over my shoulder.

He's staring with appreciation at my back view. He grins mischievously, raises his tankard in salute, and winks.

2

'A Goodly, Grave Gentlewoman'
8 April 1665

Dorimant: What kind of woman's the mother?
Orange Woman: A goodly, grave gentlewoman. Lord, how she talks
against the wild young men o' the town! As for your part, she thinks
you an arrant devil; should she see you, on my conscience she would
look if you had not a cloven foot.
—George Etherege, *The Man of Mode; or Sir Fopling Flutter* (1676),
a play based partly on the courtship of Betty and Rochester

All the way home I've wondered at Mama's silence. But then, I find,
she's like a water-clock: unmoving whilst the tube fills slowly up; but
then, with what a bang the top plunges down!

In the drawing room of our lodgings off St John Street, Grandpa sits
in the plump chair,' his lap spread with papers as figured as an
astrologer's forecast. No doubt this absorbing text is a comparison of
whose father's offered what bribe for me; or some long, dull list sent
by my stepfather in Somerset, itemizing all the cheeses on the estate
and recommending how to save a ha'penny in their setting. Grandpa
would never read such frivolities as made-up stories – unless, perhaps,
a chapbook of *Mistress Money: Her Death and Burial*:

Whether I do sleep or rest,
Pluto still defend my chest.

Whate'er the papers, Grandpa clutches one in a brown-splotched
claw. His eyes pop, and his white hairs stick out as if he'd borrowed
fashionable wires of the Lady Sandwich. More for politeness, no
doubt, than interest, he asks (without looking up), 'Adod, now,
Unton: how progressed your business?'

'Business, indeed!' cries Mama vehemently. She pitches her muff at
a stick-chair: Mrs Davenport the actress cannot have done so tragical a
gesture. 'The business is, I'm out of sorts, Father; I'm cross-grained,

I'll tell you that. I've just spent above a quarter of an hour in the company of the lewd Sedley and his entourage; Betty encouraged 'em over on a freak of mischief.'

Grandpa looks up over his spectacles. 'What of Sandwich's son? Hinchingbrooke?'

I pull a face, as if to swallow a toad.

'Well,' says Mama, 'he gave not a very promising account of himself today, but they're going to send an offer round.'

She yanks off her gloves, a finger at a time.

'Was there nobody else?'

She grimaces. 'Some fop, who was more girlish than Betty – somebody Popham.'

Grandpa's eyes glaze. 'Popham, Popham: egad, not our next-door neighbours in Enmore?'

'I'm sure I can't know,' snaps Mama. 'I could say little enough to such a stinking fanfaroon.'

I titter behind my hand, then pull a straight face and say, with mock solemnity: 'Indeed, Mama: didn't you think him handsome, the way his ribbons rustled?'

'Oh, Lord.' Mama fans herself. 'Father, you should have seen him – what a spindly-shanked, mincing rascal.'

'Egad, Unton – was there no one else at all?' asks Grandpa plaintively. For 'twas his inspiration to bring this prize sausage to market, to dangle it before the bidders.

'No one at all,' she says, loosing the clasp of her cloak.

Now, this is indeed the height of blindness.

Making a shift to sound casual, I say, 'That friend of Sir Charles Sedley's – Lord Rochester – he was mighty well-bred, Mother.'

She shrugs, a guarded look in her eyes.

I prod her a little. 'Did you not think so?'

She hesitates, as if making a shift to sort out her feelings. Then she replies, 'He seemed a bit suave for his years. There's something about him I don't trust.'

I stick out my neck a little farther on the chopping block. 'Why, Mother – you abuse him for his politeness? That seems unfair.'

'I abuse nothing.' Her eyes shift away, and she deposits her cloak on a chair. 'I only say, he's mighty smooth for someone who puts himself in the barber's hands but twice or thrice a week.'

Grandpa removes his spectacles. His eyes glint with the glaze of guineas.

'Rochester, Rochester. Egad, this would be the son of the first Earl, Unton. You know, the Cavalier general that saved the King's life and sat his council at the court of exile. Didn't he die penniless? I fear there's no business there.'

'Business, business! I'm sick of it!' complains Mama. 'Why do we not close with the Lord Ormond and have done?'

Grandpa's eyes bulge. He looks like a frog that has swallowed a disagreeable dragonfly.

'Daughter, you astonish me – adod, you do!'

'Why?' Mama puts her hands on her hips. 'I can't think of anyone I'd rather have as a son than the Lord John Butler. I know he and Betty agree, and his family –'

'His family, curse 'em, have made no final offer!' Grandpa rattles his papers in emphasis. 'There's been no putting up, Unton, no putting up, I tell thee!'

'But there will be,' points out Mama, 'as soon as the Lord John arrives in town from Kilkenny Castle. Didn't they say so?'

'Aye, shifts and policy, if you ask me,' says Grandpa with a snort. 'Best have more than one iron in the fire.'

Mama waves her hand. 'Stuff! They'll go as high as you wish, Father.'

'Then let 'em put up, adod! What hinders 'em? What stays the putting up, that's what I'd know!' He rattles the papers and snorts like a dressmaker with a crooked stitch.

'The Lord John insisted. He would speak with Betty first –'

'Shifts and policy! And mighty feeble ones – I saw him speaking plenty at Tunbridge last June; he spoke enough, adod, to court some thousand wives – why, he spoke more, Unton, in three weeks than I spoke to your mother in twenty years! Speaking!' Grandpa snorts. 'Delays – shifts and policy, adod: what's more to speak? Do they like one another, or don't they? – Come here, little hussey.'

I look at him vaguely. 'Sir?'

He gestures toward me. I dimple prettily at him, acting Grandpa's little girl: wiggle to his chair, sit on the arm, embrace his shoulders and beam.

'There's my girl!' He tweaks my cheek. 'Do you like the Lord John Butler, child?'

Marriage. How to sort my feelings out? For years I've dreamt of a husband and children. For months I've thrilled over this trip to London, this chance to shine at court and pick a husband. Now – I don't know. The man I would pick is not yet an approved suitor.

But there's no way to voice such a strange thought, and the Lord John Butler is an agreeable, well-looked gentleman.

So I beam. 'Of course, Grandpa.'

He chortles. 'There's my little lass – my little wanton!'

But I'm not your little wanton, Grandpa. Is something the matter with me? Women are supposed to be so lustful, their virginity is the close care of guardians till marriage. (Was it not Eve's fault that Adam, the more rational of the two, fell?) Now I cannot think of myself 'twixt the sheets with the Lord John Butler. And he is a well-favoured gentleman, polite. We have all the ingredients the world would approve for a successful marriage: mutual respect, a commonality of backgrounds and characters, kinsmen pleasantly disposed to one another.

Mama gazes on me fondly. How can I explain that this fine marriage, cooked up with the most careful ingredients, seems odd, foreign? How can I be so ungrateful?

Except – I could be wanton, I think, with a dark-eyed slender man, whose voice is like a lute. For a moment I suffer my mind to linger in a darkened chamber, with the warm touch of a particular lean, hard body without any nightclothes against my rounded nakedness. But sure, till my guardians put him in the category of husband, this sort of thinking's a dangerous delight. Then I start. For the conversation, meandering down its own riverbed, has lined up with my own thoughts.

'Well, I don't like that Rochester!' Mama says vehemently. 'He took too much care with his person and manners.'

Grandpa chuckles. 'Quite a charmer, eh?'

'I was not so charmed,' snaps Mama; but she was, at first, could she have but seen herself. 'Father, I swear he must have bathed; the only smell about him was of rose-water.'

So now this will be held to his discredit: that he doesn't reek like a goat.

Grandpa picks up one of his papers again, as if to signal the conversation is done. 'Well, we'll do a little looking-out of his prospects. No harm done. He may not even offer.'

'If he does, he's never getting *my* daughter!'

The tone is so violent, both Grandpa and I gawk. Mama glances at the floor and mutters, 'I mean, he has the look of a fortune hunter.'

'Well, we'll see what he has to put up,' says Grandpa genially. 'The putting-up's the thing, Unton.'

'That's *not* the only thing, Father!' Mama quivers in outrage. 'This boy's a famed whore-master, and I'm certainly not going to hand Betty over to him, that he may make her miserable.'

I stare at my mother. 'You *knew?*'

'How, I wonder?' Mama returns. 'For I'm one-and-thirty; I'm utterly stupid; anyone can make mouths in my presence, and I'll not see. Father, you should have seen 'em, all talking of some famed lecher at

17

court – and all the while, rolling their eyes at that Rochester. You should have seen Jemima Sandwich and her son blanch; you should have seen Betty and that Sedley: they thought it great sport.'

Grandpa ponders. 'Egad, now I think on't – I have heard some talk of him.'

'Lord!' Mama shakes her head. 'That clean-scraped baby face – what wicked times we live in! How could he?'

Grandpa looks at her over his spectacles. 'With a good deal of help, Unton. The talk I heard was, the women send *him* notes.'

'Lord!' Mama clutches her breast. 'That a woman would post to her own ruin!'

I put in a cautious oar. 'Let's not be too quick to judge, Mother. If the women chase him, can he be blamed?'

'For setting 'em on so cunningly, he can. With his remarks and looks and stances. With his hip thrust out just so, his eyelashes at such-an-angle. He makes 'em do all, from sheer laziness, that he may have the greater sport.'

I dare not say more. 'Tis plain the more she talks, the more she loathes him. Why? Because he's dangerous? But there's a sparkle in him, an aspiration: the sense of no challenge being too great, no obstacle too difficult. 'Tis as if his inner being is an incandescent star, and to be around it is to bathe in sprinkles of glory.

I remember the comet that came to stand over London. The country folk say 'tis a portent: a warning of God's wrath at the murder of the last king or debauchery of the present one: that the prophecies of Revelations are being fulfilled; and a twelvemonth hence, when the year of the treble sixes comes, we'll have pestilence, fire, and sword.

I shiver, touched by the cold breath of some future fate I cannot understand.

3

'Lord Orville'
23 April 1665

The conversation of Lord Orville is really delightful. His manners are so elegant, so gentle, so unassuming, that they at once engage esteem, and diffuse complacence. He is most assiduously attentive to please and serve all who are in his company, and though his success is invariable, he never manifests the smallest degree of consciousness.

His remarks upon the company in general were so apt, so lively, so just.

His conversation was sensible and spirited; his air, and address were open and noble; his manners, gentle, attentive, and infinitely engaging; his person is all elegance, and his countenance the most animated and expressive I have ever seen.

—Fanny Burney, *Evelina, or The History of a Young Lady's Entrance into the World* (1778)

I awake before dawn. Haggard from want of sleep, I make a shift to read *Romance of Arthur*. But I can't focus on the characters. Then I sit at my secretary to write. A throbbing shadow of romance and beauty moves over me – some half-glimpsed story I'd tell – but my quill only marks absently on the paper. So I sit on my balcony and watch the sun rise over the leads of inns and cook-shops. The day is streaked with smoke. Early carters whistle to their beasts, wheels rumble over cobbles, and with a splatter and a 'Gardy-loo!' the contents of someone's chamber pot hit the pave. I listen to the London street music: the clattering cacophony of cartwheels, the clip-clop of nags and the cries of vendors.

'Ballads! Who'll buy my ballads?'

'Thyme, sweet thyme!'

'Cherry ripe!'

'Sparrowgrass for salads!'

I stare at the grave antique street, all the domiciles brown-striped and white-plastered, sticking out galleries like grim jaws.

19

Why have I this urge to see him again? 'Tis the sort of push I had to get to London: a shout in the head, a voice directing me. Peace, voice! I'll see him again; I know I will. *But when? Don't wait too late!*

Or what?

The voice is silent then. *Don't wait,* is all it will say. *See him now.* But how?

Write him a note.

A note? Are you mad? Women don't write men; 'tis the men who write to plead, to offer poems and plaints and treats; the women, who wait like Sultanas for the tribute, Heras for the burnt offerings.

You'll be waiting without a tribute, advises the voice sternly, *unless you write.*

So here I sit, like a tragedy-queen, my breast torn 'twixt love and honour, passion and reason.

What will Mama say?

Nothing, for you won't tell her, says the voice. *And do you think he will?*

No, indeed. But what will he think of me?

That you've a mind to see him. What better way to soothe up his vanity?

Yes, and seem easy, like all the others. I can't do this!

But you must: for I'll hare you till you do.

Beyond this last I do not think. I flounce through the balcony windows to the secretary, and claw out quill and writing paper. For the voice has nagged me to a paleness and a half-fast this whole fortnight.

I write:

My Lord,

So pleasant 'twas to gull my mama at Whitehall Palace, I perceived upon an inspiration that we might have a go at it again. She takes me forth today, to the Great Exchange, for buying of silks and satins and such. Would it not be great sport if your lordship could be there and we could jest again? I remain, sir,

Your Most Obedient and
Humble Partner in Crime,
Elizabeth Mallet.

Upon sending for my maid Nan to find the Lord Rochester and take the note to him, I am asked, 'Madam, where is he?'

I snap, 'How should I know where he is?'

This is a tender conscience speaking. For indeed, why should I not know where he lodges, as much intelligence of him as I've gathered?

I've pumped Frances Stewart – the King's favourite, that celebrated *belle* whose weightiest part is not in her cranium but on either side of her breastbone. From Frances I've learnt his background. His father, the famous Lord Henry Wilmot, was created First Earl of Rochester after his daring rescue of the King, when the countryside was roused to discover His Majesty's hiding place after that last Royalist disaster, Worcester fight. Lord Wilmot, with his wit and flair for disguises, dressed the King as a servant and smuggled him out of the country, then became a close friend of His Majesty at the court of exile, where they drank and chased women.

From some of the reverend antiquities at court, I've heard a saying about Lord Wilmot: 'So great a scholar, he could give the best advice; and so good a soldier, he could follow it with the best of any man in England; none more valiant to return an affront, none more popular with his troops.'

But not so good a husband. His sour-faced Puritan wife, whom he had married for her fortune, he left at Ditchley, Oxfordshire, to rear their son. She is at Ditchley yet: the Protector did not seize her estate because she inherited it from her first husband, Sir Henry Lee, who, like her, was a fanatic.

But Lord Wilmot's estate was seized and parcelled out; so all his son has inherited, besides his charm and title, was a manor house at Adderbury, Oxfordshire.

Then, upon his Restoration, the grateful King financed the son's Tour of Italy and France and awarded him a pension of five hundred a year. And since Christmas, His Majesty has come to enjoy the son's company as much as he did the father's.

So from Frances and some several others I have learnt enough to know my kin will never approve him. Mama loathes his reputation with women. My grandpa and stepfather will loathe – as soon as they find it out – my lord's poverty.

The current bribe asked, to begin nuptial haggling for me, is ten thousand cash. And why not? Am I not the richest heiress in the land? Have I not beauty and wit besides? And I know Mama looks for a sum to set up my little half-brother Frank; and I so pity the poor creature, with that cold-blooded carp Sir John Warre for a father, I'd help the little fellow if I could.

My stomach feels hollow. Then it stabs with guilt. For I should be grateful: I have a doting mama and worldly-wise grandpa, eager to choose the best husband possible. Yet I thank them by sneaking behind their backs, writing to a man of whom they disapprove.

Mama finds me at my toilet-table, brow in hand, fingers leaking tears.

'Why, Betty! What's the matter?'

Then I dissemble: say, I am melancholy for being shut in; and may we not go to the 'Change? Oh, shameless! – For as soon as consent is given, my pangs and sinkings are gone, and my gut is all fluttering excitement.

Nan has found out my lord: she says he lodges in Covent Garden and that he received the message with spirits and attention, saying, 'twas just such a purpose as would draw any gentleman out; and: 'Tell your lady I'll see her at the Great Linen Draper's, the blue sign, and I'll leave within the hour.'

She also reports well of him, as a most discreet gentleman. She is surprised, he bespoke her as considerately as if she were Quality: stood in her presence, offered her a chair – marvellous genteel for an earl! She had been resigned to fighting his hand out of her bosom during the whole transaction, yet he never offered to touch her. Then, at the end, he asked if she had a chair or coach waiting or man to convey her through the streets.

My conscience stabs, to think of my ill-usage of Nan: first the haring of her, then the sending her on such an errand, in such a lewd town.

I scan her. At fifteen, she's pretty and ripe, with brown curls: what might she have suffered? He thought more for her welfare than I, her mistress.

But 'twas ignorance on my part. So protected as I am, I forget what women of the lower orders are resigned to suffer, after the way of things. And I am grateful to him that his manners were so much better than his reputation – at least with my woman.

I apologize to Nan for my want of foresight and ask if she had any trouble on the journey. No, says she, for she took a chair-man that waited, then conveyed her back; and one of the Lord Rochester's men paid him. I beg her pardon again; and, having no silver about me, offer her a choice of any of my old gowns save the yellow or blue.

She bobs a pretty curtsey; and, eyes shining, says she will do such an errand for me any day, thank you, madam.

So off jog Mama and I in a hackney coach: down St John Street, through Smithfield Market and St Paul's churchyard with the book-stalls and the church spire struck off to a box by lightning.

At last, in the merchants' district at Threadneedle, Cornhill, and Lombard Streets, there looms the Great Exchange. This three-storied building, shaped like a horseshoe with sharpened curves, has made London the centre of world trade. Sir Thomas Gresham built it some hundred years before, that the merchants would not be forced to walk the streets any more like peddlers to show their wares.

Alighting from the coach, I gawk up at the grasshopper on the column, and Mama grasps my hand. For we must traverse a square peopled with that dangerous beast, man! Divers specimens of him lounge about, here smoking a long pipe and reading a gazette; there buying a broadside from a vendor or reading a bill stuck up on the colonnades. And they all pay very little attention to the prize she parades or her apprehensions about its display.

I lead my mother like an ox in tow to the Great Draper's on the third floor. We're at the back counter, poring over bolts of cloth, when he enters the shop.

I had thought myself prepared to meet him, but I had forgot what an impact he makes on first sight. He enters with a gallant gesture of sweeping off his plumed hat and making soft, sly bows to the ladies that turn away from him to blush. His suit is plain again – chocolate brown velvet with no garniture – with the audacious accent of boots: the touch that converts him into a cavalier about to storm a wall after an imprisoned princess.

My heart leaps to my throat at the sight of him; and, my face hot (oh traitor blood, called up at his every approach), I turn away and frown, as if displeased with the cloth I inspect. I pretend to ignore him, though so conscious of his nearness, the prickles of my nerves stand up: my hair ends and spine sense the breath and heat behind me.

He almost grazes me now. I feel the heat of him in my back and inner thighs, smell the tang of jasmine, notice the furtive glances of the ladies at the counter. The bolts of cloth are as blurred as the shop noises: the linen-draper thumping a bolt and a lady's voice fuzzily taking note of its shago nap; a child dropping something to the splintered wood floor; Mama asking about a yellow silk – all part of a distant world wrapped in wool, its corners dulled, and the sharp senses of me drawing in intelligence from elsewhere, direct to my nerves.

'Lady Warre,' says that soft, sweet voice, 'how very good to see you again.'

She nods in his direction. 'My lord.'

'You have come to an apt place for choosing of your cloths, Lady Warre. We keep hereabouts the grandest selections from all the coffers of Europe. We are the North Star to which every ship sails.'

She nods. 'We're finding an ample supply to look at, my lord.'

Sidling over to my right, he leans his elbow casually on the counter; and, turning his hat in his hands, he looks over at her with melting earnestness and exudes that incredible physical presence from his eyes and smile. Merely viewing him with sidelong glances, I yearn to fall desperately upon him and cover his face with kisses; what a devil he is – I wonder how he learnt to send out such messages with a mere look.

23

Mama turns away and grows absorbed in haggling with the shopkeeper.

This leaves the rabbit for coursing, so our brisk hound turns to his game. 'Permit me the boldness to say so, madam, but choose not that brown.'

I look up at him. 'And why not, sir?'

'With that shade to enhance your eyes, I'll have no chance at you at all; your lodgings will be so crowded with suitors, I must languish out in the street.'

I open my eyes wide, the better to show 'em. 'Indeed, sir: you say what will give me a mind to it.'

I smooth a yellow velvet with my hands. He takes up a length of its end. 'What say you to this gold?'

Steadily, just as if I weren't thinking of his fingers on the same cloth, I say, ''Tis over-sallow with my complexion, methinks.'

He tosses it carelessly aside. The linen-draper looks resty but says nothing; what shop-man would chide a lord? – E'en when the lord next says, 'This is hard, dull work. What say you we step over to an inn I know nearby? I'll have something sent up from a cook shop.'

I am dubious. 'My mother won't, I'm sure.'

'All the better.'

'Oh, you! – My mother, I know, will say we should be about our business.'

'Being about one's business all the time is dull. Being dull often hampers one's business. I say we have got dull looking at so many things and need leisure to consider what you shall buy.'

'Indeed, I couldn't agree more.' I look up, round-eyed, at him.

'And as we sit, you can tell me your life story, and I'll tell you mine. Because it's damned absurd to feel I know someone so well and yet know so little of her.'

'There's little to tell of mine,' I murmur. I think: it began when I looked into a pair of dark eyes.

'Then we can speak of little and spin it into much. 'Tis a courtly vice; so we must both learn it, to keep in fashion.'

'What can you tell me of yourself?' I ask, just as if I hadn't prodded the details out of everyone else. But I'd hear him say them all. I'd relish the new twists he'll give to common information and delight to hug to my heart the precious new comments I can file with the others inside, for turning over and recollecting. My old cache of statements is pretty nigh worn from handling.

'Well, to say truth, I was born April First. That about sums me up, for I am ever fooling.'

'Oh, be serious!'

'But I tell you I cannot – I'm astrologically inhibited – I come from near Oxford, where I attended the university.'

'And fooled there, too?'

'No more but so – I got my M.A., I think, because the King got restored that year; 'twas the year for handing out meaningless honours to fools.'

We both titter at this treasonous joke. 'You're awful!' I cry.

'Only fooling – Then I toured Italy and France some three years.'

'There's a place for fooling indeed.'

'Remarkably enough, I learnt much more there than at Oxford –'

I pout at what seems a reference to courtesans; so he grows serious. The vigour, the animation of his countenance remain: the force of his presence, the aptness of his speech, the expressiveness of his manner just the same as when he talked nonsense. But now he explains about the great poetry and art and learning of Italy: about Dante, Boccaccio, Petrarch, Ariosto, Michelangelo, Pico della Mirandola; about the new learning and the academies, the University of Padua and libraries in Rome. And most of it is beyond my depth: all I can think of is how beautiful his big dark eyes are and how marvellous he should be this learned, too.

I feel a stab of regret, that I have so little education to attract him; and with my whole heart long for the schooling would make me a fit companion for him.

The longer he talks, the more his eyes sparkle with passion. 'We are on the threshold of a new age! Medieval superstitions are being flooded with the light of reason; things that before were the result of credulous ignorance are being subjected to experiment. Perhaps someday soon, we will find and weigh the soul.'

My eyes widen. 'Can we, think you?'

'Why not, if it exists? Is not the world matter?'

My brow furrows. I have no learning or experience with reason; the most I can do is sometimes sense what will happen or what people think.

'I don't know. But if it were, would not the soul perish with the body?'

'Perhaps it does,' he says, 'or floats off to another sphere.'

'Betty,' thrusts in Mama, 'are you done?'

Does she think the conversation blasphemous? Or is she simply weary and fretful? Or does she wish to drag her naughty child from the sugar bowl? I scan her; she is definitely in one of her fidgets.

'Mama,' I say, eyes pleading, 'the Lord Rochester has invited us round to an inn nearby, to take some refreshment.'

Mama grimaces in an attempt to smile as she takes my hand. 'What a kind invitation, my lord! But I fear we must be gone.'

'But why?'

Mama turns to the linen-draper but never leaves off clenching my hand. 'When can you have them sent? We are only visitors, as I told you, and I'd like to have the gowns fitted for my daughter as soon as possible, for her use in town.'

The shop-man promises to send a 'prentice round to our lodgings that night, as soon as the shop is closed.

'Madam,' cuts in my lord boldly, 'I'd be much obliged –'

She trains on him a Medusa stare. 'I'm sure you would, my lord. But you do yourself more credit to keep to your previous means of application. I am sure they will sit better with our eventual judgment on your suit.'

He inclines his head. 'Your reproof is just, madam. Forgive the eagerness with which youth and passion –'

'Suit?' I cry. 'What suit's this?'

Indeed, which of us is the fitter study of 'youth and passion'? Seldom could someone so full of these two qualities think to call on 'em as coolly as he.

Mama frowns – first on me, then on the enemy.

His eyes burn. 'She has not told you?'

'No,' I cry, 'but you tell me, now!' My lips part and eyes shine up at him.

He opens his mouth, then clamps it shut and turns, with a tight-lipped smile, to Mama.

She flushes – looks away from him and says crisply, 'I didn't think it worth telling. The King has writ, some few times, to recommend my lord's suit for your hand.' She shrugs, then adds defensively, 'Well, why stir you up about this suit or that? Nothing's settled yet, and there are a great many prospects. Why mention it each time a new one applies?'

'Well, why mention it, indeed?' I cry, inflamed. ''Tis only my life: why should I know?'

'Betty,' says Mama with a sharp look and firm tone.

I cast down my gaze and mumble, 'Forgive me, madam.'

Mama smoothes a curl off my neck. I shiver; I'm so sensitive to touch: my skin purrs 'neath it.

'Betty, with your passions, you'd be agog each day, did we tell you about each new suit. That's your grandpa's business. You know we'll tell you when we've settled on a contract. You will meet the young man then, and you will have your negative.'

I nod, looking at the floor. 'Yes, madam.'

''Tis not proper,' she says coolly, 'for any of your suitors to be courting you until the contract has been signed.' Then she leaves off – perhaps realizing how harsh her voice sounds – and adds in fairer tones, 'Not that I think, my lord, you meant amiss. I am sure you were acting well within the bounds of propriety for your age and set. But I must warn you, we'll not look kindly to such another too-coincidental meeting.'

I flush: she's blaming him for what I did.

He murmurs, 'Forgive me, madam.' He shoots me a glance as he adds, 'His Majesty forbade me courting the young lady in my own person.'

My heart swells. How noble of him to draw the blame to himself! He also lets me know why he hasn't writ.

Mama nods stiffly.

'Mother,' I cry, 'I'm surprised at the King.' I'll wager he does little enough of his own wooing by proxy (as indeed I have bitter cause to know).

'Well,' says my mother, 'things are different at court, dear, from how they are with women of virtue usually brought up in your class. Young people are thrown together without adequate attendance. I am sure my Lord Rochester is accustomed to holding conversations with young ladies in relaxed surroundings, and so he acted on impulse and saw no wrong in what he did. But His Majesty understood that manners are not so free away from court, and tried to warn his lordship.'

As Mama continues to lift back my curls and smooth them off my neck, I shiver with pleasure and gaze into my lord's eyes. They say he wishes he had the right to caress my neck, and that the moment the accursed contract gave him leave, he'd show me true pleasure. Not for him to give the first kiss in the nuptial bed, as 'tis prescribed by the old rural forms; he'd sweep me to him before the ink was dry: why, forsooth, he'd do it now, were we without this wretched audience. And would I resist those soft-looking lips?

'Mama,' I fret, 'why must we be so antique? Why can't the young men court me in their own persons, instead of through grandfatherly messages?'

'Because, my pet, your affections might become engaged, and then the suit might not work out. You see –' She leaves off fussing with the curls but lays a hand on my shoulder '– we love you, Betty, and understand you might choose a husband for other reasons than older and wiser heads would.' She flushes here and deliberately, it seems, does not look at my lord.

I look down at the floor and wonder if he is looking, too. That would make the whole trio gazing downwards.

'You suffered me to converse and dance with the Lord John Butler at Tunbridge last June,' I point out, resentfully.

'Well, perhaps that was wrong. I think it was. It gave you a taste of freedoms not ordinarily proper – but 'twas a watering place, a place of liberty. I saw no harm in the dances, and, once there, no harm in your having one partner more than the others, nor in conversing with him 'twixt turns. But I was mistaken; I own it; and the mistake will not be repeated. There will be no balls at Whitehall before you're contracted.'

She is not being honest with herself. She saw no harm if I conversed with *her* candidate; this one she would keep at a distance.

I look up at my lord and can tell he's thinking the same thing. I often know what people think, and his thoughts are easier to get than anyone else's. 'Tis as if he shoots 'em to me.

'Well, Lady Warre,' he says pleasantly, 'what fate has ordained, or heaven will allow, will be.'

She gives him a penetrating look, then tugs my hand to pull me off. I incline my head to him; and the last sight of him I see's his long, slender form leaning against the counter as he whispers confidentially, then bursts into a long, merry peal of laughter against the linen-draper's loud guffaw. How well-bred he is, to think of being pleasant to a shop-man.

In the coach, I can see Mama trying to concoct some sage motherly maxim.

'It wouldn't do to let your affections become engaged with him, Betty. He has only five hundred a year; and, I am sure, if he had you, he would undervalue all your virtues.'

'You think he's after my fortune,' I say, looking down at the hands clasped in my pink silk lap and making shift to keep the quaver from my voice.

'Isn't that the most obvious conclusion? Not that you haven't many other things to give, dear: you have. That's just the point. You're better off bestowing them on someone who will appreciate them.'

Lord John Butler, she means. And she's probably i' th' right.

'The Lord Rochester has a taste for women and expensive suits,' she points out, 'and little money to support either. The King's scraping the bottom of the Treasury, and he's always looking for ways to pay off the heirs of old favourites by other means. This is no doubt why he presses the suit.'

I look bleakly out the window at the street going by.

'Who knows?' continues my mother. 'It may even be that the King is the chief mover here, and his lordship is only obeying orders.'

All at once something in that last statement gives me pause. What is it the King might get by marrying a dependent to me? And what might the dependent get in return? More than five hundred a year, I'll warrant.

No! I can't believe either of 'em so sinister, especially my lord. There is a gentleness and protectiveness in his carriage to me – a frank affection and tenderness in his eyes.

Ah, says reason, *of course there is: can he not 'read any character, play any role' – adapt his manners to charm any woman he has a mind of pleasing?*

But only for the sport, and then in a laughing way, as he did with my mother at court! Not in so diabolical a way, giving me looks of friendliness and admiration, so's to secure my money for himself and my person for the King.

But how do I know that? Everything I've heard of him warns me to beware.

And why do I think of marrying him anyway? 'Tis plain my relations will never have him.

My head aches. What is this bond I have with him, and why does it resist all reason? Mama says that love grows after marriage, from mutual respect and common concerns: that it springs from a commonality of character. By all rights, then, I should be expecting to love the Lord John Butler, not someone so different from me, so full of poetry and mischief and learning and reason and aspiration.

What is this force that made me feel my Lord of Rochester before I ever met him and that now draws me to him as if we were two raindrops on a pane?

It is something deeper than marital affection, deeper than character. My lord draws me as I draw breath.

And I seem powerless to resist.

4

'Wherefore Art Thou Romeo?'
Late April and early May, 1665

Juliet: O Romeo, Romeo, wherefore art thou Romeo?
Deny thy father and refuse thy name;
Or, if thou wilt not, be but sworn my love,
And I'll no longer be a Capulet.
—William Shakespeare, *Romeo and Juliet*

He runs in my head as London did the night before we left the country.

Some days I yield to the impulse of thinking on him. I lie back against the bolster pillow, think on what he said and how, and what he surely meant, if only he meant not this or that other. I pump up our few brief words till they strain, great-bellied, and are like to pop; and each character of 'em, looming, is a sign whose significance must be tweezed out, like an ill-grown hair lying above a brow.

Indeed, our meetings are full of signs that tremble through mute objects, straining to make themselves known: the places he stood or leaned, the words he spoke – are these not something more than they would first appear? So there's much thinking to do, to find out the signs and tweeze the meaning from 'em.

But other days there's even more thinking to do. I must not only strain out the meaning of gestures, words and objects that were; I must also indulge my wicked fancy in presentiments of what might be.

On these days I bar reason from the door. For here we are married (never mind how); and though there are so many scenes to this play, my favourite is always the one that begins when the last wedding guest has tormented us abed with the customary ogling, and Nan has drawn the curtains and left us alone.

He leans on an elbow – somehow, though in the night, I can see his intense dark eyes – and how I blush to see his passion! – but tremble at what I feel, too. And then he touches me for the first time – really touches me – sometimes he takes my hand that rests on the counterpane, sometimes runs a finger across my cheek. But he always says, 'Well, we're alone now.'

'Yes.'

'Frighted?'

'No,' I lie.

Then he lifts my fingertips and kisses 'em gently. And all my fears dissolve into longing: I sigh and move in toward him.

'I love you,' he says. 'I loved you from the first moment I saw you.'

'I love you, too,' I whisper.

He bends down to kiss me; and as my arms reach up, he takes me to him hard; then we dissolve together.

I sigh, for the next part is always dim. And, oh, what's the good of entertaining such wicked thoughts when there's so small a chance of their becoming reality? For to marry me, he must please Mama and Grandpa; and to do that, he must have unblemished virtue and ten thousand pound; and to produce these inducements, he must be Jesus with the loaves and fishes; and Jesus he is not.

Nor can I find my kinsfolk much in error. Would I have my daughter marry a profligate and fortune hunter? What have I to plead in his defence (e'en to myself) that's relevant to marriage?

'Mama, Grandpa,' will I say; 'will you hear me, please? I lied; there is a reason I've had no appetite these ten days, nor have rested well; now I'll tell it you.'

I picture the scene; but as soon as I think how I'll begin my confidence, or what arguments I have to plead in defence of it, along with (though I have the eloquence of Cicero) how the whole is certain to be received – with what a mixture of horror, incredulity, and dismay – I realize how hopeless my cause is. In the stark light of day, I see my thoughts for the shameful things they are: how much sooner will my guardians see?

If only I felt this way about the Lord John Butler! Every day the talk is more of his suit: how he will come to London soon, how irreproachable his character is and how well suited his temperament to mine, how seductively his father's moneybags jingle.

I decide the only course to be taken is to write out a balance sheet, with the virtues of one set against the vices of the other; and so argue myself into reason.

Lord Butler:

> **Item**. Good sense, for comfortable conversation and the dependable ordering of our lives.

31

Item. Temperate habits. Virtue and honour without prudishness. Will stay home nights and be as faithful as any man can be expected to be.

Item. Good nature, with a generous spirit. Will share my estate with me and not stint me.

Item. Well-favoured. Handsome face, agreeable and tastefully dressed person.

Item. Safe.

Item. Family man. Grew up with a large, warm, close family, will delight in children and wife as his brothers and father do.

Item. The above show that the Lord Butler will be a good father: strict, warm, and kind.

Lord Rochester:

Item. Scintillating wit, which he will use to deceive me or rail against wives.

Item. Utter want of virtue and honour. Will spend nights with whores and drinking companions, break his marriage vows once and twice in a day.

Item. Lives by Hobbist principle of self-interest. Will spend all my money on himself – indeed, courted me to get it.

Item. So pretty, I can expect the women always after him, even did he not delight to encourage 'em.

Item. Dangerous.

Item. Leader of a pack of rogues that get clear of their families whenever possible. Reared without ever seeing mother and father together.

Item. The above show that the Lord Rochester will be a miserable father: absent most of the time, impatient the rest, and very handy to solve all problems with a beating.

This last item, I admit, is mere supposition; but any person of wit, seeing what flower grows in what soil, would judge the deductions very probable. A man who delights in the company of his family will be more patient with the little ones, more prone to understand and excuse ordinary infantile follies: to a rake and a philanderer, every fidg in the chair or bellow in the cradle will be a nerve-grating intrusion.

I read the list again, determined to fix it in my mind as an antidote against passion; but though 'tis a good list, with much of reason and judgment in it; and carefully wrought, with all probable truths laid out, it has an effect on me the opposite of what it is supposed to. It makes me melancholy enough to cry.

So I determine to read it again. But then I find a flaw in it: it has not the full effect, simply because I was too severe upon my lord, too unreasonable; so how could a thing so biased make a fair appeal to my reason?

First I'll blot out the stuff about the fatherhood; that's most unfair; for all I know, he loves little children and will be most tender with his own. There.

Now the stuff about the prettiness: is he to be blamed because he has long eyelashes and the face of an angel? Will this not be a virtue, to make him easy to look at, slow to pall over the daily dinner?

So I change that part – 'So pretty, I can expect always to love looking on him.' There. Are people to be blamed, after all, for the faces the Lord gave 'em?

Now, the other part that bothered me was the setting down of wit as a fault. For I knew very well, even as I set it down, 'twas the virtue in him that created that feeling of comfortableness as we spoke to one another in the same language, our minds moving together.

What is this underneath? *Utter want* of honour? Nay, that's too hard indeed. Modish habits, let us call 'em.

'Lives by Hobbes': that must stay, in all justice. But do our principles always determine our acts? He may read Hobbes, speak Hobbes, absorb Hobbes: but does it follow he will be a Hobbist?

I heft up quill to strike out that part; then I realize in dismay what I've done these three minutes, and I feel more like hanging myself than ever.

Resolutely I make a new list, full of the old, hard strictures; never mind that it may be unfair in part; I can count on myself to call up all the excuses as I read, without black-and-white characters to ratify 'em.

This done, I shred the first list into tiny pieces, lest anyone find it and be horrified to suspect what it is. Then I lock the second list away in my secretary, for future study; and I sigh, staring out the window, my fingers playing absently with the quill.

Here's an R, and an O. What would it feel to write a C?

My fingers itch to form the third character; but I restrain 'em, just as if they were legs that carried me a step farther down the slope into the fiery pit. And I shred this piece of paper, too; for 'tis even more dangerous than the other.

But then, not writing, I am left to think. What will his first kiss be like? Will he gather me into his arms in a sudden movement I'll be too overwhelmed to protest, then cover my face and lips with hard kisses? Or will he love me first with a series of slow looks so that I move to him face upturned, eyes closed?

Mayhap he'll carry me off: pull me onto the front of his horse and spirit me to the back entrance of his lodgings, then carry me up the stairs and throw me onto his bed. 'Now,' he'll say with a smile most devilishly handsome, 'I've got you where I will not take "no" for an answer.' Then he'll fling his cloak swirling to the floor; and, removing his rapier, pulling out his shirt (so's I can touch his warm breast), ease himself down beside me.

Oh, dear. What thoughts are these? Why, they are worse than the marriage scenes.

What shall I do? Oh, what shall I do? Why can I not love the Lord John Butler as I ought? What is my lord doing; has he given up the suit, or do they conceal his applications from me?

I do not e'en seem to care, any more, whether he'd wed me for my fortune or the King's pleasure. And if I take not greater heed of my thoughts, soon I'll not care whether he wed me at all, so long's he'll be kind enough to debauch me.

What shall I do? Oh, dear God, help me.

5

'I Take Thee At Thy Word'
Early May, 1665

Romeo: I take thee at thy word.
> —William Shakespeare, *Romeo and Juliet*

Mayday – and time to lie beneath a cedar in the mist, make plaits of jonquils and white hawthorns to put in my hair. Time for me and thee, on a blue-grey morning, to awake with the dew that trembles on the rose and chase each other through the steep lowland meadows, dotted with daisies and daffodils. Time of emerald-carpeted fields; of jewelled butterflies, beating their wings on the currents that race across the lightening sky. Time to read John Donne, who heightens reason with passion:

> But oh, alas, so long, so far
> Our bodies why do we forebear?
> They're ours, though they're not we, we are
> The intelligences, they the sphere.

So guilty are my reflections, I jump when Nan appears in my doorway. Grinning, she parades hither, bobs a curtsey, and places a sealed paper in my hands.

'This was sent you, madam, by a man in livery. He's been waiting in the street ever so long and would put it in no hands but mine.'

My heart thuds as she bobs again and withdraws.

'For Mrs Mallet', reads the bold superscription, each M standing huge and curvy with circled tails, the other characters angular and crowded. The seal's red wax, stamped with a little lion rearing up, front claws extended.

Afear'd to open the note, lest it not be what I hope for, I linger. Then, unable to bear the suspense, I rip the ends from the wax and read, 'My Lady.'

'My lady!' How thrilling that salutation with the big bold 'M' – ah, what might be implied, in his beginning thus instead of 'Madam'? (For 'tis he; I've already scanned the name, so's I can fetch breath again.)

My Lady,
    I have applied these weeks to your guardians without success. Now I apply to you. Would you find it in heart to meet me somewhere, where we may be private and discuss our future and our fate? There's a sycamore grove in St. James Park, just beyond the artificial lake. If you can coax your mama thither, at three of the clock today, there you will find
    Your Most Eager and Humble Servant,
    Rochester

Oh, what dissembling must I do, then, to shake Mama!

There's nothing but to exhaust her: so I begin early, about one of the clock: 'Come, Mama, let us go' – and as soon as we arrive at the park, I go a-running and a-playing, feeding the ducks and chasing the peacocks and butterflies till I truly exhaust myself, too, as tight as my busk is laced. And all the while, she makes a shift to follow me, as a good mama ought; but as she huffs from the artificial lake to the mulberry grove, from the gravelled walkway of the Mall to the red brick wall of the palace, I always bouncing before her like a will-o'-the-wisp, she pants and marvels at my unwonted exertion: 'Lord, Betty, where do your spirits come from?'

Then, as she commences to pant and sweat, and I give her not leave enow e'en to pause and fan herself, but gambol now across the green like a wicked and frolicsome lamb, she pleads, traipsing behind, her skirts held above the mud, 'Betty, let's go home.'

'Oh, Mama! Let me walk about a bit; 'tis so *beautiful* here!' So forth I frolic, running and plucking up flowers, the yellow silk gown whipping behind me and yellow ribbons trailing from my Mayday garland of white sprigs and daisies, my white-gloved hands holding up skirts.

As I bend o'er a patch of lavender wildflowers, I discreetly pull out my hanging pocket and check the gold watch on a chain. The dial tells three of the clock.

Mama staggers toward me, her breast heaving and hairs straggling all about her sweaty brow. 'Betty, let's go now.'

'Oh, Mama! There's the loveliest wood – I'm going just for a short walk. Will you come along?'

'No, no. But mind you be back soon.' She fixes me in a baleful glare. 'Mind, now.'

'Yes, Mama.'

She gives me a dubious look. 'And as soon as I catch my breath –'

But already I'm gone. I bounce away to the copse of trees that I hope for the Lord's sake will be the sycamores of which he spoke. And I step into a cool and shadowed world where birds twitter and bees hum.

A wood lark darts with a 'dwiedelee' through the twisted branches, and Herb Paris carpets the ground in green leaves and mustard flowers. Columbines, called into bloom by the unseasonable heat, grow in patches amid violets; gnats buzz in silken clouds where primroses scent the chequered shade.

I stride about a few moments, my little satin shoes hurting and making the twigs below 'em crackle. He's not coming, I think. This is not the grove of which he spoke. No, 'tis the grove – but so large, he'll never find me.

All at once I feel someone close behind me. My heart thunders in the quiet of the glade; I am certain he must hear it, especially since I have stopped breathing.

I feel a soft breath ruffle the loose hairs on my head and smell the hint of a delicious floral essence. A sweet, low voice behind me utters, close to my ear, a verse from Waller:

'To welcome her the spring breathes forth

Elysian sweets, March strews the earth

With violets and posies.'

I turn slowly about; and there, of course, is my lord. He looks on me with such passion and intimacy, I know not how to maintain a proper distance. Then suddenly I think how bold 'tis to meet him without attendance, and I feel a blush creep up my face.

I turn away, to hide my bashfulness and confusion; and all at once, he takes my hand and draws me closer.

He finishes the verse.

'The sun renews his darting fires,

April puts on her best attires,

And May her crown of roses.'

If I felt faint before, this is enough to make me swoon almost, to feel him touch me at last. Though still looking away, I'm giddy, confused; the warmth of his hand both comforts and thrills. I wonder if I should get my hand back. How much can I grant and still retain his respect?

Then I look up into those lash-ringed eyes and see that same passionate, compelling look. I know how much my face must be revealing now, but I cannot help myself; he still clasps my hand – now he raises it a moment to his lips. A tremor runs through my body. I long to throw myself into his arms, and I can tell, by his face, he fain would fly at me likewise.

'La,' I say in a small voice, 'why, here's a lover come to ambush me in the park!'

He grins as he kisses my fingers one by one. 'You're surprised, I know. You women always pretend to be surprised when you invite us forth to what you pretend to be surprised at.'

My sally has cut the cloud of passion – but not much. I speak lightly, try to ignore the tingling in my fingers. ''Twas your invitation this time. What have you to say to me?'

He turns my hand palm up and kisses tenderly – first with soft caressing lips, then with the tip of his tongue, swirling. I shudder; somehow I think, when the rule was invented that hand-kissing was not so dangerous, no one had thought to do such indecent hand-kissing as this. How grateful I am that we are outside, more or less in the public view; for my will gets weaker by the moment.

He murmurs, looking up from my hand to fix my eyes with his, 'Only something that can be said a little deeper in the woods.'

A warning bell goes off in my mind here, but I'm too faint with desire and hope to do much about it.

'Very well –' I toss my curls '– but not too far, lest my mama descend upon us like a pack of furies.'

He lets go the hand and grins. 'If she descends upon us at all, 'twill be that way. Better she have farther to go to find us.'

Indeed he has plucked an apt fruit there. No doubt she already fidgets.

We tramp farther along the path, I holding up yellow skirts and he supporting my elbow with a warm hand. E'en this light touch makes the blood course to all the wrong parts of me, so I consider how to feign tripping and fall against him, then scold myself for such wicked thoughts.

As the leaf canopy above us thickens, we walk on a carpet of wood avens mixed with red campion, the small yellow flowers meeting the bright pinkish blooms in patches of love children that reveal everywhere their mixed parentage: yellow long bells, small red ones, tiny livid flowers, large dark ones: all unashamed, in nature's way, to show the delight they've had in mingling.

A doe bounds across our path, her fawn behind. Through the array of brown trunks fading in the distance, I glimpse a brace of pheasants stalking, the brown-breasted female with her little ones and the proud gold-breasted lord of the brood.

We halt at the bank of a plashy pond. Before us a chorus of ducks honks from the lake – the meek wives brown and soft but the proud husbands brightly suited – and all sailing along, necks pumping; or tottering as if on tiptoes to flutter their wings above the flood.

We stand facing one another on the bank. I look up at him keenly.

'Now, my lord. What is it you have to say to me?'

'Only this. Your guardians will not have me. Will you?'

I look down, blushing, in confusion. 'My lord, I – I scarce know what to say.'

'Come, no ladylike airs. This is serious, and I know you're more sensible at bottom. No coquette's airs, no court stuff. Tell me. Tell me true.'

His tone is sombre; his speech, plain. That barrier betwixt us has collapsed, that man-woman division that makes us peep o'er the siege walls and shoot the fashionable cant at one another i' th' infected air of the town.

'My lord,' I say, and look straight up into his eyes, 'I will have you, despite all they can do, despite any contract they may make – and, may God help me – despite all reason and duty.'

He reaches out and takes my hand.

'What do you do?' I ask in a very small voice.

'Seal the contract.'

He leans down.

I close my eyes and tilt up my lips in a rapture of expectation.

This is all the hint he needs. He drops my hand and gathers me into his arms. I feel I've fallen into an ocean of the sweetest imaginable sensation: I know not which is better, the smell or feel of him. I bury my head into his warm breast and utter a low cry. How have my arms got about his waist? For all my other bones are gone, and my will with 'em: I feel as limp as an eel in a pickle.

It seems the earth stands still, trembling on some verge; for every voice in the forest is suddenly stilled: even the ducks with a loud quacking have fluttered away, and the gnats have scattered, to leave us alone in the golden heat.

His hand moves to my chin to lift it. I feel his warm breath draw near my lips, and I lean forward. The sensation of almost but not quite touching down there makes me tingly-warm and wet.

All at once there's a crashing and crunching of the underbrush – then a terrible shriek.

We start and jump away, to see my mother charging at us from a thicket, like a crazed bear. Oh, to be so close to Paradise and have it snatched away! His lips were but the merest breath from mine.

'Lord Rochester!'

He releases me and smiles on her. But no politeness will save his bones from this stew.

She bolts for me and seizes my arm, pulls me from his proximity as if he had the plague – and, only when I'm a decent arm's length from him, expels her breath and lets go my arm.

Then she glares on him and utters stiffly, 'Lord Rochester, you forget yourself.'

He smiles. 'Nay, madam: my self is what I do not forget. My self was behaving very naturally.'

Mother does not join me in laughing at so much delightful wit. She yanks me a little farther from him. In her eye is murder: I can tell she's seeing his head on a platter, though ne'er was there an unlikelier Salome and John the Baptist.

'Mother,' I cry, prying her clamped fingers loose from my arm, ''twas my fault as well as his!'

'Your fault, a fig!' she says crisply, letting me go again but keeping an eye cocked on him. 'An innocent girl, who's been attended all her life, cannot be expected to protect herself. But a gentleman takes it upon his honour to protect her.'

She puts an emphasis on the words *gentleman* and *honour* here – as if her adversary were getting two new words for his vocabulary. And all the while, she glares on him so, she could fright a fury.

He smiles a genteel, imperturbable smile as I defend him: 'We have done nothing wrong! He has behaved honourably to me.'

He adds, 'Only a little pleasantry, madam, and the chief part of it was conversation.'

'His hands were on you.'

She makes it sound so lewd. 'Oh, Mother, really!' I retort.

He smiles sweetly . 'They were a gentleman's honourable hands.'

He had better hold his peace. What good to stir her stew?

I try to pacify her with one of my little-girl melting smiles. 'We only hugged a little: why, you have done as much, Mother, with evil-smelling old men of a Christmas time, when they leave your open houses.'

She stands stiffer. 'Lord Rochester, we shall bid you farewell now. I hope that if we meet again, I shall have no cause to deplore your carriage.'

If! What a doleful sound's there!

'I hope so too, madam, on both counts,' he replies genteelly. 'For I am as eager for meeting you again as I am for securing your good favour.'

Thank God he's got a grip on his temper, though I know not what good 'tis to put out the fine silver when the meat's rotten.

He turns on her that devastating smile and oozes friendliness, so she grimaces in return and pulls me off.

Now could I wish, for the first time in my life, I were in trouble, to draw some of the blame off him. She lays it on him as if he were a brick to be mortared.

Back at our lodgings, Grandpa makes shift to listen at first, then begs her to have done, from being so sick of the business.

'Egad, now, Unton. I've heard nothing so very profligate.'

'Nothing so profligate? Had I not timely come upon 'em, he would have kissed her!'

No thanks to you, Mother.

'Young folks have been kissing since time began, and nobody's going to get them to leave off, I think,' says Grandpa philosophically, with a rattle of his papers.

'All the more reason to guard her closer.'

Grandpa shrugs. 'As you please, Unton. You know I leave these matters to you.'

But Mama will not leave the matter to her; she worries it like a dog with a bone.

'I don't blame Betty. She has been very protected and enjoys her romantic dreams and her books, and these things go on with her Lancelots and Chretiens de Troyes. She has no earthly notion what trouble it can get her into in real life. She only thinks how nice it would be to be kissed. All girls her age do. This is why they must be guarded, for their protection.'

Grandpa nods but continues to peruse his papers. I think he has finally managed not to hear her: would he would tell *me* his secret.

'There's a deal of this indiscriminate kissing goes on at court,' says Mama with lips pursed, 'and you know where that gets everybody.'

'The King tried to kiss me once;' I say slyly.

'There!' cries Mama triumphantly. 'Didn't I tell you?'

Whilst we both wonder what it is she told us, she tells us again: 'Let a young girl loose, and she is everyone's prey. When was this, Betty?'

I know not I like the use she's made of this fish I threw her. I had hoped to draw her off my lord and onto another scent, but she takes it in mind instead to issue a general proclamation against my liberty.

But I say, 'At Tunbridge. He got me in a dark corner during the dancing.'

'Oh, Jesu! This, from the man who should set the realm an example! I dare swear his father is rolling in his grave and weeping in heaven.'

I let her make someone roll in his grave at the same time he weeps

41

in heaven, and that a dead man, too: for I still have hopes of drawing her off the scent.

'How behaved you, Betty, when he did thus?' she probes.

'I smiled my best smile and stepped under his arm and got away. 'Twas easy: he's very tall.'

'There, now, Unton!' says Grandpa, who seems to have heard this last. 'She can handle herself.'

Mother looks dubious. 'I saw no stepping under arms today, for all the tallness there was.'

'My Lord Rochester is younger than the King,' I point out frankly, 'and vastly more attractive.'

'Well,' says Mama grimly, 'at least no one can call her mercenary.'

'I wanted him to kiss me: I looked on him as much as to say so, too. 'Twere a blockhead wouldn't have got the point, and 'twere no gentleman to have ignored it. Why, it would have been an insult to me. I'm sure he was just going to give me a little kiss.'

'I wish I could be so sure,' she says grimly. 'As for you, you are altogether too sure for your own good. Your sureness is going to get you into big trouble.'

I pout. 'There are so many pretty gentlemen in town, and you keep me locked away from all of 'em.' (Is this not clever, to draw her off the scent?)

'Thank God for that. Father, you hear how she talks. Can we not close with someone, make an end and get her married? She's at an age now where she's all curious for the experience; and if we don't keep an eye out, she'll get it the wrong way.'

'So keep an eye out,' says Grandpa, turning to his papers again. 'That's what you're here for. That's the first duty of mothers. My duty is to get her the best match, not hurry her to the altar.'

'Well, no one can accuse me of shirking my duty, I hope,' begins Mother.

'I think you do it all too well,' I inform her. 'I could have done without your Eye-Out today.'

'And had your hands full in two minutes flat with that young rake, as willing as he saw you were! He looks the type that knows how to make use of an advantage.'

'What could he have done in the park?'

'What, indeed. By that question you prove my point about your innocence.'

'Mother! In the *park*?' I shriek. She must believe us rutting rabbits.

She stalks o'er to Grandpa's chair and places imperial hands on her hips. 'Mark my words. If we linger in town, we'll have no end of trouble. I say we stay to receive the Lord John Butler, then be gone.'

6

'The Valiant Paris'
Sometime the second week in May, 1665

Lady Capulet: Well, think of marriage now.
The valiant Paris seeks you for his love.
Nurse: A man, young lady! Lady, such a man
As all the world – why, he's a man of wax.
Lady Capulet: Verona's summer hath not such a flower.
—William Shakespeare, *Romeo and Juliet*

'Betty, Betty!' cries Mama in a passion. 'You have a visitor; make ready your hair and your gown.

At the word *visitor*, my heart leaps to my throat. But, no. That word, though it mean hope to me, sure would not mean such happiness to her, if it meant what I hoped for.

I look up, lips parted, eyes round o'er my book, where Guinevere agonizes whether she shall abjure duty and yield to Lancelot.

Mama nods happily. 'Yes, dear. The Lord John Butler.'

Oh, Jesus. I am not up to this interview; truly I'm not.

But how can I refuse? This fine and amiable gentleman has come all the way from Ireland to see me.

Ah, what in the name of God can I say? This is one of the last men on earth I'd hurt. And then there'll be Mama and Grandpa, too, sniffing out each twist in the speech and looking for a Rochester at the end of it.

But, sure, the Lord Butler cannot love me. He has always been restrained, never offering any intimacies, never speaking of burnings or heartthrobs, but always carrying himself like a well-bred friend. Why, if he loved me, he'd never have been willing to part from me with a smile and then wait eleven months for his parents to arrange his brother Arran's marriage before he called on me again. He would have been so on fire, he had been in Somerset by last August, not waiting till I should come to town and he should be there, too, and all his older brothers be wed beside. Ah! – I know somewhat of love, now:

44

'tis not the calm agreement of humours of which Mama spoke. Every day without the lover is slow torture.

So why is the Lord Butler here? Well, 'tis time for him to marry; he recalled our conversations, no doubt, and would have a wife who reads and thinks. And he's too much the man of honour to let the grandfatherly supplications settle my fate. He would hear my consent from my own lips.

Ah! – but that's one thing only another John will hear, and am I not promised to him now?

The knowledge of that promise strengthens me, but still I'm miserable as I lift up pink skirts to follow Mama into the sitting room, her skinny back before me like the standard that precedes Cleopatra to Antony or the Maypole that announces the dance.

Grandpa is plunked into his usual chair, like a raisin in its dough. Standing, looking out the window, is a tall figure with a broad back and shoulders: his height about my John's but his person filled out and sturdy rather than willowy: his waist and thighs thicker, solid – his being of earth rather than fire and air. He wears powder-blue velvets draped with a red-and-white sash and holds a red-plumed blue hat.

Yes, 'tis he: quiet but tasteful dress, fair periwig to his shoulders.

He looks about and smiles, his clear blue eyes lighting up with pleasure. 'Mrs Mallet.'

I curtsey, skirts spread, head down. 'My lord.'

'Come, not so formal,' he says gently.

He strides across the room, upraises me by touching his fingertips to mine. Mother trembles with excitement like an infant on the eve of its name-day. This is going to be dreadful.

I wonder how to get my fingers from his damp ones, but he releases me as soon as I rise. I keep my eyes on the floor, though, for I begin to be afear'd what his expression will tell me.

There's an uncomfortable pause. At last Grandpa says in exasperation, 'Well, lad, speak! You came to speak, adod, so do it!'

Poor Lord John.

'Mrs Mallet,' he says softly, hesitatingly, 'I – that is – you know why I have come?'

Eyes still cast down, I murmur, 'Yes, my lord.'

Another silence falls. Poor Lord John. I wish I could help him out. We all wish we could help him out; I can see my mother straining forward, her needle nose pointing the way, her lips yearning to mouth the words for him. Grandpa looks vexed and pronounces several 'harrumphs' of disgust.

'Mrs Mallet – I – that is, come in my own person – to ask – if you could like my father's suit?'

Eyes still cast down, I murmur as if in ladylike abashment, 'My lord, I scarce know what to say.' This is a dreadful thing to do to him, but indeed I know not how else to retreat whilst still keeping cover.

Another silence falls. Not for this gentleman to chide and push a lady, 'Come, no coquette's airs.' He will yield the lady what subterfuge she wishes, no matter how uncomfortable it makes him.

At last he says desperately, 'Lady Warre – Lord Hawley – may she not speak with me privily?'

Grandpa throws up his hands in disgust. 'Speaking! Speaking! Speak where you will, adod, but do it, lad!'

'Father,' says Mama severely. Then she beams on the Lord John, extends her hands: which he, smiling, grasps. 'Of course, Lord John. My father and I'll leave you here. You call us when you'd have us return.'

What a change of humour's here! Mama leaving me alone with a man.

She squeezes his hands. 'We won't listen,' she promises.

Then she lets him go and picks up skirts. 'Come on, Father. I said, Come on. Do you want this business settled or no?'

He grunts, heaves himself from the comforting arms of the chair, and waddles off behind her. Lord John expels a breath as they disappear.

'There, now,' he says softly. 'Not afear'd of me, I hope.'

I shake my head, miserably. I study the floor as if 'twere painted with the most absorbing fresco.

'Then –' He pauses. 'Mrs Mallet, I hope I have not presumed – that is, your carriage last June, and that of your mother, gave me cause to hope –' He stops, miserably, and I could swear he says to himself, *Oh, damn.*

I decide I *must* help him out a little. I look up keenly into that refined face with the planes and angles, into those frank and troubled blue eyes ringed with the gold lashes.

'Lord Butler, I am not being fair to you. But I'd have you know that I have always thought you a most gallant and worthy gentleman. You are the only – that is, almost the only – suitor that has considered my feelings as well as my grandpa's.'

Now he has got *me* saying 'that is'.

He looks down on me, his thin lips pinched together. The eagerness I first saw in his face is gone.

'You praise me too coolly to love me.'

I look down unhappily. 'I have tried – I had thought – Mother has always said, love comes after marriage.'

'And now you doubt that?'

'I – I think it may be true for some.'

'But you fear you cannot love me? Is it something I have said, or done –'

'No! – Oh, Lord Butler – how can I say this? – It is nothing to do with you. I – I – have an affection for another.'

At this last I look up to see how he takes it, but now he is looking down, watching the broad hands that play with a white tassel on his sash.

'I see.'

Another silence falls. There are more interludes than lines to this wretched play.

At last he looks up again, his handsome square face thoughtful. 'Do your guardians know this?'

'No! – Well, sometimes I wonder whether they might not suspect.'

'But you have not told 'em?'

'No! – He's their aversion.'

'So what will you do?'

I bite my lips, the tears starting in my eyes. 'I wish I knew.'

'May I be of assistance in some way?'

I gawk at him. 'You would help your rival?'

'I would help someone you love.'

Now the flood flows in earnest. 'My lord, you're too noble for me by half!' I hug my sides and weep.

He pulls a handkerchief from a fob, presses the little square of laced linen into my hand.

'Don't talk nonsense. May I ask who he is?'

I wipe my eyes and lower my voice to a whisper. 'Lord Rochester.'

'I see,' he utters gravely again, and I can't say I like the way he says it, nor what I imagine he must be seeing.

'He loves me too!' I cry, defensively. Then all at once I realize I never heard him say so, and I wonder if the realization is writ on my face.

'And he has promised to marry you?'

'Yes! – Well, in a way he has.' Jesus, my case is sounding lamer by the minute. 'Well, he has! He's asked if I'd have him, and I said yes.'

'I see.'

Why will he say nothing else? Because he's too much the gentleman to say what it is he thinks he sees.

His eyes narrowed, he says in serious tones, 'Mrs Mallet, I repeat my offer of protection and assistance.'

'What can you do?'

He looks on me and says nothing. But his voice in my head says, *Fight that bastard if he ruins and abandons you.*

In even tones he says aloud, 'I have no idea. But there may come a day when you need a friend. Pray consider me one.'

I sniffle. 'I do. Lord Butler, indeed.'

'I will tell your guardians my suit is withdrawn.'

'But how will you explain –'

'I won't. Or if I must, I'll simply say we couldn't agree.'

'That won't satisfy 'em!'

'Probably not. Have you a better idea?'

'No.'

Another silence falls. In a voice that struggles to maintain calm, he says, as if casually, 'Of course , my suit will remain open to *you.* You will let me know if your affections change?'

I nod. 'Yes, of course.' But I pray he doesn't wait for that event: 'twill be like standing on Tower Hill to await the Second Coming.

We agree he should slip out, leaving me to make his farewells and face the explosion alone. And explosion 'tis, indeed.

'Mama,' I cry, 'you can come out. 'He's gone.'

She scurries in, eager but bewildered. 'Gone? Why? Where?'

'We thought it better. He sends his regards, but he withdraws his suit.'

She sinks down, puzzled and unhappy, into a chair. 'He what?'

'Withdraws his suit. And send his regards.'

'But *why?*' I assume she means the suit rather than the regards, which she has got before.

'He said to tell you we could not agree.'

'But I thought 'twas all settled!' All at once she looks on me accusingly. 'What did you say to him?'

I regard the interesting floor again. 'Mother, I cannot say. We had our conversation apart for a reason.'

'Was he coming to break off his father's suit? Was that why he spoke in his own person, privily?'

'I cannot say, Mother, except to urge you not to think ill of him, for I found him to be most noble.'

'Has he engagements with another woman?'

'Mother, I pray you.'

The old unfriendly silence creeps in again. Indeed it has found a most hospitable lodging here today.

'Well, I don't like this,' she says at last, in dire tones.

'I know, Mother. I grieve for it.'

Silence says his piece again.

'Has it anything to do with that foul fiend, Rochester?'

I wince and flush and dare not, for the life of me, look up. 'Why, no, Mother,' I lie. Then I feel like throwing myself from the window and begging a carter to run o'er me, for I've never lied to her before. Sure I cannot be making a very good job of it. I wonder what she reads in my quavering tone and blush.

'Well, you're a little fool if it does! I hope to God you've not turned down the finest match in the land! Or – I just hope you end up with that Hinchingbrooke instead; that'd serve you right.'

I look down, say nothing.

'Well, you haven't heard the end of this! You may not talk, but you can wager I'll be writing to the Duchess of Ormond!'

7

'That Same Villain, Romeo'
Mid-May, 1665

Juliet: What villain, madam?
Lady Capulet: That same villain, Romeo.
— William Shakespeare, *Romeo and Juliet*

Lady Woodville. He's the prince of all the devils in the town.
— George Etherege, *The Man of Mode* (the heroine's mama raving about the hero, modelled after Rochester)

I must begin to wonder why everyone else about me has a different opinion of the Lord Rochester from mine.

I could dismiss Mama's ravings and vapourings, her renaming him 'the foul fiend', screaming how he hunts my fortune till the cows two blocks hence in Smithfield Market lay back their ears. I could dismiss perhaps Grandpa's dislike of a suitor that courts not like Jove, in a shower of gold.

But I was given pause to see the dismay on the Lord John Butler's face when I named the man I loved. 'I see,' he kept saying. Oh! what a world of doubts hid behind that. 'I see' – that sombre tone, those dubious eyes.

I could tell myself the Lord John was determined to disparage a rival – that he was slyly bent on making me have the thoughts I'm not having. Only the Lord John's not a dissembler. What's worse, I could feel his thoughts – especially, *Fight that bastard if he ruins and abandons you.* The Lord John thinks not e'en so much of my lord as Mama does. At least she believes 'the foul fiend' would wed me, if only for my fortune: the Lord John, who visits the court and has all the right to know my lord better, apparently sees not e'en a church at the end of the deception.

What was the 'protection and assistance' he offered me? Perhaps even a hint that he would have me, ruin't or no? 'My offer remains open to *you*,' he said, with a straight look, an emphasis, that added, *No matter what.*

I fear this means the Lord John loves me. But how could I have recognized such a love? 'Tis of a different species from mine – so rarefied. It appears he will sacrifice all for me, even what he wishes most: myself. And I know not how to deal with this sort of devotion: I know I don't deserve it. And I feel sad, really sad, that I can't love him; for my guardians would be happy, and all my problems would be over.

But, no. In my depths I cannot wish to love anyone but my lord. For loving him is woven into my pattern, part of my soul.

But, oh! What I feel and what is! What's the difference there? For I feel my lord's devotion when in his presence, when gazing into those eyes so full of tenderness and intimacy.

Oh, but when I'm away from him – then the doubts begin. And I set that feeling – which cannot be weighed nor measured – against all the opinions of everyone else I know, and against – I admit it – the arguments of my reason – and it seems a feeling is not very much to hold up the balance.

I know how I look – indeed, will always look – to everyone else. They believe me deluded. So who's to say they're not i' th' right? I would be the last to know if I were.

And then the other possibility I don't think anybody but me has considered. The possibility that this is all a scheme of the King to get me to court: that he is the engine, the *Primum Mobile*, advising my lord, pushing him on, to marry this woman His Majesty has a mind to, bring her to court, the wife of a favourite and dependent – and all the better that the wife be so in love with the husband that she would do what he would ask of her.

Oh, now, let me think on that! What agony should I go through, so deep in love with such a husband, if he should require such a sacrifice of honour of me?

Oh God, which would be worse? A marriage like that – in which he shows his contempt for me, spends my fortune, gives me orders to bed with the King, runs after whores? Or simply being ruin't by him and cast off, then creeping shame-faced to the Lord John Butler? Or watching the Lord John fight the Lord Rochester and get killed in a duel? – For my lord is, I have heard, a very devil with a sword as he is with a woman.

Oh, what a mess this all is! And I can see no end of it!

Especially now that Mother's become so chary of letting me out.

I've not been suffered to visit the Spring Garden, for strolling and buying of cheesecakes; nor the New Exchange in the Strand, for buying of scents and ribbons. I'm banned from London Bridge, with the shops and Nonesuch House and the watermen shooting the rapids; I've barely e'en seen the Tower. I've been sequestered from court – from suppers, card-parties, promenades on the Mall in St James Park, rides about the Hyde Park ring, visits to the Queen's Presence Chamber. I've not e'en enjoyed a ragout at Locket's or a dish of coffee at Wills. ('Will's!' Mother rolls eyes heavenward. 'Oh, Lord, that's in Covent Garden, where the rottenest beaux of the town live.') And when I ask to go to the playhouse – just once – 'Where women are suffered to act and show their legs? And decent folk daren't sit except in boxes, for the brawls and traffic in lewdness? Oh, Lord, no!'

And she raves to Grandpa, 'It's enough for me! I have done with it! If she wants to go anywhere else, *you'll* be taking her. I've done with being the goat, the pigeon, the bubble! I'll not tote her about any more to these too-coincidental meetings with that penniless rake.'

I suppose I should be grateful I have not the sort of guardians some girls do. Were I in some other household, I'd be put to bread and water or the birch till I persuaded the Lord John I were willing. All I've suffered is a closer confinement – but, indeed, that's as much to keep my lord from me as to punish me. For, says my mama:

'That devil pops up everywhere, like Punch behind the curtains at Judy! You never know where he's going to be next. For all we know, he may lurk in the streets waiting for us to advance outward. For all we know, he may have a gang of cutthroats waiting to seize her.'

'Oh, Mother!' I cry.

'Now, Unton,' says Grandpa, 'give him credit for some sense, after all. Abducting an heiress is a capital crime.'

'Well, I wouldn't put it past him! I wouldn't put anything past him. He's a devil, and if Betty had any sense, she'd know it.'

Grandpa takes no part in these outbursts. His brain is too full of guineas to hold any other thought. All he'll say about the business – and that, when pressed by Mama – is:

'Well, well, well. We'll see what the Duke and Duchess of Ormond have to say. Now, Unton – we'll see what Lord and Lady Sandwich have to say. The business is not over yet. Who knows but that we may find a better? Calm thyself, daughter. So 'tis possible she has a fancy for a penniless young charmer. What's that? Girlish fancies pass. This one will, too, when she sees it gets her nowhere. We could have used some more time to pump up our business, anyway. In the end, the Duke's man may offer even higher.'

Mother curls her lip in disgust and huffs from the room.

Oh, 'tis a misery now not to be the bauble, the jewel, the pet of the household, but instead the pariah, the dog! So wroth is Mama, she leaves off no occasion to twist the knife of guilt in me: to refer obliquely to disobedience, to foolishness – to launch into orations on the villainy of my lord till I feel my whole mind is a wound and cannot begin to staunch the many places it bleeds.

Oh! 'Tis like living in the centre of a coal burner's hut, with all the black clouds that hang in the air. Then in the midst of all this fret and fury, an invitation from Frances Stewart comes, to a supper at Whitehall Palace.

'Well,' says Mama, 'I don't think we should go. 'Twill be just another time when that Rochester will come about us. Why, the palace is his haunts! That's where he hangs about and does his deviltry.'

I'm finally out of patience, listening to her. 'Oh, Mama! You make him appear a djinn or a devil that haunts about and goes poofing at the last minute.'

'Well, all I can say is, the way he appears on the spot every time we exit this place, 'twere a miracle to me. I'd say, he knows black magic; I'd say, he has the Devil at his elbow.'

'Mama, I told you and told you, 'twas not the Devil, 'twas I! Each time we met him, I had writ to draw him forth. And still you persist in blaming him for what I did.'

She gives me a look that lets me know she suspects a lie; but, 'deed, I only lie about the last time.

'Adod now,' says Grandpa, puzzling o'er the invitation, 'I think we should keep up our court contacts, Unton.'

'Well, *I'm* not escorting her to the very bowels of that devil's haunt, you can be sure of that! And she's certainly not going alone. And as far as this town business of a young girl being allowed forth with just a maid to escort her – why, that Nan would be no protection at all. So as far as I'm concerned, she's not going.'

Grandpa keeps staring at the letter. 'Adod now, Unton. Such an invitation from the King's favourite is not to be sneezed at. Who knows but that this may be a way to a better business?'

'Well, then, *you* go with her! For I'm sure *I'm* not going into that devil's very den! I've had enough of your courtiers; you cannot get me back to Somerset fast enough.'

Grandpa looks on me. 'What say you, little hussy, eh? Would you go to supper?'

I shrug. For indeed I care not. I've got so jumpy, any outing would be a treat; but to listen all evening to Frances, who has not two wits to rub together – ah! – that would be like paying out all one's silver to see a wretched play.

'So? You have a mind to go or don't you, little hussy?'

'I don't care, Grandpa.'

''Tis done then. There, now, daughter. Have no worry: I'll convey her there and back; and you may be sure, if that Rochester makes his appearance, I'll draw her forth promptly.'

'Well,' says Mother, 'you don't know him as I do, Father. You haven't been thrown together with him as I have. If you ask me, this smells like something he's cooked up.'

'Oh, Mother!' I exclaim. 'Really, now. Next you will have him down in hell-pit, directing the business of the town.'

'Well, I wouldn't put anything past him. And, Father, if you take my advice, you'll add a condition that the supper be just the three of you and the doors be locked up fast. For I don't like this one bit.'

8

'They Stumble That Run Fast'
26 May 1665

Friar Lawrence: They stumble that run fast.
— William Shakespeare, *Romeo and Juliet*

Frances' supper is cold, for her kitchen is far from her apartments in the Aviary Court; and by the time the fare is brought in, the fowl – whatever 'tis – lies greasy and congealed on the plate: as unpalatable as Frances' wit. And the wine's insipid, sickly sweet. Oh, how dull the conversation is! And, I think, Grandpa must ask himself what he ever hoped to gain, from sitting of an evening clapped up close with Frances, listening to her inanities, her chitter-chatter clump-wits.

I've already pumped her of everything she knew about my lord. And at any rate, e'en if she were to know some new scrap of intelligence, I dare not pump her in front of Grandpa, so suspicious has the household grown.

But 'tis as if I can't go the whole evening without hearing his name spoke. For I wish perhaps to hear the dear word out loud: 'Rochester.' Or to tingle inside from the dangerous delight of speaking that word when I know 'tis an evil to Grandpa and peril to me. So I bring him up backwards: I back in hind first, like a crab waving claws.

'Well, Frances, 'twere a marvel we're here at all, so resty was Mama o'er the thought of letting me near "Rochester's haunts", as she calls 'em.'

Frances turns on me those cow-eyes and blinks, as she often does to fill up the gap in talk while she tries to think. 'Tis oft a surprise to me that Frances speaks, so like a toy is she: round and white and soft, her yellow ringlets bobbing at contrived angles like springs, her blue eyes blank in a chinless face, her head stuffed with horsehair.

'Oh, 'deed, Elizabeth! Why, he said he would not be here.'

As casually as possible, I pump, 'Well, when was this, Frances?'

'Why, when we talked of setting up the supper.'

Oh, ye gods. Mama was i' th' right. I dart a glance at Grandpa.

He looks grim. 'Adod now, little lady. You mean to tell me us – this supper was the Lord Rochester's idea?'

Frances looks blank-eyed upon him. 'Why, la, yes, 'twas, now I think on it.' Now she thinks on it. What a difficulty were there.

She sits, blinks, leans o'er the table, the better to display her double-puffed advantages. 'Why, I think he – he did not set it up, actually. He simply said, what sport 'twould be, Elizabeth, if you and I were to sup together. And. Let me think.' That were a difficult enough business to keep us here the rest of the evening. 'Ah – he said that you were locked up so – let me see. 'Twere mere friendliness and charity, someone could issue an invitation to give you a little pleasantry, that's all. That – for all he could do, he could not manage it, neither in his person nor that of any of his friends. So – as one who had a care for your well-being – ah! Now I think on it, he did not actually set it up; he phrased all this, so I made the offer myself.'

Grandpa looks more dubious by the minute.

'Grandpa,' I break in, 'he's not here, anyway! Perhaps he was just speaking from common charity.'

Frances blinks her blank eyes. 'Why, la, yes. He was that concerned, Elizabeth, and bade me be sure to tell him when I'd set it up.'

Grandpa trains a black look on me.

I cry, 'Don't look on me so, Grandpa! He's done nothing; I've done nothing. Why must you be like Mother and persist in thinking he's a djinn that can poof out of any corner cabinet?'

'Well,' says Grandpa in his role of Eye-Out, 'perhaps we should be gone. And if we should meet him, little hussy, mind you don't tell your mama.'

I look round-eyed on him. 'Grandpa! Think you I'd be so stupid?'

We then issue our thanks to Frances for her wretched meal and conversation. And her little blackamoor unlocks the door for us that we may leave.

And stepping out in the Aviary Garden where the birds are stilled in the midnight air, we see the fog roll in.

It covers everything – a grey veil, a cold white hand, clammy against my skin. It rolls in off the river, chill as the breath of Satan, black with soot and the smell of evil.

'Grandpa,' I cry, 'I'm afear'd.'

'Nonsense, nonsense,' he huffs. 'Come on, now, little hussy.'

But he takes my arm 'twixt his two fingers almost hard enough to hurt – shepherds me forth, back to where the hackney waits.

The fog is so thick we can scarce see two paces ahead. As we climb into the coach again, Grandpa expels a breath.

The coach starts up – past the palaces on the Strand and towards Charing Cross. Snatches of song drift from nowhere, out of the grey haze of soot and river mist: disembodied voices call to one another on hidden paves. Now and again a ghostly clip-clop rings, distorted; or the long, rolling grunt of a frighted mare, urged forward in the thickness – her wild head, white eye, and tossing mane suddenly at my coach window, causing me to draw in an arm. Then, just as suddenly, the greyness closes about her. The drifting clouds, like smoke from an enchanter's basin, dissolve her to a nicker and a clatter, into that smoky abyss where all the bodies of the world seem buried.

Unseen we ride, though in the heart of Westminster, with revellers and strollers, taverns, cook-shops and palaces all about.

The low brick wall of Whitehall Palace emerges and vanishes on either side King Street. The elven smoke now parts, to disclose the sign of the Rose tavern; then closes again about the towers of Wallingford House, where the Duke of Buckingham lives.

We jog past the intersection of Pall Mall and Charing Cross. I pull my cloak about me to close out the grey phantoms and listen to the doves coo-coo-rooing from the countless eaves.

The bells of St Martin-in-the-Fields ring midnight.

All at once I feel our coach slowing.

'Make way, ho!' The boy that lights us waves his link. In the gloom ahead it dances like a yellow will-o'-the-wisp empowered suddenly with speech.

Our coach bounces to a halt, swaying on its straps. I peer out into the haze. Muzzles and white eyes appear here and there; swords clink, and men's pale faces loom in and out.

There's a clang and clip-clop, a champing of bits. Another town-tangle of carters and coachmen, I think, all refusing to give way in the narrow streets.

Then suddenly as I lean across Grandpa's belly, to peer from the window on his side, I see a figure break from the mist – a huge black horse rolling its eyes, red nostrils flaring, mane tossing; and on its back, a tall figure, all in black, too: cape swirling about him, broad-brimmed hat on his head, little mask on his face.

'Grandpa, Grandpa!' I shriek. ''Tis a highwayman!'

With one hand the outlaw holds the horse's rein; with the other, he cocks a pistol toward the sky.

'Stand and deliver!' he cries.

'Oh, God, oh, God!' roars Grandpa. 'In the very heart of town!'

I am amazed myself, for I had thought they only dared watch the heath out of town.

I think of slipping my rings into my shoes – but everything happens too fast. The highwayman ambles his horse slowly, clippety-clop, over to our coach; and one of his men – a rough-looking villain, grinning with split yellow teeth – has a rapier thrust through the window and lightly touching Grandpa's paunch.

'One scream, m'lord, and it'll be your last.'

He pricks Grandpa's waistcoat, and the poor old goat paws his pockets, as if his life's humour were delivering instead of hoarding.

The highwayman leans down, grinning, cocks the pistol up against his hat, and says, in low, melodious tones:

'I have no wish to steal your gold, Lord Hawley: only your jewel.'

Grandpa leaves off his pawing to stare up blankly, Frances-like, as if wond'ring what this sally means. But, ah! My hand goes to my throat. For I've recognized the voice.

'It's the Lord Rochester!' I cry.

And then immediately I could bite my tongue off for the outburst. For perhaps I should not give him away.

My lord grins. And, transferring the reins to the hand that holds the pistol, he blithely rips off the mask.

'At your service, madam. It seems you've had a dearth of outings. So I've come to oblige you with one.'

Grandpa gapes like a carp beached.

My lord, however, has his usual command o'er his tongue. 'Help the lady from the coach.'

I am jarred when the door beside me opens. A man reaches in his hand to help me out; stunned, I put my hand in his and step down.

Grandpa then bellows, 'Adod now, little hussy. Stay here! Stay here!'

I stand, torn – my hand still in the grasp of the man that helped me. Should I obey my grandpa or go with my lord? What are my lord's intents?

That sweet voice floats from the other side of the coach. 'She has no choice, Lord Hawley. Remember, whatever happens, no blame is to be laid to her. I raped her away by force.'

Whatever happens! What a doleful sound's there!

'My lord,' I speak up, 'what does happen? What means all this?'

In the interim he must have swung down from the horse, for he strides about the back of the coach and extends his arm.

'Come, madam: only a pleasant outing, as I said.'

I know not what to reply. It seems to ask him if he carries me off to be married would be too forward. And to ask him if he plans to force me would be too disgusting a want of faith in him. And – sure, he cannot get my estate, wedded or no, without my guardians' consent to a contract.

Hesitantly I put my hand atop his arm, and with that warm tingle there, going from the connection of his arm and mine, I melt.

I look up at him in the moonlit mist, and he's so wicked and handsome, just like the highwaymen in romances: the irresistible rogues that steal purses from aldermen and kisses from young ladies.

And I know with a surety that our fates are linked, and I'd follow him into the grave.

I suffer him to lead me off, into the mist.

'My lord, where go we?'

'Only where we can converse and be private. For your guardians will not vouchsafe us so much as one word together.'

We come upon a coach he has waiting nearby. All of a sudden a dire thought strikes me. 'My lord! You've intercepted me by force, and you're carrying me off.'

He grins. ''Tis observant in you. We must show you at the next fair, for your intuitions and foresights.'

'No, my lord, you don't understand. I heard Grandpa say, there's a law against abducting heiresses. 'Tis a capital crime!'

He leaves off grinning then but makes no reply. By then we're upon the coach, where wait two ladies, by their plain dress looking to be servants: one a fair sweet child, t'other a red-faced Hercules that e'en Mama would deem an Eye-Out.

'These are Gill and Doll. They will attend you, so that you need not entertain any fears your mama may have put into your head about my honour.'

His voice sours when he names her; and I could laugh, to see how equally her affections are returned – save for my fears, which have settled into a clench at the throat and stomach.

'But, my lord!'

By now he's helped me into the coach. I lean out the window.

'Did you not hear me? This is a capital crime!'

Now he grins again. 'Well, all the more exciting. That's all the adventure wanted, to give a spice to it. I had feared the mischief would be deadly dull, so I dressed up to enliven it. But now I see it will have its own excitements.'

'My lord, you're dancing on the brink of danger!'

'What better brink to dance on, to stir one's blood? – Come, now: all will be well.'

He smiles, picks up my hand on the window edge, kisses the fingers softly as he gazes into my eyes.

All at once a lackey runs up, the big black horse in tow.

'My Lord, the King's Life Guards come.'

'Oh, ye gods!' I shriek.

Swooping onto the horse, my lord informs him, 'Take the back roads, all of you, and escort the lady. Cut over toward St Giles Fields and on to the Holborn. I'll draw 'em off along the Strand.'

'Help! Ho! Rape! Robbery!' shouts Grandpa.

'Stop in the name of the King,' a voice replies.

I lean out of the coach window, my heart pounding. I'd fain tell him I love him, but I only say, 'My lord: have a care.'

The moon breaks through the mist, highlighting him in a silver shaft. Then the coachman whips up the horses, and off we clatter, a footman with a link racing ahead in the narrow alley to cry, 'Make way! Make way!'

I lean out for a last glimpse of my lord. But the mist closes around him, and he is gone.

9

'She Yields'
26–28 May 1665

Sab: Lost
She yields, she yields! Pale envy said amen;
The first of women to the last of men.
Just so those frailer beings, angels, fell.
There's no midway, it seems, 'twixt heaven & hell.
Was it your end, in making her, to show
Things must be raised so high to fall so low?
Since her nor angels their own worth secures,
Look to it, gods! The next turn must be yours.
You who in careless scorn laughed at the ways
Of humble love, & called 'em rude essays,
Could you submit to let this heavy thing,
Artless & witless, no way meriting
　　　　　　　　　　　　—John Wilmot, Earl of Rochester

Our coach careens o'er the cobbles; dark buildings rush by the window, and Doll keeps thumping into my lap like a sack of melons.

'Law bless us, law bless us: oh, my lady, sorry!'

We wheel past the western side of Covent Garden at a gallop, behind three rows of houses, then up an alley, left, and on to St. Martin's again.

'Law bless us, I am shook to a jelly! Oh, my lady – sorry!'

St Giles Field rushes past; now the footman has dropped behind, to leave us in darkness; but the High Holborn is just ahead, then Tyburn Gibbet and the Oxford Road.

I bump and bounce till my head 'most hits the top of the coach. My hair, pinned up with little wreaths of baby's breath and tiny white trailing springs, straggles down in tendrils.

But I feel a strange passion of excitement. *He's taking me away with him! He's taking me away with him!* The ruts jar the words, beating in my brain; the wheels clatter on cobbles, the rhythm of the swaying coach-box beating out the refrain. *He does love me enough! He's taking me away.*

And, oh, the excitement of the open air, blowing through the window of the coach – against my burning cheeks and flying curls – the little flowers flying off my hair, one by one – the scenery speeding past, the whip cracking. Life has never seemed so full of passion!

Doll, who must feel in charge of my comfort, grabs off her laced cap and fans me: 'There, there, there: pretty little ladyship, poor little lambkin; 'tis a crying sin, that's what I call it, to put a lady through such a coil! There, there!'

'Doll,' I inquire at last, 'where go we?'

She grunts, claps cap to grey curls at a teeth-jolting jar. 'To his lordship's manor at Adderbury, my lady.'

I yearn to ask, *Are we to be married there?*, but to beg intelligence of a servant seems a lowering of degree.

The little green-eyed creature across from me smiles sweetly. 'We'll care for you, my lady, just see if we won't. All will be well.'

Anon our pace slows. The road becomes a nightmare: one sleepy village after another; and so thick the dust, it chokes me. Doll clucks, offers me refreshment from a flask, which I refuse as politely as possible, and from which she takes great swigs.

We gallop past Hounslow Heath and into Slough. There's a fresh team waiting up the road at Maidenhead; and as the hostler backs the horses betwixt shafts, I perceive the greyness of early dawn break upon the countryside.

The coachman does not use this team so hard. Looking repeatedly down the road yet seeing no pursuers, I begin to hope we've shaken off the King's Life Guards.

Anon, it being noon, we halt at an inn on Henley-at-Thames to have a bite to eat. 'Tis a pleasant black-and-white cot with a thatched roof and dark polished wood tables.

After I relieve the necessities of nature, Gill accompanies me to a back room and does what offices of a lady's maid she can – brushing the dust off my skirts with a hard, brisk motion; tucking in the wandering tendrils of my hair (though I've lost all the little flowers now); and holding before me a glass, that I may view myself and see what else she'd have me do.

I am a grimy, gritty mess, all over dust and hair flying a thousand ways. 'Jesu,' I groan as I catch sight of the frightful apparition in the glass, 'I begin to be glad he rides not with us.'

And she says, 'Now, mistress, we're not to hear that talk from you! For you're a real lady, anyone can see that, be there never so much dust – and a beautiful one, too: anyone can see why his lordship loves you as he does.'

She moistens a cloth in a basin and cleans my face and arms and hands but will suffer me to do no offices for myself.

'No, indeed, mistress! For his lordship gave me strict instructions, I was to be your maid.' And she seems proud with this charge laid upon her. I suppose it must be a promotion from the pantry or upper stairs; for all women in households yearn to be ladies' maids.

Doll has ordered a dinner for us – such as the house affords: brown ale and bread and cheese. 'Tis well for me: I love 'em all.

But my hollow stomach throbs so with excitement, I can scarce nourish it, for the thrill that my lord is carrying me off.

Surely 'tis to marry me! What else could he do with a highborn heiress? And, after all, I've a fortune to be won only in marriage; and if we wed not fast, there's the law he's broken by carrying me off. And did he not ask me if I'd have him?

But uneasiness creeps in here – as I recall he said, 'Only going to talk a bit, where we can be private.' Sure he did not mean so, though! All this, just for a talk? Sure he meant such a talk as the Lord John Butler wished with me: a renewal of the contract. And has not my attendance by these two ladies shown his good will to me?

I giggle to myself o'er the ale till I snort the bubbles up my nose: silly, giddy laughter that causes Doll to look puzzled on me, her brow furrowed and grey hair straggling from 'neath her cap. Gill just smiles her sweet, happy smile, and I titter the more, at being abducted by the foremost rake o' th' town and feeling not one jot of fear.

And then I laugh again, snorting up the more bubbles, when I think how Mama will rage – nay, how she rages already! And how I pity poor Grandpa when he returns home without the jewel, the bauble that was stolen by th' thief i' th' night. Oh, then, what recriminations will he hear! How the chamber will ring with 'I told you so!' Why, has't not been ringing so all night long? Oh, dear, poor Grandpa. How carefully he enjoined me, lest Mama find out my lord had planned the supper. And if he feared her wrath then, what must he be experiencing now?

'Deed I feel sorry for 'em both – but cannot but laugh. For Mama so little trusts my lord, probably she has seen me thrown down in some bed and ravished ten times over already. She must think her worst fears have sprung up to haunt her, as if she's wished 'em into truth by thinking on 'em so much.

Oh! Dear! And how they'll fuss that I haven't made a wealthy marriage. I wonder if they'll withhold my fortune; I wonder if my lord knows 'tis entailed on their consent.

My two travel companions stand at the long darkwood bar, Doll paying some silver out of a little purse she draws from her inexhaustible bosom.

'I like it not,' she mutters. ''Tis plenty of time, especially as long as we've dawdled here.'

Doll, silent, her coarse fair curls tight under the laced cap, her green eyes wide and small pink mouth opened a little, stands hands clasped before her brown skirt and one leg cocked back akimbo, so her tiny black shoe rests only on its toe, and a troubled frown creases her cupid face, from brow to downturned lips. She never speaks to the old despot but seems in awe of her. I, however, giggle to myself. 'Tis so like a grutchy old antiquity, like Doll, to utter blacknesses and believe the worst. To think that my lord could be catched by any stupid old guardsmen – why, 'tis too absurd. A hero, a wit, someone who can ride and think like he – why, of course he doubled back or took another road to cover his tracks!

'Come, my lady. If you're finished, 'tis time to go.' The commands of Doll, our journeymaster, startle me from my broodings o'er the breadcrumbs. As we leave, the ale-wife nods pleasantly and bobs a curtsey, hands clasped before her, and her husband-helper nods, smiling, whilst he polishes a clear glass.

We emerge from the coolness of the inn and into the glare of beating sunshine. I open my handkerchief and scatter crumbs for the little brown sparrows who hop about my feet, chirping. As the coachman assists me up the fold-down stairs, I feel how achy-tired I am. And soon, with the renewed swaying of the coach, I fall into a light slumber.

A rut in the road jars me awake. 'Lord. Where are we?' I ask. *The Chiltern Hills*, says Doll. Up a hill and down another, all of 'em green and sheep-dotted; past a red and green forest, then a thatched cottage, then another: all grey stone and brown and white wood; then the little inns, all alike, only the signs different: this one a rose and crown, t'other a bell, but all of grey stone with thatched roofs and horses and wagons drawn up outside.

I doze again on the way into Sandford-on-Thames, Doll and I leaning together and she snoring like an elephantine hornet. A bump jars me broad awake, my eyes crusty and raw, as in the coolness of night we pull into Oxford: clitter-clatter, on the narrow cobbles, around and around. Turning past the yellow brick buildings of the college and onto Cornmarket, bound for Banbury Road, we get into several tight squeezes, and some of our bone-weary men have much ado to hold in their tempers, to avert a quarrel with this muscling carter or that drunken student.

But at last we are out of Oxford and onto the road north.

I fall into a troubled sleep and am jolted awake to broad day. We are pulling into the village.

I love it at once – from the forest on the edge of town to the meadow on the opposite end. We wind past cots of grey-brown Cotswold stone with thatched roofs; and, around a bend, climbing upward, to a venerable churchyard, o'erhung with yew and low-drifting mist, where echo the cries of doves: 'Coooo-curoooo.' The fence all about it is in ruins; weeds choke the broken headstones, and a clock juts from the bell-tower.

'There's me mum's house, me lady,' cries Gill and points to a wretched hut no different from any other. So he recruited her from his village: why, I wonder, when women a-plenty seek employment in town?

I gaze upon her oval face and pink rosebud lips, then her neat slender person. Why, indeed. I lay my life he hires not his women for their strong backs and calloused hands.

We trot slowly down the High Street; then, turning at the end of it, the coachman seeming to know the way, we pass one thatched cot after another. Gill, proud to be seen in such refined company, leans out of the window and cries, 'Hey, Alfred!' 'Hey, Meg!'

Anon, up and down enough alleys and back roads to make me giddy, we come suddenly upon a honey-grey house set off by itself and enclosed by a red brick wall. On either side of the entrance are set two knob-topped brass newel posts, each a globular bottom o'er-topped by a knobbed triangle. And a lion – the beast of his seal – turns round to roar in a white plaster circle set below the newel posts and engraved, 'Nadie me tergit'.

We drive through into a lovely green garden, the road winding past a rosebush on the right, plots of flowers lifting their violet and gold heads everywhere, a willow trailing its whispery green hair to the left. Ahead broods an ancestral mansion, and at its doorway stands a great tall woman in a severe black gown, her arms folded as if to say, 'Well. What do you want here?'

Her very presence makes me most uncomfortable. I s'pose she's the housekeeper, vexed that someone has violated her domain.

Gill and Doll, observing her, exchange a pregnant glance but say nothing.

Suddenly the coach door opens; and, jarred from my contemplations, I step out and down the fold-down steps, the footman holding my hand and I holding up grimy yellow skirts. The old harpy still stands in the door, as if she would block my way, her arms crossed, and as she looks me up and down, I hear in my mind, *Well! You're a fine little mess.*

My cheeks flush hot. How dare she? Then I recollect she did not really say the words, so perhaps I only fancied she thought 'em.

I saunter o'er to meet her. Somehow, 'neath her baleful glare, my wiggle-hipped walk feels too seductive; I find myself trying to mend my gait, to walk more straightly and plainly; then I am angry that I do so.

As I sway towards her, she moves directly before the doorway. So I halt, uncertain, so commanding and fearful a presence has she, and I so much smaller, I come only up to half of her upper arm, the way I do on my lord.

She glares down on me, her lips turned down with grim displeasure, her dark eyes slitted 'neath the severe white cap with the two upturned ends. So there we stand, she grimacing downward, I gawking up. At last she steps aside (having held me there long enough that I may feel her threatening power), and with a sweeping gesture of her arm, barks to a lurking footman, 'Take her within.'

Numbly, not knowing what else to do, I follow the footman inside to a cool antechamber with a polished wood floor, a suit of armour ahead to the left and a great oaken staircase beyond it, leading up to a landing, a faded red and blue hanging above it; then a twist of the stairs to the right, and the whole banister. It is a quaint old-fashioned structure, wood filled in top to stair and carven with curious designs and holes.

She creeps up behind me so I jump, and barks, 'Have you any trunks?'

I dumbly shake my head. Then the absurdity of the situation strikes me, and I giggle – at which one of her thin black eyebrows goes up. Frivolity, I see, does not please her; but so vexed at her am I, I care not what pleases her – indeed, would displease her rather than anything else. Given the rigidity of her carriage, the threat of her lowering brow, any person of spirit would fret and raise a rebellion.

So I say pertly, 'Nay, my leave-taking was rather sudden, madam.'

She grimaces at me. Then she turns, arms crossed (as if she were wired permanently in her pose of body-tight disapproval), and snaps to a hovering footman – who looks eager to repent of something if she will only tell him what – 'Show her up; show her up.'

He scrapes with much obeisance, as if to the Grand Mogul. Then the old harpy turns to me. 'Your quarters will be the second door on the right.'

The footman looks as eager to be rid of her as I; both of us frisk up the stairs, he leading the way.

The door assigned me by my dungeon-master is ajar, and beyond it stretches a gay, frilly chamber, the curtains and bed-hangings and counterpane all yellow and edged with ruffles. I collapse back downward on the bed. Oh! – it feels so good.

I'll rest my eyes here just a minute, then arise to wait for my lord.

The next thing I know, I start awake from a deep slumber. The shadows of late afternoon crawl across the ivory walls; bright-sparkling sun rays no longer glare through the windowpane.

Looking about for that convenience concealed in all bedchambers, I find no close-stool but a little bowl chamberpot 'neath the bed: another old-fashioned touch.

Then, knowing how ill I look, shuddering at the image in the glass, trying to tuck a few trailing tendrils of my hair, yearning for a maid, moaning at the dust and grime all over my yellow moire, the dirt streaks on my white stomacher, I head at last down the stairs and hear the old harpy berating someone.

'He should have been here by now! Where is he?'

'Madam, I cannot say,' a footman is replying. As I come straggling down the stairs, she stands below at the foot of 'em and casts me up a grim look.

'If he's in trouble, this is your doing.'

I gawk at her. '*My* doing, madam? I did not ask to take this holiday. It was forced on me.'

On the footman's face relief is writ large, that someone has arrived to take the heat off him. It boots not that the poor man was at Adderbury, attending to his duties the while this adventure occurred: a bully is not reasonable about selecting victims.

This one glares on me the harder, then responds with heavy sarcasm, 'So. I see. 'Twas forced on you. You had no desire to come. Well. 'Tis all the worse. For it means you feel no affection for him.'

'That's not so!' I cry. 'And, anyway, who are you to berate me?'

She glares me straight in the eye. I halt on one of the steps, quiver, become vexed that I quiver, notice my hand clutches the banister.

In a voice heavy with malevolence, she says, 'His mother.'

10

'An Intense Parental Effort'
28 May 1665

It has often been noted by writers on the Puritan family that the prescribed and common personal relationship between parents and children was one of restraint and even aloofness, mixed with – as we have seen – an intense parental effort to impose discipline and encourage spiritual precocity.
—David E. Stannard, *The Puritan Way of Death*

Oh, 'tis as if an arrow had been shot direct to my heart! Of course, I say to myself. Why did I not see the truth before? Had I not been told she was a sour old Puritan? And yet when I saw this sour old Puritan before me, I could only think she must be some disagreeable housekeeper.

To cover my confusion, I blurt out, 'I thought you had been at Ditchley, madam.'

She glares tight-lipped upon me, and I notice she has dark eyes like his though without the long lashes. 'And suppose I should take a notion to come see my son's estate? That affronts you, does it? I should stay put in my home to please you?'

I flush again. 'I said nothing of the sort, madam. I only expressed my surprise at your being here.'

Ooooo, I think, what a fine little war we will make of it after the marriage! Such instant dislike had passed betwixt us, and, on my part, a strange desire to seize him away from her, lest she do him hurt: to protect him from her.

Oddly, I feel that this great jealous and possessive love burning from her is equally mixed with some inexplicable hate; that the cold rigidity and sternness is but a clamp-down on boiling passions within – black passions.

'We will eat now,' she says in clipped tones.

'Tis a cheerless meal, sitting across table from *her*, with the footmen stepping in and out, silver trays on their liveried arms, and no conversation passing our lips. What a contrast 'tis, the silver plate and candlesticks, the snowy tablecloth and dainties of fruit, bread, cheese, sparrowgrass, pullet with onion; then the black cloud so billowing from her presence, I almost choke on every bite.

The whole while, I yearn to ask her, 'What will his lordship do with me?' But indeed I dare not. Partially because she's the last person on earth to confide in – partially because even more before her, I'm ashamed to admit I know not his intents.

Oh, what a long, dread, dull evening! For after the gut-knotting meal, we adjourn to the sitting room, where she and I, ensconced in antique chairs, proceed to a wordless glaring session some hours. Fortunately, a younger lady (who has had the sense to eat in her chambers) awaits us in the sitting room and makes shift to keep up a cheerful conversation. She presents herself as wife to Frank Lee, the younger and only surviving son of the old harpy's two offspring from her first marriage.

Perhaps a silent sympathy springs up betwixt us, as one who already suffers harpydom and one who is like to do so (both of us finding a witch's face o'er the nuptial bed), for she speaks to me most kindly, tries to draw me out, as the harpy and I glare at one another across her cheerful conversation.

Here, both within the same spring season, have I had two such strong and violent reactions to first meeting people: that instant gush of love upon first meeting my lord, and equally as quick a gush of opposite emotion upon meeting his mother!

Mrs Lee sits knotting, with long needles that click in and out: makes loops, pulls the weave tight. The old harpy bends hawklike o'er her sewing, her nimble needle flashing in and out (the thread would not dare displease her); and I, the only non-needle lady in the group, feel very much out of pocket, branded the learned lady: as with the few glittering harpy-glances cast my way, she knows a sewing basket is as foreign as a musket to me, and I'm that rarity despised by my own sex – the devourer of books, the one more at home discussing poetry with the men than creating laced caps with the women.

So we sit in frosty silence across from one another till I yearn to creep to the kitchen and seek out the comforting company of Doll and Gill – except it not be seemly.

Even this sitting room makes me jump, somehow. I stare at the fireplace with its marble lintels, the damasked lounge chairs, the chequered walnut table 'neath the window, and my flesh creeps. And finally, the dread evening being over, as I'm about to ascend the stairs, Mrs Lee catches my arm.

'A word with you, dear, if you please.'

I acquiesce. She leads me 'neath and behind stairs, down a passage toward the back of the house, and into a lady's sewing closet. I think, here's a hidey-hole from harpydom.

She opens the thick wood door, and we enter. She turns smiling to me, her face gentle 'neath the doily-cap of lace, her gown of sapphire silk topped with a modest pinner at the bosom.

'I'd apologise for her ladyship, dear. She's quite worried, you know, and so cannot be very civil.'

I look blankly on her. 'Worried, madam? For what?'

Mrs Lee looks surprised and pitiable on me here, as if to say, what a child, what a little fool you are. She grasps me by the two hands and says, 'Sit down, dear,' and, she still clasping my hands, we sit: she on a backed chair, I on a nearby stool at her feet.

She says, 'Have you not wondered why he has not appeared yet?'

My eyes widen. 'Why, I s'pose he's lying low, hiding from the guards, doubling back and forth across his path. Why, sure, you cannot think any harm has come to him!' My voice shows my incredulity.

She gives me a level look. 'Has it never crossed your mind that he could have been apprehended?'

'Why, no!' I stare on her innocently, then blurt out, 'For he can do anything!' Then I blush. 'I mean – that is, madam –' I stop in confusion.

She looks on me kindly. I can tell she knows how I love him. 'Well, her ladyship sees him from a different perspective, dear. She does not believe he can do anything. She recalls him as a boy who could get in a deal of trouble, and she fears he's in it up to his ears right now.'

'Why, what thinks she has transpired?'

'She believes he's been apprehended.'

'Why, no! 'Tis impossible!' I blurt out.

'And why is that?'

'Well, why – he has far too much wit. Why – and courage, too. There's nobody can take him unless he's a mind to be taken!'

She gives me a pitying look.

'Well, dear, I hope for your sake 'tis true.'

'It is. I know it! Why – he's the greatest wit, the greatest swordsman – why, never for a moment could I believe he could not handle any situation.'

'Very well, then.' She stands, drawing me up with her. 'Come, let's to bed then, dear.' She puts an arm about my shoulders. I look suddenly up at her: like everyone else, she's much taller than I.

'Madam, I'm glad you came.'

'And I also. When John writ to request his mother's presence at Adderbury and mentioned the reason, I thought I had best come, too, knowing her humours, and –'

'John writ?' I interrupt. 'Is that why the old harpy – that is –'

Mrs Lee bursts out laughing at this apt pseudonym.

I blush. 'I mean – is that why her ladyship is here? He writ to draw her hither?'

'Why, yes, dear. How did you think she knew to come?'

Why, I supposed that, like God, she'd had a great goggle-eye upon the countryside. Sure, I never dreamt anyone would invite her to make up a party anywhere: 'twould be like inviting the plague to a ball.

But this is scarce an apt response for a future daughter-in-law, so I respond, 'Why, I don't know, but – what said he in his letter to draw her forth?'

Is this not sly of me? Now I will hear whether there's been mention of a marriage.

Mrs Lee replies, 'Only that there was a young lady of quality coming to be his house guest for a time, and as her nature was one of innocent sweetness, he would be much gratified if her ladyship would vouchsafe to provide the necessary supervision that the lady might not feel uneasy as she might, being under his guardianship alone.'

Well. I cannot say whether I like this or not. Sure, it bespeaks of his honour to me, but it smells not very much like a wedding, if we must have a supervisor over't. I daresay he wouldn't want her supervising our nuptial bed.

But Mrs Lee has so drawn down my guard, I let my feelings slip and say, 'Why, do you mean he brought me here just for a visit, just to be my host?' She must hear the disappointment and dismay in my voice.

'As far as we know, dear, yes.'

'But – but I thought sure, that is – why, he's committed a capital crime; he's broken the law against abductions!'

'So we were to find out, questioning your men, when we saw in what a state you arrived.'

'So you did not know?' I cry.

'No, indeed, we thought you a house guest of some sort, perhaps someone's homeless ward.'

So that's why the old harpy looked me up and down when I came in dirty and without baggage. Indeed, she might have had justification for her wonder: I'm sure I looked a sight.

'After you came in, dear, her ladyship was questioning the men that brought you, and she was mighty angry, let me tell you, when she found out the true facts of the case.'

71

'Angry that he wanted me enough to carry me off?'

'Perhaps – angry also that he had acted rashly again and got himself in more trouble.'

'Again? Is this like him?'

'Oh, dear me, yes.' Mrs Lee folds up a handkerchief and lays it in a little purse dangling at her skirts. 'Why, there were a million pranks and more that he pulled: I cannot tell you all of them. But how my husband has had me laughing sometimes!'

I giggle a little too. 'What were some of the things he did?'

'Come, 'tis late. You should be getting in your bed.'

'Oh, Mrs Lee, just one, if you please.'

She smiles indulgently as if she were a fond mama with a baby. 'Very well. There were the fishes –'

'The fishes?'

'Yes. On a day when he was to be studying, he went traipsing down to the pond – this was at Ditchley, you know – and caught a brace of big fishes and was too proud of them to throw them back but did not dare show them about her ladyship, and when he brought them in the house was considering what to do and, hearing her coming, thrown into a fit of fear, he stashed them under the settle-cushion in the sitting room.'

I burst out laughing. 'Oh, ye gods, what happened?'

'Oh, madam, 'twas such a thing! Her ladyship, then coming into the sitting room, remained there the rest of the afternoon. 'Twas a very hot day –'

I laugh. 'Oh ye gods! Say no more: I can smell 'em.'

'His mother was going all about the room, sniffing and hollering, hectoring to the help: "What's this vile, foul smell in here? Why have you not cleaned my place properly? Someone is going to get a scouring over this."'

I giggle and titter 'most to death. 'Did they ever find the fish?'

'Finally, I think – for by using their noses, they found whence the odour emanated. And someone got a scouring, all right.'

I sober here, for, 'deed, 'tis hard to think of him being hurt.

Suddenly I think of what I felt when being told this harpy was his mother – about how I feared she would hurt him and not love him properly, so I say: 'Was he beaten often?'

'Oh, dear, yes. I'm afear'd so. Come.' She puts an arm around my shoulders, and we walk out of the closet. 'You see, he had an indomitable spirit, and so had her ladyship. And people that lived with them together in the house talk of what a pain it was to see the battle joined the way it was, day after day, and her ladyship, I fear, knew no other cause than one to tame his spirit. All of her theory books on bringing up children stressed the importance of crushing the will and making the child obedient, and she simply could never get a handle on his compliance, no matter how she tried. It pure enraged her. But she could not break his spirit, for she had to end always before she utterly broke his body.'

I shudder. 'Were his elder brothers beaten so?'

'Not at all. But rarely – and that lightly. My husband says they were wont to creep to the door of the study and listen, fearful, as the blows fell on John. They felt guilt at their usage being so much kinder than his.'

How stupid she must have been as well as cruel! Any person of sense, seeing a child of pride and mental acuity, would resort to reason before the rod; or at least, seeing the rod made him more stubborn, would know to change her tactics.

'How stupid she was.' I say my thoughts aloud.

'My dear, never believe it for a moment. She is the canniest soul I know, male *or* female. Have someone tell you, some time, how she wrought upon both Royalists and Roundheads to increase her land and fortune.'

'Then why beat a child who'll not be mended by blows?'

She answers, 'Henry and Frank were the fruits of a happy marriage. Her husband Wilmot saw her ladyship so little, there was much wonder at the birth of John. For a while he was rumoured the son of Allen Apsley, her ladyship's brother by marriage.'

I gawk in amaze and cannot imagine a whorish harpy.

'Not true, of course: the older he grew, the more he had the spirit and look of his father. My husband thinks that likeness aroused her rage, which she worked out with rod and birch. Come, dear, up to bed now.'

I see a footman waiting with a candle.

'Mrs Lee?'

'Yes, dear?'

'Do you, truly, really fear something has befallen him?'

She tries to smile encouragingly. 'Let's not think about it, dear. There's nothing much we can do, nothing but wait. You love him very much, don't you?'

I feel the truth shining out of my eyes. 'Yes, I do.'

'Well, I hope he makes it here, dear, soon – and marries you, too.'

Jesu, is my love writ that much on my face – the hope of what he brought me here for and the downcast look, no doubt, when I found 'twas not what I hoped?

'I – well – it' s just that I – couldn' t see why he would have brought me here – unless he –' I make a stop, but she understands anyway.

'My dear, John does many things on impulse before he stops to think of the results. Especially when there's a chance to defy authority. I've no doubt he's attracted to you, or he would not have done this mad act, but I also doubt he meant immediately to marry you if he had not told us to have a parson here. I think 'twas just another of his mad pranks to divert himself – like hanging a little straw poppet from the rafter, that anyone who walked down the way might scream and fall back, and he watch their reaction – just another mad thing.'

'I see.' I look down, turn about, lift up my skirts. And I think, so – he's risked his life, got up my hopes, grabbed me from my guardians so they'll lock me up the closer – and all for a mad prank.

Oh, now as we ascend the stairs does Mrs Lee's uneasiness begin to seep into my bones. I perceive the ladies in this house don't see him quite as I do – the ideal knight for whom nothing is impossible.

And for the first time, I wonder if 'tis possible he has been captured.

11

'Almost Terrifying Intensity'
29 May 1665

... virtue in the seventeenth century was a positive force of almost terrifying intensity. It hung over children, especially, like a cloud, and when they were amenable to its influence, utterly dehumanized them.

—Vivian de Sola Pinto, *Enthusiast in Wit: Portrait of John Wilmot, Earl of Rochester, 1647–1680*

Passing the night in quite a troubled sleep, meandering in and out of a doze and suffering dreams of I scarce know what but mist and weeping, I awaken early, for there's a tremendous row, a broil, that sounds to be right at the foot of the stairs.

My eyes burning from want of sleep like two peeled grapes, I arise and cover my nakedness with a blue velvet dressing gown Mrs Lee has lent me, for the servants are to clean off my yellow moire this morning. I draw the oversize gown about me as best I can with the two drawstrings. The shoulders come partway down my arms, and I stand on the hem.

Gathering up the excess billows as well as I can, I half stagger, half creep from my bedchamber to the top of the stairs, to listen.

The argument isn't at the bottom of the stairs, as I'd believed, but floating in from the left, from some rooms past the dining room, an area I've not visited. But so loud is the noise, I can hear the words quite clearly.

The old harpy is yelling, 'I knew it! I knew something would be amiss. I just knew it all along; this had a bad smell about it!'

Mrs Lee's voice is raised in reply, but so much softer I cannot hear what she says.

The harpy tones then boom, 'Well, no one can blame me for any of this! Heaven knows, I did all I could.'

Mrs Lee's voice is a little stronger and louder here. 'Your ladyship, I'm sure no one can accuse you of want of duty toward him.'

'I did everything I could for him, Lord knows! I saw to his education! I gave him more Bible lessons than the majority of children have and examined him to make sure that they had taken and he understood them, too! No one can say I was not careful with his rearing.'

'Your ladyship, no one is going to say anything like that.'

'No one can say I did not do my best, even without a father here to help me along! No one can accuse me of too much maternal softness.'

'No, your ladyship, I'm sure not.'

'"Just be sure you don't rear up a mama's boy," my lord kept repeating in his letters. At least no one can accuse me of that. I was very firm with him. I would brook not the slightest disobedience, not even in a look of his. And now all this has happened! Indeed, I know not why. I believe some children's natures just cannot be bent, no matter how severe the measures taken.'

'Yes, your ladyship, perhaps that's so.'

'But he's not a bad child! Indeed, he was such a pretty boy that all the ladies that came would dote on him. And so polite, so full of charm, they would remark upon it when he made his bow and left the room. Oh, he's a good boy at bottom, I know it! It is only – it must have been that crowd he fell in with at Oxford, that gang. His tutor writ that he was debauched by some lewd older fellow who doted on him and took him out drinking and did – Lord knows what else.'

'Calm yourself, your ladyship. Indeed, you look not well.'

'And for all we know – oh, this is all her doing! That little pint-pot of trouble.'

My cheeks flush hotly at this summation of myself.

'Your ladyship, Mrs Mallet, I believe, bears no ill will toward him nor would wish him in any trouble. I believe her only culpability in this whole business is to love him dearly – a factor which might have encouraged him to carry her off.'

'Well, if she loves him dearly, so much the worse for't!' rages the harpy. Indeed I cannot please her. For t'other day, when she expected I loved him not, she was equally ill pleased.

'For the little wench no doubt has no notion what love is. She has doted on his cravat or his pleasing manner, and so she has got him in all this trouble.'

'Mother,' says Mrs Lee, 'to be quite fair, Mrs Mallet, you know, was taken off suddenly by his men by force and had no actual choice in the matter.'

'Oh, she says so! But you can bet there was some sort of collusion betwixt 'em before he would have carried her off. Your point about having coaxed from her notions of her "love", as she calls it, would explain that. No doubt the baggage has inveigled him to do this, that she may be th' talk o' th' town, everyone know her attractions – and no thought of what trouble she's going to get him in.'

Mrs Lee sighs deeply. 'Mother, to be fair, you know you writ to your cousin Castlemaine and bade her rig the King, that John might wed the wealthy heiress of the West.'

My mouth pops open in amaze.

Her harpyship says bitterly, 'And as soon as that creature flounced here, all pertness and vanity, I got down on my knees and begged the Good Lord to forgive me for such a petition!'

Mrs Lee sighs again but makes no response.

'She has ruin't our family name. No, I tell you, he would not have hit upon this by himself! I took great care when we were living in France with the court in exile, awaiting for my lord to come back from Bruges or Germany or wherever he was, that this boy would be too frighted of executions ever to defy the law. Each time there was to be an execution in the city, I took him there to watch, and then to be certain the lesson had taken, him being brought home again, I got out the rod and gave him a good sound beating and told him, 'There! Now you will remember what happens to bad boys when they grow up.' I would have thought such a lesson would have took! And yet here he goes off and does the very thing against which he had so many childhood warnings – commits a capital crime! 'Tis as if he throws defiantly in my teeth the very thing I warned him most against! I cannot make it out, I cannot!'

My skin has crept cold at this last narration. I've heard stories of parents so cold-hearted that they beat their children at executions or lessons not for faults but to jog their memories – but I never knew anyone that actually did it.

I see another angle on this carrying-off of me now. I think the old harpy partially hit upon it, for someone with his spirit, being told so positively not to do something and being so severely punished for no good reason, would have a secret motive to do the very thing he was enjoined not to do and so throw it in his torturer's teeth.

The more I think on this carrying-off, the more angles to it do there seem. I know not why any more I felt such sureness of his love at the beginning.

The one thing I share in common with the harpy is my fear for what has happened to him. Indeed it has taken him overlong to reach this place, no matter what road he takes, no matter what doubling back he's done, no matter e'en if he's lain over the night at some inn. And anxiety knots my stomach and throat.

The Grand Inquisitor is raving again. 'No one can say I did not do my duty by him, no one, no one! I dared not be any stricter with him; he was too frail. I did my duty, I say! Even his tutor, Mr Giffard, would warn me to let up on him, lest he be too ill to do his lessons.'

The more I hear, the more does my flesh creep. Jesu, what a childhood he must have had! I knew not how lucky I was, being checked only with frowns and injunctions. I vaguely remember being whipped once or twice with a little stinging rod, but I was very small at the time and can neither recall what I did nor what the occasion was – and grew up without any fear except that of guilt, of displeasing those that saw to my welfare.

I know boys are treated more roughly – but still, even my poor little half-brother Frank, with a cold-livered hawk of a father, is beaten only occasionally. But then, he has Mama and me to protect him. And this old harpy strikes me very different from Sir John Warre, who is but a bird of prey with his beaklike nose and money running in his veins. Anyone that keeps clear of him is let alone – whereas this old Medea, I now begin to understand more than ever, has black, hot passions boiling in her, and the rigidity of her backbone and of her clasped hands is merely the last device to clamp down on a boiling rage.

My knuckles are white as I grasp the banister, for it makes me sick to the point of falling down to hear hints of how he was used. Something swirls in my stomach area, as if a hole in my stomach wall opened, and a black wind whirled in, to make me dizzy – I feel all of his pain, the mental anguish more than the bodily.

I get a big hit at the pit of my belly, a feeling of not being loved and of dealing with it by pretending it doesn't matter, but deep down hoping for a sign of love that never appears. I grasp the banister harder to keep from pitching down the stairs head first. And the tears pour from my eyes. And in that moment, such a deep hatred of that woman is born – such as I never knew could exist in me.

And all the while she yells so self-righteously down there, as if she had done her duty! How no one could fault her discipline: how he got it for looking at the floor or for looking her in the eye – or eating at the wrong time or not eating at the right time – or before church or after church – indeed, the old hypocrite has deceived herself and sees not what she must have done to him.

My head spins in the whirlwind spiralling up from my stomach. I sink down at the top of the stairs, sitting before I pitch downward in a faint.

A footman walking through the vestibule stares up at me. 'Mistress, are you well?'

'I am a little faint, thank you.'

'Would you have somewhat to breakfast on, now, miss? We can get some hot-cross buns and some marmelotte ready in a trice.'

'I – no thank you.'

''Tis orange marmelotte. Made on the premises, miss, and very good.'

He reminds me of my mama. I smile weakly at him. 'No, thank you.'

'Some chocolate then? Or another hot drink? Ginger or cinnamon water?'

I shake my head.

But now Mrs Lee stands in the doorway of the dining room to the left. The man addresses her.

'Madam, the young lady looks not well, and I was offering whether she should eat something, but she would not.'

'Thank you, James.'

He bows then and exits 'neath the stairs, moving to the left of 'em, towards the kitchens and servants' quarters.

'My dear,' says Mrs Lee, 'are you ill?'

I shake my head, but seeing her stolid figure, hands clasped before the black silk gown, brow furrowed in sympathetic concern 'neath the white cap, I at last manage to squeak (for her kindness toward me deserves some response): 'I – hearing how he was hurt in childhood – could not bear't.'

'There, there! Children do get punished you know.'

'Not punished like that!'

'There, there, 'twas all long ago; 'tis past.'

That argument has always seemed inane to me. The past is as real as the present – realer sometimes. Nothing in my own life has ever gripped my gut so.

She ascends the stairs, grasps my shoulder. I lean against her, and with my knees watery and her hands about my shoulders, she supports me down.

'My dear, you've no strength in you at all! Are you sure 'tis only passion has made you so weak?'

I nod. 'I – I am a very passionate woman. Emotions hit me hard and disorder my physical being. When I feared for him and hurt for him, 'twas as if all the strength had left me and I were under violent attack.'

'There, there, there, my dear! You must not open yourself so.'

She supports me down the staircase, my curly fair head leaning against her armpit and her left arm about my shoulders, our right hands clasped together hard.

'There, come down now. Go off to the left.'

Through the sedate dining room of dark polished wood is a garden solar, window-wrapped, through which sunlight streams. Mrs Lee, still supporting me to the point she almost carries me, deposits me in one of the new French wicker chairs, yellow with green cushions.

Her ladyship looks on me with as much hatred and disapproval as I must have mustered for her.

'What's the matter with her?'

'A qualm, your ladyship, that's all.'

The old harpy stares on me coldly and then says something that so astonishes me I almost faint.

'You're not with child, are you?'

I am so amazed I know not what to say. My mouth falls open, and I gape at her. How can she be so brazen? She trains on me a cold, calculating look.

'Why, madam! How can you speak so? He and I are not married.'

Her eyes narrow the further. 'Aye, but in town that does not matter so much, does it?'

'It does with me!' I snap. 'Anyway,' I add, seeing that she still eyes me dubiously, 'even if I had the inclination, I would not have had the opportunity – for this is the first time I've ever been out of my home without my mama at my arm.'

She looks more satisfied. 'Well. If that's the case, madam, I trust more to that than I do to your virtue.'

My mouth flies open again; she stares on me smugly, her eyes narrowed to slits, the corners of her lips turned upward in a pleased smile, as if she's accurately branded the Whore of Babylon.

'You've no cause to insult me so, madam!' My hand clutches the whole of my belly area, which swirls and spins and hurts with the passions pouring in there. 'The main reason I grew so faint was to hear what you said.'

'What I said?' She stares with astonishment on me.

'Your ladyship,' Mrs Lee makes shift to interpose, 'pray let's –' She looks very uneasy, but I go bursting through her conversation, as if I were a runaway horse and wagon careering down Ludgate Hill, and once I've begun, everybody get out of the way, for there's no crying me halt!

'Yes, you! I almost fainted on the stairs to hear how you ill-used him when he was a child.'

Mrs Lee sinks back in her green and yellow chair.

'*I* ill-use him!' Now 'tis the harpy's her turn to gape. 'I cannot see what you mean: I'm sure I took much more care with his education and training than most mothers do. I got him a tutor, then sent him off to grammar school, then to Oxford, and wrought upon the King for money for a tutor and Tour. I'm sure I was rigorous to obey his father's injunction, not to let him grow up soft and spoilt. And anyway, even if I'd kissed him and petted him and taken him in my lap and fed him sweetmeats and done all the wrong things like that – sure I could not hear my duty being read to me by you, a mere slip of a girl! What impertinence indeed!'

I fling back at her, 'I'll be impertinent as I like with you, for you can't beat *me*! And as far as all the things that you mentioned, those are the very things you should have been doing, and if you weren't doing 'em, so much the worse for you, and so much the worse for him now!'

'Ladies, ladies, please, I pray you,' interposes Mrs Lee. 'All this is nothing to the purpose.'

We quiet now but glare our hatred at one another across her. And now that that hatred is out in the open, it seems an even blacker cloud billowing 'twixt us than over the silent, choking supper the night before.

'Well, miss,' she snaps. 'If that's your notion of rearing a boy, God help you: I hope you never have one.'

'You used not the Lees so.'

'They were good boys! Obedient! With a godly father. They'd no devil to be beaten out of them.'

'Madam, you're a hypocrite. And I would laugh in your face were I not hurting so much over every blow that he ever felt in his body!'

'You are the most brazen –'

'Ladies, ladies, I beg you, if you please,' interjects Mrs Lee. 'There's much more to the purpose to be concerned about now.'

This statement draws me back to the present. All around me is a cheerful yellow room, its enveloping windows streaming sun on yellow and green French furniture – so why feel I this black grip of fear at my throat?

'Why, what is't, Mrs Lee?'

She reaches over to take me by the hand. 'Dear, we have had some visitors this morning.'

Her harpyship bursts in. 'Two of the King's Life Guards have come here, miss, with a pretty tale to tell! My son is in the Tower, and it is all your doing!'

'The Tower!' I shriek.

'Aye, and under sentence of a capital crime. What make you of that, miss? Are you so bold and brazen to my face any more?'

'That has nothing to do with what we spoke of! If he's in the Tower at all, 'tis *your* doing.'

'*My* doing! Why, I did everything I could to avoid it.'

'You did everything you could to send him there, when you treated him so unjustly. Why, any person of his spirit would have done everything to throw it in your teeth.'

'You talk no sense at all.'

'I talk perfect sense.'

'Ladies, ladies! Are you so intent on pursuing your quarrel, you cannot be rational to see the present circumstances of the one you quarrel over?'

Indeed, she's i' th' right. She's the only reasonable one in the group.

'Mrs Lee, you're i' th' right,' I cry. 'I pray you tell me what's become of him.'

'He's in the Tower! My son, in the Tower. I am disgraced! And because of you!'

I long to rise to the bait but resist. 'What else know you?'

'Nothing, dear.'

'But the guard might! Can we not bring 'em here and question 'em?'

'My dear, they arrived quite early this morning and have been questioned already. They know nothing else. They've only come to fetch you back to your guardians.'

'But why did you not wake me?'

'There seemed no cause. Now that your dress has been wet and cleaned, we must needs wait for it to dry. And the men are resting. They had little sleep last night, for they were bade to make haste, to search first in Adderbury and then in Ditchley.'

'I would go now! I would go back to town now, to see what's become of him – perhaps plead his cause to the King.'

'Yes, well you might,' snaps her harpyship, 'having got him into this coil yourself.' She gives me a look that says, *Well might such a one as you plead with such a king as this, whose concern is with his cod.*

I whirl on her. 'Madam, I have told you and told you, I had no part in this but to love him and tell him I would marry him. It was his decision to carry me off.'

She glares back, folds her arms. 'Aye, and what encouragements you must have given him, too.'

I see there's no arguing with her. She will believe me a trollop despite all reason; she will believe that somehow I have performed the act of love before my mama's eye.

I turn to Mrs Lee. 'Is he – under sentence of death?'

There is a pause. Her harpyship scowls and looks away, and I swear, as hard as she is, there might be a tear she would not let us see have fall, to spoil her character before us.

'The men said it was a capital crime.'

I burst into tears. No harpy rigidity for me. I will let all out. I hug my sides, every nerve in my body exploding and the tears bursting and leaping and rolling out.

The harpy says in clipped tones, her head turned away, 'Have you no control?'

'No, madam, I do not – not in such a cause as this!' I weep bitterly, hugging my sides, my stomach tumultuous.

'There, there, dear.' Mrs Lee puts an arm about my shoulders; I lean my head against her arm and weep. 'There, there, there.'

'This is disgusting!' mutters the harpy. 'No self-discipline at all.'

I gasp between tears, 'I know not what you mean, madam, by self-discipline, nor why it is such a good.'

'Self-discipline,' she snaps, 'is the greatest good in God's sight. He tells us that we are to govern ourselves.'

'Indeed,' I burst out, gasping and shuddering and scattering tears, 'I saw not that in any of the Commandments!'

'Come, come, come, the two of you!' says Mrs Lee. 'Really. You make me tired, both of you. Why, you're upsetting yourselves the worse, clashing with one another so! Indeed, though you be of such different philosophies, can you not at least support one another in the common cause of sharing your love?'

No, we cannot, for that is one love we refuse to share. We are each of us engaged in pulling it to ourselves and pushing the other off from it. That love Mrs Lee speaks of, each of us would take as a bauble to her own self and hide in a hole with and claw the eyes out of the other that wanted even a piece of it.

To her I'm the trollop that's no doubt with child, that has no self-governance, that has drawn him into her toils. To me she's the absolute preternatural form of vile brutality, everything that a mother out of a tale of horror should be: Medea wreaking her rage on the innocent babe of absent, straying Jason. So, no, Mrs Lee. We cannot support one another, indeed. We can only do our best to claw one another to pieces, and this you will notice e'en more when we are both upset and worried.

'Where are the men?' I sob. 'I would go now.'

'Dear, the men are lying down to rest. And you're going nowhere till your gown is quite dry and you've had somewhat to eat.'

'I'm not hungry.' I sniffle.

'Aye, aye, that's the way,' snaps Medea. 'That's where we're going – refusing the good food that's put in front of you. He would do the same thing.'

'Maybe he wasn't hungry either. Who could be hungry sitting across table from *you*?'

A groan escapes Mrs Lee's lips.

'Madam!' she hisses 'I can see that your mother did not do her duty by you, to teach you to respect your elders.'

'I respect people who deserve it. Not people who hurt and ill treat their dear sons and make 'em miserable.'

'Will you listen to her?' rages the harpy. 'Will you listen to her addle-headed nonsense? God help her if she ever has children! For they'll tear the house down, brick by brick, before she will take any trouble with them.'

'Ladies, I beg you.' Mrs Lee turns to me. 'Will you let me take you off and get you something to eat?'

'I'm not hungry,' I moan.

'Come, then, sit at table with me and talk.'

She puts two hands on my shoulders and leads me off – I think, simply a device to get me out of the harpy environs more than anything else.

'Oh, what if they're having him tortured? What if he's on the rack?'

'Now, why would they do a thing like that?' soothes Mrs Lee.

I lean against her and tremble; she supports me into the dining room.

'Perhaps the King tries to get out of him where I am.'

'Well, I don't think that's likely if His Majesty bade the men search. Anyway, the nobility are never racked. And John keeps company with the King's friends. Come. Sit.' She pulls out a chair, deposits me in't.

'I'm not hungry now, madam.'

'I know, I know, but let's just see if you can take a little down – just to keep me company, dear.'

She snaps her fingers; a footman bows, exits, and returns with a silver platter covered by a dome.

'Please take a little. A hot-cross bun, dear, just to please me, just to see't on your plate.'

I sniff and take a bun and put it on my plate.

Another footman passes round the orange marmelotte with the orange strips in't.

'Just take a little, dear, and put it on the side of your plate. You don't have to eat it if you don't care to.'

And so bit by bit she coaxes me into taking some nourishment. I doubt that the harpy, being faced with my lord's queasy stomach, adopted such measures to make him eat. Indeed, she earlier hinted what measures she adopted, certain to make him queasier.

I drip tears on the plate but manage to get a little food down.

Oh, and the rest of the morning's pure agony! I pace to and fro, hugging my sides, and Mrs Lee has much ado to keep the harpy and me in separate rooms, as if we were gamecocks in a fine mettle.

At last the Life Guards arise from their rest, take a little more food and say they're ready to go, and my gown is pronounced dry too, and donned.

The Life Guards are kind gentlemen, treat me with all respect, ask me if I do well, have I been frighted on my journey, has the earl done anything to upset me? I can see the question that would have been my mama's uppermost in their eyes.

I blurt out, 'Oh, 'deed, gentlemen! What upsets me is fear of what may happen to him! I pray you let us get back to town speedily, that I may plead to the King for him!'

They exchange pregnant glances. I can hear 'em thinking, *So that's how the land lies.*

The journey's a nightmare, the green hills of Oxfordshire rolling past my window, the hooves of the horses beating, faltering ahead on the rutted road.

When we break our journey at an inn, I am disordered to the point of madness. In one part of my skull, through some secret intelligence to the feeling part of me, I can literally hear him cry out, and so frantic am I at this distance betwixt us I shake over all in a fit, as the blast of passion thunders to me down the London Road. It screams out at me, a bolt of pure pain and feeling – cleaves me in two, shoots through me like an arrow, splits me like an axe; it vibrates as strong and loud as the blast of trumps in hell; it pours in at my open belly and swirls upward to yell in my brain; I hear it, I feel it: he calls to me and I can do nothing, nothing!

Oh, that I could send out a part of my mind to town – that I could be a man, now – one of his circle – to hear what is said, see what is done – take the initiative and plead with the King!

Sure, if anyone could sway His Majesty, 'twould be Buckingham, reared with him in the royal nursery; or Sedley and Buckhurst, whom His Majesty has pardoned afore; or that well-looked Lord Ashfield, whose tenderness of heart is all the talk.

Oh, if I could but be there in London, to hear 'em now!

Part II

'The Measure Of An Unmade Grave'

Robert Blair, Earl of Ashfield
May–July 1665

Friar Lawrence: Romeo, come forth; come forth, thou fearful man:
Affliction is enamour'd of thy parts.
And thou art wedded to calamity....
Thy fault our law calls death; but the kind prince,
Taking thy part, hath pushed aside the law ...
Romeo: 'Tis torture, and not mercy....
Thou canst not speak of that thou dost not feel:
Wert thou as young as I, Juliet thy love ...
Then mightst thou speak, then mightst thou tear thy hair,
And fall upon the ground, as I do now,
Taking the measure of an unmade grave.
—William Shakespeare, *Romeo and Juliet*

1

'The Court Wits'
27 May 1665

Shortly after the restoration, the serious-minded cavaliers at court noted with dismay that the King was to be found more and more in company with 'the men of mirth', as dour old Chancellor Hyde called. Them. These were sprightly young fellows who ... cared nothing for laws civil and ecclesiastical, and who could and did droll at anything under Heaven, including the King's own Majesty. These men formed the nucleus of the group that came to be known as the Court Wits.

The name was as loose as the morals of the assemblage. A Wit was anyone from wild, malicious Harry Killigrew ... to George Villiers, Duke of Buckingham, the last splendid playboy of the fading Renaissance....

To him [Dryden], wit was the perfect blend of fancy and judgment.

—John Dover Wilson, *The Court Wits of the Restoration*

I, Robert Blair, Earl of Ashfield, being in my twenty-second year of age and fifth of drunkenness (yet being of sound enough mind, too, to have got clear of my estate at Wiltshire), do stand amazed, that I can find naught better to do with my life than hang about this town with my old school chum, Buckhurst.

So I drink, that I may not think; and being awoke with a belled head, think to drink that off, too; or drink to raise my wit; and, being sick to the very blood of drinking, I take a turn with the women; and so to the wine-butt again.

For this mad mob that Buckhurst consorts with hath fingers permanently wrapped about tankards, as if a marvellous growth protruded from their palms. And Buckhurst ne'er grows witty till he drinks; and I, by drinking, believe I'm witty: which is all the same to me; and to those about me so drunk they know not what they hear neither. And wine, as everyone knows, will make the rottenest doxy look like Venus.

89

So this morning to Buckhurst, the best-natured man alive, who, though he speaks little by reason of his phlegm, hath, it being heated well enough by wine, a nimble fancy; a wit raised, too, by the mad mob with which he keeps company; others enjoying his patronage being, viz., George Etherege, grandson of a rich vintner, made known to Buckhurst by his comedy *The Comical Revenge; or, Love in a Tub*; and Fleetwood Shepherd, whose ribald farces are ever most welcome, and who was given a living as Buckhurst's steward. In truth, the steward is more aptly his shadow, like antitheses ever together that make a whole: the lord, heir of the Earl of Dorset, round, pop-eyed, good-natured; his shadow rangy, sparrow-eyed, rollicking with ill-natured drolleries. Where the mob is, they are; and much enjoyment, too.

So this morning I arise in company with my belled head and think to take it with me to dinner, where the mad mob is to make up a gang at Locket's. And being arrived there, I see a heated commotion, all of 'em exclaiming at once, to the diversion of the waiting-wenches and the vexation of the few patrons more sober that have blundered through the open door, on a mistake, in hopes of a quiet meal.

As I negotiate my way past the wench that carries tankards t'other direction 'twixt the oaken tables, I see Sedley (or Little Sid, as we call him) holding court o'er the whole gang, orchestrating (as is his wont) some new tidbit of gossip:

'Complete with a black cape and pistol: I wonder he did not stage-manage it on Hounslow Heath, for the better effect.'

'What's this?' I query. 'Has someone been robbed?'

Buckhurst pulls me down on the oaken stool beside him and fills a waiting tankard, from a butt of sherris-sack. 'Lord Hawley.'

Shepherd chortles, 'Of ten thousand guineas and more.'

The whole table rollicks with laughter. I sip sourly: 'tis plain they're some few hogsheads ahead of me, to find so much diversion in a robbery.

'Then, too,' muses Sedley, his small black eyes sparkling 'neath the mountainous periwig, 'there's the capital penalty – this he would take as a spur rather than a curb; for you know what a dash he would make, to please th' admiring crowd, on the ride up Tower Hill.'

The table roars with laughter again. George Etherege, who dresses but plainly yet well enough, in periwig of light brown, simple tied neckcloth, white cotton shirt, and black velvet jackanapes coat and breeches, remarks, in a wry voice with the hint of a lisp, hoisting his tankard, 'Here's to making a good end!'

Good-hearted Buckhurst slaps his colly's shoulder. 'He will, George: anon his majesty will laugh at the frolic.'

'My lord,' says Etherege, 'not all have your good fortune with the law.'

'Why,' says Shepherd, 'he'd be laughing, too, an he were here! Gad, can you think what jests he'd crack?'

I yell, vexed to the very blood, 'Will someone tell me what in God's name the joke is?'

Etherege extends a palm to Little Sid. 'You tell, Sir Charles: gossip is your province; we'd not deny you the thrill of repetition and enlargement.'

Gulping plenteously to fortify himself against the marvels of the tale, then straightening with an air of importance his ruffled neck-cloth, Sedley orates:

'Last night, about the stroke of twelve, Elizabeth Mallet took leave of the palace, and Rochester of his senses. He lay in wait not fifty paces from here, with a band of armed men; stopped Hawley's coach; and raped away the lady.'

'Oh, no!' I cry.

So that's why our Boy Genius is missing. I'd but thought he was late as usual, sliding us 'twixt his morning levee and afternoon enjoyment; waylaid in the streets by a wench with her mistress' billet-doux or a notion of her own.

'He is the news item of the day,' cries Shepherd, narrow eyes dancing. 'If de Ruyter sailed up the Medway and took Whitehall, he could not make a greater coil.'

'Rochester and his adventures,' I mutter. 'I only wish to God he'd take it in mind to do something less dangerous, like go to war.'

'Faith, he may honour your request,' says Sedley drily, 'as soon as he finds an eyepatch and cutlass, that he may masquerade as a pirate.'

I sit glumly o'er my tankard. 'This is all my fault. I taxed him o'er his want of honour to the lady, when we sat in our cups and he talked his usual hard talk. "No man of honour," I told him, "would so engage a lady's affections and then sit idly by, whilst her marriage was being arranged to someone else."'

'No,' protests Shepherd, 'we think 'twas more the passion thing.'

'A heat in nature,' says Buckhurst.

'He is all pr—k and no brain sometimes,' augments Shepherd.

'Oh,' rhapsodizes Sedley, 'for the resty pr—k of eighteen again, that waking will not let thee sleep, that drives thee on from hand to whore – faith, 'tis the happiest memory of my childhood.'

'Conjoined with a drunken fancy and an opportunity, unhappily met.' Buckhurst exhales and blows out his fat cheeks at the unfortunate conjunction. 'Jesus.'

This comment awakens their drunken muses.

'Absent from himself,' says Etherege, 'and his better judgment.'

'Beside himself, with his better judgment on the wrong side.' Buckhurst nods, tossing off his pint pot.

'Saw you, my lord, those new suits he had made up?' asks Etherege. 'A hundred pound each, ne'er stir, and that excepting the fine silk hose and shirt and point de Venise cravat.'

'You would know, George,' says Buckhurst.

Etherege nods. 'I have marked his dress at the top of the mode, though on five hundred a year; marrying an heiress was his only hope of salvation, not but that she was an angel herself, sent for the purpose by a benevolent Providence.'

Buckhurst replies, 'He was heated.'

'But no doubt cooled, my lord, when he came to himself in the Tower' says Etherege. 'And now has very little hopes of the lady herself, nor of all the others he juggles at the palace.'

I sigh. 'More like playing at ninepins. A score laid low at one toss. I wish I knew what he did.'

'He must be as clever with his hands and pintle as he is with his verses,' muses Shepherd, filling my tankard.

'And always after the coldest or most inaccessible women.' I shake my head.

'So 't be hard,' pronounces Sedley, 'he does 't; so it be impossible, he willingly risks his neck in the venturing of't. But he's done 't now. That old screw Hawley has been at the palace already today, screaming for his pound of flesh; and from what I know of the man, he'll get it.'

Now a pert wench makes bold to come to our dangerous table. And a frisky little colt she is, too: bold, inviting eye; bosoms like melons; a skirt that clings to her thighs.

She winks and smiles. 'You gentlemen look mighty dry.'

'Only, Kate, for want of thy sweet nectar.' Buckhurst enfolds her about the waist.

Kate puts her arm about his shoulders. 'Law, sir, your lordship was ever such a one: no woman could preserve her virtue about you.'

Buckhurst puts on a pretence of horror. 'Virtue? Let us hear no such unlucky words betwixt us, Kate.' Then she puts her round mouth down over Buckhurst's, which business I watch gloomily.

She departing richer by a few coins, Sedley observes drily, 'We need never fear Buckhurst putting his head into the wed-lock: he's too fond of the lower kind.'

My chum's fat face splits into a grin. He raises his tankard in salute to his favourite bawd. 'Give me bonny black Bess any day, and hang all the fine prudes at court!' Shepherd raises his tankard, clanks it with Buckhurst's.

Etherege says, 'For an heiress, I'd not stick at marriage.'

'Marriage!' Buckhurst shudders at the dreadful thought.

Shepherd augments, 'Gad, Etherege, that old lady of hers would not have suffered a marriage – not to one of us. She thinks we ravish ten nuns each day before breakfast.'

Sedley lowers his tankard, wipes his lips. 'We need not worry about enlarging our reputations: the good-natured town does't for us.'

I look up at once to see the grand figure of Buckingham bearing down on us, his white velvet suit slashed ruby, his scarlet plumes waving, his head nodding haughtily here and there to those that gape at the great man. Kate breaks off a jest at a nearby table, shoves a tankard at the man there, and lopes for the bar.

Buckingham (Bucks, as we call him) settles himself grandly on a stool t'other side of Sedley, holding his hanger to one side, and looks over for the wench. He holds up a hand to snap his fingers, but she's already at his side, swooping a tankard before him.

Our table has reverently quieted, but at last Sedley says, 'How now, what news?'

Bucks nods significantly at the butt, and the wench gallops off for another. Then, pouring the last of the sherris-sack into his tankard, he says, 'Still at large, they know not where.'

A respectful silence descends, to give Bucks leave to speak more.

He tosses off a draught. His hand sparkles with rings curious: one an emerald, one a seal, one engraven with pearls after the signs of the zodiac.

'I've just left the King. He's mightily vexed. It seems he had written to the girl's guardians to plead for Rochester, urged him to be patient – warned him against any sort of rashness~~but that Rochester had been getting resty. You know his hot blood.'

The wench returns with another butt, deposits it on the table, takes her leave.

'What will happen now?' I ask.

Bucks shrugs. 'The King has secluded himself in the Whitehall laboratory, to soothe himself by working chemical experiments. He's left word, directly they're found, that Rochester be sent to the Tower.'

Now that ape of a Killigrew bounds up ('Lying Harry', we call him), his hanger clapping about his legs like a tail. 'Ha! Have you heard what Rochester's done?'

Our bleak faces would tell him we have. Killigrew drapes a cloak o'er his head like a woman's hood and mantle, then, mincing about with his hand up, raises his gravelly voice to a shrill one.

'Oh! My! What would your lordship have of me?'

Hoots and catcalls greet this performance. To scattered applause, Killigrew makes his grave curtsey.

'This is not so diverting,' I snap. 'His Majesty is mightily vexed.'

'Not everyone is so fortunate with the law as our friend here.' Etherege nods toward Buckhurst.

Killigrew whips the cloak from his head, throws his long limbs down t'other side of Bucks and reaches for the bottle. Bucks turns aside with a faint air of contempt and draws his cloak about him.

'The law! Better and better! By Gad, that youth knows how to lay a plot to divert the town.'

I glare at him as he holds the bottle o'er his mouth, the honey-brown arc splashing onto his tongue. 'Killigrew, this is a serious affair of honour – and all my fault.'

'Ballocks!' cries Killigrew in disgust and smites the table with his fist. He screws the top on the bottle again and sets it down. 'His life had got too quiet, that's all! He wanted an adventure; and what better time than just before His Majesty's birthday, when there will be large gatherings at which his daring is sure to be cried up the more?'

Etherege shakes his head. 'Killigrew, the Quality have a place to maintain and no concern for what it costs.'

'An' he were in desperate straits for a fortune,' argues Killigrew, 'think you he would effect the solution in costume?'

'It's of a piece,' says Etherege, 'with his dressing for the occasion.'

Shepherd breaks in, shaking his head. 'No, he has gone into a breeding frenzy.'

'What, for one woman? Elizabeth Mallet?' I demand, still not to be swayed from my judgment of the facts.

Sedley smacks his dirty pudgy fingers to his lips. 'A bosom that would tempt a saint – a waist a faerie could span with two hands – and eyes! Such wide-eyed innocence, sweetly demure – then suddenly, such a naughty sparkle – such an untouched rosebud that says, "Open me sir" – and those pouting lips –'

I consider. 'And a mind and will of her own. This, to Rochester, would be irresistible.'

Little Sid, sipping, offers his view of the business: 'I credit not the irresistibility of his impulses as some of you do. I think he made a decision in the cool light of judgment.'

'Judgment?' cries Shepherd. 'He got so hot he grabbed her in the face of the axe; what sort of judgment is this, that thinks with the pr—k?'

'I say he thought with his head,' says Sedley, ticking off the list on his fingers: 'Twenty-five hundred a year, a lady suited to his humour, beauty enough to keep him interested in returning to her bed. He knew he had found the best wife available; he rationally contrived the best scheme to win her, given her guardians' intransigence.'

'Rochester is not that cool,' protests Shepherd. 'If his reason were as much in control as you say, Sedley, he would not be drunk so often.'

'He is drunk,' argues Sedley, 'because wine so heightens his wit, we all refill his tankard; and because any man of reason is determined to soak up all the pleasure he can, life being nasty, brutish, and short. I wish you had seen him Sunday last, after the sermon at Whitehall chapel, hacking religion to pieces over a chine of beef at Long's. He disputes as incisively as a bishop, and he never loses control as he rips his opponent to shreds. I have never heard such logic.'

'So,' I muse, refilling my tankard, 'here is one of us to say his ruling passion is passion; t'other to say it is reason. Bucks, we still have not heard from you.'

Buckingham has been sitting quietly through this debate and looking diverted, as if he had some secret knowledge. Smiling in his imperturbable, polished way, he says, 'It was not the woman he thought of, nor her fortune. He was striking out at the King.'

'The King!' we all cry, astonished.

'Absolutely. Observe, if you please, the timing of this little adventure: sure to divert the King from his birthday cheer.'

'Well,' bursts in Shepherd, eyes wide, 'I see not why anyone would deliberately anger the King!'

I nudge his ribs. 'Rochester is not silenced in awe by majesty as Buckhurst is by women of virtue at court.' My chum grins.

'Nor,' explains Bucks, 'do I hold to Sedley's judgment that Rochester is the man of reason. I think there is a deal of the frustrated little boy in him. Anyone can see't the way he runs for all the sweetmeat trays in town and gorges himself sick. His Majesty has dangled a very desirable woman before Rochester and urged him to try for her, then caused him to work with so many restrictions that he is frustrated at every turn. It is rather like the father that tells his son he may have a pony if his lessons are good but then picks out the smallest vagary in his translation as an excuse not to fulfil the promise. He does what youth has done from time immemorial: he rebels.'

I regard Bucks dubiously. 'Your judgment is no doubt good of boys and fathers, Bucks, but this is the King we speak of.'

Bucks smiles his imperturbable smile. 'You should have seen Rochester's anger when I conveyed His Majesty's last message, which was to command him to cease suing for a time. "By Gad," Rochester exploded, "he thinks to divert himself by watching my alternate throes of hope and fear. But I'll show him I'm no helpless schoolboy, to proffer anxieties for his enjoyment." All of you forget his age because of his wit. He is barely eighteen. Buckhurst, you and Ashfield are five years older; Sedley is six-and-twenty, and Killigrew two years older than that; Etherege is already thirty, Shepherd some two years older; and the King and I, but some few years short of forty. He may see us as fathers as well as friends. '

'Then the more fool him,' groans Sedley. 'I am not prepared yet to play father to a fractious youth; I have one problem child already; that's enough for any man.'

We all laugh at the truth of this last.

'And I am not ready to be a father neither,' complains Shepherd. 'I have enough trouble controlling myself.'

'The time will come, Shepherd,' Sedley predicts, 'when the efforts you have made to control yourself are as naught, compared to the task of bridling a she-wildcat.'

We all laugh at this apt tag for the little Lady Katherine Sedley.

'It seems to me,' I muse as Shepherd utters an amiable curse or two in Little Sid's direction, 'that Rochester is more to blame for influencing all of us. It is he that writes the lewdest verse and gets drunk most often and requires the most women to satisfy him. He admitted himself that he was a drunkard at the age of twelve at Oxford.'

'He was a drunkard,' says Bucks, 'to please that older fellow Whitehall, who took an interest in him and dragged him to the taverns and stews.'

'Rochester was hardened in sin before we knew him,' protests Shepherd. 'The minute he was presented at court, he was swearing and cracking obscene jokes with the best of us.'

'He always adapts to the manners of his company,' says Bucks. 'I have it from His Majesty, who got it from Sir Andrew Balfour, his tutor on the Tour, that Rochester was a quiet and scholarly youth, who never so much as took the Lord's name in vain; who drank but seldom and burnt candles at night studying late; and that his only flaw was an insatiable craving for the embraces of women.'

'That last rings true,' quips Sedley.

'Sir Andrew told the King,' continues Bucks, 'that when the Tour ended last December, Rochester begged him, with tears in his eyes, not to go back to Scotland but to stay in town and make his home with him".'

At this revelation our eyes pop.

'Lying,' says Killigrew, 'to puff his accomplishments.'

We are silent a moment.

'It seems to me,' I muse, 'that we are still not very successful in understanding Rochester. I think he has shown a different side of himself to everyone he meets.'

'And it seems to me,' mocks Lying Harry, 'he has enjoyed fooling every one of you, no doubt that you might be brought to this moment. He is a man of a thousand masks.'

'Then I daresay,' Bucks snaps, 'the light-hearted mountebank he plays for you is but one of 'em.'

Killigrew has no proper answer but to retort, 'I hear that Your Grace still has not taken my advice to enjoy the Lady Shrewsbury. Or can it be that your noted charms and stratagems have proven powerless, in the face of her attraction to her other lover?'

Here we go at last. I much wondered at how Killigrew had restrained so long his lying tongue from its current game of pretending to enjoy the Lady Shrewsbury, itemizing her supposed naked virtues, urging Bucks to enjoy her, needling him for his want of success.

Bucks returns amiably, 'When I see her old husband, I'll inform him of the interest you have in the matter, and he can answer you himself.'

Nervously I plead, 'Let us have no more affairs of honour here; I have enough to regret at having pushed Rochester o'er the brink.'

'I repeat,' emphasizes a sipping Etherege, 'you pushed his lordship no more into it than the rest of us, who looked to him to lead the mode.'

'And I repeat,' says Sedley, 'no one pushes Rochester into anything.'

Killigrew slaps the table. A grin splits his ugly monkey face. 'Very true: y' have hit it! He has the Devil's fancy; 'tis his business to play at controlling others.'

'He may control others,' puts in Shepherd, 'but, like me, he is not very good at controlling himself. How about you, milord?'

He nudges Buckhurst. And my chum so broods o'er his tankard, I wonder if he recalls the drunken frolic of exposing himself half-clad on a balcony with Sedley, or the other freak that turned tragical, wherein he and his brother, thinking to play at catching robbers, ended up shedding blood.

'He was drunk,' says Buckhurst, 'and woke up sober in the Tower.'

'Buckhurst's arrow has hit the mark,' agrees Bucks. 'Rochester is still not quite grown: no matter what his wit, he is still prey to the rash passions of youth.'

And so the debate proceedeth, 'til the second bottle is drained and we advance to our dish of mackerel and pease. There must be as many Rochesters as there are Germans on the Rhine; doubtless none of us has the complete truth; and that, were there another voice to add to the debate, 'twould be raised with a yet more startling judgment. 'Tis reasonable to assume that Rochester had a good many motives for raping off the lady: that a prank seeming on the face of it outrageous must have been a cause to satisfy not only honour and reason, but passion too. And no doubt were we privy to all of his thoughts, there were yet other motives none of us could begin to guess at.

Perhaps we will hear more at the King's birthday.

2

'The King Mighty Angry And The Lord Sent to the Tower'

29 May 1665

Thence to my Lady Sandwiches.... Here, upon my telling her a story of my Lord Rochester's running away on Friday night last with Mrs Mallet, the great beauty and fortune ... who had supped at White-hall with Mrs Stewart and was going home to her lodgings with her grandfather, my Lord Haly, by coach, and was at Charing Cross seized on by both horse and foot-men and forcibly taken from him, and put into a coach with six horses and two women provided to receive her, and carried away. Upon immediate pursuit, my Lord of Rochester (for whom the King had spoke to the lady often, but with no success) was taken at Uxbridge; but the lady is not yet heard of, and the King mighty angry and the Lord sent to the Tower. Hereupon, my Lady did confess to me, as a great secret, her being concerned in this story – for if this match breaks between my Lord Rochester and her, then ... my Lord Hinchingbrooke stands fair, and is invited for her. She is worth ... 2500*l*. [pounds] per annum ... But my poor Lady, who is afeard of the sickness and resolved to be gone into the country, is forced to stay in town, a day or two or three about it, to see the end of it.

—Samuel Pepys, *Diary*, 28 May 1665

With a stir at the door, His Majesty enters his birthday celebration. Nodding graciously, throwing out his long bony hand in genial flourishes and waves of salutes, he strides into Barbara Castlemaine's wainscoted music room, the little black-and-white spaniels yapping at his heels. Ladies lining two sides of his pathway bow low, hands spreading skirts, eyes modestly down; and as he passes, his eyes shoot down toward their bosoms.

The King, tall and slender, his long, dark face creased with lines from the huge nose to the little moustache, his brown eyes sparkling and thin lips curved in a smile, nods to the right and left, one fist on a hip so the ermined cape with the Garter is slung over the thin

shoulder. In his wake hath followed two guards with rods and hal-
berds, to station themselves on either side of the door.

Fiddles and flutes strike up the merry strains of 'When the King
Enjoys his Own Again', and the lot of us sing and clap.

The King, still nodding, still flourishing his hand and saying, 'Bless
you, bless you,' saunters across to where Barbara kneels, her skirts
spread out, her auburn-curled head bent down. He raises her up with
a bejewelled hand. 'Thank you, my dear,' he says vaguely, his eyes
darting about.

Barbara stares up at him with a cat's eyes: eager, possessive, her
hand over her childfull belly swollen out under the blue watered silk.
But he heeds not the mistress he hath got with so many children; he
looks for the one that hath not yielded to his blandishments.

Suddenly his face lights up. 'Ah, there's my pretty pet, my *mimeaux*.'

He looks dotingly upon Stewart, who waddles up, her head at a coy
angle and her lips pursed in a pretty mouth.

'Oh, tee-hee, Your Majesty!' She turns to blink on the King, puts a
coy finger to her mouth, tilts her head. 'Now, I wonder if I should kiss
a king on his birthday, indeed I do!'

The King regards her fondly. 'Kiss not the King, my dear, but the
man who loves you.'

She squeals, claps her hands together, and stands on pretty tiptoes
to put her mouth on his, both of 'em clasping hands.

Barbara's face hath gone pasty white. 'Your Majesty,' she murmurs,
and with another curtsey and crisp nod, scoops a goblet from the silver
tray held by the black houseboy and taketh herself off to disappear in
the crowd.

My heart wrenches for her. But a year or two ago, she would have
made one of her inimitable scenes: raged, stormed, threatened, made
off to her uncle's house in Richmond till the King once again got
down on his knees to beg pardon. Now she bites her lip and holds in
her famous temper. For were she to post off to Richmond, the King
might not follow.

As the King and Stewart break mouths, I sidle closer, on a pull to
introduce the topic of Rochester; but I am mowed down by a score of
other toadies, yapping like the little dogs.

The oily frog, the Comte de Gramont, raises a goblet. 'Huzzah! Let
us drink to the thirty-fifth anniversary of royalty and the fifth of
justice!'

The King regards him drily. 'Monsieur Le Comte is as politic as his
royal master.'

The other bowers-and-scrapers burst in, each delivering the polite compliment or jest that hath been polished all day as one sat to picture, another beneath the barber's hands or at cups.

'I drink to Your Majesty's birthday in the open, now, instead of in the dark!'

'May the next five years bring Your Majesty even greater health and fortune!'

'May Your Majesty soon bring the nation peace, as he hath already restored it to happiness!'

The King looks vague, waves his hand. 'Bless you – bless you!'

A toady plucks the King's sleeve. 'Your Majesty – about that place for my sister with the Duke of York –'

The King, eyes scanning the corners for a convenient nook, waves a hand. 'Bless you – see my brother about that.'

One at his elbow shouts, 'Your Majesty, the commission still has not come through for my son. You remember –'

The King waves hand again. 'Bless you – see Mr Pepys in the Navy Office.'

'But, Your Majesty, I already have –'

The King's eyes light up a second time. 'Ah, here we are.'

The tall, stout figure of his brother the Duke of York marches up, grasps him by the two arms, and embraces him heartily with cheek laid to cheek on both sides.

'Jamie, 'tis good to see thee!'

'Happy birthday, sire, and may you enjoy many more.'

The King fondly stares on the hulking, stolid figure before him. 'Now, there's a kind sentiment to come from my heir.'

Laughter and applause greet this sally. The King smiles, flourishes a hand at his audience, darts an eye towards a corner where two velvet chairs sit drawn up, and leans down to whisper to the eye-batting Stewart. I open my mouth to plead for Rochester, ere the King disappear with his toy, but then the Duke of Monmouth bounds up.

With his long, slender form and delicate face, he is said to resemble his mother, Lucy Water, who took the King's mind somewhat off his exile.

'Happy birthday, Father! I've brought you a gift.'

The pretty youth hands over to the swarthy, horse-faced father a small box with a ribbon tied round it. The disparity in looks 'twixt 'em hath given His Majesty the affectionate tag-name 'Old Rowley', after the ugly old stallion in the Mews that sires beautiful offspring.

'Why, thank you, James.' The King gazes just as tenderly on him as he would if the boy's birth had been legitimate. They embrace.

The toadies crowd round, clamouring in mingled voices. The King,

101

ignoring 'em, makes to pull on the ribbon and open the box, but then suddenly turns round behind him and crooks an eyebrow. One of the guards marches up.

'Keep this for me till later.'

The man bows, backs to the door, and stands with the halberd in one hand and box in the other.

'Father, why could we not have had a ball to celebrate this day?'

The King smiles drily. 'Too great a threat of contagion, Jamie, given the plague – and of expenditure, too.'

No doubt Barbara can afford more entertainments than the King: she's always bleeding the Privy Purse.

As the King's eyes roam to the corner, no doubt looking out the properest place whither to retire for fondling, I shout above the clamour, 'What can Your Majesty tell us of the Lord Rochester?'

He turns on me that bemused gaze, the constant look of cynical enjoyment with which he watcheth the parade of human folly. 'That my favourite spaniel has bitten me.'

'Your Majesty!' shout the voices. 'Your Majesty!'

He waves his hand at the throng and sweeps 'round him a stern look. 'Give us leave, good people.'

They fall silent as he strides to the corner, the plump white hand of giggling Stewart on his arm.

Around me then the talk buzzes on Rochester's madness. Why would he so fright a lady that he barely knew and anger her guardians? Why would he inflame the King, who'd been pleading his cause before?

So resty am I, listening to the ill-informed nonsense, suffering from the great heat, I sweat like a very devil on a bed of hot coals and fan myself a little with the sides of my heavy jacket that fashion will not suffer me to put off.

Then I remember Barbara is Rochester's distant kinswoman. Perhaps her charms will count for more than mine in wheedling intelligence or mercy from the King.

I meander over to where she guffaws, her mouth open, her hand twirling the goblet. I tap her invitingly exposed shoulder.

'Barbara, I'm worried about Rochester.'

She tilts up her goblet, drains the contents. 'Best not to press Charles on that subject.'

'So I noticed. Can you do anything?'

She shrugs, her eyes glazed with drink. Then, with a grimly wry look, she nods forward to where Stewart makes a colloquy with the King in the corner.

'Better not ask me. Ask that tight-c—ted little goose.'

I had been engaged in a lusty swig from my goblet. Now I laugh so uproariously I spray wine all o'er my cravat.

Barbara slings her goblet on the tray presented by the black houseboy and grabs a full replacement. The crowd titters, for it is all the talk how the King visits Stewart's chambers each morning after breakfast, then leaves languishing and sighing because the lady holds the line against granting the final favour.

'What know you of Rochester's fate?' I press.

She shrugs, tilts up the goblet. 'He's in the middle storey of the Beauchamp Tower. The King told George' – she alludes here to her cousin, George Villiers, Duke of Buckingham – '"You yourself have lived in worse rooms in Holland."'

'But think you the King will exact the legal penalty?'

She shrugs. 'Unlikely, given his easiness. But he's under pressure from Parliament, and he knows he rules by their good grace.'

A liveried lackey stands in the threshold and announces supper. The crowd drifts, chattering, fanning, towards the doorway.

'I'll do my best, Ashfield. But my best isn't much good any more.' The last words she delivereth bitterly, with a glance toward the King and Stewart, sweeping from the room together, his red velvet cloak trailing beside her pale blue moire.

I take poor Barbara in, feeling as sad for her as I always doth for the poor Queen (notably absent tonight).

At the supper I am seated beside Etherege, who is clad in a fine suit of black with white garniture, and who cultivates the most important notables within earshot, his remarks apt and polished, his carriage full of delight and wonder that he attends the King's birthday dinner. During a break in his toadying to the other nobility, I insert the news that we may be assured of Rochester's comfortable confinement.

He replies, separating the pieces of his lark, 'I am not much feared His Majesty would injure his lordship. What I worry about most is the plague.'

'What, is't so bad?'

He nods soberly. 'His Majesty thinks of leaving town, should the cases continue to multiply at this rate.'

I sit with tear-filled eyes o'er my supper as fancy paints my friend stricken by plague and heat in the Tower ; then I set my lark's wing down, to wipe my fingers on the napkin. The candle before me is a dancing blur.

'His Majesty thinks of leaving town,' I observe in a voice rather choked, 'but he confines Rochester to the Tower, which is sure to be the most unwholesome place of all.'

Gentle George, as we call him, seeks to cheer me: 'He does no such thing! I am sure he will release my Lord of Rochester as soon as we all leave. Now eat your supper, if you please, my lord: it cools.'

I stare glumly at the doomed lark, now but a pile of meat and bones. 'I cannot eat, not with Rochester under sentence of death.'

'Come, my lord: speak not so; no one believes the King will injure his lordship.'

I mechanically pick up the lark wing and nibble a bit on the juicy crunch of't. 'I know what *you* would do, if you were king,' I retort, mouth half full. 'Make him Lord Chancellor. But we speak of Charles Stuart here, not George Etherege. And there is still the plague to consider.'

'My lord, it is early days yet, both for his lordship's arrest and for the plague. I'm not happy about the situation, but we perforce must wait it out.' He swallows a gulp of fine Rhenish. 'I think the King's giving my Lord of Rochester such humane confinement is a sign His Majesty loves his lordship and will not let him come to harm.'

I peer down the long row of elegant diners to the head table, where presides the King. One moment he appeareth melancholy and pre-occupied; the next he bursts into laughter to make a spry retort, ironic eyebrow lifted.

Etherege plainly does not wish to consider the worst lest he be moved to bestir himself to prevent it. Sedley and crew seem not even to care: they laugh, jostle one another with playful elbows, burst into snatches of song, gossip on one another's follies. Barbara, clearly a less competent ally than she would have been a few years before, sits at the King's side, reading every muscle in his face, laughing raucously at his every joke, and applying herself heavily to the goblet before her. The King pays her polite heed but plainly dotes on Stewart, t'other side of him: feeds her bits of lark, wipes her chin, &c – and laughs delightedly at all, as if he be a mama with a new infant.

After the supper, which I feel guilty eating, Etherege gathers up the broken breads for feeding of birds, and thence we progress to the music room, where the fiddles, trumpets, horns &c are prepared, and chairs have been lined up in stiff rows. The Devil take me if I know why no supper is thought complete without the obligatory boring set pieces. I much prefer Rochester's method, to have in a fiddler that plays sprightly airs and drinking songs that are to be talked to or provide an opportunity for lively singing.

But in these formal consorts one must sit straight-backed and attentive, though so full of lark and wine and oysters, and usually by then in want of a piss but unable to skulk off to find a close-stool or window. At Bucks' consorts everyone talks openly and swills brandy, and Sedley has been known to piss out of a window, but tonight everyone seems constrained by the gravity of the King's presence, the occasion of his fifth-and-thirtieth birthday, and the knowledge of his vexation with Rochester.

The musicians are more constrained than anyone, and rather than rousing us with a Civil War ballad, must needs stride solemn-footed through an entire suite of Lully, with processionals so grand I can almost picture the French Machiavel Louis a-strutting: Gramont's royal master, as the King so aptly and drily tagged him. I squirm in my chair, longing to piss and thinking of what I'd do with a whore, could I escape – every bit as if I were in church.

Barbara has somehow pried the King loose of Stewart, and she sits with His Majesty behind me. They, unlike the rest of us, have the bravado to talk – and as the strings lift into a sprightlier crescendo, their voices rise too, in what sounds like strife.

Pretending to drop a handkerchief, I lean down to retrieve it, a gesture which enables me to glance behind and see that Barbara looks none too steady. Her eyelids droop, her face puffs, and her famous person, once designed alone for Venus' follies, sits askew, the belly swollen out and the once-famous breasts a little pendulant.

'How can you be so unkind, Charles, to a pair of lovers?'

The King's brow furrows, the black eyebrows pointing down in vexation, the lines about his mouth tightening. 'Get a command on yourself, madam.'

Barbara hiccups. I try to shoot her a pleading glance, to let her know this is not the best time or method to argue Rochester's cause. Indeed, what she is like to do is inspire His Majesty to some brutality against Rochester, as she herself, when angry, is wont to take the birch to one of her babies.

'What's the good of being king if you must obey the law?'

The trumpets blast and the strings sing, and the presence of old Louis seems to frown on this insult to sovereignty. I much wonder that Etherege has not fainted at it, especially at the address of 'Charles'.

His Majesty mutters an indistinguishable reply, in which I catch the words 'Hawley' and 'Parliament'. A few ladies seated across from us dart looks in our direction, giggle, and raise fans to confer. I long to turn about and look again but cannot contrive another means to do't. Even I would not drop a handkerchief twice in a row.

'You do not give a Goddamn about him or me either one!' her voice blasts over the trumpets. 'All you care about is that insipid fool Stewart, that empty-headed little goose!'

The urge to laugh at this apt description of her character is very strong; nor does everyone who hears it forebear the delight of so doing. Stewart sits across from us wide-eyed and big-boobied, blinks a few times, understands naught.

Then pretending to shift in my chair, I cast a backward glance at His Majesty, whose sweat-beaded brow darkens with vexation. I sweat a little more myself in the stifling crowd, the hot bodies so close packed in the thick air, and feel the shirt stick to me in clumps beneath my heavy wool jacket. I hope Rochester is not as uncomfortably hot as I fear. I hope e'en more that Barbara will not provoke the King. I try to catch her eyes with mine to warn her off, but she is too absorbed in the text of her own grievances. She has, moreover, that thunderous expression which always signifies her imminent eruption into a threatening speech. Then, as I turn back around, the cone of the mountain breaks, and the fire pours forth.

'I'll throw your children in the street! I'll break their legs and set 'em out with bowls to beg! I'll cut 'em in pieces and serve 'em to you in a stew! I'll fire your apartments and let all your horses and falcons out of the Mews – Charles! Are you listening to me?'

All at once the music ceases, and a great mingled rumble and gasp go up. I turn about to see that the King has arisen, white-faced and trembling. With a great rustle of skirts and coats, we all stand.

'Madam,' he thunders, 'I leave you here, to recover yourself. And I advise you to beg no more for your young cousin, lest we all wonder what your interest be in him!'

And then the King sweeps from his chair, knocking it over in his haste, and lopes for the door, the spaniels yapping at his heels, everyone bowing or curtseying at his passage.

'Charles, you forget my great belly!' she screams with a hand on it. 'Charles!' Then, as he continues to stride, she, seeing that dodge helpless, cries out, her voice quavering in fear, 'I'll take my plate and servants again and go to my uncle's house in Richmond!'

The door slams on the other side of the apartments; Barbara collapses in her chair and begins to blubber, after the fashion of some drunks; and, seeing how much older and less lovely she looks, with her drunkenness and rage, her spoilt pasty complexion and swelling womb, I feel sorry for her. She's no longer the termagant that rules Whitehall with her capricious temper. She's a poor lady who's lost power, beauty, and love alike.

As the music strikes up quickly again, I push my chair out of alignment and go to His Majesty's chair, which I pick up from the polished floor. Then, sitting next to her, I put an arm about her shoulders to make soothing noises the best way I know how.

'He doesn't love me any more, Ashfield,' she blubbers loudly, almost drowning out the music, leaning against my breast, impervious to all the eyes that watch her.

'Of course he does,' I protest. With an arm still about her shoulder, I dig in my waistcoat for a handkerchief, on which she blows her nose heartily.

'He doesn't love me,' she insists, as the fiddlers take up a sprightly counterpoint. 'He would never have walked out a year ago. 'Tis that damned Stewart.'

I glance over to where Stewart blinks, surprised; and I long to tell Barbara that her quixotic humours, as much as her rival's young charms, must be the cause of his ardour cooling, but I have more sense than to rub salt in a raw wound. So I merely lie, ineptly, 'He loves you, Barbara. I know he does.'

She looks up red-faced and puffy-eyed as the strings commence a long slow march. 'Does he truly?'

I nod, trying to feel for another handkerchief but unable to locate one. The Lord Richard Butler presses one into my hand, at which I smile gratitude and give it her.

But then she asks a question I had little anticipated: 'How do you know?' And her eyes are set deliberately on my face, to read the truth of my answer.

The strings undulate in a slow, lazy pattern, and everyone stares at the diverting scene we make, whispering and nudging, so that I feel like the elephant in the Tower menagerie.

'I can tell,' I reply lamely. Then, seeing how she stares at me, I add, 'Does he not continue to support you lavishly?'

'Yes,' she snuffles, 'but 'tis much of it guilt, or the reluctance to incur a scene, I know.'

Seeing that she is about to break into fresh tears, I think until my brain bursts, and I get an inspiration.

'His Majesty said but recently he was convinced anew how much he loved you.' She clutches Butler's handkerchief, and hope leaps into the green eyes that search my face.

'He did? When?'

I cudgel my brain. 'Not long ago – just after Mayday. The gang was sitting with the King at cups, and he and Rochester were exchanging some witticisms about marriage.'

But my happy intelligence has not the fate I had hoped. She regards me warily. 'What precisely did they say, Ashfield?'

I sweat even more in the close, hot air. 'Oh, it was some silly stuff about rivals and husbands and cuckolds. What I do recall, Barbara, is that the King remarked all husbands should be as pliable as yours – then commented, the full fruits of his love for you had recently come home to him.'

She collapses against my breast and shudders with a new spate of tears. 'That was one of his dry ironies. We had fought on Mayday over his attentions to that – My God, why didn't I think of it before?'

'Think of what, Barbara?'

She sits up, her tears forgot at this new inspiration of jealousy. 'It is that pert little pout-mouth of a p—k-tackle! God, why didn't I see't before? And here I wondered why the King was so angry.'

My heart stops at this last. 'Barbara, of what do you speak?'

'That sly little baggage from the West Country! Charles's mouth watered when he saw her at Tunbridge last June – and you can bet he's let Rochester know it, too! Ha, pliable husbands indeed! They were trading barbs about her future.'

I stare at her aghast.

''Tis true,' she insists. 'You should have seen the gleam in his eye. He's issued some score of invitations to her, and the guardians turned 'em all down. It seems the invitations were worded to hint that she come alone. It was that we fought over.'

I continue to stare aghast at Barbara. Finally I sputter, 'I cannot believe it of the King, Barbara – not with a little miss he tried to secure for a young friend. No, I will not.'

'Turds!' sniffs Barbara, wiping her nose. 'You think too well of everyone, Ashfield. 'Tis your gravest flaw. We all love you for't, but no one would pay much heed to your judgment of anyone's character.'

'Well, all of you err too much on the side of cynicism!' I protest. 'I'm sure the King only tried to plead Rochester's cause.'

'And I'm sure I know how to interpret that gleam in the King's eye. God knows I've seen't often enough before.'

'Barbara –'

'Not that he'll do aught, her not being by; for he never exerts himself too much – he'll chase some handier skirt,' she adds cynically. 'To hear you tell it, though, he but 'joyed himself in fencing wits with Rochester, and neither of 'em was much concerned about the woman in the case.'

'I heard it not that way.'

'But you're not a woman. You're not accustomed to being itemized, possessed, and cast off after use.' Her voice is bitter.

The musicians play the last long trill and then rise, to bow to applause.

I determine that she broods on her own ills and cannot consider another's; so I bow, express my thanks for her supper, and join the throng crowding for the door.

3

'Venus Smiles Not In A House Of Tears'
6 June 1665

... so to my Lady Sandwiches.... She tells me my Lord Rochester is now declaredly out of hopes of Mrs Mallett, and now she is to receive notice in a day or two how the King stands enclined to the giving leave for my Lord Hinchingbrooke to look after her.
—Samuel Pepys, *Diary*, 6 June 1665

Paris: Immoderately she weeps ...
   And therefore have I little talked of love,
   For Venus smiles not in a house of tears.
—William Shakespeare, *Romeo and Juliet*

More than a week hath passed. Rochester, who hath a fanatic conceit for cleanliness and washes himself all over with water, sometimes once and more in a day, lies in the Tower, in the midst of the worst heat wave in memory, with no means to wash himself or shift his shirt and linen; with no occupations for his active fancy save thoughts of the axe and the loss of love and royal favour; with the plague increasing daily, more and more houses being shut up and their families, sick and sound alike, left within to languish.

The talk that runs through the galleries is bad. Mallet hath been found and verges on a marriage contract with Hinchingbrooke. The King will say nothing of his intents toward Rochester and will suffer nothing to be brought him, not book nor writing paper nor water for washing, though allowing him good measure of meat and wine. Hawley pressures for the death penalty.

As for Rochester's friends, that heartless mob, they disport themselves (and I with 'em) playing of bowls on Whitehall green or taking water to the Spring Garden; delighting over Rhenish and oysters to the usual gossip, what the factions are and who and who's together; taking water or coach to Dorset House, to scare up Buckhurst for a party to Black Bess's; or watching another party sit to cards.

But Barbara being so ineffectual a pleader, and the rest of us doing no better, I determine to call upon the Lord Ormond's clan at Whitehall, to see whether anyone there may be moved to do aught for the Boy Genius.

As Lord Lieutenant of Ireland, Ormond hath an influence as vast as his wealth, and a moral sway no less. With his leonine head and gruff grandeur, he hath outfaced two kings now; once he and the present monarch quarrelling, Bucks joked, 'Was't the Duke of Ormond out of favour with the King, or the King out of favour with the Duke of Ormond? For His Majesty looked by far the more out of countenance of the two.'

Then there is his indomitable, high-principled lady, of whose moral influence, Cromwell said, he was more frighted than of any Stuart army; for that she could raise a rebellion with the mere lending of her name to a cause.

These two hath given birth to a brood more full of honour than a meeting of Knights of the Garter. The father and numerous sons would be racked rather than stoop to low associations or tell a lie; the eldest son, Lord Ossory, I think has never so much as lain with a whore, even before his marriage; and the greatest marvel is, no one jeers him for marital fidelity, no doubt being afeard to encounter his sword.

So, after sleeping but ill by reason of the great heat, I take coach to Whitehall and call upon the Lord Ossory at his section of the Duke's apartments.

He asking what I think on the sea war with the Dutch and I thinking very little but how to begin talk of Rochester, I make a polite answer when his lady joins us with a few of their babes. His little ones are so polite and well-bred, one can sometimes pay 'em the compliment of forgetting they are children.

I watch the pleasant family: the flaxen-haired, slender lady, her heart-shaped face glowing simple sweetness as she runs her stubby fingers through a little boy's hair; and the proud, stiff, formal father, his back straight, his large lantern jaw set and his gaze lofty, his warrior's breast swelled out with pride. Almost a softness comes o'er his stern countenance as he watches his brood.

'Lord Ossory,' I say, 'I might e'en consign myself to marriage had I hopes of such bliss as yours, and 'tis on marriage I've come to speak today. I'm very concerned about a friend of mine, and I wonder if you or your father might help somehow.'

Ossory nods, his head high, his gaze sombre. 'Speak, my lord. If it is consonant with honour, all who are Christians are enjoined to help those in distress.'

'It is about my friend Rochester.'

A run of bubbly laughter interrupts my thoughts. Into the threshold bounds Ossory's sister the Lady Chesterfield, leaping and galloping, squeezing her brother John at the waist as she flits to his side. He smiles down on her.

'You've outstripped me, baby brother! But I will ever be wandering by the way to gossip, and you'll not wait. Ah! – I've a mind to tickle you for going on ahead, impertinent creature, and make you giggle as I did when you wore skirts.' She flounces at him, her hands out.

Butler, laughing, wards off her sudden attack. They wrestle a moment, her tiny dainty hands ineffectual against his large broad ones. Ossory frowns on their frivolity.

''Nuff ! 'Nuff!' cries the lady at last, at which he releases her wrists. Then she, tilting her lovely oval face at an angle, her dark curls tumbling, winks at Ossory. 'Thomas, what d'ye think? I've disobeyed my husband and gone out – been riding, and that, with my favourite man, too.' She punches Butler affectionately in the ribs. 'Think you my lord will post back to the country with me again, to remove me from my lovers?'

'Very like,' says Ossory grimly.

'La, la! What a grave puss we have!' Lady Chesterfield flounces over to a chair and flings herself down into it; legs sprawled, she removes the green velvet monteer from her head and commences to fan herself. 'You men – well, I suppose if he could be jealous of my cousin James, why not my little brother? La, Thomas! How some men never love a woman 'til she cuckolds 'em.'

She babbles after her sprightly fashion, cooing to the babes that have toddled over, patting a small head here and tickling a chin there; unfastening the top two buttons of her man-tailored riding jacket.

Ossory frowns and looks at his lady, who eyes the little ones as if considering whether to send them away from conversation so free.

'John, what ails you? – Scandalized, I suppose, just when your sister's found *such intimate favour* with the Duke of York! La! You are more Tommish than Thomas, as grave as a thousand Papas – Oh! You hang about this stiff-lipped gang too much. I must on with my plot to get you a wife as giddy as I: she'll lighten your humour.'

Butler's hand clenches where it rests on a chair back. 'I've told you, Betty, I have no plans to marry.'

'La! Still o' th' sour humour, I see! Indeed you've talked to my lord: you fear his fate.'

Stiffly, Ossory says, 'The Lord Ashfield is here, Betty, out of concern for his friend Rochester. I've told him we cannot do aught to help.'

'Ooooo,' she says knowingly, her small pink tongue flicking at the side of her mouth.

'I was about to tell his lordship,' interrupts Butler, 'that I plan to speak to His Majesty on the subject.'

Butler and Ossory stare stonily at one another.

'Ooooo, better and better!' cries the Lady Chesterfield, lazily fanning herself with the monteer. 'Well, do what you will, baby brother: that's nothing to the purpose here.'

'Agreed, for I will not marry.'

He stares firmly at her; she rolls up her blue eyes.

'Lady Chesterfield,' I break in, 'as I'm mightily obliged to your brother here for his kindness –' He inclines his head politely '– I feel bound to take up for him. There are many of us not eager to embrace marital bliss.'

With such droll irony do I produce the last few words that she trills a run of laughter and cocks her head at me, her black eyelashes fluttering, her tongue tip showing.

'Yea, Lord Ashfield – but not my bonny brother here. Mother and Father agree with me. Emilie, what say you?'

The Lady Ossory smiles at her husband and announces, with a voice that bears a trace of her Dutch origin, 'That ve must all hound John to get a vife.'

'Not I,' he protests, his mouth in a grim line.

'La!' cries the Lady Chesterfield. 'A young man soured on wedlock, and his big sister, I vow, to blame! But no one would cuckold you, John, as I do my Lord Chesterfield, to requite his womanizing!'

The little ones have crowded about the two ladies to tug at skirts or crawl into laps. 'Tis plain their parents take more care and thought with 'em than most do. Buckhurst and his brother were suffered to run wild in the nursery with an indulgent and lazy nurse, and every now and then, being detected in one of their more incredible pranks, they had the indignity of their father ordering 'em a birching by a footman. But Ossory and his lady offer loving, firm guidance.

It doth the heart good to see 'em caress one another with their glances and the little ones cleaving so trustingly to her side. I note they do not approach their father; but then, who at court is not a little awed by Ossory's mien of quiet, intransigent honour?

All at once the smallest boy bursts out, no doubt in mimicry of his elders, 'Uncle John, you need a wife,' whereat a general laugh goes up and he looks not a little pleased with his performance.

Ossory gives him a severe look. 'James, children may remain to hear the conversation so long as they do not speak.'

Lady Chesterfield rolls her round blue eyes at me, and indeed this reprimand does seem a little strict, for he had interrupted only once. A silence falls, during which the little boy hangs his head, obviously ashamed to the blood: at which Ossory, seeming to relent a little, says in gentler tones, 'Come here, child,' and the boy doing so, the father smiles and ruffles his hair a little: a gesture to let him know he is loved. The boy looks up into his father's face and smiles, and for a moment I expect he will climb on his father's knee, but he does not: he covers his blushing face and runs to Mama to bury it in her skirts – whereat she smiles and pats his head.

The Lady Chesterfield gives her favourite brother an earnest look. 'We only hound you, dear, because we love you, and we know your feelings. No good, you cannot hide 'em, you never have: that face has ever told all. Now, you know you cannot leave her with that wooden-headed prude; you know her affection for you; and Papa has promised you need not haggle. He'll send Nicholls. Your part, bonny brother, is to appear later: the charming lover.' She smiles.

Fretting, Butler pulls at his tight holland-band. 'I am no charming lover and will not masquerade as one. I cannot write verse or even quote it; the only language I speak well at all is my own. I am a plain ordinary man of sense, without any great wit or special attractions; and I will not be compelled into the absurdity of playing some role I must perforce fail in.'

She shakes her head in dismay. 'John, look in your glass. You know not your attractions –' On a sudden she turns to me. 'Nor do you, Ashfield – ah, he colours: – what a sweet baby 'tis, with its shy manners and green eyes – and how I long to pinch its rosy cheeks and make it blush the more – no, I'll not – I'll pinch my Dickie instead.' And she tweaks the little boy nearest her, who bursts out laughing; and then cuddles his squirming body to her breast, but with her eyes looking a very plain invitation to me over the child's head.

Now I grow very uncomfortable; for despite this lady's beauty and wit, I have no desire to tangle with her jealous husband, who may be soon enraged enough to begin quarrelling over her. I have never been called upon to draw my sword yet, and God help me if I ever am.

Then the Lady Ossory, whose own happiness causes her to incline to matrimony, offers up, 'Ve must get Ashvield a vife, too.'

'Not I!' I cry in a horror that would have done credit to Buckhurst.

Butler laughs. 'Ashfield, we must concert an alliance against the ladies that would cajole us to the church door.'

I am about to agree when Ossory breaks in, his long jowls grim, his voice authoritative. 'John, now you listen here. Father and I have both

agreed on this business; and I know that you'll thank us later, for
forcing you, when you consider –'

I am surprised at the violence with which Butler turns on him.
'Thomas, I am a man now and will take no more lickings from you in
Father's absence.' Seeing his brother's hurt expression, he adds hastily, 'I know your motives are irreproachable. But if you love me, you
will desist from coercing me into another futile and humiliating
contest; I have competed already a whole lifetime with a father and a
half score elder brothers who excel in every accomplishment.'

We all stare at him aghast, incordiality being such a rarity with him,
and loving kindness being the usual mode with this family. Though
often envying this large clan their warm, noisy happiness with one
another, I never till now thought on how it must feel to arrive as the
youngest male in a household so brimful of accomplishments. Indeed,
everyone speaks of Ossory's nobility, Arran's sportsmanship, the
Duke's magnanimity, &c; but no one mentions Butler much at all,
though he is such a well-bred and thoughtful gentleman, in another
family he might be its chiefest ornament.

Ossory speaks up at once. 'John, I am distressed at your attitude. It is
my conviction –'

'No speeches, Thomas, I pray you. And if you vex Mother with any
of this, I promise to beat you with my fists.'

'I would e'en let you do't,' replies the gallant elder brother, 'if you
stopped this silly talk of competing.'

'I will, then,' he agrees, 'as I have long renounced any hopes of
accomplishing anything thereby. I've done fencing with you, or
shooting with Arran, or guitaring with Richard: all of you had first
claim on the family titles and talents; when I came along there was
nothing to be granted but a modicum of the family looks.'

'Stuff!' cries the Lady Chesterfield, smiting her boot with her riding
crop. 'Can you hear him? Thomas, make him go to the glass and look
at that face; then name any woman that will scorn it!'

'Richard's the lover in the family,' protests Butler.

'Richard has the flair,' she argues, 'as shallow water sings louder. He
has the guitar, the verses, the pretty speeches – but you've ten times
his mind.'

'Call me the family intellect, then,' acquiesces Butler wearily. ''Tis
tame enough, when you instruct me to compete with a compendium
of your wit, Richard's charm, Arran's agility, and Thomas' daring
honour – ah, yes, and we must add James's scholarship, into the
bargain! – I might as well compete with Father, who is the compendium of all the virtues.'

'You cannot make comparisons with Father here,' argues the loving sister.

'Why not? Did he not get Mother away from Lord Holland, who was marketing her to the highest bidder and refusing her the man she loved? Where would she have been with someone as impotent as I to rescue her?'

'Butler,' I object, ''tis part of the cross we must all bear, to be compared with our fathers or brothers or even friends. But though anyone would find in your relations much to praise, he would not find you therefore wanting. You are simply a different person.'

'Yes,' Butler returns sardonically, 'I have a sword I do not use and a wit that arrives at rejoinders an hour after the occasion has passed.'

'And a deal of other virtues,' says Lady Chesterfield, 'that he does not.'

Butler smiles bitterly. 'And all of 'em very dull – though pleasing to my mother and sister.'

'And to your vife, too, John,' breaks in the Lady Ossory, stroking her son's head where it lies in her lap. 'A voman vants a man she can depend upon.' And here the lady and her husband exchange a touchingly tender smile.

''Deed, yes, Emilie: you say,' exclaims the Lady Chesterfield passionately. 'Here is one, John, to tell you – who thought she married for love – dazzled by a dazzler – who was after my father's money. Now see how happy I am – love, la! Love is what she will end by feeling for you. Father has writ this day from Kilkenny, as Thomas says, and he agrees with us.'

Butler seems so plainly distressed by this entire business, I refrain from intruding to ask who his lady is. He returns, 'Then I must write to Father myself. I have given a promise that honour demands I keep.'

'"Honour" – sooth-la!' breaks in the Lady Chesterfield passionately. 'Think of this angle a while: which of her two approved suitors would "honour" her person and her feelings?'

Butler flushes and stares at the hands working in his lap.

'Which would be likelier to force her affections on the nuptial night? Which would "honour" her sentiments, be nicer about restraining his passions until he receives encouragements they are returned?'

Butler stares at the large square hands clasping and unclasping in his lap. 'Betty, I beg you to drop a subject which is painful to me.'

She smites her boot impatiently with the riding crop.

'You are too reticent and humble, John. But we will do your wooing for you.'

I take polite leave of 'em then; but, considering what little I've done for my friend Rochester, feel more in despair than ever. What boots it that some youth no older than Rochester hath promised to plead for him?

I decide there's only one cure for my melancholy, and that is, a good debauch. 'Tis the court medicine: no matter how temperate a man on coming here, the manners soon draw him ever deeper into drink.

And I – who arrived here five years before almost dry – go now a-rowing on an ocean of sack, 'til the next two days pass in a blur.

And I awake to a world far worse than the one I sought to leave.

4

'Lord Have Mercy Upon Us'
9 June 1665

... it being the hottest day that ever I felt in my life, and it is confessed so by all other people the hottest they ever knew in England in the beginning of June.... This day, much against my will, I did in Drury-lane see two or three houses marked with a red cross upon the doors, and 'Lord have mercy upon us' writ there.
—Samuel Pepys, *Diary*, 7 June 1665

Lying in the morning with eyelids closed, I hear the bells go ten, at which I begin to consider where I can be, that they seem to chime the hour so close, the Chapel of St Paul's, Covent Garden not having a set so loud and lusty, nor so skilful a change-ringer to peal the varied sounds and positions. Nor doth the bed beneath my sweaty back seem fit – a great lump poking me beneath the kidneys.

Then, daring at last to open my eyes, I see a close, filthy chamber little like to joy me: the sunlight streaming through cracks in the eaves and splintered boards, a window curtainless and unglazed. The warped door leans on its joints, with a rope for a knob to secure it (no new-fashion knockers here); beside it leans a splintered table, listing to one side on a broken leg, and with no chairs.

'Awake, are you, sweetheart?'

I turn, a little stunned, to see a filthy woman beside me in the narrow bed, her mouth painted cheap red. Somewhere within the bowels of the dwelling rats skitter and squeak.

'Tis plain I have fallen to the stupidest of all follies, for which I am ever scolding Rochester, and from which I have ever held myself too high to practise: which is, enjoy one of the lowest women of the town.

I try a pull at recollecting what could have happened last night, but cannot ever recall leaving the Bear at Bridge-Foot, where we all disported ourselves with oceans of sack.

Then, a throbbing pain stabbing me in the lower jaw, I, feeling with

118

my tongue, discern I have a cavern there where a perfectly sound tooth used to be.

This is enough to make a man believe his sovereign reason is not what the philosophers tell him, if drink could so easily wipe it out. Here I had apparently been a beast last night, and lost a tooth God knows how, yet can remember naught of't; no doubt I have the pox by now, or at least a thousand fleas; and have been very likely robbed into the bargain.

Dejected, enraged, sick of myself and the whole human creation, I begin to fumble with the laced linen shirt I have dropped to the floor.

'How about another go, sweetheart?'

With a glance over my shoulder at the wretched creature I must have embraced in my drunken longings, I refuse as politely as possible and clap my elegant fair periwig to my head – not without wincing to think of how oft my class flies to art whilst the bulk of the town lives in the ragged bowels of nature.

Her eyes flit to the bulging purse I scoop from the floor. 'You wasn't to stay, you said; so that'll be –' She considers, then regards me with shrewd, hopeful eyes '– five shillings again.'

I see plainly she believes she cheats me, but the sum of five shillings means naught to one of my means; so to so mild a form of robbery I cannot find it in heart to complain, as Sedley would, for the jest: the marvel is she left me any purse at all rather than robbing me blind.

Fumbling in my purse, I come across a pistole, worth more than three times what she has asked, and toss it to her; then, looking about for a chamber pot, which there is no evidence of, and wondering how in the circumstances to ease the morning demands of nature, I feel her tug on my arm.

'Stay about, sweetheart. We'll send down to the Three Cranes for a bit of bread and cheese.'

I glance o'er my shoulder to see how shrewdly she eyes me, her brows a little narrow and her red lips parted. 'Tis plain she has me marked as a fruit ripe for the plucking and no doubt makes shift to hold me here 'til her gentleman-housebreaker comes to cudgel the rest out of me. I, shaking my head, fumble into my breeches, then make shift to slip on my boots, standing up and without aid – which, having never attempted before, I go hopping about in my haste and agony, almost fall on my arse, and look very little like the noblest creature of creation, the so-called rational animal.

All at once my eyes stray to the floor, where I am horrified to see a little girl lying on a straw-tick pallet near the filthy bed wherein I suffered my fall.

She is frail and sickly, with large blue eyes and skinny limbs. She is clad in naught but a short, torn smock, and I am sickened to see the bruises on the backs of her legs.

I stare at her in horror; she but regards me with solemn, precocious eyes that tell me plainly she knows me for the beast I am. Then turning away, as if in weariness and disgust, she rolls her listless eyes toward the bed again whereon reposes the punk, and offers up in a voice faint and meek, 'Mama, I am so hungry.'

If I felt sick before, this is enough to make me wish to hang myself; and, with not a little shame, I recall the enormous supper I had last night of pullet, oysters, and hare pie, half of which went uneaten.

'Stop your mouth, you little bastard,' snarls this sign of mother-hood, 'or you know what you'll get.' Then she smiles on me sweetly, showing a mouth full of broken yellow teeth. 'Now, let's not be in such haste, sweetheart.'

I watch with a broken heart as the little child huddles down on her pallet again, crossing her arms round her thin stomach, as if to push out the hunger. Within the woodworks a rat snuffles and shrieks.

Sick to the very blood, I draw on my rapier with the black enamelled hilt, then my fine plumed hat, and plunge from the door. Pulling twice on the rope before the warped boards will give way to any pressure, I stand within a close alley, which stinks with the piss and offal of the clogged kennel-channel. At my feet a dead dog lies but half-decayed, the flies buzz about the red-and-white stench of its corpse, and a mammoth grey rat skitters across the polished leather of my boot.

Ducking into another alley against the attempts of my doxy to find me out, I take a long piss against a tumble-down shack, to the delight of a ragged little boy who watches with mouth open the amber arc. The demands of nature eased, I then plunge up and down a few more alleys, dodging the dogs that snap and growl at my feet, past the contents of a chamber pot (yellow lake with the foul brown islands in 't standing flies), and then an indeterminate rotting heap that stinks most gloriously sour-sweet in the baking sun, and from which I hear a squeal and the hiss of fangs bared.

Arriving at last at a cook-shop near the Old Swan, off Fish Hill Street, I pay out an order of several meat pies and three loaves of trencher-bread new-baked, and direct that they be sent presently to the little alley abutting Leadenhall Market and Gracious street, hard against the sound of St Dionis Dells, and due east of the Great Coffee House, joining Cornhill and Fenchurch Streets: the easternmost alley and the third hovel to the left, with a poor wretch of a dog decaying outside and a starved child and her mother within.

This errand done, and many assurances conveyed to his lordship that all shall be done as is ordered and that by present runner, I proceed down an alley to Thames Street, with a mind toward passing the Steelyard and going to take water at the Three Cranes, westward-ho, for Somerset Stairs.

I make a shift to dismiss the little girl from my mind, my reason telling my passion I have done more for her good cheer than the majority of gentlemen would: but still cannot put off the little-decayed image of her great suffering eyes, thin limbs, and bruises. My gnawing sense of guilt tells me that some several of pies and three loaves of bread will not hold off hunger for ever, which is an ever-growing thing like a weed; nor can I stop the mother from beating her, nor some brute soon from ravishing her innocence from her on the wretched straw tick: that is, unless someone already has.

It little matters, as my reason tells me, that there are children like this one in every hovel in town, from Sir William Warren's shipyard to Blackfriars Stairs: for this is one I have seen; and the senses being so much more palpable than fancy, I cannot wrest the thought of her from my mind.

All at once I hear a horrible cry: the anguished shriek of mere horror and agony, as if the very tortured soul of a man be whipped out of him on the acrid, foetid air of town.

I stand sweating in an alley, my head almost overcome by the sweet-sour stench, my armpits pouring and my hand on the enamelled sword hilt. My eyes burn from the sooty haze that hangs beneath the rotting timbers that jut above my head; not five paces away a heap of stinking refuse moves, a long pink tail disappearing within it.

A man dashes toward me down the winding narrow alley, his arms held out as if in supplication. My fingers tighten about the rapier hilt, and I sweat the more, wondering what pursues him. Then he drawing closer, I note with amaze he is stark naked, his head thrown back and arms outstretched, like some ghastly apparition of the damned from some old hanging.

On his groin he bears two large swellings, the size of duck eggs: the black tokens of the plague.

I draw back in a horror, cringing against the splintered wood of a nearby hovel; the man passes so close, I break out into a colder sweat, to see such nearness of so horrible a black decay. If I have not got the pox, I have got the sickness for certain now: those miserable creatures exude an effluvia that contaminates the air about 'em.

My knees shake, and my sweaty velvet breeches feel cold against my clammy skin.

'John! John!' I hear a woman shriek.

Looking down the twisting close corridor of the alley again, I see a woman, fully clad and appearing quite sound, come flying toward me. She weeps, stumbles, falls, picks herself up again, then continues to run, whipping past me, holding her skirts and crying out.

'Tis plain she pursues the wretch that hath stripped himself naked to run out and die in the filth of the town kennels. Though how she can have got out of her home, which must have been shut up; nor why she must chase a dying man, rotted away inside by the anguish of the black death, is more than I can say. 'Tis plain he is doomed and neither of 'em can do aught to save him.

I stand against the wall, my knees quivering and my face pouring cold rivulets. I take off my hat and wipe my forehead with a soaked sleeve; suddenly I shake violently all over, and my stomach turns. Have I got it already? I feel the scene begin to go black before my eyes, but this is no place for a falling-fit, where anyone is like to slit my throat for my purse and gold buttons.

I stumble to the end of the alley, past a door with a gruesome red cross painted on it and the pitiful slogan, 'Lord have mercy upon us'.

Staggering as if in a dream, I come at last upon the stream of traffic and shops on Thames street; and cutting over past the Steelyard, the bells of All Hallows the Great and Less going eleven, and heading down toward Skinner's Hall, my stomach lurching and the crowds surging against me, I jostle against a man in a green waistcoat and cloak, and turning about weakly to beg his pardon, see another man – a gentleman of fashion, plumed and cloaked, cleanly and well-bred – get a look of surprise on his face, then drop down dead in his tracks.

The crowd parts about him, the women shrieking, and the men taking charge with cries of 'Stand back! Stand back!'

And now violently a-tremble, I lean against a wall. 'Tis horrible enough to see a man raging and screaming in his anguish, but this is the most ghastly kind of sickness imaginable, that works inside the bowels of a man almost without his knowledge, to rot out his hidden innards one by one, whilst he walks about finely garbed and those about him believe him whole.

Somehow I stagger to where the watermen wait at the Three Cranes; and barely noting the cruise at all, not the customary gibes of the other watermen ('Hey! See Frenchie in his plumes!' 'God's beard, a peacock taken to water!' &c), nor the chatter of the man and his other passengers, all of the black death, and houses newly shut up, and this

122

one dead, and another fallen ill, and what a crying shame it is, and how the wife is home, putting up the china and silver against their flight from town, their maid-servants having run away to the country already, I alight at Somerset Stairs, thence on shaking knees over to the Strand, where, hailing a chair, I am toted to Covent Garden, my bones aching and stomach spinning.

Edward bundles me, slung o'er the brawny arms of two footmen, to bed. He then sends for a stiff draught of Malaga from the hogshead newly opened, then for the surgeon, who draws above 19 ounces of blood from my arm, at which I feel e'en giddier: which seemeth to be a bad omen. Then, taking a strong draught of the surgeon's own mixing, I fall into a fitful slumber, my arm throbbing where the blood hath been let and my jaw pounding likewise for want of the tooth. Awaking in the swelter of afternoon, with the sun lowered in the sky, I find myself better though still very weak, and have a mind to lay my indisposition to a weakness of nerve and the heat.

Now I am ashamed to the blood, for I recall the little girl I saw, who hath such a worse time of't; and, calling for Edward, I dispatch him to make what offer of coin he will for the child; for I believe her better off as one of my scullery-maids than she would be in her present state. I see by the look he gives me he thinks me capable of debauching a child of nine years, but let it go; why should I be concerned what my footman thinks?

The notion of debauched children leads to an association with Rochester, and I begin to brood on his confinement in the Tower. The sickness indeed doth appear to worsen; already I have seen carts piled high with possessions, all taking the Holburn or Bishopsgate out of town; and the heat wave continuing, as it is very like to do, the effluvia of the sickness will spread even faster on the air.

At any time someone may be committed to the Tower with the tokens of the black death upon him; and should Rochester fall ill in the heat of the place, with no one to nurse him, he will not only suffer the extremest agonies; he will almost surely die. I must find out a way to cajole the King into his release. The lad hath languished there two weeks almost already, at the height of the worst heat wave in memory, with no water to wash himself and no occupations for his mind save that of the axe and all he hath lost; by now he must be stark mad with worry and violently sick in the close, airless oven to which he is confined.

But how to soothe up the King to work for the lad's release? His Majesty hath been very short with anyone opening up the topic; and there is good reason to believe him so vexed, so hounded as well by

Parliament, that any additional pressure might inspire him to sign the death warrant: which I dread every day lest he do. Barbara, so eager as she is now to be all affability to the powerful lover whose ardour is cooling, will provide me no help; nor is there much chance of his so-called friends bestirring themselves for aught that consters not to their own pleasure.

Very hot and nervous, with a throbbing arm and jaw, I pace in my stifling library: whither at last Edward shoos the child. He first pushes, then drags her by the hand to me, her face pale with terror; and with a pang it suddenly cometh to me, that this child, witnessing every night what her mother is subject to, believes she is about to suffer the same fate.

Edward does no good by offering up, 'Here she is, Your Lordship, though why Your Lordship would fancy such a skinny dirty creature, I cannot say. Your Lordship can get better every day at court, and this little bitch cost Your Lordship fifty pound: 'twould be easier to go round to Black Bess's or Mrs Bennet's.'

I glare at Edward. 'Stop your wagging tongue, you fool. You fright the child to death.'

Then I smile as encouragingly as I can at the filthy waif that stands bare-footed beside the red velvet hangings at the window. 'Will you come a little closer, child?'

She hangs back in terror: whereat I see, blockhead that I am, I have confirmed her worst fears. I urge her, 'I mean you no harm, child; I would not take advantage of your misery. You need apprehend no attack from me.'

She eyes me dubiously, one black-fingernailed hand playing with the gold tassel at the window-hanging, whilst I coax, 'Will you not approach and suffer me to speak with you?'

Edward gives her a sharp poke betwixt her poor skinny shoulder blades. 'Hey, move forward, girlie, when His Lordship what bought you gives the order.'

I can see plainly what a disadvantage Edward will be in this business; so I order him from the chamber, on the pretext of seeing whether the footman be arrived from the tobacconist's with the roll to chaw as a plague-preventative.

Then I step over to the child myself. She shrinks back a little; I pet her head comfortingly and see't crawling with lice. I forebear as best I can shuddering and say a silent prayer that this child has not got the plague and ask her, 'Had you the victuals I sent?'

She nods but still continues to watch me with great dubious eyes.

'We will have you washed with some water and then give you some venison or mutton or whatever we have about. Would you like that?'

She makes no answer, not e'en a nod this time, but continues to train on me those anxious eyes. I search frantically for something comforting to say and wish I had Rochester's wit, or at least his smile, for he could soothe a child like this in a minute, I know. I think to pull a handkerchief from my fob and make a poppet with it, the way he doth to lure the fear from Castlemaine's children, so that they all crawl about with a hand to his knee or a head tucked to his breast; but I know not how to proceed to fold the thing, much less invent the drolleries he always hath it speak; and this child looks a bit world-weary to delight in such a toy.

Then I remember me one injunction of his for children: 'Do you not address 'em from your full height, so that your voice booming down sounds like God's.' So I squat to put my head at a level with hers, and she looks a little easier. 'What is your name, child?' I ask, this being the only means I know to approach intimacy.

'Jane,' she replies but still watches me carefully.

'Jane, I have brought you here that you may help in the kitchen. I am sure that in time you will learn to trust me. For the present I would have you get some victuals and washing and sleep; and if anyone ill treats you, I would know.'

She still regards me warily; but seeing I can do no better at present, I arise and summon Edward again and order that the child be put in Mrs Marshall the cook's hands, for cleaning and feeding. As he leads her forth, the boy coming to me says that Sir Charles Sedley desires to know if he may walk up.

I granting acquiescence am soon in the presence of our diminutive great-wigged jester, who asks me how my tooth does.

'As ill as can be,' I complain. 'What the devil went on last night?'

The boy hands us round some wine as we sit, and Sedley, putting his feet with the soiled pumps on the polished walnut of my writing table, informs me he hath taken vengeance at last for the time we all agreed in a drunken fit to sacrifice something, and Buckhurst insisting on cravats, he watched weeping as his best pile of lace and ruffles went up in flames, to our concerted merriment.

'If we all did it,' I point out, 'at least I have the comfort, Sedley, of knowing your mouth is as sore as mine.'

'Yes, but I had a rotten tooth. I but cozened everyone else into sharing the pain I had no hope of escaping. What's the business with this guttersnipe at the end of Edward's fastidious fingers?'

Flushing a little lest he guess my purpose, I reply evasively, 'We were in want of a scullery-maid.'

He chortles, his small, merry eyes dancing. 'With everyone dismissing help to retire into the country from the plague? Ashfield, you are as tender-hearted as Price.'

I flush yet the more at this comparison of myself to the man-hungry, lumpish Maid of Honour that is the jest of the court.

Making a shift to change the subject, shaking my wet shirt 'twixt thumb and forefinger where the linen lies damp against my chest, I ask, 'What have you heard of Rochester?'

Sedley sips. 'The King still chafes at the affronts done him and is little like to consent to any release soon.'

I stare glumly into my goblet. 'The plague worsens about there, Sedley. Dozens of houses have been shut up, and people die right and left.'

'*C'est la vie.*' Sedley shrugs. 'The death's head is ever dancing on its hinges at all our elbows. Faith, I may drop before I leave here, or you may: why worry about anyone else?'

This is in a measure true. But still I cannot help but think Rochester in far greater danger, confined as he is, and closer to the heart of the pestilence.

'Sedley, he is much closer to the infected zone than we are, and no doubt weakened with his discomforts and troubles. Can you not help me soothe up the King? Rochester is supposed to be your friend.'

'Faith, of course he is.' Sedley, imperturbable, holds out his goblet to the boy, who refills it from the pitcher. 'But let us not load too many logs on the burthen of friendship: 'tis a porter whose back easily bends; 'twill not bear the angering of a king.'

'Then it can be a very weak porter. For my part, I can think of little else but how he suffers in that airless chamber, awaiting death.'

'Tsh!' Sedley waves a laced handkerchief at me. 'You thought of't very little last night, in your cups.'

This accusation stabs me to the heart. 'Then I am becoming as great a beast as all of you. Something should be done –'

'What? You are like the man that would scour the streets for new virgins, up from the country, when Madame Ross hath already met the coaches. What His Majesty will do, he will do, no matter what you and I will say; what he will promise to do, he will seldom do anyway, unless he hath already a mind to do't.'

This is true enough.

Reluctantly, I gulp and admit, 'I grant the justice of that, Sedley. Still, if we're Rochester's friends, we should make a show of support.'

126

'To what end: His Majesty's diversion? Ormond's youngest son, the Lord John Butler, hath provided that in plenty. He having pled Rochester's cause and then made a pretty leg and taken his leave, know you what His Majesty said?'

'No.' I sulk into my goblet.

'He said, "There's a type as rare as a merman: your basic man of honour." He was mightily diverted.'

'Well, I think 'twas noble in Butler.'

'You would. You are another such, the upside-down of sense. You are not in love because you have not yet been sure of a rival whose cause you can plead.'

I scowl. 'Well, even if Butler were, for the sake of argument, a rival –'

'"For the sake of argument"? Is this something else you wot not of, Lord Butler's affection for Mrs Mallet?'

Loftily I put on an indifferent mask that I hope showeth not my surprise. 'Of course I knew of that. I think 'tis all the more noble in him – and looks all the worse in us, Sedley, being Rochester's especial friends yet doing naught.'

He looks on me merrily o'er the goblet, then smiles and claps my back. 'Ashfield, you but seek to stay the rod that would instruct a very deserving boy.'

I might have known. Sedley would no more comprehend why I'd remove Rochester from the Tower than he would understand why I have bought this miserable child off her mother. He's not a bad man: he's simply the usual sort, with little heart to see how others suffer. His imagination extends only to his own experiences: he can conceive and extend his sympathies to a morning-after headache, but not to a hovel or the Tower.

The simile of the rod, which he thought to fling in my face, but proveth my point. Recalling how much pain I felt after every brutal encounter with Dr Busby of Westminster School, I much wonder at the common notion that a boy must be running blood or pounded with bruises before any impression can be made on him. It has always seemed to me, a little pain will teach the lesson as well as a deal of 't; and a few days in the Tower, in the midst of a pestilence and heat-spell, would have been sufficient to a thousand sermons. Rochester hath been there two weeks already, and carrying with him a mind of unusual passion and fancy but without even a book to distract him.

Granted, he made a foolish mistake; but I am sure he has suffered more than enough already; one day in that place would be sufficient to teach me a lesson, and I have not Rochester's mind by half.

I know not which to be more concerned for: the discomforts of his person and mind or the threats to his future life. The black plague spreads more with every hour.

So I determine to do something. And behold, Sedley, how when you will not help, I can really make a botch of the business.

5

'The Town Grows Very Sickly'
10 June 1665

Her figure was more showy than engaging; it was hardly possibly for
a woman to have less wit, or more beauty.
> —Sketch of Frances Stewart in Anthony Hamilton, *Memoirs*
> *of the Count Grammont*

The town grows very sickly, and people to be afear'd of it – there
dying this last week of the plague 112, from 43 the week before –
whereof, one in Fanchurchstreet and one in Broadstreete by the
Treasurer's office.
> —Samuel Pepys, *Diary*, 15 June 1665

Awaking in a sweat-pool, I wash myself with water, which but briefly
cools me, then put myself in the barber's hands, to hear impertinent
talk of his daughter that would be a lady and wife that would leave
town to flee the pestilence. The shoemaker calls with the pumps of
new-fashion satin and begs present payment; the tailor Darvis calls to
take a fitting of little Jane. Divers other lackies, alerted by him, descend upon me with a show of girl gewgaws, laced caps and shifts, &c
&c.

To William, who hath dressed me as they clamour, I recommend the
whole mob. And so I leave him to pay the bill of the one and call up
little Jane to be harassed by the others, to choose what she's a mind to;
and, clad in silk shirt and breeches, I step from my oven and out
through the colonnade and into Covent Garden piazza, where the air
(though stirless) is at least cooler.

In the piazza some babies play under a nurse's eye. Strolling with-
out, past the colonnades, nodding and speaking to whomever I know,
I try a pull to stir up my brains, to think of what I might do for
Rochester.

I prick up in my mind a list of his friends, to see which of 'em I
might engage to help me, and arrive at very little of comfort. Sedley,
having run up the flag of allegiance to My Own Dear Self, is palpably

helpless; Buckhurst, who might be tender enough to exert himself in small degree, hath gone into the country, to Knole, with his family, the elegant Lady Dorset having decided she'll suffer no proximity to nastiness such as plague buboes, so exited in her new-fashion glass coach, pulling on her long white kid gloves, her chin a little elevated and her plume trailing from her Le Gras hat, with a footman to open the gilt door for her and her men trailing awed in her perfumed wake, son Edward holding her gut-windy little lap dog, and she halting a moment to peck me a chilly buss of decorous affection on the cheek, and extend an invitation to come to them whene'er I please and stay as long as I like with dear dear Charles that so depends on you.

So that's useless. What else?

I pace past the four-columned front of Inigo Jones' neat little chapel.

Bucks, from what I have heard, has a deal of affection for his cousin Rochester and might be brought to do something for him. But I confess I, like most people, am a little in awe of Bucks. 'Tis not only the grandeur of his title nor the knowledge he was reared more or less the King's brother, nor e'en the vastness of his fortune: but the commanding air and regality of his carriage and the acidity of his tongue (which a man must ever fear) and the slyness of his wit, the cold-heartedness with which he is wont to probe an inferior's weakness and then, affably smiling, expose him.

Though he hath never given me the business as often as Sedley and Shepherd do, yet their rallying is the open, friendly sort. I am uneasy in Bucks' presence and tend to stammer as those cold, shrewd eyes appraise me: from which, I am sure I could not summon up the effrontery to ask aught of him. It hath been my life's marvel that Rochester seems to have forged such a warm friendship with him, Bucks not showing such human warmth to anyone else I know.

Thinking of Bucks, one cannot but turn the mind to Killigrew, his sometime cohort and sometime annoyance. But I would as soon concert a plot with Killigrew as I would take a snake to my bed. I have never liked the man, and I see not why Bucks, the King, and Rochester get such a deal of diversion from his scurrilous lying tongue and rascally pranks. For my part, I think the man borders on being ripe for Bedlam, and I trust him not so far as to pour out a draught for me in all due seriousness, much less plead to save someone from death. I pace about the western colonnade now and turn to stride past the garden-wall of Bedford House.

The only other member of our immediate gang is Etherege, who, I am sure, would dance upon a rope above London Bridge if he thought it would do aught to help our Boy Genius. But Gentle George never speaks to the King – only sits awed in The Presence and collects minutiae with which to awe lesser folk, such as the richness of Bucks' vest, the quality of the wine, the thousands of pounds everyone must have spent on a supper or a suit; and how you can tell the Quality by their shoes; &c &c.

The only other solution would be to engage a female favourite of His Majesty to help us out.

Fretting, I stroll to the painter Lely's house: where, knocking up his man, I see some of the portraits, which are very neat and fine, and begin to repent me I had some other coxcomb do me but for less of a fee. I see plainly this Lely hath a skill at catching the particular beauties of a face or character of a subject: unlike the impertinent fellow I engaged, who did but meanly, making of my short blub nose a bulb; and who, doing Rochester as well, took the face of an angel and made such a botch of't, besides missing all his sense of presence and painting him in armour (which is the dullest thing that ever I heard of, for a lover and gentleman-scholar), that his mother the old Countess, who ordered it done, must have been amazed and vexed her money was so ill laid out; or believed her son had grown a new nose and chin.

Scanning the portraits, I think on what lady might be able to plead for poor Rochester. Barbara is the obvious choice: she being not only Rochester's kinswoman but notoriously soft to all well-favoured and charming youths. It runs through the galleries 'twas she that rigged the King to secure Mrs Mallet for the Boy Genius. And who knows? Rochester may have claims more than distant to her affections. For passing through her sheets at least once hath become, for all new and well-looked youths, the court rite de passage: as I have cause to know.

But Barbara's influence hath sadly waned. His Majesty hath wearied of her towering rages, impossible demands, and caprices: not to mention, her numerous infidelities.

This leaves Stewart.

I stare at Lely's picture of her: the sweet vapid face framed by trailing curls; the fine eyebrows, thin and long, above the Roman nose; the plump white arm seductively gathering back a sensuous satin skirt-fold; t'other hand coyly bearing a bow of Artemis, to signify her pre-cariously maintained chastity. She is all innocence in this portrait: the famous little globes, usually exposed at her bodice top, are severely reined in with tight corseting that leaves her straight, from bosom to thigh; a modest furbelow of white shift o'ertops her bodice and billows in puffs gathered below her trailing sleeve. The eyes are so vacant, the little mouth so wanting in character, I determine she might be easily swayed.

Striding to my lodgings again, I dispatch a note to Stewart asking when I may wait upon her; then, with the craft of the fox (unusual enough for me), I take the coach to the New Exchange in the Strand, where I purchase some lavender-scent for her, along with a lovely light bird's-eye that, catching my eye, I think might be fashioned into a gown for little Jane. Then, leaving the mammoth ugly columned structure, with its three tiers, and returning to my lodgings, I find I am answered: Stewart will be within and receiving all afternoon, and I may call when I will.

This is as pat as may be: with full mouth to the business, I tell Edward to send the bird's-eye round to Darvis; then, climbing into the coach again, I jostle around the piazza, down the alley, over to the Strand and on to the palace street.

Leaving my coach and horses to wait before the Banqueting House, I pass through the palace gate at its left and into the brick court: thence down the crooked corridors 'twixt the southernmost buildings on the river, past the seven apartments at the Privy Stairs and belonging to the Duke of Ormond, then to the rooms of the Maids of Honour, along with Lady Sanderson, Mother to the Maids: all of 'em ringed about a brick court where is housed the aviary.

Knocking at Stewart's door, I am answered by the little black houseboy, who shows me into the wainscoted sitting room, where I am pleased to stare at the simpering shepherdesses above the fireplace till Stewart waddles in from her bedchamber: at which I stand politely.

'Oh, Lord Ashfield' – and she bats her round eyes – 'this is such a surprise, indeed it is.' She comes to squeeze both of my hands and gaze earnestly up into my face, but then, encountering the scent, recoils back for an instant in surprise – but only an instant – then cries, looking up with eyes sparkling, 'Why, my lord, such-a-one as you are; why, you sly, wicked thing, you've brought me a gift, indeed you have.'

Somehow I can be more sprightly than usual in Stewart's presence: mayhap because I feel more the wit here than in Sedley's.

''Tis not half so sweet as you, madam: but I hope 'twill divert you in making yourself sweeter.'

She squeals, claps her hands, regarding me all the while with her tongue a little showing through her white teeth and her head at an angle. 'Indeed I shouldn't trust you! What was it that someone told me once about bearing gifts? But I am a bad girl; I've forgot the lesson – so I will take it.' Unclasping her hands, she suddenly seizes the lavender scent from me, her eyes for the barest instant gone hard and greedy.

A great squawk arrests my attention: at which I note that her little grey parrot hath been brought chained to its perch to bask in the sunlit air near the window.

'Hush now, Poll.' She puts a lovely finger to her lips, then wags it at the bright-eyed creature. 'Mustn't be a naughty Poll with Mama's guest.' Now she turns to me, her long lashes fluttering over the large shallow eyes, as if in anticipation.

'Does it speak?' I ask nervously, tugging at my holland-band where the sweat trickles down it, with a pull to make a little conversation before we come to the point.

''Deed yes, oh, it speaks ever so much night and day, Lord Ashfield, and diverts me so – only I can't understand a word of't. Come, let us sit.'

Suppressing the urge to laugh, I suffer myself to be led to her settle against the wall by the fireplace – and thus am seated on some plump stiff red stuff that feels to be shago stuffed with horsehair.

'Sir Charles Sedley says it speaks Portuguese,' she cries, her eyes wide, 'and he says it curses, oh most dreadfully, 'deed it does, and makes improper suggestions; he said he would translate if I wished, but he is a wicked thing.'

I burst out laughing now: on which she laughs too, she knows not why, and blinks twice.

'He is indeed, madam,' I explain. 'For I can assure you, were't Portuguese, he would understand naught of't himself, and all the suggestions would be his own.'

'He is a *thing*,' she pronounces firmly, this cant word having apparently replaced *such-a-one* in her week's vocabulary. 'But don't let's talk of him; let's talk of us.' She bats her eyes at me.

I had been concerting in my mind the best way to begin talk of Rochester, and this advance catches me entirely off guard.

'Us?' I blurt out, and give her an astonished look.

She bats her blue eyes and rests a delectable plump white hand on my arm. 'Oh, my lord, why, you are the wickedest of 'em all, indeed you are: you are the slyest thing!' She giggles, removing the hand that she may put a white finger to her teeth, and with the other hand sets the little bottle down on the edge of the Japan corner cupboard nearest her. 'Isn't he the slyest thing, Poll? But I know you, my lord, you see: you're none of you to be trusted; no, indeed, you're not.' She leans a little forward, her lips parted.

I break out in a sweat whilst I consider the choices open to me.

Imprimis, I can start in with her, in hopes, perhaps, of helping Rochester and no doubt end up so enraging the King I am the next one in the Tower. *Item*, I can bluntly refuse her and lose all hopes of her friendship and help: which, besides being the act of a booby, would earn me an eternal niche in all lampoons to be writ ever after, and a permanent spot in the comedy orations of Sedley, to whom I would ever after be 'Joseph'. *Item*, I can pretend I cannot understand her – which, being the safest way out, and also a possibility she is likely to accept, so dim is she herself, I presently take it: though the flesh is weak, I confess, and as she leans over, my eyes travel irresistibly down into the rich cleft 'twixt her milky breasts: she hath no modest shift up-pushed as in the portrait, and I can see two neat oranges formed for love.

Her eyes have gone half-closed in a languor that can only signify desire; she draws a long, plump white arm over the back of the settle. 'You are a wicked thing, my lord, 'deed you are, – isn't he, Pol? – to call on me alone thus and bring the scent – you think I'll kiss you, my lord, don't you?'

I sweat a little harder at the double-edged sword that hangs over me: there is no possible answer to such a question. To say yes is to besmirch her honour; to say no is to commit the worser folly of ignoring her beauty; and either way, I must conclude at last by kissing: which I begin to be mightily afear'd I've a mind now to do.

Helplessly I reply, 'I do not know, madam, what I think, but I hope you will not believe me impertinent.'

She giggles, cocks her head at a coy angle, and with eyes snapping, pokes a lily-white finger at my arm. 'Oh, you thing of a lordship: impertinent – why, of course you are, indeed. Why, what else should Your Lordship be? – But you may kiss me if you like.'

And she closes her eyes and holds up her face expectantly.

I begin to believe we get further away from Rochester with every moment, but there is no way a gentleman can refuse so pointed an invitation, be the lady never so ugly; and this one is so far from that, I confess I am not entirely dismayed to do what politeness requires of me. I lean forward, getting both arms about her curvaceous form, and she goes eagerly into my arms with her mouth open: upon which we crunch close, our tongues battling a long while. Anon, as I run a hand up to her bodice to touch her breast, she sighs heavily and rubs my hand over the thick-fitted bulge where her tit is no doubt hid.

At last she pulls away. 'You wicked thing, you: to take a woman so by surprise.'

Now, this is a speech which, with more propriety, might have been made by me. But I grin sheepishly, all gentlemanly acquiescence to the unusual notion of myself as an irresistibly clever stormer of maidenly citadels.

'Next Your Lordship will ask to go to my bedchamber,' she predicts, batting her eyes, 'you wicked, handsome thing; but I'll have you know, bad man, that I am a woman of honour.'

'Yes, madam,' I agree dutifully. 'I know you are.' And indeed it is all the town talk how she preserves her maidenhead, though I begin to wonder how.

She giggles with one coy finger to her mouth. 'I know what you think, you bad man, you.'

This is more than I can know, but I only smile as genially as may be and reply, 'You do, madam?'

''Deed, yes,' and she gives me a seductive sidelong glance, 'you think I will let you do what my Lord Rochester is said to do, you bad man.'

We have at last got round to Rochester: though by such a side road I know not how any more to take the front gate.

'Indeed, madam –' I stammer. 'I never – that is –'

What the devil would she mean? The one thing Rochester seems all the time doing would not leave her with that jewel she guardeth so closely.

She regards me with head cocked and eyes full of craft.

Why the devil did I think she wanted wit? Mayhap she's like a spaniel or monkey that hath learnt one trick supremely well. With her tongue a little out betwixt her teeth so that the pink tip showeth forth, she breathes, 'I let His Majesty do it. Shall I let you, I wonder?'

She takes my hand and puts it on her bodice again where I had touched before and, with her eyes half-closed, begins to rub my hand back and forth. 'Would you like to play *le precieuse* game?'

'Madam?' I ask helplessly.

Her eyes open wide; her voice shows a trace of irritation at my stupidity. '*You* know. Rub and feel of me all over.'

If I hadn't thought of accepting her invitations before, nature has long since taken over, and reason by now assures me, doing its usual office for passion, that I can help my friend far more by getting on her good side. And it helps, too, that I now know what I'm invited to enjoy. My answer is to lean forward and take her mouth again, hard – and rub the harder on her bosom.

'Ooooo, you wicked man,' she cries, pulling back a little. Then, her eyes shrewd, she announces, 'Well, la! I think I shall retire now, 'deed

I will, and 'tis so dreadfully hot, I know I shall be all naked within the next five minutes.'

She flounces through the back door again, not without a seductive smile over her shoulders, and closes the door to the *sancta sanctorum.*

Helplessly I wait, and in the interim my blood cools enough for me to ask myself an hundred times how the devil I ever got into this coil and what I will do if the King calls and finds us together. E'en more, I have never done what it is she obviously expects of me, being an all-or-nothing man myself; but I suppose I will have to play as I go. At least I am far from innocent.

But I admire much anyone would wish to start the thing and not finish it. Though a man can spend easily enough, a woman, I should think, could find little joy in simply watching him do't. And I wonder much that the King and Rochester can joy themselves of such an insipid pastime.

Anon, the minute of my doom arriving, I feeling the full ignominy of having been outwitted by Frances Stewart, and wishing e'en more I had something to drink, I turn the knob of her door as nervous as if I be a bride-man awaiting a strange virgin.

'Ashfield, what in the name of all the blue blazes of hell do you think you're doing?'

I turn about to see Barbara at the outer door.

'Barbara,' I say helplessly, 'I hardly know, except that I know not how to get out of it.'

She sweeps into the room, her blue taffeta skirt trailing. 'Shoo! Out at once! His Majesty comes –'

I utter a foul expletive and look round the room in desperation.

'Out, I say. I'll disrobe and hop in beside her; His Majesty will be delighted to have two instead of one.'

I clap hat to head and bolt from the chamber, like a gelding from a barn, and almost collide with the guard escorting His Majesty.

'Ashfield!' The King's mouth quirks. 'Visiting the Maids of Honour, I see.'

'Ah, yes, Your Majesty.' I make my bow and back away from his presence.

As I return to my lodgings that night, e'en though I ne'er venture again into the infected zone, I cannot help but mark what signs of confusion and disarray are there already in town.

Wagons, packed high with virginals, silver, family portraits, and garments trundle westward down the Strand. Some five carts block our progress in the fashionable alleys around Covent Garden, here a maidservant trundling up to one of 'em with a bundle, there a brawny groom porter hefting a table onto his back and a boy behind him carrying a chair to it. Children cry in sleepy protest as nurses drag 'em to coaches and carts; gentlemen of fashion linger in the streets and, stripped to their shirts, holler orders to scurrying underlings. A lady with ruffled sleeves sticks her head from a window and calls that the silver is new packed; a nurse darts into the street, a bundle held in one hand and a child by the other. Carters curse, cracking whips or backing their teams with a brawny hand held to the bridle; link-boys stand two or three to a street, so that the darkness appeareth almost as bright as day.

So crowded are the streets, we must perforce down several pathways before finding out a clear progress into Covent Garden piazza, which abuts my lodgings. But at last I knock at the door, and Edward greets me with news that the effluvia have spread westward on the air and red crosses hath been seen in Drury Lane, but a few blocks eastward: the wretches within doors pleading to be let out and the guards patrolling against their possible escape, to spread the infection.

I, hearing this dismal news, issue the order for which he hath waited: that he may begin to arrange our belongings against a hasty departure. There's naught else I can do, though Rochester lie trapped like a rat in a black hole, shut in with the stifling heat and his own fear.

I climb up to see how little Jane fares in her attic below the eaves, where she's been put to lie in a truckle-bed.

At first inspection she appeareth to sleep, so that I try a pull at closing the door, but a small voice asks, 'Sir?'

'I came to see how you did, Jane. Does everyone treat you well?'

'Oh, yes, sir. And it is ever so fine. I – would have come to Your Lordship – but –' Her voice trails off.

'What is it, Jane? Be not afear'd.'

'To thank you for the new things.' Her voice comes forth in a bashful rush. 'I never had such things before.'

'You are very welcome to them, Jane. You must never be afear'd to come to me – especially if Mrs Marshall shows herself grutchy.'

'Yes, sir,' returns the small voice in tones of awe: whereat I am conscious that I am as great to this child as if I had been the King himself. 'Your Lordship?'

'How's that, Jane?' I encourage her. 'Be not afear'd.'

Her voice tumbles out in one lungful of breath. 'It is all the talk, sir, below stairs, that Your Lordship must be away soon by reason of the sickness.'

The breath being done, the nerve is too, so I probe in fair tones, 'Yes?'

'I thought – that is, sir, though it is not my business –'

'Yes?'

'Will Your Lordship take me with you?'

All at once I wonder whether this ill-treated child could wish for her mother. 'Don't you have a mind to go, Jane?'

'Oh, yes, sir! – But – some of the girls was talking, my lord; and they said the other Quality, fleeing from town, have let their people go, and they have nowhere to get work.'

I am horrified to the very bones. 'They have turned their servants loose to the plague, without bread or shelter?'

'Yes, sir.' The little voice grows stronger. 'Some of 'em have got places with the government. The men watch houses that have been shut up, and the women are took on as nurses. But that sounds dreadful frighting, sir, and we are afear'd.'

Now here is the final proof I had wanted that men are beasts. I reassure the poor child, 'You may tell everyone, Jane, that I will let no one go. Everyone will be put to lodge at my estate or at Hampton Court.'

'Yes, sir,' returns the voice in tones of awe. 'I thank Your Lordship.'

I close her door and shudder. How can men of my class have so little conceit of their responsibilities? Now, this is a fit conclusion to a week that has seen a child beaten and starved by its mother and a charming lad left to rot in a black hell of heat and disease whilst those that love him take flight.

Sick at heart, I call for the maidservant that is eager to serve in bed; and she gives me a good, simple, hearty f—k that hath more of good nature in it than I have seen these two year at court.

But though I ought to have full joy of her, being so lusty and simple an animal and going at the business of serving my flesh with such a will, I find myself at her leave-taking yet the sadder, with a gnawing in the spirit like a hunger in the belly, though I cannot say what I am in want of.

Here I lie pampered, my needs sated with good meat and womanly comfort, and put to rest in the finest of four-poster walnut-tree beds, complete with hangings of Hungarian lace, very handsomely worked on red velvet stuff together with bolster pillows and a counterpane of the like; there a fireplace in pink marble with sconces to it of polished neat silver, fine and brave, and above it a portrait inset (though in darkness now) of the dear ones whose love brought me into being, but who, drowning so long ago, I can scarce recall.

Brooding in the dark on my parents, who my grandma said had such joy in one another, I almost have a month's mind to be married myself, on a pull to secure such happiness as Ossory seems to enjoy. But whom shall I marry? The sweet ones like Lady Ossory are so stupid; and the witty ones, so flighty.

And 'tis the age of marital misery, as prominent examples show: the King shackled for reasons of state to a Portuguese reared in a convent; Bucks wed (craftily, as he thought) to a Roundhead general's daughter, as like him as porridge to peacock; the Duke of York wed secretly on a whim of passion to the lowborn offspring of Chancellor Clarendon, then eager to disown her but stopped by the ashamed, good-natured King; Sedley wed on a similar whim to a woman who turned mad with his neglect; the Lady Denham, married to an old *jealoux* out of comedy; the Lady Chesterfield, first enraptured, then disappointed by a rake who proved after her fortune. And most of 'em committing adultery as if they'd never been married at all.

And what would I do with the children I'd got? My conscience would ache no matter what mode I followed: the sternness of Ossory, the negligence of Buckhurst's father Dorset, or the inconsistency of Sedley – who rules his daughter by alternating tastes of the rod and disappearances with a tankard.

No, 'tis better to seal up the gaps in my spirit with a street urchin or whore – and friends, I have no doubt, that will keep company with me as long as I'm in no want: that will debauch with me, bludgeon me with their wit; then, having seen me drunk, get a tooth yanked from my jaw in jest, though the thing be sound, and though I be put to grief for two days and more thereafter.

For what, goes the common philosophy, is a little pain, so long as I suffer none myself? What is the grief of another living creature, so long as I am thereby served, whether it be a lean horse whipped up Ludgate Hill with a load too heavy, or a satined maid undone in her court apartments; a maid-servant brought to such persistent coercion of mind and person, we enjoy her in a posture but little short of ravishment; a child sold into a miserable marriage, that we may enjoy gold for our pleasures; or whipped bloody to work out a violent passion against its father, who has but lately vexed us?

And here, no better than the rest, lounge I, unable to stir my lazy limbs to present action, to save a friend.

But ere long a message cometh, to propel me dead centre into the holocaust of Rochester's misery.

6

'This Day's Black Fate'
12 June 1665

Romeo: This day's black fate on more days doth depend;
This but begins the woe others must end.
—William Shakespeare, *Romeo and Juliet*

William, drawing back the bed hangings this morning, relates that Darvis is below stairs, with an armful of gowns and gewgaws for a girl-child, these having been made for one but recently dead of the sickness; and will his lordship have them for the new wench, against the preparation of the bird's-eye? He will make a very good price, &c. I giving assent, Edward conveys these tidings to the sharp wretch at the door, who must get up his crumb o'er a child's grave; and I set to opening my messages.

Buckhurst writes from the country that all is deadly dull, and he would give another tooth for a debauch: indeed, things are brought to such a sad pass with him, he e'en regrets the loss of Etherege; he eats each afternoon and night with his parents, so that his nerves are raw from excess of politeness; and will I come into the country to stay with him until he can contrive an excuse to be gone to Hampton Court?

This is as pat as may be: another friend of Rochester's thinking only of his own comfort. I write back that I can little think of posting off to Knole whilst Rochester sweats in the Tower, awaiting the plague or axe; and I suggest he ask Sedley, who will be delighted to get all the waiting-women with child, then leave as they begin to swell and curse Dame Fortune.

Then idly reaching for the next in the pile, I see the lion and unicorn in the wax: which must signify, I think, the King's sending orders against our present removal; but opening it, I read:

THIS DAY'S BLACK FATE

My Lord of Ashfield,

The bearer of this leaves behind an earlier one to the Tower, which is a commission to Robinson to provide for Rochester all the writing implements he may desire. Should he feel a nudge toward repentance of his misconduct toward us, he will then have free hand to write an apology. Anyone who calls himself my Lord of Rochester's friend would not be amiss in paying him a visit to urge repentance. Robinson has been given leave to admit visitors, though they may carry no gifts of comfort other than their words.

I hope this finds you in good cheer.

C.R.

So full of craft and policy is this, I must needs read it thrice to be certain what it hints of; but at last the intelligence is clear, that our Machiavel of a king, being grieved by the pangs of good nature, wishes to release Rochester, though he know not how and save face; that he feels himself too injured to address Rochester himself or admit positively that an apology will secure a release, so he wishes me to do the office for him.

I holler for Edward, that he may ready my person and coach, and anon I am jolting from Covent Garden piazza, down an alley for the Strand, and thence by Fleet Street about St. Paul's and for the Tower. Half an hundred times I repent me that I had not taken to water, the streets being so thronged with carts and burthens; I fret and jostle in my white cushions, leaning out the window each minute to holler haste, the footmen ahead of us sprinting, batons in hand and voices raised, 'Make way! Make way !'

We jostle o'er the nasty sluggish stream of Fleet River, past the mammoth long, spoilt nave of St Paul's and the Old 'Change. But now at last we pass Fishmonger's Hall and St Dunstan's in the East, Pudding Lane, and so onto Thames Street. And the brooding walled mass of the Tower looms before us, its turrets scraping the sky.

Leaping from my coach almost without assistance, I hasten through the round black-lichened wall of the Bullwark Gate, being nodded forward by a beefeater with pike and red coat; but then, speeding past the Lion Tower and down the close passageway to the Middle Tower, a guard 'twixt the two round turrets there halteth my forward progress and says, would I go any farther, I must have permission of the lieutenant.

Nigh to a fit of the mother, I beg he be summoned; which the guard on duty departs slow enough to do; and whilst I sigh and fidg and fret and sweat with the immoderate heat, even worse betwixt these close heavy walls, at last we have the lackey returned again to relate, as I am a gentleman, Lieutenant Robinson will be very pleased to offer me a glass or two of wine at his lodgings, down the passageway to the left past the Byward and Bell Towers, and hard upon Tower Green.

So I am escorted to a handsome large brown and white wood house, looking to be of the last century, gabled and delicately patterned with a neat trim. And there I am left to the veriest ninny of a man, barrel-bellied and moustached, who effuses o'er the honour done him; will say naught a word of business till I have proceeded to a draughty hall, to a mammoth table of oak wood to stare at antlers and old hangings; then I pressing him with the urgency of the business, he maketh no more move toward it than a dog would from the sun, but only thinks to discourse on't.

'Well! That's several visitors the earl's had today, I must say, my lord. Sir Charles Sedley and the Duke of Buckingham have just walked up; the duke came first; but I warned 'em, the earl seemed rather in too foul a humour to consider good advice. He rated from the door the clergy that were good enough to call 'on him. Said he'd a mind to fry rather than recant, and they should cozen their wealth from the gullible: they'd get naught from him.'

'May His Lordship be seen now?'

'Of course, of course. I'm the King's servant; I follow his orders, eh? Would you see the lion and elephant in the menagerie first? The children love 'em –'

'No –'

Guilty now o'er my want of cordiality, I slink behind the beefeater he hath summoned, who leads me from the cool corridors of the old Elizabeth house (bristling hangings and antlers and breastplates and pikes) out onto the brilliant sunshine of the green.

I fan my wet shirt against my sticky bosom as the beefeater points out the round yellow Beauchamp Tower, hard across the green, and bids me walk up.

The way up is cool, with stairs that wind in dark dampness through the bowels of the tower. Passing a storey with small chambers opening off it, I arrive at last at the third storey, where another beefeater guards a thick wooden door behind which Sedley's laughter sounds.

Laughter in such a place! I admire much that Sedley can have so little sense.

With a rattle of keys, I am admitted.

Beside a great fireplace lounges Bucks, his arm slung o'er the mantel and a stool beside unused. Sedley, ensconced on the bed, waves both hands and talks.

Beside a window cut into the stone, a wan, thin figure, clothed in black, leans on a chair with its two legs against the wall. His soaked and grimy shirt hangs on him as if it belongs to someone else. His dark eyes are haunted, though a cynical smile curves the boat-bow lips on his pretty oval face.

'Well, Rochester,' Sedley is saying, 'it appears you've discovered a way to get more support from the King. I've a mind to join you here, to diet free of charge awhile.'

Rochester regards him glumly, sardonically. 'I advise you not to speak, Sedley, about matters of which you can know nothing.'

'Says the one who claims to know so much about children. Come, let us not be so grutchy and resty of temper. I but try to wheedle you from your ill humour.'

I gawk about the room.

'Sit, sit, Ashfield,' invites Sedley, as if he were the steward and this a drawing room. 'His Grace has a mind to stand.'

Bucks nods graciously, to condone the breach of decorum.

I stagger stupidy about and at last settle on the bedclothes beside Sedley. Rochester continues to sit at an angle, his chair rocked backward by a window looking onto the ramparts. Nearby is hacked the melancholy inscription, 'Iane'.

'It seems to me,' I point out, 'that you would be well rid of this place.'

Rochester smiles grimly. 'Then you must apply to the host that invited me.'

'I have. He has hinted that an apology will secure your release.'

Rochester makes no reply but only stares grimly ahead of him at a wooden table whereon repose a quill and ink and writing-paper.

Bucks, still leaning on the mantel, says gently, 'Come on now, lad. You write, and I'll carry the message.'

'Why? So he can laugh at my humility?'

'No, so he can let you out and save a little face.'

'We don't know he'll do that.'

'I know. I guarantee it to you.'

Rochester continues to stare moodily ahead – so thin and white, he looks a very spectre of himself, the filthy shirt clumping in wet patches at his breast and armpits.

What shall I say to move him – that a hundred and twelve deaths were recorded on the bills this week? That the King hath been most gracious, given the injury done him and the pressure exerted by Parliament to hold a trial? That the little lady who loves him would be broken-hearted to hear of his demise in her cause? That his mother is no doubt distract with worry by now?

Taking my wet shirt 'twixt thumb and forefinger, I fan it against my breast. It is as hot as the bowels of hell in here! I'd be writing an epic in twelve books were it to secure my release.

A silence descends. Bucks and Sedley look at one another.

'You look not well, lad,' says Bucks, his square, florid face furrowed with concern. 'You've dark hollows under your eyes.'

Rochester shrugs. 'I've had nightmares.'

'Shall we see if His Majesty will order you a sleeping draught?'

'No! No draughts. I'd at least keep my wits about me, what little of 'em I have left. 'Slife, I believe the terrors of this place hang i' th' very walls and wait to invade a man when his reason leaves him in his sleep. I can almost believe that ghosts creep out at night and transfer their memories to a man when his control is down.'

'Aye,' sympathises Bucks, ''tis amazing what power a place can have over one's spirits.'

'Can you not wheedle from His Majesty some water for washing? I've gone almost wild these weeks with smelling myself.'

'I can't smell anything,' I say generously: which is true enough.

He smiles savagely. 'That is because you smell the same.'

'I'll try again, lad,' says Bucks. 'But I think His Majesty would make you uncomfortable so that you'll be out the faster.'

As Bucks speaks Sedley consoles me: 'My lord has the nicest nose in Christendom. I wonder he does not leave us, to fly up and keep company with the angels.'

Before he's done Rochester is railing, 'Then bid the damned King have me confined to Little Ease, my knees jammed up under my chin and my wrists manacled to the wall! At least I'd have more of distraction than my mental torments.'

We all exchange glances.

'Well, come then, let us go,' says Sedley, 'and leave him to ponder on the wording of his message.'

''I'll be back in a day or two, lad,' says Bucks. 'If you've not writ by then, I promise I'll not leave without carrying a message myself.' He strides over to embrace his young cousin, and they cling. 'Take care, lad.'

Bucks leaves abruptly before us, rattling hard on the door and cursing the guard for his tardiness, then quickly swiping his hand across his eyes. I walk forward to embrace my friend at parting; he claps my arm, 'Take care, Ashfield. Best be gone before you find yourself in bed with a bubo.'

I wince at his idea of a jest. 'Are there any errands I can do for you?'

'You can wait upon my cook-maid Mrs Doll. See how she does in ordering the household for a removal to Adderbury.'

I pick my way down the dark stone staircase; Bucks waits for me on a step below, his face grim 'neath the blue plumes.

The coach that takes us away eventually slows, and I mark we've arrived at St Martin's Lane, with the fair row of houses belonging to Lord Salisbury.

Sweat pouring down my neck and back, I am helped from the coach: whereupon, dodging a carter, some few coaches, and a chair, I cross over to the genteel lodging, white-columned and red-roofed, that I know to be Rochester's.

I knock briskly, then wait, not a little vexed at the delay. Sweat pools on my neck, to swelter and steam 'neath the fashionable periwig. Sure some devil breathes over the town with his scorching exhalations; with his clawed hand raised, he stills all breeze; and with his pitchfork he pricks up the soul of Rochester.

I am answered at last by a dull groom-porter, who knows but to say that His Lordship is out.

'I know that, you blockhead. I've just left him. He's asked me to look in; have you a mind to refuse me?'

'No, Your Lordship. But His Lordship is out.'

'You fool! Let me speak with whoever's in charge.'

He filters this request through the layers inside his skull. 'That would be Mrs Doll. Your Lordship would speak with Mrs Doll?'

Sardonically I reply, 'Only if she's receiving this afternoon.'

'Oh, yes, my lord. Would it please Your Lordship to step within?'

I am left, against all laws of politeness and decency, to cool my heels in the vestibule; but soon the coxcomb returns, and I discover I am to have the honour of being received by the cook-maid.

Pursuant of this solemn privilege, I follow him up the winding stairs, where all is hurry and confusion, the maid-servants running hither and thither, their arms stacked with cloaks and shirts; and so into the bedchamber, where Mrs Doll, as befits her elevated status, sits on the great bed, to supervise all.

This worthy urging me to come in now, pretty chick, and tell old Doll, she'll handle it, I observe lamely:

'The Lord Rochester asked me to look in to see whether I might be of assistance.'

With an angry eye cocked on the maid-servant malingering in the threshold, Mrs Doll barks, 'Get them there books a-packed at once, or you'll be gone without wages, that I promise you; for I'm in charge

145

now, I'll tell you what's what, and I'm a-telling you now: no time to malinger and be ogling all the men in livery. We have got to be gone, come the middle of the month; for there's rent due, and no money to pay it; and I've got the key to the table-book – His Lordship knows who's to be trusted – so go without wages now or help in the library – 'tis all one. Law, law, so much to be done: characters to be writ for those to be put away, and wages to be paid, and decisions to be made on who goes to Adderbury; and these sluts here – why, not a one of 'em'd pass a sponge over the floor, Your Lordship, unless I was at 'em night and day; they try to get around in a young gentleman's household with a simper and a leer, and never take no heed to clean the chimbley, any more than if it was the high road to Canterbury.

I commiserate with her on the unreliability of help.

'Hey, you, there, mind you have a care with Her Ladyship's portrait.'

A girl trundling past the doorway a portrait too large for her, in a great gilt frame wrought extreme fine, I scan the likeness of Rochester's mother, poised a moment without the threshold. And so I gaze into the pensive, soft brown eyes of a lovely young woman, who looks to be no more than my age, her red curls tumbling in a cloud about her head, her fine lips curved in a sweet modest trace of a smile; about her neck a string of pearls, and about her shoulders, a gown of rich blue taffeta with a pinner of white silk and withall, and a mien of womanly tenderness and beauty, from the gentle curves of her white neck and bosom to the shy, winning smile. How fortunate is he, that his mother still lives!

Seeing that the cook-maid hath the business well in order – indeed, far better than I could order't – I take polite leave of her.

'Well, get along then, Your Lordship, pretty little chick; but mind you stop at a fortune-teller's, for a plague antidote: there's no taking chances. And mind you hurry out of town soon; there's talk of sealing up the roads.'

So I take my way, along with her advice, into the coach again, bound for my lodgings t'other side of Covent Garden piazza.

There I pace up and down the gilt winding stairway, to the vexation of those that would bear burthens against our departure – I bump into maid-servants with portraits and sconces, tread on the toes of groom-porters that would seek to come downstairs, their shoulders straining 'neath the load of the ancestral bed; and anon, descending to the marble hall, stumble o'er my footmen John and Edward, who direct this group of trunks and hutches to Wiltshire; t'other, to Hampton Court.

The terror of the moment grips me. Here are all of us fleeting town, leaving Rochester – to what?

I recall the terrible city images. a cart rattling down Thames Street, a few long burthens in back with sheets thrown o'er 'em; straw littering the streets before fashionable doors adorned with new-fashion knockers and, painted in garish red, 'Lord have mercy upon us'; the guard on patrol without each shut-up house, whether mansion or hovel, lest any of the wretches within (sick or sound) escape; the softer clickety-click of my coach wheels on cobbles muted by straw; the aromatic vapour of vinegar, plaster, and fume pressed tight in a cloth to my nostrils, to keep out the infection.

I recall the cynical and bitter eyes of Rochester in the Tower and the pitiful inscription hacked nearby, 'Iane'. I cringe as a blow resounds, then a shriek: some child's being beaten by an upper servant below stairs.

'Your Lordship,' cries a maid-servant, coming to pluck on my sleeve, 'the pickle in the sturgeon must have gone stale. In it are many small worms creeping.'

The whole world's got the plague.

7

'Despair Bolts Up My Doors'
18 June 1665

...my thralled mind, of liberty deprived,
Fast fettered in her ancient memory,
Doth nought behold but sorrow's dying face....
Despair bolts up my doors, and I alone
Speak to dead walls – but those hear not my moan.
　　—Sir Walter Raleigh, confined in the Tower after his secret
　　　　　　　　　　　　　　marriage was discovered

'Tis three days now that we've been settled at Hampton Court, and not a word of Rochester.

This morning, the astronomical clock above Anne Boleyn's Gateway stares at me with such a prescience of doom, the hands creeping like pestilence about the black-ringed face, the dome-topped bell above looming sepulchral, the crenellated turret on each side hinting of Beauchamp Towers, that I take a resolution of catching the King after his constitutional, to plead with him again.

Pacing about the long Communication Gallery, hanging at its windows, I watch the King run mad circles in the privy garden below, the little dogs snapping at his heels; and, wiping my brow, I much wonder that anyone can so bestir himself in this heat.

Another melancholy petitioner in this gallery, Queen Catherine Howard, is said to have broken from her guards and raced, on a fruitless pull to reach the chapel and plead mercy of King Harry there. The superstitious believe her ghost haunts this gallery.

But sure, 'tis tragedy that haunts this salubrious pleasure-palace, built for Wolsey and relinquished to the Crown some one hundred and forty year ago at his fall; this red-and-white-brick sprawl of turrets and courts laid on the Thames; the garden-set honeymoon place of Queen Anne Boleyn, whose initials the doting King caused everywhere to be carved – and then later effaced at her execution, save the forgotten 'AB' under her gateway.

The present monarch, done with his exertions, appeareth at the end of the gallery by the back stairs; and having been left in peace, as I suppose, by Catherine Howard, is accosted nonetheless by me.

'Your Majesty.' I bow, though 'tis not easy to observe formalities before a man whose linen shirt sticks to him in wet clumps and whose spaniels yip and fight at his feet.

His eyes twinkle. 'You are late, Ashfield. I am already done.'

Ignoring this customary irony on my sloth, I ask, 'Your Majesty, has Rochester writ out an apology yet?'

He calmly towels his face. 'Not yet, but he will. Hush, hush, Colette.' The little dog thus reprimanded yaps and wiggles, then stares grinning, tongue out, up at the King, so that he stoops to pat its black-and-white head.

'Your Majesty, Rochester is a very proud youth. He would die rather than apologise.'

The King's brows knit with vexation. 'Oh, prisca fides, Ashfield: no one is that proud except he be on stage.'

'And where else has Rochester been, ever since we've known him?'

The King hands the towel to a footman, who bows; then he begins to walk with great bold strides down the gallery towards the state apartments.

'This will be another very hot day. I think we'll make up a party to dine along the riverbanks.'

I lope along beside, suppressing with difficulty the urge to pluck at his sleeve. 'Your Majesty, I beg you!' He halts so without warning that I almost tread on the royal heels.

'You would do better to beg Rochester.'

'Your Majesty, he'll die first!'

The King gazes thoughtfully from the window o'er the garden below, whither in his absence the Queen and some of her ladies have repaired with cushions and embroidery, jointed stools and baskets for gathering the red and white roses. 'Life, Ashfield, is a great dispeller of youthful ideals and heroics.'

'Your Majesty, he looked far from well. I think of the lines from Hamlet. 'There's something in his soul,/O'er which his melancholy sits on brood.''

Leaning against the window sill, the King stares out as if in thought at the Queen seated on a stool below, her feet cushioned above the grass and her busy hands working embroidery.

'Give him a little time, Ashfield.'

The rest of the afternoon finds me brooding in the gnat-clouded heat by the river.

'My Lord Ashfield!'

Startled, I look back towards the green expanse of lawn, to see through the files of shaped yews, and with the red-and-white grandeur of the palace as a backdrop, an elegant figure in white puffed sleeves and black satin knee breeches, his head waving white ostrich plumes. The feathered prodigy turns into Etherege, who hath lectured me more than once that black looks well with anything.

Fishing my stoppered ale-bottle from its string in the river, I unstop it and offer him a swig as he plunks, hanger clanking and plume waving, onto a perch beside me on the sloping riverbank.

Carefully removing his spotless new black silk shoes with the white butterfly bow, he takes a swig and says, 'I would have thought Your Lordship would have dined with His Majesty today. We took water to go and eat among the flowers. You might have worked on him some more about my Lord of Rochester.'

Glowering, I seize back the bottle and re-stopper it. 'I have worked on him so much that I'll soon be joining Rochester in his quarters. What the devil have *you* done?'

Etherege wipes his chin and smiles friendly. 'Good ale, my lord: not the local swill.'

'I got the merchant's name from Buckingham.'

Etherege is silent in respectful awe whilst the table-book in his head calculates what must have been the cost. He then answers, 'I have done my best. I've writ to my Lord Rochester in the Tower and my Lord Buckhurst at Knole.'

Etherege opens a handkerchief and tosses some crumbs out towards the water. The fish strike, making ripples.

'What about Sedley?' I ask, lowering my treasure on the string down into the cool gurgling depths again.

Etherege tosses some crumbs to the tiny brown birds that hop nearby. 'Sir Charles thinks the sooner we all let my Lord Rochester alone, the sooner he will be bored and decide to apologise: that by pleading with His Lordship, we only put him where he would be, on centre stage.'

This interpretation makes some sense. Knowing Rochester, he is delighted to await what visitors or messages High Tide may bring, then assume dramatic poses in his well-phrased replies.

But I protest. 'There's some truth in that, Etherege,' I admit. 'Still, his friends should continue to plead, 'til his vanity has been soothed up enough that he can afford an apology.'

150

We both sit hugging our knees. Etherege, his largesse being distributed, runs a hand in the cool ripple of the water, and the sun glares down, drawing sweat from all my pores. What the Tower must be like in this heat, I can scarce conceive.

'What have we here?' greets a hearty genial voice. 'Angling fit for a gentleman?'

I stare down at the string, with its catch of ale, then up at an impeccably plumed and tasselled Buckingham, in Venetian gros point lace and white velvet, hand on hanger hilt.

Etherege pops up to bow like a puppet. 'Good afternoon, Your Grace.' He has a slight lisp on 'Grace', and his 'Lordship' always comes out 'Lor'ship.'

Bucks nods graciously, then seats himself beside me on the riverbank and, uninvited, hauls up the string.

Etherege seats himself again. 'Heard you aught of my Lord Rochester, Your Grace?'

'The damned young fool. No, but he's writing today, whether he will or no.'

'But the King has not promised anything specific,' I point out.

Bucks stares straight ahead. 'That's merely his evasive way. Why appear the dealing merchant when he can be the suddenly merciful monarch? Why open himself to talk that Rochester wrote from cynical self-interest rather than honest repentance?'

This last rings true.

'At any rate, I'm taking water today to force the obstinate child to the task and then bear the message back.'

'But what sort of force can Your Grace use?' prods Etherege respectfully.

Bucks gives Etherege a dry look. 'Reason and self-interest, of course. But I've a mind to jostle his iron dignity with a crack from the end of my cane.'

Etherege looks horrified by the ignoble suggestion.

'Though,' adds Bucks, 'I'm not so certain, faced with a gentleman that looks so polished and well grown, I could find it in my heart to ask him to bend over. It's just that I can recall clearly when he was much smaller.'

Etherege is surprised. 'I had not known Your Grace acquainted with his lordship before this year.'

Bucks runs a finger o'er the side of the bottle. 'Not the Rochester we know, but a timid and sickly little boy. His mother brought him to Paris in his sixth year, where we kept up the court in exile.' Bucks stares across the river again toward the green copse of trees in which a hind leaps. 'They stayed a year or so, till at last they returned to Ditchley, when it became apparent that Harry Wilmot would absent himself on spy missions till they left. She was very angry and complained often to me, as his friend and her kinsman.'

'But had His Lordship's father no interest in him, Your Grace?' asks Etherege, astonished.

Bucks shrugs. 'But little. He asked me to look in on the boy, to be sure his mother wasn't spoiling him. She wasn't.'

'Well, that's good,' I say cheerfully.

Bucks trains on me the bemused, contemptuous stare he reserves for ninnies. Whilst I flush without knowing what the devil I've said, he proceeds cheerfully, 'I did my best to spoil him a little. In the end I think he trusted me, which was quite an achievement.'

'Why, Your Grace?' asks Etherege.

'He was not a very trusting little boy. He still isn't – observe, *si vous plait*, his reaction to the King's offer. But perhaps I can work on his earlier trust and get him to send a message by way of me.'

8

'Your Petitioner'
19 June 1665

From his prison the young earl addressed a contrite petition to the King, which:

Sheweth
That noe misfortune on earth can bee so sensible to yr Peticoner as ye losse of yr Maties favour.
That Inadvertency, Ignorance in ye Law, and Passion were ye occasions of his offence.
That had hee reflected on ye fatall consequence of of incurring yr Maties displeasure, he would have rather chosen death ten thousand times than done it.
That yr Petitioner in all humility & sence of his fault casts himself at yr Majesty's feet, beseeching you to pardon his first error, & not suffer one offence to be his Ruine
And hee most humbly prayes that yr Majesty would be pleased to restore him once more to yr favour, & that he may kisse your hand.

It was not likely that Charles would turn a deaf ear to such an appeal as this, and on 19 June an order was sent to the Lieutenant of the Tower authorizing him to discharge his prisoner on condition that he gave 'good & sufficient security' and promised 'to render himself to one of his Majesty's Principal Secretaries of State' on the first day of the next Michaelmas Term.
—Vivian de Sola Pinto, *Enthusiast in Wit*

Bucks hath done't. Gazing this afternoon from the window of my apartments, who do I see striding across the grass of the Base Court but our Boy Genius.

But he looks not well. Gaunt as the genius of famine, his filthy shirt and breeches hanging on him, he walks slowly, the arm of a white-and-gold-brocaded Bucks about his shoulders.

My heart wrenches at this suggestion of using support to walk. The lad seems e'en younger than his eighteen years: dwarfed by the

ROBERT BLAIR, EARL OF ASHFIELD

imposing figure of Bucks and the red-brick walls of the Base Court looming on all sides. Clearly, they've arrived not by water at the gardens in the back but at the great West Entrance, where the two files of white heraldic beasts guard the turreted front archway.

They cut eastward across the green square below, toward my apartments near Anne Boleyn's Gateway and so into the inner Clock Court. I lean from my window, yell, and wave.

Bucks looks up, vexation lining the strong-lined face with the large chops. His arm still supports Rochester, who looks not up, only halts as his companion doth.

'Hold up a minute!' I yell.

They wait for me to scramble down from my second-storey perch near the octagonal turret by the Base Court clock.

Not too long, now,' warns Bucks peevishly as I embrace his charge heartily. 'I've a bath laid for him at my apartments.'

'Rochester! The Devil take me, but I'm glad to see you! How the devil d'you get out so fast?'

Crushing him to me is like embracing a starved chicken; he's all bones. In a low, listless voice he says, 'Thank Bucks.'

'Tush, tush,' says Bucks. 'I'm but the messenger boy in this sad business.'

'My Lord of Rochester!' cries a joyous voice.

I look about to see the toady Etherege, who falls upon Rochester like a great bird upon a small starved beetle and almost knocks him down.

''Pon my honour, but 'tis good to see you, my lord!'

'Come, let him alone,' Bucks says sternly. Etherege falls back with a repentant and hangdog look.

Bucks relents: 'Come, 'tis only that he's weak. I've a bath and dinner laid for him, but I promise to show him at His Majesty's apartments tonight.'

'My Lord of Rochester,' says Etherege, 'will then hear how His Majesty and the rest of us have missed his merry company.'

As Bucks, yellow plumes waving, supports the lad through the archway 'neath the clock, Etherege leans over to me in that foppish, confidential way he hath, holding up a handkerchief as if to conceal his confidence from any audience: 'Gad, but I never thought to see His Lordship look thus.'

I scowl. 'He had not his laundresses and wardrobe with him.'

Etherege cocks an eyebrow at me. He knows I rail on his fashion sense: whereat I feel guilty and flush. He takes not raillery against him as lightly as the others do. He will not give back as good as he gets but only looks unhappy.

At last he says, 'His Grace was with His Majesty all yesternight: I warrant, pleading how fast was Rochester's decline. Sir Charles says, His Grace was all the afternoon arguing with my Lord of Rochester, and all the night with the King.'

'Sedley has an ear at every keyhole. I wonder he can use such energies for tattling and gossip yet lift no finger to help his friend.'

'He means no harm,' says Gentle George. 'Gad, but His Lordship looked ill. Sure His Majesty did not have him put to the torture?'

I stare upward at the red walls, looming on all sides with crenellated tops and octagonal turrets.

'No, I think the torture's in his mind.'

9

'The Art Of Loving'
20 June–5 July 1665

The anima is a personification of all feminine psychological tendencies in a man's psyche. . . . the character of a man's anima is as a
rule shaped by his mother. If he feels that his mother had a negative
influence upon him, his anima will often express itself in irritable,
depressed moods, uncertainty, insecurity, and touchiness. . . . Within
the soul of such a man the negative anima-figure will endlessly
repeat this theme: 'I am nothing. Nothing makes any sense. With
others it's different, but for me . . . I enjoy nothing.' These 'anima
moods' cause a sort of dullness, a fear of disease, of impotence, or
of accidents. The whole of life takes on a sad and oppressive aspect.
Such dark moods can even lure a man to suicide . . .

—M. L. von Franz , 'The Process of Individuation' in *Man and*
his Symbols, ed. Carl G. Jung

Hysteria, alcoholism, inability . . . to cope with life realistically, and
depressions result from mother-centeredness. The ability to love
depends on one's capacity to emerge from narcissism, and from the
incestuous fixation to mother . . .The practice of the art of loving
requires the practice of faith.

—Erich Fromm, *The Art of Loving*

In the weeks that follow I watch Rochester come to pieces.

Fitfully he acts the life of pleasure. He arises to the King's levee,
looses a falcon or runs down a fox in Bushy Wood; presents himself
prettified and washed for Barbara's consorts and card-parties where
she lodges in Wolsey's old apartments; undoes some maid-servant that
pants to know his full charms. And all the while, he downs hogsheads
of wine and stares about with haunted eyes.

'I run mad here!' he frets, then begs His Majesty for a commission
to join the sea war against the Dutch.

The King – loathe, as I believe, to part with the charming lad – says,
'Tarry with us a while, my lord.'

So then the Boy Genius lashes out at us. By what reason can fortune condemn some of us to be born in squalor and hunger, then left to rot of infection, whilst the rest of us sojourn in this pleasure-palace? Why doth the pestilence spend itself in one corner of the globe, then repair to another? Anyone that can see these things and still believe in a big Papa God is a fool.

He rails to us on some of the ladies who hath repaired to the Chapel Royal to kneel below the gilt gesso and gold pendants, hung with angels blowing the last trump, and pray for the beggars left in Blackfriars. He asks us: Do they not see their hypocrisy? Had they truly consciences, they'd repair like the Lord Craven to town, lay out money and energy succouring the diseased, wipe the fever-sweat from brows with their own hands.

'Rochester,' I say, 'we do not notice you doing these things.'

'No, for I admit what I am. But they will not do what their faith demands nor admit they refuse to live it. They are neither hot nor cold, and their God spits them out.'

Those of us without faith he rails at also as we disport ourselves merrily amid the pleasant walks and alleys; down a pipe of Hippocras; or enjoy a supper of bread and cheese at the riverbank, Pond Garden's end, with torches lit on the lawn for a set of dances from *The English Dancing Master*. He puts to us savage questions, as: Is't not merry to be a gentleman of fashion: that is, reason and no conscience? Does't never bother us to know our lives are meaningless? Feel we not the pettiness of our species, crawling 'twixt heaven and earth: so many worms, who strut upon their blind sticks and await their dissolution into dust; who dream the dreams of an hour, then expire with 'em into nothingness; spin with infinite pain the webs for another generation to unweave; toot, with much magnificence and little sense, their pitiful symphonies: deaf to the music of the spheres, vexing the faceless heavens with their clamour and pretense of worship, and rolled unto Time Everlasting through the predestined cycles of a vast *Primum Mobile?*

Etherege admires the lad's tropes and figures. I, however, believe his mind unhinged in the Tower.

But Buckhurst, who hath got clear of the family clutches to join us, only shrugs. His shadow Shepherd, however, pronounces cheerfully, 'You're mad, my lord. All the talk is, how merry Rochester is and free from cares.'

'How much wine he drinks –'

Buckhurst trails his hand in the water. We float down the river in a canopied barge, a boy in the stern playing airs on the angélique and a waterman rowing.

Shepherd says, 'Everyone drinks.'

'Not the way he does now, to wipe out his mind.'

My chum scoops up a handful of water and splashes it on me. I laugh and splash back at him.

Shepherd says, 'I've seen you two milords with your mind wiped out, a time or two.'

I retort, 'I'm not proud of it, but I don't court it as he does.'

Buckhurst holds out his tankard, and I pour him more of my sherris-sack.

I remind my chum, 'He drank but little until you and Sedley and Etherege took to refilling his tankard and urging him to take more. You knew he foreswore wine because it made him so sick at Oxford; and you three encouraged him, to hear the wit of his drunken fancy.'

Buckhurst shakes his head. 'Jesus.'

Shepherd says, 'What is't with you, my Lord Ashfield? We came here because my Lord Buckhurst thought his mother's nagging was bad, not to get another such sermon from you.'

'Well, 'tis a fair remark,' I admit. 'I only worry about Rochester.'

'Anyway,' says Shepherd, pouring more into my goblet, 'His Lordship will be off to sea soon.'

'There's little drinking there,' says Buckhurst, now in his cups. 'I recommend't for sobriety and chastity and wormy biscuit.'

'Rochester and his adventures.' I sip glumly.

'My Lord of Rochester says,' explains Shepherd, 'he's a mind to get some gold and silk shirts.'

Buckhurst shrugs. 'And glory. I warned him, though.'

'Someone should go with him to war,' I brood. 'He is such a rash youth, he will kill himself attempting some stupid feat under fire.

'You go,' says Buckhurst, nudging me. 'I got a bellyful, December last.'

'I just may –'

'You?' Buckhurst stares. Then he laughs. 'Best carry some several bottles with you.'

Shepherd shakes his head. 'He'll go nowhere, my lord: not when the wine and comforts are here.'

Buckhurst shakes his fat chops. 'Hercules would sooner dance the courante with a coronet of posies.'

This insult vexeth me to the blood. 'Buckhurst, from anyone else that would require a challenge. As it is, I've a mind to bash you where you sit.'

'I mean no harm,' he says cheerfully. 'But an Achilles, you are not.'

I chafe and sulk. 'Nor are you, neither, for all the tales we've heard, three parts of which I am sure are mere fancy.'

He grins, needling me. 'Wait until the cannon boom, and the bullets –'

'– go whizzing in the sails; I know, I know. By God, I've a mind to go, just to silence you both.'

'You'll never do't, my lord,' predicts Shepherd, downing more of my sherris-sack in a manner most cheerful.

I stare at the far bank, where the maids of honour, dressed as shepherdesses, pluck up daisies and pinks. Now more than ever have I a mind to the business: not only to watch over my rash young friend, but to prove myself before the complacent one. It cannot be so dangerous, after all, if Buckhurst would do't.

I am still turning the business over in my mind on 5 July when a message arrives from Bucks, announcing Rochester's departure on the morrow and inviting me to a celebratory debauch.

The entertainment he provideth is most brave. The Haut-Brion flows in floods, and half a score of beauteous punks, well-culled for wit, and no doubt fee'd to a marvel beforehand, wander about with full mouth to do what we list. Buckhurst, Shepherd and I, a little gone in the grape, build card-castles, unsteadier e'en than ourselves, which falleth down time upon time: whereat we laugh uproariously, and our whores, being good whores, laugh too.

We circulate Rochester's comical lampoon on Price. Shepherd thrusts the paper on me. 'She's been enjoying Chesterfield in a glade up the river and sent him a packet of Italian gloves.'

I read:
'When you this packet first do see,
"Damn me," cry you, "she has writ to me.
I had better be at Bretby still
Than troubled with love against my will.
Besides, this is not all my sorrow:
She's writ today, she'll come tomorrow."'

I am not much diverted by this cruel entertainment, as all the others at court are; but I produce an obligatory chuckle. The Boy Genius himself strolling up, goblet in hand, we commend him on the verse.

'It will take more than verses to get His Majesty's full approval again.'

'So you hope the sea will wash out his memories of your little jaunt with the heiress', says Shepherd.

'I intend it shall; and, opportunity presenting itself, will think of nothing but acting with that intent in mind.'

'Rochester,' I say, asking the question that hath been uppermost in my mind these last weeks, 'why'd you do it, anyway? What had you hoped to accomplish?'

He smiles lazily, tossing down a draught of wine. 'To play with her, to see how she'd play back at me.'

'To *play with her*?' I ask, amazed.

'Of course. What else do we live for but for pleasure?'

Gentle George objects, 'But to use such a lady for pleasure –'

'Not as you think, but in conversation. She's as witty as any of us but more pleasing to watch.'

I am exasperated. 'But surely, before you act, you must consider consequences!'

He shrugs. 'Why think beyond the present moment if 'tis pleasurable?' Seeing my vexation, he adds, 'I was ignorant of the law.' Then his eyes sparkle with mischief. 'I knew she'd enjoy it.'

'She would not have enjoyed being ruin't and cast off,' says Gentle George, 'after Your Lordship had wrought upon her, alone in the country.'

'*Alone?*' Rochester is as amazed as we were before. 'You think I took her alone, to give her a fright or besmirch her reputation? Never believe it: I'd some formidable ladies prepared to receive her – and Mrs Doll, if you please, not the most terrible of the lot. Think you I'd run off with such a treasure and not provide dragons to guard it from my plundering hands?'

'Plundering is more in keeping with your reputation,' I point out.

'You know me not so well as you think. She knew me better and put her hand willingly on my arm. Why would I offer harm to such a lady so innocent and trusting, so breathing the very apophthegm of *sweet and beautiful?*'

'It is your usual pastime.'

He smiles enigmatically. 'Not so usual as you think. But after you've unlocked my secrets, Ashfield, mind you show me the key.'

He strides off.

Etherege leans to my ear and mutters, 'He is in love.'

I watch the Boy Genius draw a punk to his knee and utter some speech that makes her laugh and flush in delight, then bend over his mouth. If he's in love, he showeth it not as I would.

Anon we all commence to compose a brilliant drunken verse, mimicking heroic plays, whereat our own vinous wit so transports us with merriment, we roll and stagger laughing o'er Bucks' grand sitting room. And as drunks do, I stand outside myself, thinking, *Who is this fool? How can he think he enjoys himself when he staggers and slurs and prepares the next day's headache?*

'Buckhursht,' I enunciate, 'I'm going, too.' He pats my back.

Some of 'em act out the verse just writ. Killigrew ties up his periwig, minces about with wrist up, then wraps the red window-stuff about him like a gown and trills in a high voice:

'First virtue urges honour that I pick,
But passion after urges me to p—ck.'

We all roar our encouragement with laughter and applause, along with many comments pointed to the business: 'Sayest thou so, fair one?' 'Come, give us a kiss, sweetheart', &c., so that Killigrew wallops us with his fan, to cry, 'La, what beasts you men are!'

Rochester, as befits his amorous humour, playeth for us the heroical lover, waving his hanger and speaking sublime nonsense: all arguments of love against honour, passion against reason, as if this be a tragedy of the age:

'*Rochester.* As monstrous comets flame the skyey dome
And fire the chilly womb that gave 'em home,
This way, a flaming sun; behind, a trail:
So honour fires my head and love my tail.
Killigrew. Your honour calls you, warrior, to the front.
Rochester. But your fair charms incline my heart to c—t.
Sedley. His honour fires him on to feed his pride;
Bucks. But reason says to run away and hide.
Killigrew. As the kind cow goes lowing to her sire,
With amorous thoughts your yielding heart I'll fire.
Rochester. Oh fair F— killa, wound me with your eye,
And off the field I'll be content to die.
Like piglets twain we'll wallow in the mud.
I'll stick; you'll squeal; my staff will rise with blood.
Kind dirt! Methinks you smile upon our love.
Sedley. As naked cupids twine their limbs above.
Rochester. My brain is but a bubo of desire:
Swollen with love, raised with feverish fire,
Till reason's lancet make a prick on it
Bucks. And, being exploded, outruns all his wit.'

We of the audience applaud with many a 'huzzah'. Then, passing to a quieter drunken phase, we toy with the punks, speak more sombrely. Etherege falls on Rochester's neck and bids him take care; Buckhurst, Shepherd and Sedley clap his back; Bucks embraces him hard enough almost to crack his skinny ribs: 'Take care, now, lad.'

And I, embracing and blubbering with the rest, am more determined than ever he shall not go alone.

The whores accompany us friendily to our separate apartments, but first a gang of us must needs tote Rochester to bed, his versifying having been followed by an utter collapse.

Etherege takes one arm and I, another; Sedley shoves from behind; Buckhurst and Shepherd lead the way. The whores dance about offering advice.

We haul him down a long gallery and into his apartments, past a pleasant sitting room with its long looking glass in black frame and table and candlesticks of like stuff, past some square stools which almost trip me in the dark, and through a panelled withdrawing room, the chairs lined up against its wall and lined with figured velvet; then anon into the bed-chamber.

'How can someone so skinny be so heavy?' I complain. But at last we sling him, like a dead sack of meal, into the great bed with valence of Venice lace and red velvet.

A few of the whores pile into bed with him, pronounce him a 'poor thing', and rub his brow and untie his cravat. As we pull off his boots I watch Buckhurst, who hath two heads that keep merging and dispersing.

'Light a candle,' orders Sedley. 'We all bump into one another like ragamuffins at a house-breaking.'

I wander a progress back and forth through the dark bed-chamber and at last bark my shins on a table, whereon reposes a candle; then stagger into the sitting room with it, to light it from one that burns in the sconces there.

As I hold the wick of one candle to the flame of t'other, I glimpse on the table below a scrap of verse, scrawled in Rochester's angular handwriting. The title I cannot make out at all, but the matter is plainly his lady, who yielded to his abduction.

Sab: Lost
She yields, she yields! Pale envy said amen;
The first of women to the last of men.
Just so those frailer beings, angels, fell.
There's no midway, it seems, 'twixt heaven & hell.
Was it your end, in making her, to show
Things must be raised so high to fall so low?
Since her nor angels their own worth secures,
Look to it, gods! The next turn must be yours.
You who in careless scorn laughed at the ways

Of humble love, & called 'em rude essays,
Could you submit to let this heavy thing,
Artless & witless, no way meriting.

The figures puzzle me. Why doth he see her as an angel, 'the first of women', and himself 'the last of men? He seems to feel his love will soil or debase her: 'Things must be raised so high to fall so low.' In choosing him, she falls like Lucifer from heaven into the pit.

He also despairs at having to conceal his passion from the jeering mob at court, 'who in careless scorn' would make a jest of his feelings, as they do Chesterfield's or Price's. But he challenges them, not even they could stand idly by to see this angel fall to Hinchingbrooke: 'Artless & witless, / No way meriting.'

Sedley strides into the room. 'Well, we've left the women with him.'

'Though so drunk is he,' proclaims Shepherd, 'they'd have an easier job raising Lazarus.'

I blow out the candles. A hymn, to love! It keeps out the cold, more or less.

Part III

'This Stage-Play World'

Robert Blair, Earl of Ashfield
July-September 1665

At his execution, as at other crucial moments of his life, Ralegh [*sic*] displayed the talents of a great actor. Again and again we see him performing a brilliant part in what he called 'this stage-play world' ... reciting his splendid lines, twisting facts for dramatic effect, passionately justifying his actions, and transforming personal crises in to the universal struggle of *virtu* and *fortuna*. Emotions are exaggerated, alternatives are sharpened, moods are dramatized. Ralegh's letters, like his actions, reveal a man for whom self-dramatization was a primary response to crisis.
> —Stephen J. Greeblatt, *Sir Walter Ralegh: The Renaissance Man and his Roles*

1

'For Gold, For Glory, And For Power' 30 July, 1665

Ralegh [*sic*] ... voyaged for gold, for glory, and for power.... there is in Ralegh's cold brilliance, a heroism more pagan than Christian.
—Stephen J. Goldblatt, *Sir Walter Ralegh*

Well, here we be, on a ship called the *Prince*, somewhere near the Norway coast: a stupid way, did mortal have any, to avoid the plague by running arms open into the jaws of a surer death. I repent me an hundred times as I watch the lap-lap of the blue wave without the porthole.

The Dutch Admiral De Ruyter, with some 12 sail and more, hath sneaked homeward from Guinea, laden with treasure; and they are hid now in the port of Bergen, just north to northeast of us about a day's sailing. His Majesty hath concluded privily a treaty with the Danish king (whose port it is) to suffer our passage thither and then act as our allies. The plan is, we firing on the Dutch India-men, the castles and forts on shore will answer with powder only and no shot, to put up a show of neutrality: after which, we and the Danes will divide the rich spoils. Hence our commander Sandwich hath determined this day to send into the harbour of Bergen some 20 sail, the whole of which is to be commanded by Vice-Admiral Sir Thomas Teddeman.

Rochester, of course, is determined he shall go with Teddeman and risk his neck.

'And you?' he rallies. 'Have you no stomach for gold and glory?'

I scowl. 'I'll go, I'll go!'

So, both of us having taken a resolution most manly to kill ourselves, we take another vow to debauch; for as the song saith, 'There is no drinking after death.'

I had not thought to bring wine; but Rochester says he is friends with a veritable cooper who hauls his own tun with him wheresoe'er he goeth; and in his company and that of some others, we will celebrate our departure into battle. Whereupon I see, the dog-watch being done and night bringing on the debauch, that Rochester was pleased to make one of his sallies: this new comrade carrying the tun before him in the form of a very large belly.

Rochester presents him: 'Mr Henry Savile.'

The fat boy bows with the flourish of an arm. Then, holding his massive guts, he winks and adds, 'And Monsieur Belly.'

'Both brave enthusiasts,' says Rochester slyly, 'though the second more eager to be tried in battle, its business being with a haunch and hogshead.'

'Ho! And here is my lord the Genius of Famine, set to dance the shaking of the sheets with his sickle and sockets out. Shove him fairly and listen to his bones rattle.'

Savile shoves; Rochester shoves back; they both laugh.

Anon, the topic being brought round to the present engagement, we all discover a resolution to go – except Falstaff.

'What! An I should show this belly to a twelve-pounder, I'd have twelve extra pound in it; nor bullet nor shell should miss this bloat ketch here.' He pats it fondly. 'Let all of you go who by turning sideways shall vanish.'

'Nay, Mr Savile,' urges Rochester, 'go, prithee, that we of little faith may see how fast a mountain can remove.'

'Why,' drolls Savile, 'an your lordship saw it, 'twould be but policy; for then I'd sound like a whale beneath a scurvy frigate full of Hollanders and scatter 'em to the seas; I'd crunch their decks like lark's bones – and leave the remains to be picked up by all you little men.'

We laugh heartily – Savile, too. But then he puts a haunch-sized hand on Rochester's thin arm and says seriously, 'But say, my lord – can't we get you to remain with us here?'

Rochester stares with troubled dark eyes on him; and the merry fat boy, laughing, slaps the arm and removes his hand.

'What if you should catch a bullet or the end of a blade? You can't spare any flesh.'

'Nay, Mr Savile, what I can't spare is time.'

'Ho, time? With that baby face? I should think you on the right side of it – in faith, that you lie in its very bosom.'

'Nonetheless, "at my ear / I hear time's winged chariot rushing near".'

'Spoken truly, i' faith! And so I'll let no wine before me go unsampled,' vows the fat boy. 'Now let's have a song, and we all break out in "Loath to Depart".'

We all sing:

'Sing with thy mouth, sing with thy heart

Like faithful friends, sing loath to depart:
Though friends together may not always remain,
Yet loath to depart, sing once again.'

2

'Still Climbing After Knowledge Infinite' 31 July 1665

Nature, that framed us of four elements
Warring within our breasts for regiment,
Doth teach us all to have aspiring minds.
Our souls, whose faculties can comprehend
The wondrous architecture of the world
And measure every wandering planet's course,
Still climbing after knowledge infinite,
And always moving as the restless spheres,
Wills us to wear ourselves and never rest ...
                    —Christopher Marlowe, *Tamburlaine*

We having got aboard the *Revenge*, a third rate bearing Sir Thomas Teddeman, and sailed with our small fleet into the haven Cruchfort, our spirits are sobered this night. For on the morrow we sail for Bergen, some 15 leagues away, for our several fates with the enemy.

We keep watch with some bottles and tankards, sent by the jovial Savile; and with us are some other of Quality that have volunteered: Edward Montague, a pleasant and fair-spoken goodfellow, large and florid of face; and Mr Wyndham, a gentleman of reason and learning, lean and long-visaged.

'We want Mr Savile here,' I complain, missing his drolleries.

'He's sent his friend to hold a place for him.' Rochester winks and hefts a tankard.

'Well,' says Wyndham after a pause, 'I've tried wine, and I've tried women. But for me, the real elevation comes in the word of Our Lord.'

Rochester sets his mouth in a grim line. 'That seems to me pure cant, and I can see no reason in it.'

'You are young, my lord,' says Wyndham gently.

'Yet old enough to see all the evil and the injury that is done in the name of religion,' says Rochester.

'We none of us argue the all of its practitioners are blameless, my lord. It is the principles that we all honour.'

'That were a neat trick to have oneself commended,' says Rochester. 'For the principles without the practice hath been the making of many a fine hypocrite.' Wyndham's mouth growing tight, Rochester hastens to add, 'Not you, sir. I am sure you are a very honest gentleman. I but spoke in generalities. I know too many of the other kind, their mouths crammed with Scripture and their hearts with none of its charity.'

'We are all of us poor creatures, my lord, and sunk in sin.'

'That I'll not believe, neither,' shoots back Rochester. 'I'll believe that man is frail, wanting in courage and parts to carve out his own place in this bewildering universe. But I'll not believe him evil, sunk in some natural depravity that even a poor innocent babe must have lashed out of him.'

'We are taught, my lord, that Adam's fall was the undoing of all of us.'

'Aye, and a neat trick it is, too,' says Rochester, 'that we may have a handy way, then, of blaming anyone we've a mind to abuse.'

'How so, my lord?'

'Why, then, all the good he does is for naught, and all the evil he does apparent even though he strive to do good. He is condemned without being heard, sentenced without being tried, and all because someone else was silly enough to mind his wife after she ate an apple.'

Montague says gruffly, 'I don't know that I care for this sort of fooling.'

'Many people do not,' says Rochester with a shrug of his thin shoulders. 'But I please myself. Anyone that would hang about with me must be prepared to endure my silliness and sin. Whether 'tis original, I cannot say; but 'tis gone on long enough, I'm original in it now. And the blood of the lamb will not wash it clean, so I drown it in sack instead.'

Wyndham touches Rochester's arm. 'My lord, I've watched you, and you have a good heart. I would ask you to consider that not all religion is severity and judgment.'

Rochester getting a pained expression, Wyndham finishes gently, 'I think your scepticism comes not from your heart, and I will pray for a way to unfold God's mercy to you: that by His agency, He will show you, if you will accept it, He tries to give you His love.'

Mr Montague says abruptly, 'Let's take care how we use the Lord's name; for I've a presentiment I'll never return to England.'

The glow of the lamp suspended above illumines our space but faintly, so that the shadows creep at the outer edges of the cabin and throw our faces into partial darkness. There's no sound but the lapping of the wave outside, nothing but quiet and dark, like a moment stalled in time.

Rochester – thin, pale, oval-faced, a brown curled periwig down to his shoulders, cravat and cuffs prettified with fine lace, the space betwixt his brows furrowed with thought, his nose long and fine like a Grecian statue's – has a dagger in his hand and nervously throws it at the hardwood table and picks it up again. To his right's Mr Wyndham, with an open-throated shirt, periwig less curled, small moustache: lean, thin, horsey face with thoughtful eyes, thin-etched brows above 'em. To his left's Mr Montague, a fatter, rounder gentleman, florid of face, bulbous of nose, his fair periwig not curled but in bumpy rows.

Wyndham says, 'Aye, what of it? I've the same presentiment, but we're all in God's hands.'

The youth in the centre glares up, his dark eyes piercing, thoughtful.

Wyndham says, 'It's fanciful, I know, and who can be sure of anything in this world?'

Both then glance at the brooding Rochester.

'Well, then,' says Wyndham, 'what think you, my lord, you who've been to Oxford, studied at Wadham College – the centre of the new learning – you who've read Hobbes and Descartes and all of the new philosophers of the age?'

Rochester, inspecting his long slender fingers, thrumming 'em on the table, says, 'I think we should make experiment here.'

Montague, round-faced and red-cheeked, stares at him seriously and says, 'What sort of experiment, my lord?'

Rochester leans over in his chair so one elbow is on the table, and inclines his face thoughtfully on a fist. 'It appears we have a case of something non-corporeal, non-material communicating intelligence to you and Mr Wyndham. If you have been given notice that you are not to survive the coming battle, to what part of you is that notice given, and what agency delivers it? This is what I'd know.'

Montague grunts and lifts the tankard again in his huge ham-fist. 'That's not so easy a task to find out.'

'Isn't it?' Rochester looks thoughtful. 'By the time of the battle, we'll know whether your prediction is true or not. Then, it seems to me, we'll know whether we're dealing with a flight of fancy, induced by a heat in nature, or with a reality beyond what we can presently conceive.'

The shadows creep in from the yellow pine boards about the porthole.

172

'What sort of experiment would you have, then, my lord?' asks Wyndham, setting down his tankard, his face long and grave 'neath the dark periwig.

'Suppose we enter into a pact, that any of us not surviving the battle should return to give the others notice of a future state?'

'You may let me alone for that,' bursts in Montague. 'It smacks too much of demonism, black witchcraft.'

Rochester shrugs, his shoulders thin beneath the linen shirt. 'It's experiment, Mr Montague. The spirit of the new age. It is the attitude of the new philosophy: weigh, measure, test, prove.'

Montague grunts. 'I had thought the new philosophers were atheists and believed the world matter.'

'Yes,' says Rochester, 'but the best of 'em believe the evidence of their senses and their experiments as well. And if I have proof of a soul, I'd be of a mind to believe it, being a man of reason, a man that regards the evidence of his senses and draws conclusions from 'em.'

'Well,' says Wyndham, 'I don't care. I'll enter into such a pact if you will. For I do believe there's a soul, just as I believe mine is not longer for this earth, and I'd fain give evidence to silence all the sceptics.'

'Of which my Lord of Rochester no doubt is one,' grumbles Montague, his large lips still over the tankard.

'I am,' says Rochester, 'but not no atheist, neither. I know many things without knowing how, and I have intimations my reason cannot wholly comprehend. I have feelings without knowing their origin, attitudes without understanding how they came into being. And I am perfectly willing to believe I have some sort of substance that survives death if I can find some proof that will tell me so.'

Wyndham reaches from below the table and pulls out – no doubt from a cloak or pocket somewhere – a small Bible, which he places before the candle. 'Let us all three lay our hands here now,' he says, and places his hand on top. Rochester quickly follows suit. Montague goes to lay out a chubby hand but then suddenly draws back and shakes his head.

'Not I. It is too much like witchcraft to suit my pleasure. I cannot but remember the injunction, "Thou shalt not tempt the Lord thy God."'

'Very well,' says Wyndham. 'My Lord of Rochester and I will vow alone. Would you care to phrase the oath, my lord, this being your experiment?'

'Very well,' says Rochester, his long, slender hand still laid across Wyndham's. 'I here decree that both of us vow, should either meet death in the forthcoming engagement, that he will return to give the others notice of a future state, and that the matter of this evidence shall be such as to admit of no doubt.' Rochester then looks up quizzically. 'Is this all you wish, then?'

'Should we not have some ceremony of religion?' Wyndham asks. 'To give protection and ask divine blessing for this our enterprise?'

'You say it, then,' says Rochester.

Wyndham clears his throat. 'Very well then. In the name of the Father, the Son, and the Holy Ghost – amen. We here assembled beg, in the sweet name of Jesus Christ, and of His body and His blood, shed for us, that our enterprise find favour, and whosoever passes over to the other side may not be hindered, in the giving of evidence to those left behind, that all the doubters and sceptics of the world may take notice and have their faith renewed. This we ask in His name Who died for us, amen.'

Rochester and Wyndham then remove their hands from the Bible and look sheepishly at one another.

We all apply ourselves to our tankards again, and a silence falls. The cabin is solemn, its air changed somehow, our voices low and constrained thereafter. Rochester looks exceptionally thoughtful and is the first to break the silence.

'If the soul is matter, it may not survive the death of the body. And this I would know.'

Montague, looking down into his tankard, says, 'It may not be so good to know these things. It may be that God has stopped our ears for a reason.'

Rochester's dark brows knit together. 'I cannot believe there would ever be a good reason for staying of knowledge, which is a sacred thing, and the royal road to any God that may exist.'

At this last phrase both Montague and Wyndham exchange glances.

'No, gentlemen, I am not an atheist,' Rochester repeats. 'But what is out there, what moves the universe, I fain would know – how its messages reach us – if they do, and if there are any; I would know, too, what parts of the messages we think we receive we can depend on, and what are mere fancy. For if we could know all this, gentlemen, we would have no need of the philosopher's stone.'

3

'I Hold The Fates'
1 August 1665

I hold the Fates bound fast in iron chains,
And with my hand turn Fortune's wheel about,
And sooner shall the sun fall from his sphere
Than Tamburlaine be slain or overcome.
So looks my love, shadowing in her brows
Triumphs and trophies for my victories;
Adding more courage to my conquering mind.
Then, after all these solemn exequies,
We will our rites of marriage solemnise.
            —Christopher Marlowe, *Tamburlaine*

Rochester leans on the railing, his elbows bent and his long, slender hands clasped, his eyes gazing out at the expanse of sea. 'There's a feeling of peace here, of transcendence, one never gets on land,' he observes dreamily.

Montague, stepping up behind him, says, 'It is a calm day – but perhaps 'twill not be so tomorrow, eh?'

Wyndham goes to lean on the rail also, his long, gaunt face thoughtful. I wonder if he thinks of his premonition. 'I suppose all a man can do on the eve of battle is make his peace with his Maker and go in with a serene heart.'

'Or make his peace with himself,' says Rochester, 'which is the harder thing – my Maker, I think, being not so demanding, nor so foolishly divided from Himself and His purposes as I am sometimes wont to be.'

Anon, about six this evening and the sun still brightening the billows, we are come into the port of Bergen, the castle looming south by southeast ahead, and the masts of the merchantmen rising straight and clear by the southwest. Our ship making about, to present stern forward and starboard side to castle, I descend to the cabin to read awhile; and when I return, a shallop is being dispatched to the ship.

'What transpires?' I ask.

Rochester leans toward me. 'Some French fop, whose fashion sins would set Etherege to roaring. He's been ferrying messages to and from the shore.'

'What it is,' says Montague, 'we'll discover presently.'

And so we do, the dog-watch being done and bringing us to supper with our commander.

'My lords,' says Teddeman, his big thick mustachios twitching, 'we've a problem here, a problem. It seems this French gentleman carries us word that the Governor General of Bergen is loath to admit us as friendly company.'

'What's that?' Clifford looks up, startled, his broad, long face with the amber brows knit. Teddeman's mustachios quiver in outrage. 'I told the man and told him, that his master the King is friends with the King our master, and they have concerted in a treaty to admit our warships to his harbour; and that we will not fire on his forts and castles but only on the ships of the Netherlanders that are our enemies. But he persists; he sends the same message: what do we here, to bring above five ships into his harbour? It is a hostile act. We must put out all but five of our ships, or he must open fire on us.' Teddeman shakes his head. 'I cannot make it out.'

Rochester, his oval face looking young and thoughtful, says, 'Do you believe this portends any deceit, sir?'

Teddeman shakes his head. 'I know not – I like it not.' With a spoon he shoves some pickled peas 'twixt the great mustachios. 'Eight days, mind you, they've asked, to send a message to the Danish king their master, to ask for orders!' He snorts. 'It wants no eight days to go to their master and back.'

We exchange worried glances.

After our meagre supper – pickled peas, biscuit, and hard cheese cut off a large wheel – we stand on deck once more and gaze at the stars and the many wee lights winking on the shore.

'What's that?' says Rochester at once.

We strain eyes into the darkness.

'Look, there it is!' cries Wyndham, pointing.

All at once I see, in the darkness across the bay, boats riding low in the water: huge, dark shapes in 'em. 'What can that be?' I cry.

'We'll see,' says Rochester; and, taking his prettily shod foot off the rail where he had leaned it, he walks down a few stairs into the main deck, disappears into a nearby cabin, returns with a long telescope, shoves it out and stares through it.

'What see you, my lord?' asks Montague.

'Little enough, in all conscience, in this dark. See what you can make out.' He hands the device to Montague.

'It looks like –' Montague pulls the telescope down, stares at us gravely. 'Looks like cannon to me.'

He passes the telescope back to Rochester, who takes a look through it, says nothing, but passes it on to Wyndham.

'May God have mercy on us all,' says Wyndham. 'They're fortifying the shore. The Dutch are sending their guns to the forts and castles under cover of night, and they'll be trained on us, come the dawn.'

Rochester wheels sharply on his heel.

'Where go you?' cry Wyndham and I at once.

'To Teddeman. He should know of this.'

Leaping down three stairs at a time like a small child, his hand sliding on the banister, Rochester descends to the lower deck and strides to knock on the door of our commander's cabin. I ramble behind him, as is my phlegmatic wont, and arrive at the door just in time to see him bent over the table, leaning two fists on it, then slamming a palm down. Before him sit Teddeman and the oily, smirking frog with his cold eyes and wavy plumes.

'We've seen cannon out there! The Hollanders run cannon to the Danish shore. What excuse make you to that, Monsieur Tolor?'

The frog shrugs, titters, rolls his eyes. 'Why, la! It is as I have said, gentlemen. You make into ze port wid ze many warships. Ze Governor General of Bergen, he grow uneasy. He ask his friends ze Hollanders for ze support on shore in case it come to anything, eh?'

'Lies, all lies!' Rochester again slams his fist on the table.

Teddeman shakes his head and frowns.

Rochester subsides.

Teddeman then turns to the frog. 'Monsieur Tolor, we have told the Governor General of Bergen we will not fire on his forts and castles. We fire only on the ships of the Hollanders that are our enemy. He does us an injury.'

The frog shrugs his shoulders, runs the handkerchief betwixt his long, skinny fingers. 'Waaalll, I like not dis. I cannot say how it will end, I cannot say.'

'You dog!' explodes Rochester. 'You can see't very well.'

'My lord,' says Teddeman sternly, 'I must ask you to leave if you cannot contain yourself.'

Rochester bites his thin, bloodless lips, his face white with anger.

ROBERT BLAIR, EARL OF ASHFIELD

'Monsieur Tolor,' says Teddeman, 'I must tell you we consider it an unfriendly act to fortify the shore; and if the guns are not withdrawn immediately, we open fire with sunrise.'

4

'Devilish Shepherd'
2 August 1665

What means this devilish shepherd to aspire
With such a giantly presumption,
To cast up hills against the face of heaven,
And dare the force of angry Jupiter?
—Christopher Marlowe, *Tamburlaine*

I will wear a garment all of blood
And stain my favours in a bloody mask,
Which, washed away, shall scour my shame with it:
The long-grown wounds of my intemperance.
—William Shakespeare, *Henry IV Part I*

Five of the clock this morning, the Dutch having all the night carried some 300 cannon into the forts and castles of town, their marksmen perched high on the walls sighting down into these our cables and decks, the Governor General of Bergen having carried all the night delays in a shift to play us the cheat – five o'clock this morning, the sun rising red to spatter the Norway haze, the seamen at our gunwales below, Teddeman standing at the bowsprit with a telescope, and the rest of us brave comrades at starboard, our rifles ready and I sick to the very blood for fear – up run the fighting colours on the mainmast. For one instant, no sounds but the lapping of water at our hull and the whistle of the hard north wind – and then, from the *Happy Return*, explosions and grey clouds of smoke; then, all about us, as if Hell had opened to vomit forth shot, an explosion from every quarter: a long rat-tat-tat-BOOM from the *Prudent Mary* just before us; and an echoing blast from our decks below, a pealing like thunder from bowsprit to stern.

The blast rings back and forth along the half-moon string of ships, till my ears shatter and I think I've fallen from this side hell into the bellowing maw of the Devil himself. The smoke rises from the sun-tinted water; and it rolls north, hard and fast, on a brisk wind that whips the linen against my skin and carries the smell of powder and dull sweat. And then, as the echoing thunder rolls from heavy to light below us, an answering volley from the Dutch gunwales, and a greater tumult yet from shore – a boom from the castle and a puff of smoke, then an echoing blast, one boom hardy and heavy upon another, as if all the bells in heaven pealed change-shift for the Doom.

Now past my ear I hear a ping, and over my head another. I, looking at my sleeve with a kind of admiration, do see a little black hole there.

All at once it comes to me that I am being fired upon with live shot, and some scurvy Dutchman up there on the curtain has a mind to kill me.

I drop to a crouch, the pings and whistles continuing still above my head. This sort of inspiration in which I am made aware of what is obvious never fails to divert Buckhurst; on this occasion, however, it brings me to myself so that I know my surroundings. This is it, I think; and I wish to Christ I were sailing instead on a Hampton Court barge with Sedley or even had the sense to be back on the *Prince* with Savile.

Huddling a moment chilled, I watch what Rochester does farther down the starboard side – whereat I see he behaves with courage and restraint, as if he hath done all his life the office of war: stands up high, brave, and unconcerned to aim his rifle and shoot – then, the shot being discharged, ducks down again to reload. Think I, that motion looks not difficult; should anyone come along that might take notice of my carriage, I had best be seen doing't, too; and scanning down the deck, see Clifford so comporting himself at the stern; and on either side of Rochester, Montague and Wyndham busying themselves as well.

Think I, that looks not so very difficult; so with a comfortable happiness to think of how all this may be related to Buckhurst with the best possible flourish, I hop up, throw the blunderbuss to my shoulder, and blam away at the shore, then duck down again to ram at the barrel – having done hurt, I am sure, not even to a passing albatross or gull.

'Tis strange how custom lends to the business after a time a certain easiness; I jump up, throw rifle to my shoulder and blam, then hop down again to ram powder and shot to the barrel and fool with powder and pan; and all the while the bullets whizzing, the cables and rigging above my head unravelling; the long rolling boom shivering the timbers below my feet – but all seeming naught but a stage-battle out of Dryden or D'Avenant or some other tragedy. I rehearse in my mind how to narrate it all to the ladies that will clasp their hands to their white bosoms for fear.

Rochester stands on deck, blasting away with his flintlock. Wyndam stands to his right; Montague, to his left.

Then the deck explodes. With a terrific shock and boom, Rochester, being slender, is tossed to the left and slams his head against the cabin wall. Lying back, his long legs sprawled out, his, eyes dazed, he rubs the top of his periwig to feel for the hurt.

Suddenly a look of horror comes over him. I glance up, following his gaze.

Sailing through the air is another cannonball; and Montague and Wyndham having moved together to close up the space that Rochester hath left, the cannonball falls directly on the both of 'em and explodes.

I stand frozen, my reason stunned at the play of random fortune that hath made their prophecy seem true. Rochester lies sprawled still against the cabin wall, his eyes wide in horror as he beholds the hole in the deck where but a few instants ago he stood.

I stare fascinated as once I did to see a hare gutted and marvel at the hidden world inside, so shiny, bright, and strange, that keeps a man this side of mortality: a backbone bleached white like a china dish, a red heart-muscle webbed in white. I stare, the shock of seeing so great, I feel as yet no community with these pieces of flesh and blood that were so lately comrades.

Speechless, staring, face white, Rochester staggers upward, sliding his person up the wall behind it. O'er the din of gunfire I scarce hear his soft words.

'They *knew!*'

A shot going by my ear, I turn about, blam again with the blunderbuss, and crouch down to reload.

'They couldn't have,' I yell over the din. ''Tis mere chance.'

Rochester still stands exposed on deck, his back to the cabin wall, but now he averts his stare from the carrion mass and, shading his eyes, sweeps his gaze from right to left.

Clifford comes bounding up from his right, jumping down the stairs from the poop deck and running to seize Rochester's skinny arm and give him a shake. They stand there a moment in tableau: the thicker, coarser Clifford, broader of face, stouter of frame, a few inches shorter in stature, his sturdy hand curled about Rochester's thin upper arm.

'My lord, look about you! Take notice! You're under fire. Get hold of yourself, now.'

With one more good shake, Clifford lets him go, drops down to his knee, fires at the shore.

The shaking hath pulled Rochester to. He wobbles his head to and fro, looks as if he makes a mighty effort to bring himself round from whatever dream-world he wandered in, and slowly drops down to a knee, places his hand upon the rail, puts the rifle atop it, and then fires. The recoil sends him back as if he shot a cannon.

Clifford claps him on the shoulder. 'Death is not a pretty sight, eh, my lord?'

Rochester shakes his head, pulls the rifle back down again, cocks its barrel down to reload, fumbling with powder and shot. Right frail and pale he looks, in his satin brocaded waistcoat, white stockings, buckle-shoes, and laced sleeves.

'Your Lordship will be well soon,' says Clifford kindly.

'I *am* well,' retorts Rochester. He holds the rifle to his shoulder, squeezes the trigger, then gives Clifford a hard, speculative look. 'It is just not what I expected.'

'Aye, well, it never is,' says Clifford, sighting down his barrel.

Then, having reloaded, Rochester wheels about, drops to a knee, puts the rifle level on the ship's edge, and fires again on the shore.

Anon, Rochester throws the rifle to the deck and mutters, 'This is bootless: I'm going up top in the riggings, to see what intelligence may be got of the battlefield.'

Clifford stares aghast at him. 'My lord, that's certain death!'

Rochester shrugs. 'If it were my day, I'd know it.'

Then, taking not so much as a pistol, he strides across the deck, over to the mainmast, puts a foot to the prongs that stick out and spryly climbs up the pole. Clifford stares up astonished at him as, foot by foot, hand by hand, he ascends the mast.

'Great God Almighty!' yells Teddeman, thick-bellied, mustachios yet again twitching, smoking pistol in his hand as he runs up. 'What the devil does that young fool up in the mainmast?'

Eyes still cast upward, mouth agape, Clifford says, 'He goes up to scan the field of battle.'

'My lord!' cries Teddeman. Rochester, looking down, pauses in his progress upward. 'Get the devil down here at once!'

Rochester smiles, then casts his eyes upward and begins anew to climb.

'By God,' says Teddeman, 'I'll command a fleet again, if His Majesty wishes me; I'll sail into the jaws of any doom; but I'll think twice again, you may be sure, before I play nursemaid to any of his boy-companions! Well, let him kill himself if he's a mind to. But I know not how *I'll* answer for it.'

And, wheeling about on his heel, he stomps off, pistol still in his right hand.

Rochester climbs to the top of the mast, like one bent on his own doom. Anon, at the very top where the banners pop to the breeze, he stands on a high, swinging post, one foot on each of the bars that stick out, holds up a hand and stares at the shore, then at the ships. All about him bullets ping, cutting our cables, ripping our sails. And I watch, expecting to see any moment him crumple up, clutching an arm, or bend over, holding his stomach, and plummet like a cannonball into the deep blue wave lapping below.

The cannon on our ship boom, rocking backward on their stays. All our lower portholes are open and the hatches up, and the seamen below briskly do their office, pounding away.

Rochester yells something, his hand shading his eyes, but the breeze carries his words from us. Anon, he, having enough, scampers down the pole again, blithely and briskly, just as if he danced about a maypole; and, hopping down to the deck, brushes off his fine suit, looking down with vexation where a bit of tar got stuck on the fine brocaded satin of his waistcoat.

'There's another one ruin't!' he mutters. 'I should have a care how I fight or drink in my fine gear. I have little enough, in all conscience, to have more suits made with.'

One would swear, for all his attitude, he were strolling down the Strand.

Clifford shakes his head. I mark how differently the two men are dressed: Clifford, his straight fair hair to his shoulders, his shirt open, and a pair of large breeches belted at the waist; Rochester, periwigged, perfumed, with laced sleeves and fine silk hose, which he now curses and brushes a dirt smudge off it.

'Here's another one spoilt, and no laundresses with us!'

Clifford shakes his head, turns round to the ship's side again, hauls up his gun, and fires.

'Well, I'll to Teddeman now and tell him what I saw,' says Rochester, cheerfully strolling down the deck, as the shot beats all about him.

Meandering to the bow where Teddeman crouches down in its shelter, holding up a telescope, Rochester taps him on the shoulder. Through the din of the cannon I can just make out their conversation, for Rochester shouts to make himself heard.

'Sir Thomas! There are some warships down there, to the south.'

'Eh? What's that my lord?'

'Warships, down to the south. They have trained their guns broadside on us, and that is why we take such a beating.'

'Warships! Why, we were told there would be only India-men in this port.'

'Nonetheless, there are warships. I have seen 'em from my unsteady perch. It appears what we have been told is not what we find through this whole business. I suggest you move about the ships that are to our northwest, for they catch a very devil of a fire and, sure, know not whence it comes.'

Teddeman's great brows go down in an angry frown. 'Ay, 'tis well you say, my lord. But who'll carry a message in this fire?'

'I'll go.'

Teddeman, standing still with the telescope half shoved out and held in both hands at an angle 'twixt his chin and breast, says, 'If you'll do that, my lord, you're a fool indeed. 'Tis certain death.'

'Suffer my foolery, then,' says Rochester, 'to your own self-interest.'

Teddeman slams the telescope closed and stares at where the two ships in question are being cut to pieces, their masts falling over, rigging cut, sails ripped up.

'Go, then. But by God, be careful.'

Rochester then parades down deck, as if he were walking the Mall in St James Park, and cheerfully goes to the side, to unloose the ropes on the shallop nearby where I stand.

I gawk at him, but a shot going over the top of my head, I hunch down again.

'Rochester?' I scream. 'Are you mad?'

He grins at me. 'For gold and glory.' Then, unloosing the final stay on the boat, it plopping down into the water with a splash, he clambers over the side and descends the ladder.

A bullet pings over my head, but I hop up long enough to lean over the side and yell, 'Come back, you fool! You'll get cut to ribbons out there!'

He seats himself in the boat and grins up at me. He then commences to row. In disbelief I stare o'er the side as the tiny boat manoeuvres away from the hull, then straight for the bow and about it, to disappear.

Blunderbuss in hand, other hand clasped to the top of my grand hat to secure it, I gallop to the bowsprit to lean over and watch the shallop pull away across the deep blue water toward the two ships staggered out in front. All about Rochester's vicinity little geysers spray up where the shot hits. The mad hero, hunched down but making no dramatic move to conceal himself, rows steadily in time, as if he all his life knew the use of oars. I can just make out how he heaves to the side of the *Guernsey*, throws an anchor out, and calmly clambers up the rope ladder at its side.

'Damned young fool,' mutters Teddeman, telescope to his eye as he stares in Rochester's direction.

Several seamen gape over the side of the *Guernsey* in time to pull him up by the arms over the rail.

In the battle line drawn to the south of us, our ships are beat to pieces, their cables cut with small shot, their sails loosed and torn, hanging like broken limbs on cut masts. A cold wind blows constant in our faces, bellying our topsails, whipping our silk flags, and rippling my breeches and shirt against my skin.

Anon, back our hero comes, over the side and down the ladder, to row about the *Guernsey*, the shot raising geysers about him; and disappears, no doubt bearing his message to the *Coast Frigate*.

'Damned young fool,' Teddeman mutters. 'Well, the Lord must protect 'em all.'

The ships in the line of battle float in disarray, cables cut, drifting, running onto rocks and into one another, unable to turn or manoeuvre in the narrow neck of the port.

Anon, here comes the hero's shallop, he pulling on the oars competently and strongly, to come about the bow of the *Guernsey* just as it is loosing sail for the turn.

Rochester calmly rowing about to the starboard side of our ship the *Revenge*, the shot pinging all about him, yells, 'Hey! Someone catch my tackle,' and throws up a rope with a hook to the rail of the ship.

A few seamen, stumbling over themselves, grab at it. And clambering calmly and cheerfully up the rope ladder again, he hops over the rail, dusts his hands off, and leaves the seamen to pull up the shallop and make it fast.

Then he strolls, as if taking the air in Hyde Park, over to Teddeman to report.

'I gave them the proper coordinates, sir, that they could train their guns on the warships,'

Teddeman grunts and nods, hauls the telescope down, slams it shut. 'My lord, I'd not have asked anyone to do what you've done. But I thank you, and I commend your courage right heartily. But before God now, take no other risks with your life.'

Rochester nods, grinning like a small child, his eyes dancing with mischief.

'And if you ascend that mast again, I'll clap you in irons.'

'Aye, aye, commander.'

Teddeman then grins back, as if Rochester's smile were an infection he'd caught. 'But by God, I thank you for what you've done today.'

All at once a boom rocks us.

'Name of God, what's that?' Teddeman cries out. Smoke billows from all the forts and castles on shore. 'By Gad, the false Danes have opened fire on us, too! Well, warships we had no notion of, the shore fortified, and now the Danes turning on us. Our fireships unable to be loosed in this wind –'

Teddeman slams the telescope shut, turns on his heel, wheels about. 'Well, there's only only thing to do. We must make about and leave this place.'

Rochester's face falls, his eyes widening in horror. 'Not retreat, sir?'

'Aye, retreat. For there's no winning this battle.'

Rochester grabs him by the sleeve. 'Sir, can we not –'

Teddeman shakes him off. 'Back, boy – now, back. I'm a seasoned commander.'

He strides off down the deck, barking orders for retreat. Rochester stands sulking.

Our ships have answered their challenge as best they may, cannon booming at all gunwales and above the painted galleries; but 'tis plain they can do but little, so hot is the firepower now trained on us from shore; and so quick our withdrawal, Rochester's act of heroism hath small chance to make itself felt.

'Run up the colours for retreat!' yells Teddeman.

A grizzled seaman, brawny of arm, playing with several coloured flags, attaches one to a rigging and begins hauling it up.

Now our ships limp as best they may out of port, their cables cut and sails torn, their yardarms running on the rocks and their masts and spars shattered. How they can sail is more than I can know; 'tis a miracle not one of 'em is sinking stern down in Bergen harbour.

I consult my watch. 'Tis well past eight of the clock and hard upon the twenty-fifth instant; never have three and one half hours scudded by so fast.

'Now, the Devil take him for a half-arsed commander!' fumes Rochester. 'Just when the business was going well, just when we turned the tide our way – he snatches defeat from the jaws of victory! How the devil's a man to make his fortune and win his lady with such betters as these to lead his star?'

Rochester, striding boldly after Teddeman, leaps up the stairs to the high deck two at a time, hand sliding along the rail.

'Rochester!' I yell. 'Vex him not.'

Blunderbuss still in hand, I clamber after him, up the stairs two at a time – and, my foot slipping, I lose my balance. As I drop my gun and grope frantically for somewhat to grasp, I feel a giddy rush about me falling; and before I can do more to save myself, the fear rushing up through my stomach and out, I feel myself twist and with a great wham strike the main deck, an arm crumpled beneath me.

5

'A Farther Prospect Of Felicity And Glory'
2 August 1665 (afternoon)

My lord Sandwich... did inform us of the business of Bergen, so as
to let us see how the judgment of the world is not to be depended
on in things they know not; it being a place just wide enough, and
not so much hardly, for ships to go through to it, the yard-arms
sticking in the very rocks. He doth not, upon his best enquiry, find
reason to except against any part of the management of the business by Teddiman, he having stayed treating no longer than during
the night whiles he was fitting himself to fight, bringing his ship
abreast, nor could men be landed there being 1000 men effectively
alway in arms of the Danes. But that wherein the Dane did amisse is
that he did assist them, the Dutch, all the while he was treating with
us, while he should have been newtrall to us both.

        —Samuel Pepys, *Diary*, 18 September 1665

... soe greate a disproportion 'twixt our desires & what is ordained
to content them; but you will say this is pride and madness, for
theire are those soe intirely satisfyed with theire shares in this world
that theire wishes nor theire thoughs have not a farther prospect of
felicity & glory. I'le tell you, were that mans soule plac'd in a body fit
for it, hee were a dog....

        —Rochester, from a letter

The engagement at Bergen hath cost us dear: of men 112 slain and
309 wounded, of which number I doubt not no one hath pricked
down my ignoble wound. Sure 'tis a silly business to be engaged to the
death with cannonballs and shot flying all about a man's ears, then to
be hurt dancing the bransle backwards off the poop deck, of one's
own folly: the same which he might have done any day falling drunk
from the balcony of Oxford Kate's in Bow Street.

    The best jest is, this damned spoilt arm grieves me I am sure an
hundred times worse than if I had been nicked by a bullet, yet carries
no credit to my honour: I dare not huff with it before Buckhurst, who I
am sure will give me no peace on the subject, though he did little

enough December last patrolling of the channel on the *Royal Charles* with the Duke of York.

So here lie I, like the Balcrean crane in St James Park, my limb in splints – but being a rational creature rather than a feathered one, have the sense to remain more than fairly drunk, applying myself to the good surgeon's brandy bottles till I have floated all this day in a bliss free of pain.

Rochester hath quarrelled with Teddeman and would not be satisfied, until assured we but withdrew to Jelliford the northern entrance, that we might send anew to the Governor General of Bergen and await conditions more favourable, as the arrival of some several of our ships lost on the voyage hither; the cessation of the high winds; and news from Sandwich.

These asssurances being given, Rochester hath quietened somewhat, though with a grin he confessed to me Teddeman hath said, 'Though Your Lordship's courage cannot be too highly commended, and I will so commend it to all I meet, yet I had almost rather sail with a crew of devils horned than ride saddle on Your Lordship again.'

Rightly readily can I sympathize with Teddeman. This afternoon, drifting on the edge of a sleep induced by brandy, I hear our Boy Warrior complaining to Clifford, and loudly enough to bring my eyes and ears back to the less comfortable world.

My eyes half opening where I lie on the narrow bed, I see the hero and his audience, settled at the table and chairs in the centre of the cabin, but a few paces away.

Rochester fumes like a squib set off for the King's birthday: crackles and spins and throws out sparks. He sits polishing his father's silver-and-gold-damasked pistols, though they've not seen action: I suppose, like his household gods, to which he must pay homage. His face drawn, pale with rage, his dark eyes narrow, he leans back in his chair and snaps to Clifford: 'By God, I'd have never come on board if I'd have seen the day that we'd turn tail and run in cowardice! Who is that man that thinks he has a right to command a fleet when he has not even command of his own fear?'

Clifford, looking serious, his mouth turned down gravely, sits leaning over in his chair so that his forearms rest on the table, and he clasps his hands. 'I think, my lord, it was not any personal fear but simply a knowledge of strategy, a caution that a veteran commander is like to have when he sees the field is lost. You know, my lord, if we had stayed for all our ships to go down and our men to be killed, it were no credit to him. This way, he has saved his company to fight another day.'

'Well, by God, such fighting as he does is not worth doing! A man can't simply flee the field when things grow a little hot. Why, armies have been vastly outnumbered – aye, by guns and men, too – and often it is courage and determination – or, more likely, wit – that turns the day. 'Slife, I would have helped him with the guns on shore as I did with the ones down in port! He turned too easily.'

Clifford makes shift to conceal a smile. 'My lord, it may be he would not take so much advice from you so easily.'

'No doubt, no doubt. Well, I've a mind to go home now and loll impotently with the court; for I can see, if I don't have the command where I go, I waste my efforts.'

Clifford smiles more broadly. 'Surely, my lord, you cannot believe His Majesty would hand over a command of his ships to you when you have no experience at all.'

'Experience be damned!' Rochester polishes the barrel vigorously. 'What is wanted is wit and courage and cunning. And a certain spark to inspire men – to make 'em drive on in the teeth of danger and rise up their spirits to push against hard steel and shot, simply because *you* are standing there, and you've asked 'em to do it. Because they follow your star; and, looking on your face as you show yourself to 'em, they are possessed with a thrill to go out and sweep the field in your name.'

'Well, my lord,' says Clifford with a smile, 'there are very few commanders that reach that stature.'

'No doubt, no doubt,' snaps Rochester. 'Sure, was ever such a petty-souled man sent in to command a great force? He stands in the bowsprit the whole engagement, never doing a thing to inspire or excite his men.'

'Such as climb the riggings, my lord?' Clifford smiles more broadly.

'Aye, that, or whatever else his wit or flair for rhetoric would suggest. For a good commander should act the hero so broadly, speak so movingly, that men throw down their fear and follow him into the jaws of death and hell. But this petty little nothing that we have –' Rochester shakes his head, polishing still of the pistols as if to rub a spot on 'em '– Why, he stands there with a telescope, as if looking will save the day. And the minute the firepower gets a little hot, he's for running up the colours of retreat.'

'Well, my lord, perhaps 'tis better. For I think in the end, the battle would have gone against us anyway.'

Rochester slams his fist on the table so that Clifford jumps. Dark eyes ablaze, he says, 'I tell you, victory belongs to those that court her and claim her as theirs – and have conquering mind enough to reach out and take her hand.'

Clifford smiles.

But I hear him say later, 'I cannot say what it was, but I felt I would have followed him. A skinny, scrubbed youth with a head full of ideas – but there is a glow about him, a kind of power. I saw it during the battle, when he went up in the riggings and then out to the ships. And I saw it again afterward when he talked of how he would have snatched victory from defeat, and I – damn thing that it is! – almost believed him.'

6

'For Gold, For Praise, For Glory ... To Try Desire, To Try Love Severed Far'

3 August 1665

To seek new worlds, for golde, for prayse, for glory,
To try desire, to try loue seuered farr,
When I was gone shee sent her memory
More stronge than weare ten thowsand shipps of warr.
                    —Sir Walter Raleigh, *The Ocean to Scinthia*

By noon our ships that we lost having limped in from Kors fjord, whither they were blown in error, Teddeman puts quill to paper to dispatch a packet to Sandwich, complaining of our woes and asking of advice; and in expectation of another battle, he hath determined to send back to Flamborough Head within the week all those wounded: of which, I find to my relief, I am considered one; and right glad am I to discover a good way out of this bad business. For Rochester, it seems, whom I was to come along to protect, makes a better case of protecting himself (his great daring notwithstanding) than the great botcher here could do: the which, I am sure, Buckhurst will take every opportunity to remind me.

So a packet being carried to the main fleet today, Rochester is all the early afternoon a scratching of quill to dispatch his own packet. This, think I, is a billet-doux, opening his heart to the lady for whom he proves himself. So when he is called by the bells to dinner, a tray having been already brought me, I cannot resist taking a peek at the blotted narrow characters, scrawled on the sheet which he hath left in plain sight.

I am surpris'd to read not lovemaking but a message to his mother so abject, deferential, and religious, it might have been writ to a clergyman.

From the Coast of Norway
amongst the rocks
aboard the Revenge,
August the 3.

Madam,

I hope it will not be hard for your Ladyship to believe that it hath been want of opportunity & no neglect in me the not writing to your Ladyship all this while. I know nobody hath more reason to express their duty to you, than I have, & certainly I will never be so imprudent as to omit the occasions of doing it. There have been many things past since I writ last to your Ladyship. We had many reports of De Ruyter & the East India fleet but none true till towards the 2nd of last month we had certain intelligence then of 30 sail in Bergen in Norway, a haven belonging to the King of Denmark. But the port was found to be so little that it was impossible for the great ships to gett in, so that my Lord Sandwich ordered 20 sail of fourth & fifth rate frigates to go in & take them. They were commanded by Sir Thomas Teddeman one of the Vice Admirals. It was not fit for me to see any occasion of service to the King without offering myself, so I desired & obtained leave of my Lord Sandwich to go with them & accordingly the thirtieth of this month we set sail at six o' clock at night & the next day we made the haven Cruchfort (on this side of the town 15 leagues) not without much hazard of shipwreck, for (besides the danger of rock which according to the seaman's judgment was greater than ever was seen by any of them) we found the harbour where twenty ships were to anchor not big enough for seven, so that in a moment we were all together upon one another & ready to dash in pieces having nothing but some rocks to save ourselves, in case we had been lost; but it was God's great mercy we got clear & only that for we had no human probability of safety. There we lay all night & by twelve o'clock next day got off & sailed to Bergen full of hopes & expectation, having already shared amongst us the rich lading of the East India merchants, some for diamonds some for spices others for rich silks & I for shirts & gold which I had most need of; but reckoning without our host we were fain to reckon twice. However we had immediately a message from the Governor full of civility & offers of service, which was returned to us, Mr Montague being the messenger; that night we had seven or ten more which signified nothing, but were empty delays. It grew dark & we were

193

fain to lie still until morning. All the night the Dutch carried above 200 pieces of cannon into the Danish castles & forts, & we were by morn drawn into a very fair half moon ready for both town & ships. We received several messages from break of day until four of clock much like those of the over night, intending nothing but that they might fortify themselves the more; which being perceived we delayed no more but just upon the stroke of five we let fly our fighting colours & immediately fired upon ships, who answered us immediately & were seconded by the castles & forts of the town, upon which we shot at all & in a short time beat from one of their greatest forts some three or four thousand men that were placed with small shot upon us; but the castles were not to be taken for besides the strength of their walls they had so many of the Dutch guns (wlth their own) which played in the hulls & decks of our ships, that in 3 hours time we lost some 200 men & six captains, our cables were cut, & we were driven out by the wind, which was so directly against us that we could not use our fireships which otherwise had infallibly done our business; so we came off having beat the town all to pieces without losing one ship. We now lie off a little still expecting a wind that we may send in fireships to make an end of the rest. Mr Montague & Thomas Wyndham's brother were both killed with one shot just by me, but God Almighty was pleased to preserve me from any kind of hurt. Madam, I have been tedious but beg your Ladyship's pardon who am

Your most obedient son,
Rochester

I have been as good a husband as I could, but in spite of my wish have been fain to borrow money.

Now, this is indeed a more sanguine account of our business that ever mortal could dream of; had we indeed 'beat the town to pieces', 'tis more than I could know, we looking so beaten ourselves; and did the wind carry us from the engagement, 'twere a mind backed by Teddeman's commands and the turning of sails and whipstaffs; more, that we (indomitable and victorious) lie but in expectation of a wind to bring in fireships and turn all to success, 'twould take indeed the great mercy of that God he speaks of.

There is a deal in this letter that is surprising. He appears to have known Wyndham before their meeting on ship; yet of this prior acquaintance he gave no sign. This mystery I put down to Rochester's closed-mouthed way, his gift for talking much yet revealing little: of discoursing with great intimacy on his views and philosophies yet somehow never revealing his deepest motives and feelings.

I am puzzled not only by the omissions and distortions in the account but by the references to the personal God that hath directed it: as if he be a Puritan writing a Providential history and laying the fall of a flea to the inscrutable Plan. The references to God, which usually pepper his speeches as oaths, are here adapted to a grave religious tone; but here I suppose we have again Rochester adapting his manners to please his audience, as he did with the heiress' grave mother at court.

Another tone gives me pause as well; and that is, the indefinable guilt. He presents himself as one who has done wrong for writing, yet has also erred in waiting so long to write; he even makes a desperate confession at the end, as if offering a sin for her to find fault with. Yet he signs himself 'obedient' and assures her he will never be found wanting in his duty, as is plain from the fullness of her account; so why must he beg her pardon? He hath left off his usual breezy, insouciant air, writing not with a swagger but with an air of self-deprecation. He even calls her 'your Ladyship' and never once descends, as Buckhurst and his brothers do, to the informality of 'Mother'.

Why says he so little of his crazed heroism, which must redound to his credit? Does he fear she'll think he boasts?

I scan the part about the death of his comrades. This experience would make up the bulk of my letter, were I writing to my mother; for 'tis plain the event, seeming foretold as it was, had an impact on the lad. His carriage changed first to horror, then to resolve. He first looked all about in a daze, then behaved as if he believed himself charmed. Yet this, which must have loomed highest in his mind, he devotes the least time to – even condensing it to a sentence, that they were killed 'just by me' – without mentioning the cannonball that threw him clear of the deadly explosion.

I ask, 'Why so brief about the business with Montague and Wyndham?'

He grins. 'Because I've no wish to offend my pious mother: to tell her, I've put a ghost on the scales and found him no more than a chimera; nor to tell her, I have tempted the Lord her God; and been shown that the soul, though it has presentiments of its end, perishes with the body.'

The next day I hear intelligence that the plague hath killed in town some 2500 persons in the past week alone; that the streets are full of death-carts, and the bodies piling so fast in the kennels of town 'tis all

195

that can be done to shovel 'em into the great common pits; that the churches hold day and night long services of prayer hurled up into the vacancy of the sky; that hordes of rats run wild in the town gnawing the corpses, and dogs are being shot for food; that the roads are full of starving vagabonds, who, having left their pitiful homes in town, have nowhere else to go, and who are beaten from town to town with whips and guns, those in hamlets yet clean being too fearful of the sickness to take 'em in; that camps of the starving and homeless have sprung up in every forest, to survive by poaching, and be shot by any of the fearful residents that find 'em; and that, withall, the court disports itself by the side of the sweet-flowing Avon in Salisbury, some half a kingdom away, and the common man begins to grumble that it is a judgement of God upon their Wickedness, and His hand will follow to smash 'em wherever they flee.

Rochester may brood on the meaning of life and death and torment himself that Wyndham's ghost could not appear. But as for me, I leave this engagement more determined yet to make use of the brief span allotted me before annihilation. Right glad will I be to take the ship provided for me soon and sail off toward Salisbury – and my pleasures.

7

'No Longing Remains Unfulfilled'
19 August 1665

There is no struggle of soul and body save in the minds of those whose souls are asleep and whose bodies are out of tune.

No longing remains unfulfilled.

—Kahlil Gibran, *Sand and Foam*

Taking coach at Bournemouth, and mighty glad too to find myself on solid ground (though my body rocketh still as to the swing of the waves), 'tis a good hard fifty mile and more straight out north to Salisbury, though on fine solid roads; and my manor of Westford Park lying fair in the path, but a few miles' drive from the road near Clearbury Ring; think I, that's a good inn to make for a week's rest: whereat, finding myself the first time in these five years past making my solemn entrance into this my village of Westford, my breast swelleth with pride near my broken arm, to see these my freeholders again: my mind paints to me the fancy of how they will line the High, the little girls holding daisies and the simple tenants tossing upward their caps with a 'Huzzah'.

So 'tis a little to my disappointment, entering the village path and thence onto the High, to be greeted by naught but John Fuller's dung heap, which steameth in the sun beside the Cock and Bull; and the ruin't chancel of the parish church, its windows of stained glass broke open and crosses and angels despoiled just as Cromwell's fanatics hath left it, and a sow and piglets lying beyond its broken-down fence in the shade of a spreading yew on the cool gravestone nearby.

The simple freeholders who were to cheer me hath without doubt found a better business to do, mayhap at the Cock and Bull or Joan Aubrey's; or, I doubt not, the more industrious are out minding their strips of corn and barley scattered here and there or their sheep on the village common. I might as well be a loosed gelding to be catched and locked in the manor pound, as the man to whom all owe early rents and duties, the Law personified in flesh and blood. But then, say

197

I, they had no notice of my coming, and I arrive in no coroneted coach.

The cots along the High seemeth in fine repair, many new thatched and new built. William Mercer's, which was nigh unto ruin, now intrudes cheerfully onto the High and looks to be new plastered, its roof new thatched and boasting a wooden-barred window (unglazed) to signify he hath built into the loft a chamber for sleeping. Indeed, much of the thatch along the High appeareth fresh, some with shapes of the roof squared off and others triangular, and the fences neat and mended, too.

Jostling grandly up to the front of Westford Park Manor House with its brown and white trimmed gables, I am let from my conveyance and through my door, to be scolded by my steward Frank: first, that I hath arrived without notice and nothing is ready for me; and then, that I never come half often enough: that I have poachers in my forests and anglers in my streams.

Then this is not all: I must needs hear that the new people I have sent in from town will not obey his authority, and carry themselves high as if he be a beast of a lower order: that John Ross and Edward Miller, being two footmen brought in from town, hath led a plot of all their kind to lie drunk, smoke tobacco, and catch at the women all day, and cannot in no wise be brought to assist on the manor, insisting they were bred for finer things; that Moll Smith and Mary Huddleston hath done little better, for they carry themselves before the village girls as if fine ladies, intoning of their vowels through their noses and dressing of one another's heads all day, and so snubbing the country help with tales of my Lord Rochester's kisses and my Lord Buckhurst's coins, that there is at least one hair-pulling match a day: in short, why did his lordship not leave all this town riffraff behind, as the other gentlemen did, instead of sending 'em into the country to vex the honest folk there?

I almost wonder why myself. I am sorely tempted to haul 'em over Salisbury Plain and commend 'em to the sacrificial gods of Stonehenge.

One piece of news, though, joys the heart: which is, no one has aught but praise for the staunch way in which little Jane has taken work on herself (no directions being given by anyone else), setting herself to polishing of silver, dusting of the old clawed furniture and hunting of berries for pies: whereupon being praised, so Frank relates, she hath said with a very sober look, that she cannot do enough for his lordship, to serve to make up what he hath done for her.

I am so delighted to hear this news of her, after the griefs given me by everyone else, I commit a serious breach of the proprieties and insist she take her dinner with me in the great ancestral hall: whereupon both of us, bashful, sit regarding one another with darting looks and polite remarks down the long polished length of oak. I can tell that she is as alone in the world as I, and we contrive a timid alliance, I telling her to pack her bundle against a Friday's departure, that I may carry her to court with me; and her tutor, too, who says she progresses in her letters.

Then with naught else to do, I visit the great library, though poking about the musty volumes there, I encounter naught to engage me till my hands run over the line of old school books that I could not e'en translate at Westminster, much less now. I put a hand on a thin volume of Juvenal and pull it out: whereupon I am seized with all the terror and heartache of my school days. I am no longer a man, answerable only to myself, but a boy trembling before a huge tyrant, long, thin rod in his hands, and about to take down my breeches to be whipped because my translations are not good enough but afear'd I will not be able to bear the pain without tears. I feel again the anxious hush of the schoolroom, the eyes of the other boys watching, the explosion of pain from the first stripe. Then I recall the tenderness of Grandma, who, finding on my first holiday how I was being taught Latin, said I need not return to such a place. Then I feel more melancholy than ever, thinking on her death and the drowning of the dear parents I can scarce remember at all.

With a slamming shut of the book, I determine to shake off this humour that hath descended from nowhere. Making the best horse to be saddled, I try a pull at riding about the village and estate, at first joying myself in the pleasant fields and flowers, in the new diversions of watching little girls gather pinks or sheep graze on the common, finding joy in the buxom titty-bounce of a maid that strolls thereon, a pail swinging in her hand, high voice singing sweetly.

I inhale draughts of air pure and clean, suddenly conscious of the beauty about me and wishing I could share it with someone – Buckhurst? No, not Buckhurst: who hath never been to Knole or Copt Hall but he sneers at it *à la mode*: the one is so sombre and splendid, he claims, even the ghosts fright themselves; the other is too rustic for the enduring: an a man can survive the roads, he finds himself imprisoned on a hill in a forest, with no escape from his relations, and all about him Essex-men that know not how to speak. No, not Buckhurst: whom though I may drink and sport with I dare not confide in. Then who?

All at once some depth of my mind is jarred, and up spins a long-forgotten memory. I see myself on a horse very near this spot, sitting in front of my young fair-haired father, who steadies me with an arm and asks me, *Would you feed the ducks or first ride to the Downs?* I cannot have been very old at the time; for I was but six when he died. But the picture is there, like an old miniature seen through mist; I strain harder to see his face or recall something else, whereupon the whole is gone.

Now do I feel more melancholy than ever; and, amazed that the dim past can hold such powerful sway on our emotions and attitudes, wiping away first one tear then another, I understand more than ever before what Bucks means when he says he yearns for a son.

I remember one of the few lines from the *Aeneid* that made an impression on me, Dido yearning for a *parvulus Aeneas*, a little version of the man she so adored. How I long to have a little girl on one knee and a little boy on t'other, then several older ones playing on the floor, a baby in the nursery, and a rose-cheeked lady delicate and refined to share the intimacies of my talk. No doubt I am the sort of man, like Ossory, who was born to be married; yet who am I to press into service as a wife – little Jane? Some flighty female like Mallet or Jennings? I refuse to marry out of *ennui* or simple loneliness, to discover myself in the same sinking ship as Sedley; and seeing the fever of Rochester for his lady (which is apparent as it drive him from Tower to war, work though he doth to conceal it), I have considered this may be the only excuse for a man to shackle himself for life. For custom dulls the edge of appetite, and the court air's a never-failing corrosive to the metal of the marriage bond. Would I wed in haste, to make my home unquiet with the scolding of some resty jade, who will drive me thence, amid the laughter of my friends?

Tonight, as I sit to supper in the great dining hall, and this time alone, and the footmen stepping in and out pompously with one antique silver dish after another, methinks I hear the wood creak as it settles into the ancient earth.

Making an end of the meal, I order up an enormous quantity of sack from the wine cellar, so to sack myself to bed; and taking it down in great draughts, listen to the croaking of the frogs.

8

'The Desire for Certain Pleasure is Part of my Pain.'

20 August 1665

Strange, the desire for certain pleasures is part of my pain.
Make me, oh God, the prey of the lion, ere You make the rabbit my
prey.

—Kahlil Gibran, *Sand and Foam*

Today being Sunday, I am awaked at the rudest of rustic hours by the
proprietary Frank, who hath laid out His Lordship's blue velvet suit
and doublet against the morning services: the which, he was certain,
His Lordship would not omit to set a good example by attending, and
where there was being held for him the front pew. So I must needs sit
beneath the despoiled pulpit, by a side aisle nasty where the pigs hath
slept and a shattered window, where all can see my pious attitude as I
hear how the hand of the Lord is raised against this country, in that
whoremasters and drunkards sit in the councils of state; that the
avenging angels are in the sky, pouring out the vessels of wrath –
already we have the sword and pestilence, and have now but to await
the fire – whereupon it behooveth all of us to repent of whatever sins
we may have: for the breath of pestilence will spread far over this
mighty land before the Lord hath spent his vengeance on the crimes
of the lost sheep therein.

Of course I see plainly at whom this oration must be directed, but
what am I to do? Engage in an unmannerly dispute with some scurvy
rustic whose stipend is but £4 13s 4d a year? 'Tis a dispute I would
likely lose, not being of a quarrelsome humour and not having any
excuse for my mode of life into the bargain. 'Tis better to contrive not
to see his drift, and smile agreeably, and commend his eloquence
afterward, then, tumbling out of the ruin't leaning door, go to hit the
bottle. Vengeance will be mine when I am returned to court, where I
can mimic his enthusiastic airs.

Buckhurst hath writ me from Copt Hall of a variation of this argument being preached in Essex: the King and court, the argument goeth, are blamed for the plague, which the comet is said to have announced; and the vulgar are all too ready to believe. What a simple universe these vulgar live in: the whole of it linked in cause-and-effect, with a big heavenly Papa making his displeasure so clearly known, only the foolhardy would dare to grab a titty under his disapproving ogle.

The preacher is right glad to see me returned to my flock at last, he saith, for great mischiefs hath been done in my absence. That the archdeacon's court was held here not six weeks ago, and he is sorry he must needs say, that the inquisitors appointed thereto hath been forced to present before the court numerous crimes, viz.: Edward Wilson hath been presented for carting upon the 4th of June, this being a Sunday, and Andrew Thomason hath had carnal copulation with his wife before their marriage. That Mistress Meade hath presented her husband, in that he and Madge Talbot do live together incontinently; &c. &c.

Escaped at last, I am thereupon released to spend the rest of this day in the doldrums of a rustic Sunday, the only diversion being, one Señor Rodriguez come to present himself to my service, he being a Spanish guitar master who hath made all of the neighbouring manors in the forlorn hopes of a gull. He puffeth mightily the ease with which his art may be learnt; the stunning triumphs with ladies infallibly following upon the mastery thereof; the many virtuosi he hath initiated, the last being La Linda Sotherby, whose manor lieth near Shepton Mallet in the next county. Thus am I made his latest prey, as I am to any travelling pedlar: for I stand about, hem and haw, loath to refuse 'em anything, the guilt of my vast fortune riding always on my conscience. I engaging him to make a party with me on my journey to court the next day, he is delighted, whereupon with a wink he insinuates, he knew what he was about by calling at Westford Park, being conscious that there abided the leader of the wits.

I am not much deceived at being denominated the leader of Rochester or Buckingham in wit; and I beg him to leave the honey off his tongue if we will have any business together. Right glad doth he nod briskly and acquiesce, whereupon pulling forth a cittern, with noble carved head, he doth make my skull to ache with the minutiae and mysteries of his business: these are the 4 strings, I am told, and of wire not of gut, and this the *g*, that the *b*, the others *c* and *d*: this the cittern, *don* Ashfield, hath double strings as we may plainly see; and his lordship hath chosen wisely thereupon to acquaint himself with the mysteries of the musical art, the lute being hard to hold with its round belly and the gittern being harder to tune and play; *por favor* to observe *don* Ashfield, my good lord, how it may be tuned; this the treble string we tune as high as may be, so! – but taking care, my good lord, that it be kept from breaking; for it will break my lord *sin duda* if tuned too high, and this the 3rd string tuned lower than the 4th, *vea usted*, so, and the *g* lower than the *b*; &c.

The whole of this speech being such a mighty bore, I pay little heed, but sit enrapt instead on the wonderful presages of the future, painted high by the colours of fancy, in which I will sit soon in a chamber with Arran, or mayhap his cousin James Hamilton, these two being the handiest guitar-men at court; and espying one of their citterns, pick it up, thereupon to run my expert fingers over the strings and begin to draw forth music that will make the stars dance. Methinks I hear Rochester cry, 'Ashfield, I never knew you could play guitar' (he cannot do't); methinks I even see Buckhurst look upon me with a new respect and Sedley admit there is somewhat I can do.

Mayhap I must be the butt for recalling so ill my scraps of Latin; mayhap my verse is unpolished and trite and my fencing worse; mayhap I am made sport of in my wonderful proclivity for stating the obvious or melting in pity at the distresses of others; mayhap I am the only man who, going to war and seeing a mighty battle, can return home wounded with a broken arm, and the only peer whose servants scold and manage him – but I am determined, I shall astound the whole world by my wielding the guitar: determined, like the lowly worm, I shall metamorphose myself into a lovely butterfly of song. There must be something I can do – and God knows I've tried everything else.

Tonight, rambling about the musty grand palace alone, and listening again to the frogs croak their communications down at the pond, I feel nigh to weeping; yet it is even more forbid for me to resort to tears than it was to have little Jane into the dining hall. Not until these two days have I been made so fully conscious what a lonely life it is I lead, now there's no play to attend or mob to get drunk with: nothing, to say truth, to fill up the gap in my life but the awesome and terrifying business of self-examination, of looking at my life and what I do with it: whereupon I like not what I see and yearn even more to get drunk. Is there no one at all to do't with?

On an inspiration I decide to take myself down the High to Joan Aubrey's, where no doubt the better part of the village hath gathered. So, by brave moonshine and in warm air to the warble of the nightingale, I walk the little distance down the High, whereupon coming to the sign of the Lion that is Joan Aubrey's beside the little stone alehouse, I hear a merry snatch of song:

'What though the zealots
Pull down the Prelates
Push at the Pulpit
And kick at the Crown:
Shall not the Roundhead
First be conf'ounded
Sa, sa, sa, sa, boys:
Ha, ha, ha, ha, boys:
Then we'll return
With triumph and joy:
Cast up our caps and cry
Vive le Roy.'

I eagerly pushing open the door am confronted by a merry roistering company, and one very like to joy the heart, the trestle-tables
their planks laid out and jointed stools before 'em, the wenches
cherry-cheeked going about lively with the foaming tankards, and a
pair of lovers in the corner groping and bussing; the burthen of the
song going merrily about the common room, tankards raised, caps
flying, and men a-roaring: whereupon all at once, a great gasp goeth
up and stillness descends.

'My lord!' crieth one of 'em, and hops to his feet.

'Your Lordship!'

'My lord!'

And they are every man jack of them risen to their feet, caps in
hand; even the lovers leaving off their fondling and coying, the woman
to curtsey and the man to make his bow. 'Tis of no avail to urge them
to be themselves, that we may all enjoy ourselves as human creatures
do over a tankard: the whole of the company must sit up straight,
minding their manners, like boys in a schoolroom or little girls with
the parson come to tea; they speak respectfully, thank me for the
round I order; and make a great shift to watch their grammar.

I cannot seem to put 'em at ease, as Rochester did with the seamen,
by assuming a kindly, gracious air without either condescension or
familiarity. Seeing how I dampen the cheer of the company, I toss
down a flagon and depart: whereat I am lonelier than ever, to hear the
burst of relieved merriment within, all the voices chattering again at
once. But how can I have expected these people to joy themselves with
me? They cart my hay, harrow my oat-land, reap my corn, rent my
acres, stand in my court, trade so many days of work for 7s a year or 2
hens and 20 eggs.

I am not even human to these people: I am a local Zeus, whose
bounteous charity supports the district; whose maid-servants sew for

the poor and whose fields support their livelihood; whose agent makes their laws in his absence, and who this once in five years hath descended from his cloud. Can they suddenly carry themselves to me as a fellow? Nay, and I might e'en resent the gesture did they accept the friendship I would offer.

Lonely and sad, I walk the High toward the great looming manor house that riseth ahead, dominating the countryside; and on a pull to make a shorter way, cut through the pleasant grove at the northeast of it – whereupon wandering through the elms and oaks, I almost stumble upon someone.

'Your Lordship!' breathes a soft feminine voice with a tremor.

It is the beauty I saw the day before, who hath come, by the evidence of her basket, to gather mushrooms. Her round breasts heave beneath the flimsy cloth of her low tight bodice, whereat I feel a twinge of desire.

'What make you here, pretty maid?'

She is a true brown beauty, the moonlight breaking through the leaves on her face.

'I –' She breathes and blushes so, with such wild looks of confusion, the inspiration suddenly moveth me that she is as aware of my sex as I of hers. I reach forward and gather her to me, till her high hard breasts are against my bosom, and taste long of the honey inside her mouth: which she suffereth without protest, her lips admitting my tongue and her arms taut against me, but without methinks much delight; whereupon releasing her, I see in the moonlight two tears on her cheeks and a look of pleading on her face.

It cometh to me then that I might have this woman as I pleased right here in the grove, and she do naught to prevent me, and all because of my rank; but that she is all over terror, her little brown hand trembling now in mine, to think of how she must submit to so terrible a coercion.

She moistens her lips, and, her eyes two great round circles pleading, she manages to whimper, in a small voice, 'Your Lordship –'

Every tincture of desire gone, I release her hand, into which I put an angel, and so back to my melancholy trail to the great lonely house, and the isolation in which I am suddenly made conscious all men must live.

9

'A Place Pickt Out By Choice Of Best Alive'
25 August 1665

A place pickt out by choice of best aliue,
That natures work by art can imitate:
In which what euer in this worldly state
Is sweet, and pleasing vnto liuing sense,
Or that may dayntiest fantasie aggrate,
Was poured forth with plentifull dispence,
And made there to abound with lavish affluence.
    —Edmund Spenser, 'The Bower of Blisse', from *The Faerie Queene*

Up early for a joggling ride down Salisbury Road, which is to my mind
the avenue to the sweetest town that ever anyone knew, and with the
silliest companions (to say truth) that ever a courtier brought
removing thither: the one a señor with a cittern slung over his horse;
t'other a young tutor with his hat in his lap; and the last a scullery
maid, who leaneth from the coach window in a passion at each rise, on
a pull to view the grey jutting shadow that·is the high-flung spire of
Salisbury Cathedral.

The black sweet-flowing Avon mumureth its way through this lovely
town, and from every angle riseth the spire: here half-hidden by the
sheltering branch of a yew or elm in the Cathedral Close, there rising
on a sudden grey upsweep behind the clustered shops of red-and-
white brick, or like a sudden grey shadow plummeting skyward behind
the white stone city gates with their crenellated tops. Miles out of town
it riseth through the mists of the lowlands, a Tower of Babel bent on
scraping heaven, and plainer even from afar than the older monu-
ment of faith but ten miles to the northwest of town, the Druid circle

206

of Stonehenge, monoliths lying shattered and forgot in the winds of Salisbury Plain.

'Mark the spire, Jane,' says Mr Rivers the tutor, seeing the little girl's passion. 'How high is it, would you guess?' She shakes her head. He points. 'Some four hundred feet, the highest in the country. 'Twas built in 1265 at the town's removal hither from the earthworks of Old Sarum, where St Osmond built the first cathedral in 1092.'

And here the cathedral hath spread and towered ever since, in a meadow of green close-cropped and lovely, on the two of its sides a high stone wall and on the other the sweet river, laving its banks with a swift-currented eddying flow. Here the grey stone facade hath borne silent witness, its jutting towers and lacey friezes, array of saints and deep-carven Norman archways; its spire upflung where nave and transept join near the flying buttresses; its windows of tablets, multi-foils, circles and cloverleaves all letting in the many-rayed light of heaven.

Salisbury! Why do I love thee so? The first time I saw thy spire, the heart welled up in my throat; thy river walks, thy inns, thy sights were so dear to me; and yet, thou art little different from many a fair English cathedral town.

Arriving at the speckle-stone building where John and Edward hath lodged me in Cathedral Close, I confess it is to my diversion to see with what wistfulness the little London-bred Jane doth peer from the window, shoving its chequered panes outward and sticking herself out neath the gable to stare at the cathedral. Telling her to have joy of her day as she may list, I give her a few coins for spending in the shops or inns and suggest of activities that might be a frolic to a child, as visiting the ducks and geese that swim near Harnham Bridge by the Rose and Crown inn.

The tutor waxeth eager: 'We could have a history lesson at the cathedral, my lord; she might be shown the sarcophagi, the chapels, and in the library, the old documents...'

She making a mouth at such scholarly employments, I tell the tutor that, just for today, he should accompany her where she list; and give them also the directions to Salisbury Market and recommend the inns thereabout, as the Cross Keys and the Haunch of Venison.

The tutor, Mr, Rivers, a good-hearted young man chosen for character as well as scholarship, extends his hand for her to take; and she looks a pretty and pampered child in her damask overskirt and white puffed sleeves. She learns quickly, though the sounds of her speech betray her origin. I make a sudden decision to leave off this pretence of her being a scullery-maid and to declare her my ward.

The Gothic old clock bonging from the bell-tower and making me to admire how I will sleep in such quaint lodgings as these, I fall to examining those messages that have piled up on the tray against my arrival. The most recent is a note from Buckhurst, saying, as I am like to arrive during the thirteen hours of daylight, I must join the King and court where they frolic at the great earthworks of Old Sarum, some two miles north of town on the Stonehenge Road. This I am right glad to do, though so weary from my journey: having had enough, on my life, with this loneliness into which my rank hath thrust me these several days past.

So I make the best horse to be saddled and ride to Old Sarum, where the treble ditches, deep enough to swallow one giant on another's shoulders standing, guard a sky-topping high grass bailey, which might have held the Ark out of the flood, and the whole built so long ago as to be ancient even to the Saxons – mayhap e'en to the Druids of Stonehenge.

Tying my horse at the foot of the first ditch, where a multitude of other sleek beasts graze, and huffing my way winding up a narrow path to the crest of this man-made mountain, then negotiating the planks that hath been laid across the mammoth rings of moats (now but grass and earth), I see plainly why the Normans repaired hither to these old earthworks at first instead of the valley. A race of savage giants might rampage below but never scale these towering heights, much less a scurvy herd of Saxons; to say truth, I much admire I can leg it myself, and that with planks for the crossing and no Norman bowmen trained upon me.

Who'd be mad enough to traipse hither for a frolic? His Majesty, no doubt, who hath a passion for bodily exertion unlike any I ever did see before.

Having climbed at last to the height and even got above the last ditch that circles the inner high mound of the bailey, which riseth in irregular clumps of grassy earth and piles of broken white stone, I see from my giddy perch as a crow might the valley below, blue-grey in the distance, and green fields below dotted with the roofs of farmhouses and emerald tops of trees.

All about me is pleasant recreation, Arran and His Majesty having erected on one of the mounds a tennis net, where they bat away to an audience sipping from pewter tankards: lovely ladies, their satin or velvet skirts whipping to the high wind, and gentlemen whose plumes blow.

To the north side of the height where sprawl the ruins of the castle, here sits Gramont to cards with round-bellied Castlemaine and some other gulls. On the grass plain a few feet below, where a cross-shaped outline of stones marks the nave and transept of the cathedral that rested here some 600 years ago, the maids of honour frolic with Blind Man's Buff, shrieking as they fall over the small white piles of stones and onto their lovely posteriors.

Everyone acts mighty glad to see me, so that wine and pullet and cheese are pressed on me more than anyone can swallow, though I see plainly how wearisome will be the trial of explaining my arm, everyone waiting to hear an heroical tale of a wound and laughing fit to burst at the plain matter of the truth – and none more than Shepherd, whom I discover and embrace in company with Buckhurst and Sedley, where they sit on a high-flung post of earthworks looking off into the valley.

To do me justice, I contrive to set off the silly tale of my wounding with an epical enough picture of bullets and cannon, to the which Buckhurst and shadow hath not many retorts; after which I inquire the news. After treating me to a long discourse of who and who's together, they fall into a sombre silence.

Just then a gang of giggling fair ones appeareth, to bid me stand, relate of my wound and the fleet, come hither and suffer 'em to feel of the splinted arm; &c. Good-humouredly I stand, to be teased by their leader the buxom-bosomed young Lady Denham. She taps my arm with her fan, lowers her long black lashes, talks idle nonsense of what a hero I must be, so that I gaze anxiously about on a pull to spy the whereabouts of her jealous old husband.

Sedley, sitting atop one of the tumulus grass mounds a few paces away, wiping some pullet-grease from his chin, sadly shakes his head. 'I would the Lady Chesterfield were here amongst us again. The news about her hath been preying sadly on my mind.'

News? What's this?

Buckhurst nods, blowing out his fat cheeks. 'A sad fate, poor merry lady.'

Sad fate?

'And behold her husband over there – playing as if nothing had happened,' says Shepherd.

I look toward another knoll, where Chesterfield serenely crouches, one knee up over a board of draughts which he plays at with some ladies, the fat Price included, at whom he winks.

Lady Denham, purring, links two white hands about my good forearm. 'We lodge at the Red Lion, my lord. Shall I invite you thither to walk up sometime?'

I am surprised to see Clifford strolling up across the green rock-littered tumuli. 'What make you here?' I ask.

He settling himself on the mound beside Buckhurst and Sedley, smiling at me and greeting them, tells how he hath carried a message to His Majesty.

I extricate myself as politely as may be from the teasing embrace of Lady Denham and her gossips. 'Ladies, permit me to speak with an old sea comrade. I will admire your beauty with my eyes while my ears lend their attention elsewhere.'

They whirl about and huff off in a flurry of skirts and chatter.

'What's this about the Lady Chesterfield?' Clifford inquires, sitting cross-legged on the grassy knoll, his long fair hair whipping to the breeze.

A football flying through the air comes nigh to divesting Sedley of his enormous periwig: at which, he ducking with a curse, Buckhurst catches it in both arms and with a heave-ho sends it spinning back toward a shrieking clutch of children.

Sedley shakes his head. 'Poisoned. Or at least, so the news is.'

'Poisoned? By whom?'

My comrades turn their two plumed heads to stare at Chesterfield, who moves the marker on the draughts board.

'Her husband?'

'Well, let us say, her last meal may have been seasoned to disagree with her,' says Shepherd. 'And let us say, her husband was mightily jealous – even of her brother Lord John.'

I recall with pain that sprightly air and charming staccato speech, that *joie de vivre* and sparkling blue eye – and then her comment, 'La, how some men never love a woman till she cuckolds them.'

Clifford looks down thoughtfully, his fingers plucking at the grass, his shoulders hunching. Then he looks up. 'But – has there been no investigation?'

Buckhurst nods. 'Ormond raised a coil.'

'Her body was opened, but nothing found.' Shepherd stares into the distance.

'Chesterfield hath been to Italy, though,' says Sedley, 'and we all know what subtle poisons can be found there.'

Buckhurst shakes his head at the thought. 'Jesus. Italian seasoning.'

We say nothing for a minute, the wind whipping through our plumes. But I think how tragic love becometh in this court and how impossible is the hope for marital happiness.

I look to where the Duchess of Buckingham, sitting on a ruint pile of white stone and grass, spins a top before the admiring eyes of Castlemaine's little ones, Anne and Charles. Then I look to where their mother, full of another royal child, shrieks o'er a hand and lays it down on the grass. On a far mound the Duke of Buckingham lounges beside the Lady Shrewsbury, who plucketh notes from an angélique, and whose old husband no doubt could not scale the earthworks. Anon he may become like Castlemaine's husband, permanently absent to save face.

Good Queen Catherine, small and dark as a monkey, childless like the Duchess of Bucks, sits knees up and hands clasped about 'em, her timidly adoring eyes watching the tall, slender figure of the King dart back and forth after the tennis ball, his racket batting it, his dark eyes and white teeth gleaming as he casts admiring glances at the simpering Stewart.

The Lady Denham, wind blowing her lustrous dark curls and shaping the pink satin skirt against her invitingly rounded thighs, talks to the Duke of York, who ogles her and grimaces like a monkey in his tight-curled brown periwig. The Duchess of York, double of chin and pendulant of breast, her legs like tree trunks and busk stays bursting about a Savilian belly, crouches on a green mound, the bones of done-in chickens about her. The fortunate woman hath contrived to enjoy her dinners so much she no longer minds her husband's straying. Of course, she's twice the size she was at her wedding a few years ago.

Like the Lady Chesterfield's, hers was a love match.

'What doth our friend Rochester with the fleet?' asks Sedley suddenly.

'More than he should, to keep alive,' says Clifford. 'I've never seen such a fireball in all my life.'

'We've sadly wanted him here,' complains Shepherd. 'The women are not stirred up so much to diverting quarrels amongst themselves. The lampoons are not so sharp, nor the debauches so jolly. His Majesty hath made complaint time and again of Rochester's absence.'

'Well,' says Clifford, 'he has some sort of bee in his bonnet, something driving him. I'm not sure what.'

'I think he looks for gold,' I say, 'that he may offer a bribe-price for his little lady.'

Clifford says, politely, 'That may be some of it.'

Buckhurst shakes his head sombrely, his cheeks blown out. 'Well, there's not much taking up there. The news is, she's well-nigh wedlocked.'

Shepherd adds, 'Well-nigh contracted to Hinchingbrooke. And the Duke of Ormond is making motions to secure her for the Lord John Butler.'

'Which God speed,' says Sedley, 'rather than she be given to Hinchingbrooke.'

Buckhurst shakes his head. 'It boots little whom she marries. P—k and c—t will have their way; love needs not the ties of love and property.'

Shepherd adds, 'He may enjoy her more if he's not forced to't.'

'There's a cynical sentiment,' I grumble.

'Why? 'Tis plain my Lord Rochester will not have her, and love is brief anyway. They may draw it out the longer and more delightfully if they're not obliged to't.'

I grow more and more melancholy till, the yellow sun pounding on my bewigged head and the ants crawling over my boot, I wonder what I do here with this heartless mob in the heat and my arm aching, too. But where else am I to go? And what am I to do?

And Shepherd is in the right. Possession is a certain antidote to passion around here; marriage is thrice deadly.

'Well,' says Clifford, 'no one's about to get much of a fortune at sea. The news I brought to the King and Duke was not good. De Ruyter managed to give us the slip and sail back home. The Lord Rochester was in a fury, laid it all to our withdrawing back to Flamborough Head to rejoin the main fleet. But our commander would have more instructions from the Lord Sandwich.'

'Perhaps we'll have another chance,' I say feebly.

Clifford languidly stares out at the blue-grey vista. 'Perhaps.'

But I know 'twould take a miracle to get Rochester his lady now. And perhaps, the way marriages sour around here, it were better he wed coldly, not to involve his heart in some tragedy.

10

'I Want A Hero'
15 September 1665

I want a hero, an uncommon want
When every year and month sends forth a new one,
Till, after cloying the gazettes with cant,
The age discovers he is not the true one.

—Lord Byron, *Don Juan*

'He's back!'

The cry echoes round the half-moon circle where a clutch of us sit by the riverside behind the Rose and Crown inn. I look up, startled, and bearing down upon us is Etherege, his plumes waving as if he be one of the water fowl fed by the ladies at the bank.

'Who's back?' I ask.

'Rochester! He rests in his quarters just now, with a fat boy he's brought back from the wars.'

Savile! This would portend some pleasant frolic.

I follow Etherege through the pleasant garden where roses blow and pansies wink up at my feet and so into the inn, where like a hawker for a fair he bounces before me, advertising the delight to come. 'Gad, but he looks well! And speaks most divertingly!' – so that I feel I'm to see the Three-Headed Boy from the Indies.

Throwing open the door to the *sancta sanctorum*, he gesticulates with one hand proudly, as if he be a priest unveiling a mystery. His square face grinning, eyes of blue-grey alight 'neath the fair periwig, he proclaims with a grand flourish of the arm, 'There!'

I peer through the open door to see a plain room of black timber and plaster, a great bed like any other – but in a chair beyond it, booted leg slung up carelessly on a table, person stretched out, the prize that Etherege would display.

I walk through the door that he holds open and am a little surprised to perceive, I have a train of attendants following me, as if drawn in to a raree show, some half a score of ladies and gentlemen sufficiently

213

interested in the Boy Genius to come peer and listen at his return. I wonder if Etherege has chosen his moment aright, for Rochester, though his face has good colour and his flesh is a little better filled out, looks mightily enervated, no doubt with the long journey. With two long fingers he massages his eyelids as if he would close 'em in sleep.

Across the table from him in another chair reposes a round pint-pot form rather like a pear – the which I have already grown to love.

'Savile!' I cry. 'Why, gad, 'tis good to see thee.' I go up to hug him. 'And Rochester!' I embrace him, too; he pats me on the back. ''Tis well to see thee here alive.'

The others file in after me, the men going to clap Rochester on the back as he drags his body out of the chair for a polite bow, in acknowledgement of the ladies that giggle blushing near the door. Savile stands to be presented in a flurry of introductions.

'What make you here?' asks someone in the crowd.

'Sit, sit, for God's sake, friend,' says Savile. 'You're well nigh exhausted, my lord. The ladies will not mind, I am sure.'

Rochester looks uneasy, but with a high trilling chorus begging him, he slings himself back down into the chair again. Savile hath already lowered his partridge plumpness into its nest, for only Rochester stands in the presence of ladies, as if he be a child honouring a strict parent.

Massaging his eyelids again, he answers, 'Bringing of a report to His Majesty on our fortunes at sea.'

'And how are these?' asks a gentleman.

'Ill enough, in all conscience. I wonder we do not either sail to Holland and subdue the whole foul nest in a campaign of a three days' wonder or give up the whole business entirely. But this dancing about from one latitude to another, exchanging a bit of shot and then backing off, is like a maid who cannot consider whether she will enjoy or no but keeps herself ever high strung and miserable with the excitement of the state in between.'

His audience laughs, and Rochester grins.

'My lord,' lisps Etherege, 'stay you here long?'

He shrugs. 'A while, perhaps.'

Upon my life, he looks world-weary – and disgusted, too.

'Let us order him up some wine!' cries Etherege. 'My lord, what will you have? They keep a very fine cellar here.'

He shakes his head. 'Nothing for me, I thank you.'

Etherege's eyes grow wide at this sacrilege. 'No wine? Why not, my lord?'

'I am weaning myself from the habit. I lost the taste for it at sea, as I did once before on my Tour; and 'tis a mistress I'd not court back to me.'

'Whyever not?' Etherege is amazed.

'My constitution does not bear up well under it.'

'Nay, 'tis so,' intersperses Savile kindly, for all his worship of Bacchus himself. 'His Lordship has but a queasy stomach. The seamen that cleaned the deck were right glad when my wine ran out.'

Laughter rumbles up and down the scattered crowd.

A fair lady with a clutch of sunny curls on either side her neck and a gown cut low in front, with no shift nor pinner to conceal her white swollen melons up-pushed, lowers her head demurely and, fanning, says, 'My lord, I hope you will stay with us for a while, that we may enjoy some more of your conversation.'

Rochester smiles and nods toward her. 'A bit, aye.'

'What did His Majesty say,' bursts in another voice, 'and the Duke of York, when you told him the news of the fleet?'

'I cannot say that either of them were pleased.'

'What is this rumour, my lord, about the Lord Sandwich breaking bulk?'

The space betwixt Rochester's eyebrows furrows. At last he says, 'I know not if it be proper for me to comment on the action of my fleet commander nor whether His Majesty would have me speak on that subject.'

'Broken bulk? What is this?' I cry, nor is mine the only voice so raised.

A greater crowd washes through the door, as if a swell from a North Sea, and I am crunched against a poster of the bed. So it is when a man will make shift to keep company with Rochester: he draws admiring audiences as a dog doth fleas.

This tide of persons washes toward me Buckhurst, whose nautical adventures hath no doubt qualified him to speak to our mystification.

His smaller, pudgier form at my left elbow and jostling toward me now and again with the shove of the resty crowd, he discourses learnedly, 'Breaking bulk is carting off some of the cargo before the Prize Court divides up all booty fairly.'

'What? You took some ships after all?' I say.

'Few enough, in all conscience,' mutters Rochester.

'Nay, 'tis not so!' objects Savile. 'Two fine ships, then eighteen others got in a fine, brisk battle – no Oriental treasures, sure, but modest takings, nothing to be ashamed of.'

Rochester shrugs. 'Lean pickings.'

215

I wonder if he thinks of the ten thousand pound asked by Hawley for Mrs Mallet. And I wonder if Sandwich thought of it, too. The 'heavy thing' he fathered is said to be her chief suitor now, though down with a smallpox guaranteed to lessen his already negligible charms.

Sedley, who hath crept in behind Buckhurst, augments, 'The news is, Sandwich hath carted down to his estate at Hinchingbrooke all the spoils that were to have been shared by the seamen. Some of the junior officers were to have shared in the loot –' He rolls his black eyes toward Rochester '– but not, of course, the man of honour here.'

Buckhurst shakes his head, blowing out his fat cheeks. 'Rochester: a man of honour on top of everything else.'

Rochester, leaning back lazily, grins. 'It is to my self-interest to appear so.'

Savile explains, 'His Majesty hath promised His Lordship a reward of seven hundred and fifty pound.'

The crowd murmurs.

'What,' says someone in the crowd, 'for not grabbing treasure along with Sandwich?'

'Aye,' says Savile, 'and also for his courage in the battle where we took the ships, which was the engagement at Sole Bay. Sandwich in his letter writ, "For particulars I refer to Lord Rochester, who was present & showed himself brave, industrious, and of useful parts."'

'That's an understatement, I'm sure,' I say. It must have stuck in the old Admiral's craw to praise his son's rival.

'Rochester,' cries Buckhurst, 'you're to be much commended.'

The lad shrugs. 'Little good may it do any of us, the way this war is being conducted. 'Tis like to drag on for the next decade.'

'Ho,' says Sedley, 'so you would have the command of it!'

Rochester looks at him seriously. 'And why not, if I have the tactics will win it?'

'Why, what would you do then?'

'Command a fleet over to Holland. Stock the ships with cavalrymen and gun. March in, subdue the whole damned misbegotten swamp, offer to let it be reclaimed by the ocean in two or three days, and make 'em pay what tribute I would.'

A laugh goes up.

'And if they refuse or resist?' prods Sedley.

'Trample their damned tulips and knock over their windmills and poke down their dike and let 'em be drowned in their own ocean until they give what we ask.'

Sedley comments to the laughing group in general, 'Fireball

indeed! Clifford is in the right. And so you have the campaign that would be waged by a youth of eighteen.'

I see the Boy Hero later in the small oak bar, at the bench built beneath the chequered window looking out to cobbled Harnham Road. He has no silver tankard beside him, but a silver tray littered with messages.

I greet him and ask, 'Have you anything there to raise your spirits?'

'Anyone must be pleased to have so many proofs of tender anxiety as I have got. The merchants in town stand in extreme fear of my demise.'

I laugh and pull up a chair. 'Has your lady writ you?'

'What lady?'

His reply startles me. And his eyes, dark and penetrating, watch me so closely as to make me jumpy.

'Why, Mrs Mallet. Who else?'

'Why should she write?'

I grow more uncomfortable by the minute. 'No reason. Has your mother replied to your last?'

He stares on me as if he likes this question even less than the last one. But at last he replies, 'What else would a good mother do?'

I gazing from the barred oak window and onto the cobbled street without muse on what a pleasant town this be, and how melancholy if, as the King hints, a resurgence hither of the plague may send us next to Oxford, whither today he hath posted.

'We may remove to Oxford next,' I muse aloud; then, an inspiration hitting me, I give thoughtless voice to it: 'Rochester, your mother's estate is in the very neighbourhood there. You would be able to visit her.'

He makes no reply but seems very absorbed in breaking the red seal on another message. I ruminating sadly on the golden-haired angel I can scarce recall and thinking on his mother's sweet-faced portrait ask, 'How long has it been since you have seen her?'

'I knelt and asked her blessing before leaving for grammar school.'

I am aghast. 'What, ten years? Twelve?'

He rifles through the messages as if intent on 'em, and I can tell the topic distresses him. He even managed to pack for a matriculation at Oxford and a four years' tour of Italy and France without going home.

But then, his letter so timidly and boyishly solicited her approval, I know he must wish to mend matters. I decide a visit would cure the ill.

'Rochester, if there's a breach betwixt you, I think a visit might heal it.'

'Then you know very little of the situation, and I'd thank you not to advise me out of your ignorance.'

I having signalled the wench, she parades over, twitching her rump, with a tankard of the bracing Wiltshire ale, smiles at the coins I press into her hand, then sways her progress toward the great brick fireplace, to scoop up a tankard abandoned on the mantel. We watch her undulating hillocks appreciatively.

I try again: 'Rochester, she has writ you, after all.'

'So she has. Read, that you may be satisfied – and afterward, silent.'

With an aggrieved expression, he thrusts a paper toward me, then slumps down into the chair again. I read the letter, which is writ in a bold hand, its characters pressed so hard into the paper that they are pinpricked with the quill end.

Sir,

I cannot much commend you for succeeding to the sins of your father. The drinking & whoring you had done before wanted only the flourishing your sword & wasting money to complete it. I thank God, tho', that you are out of that perpetual bawdy-house call'd a court, & you are well rid of that Pint-Pot of Trouble, that flounced hither under your protection & proceeded to insult us. Beware, sir! Such a wily trull as that knows how to get herself with child.

The talk of your being in the Tower begins to die down, thank God. Try to live so that I shall no longer be ashamed of you. Avoid lying, drinking, quarrelling, & unchastity. Let not your studies go utterly to wrack, nor your passions betray you into wedlock with some saucy doxy (just the sort one expects, when a child barely out of the schoolroom will make his own choice).

Tho' you have no respect for your reputation, sir, try to summon up a little for your title & another who bears it,

Anne St. John Lee Wilmot, Countess of Rochester

Now, here's the letter of a jealous woman, railing o'er her rival, scolding at the activities that draw off her darling's time and attention. 'Tis plain they both would fain approach one another yet know not how.

I push the letter back toward the pile. 'She sounds mightily vexed, Rochester, at your neglect of her.'

The wench twitches her rounded bum over to the great oak bar again – looks up at Rochester, blushes, looks down again. When she peers cautiously up once more, he winks. Her blush deepening, she turns about and clanks together furiously the tankards 'neath the bar.

'And the business about "flourishing your sword",' I add, 'sounds as if she worries o'er your risking your neck.'

Rochester leans back lazily into the alcove of the window and rearranges his carriage, his long legs thrust out and arm flung up, elbow crooked, on the sill. All the while he watches the wench, his eyes alight as if with reverent appreciation and lips curved in a boyish smile.

The wench hath looked up and down so many times now, a man would swear she measures a throw on a bowling green. Now at last a tentative, shy smile breaks o'er her face afore she bobs her head down again.

I continue, 'If you were to visit her –'

'Since you've an interest in the matter, pray go yourself.' Abruptly he stands and scoops the messages onto the tray. 'I'll return these to my quarters.'

As I watch him stride gracefully away, blue velvet hat in hand and the wench giving him a surreptitious glance like unto what we had given her, I know I have vexed him. I cannot but believe, however, that his mother's complaints arise from his keeping clear of her.

And I determine to pursue the business on the next opportunity.

11

'A Strong And Ambivalent Bondage'
16 September 1665

... according to Freudians, the Don Juan is fleeing from incest, from a strong emotional attachment to the mother, established in early infancy and never outgrown, the classical Oedipus complex: 'The many women whom Don Juan has to replace again and again represent to him the irreplaceable mother....Yet he must also flee from any mother figure because of the ingrained prohibition against incest. Associated with this pattern is the tendency to divide women into virginal mothers and lusty whores, those for whom one feels love (respect and affection) and those for whom one feels desire (but no respect).... The mother is at once sought and avoided.

... Biographical evidence would appear to bear out the possibility that Rochester himself suffered from the Don Juanism and psychical impotence he so often described.... There appear to have been ample opportunities for Rochester to have developed a strong and ambivalent bondage to [his] mother.

—Dustin H. Griffin, *Satires against Man: The Poems of Rochester*

Up early today by reason of a pleasant frolic; and walking through the green meadow of the cathedral close, I cross the stone bridge into East Harnham, where the Rose and Crown nestles in its garden on delicious airs from the sweet-flowing river. Threading my way through delightsome bushes blushing pink roses, I arrive whither the current laps with its eddying flow; the ducks honk; and the geese, their long necks snaking, twining, pumping, attack a jovially laughing Etherege and Savile, who scatter crumbs for 'em.

A pleasure boat awaits us: canopied, with an oarsman in back and a little page in front to play notes on an angélique.

'Where's Rochester?' I ask.

'Faith, in a pleasanter bed than mine,' says Savile. 'He left smelling like a garden last night and said he'd see me i' th' morning. But he would not reveal the lady's name.'

'He never does. But I suspect the brown beauty from the bar within; they were giving one another the eye yesterday afternoon.'

'Ho, that's a good one! I sat drinking last night with five gentlemen who said there was nothing doing with her; she kept her legs tighter closed than the Virgin Mary. What'd he do?'

I shrug. 'What does he ever do? He *looks* at 'em.'

An angry honk sounds from nearby, where a swan hath twisted its webbed foot in the river roots to hold on against the drift of the current and make free with Savile's cheer: the which, no doubt, it thinks not liberally enough dispensed. Roaring good-naturedly, he throws toward it a generous hunk of bread, the which it curves down its long neck to smack for in the water, its beak making gurgles and ripples. I mark how pleasantly Savile makes himself welcome, feeding birds with Etherege and rallying with the rest of us, and uttering his honorifics to the nobility with more ease than doth Etherege.

Anon here comes the lover, striding across the flower-decked green.

Savile embracing him rallies, 'Ho, here's someone who looks kissed out. I warrant you couldn't pucker, my lord, if Venus herself walked by.'

He claps Savile's back, then embraces me. 'I might pucker, but I doubt if I could stand to much else.'

We laugh.

'Good God,' says Savile, 'he's shifted his garb again.'

Rochester looks down in surprise at his impeccable white linen shirt and breeches and waistcoat of brown lustring. Then he looks up, amazed.

'Why, you wouldn't have me appear this morning in what I wore the night before! It wants washing now.'

'Ten to one he's washed himself again, too,' I inform Savile.

'No, the washing he did the night before; he even had a bath laid.'

'Ask him,' I say.

We both stare at him.

'Well, the Devil's in't! How could I be comfortable in company making an appearance in the sweats and fluids of last night's passions?'

'I don't believe it,' groans Savile.

I dig his ribs. 'You see: you've been on board ship this while with him, but you've just begun to know his marvels.'

The quacking and honking herd pressing closer with their complaints, Etherege scatters more crumbs; and some other feathered friends, seeing what his business is, shove off eagerly from the far shore to paddle chuckling down on the current whither he doles out his charity. He calls to them, mimicking their sounds and saying, 'Come, birds.'

Savile expresses amazement: 'He shifted his garments three times yesterday and sent out to the laundresses a pile larger than himself.'

'And as you lay together at the inns, on the journey hither, he splashed in water twice or thrice a day?'

'Aye! I wonder he does not catch a death of ague, running about half-wet as he always does.'

Rochester grins. 'I take care to frisk fast enough to dry myself.'

Anon the whole gang appearing and the two bird lovers having scattered the remaining minute crumbs to brown sparrows that hop peeping at their feet, we settle ourselves in the cushioned seats of the boat. Savile takes up one back seat altogether; Rochester and Bucks settle themselves in the next, Buckhurst and Sedley together and Etherege and I up front, and so, the oarsman shoving us off with a foot, up the pleasant river we row, against the current and away from Harnham Bridge, willows trailing at the riverside, ducks quacking all about and swimming in trails with their little ones.

Savile hath concealed in his copious bosom a flask, which he agreeably presses on everyone and from which we all swig, save only Rochester, who endures cheerfully the sarcasms upon his determination to kill himself with good health.

'My Lord Rochester,' says Etherege, 'your home is near Oxford, is it not?'

'My home's the world.'

'Ho, we are treated to the philosopher now,' says Sedley.

Bucks explains, 'His mother's estate is at Ditchley, and his manor house, at Adderbury.'

'What a good opportunity,' says Etherege cheerfully, 'to have a look at your lands.'

'Lands have I none. They were seized during the Commonwealth.'

'And he will not go to see his mother,' I burst in, 'though I have urged and urged him. Bucks, perhaps you can convince him. He is feeling rather low.'

Bucks regards me with that shrewd-eyed glance of quiet enjoyment he usually reserves for a victim of one of his pranks; and I feel myself flush a little to understand I am being appraised and found foolish. Then, his humour seeming to change, he frowns and says, sardonically, ''Twere no more certain way to make him feel lower.'

Rochester looks uncomfortable but says nothing.

'Well said,' says Buckhurst. 'Rusticating is dose enough: add a mother, and no way to 'scape her advice, mouths made o'er wine

222

consumed, and long dull dinners: when saw you me racing to the family clutches?'

Rochester grins. 'When you were mannerly and ready to take good advice? In your swaddling-clouts?'

They both laugh.

'Well, you haven't heard the last of this,' I promise him.

I am surprised to see Bucks' large handsome face frown on me 'neath his yellow plume, and I am even more surprised when the great man seeks me out that evening, where I tope a few in the King's Arms, St John Street, in the little left-hand room with the great carved oak fireplace above which is inset a portrait of His Majesty as the Prince of Wales.

No true-blue Royalist would stay in Salisbury without visiting this historic inn, where part of the King's escape from the Roundheads was planned, after the battle of Worcester. During that thrilling time he hid here and there (even in an oak tree one night, his head in the lap of Major Careless), until Rochester's father and Jane Lane smuggled him from the country in the disguise of a servant. 'Tis said the King even hid in this inn on an earlier flight to the continent when he was still Prince of Wales.

So when Bucks sweeps in through the door and makes for my small round table, I lift my tankard and say, 'Bucks! Come you hither to pay homage to this spot?'

He sliding into a chair across from my wall-seat and nodding toward the innkeeper behind the great bar, saith, 'No, I've come in search of you, whither your servants directed.'

I no doubt looking surprised, he holds his tongue till a wench scooting from the back appears to bob a reverent curtsey.

'Hippocras, your best –' She then bobbing again and departing, he stares on me gravely and says, 'I advise you, Ashfield, if you love Rochester, not to bring up his mother again with him. It is a subject that causes him great pain.'

'He brought her up once at sea, in jest,' I grumble.

'Let him. But you refrain from introducing the topic in earnest.'

The wench returning with a tankard, Bucks digs for silver and slams it into her palm. She saluting him with several leg-bobs and utterings of 'Your Grace', he waves her off with a flourish of the hand, his frown still trained on me.

'Very well,' I huff, staring into my tankard.

He hesitates, then says, in a voice kinder and more sincere than I've ever heard him use to me, 'I know how you love him, Ashfield. That's why I'd warn you off. You have so much good nature and so little sense about applying it.'

'Very well,' I say gruffly. 'I didn't understand.'

'If you knew his mother, you would. The whole year they were in Paris, I never heard her speak a kind word to him. She was ever raining blows on him, even in the public view. "Mind what I say," she'd rail, and follow it with a slap to get his attention; or "This way, sir," and she'd suddenly turn right down the garden path, jerk his poor little arm half from its socket, and if he faltered, halt to lean down and whack him four or five times and say, "Why don't you mind, you bad boy?"'

The rumble of conversation at the other small black tables turneth to a buzz, a ringing in my ears as if the scene be not real; yet I know by the stern lines at Bucks' brow and thin lips, he speaketh the truth.

'I knew it not,' I hear myself say faintly.

'Nor does anyone, save the King and the rest of us old dogs from the court at exile.' Bucks sips and continues. 'She was erratic: at times would sit and converse, he standing by her chair, and she taking no notice of him; at other times, she'd glance at him and say, "What means that look?" and give him a shake, then grasp his cheeks betwixt her thumb and forefinger to force his gaze up into hers. Often she told the company she was considering whether he had been good enough to avoid a whipping when they got home. This she said so the poor little wretch would think the rest of the afternoon what might await him later – unless her whim changed.'

My tender heart wrenches. 'That must have been an anxious existence for a child.'

'No doubt. As she dosed him again and again for digestion, I made shift to tell her, the best physic would be to let him alone; but that she could not do, morning nor night, but must fly upon his every look, and jump upon his every remark – what did he mean by this, or that? What was he about then, or why did he thus? What did he think of this thing, or what meant that look he had?' – a-probing of his head each instant, like a surgeon with a lancet that nudges the wound.'

I shudder. 'Forgive me, Bucks. I now see why he would not visit his mother.'

'The servants let me in once when she was walloping him with a heavy cane; the noise was so terrific it sounded to be workmen hammering; and as he was trained not to cry out, it went on forever before I understood what it was I listened to. She never seemed to realise that small children can be injured by repeated blows.'

'How dreadful,' I sympathise, 'that you had to stand there and listen to that without being able to do anything to stop it.'

He gives me another of those looks, long and keen, whereby I flush to understand I am being summed up and found foolish; then he responds:

'Of course I stopped it. Wouldn't you?'

I feel myself flush the more. 'Well, I suppose I would – but – that is, how did you do it?'

He takes a pull from the tankard. 'I walked to the study on my two good legs, knocked on the door, and told her I was coming in. She was sufficiently ashamed to cease without my asking her.'

'But did you say nothing to her at all?' I persist, unable to fancy myself intruding in so private a situation.

'Nothing in the face of her tiny victim. But after I had carried him to his bed, I returned to advise her to get someone else to punish him who wasn't angry; or to reach for a small switch the next time, if she had to strike so long and hard. "Switches give too little pain," she said. "Well, canes give too much," I informed her bluntly, "the way you wield 'em. As often as you lay into him, you should not strike more than once or twice at a time. Grown men have died, madam, from being cudgelled, and your son is a small sickly boy." She stared at me brazenly and said, "He is not hurt." "He is badly hurt," I told her. "He could not walk." "But he is not hurt," she insisted. "He'll be up and around in a few days." There was no quarrelling with her insane definition, but I reminded her that her husband had asked me to look in on his son, and I wasn't going to make a good report. "Everyone uses canes," she said, and huffed from the room.'

'And what did his father say to all this?'

Bucks sips, and his amber eyebrows turn down sardonically. 'What he always said: he was glad the boy was not being spoilt, that firm discipline was good for him.'

'But did you not say enough to show him the difference?'

'I did. But he could not be bothered. His mode of life, he said, did not permit his keeping a child.'

I am horrified. 'But did he care nothing of what happened to his son?'

'That would be the reasonable conclusion to draw. But then, Wilmot cared for very little, besides himself and the young king he served.'

I shake my head and settle down further into the built-in seat of dark wood by the fireplace.

'I wonder he survived, Bucks.'

'I think that was owed to his extreme docility. I would not like to see that woman in charge of a boy that stood up for himself and defied her.'

'But yet, Rochester is very defiant now.'

'That may be his natural temperament. And mayhap it broke out occasionally, but I saw none of it in Paris. He was more perfectly trained than any spaniel – would stand quietly beside her chair or at her side like a dutiful little shadow; even if children were playing right in the same chamber, he might look at 'em longingly but never offer to approach, even if they called him over. If anyone asked aught of him, he'd look up into her face for permission before replying.'

'He has ceased asking her permission now,' I observe.

'He's rejected the religion and entire way of life she took such care to pound into him. His habits are just like his father's, and I'm sure the thought gives the old woman the apoplexy.'

I grin.

'She has a prejudice against every sort of pleasure,' Bucks elaborates, tossing down another draught. 'Rochester was not even suffered to accept sweetmeats from anyone or approach 'em to be petted. Once a lady of the French court gave him a little top, and he turned it round in his hands, as if not knowing what it was; his mother directed him to give it back and said her son did not waste time with such vanities.'

'Good God, he never had any toys?'

'Not that I ever saw. He was always studying, either religion or the Classics. The few things I bought him, he insisted on leaving at my apartments. He said he'd be chastised if his mother knew he wasted time with a hobby horse or tin soldiers. And when he visited me, he would stand quietly, waiting for instructions; he'd not touch a toy or book unless one remembered each time to give express permission.'

I hunch o'er my tankard. 'I can't imagine a childhood where playing is so rare.'

'Playing! You know not the half of it. He was not even suffered to hear kind words from anyone. If someone remarked in his presence on his politeness or prettiness, or complimented him on a shrewd answer he'd made, she'd bite off the words in mid-sentence and warn, "Say not such silly stuff to him! You'll make him vain." And here he was, so eager to please – he'd glow all over at a smile or "thank you", like a spaniel that will fetch a stick till it drops so's you keep patting its head.'

'I've heard the King say the ladies admired him even then.'

'Everyone went wild over him, though his mother grudged him the slightest movement toward anyone else. And one soon learnt to approach him carefully: any quick movement would make him shy like a skittish horse.'

I shudder at the implication.

'Then one day, she coming with him to the court, holding his hand fast as usual, said that she had brought him, on a whim, to Paris, thinking his father might like to meet him – or, even more, take him off her hands; but that her lord would not leave Bruges, claiming to have great business there: and that she'd a mind to seek him there, to unburden her mind of what she thought of his neglect of her and his son. But that instead they would soon return to Ditchley: she had secured a tutor, Mr Giffard, who would assume total governance of the child, even sleeping with him in the same chamber, so that she could keep to another part of the great house and see to her business. That the child was to be well grounded in the Scriptures and the Classics: that Mr Giffard should report to her each week what the boy learned and whether he met expectations, then to notify her when he was ready for grammar school. She added that she would do her Christian duty by her son and see to his education – but that she feared so much of his father was in him, he would grow up a sinner, doomed to hell.'

I stare at Bucks in amaze, then finally say, 'What an unnatural mother!'

'Not so unnatural: you've led a limited life, Ashfield, and not seen the divers characters the world affords.'

I brood a moment then ask, 'Didn't she have two older sons by a first marriage?'

He nods. 'Sir Henry and Frank Lee.'

'Was she so severe with them?'

'Not when I knew them,' says Bucks. 'But they were almost grown up then and were married soon after.' He sips. 'They were at school in Paris and had fallen ill; her solicitude had drawn her thither, to be their nurse. We heard often what good boys they were and how concerned she was after their health.'

'I saw a portrait of her, and she looked a sweet, lovely lady.'

'An old portrait, no doubt, during her first marriage – or early in her second. Being the wife of Wilmot soured her and made her hard.'

He drains his tankard and bestirs himself as if to take leave; then a thought seems to strike him, so he pauses, hand on hanger hilt, person turned half around in chair. 'Oh, and Ashfield –'

'Yes?'

'I doubt Rochester would have you speaking of this to him or anyone else.'

'Of course, but – why? I should think anyone would sympathise.'

'I doubt he would have sympathy. He seemed ashamed of her reaction to him, as if it were his fault. He said he was a bad boy and his mother cared for him enough to chastise him for his own good. When I contradicted him and said he was a good boy, he said he did his best to be, but regularly gave offence without meaning to, which was the sign that Original Sin was rooted deeply in him. He also said his mother had told him she'd hoped to wash her hands of him by turning him over to his father; but that his father would not have him.' Bucks pauses, then adds, 'I would I could contrive to do it over, somehow, and have him be born to me.'

I have barely time to consider whether Bucks' voice hath grown husky before he is gone, sweeping off in a flourish of yellow plumes.

12

'Love, The Most Generous Passion Of The Mind'

23 September 1665

Love, the most generous passion of the mind,
The softest refuge innocence can find,
The safe director of unguided youth,
Fraught with kind wishes, and secured by truth;
That cordial drop heaven in our cup has thrown
To make the nauseous draught of life go down; ...
This only joy for which poor we were made
Is grown, like play, to be an arrant trade.
—John Wilmot, Earl of Rochester

Though faring so well generally with the ladies, Rochester seems mighty unlucky in the two he best loves. First his mother treats coldly with him. Then, the day we ride to Stonehenge, we find his mistress hath played him false.

Galloping across the chalky Downs, Rochester looks as if he were born on a horse: leaning forward, putting his cheek to the beast's neck, embracing the barrel of its sides with his knees, urging it forward with a pressure of the legs and spoken words 'til they streak as one. I joggle along behind, as much above the saddle as in, and marvel that the gang clip-clopping all about would wish to ride nine hard miles for the ogling of a pile of stones.

Topping the hill behind our Boy Genius, I see flung out below me the circle of silent monoliths, a ring alone, whistling to the hard winds of Salisbury Plain, and all about it the Downs, where lie the barrow mounds of warriors long dead.

Streaking like a comet down the hill, his hands grasping the reins and body leaned forward, the horse's nostrils flaring and his knees gripping its sides, both of 'em moving like a single force of Nature more than a man compelling a beast, he wheels to a halt at the ring of stones and vaults off the horse, to twirl its rein about one of the small rocks lying on the ground, pat its neck, and stride off.

It nickers and reaches out a head to him. He steps back to pat it some more and talk to it in a low voice.

At last we have catched him up: I bouncing along behind, the rest of 'em trotting at a lower pace, and all of us put in our divers needs to bounce, kick, wield crops, pull on bits.

Killigrew pulling to a halt, swinging off his horse, and fixing its rein to another boulder, then dusting off his fine green doublet slashed red, complains, 'Rochester, what the devil would you come out here for? Have you a sacrifice to make to the God of Love?'

The rest of us amid our dismounting and tying up laugh.

'No, I but come to peruse the mysteries of time and the perplexities of existence. Behold, they are all about us, and we walk past them as men blindfolded, custom having made them too familiar to us.'

Bucks looks about the great circle of stones. towering perpendiculars topped in pairs with slabs. 'Who d'ye think put 'em up, my lad? The Druids?'

Rochester's brow furrows. 'Perhaps – or some race older.'

'Who can be older than the Druids?' asks Buckhurst, a stout, brown-suited figure sucking on an orange.

Rochester shrugs.

He goes to stand by one of the giant, time-nicked tablets pointing upward and leans an elbow against it. His gaze sweeps up the weathered mass, to the tablet laid across its top and joining it to its fellow perpendicular. His gaze then sweeps the hard blue dome of the sky. For a moment there's no sound but that of the harsh summer wind whistling o'er the burnt grass of Salisbury Plain and through the ring of giants in whose circle we stand.

Sedley fans himself with a dainty small hand. 'This bouncing about on a horse is wont to weary a man. I think that after God invented the four-footed beast, He must have invented the coach, had He any compassion for Adam.'

We laugh.

Rochester throws him a look of disgust. 'That's the greatest exertion I've seen from you in months. I've a mind to take you to war with me.'

Buckhurst shakes his head. 'Jesus. Not again?'

'Rochester, forget this war business,' says Killigrew.

'And gold and glory?' asks the Boy Genius.

'Aye,' says Sedley. 'For we know your motives. Best give up your suit: the lady's well-nigh contracted to Hinchingbrooke.'

He glowers. 'Who said anything about a lady? But if I *were* still after

Mrs Mallet's hand – which I don't admit – the surest way to lose all chance of her would be to follow your advice, Sedley, and loll about drunk until she were given to someone else. The only way to win her is to make some motions toward that end.'

The stones loom, casting long, silent shadows on us.

'Aye, but with this latest twist in the suit, it looks as if the lady herself has given up on *you*.'

Rochester sets his mouth in a grim line. His voice is quiet. 'I wish her well, I really do, whomever she marries. Has she made another choice?'

Sedley looks even smaller, squat on the jutting block, his eyes black beads 'neath the massive curled periwig. 'It is all the talk how Ormond sent his ambassador, one Nicholls, to Somerset to plead for the Lord John Butler and the lady encouraged him very eagerly, said the Lord John was one of the few real men that had ever courted her and she would always have an affection for him. The talk is, she was well nigh flirtatious and begged to see a letter Butler had writ of her.'

Rochester shrugs, stares off into space as if he scanned the vista of stones making their arc near the heelstone. 'She is a natural coquette. She would flirt with a sunflower. It means little.'

'Well, I hope for your sake 'tis so, though for my part, it seems a bad business. I deal honestly with you, Rochester. I'd not pursue the business to such length as you have. I'd have given it up long ago.' Sedley shakes his head.

Rochester displayeth that vexed, aggrieved expression he always hath when Sedley noses into his affairs to give him brotherly advice. 'For all you know, I *have* given it up.'

'Aye. Well, don't be running off to war again, then.'

'Has it never occurred to any of you,' snaps Rochester, 'that this sort of life, lolling about, doing nothing, is well nigh to make me jump with vexation?'

Buckhurst's eyes pop. 'Why, Rochester. What should you do?'

'I don't know! I don't know! That's the folly of it, the damned frustration of it! I simply feel I must be doing great deeds somehow, making something of my life – and yet I don't know what I'm to do or how I'm to do it. But when I come to loll about with the court, I begin to feel a slow poison creep through my veins and voices whispering in my head that this is dangerous to me.'

'Rochester,' says Killigrew, 'you've wanted employment of late. Let us conspire to make an elaborate jest: expose some fool or undo some lady.'

Rochester shakes his head, puts his fists on his hips, stares down at the gravel in frustration. 'No, Killigrew. You're mistaken in my text. I only do such things out of malicious frustration, not having any other way to turn my wit and aspiration.'

Bucks, leaning against a monolith, puts in, 'So you think that battle will be a way to achieve your ends?'

'I don't know! I don't know! Some part of me thinks that it may be, but when I'm in it, God wot, it never seems the way I expected, and I can never reach the heights I wish.'

'Aye, small wonder,' mutters Sedley.

'Small wonder indeed,' snaps Rochester, 'when His Majesty won't give me a command, and I'm put to bear burthens along such petty-souled men as Teddeman, that must always be skulking back to Flamborough Head, so that Sandwich can tell him what to think! – But I don't really know if being in battle is what I want. I do know it's better than the court.'

'Better? How so?' asks Sedley, amazed.

'A man is doing something!' Rochester begins to pace. 'And he's out in the fresh, open breezes. I've never taken care of myself so, felt so good, despite the hard fare, as when out at sea. For the most part there's no wine about, and I feel much better when I'm not drinking.'

'Faith, I wouldn't know about that.' Sedley smiles. 'I've never made experiment.'

We laugh.

'Jesus, I have,' puts in Buckhurst. 'A little sea life was enough for me.'

The wind sweeps through the monoliths, makes an eerie whistle.

'This I know,' says Rochester, leaning with both hands on a stone, staring up at the blocks laid across the upthrust monoliths. 'There's some purpose my life is to have, some quest I'm to be on, and I will be restless 'til I find what it is.'

I recall what Clifford said about Rochester: 'He has some sort of bee in his bonnet, something driving him.'

The sun broils pitilessly down through my hat and periwig; it bakes into my brain and shimmers in curtains before the green rolling downs. We stand in a great circle that is dwarfed by the hard blue dome of sky above us. And I am reminded anew of what ants we all are, crawling 'twixt heaven and earth, the sport of coincidences and fates we can know naught of.

'Let's head back,' says Rochester suddenly, 'and get some wine.'

13

'Thrust On The Wrong Tack'
28 September 1665

> God wot I need not be too severe about others; I have a past exis-
> tence, a series of deeds, a colour of life to contemplate within my
> own breast, which might well call my sneers and censures from my
> neighbours to myself. I ... was thrust on the wrong tack at the age of
> one-and-twenty and have never recovered the right course since, but
> I might have been very different ...
> —Charlotte Brontë, Mr Rochester speaking, in *Jane Eyre*

'You are drinking too much,' I advise Rochester.

'Let me be!'

We stroll in the fading light through Salisbury Cathedral.

'No woman is worth it –'

He turns savagely on me so I almost tread on him. Above us stretches the mammoth nave with its vaulting of tiercon ribs.

'I care nothing for what she does! May she joy herself in the fens,
dropping honourable little blue-eyed heirs, like that Dutch rabbit.'

The fading light slants rainbow-hued past St Osmund's shrine and
to the effigy of William Longspee, First Earl of Salisbury and half
brother to King John. This worthy, his meagre likeness swathed in
chain mail and tunic, flings his head twisted toward the right as if a
silent, desperate scream cannot pass the mail mantling o'er his hidden
mouth, his eyes wide as if in anguish or fear, and the long shield
angled across his stiff form, the toes elongated as if on the rack.

Savile, waddling down the stairs from the cathedral library, frowns
on the spectacle of the fretting boy, erupting words like lava, stalking
about like an apparition with his white skin and dark hollows of eyes.

'Rochester,' I scold, 'say what you will about the lady, but
Lord Butler is very noble. He pled to have you released from the
Tower.'

The lad flashes out like lightning, 'May the road rise to meet him as he falls on his arse; may he lose himself in the corridors of Kilkenny Castle, looking for the most honourable spot to piss in.'

He whirls on his heel, drawing his cape about him, and marches from the nave. Savile hath catched up to my side now and shakes his head.

'It is a bad business.'

'Come,' I say, 'let's catch up with him at the King's Arms.'

Savile toddling and huffing beside me, I leg it briskly across the Cathedral Close t'other direction, from East Harnham and into Salisbury, on a pull to intercept our overwrought friend at the hostelry.

The small left-hand room where Bucks and I talked swarms with courtiers gaily clad, the wenches and pot-boys making haste among 'em with steaming plates of meat and sweating tankards, apologies and promises to those that would catch at 'em en route. I stand in the outer alcove, the left-hand door pushed open, and scan the crowd.

'Oh, no,' I suddenly cry.

Behind me Savile urges, 'How now, my Lord Ashfield: come, my lord, let's in and have some belly-cheer.'

'Savile!' I cry in a frenzy. 'Rochester has found out the Lord John Butler. Oh, God, there'll be bloodshed.'

'Where?' asks Savile. He nudges me forward, and we amble within, the door closing behind us.

I point to a table of round dark wood in a beamed corner, where my heart leapeth to my breastbone to see Ormond's notable Irish sprigs, Lord and Lady Ossory, pulled up tight beside Lord and Lady Arran and Mrs Mallet's gallant, the Lord John. All of 'em look up, expectant, as the wraith of Rochester hovers above 'em, eyes flashing and mouth moving.

'Oh, I see,' offers Savile. 'By the apple-cheeked lady with the yellow hair.'

'Yes,' I explain, woebegone and fearful, 'that is the Dutch rabbit.'

'Which is Lord Butler? The sourpuss beside her with the Sunday look?'

'No, that's her husband. The fair youth with the refined carriage.'

But there's no need to augment any further, for Butler tosses down his napkin and stands. I groan, half covering my eyes, and waiting for Rochester to pull off a glove to slap him with or hoist up a tankard to douse him with; but they appear to be smiling cordially, and with a brief handshake part again, Butler then seating himself and Rochester threading his way through the crowd in our direction.

Savile looks first at Butler, then at Rochester, whose progress is followed by some score of female eyes all about the room; and even in his wretched state he hath about him a lightning sparkle, and I see plainly on the double-chinned face surprise that a woman would prefer the unexceptional comeliness of the one to the gorgeousness of the other.

'Well, there's no accounting for women, my lord,' Savile says to me with a snort. 'What explanation have you?'

I shrug. 'Ormond bids fair to be the richest man in three kingdoms. And he's Lord Lieutenant of Ireland, too.'

'So she's that sort of bitch, is she?'

'I can't say. Butler's a very noble youth, full of high principles and seriousness. She may admire his character.'

We cut off our remarks then at the approach of our jilted comrade.

'Rochester, what did you then?' I burst out, pressing my person toward the left wall to admit the passage of three outgoing men.

He appeareth surprised at our anxious hovering presence. 'Carried my thanks to Butler for the kind offices he did me during my confinement, and pledged return, should he ever need my sword or voice in anything.'

'That was very noble of you,' I say.

'Not at all. I'll not have the son of a whore best me with his cutthroat honour.'

We laugh heartily.

'Come,' fidgs the lad, 'if you've enough of being my lifeguard. 'Tis plain the others bend their elbows elsewhere.'

'Aye, and are one or two ahead of us, to boot,' agrees Savile. 'Let's try the other room.'

We cut through the door and alcove and into the right-hand oak-beamed room, larger. Here Killigrew, Bucks and Etherege are smushed up about one midget of a table and Sedley, Buckhurst and Shepherd hold a larger nearby, whither we draw up stools and crowd ourselves in. An alcove beneath the beams shelters two country lovers, who toy and buss, the which we watch for a moment bemused, this sort of display being considered impolite at court, where lovers behave as strange in public as if they'd ne'er touched.

We keeping watch for one of the wenches, who run about harried and overtaxed, Rochester saith to Sedley, 'We await the tattle of Rumour, with its many tongues.'

Little Sid giveth him a sly, merry, black-eyed look; then, fussing with the stiff flounces of his many-tiered cravat, reports, 'Coventry and some others make a noise about the prizes. Sandwich's story, it seems, is that he but suffered his men to take their share before the Prize Court made the divisions. What say you, Rochester?'

The lad shrugs. Then his eyes sparkle. 'My accounting boasts not the detail of yours, Sedley.'

'So we all see! We'd starve an your closed-mouth was to supply our fare of news. Sandwich is said to have made above four thousand pound on the business and to have sailed nigh Gravesend, that he may return and answer –'

But now at last the wench bustles up – though so distracted, she injudiciously presents her plump arse in the proximity of Buckhurst's fingers.

She whirls about, and for a moment I believe she is vexed, but then mayhap recalling that such usage comes with the job, or that Buckhurst is after all a lord and generous at that, she appears to resign herself: even sports with him a bit, knocking his shoulder with her fist to exclaim, 'If you ain't the boldest thing, me lord!'

'Give us a kiss, Moll,' he urges.

Laughing, she leans over, to put her full red mouth on his. I stare at him glumly and wish I had his address.

'Keep the sack-and-sugar coming,' Savile instructs her, honouring what he believes our main business. 'Have you still the puff pasties that steam from out the little hole with the succulent smell of pigeon and gravy?' She nods. 'Three – no, make that four – of those; and two trencher-breads with some pound and a half of butter fresh churned – have you still the pickled mushrooms and hard cheese you brought me before the dinner yesterday?'

The wench regards him slyly. 'Yes, sir: I believe you left a handful or so.'

We laugh heartily. Rochester winks at the girl, and she blushes, then looks away.

'The Devil take me if I did!' Savile castigates himself. 'I must do 'em right today. – Then, for the chief dish, we'll have the pullet – bring that after the others, and don't skimp on the mushrooms – they're succulent, my lords: we'll eat all, I know.'

'How many pullets?' asks the wench, who I can see plainly strains her brain to remember the whole of this gargantuan fare.

'Four, at least – no, make that five; and five dishes of the good buttered pease, and the little orange cakes to finish, one each, with the almond jumbels.'

'Mr Savile,' breaks in Rochester, 'I know not who you believe is to join us here; but as for myself, I must fain be left with the mushrooms, should you force 'em on me.'

Savile stares amazed at this heresy: whereat we all burst into laughter.

Then our gourmet waves off the wench. 'Go to, go to; bring the sack and first dishes; I promise ye they'll disappear.'

'Rochester doesn't eat much,' I inform Savile, 'but sometimes he compensates by the amount of wine he pours down his gullet.'

Savile frowns at his slender young friend, then wags a finger in the pale oval face. 'How now, my lord: that's the certainest way to go to an early grave.' Then he looks astonished on all of us. 'And have none of you tempted him to eat? Well, we'll mend matters: 'tis plain he hath wanted a man that knew what to order.'

We smother giggles behind our hands as the wench returns with the sack-and-sugar and a dish of pickled mushrooms.

'Aha!' Savile rubs his hands with glee and dives into the plate, orating, 'This is the sublimest of pickles they use here: note just the hint of lemon peel, and the white wine vinegar they have not let overpower it, but just a touch of mace and clove. Eat, eat –' Whereat obediently we each take one, Buckhurst and I nigh to exploding with laughter. 'Eat,' he hectors again, thrusting one into Rochester's mouth.

The merriment dying down a bit, and Savile diving still greedily into the tray, opening to us the mysteries of ginger and bay leaves, Sedley launches again into his narration:

'The two East-India men in question are called the *Phoenix* and the *Slothany.* They were crammed to the timbers with such stuff as silks, cinammon, indigo, and nutmeg. Eleven other ships were taken with them on the third. 'Tis believed Sandwich will make it in to port to answer the charges.'

Now the wench arriving with a plate of good hard cheese and two trencher-breads, a pot of butter beside 'em, Savile roars with glee; and, rubbing his hands together, calls for more sack: whereat she bustles off good-naturedly, though I am sure regretting the day she ever served such a table as this.

'What say you, Rochester?' probes Little Sid, mouth full of mushrooms, hand on the jug to refill Rochester's tankard.

Rochester obliges him with a witticism: 'That I'd stay at sea, had I such a silly wife and sillier pocky son.'

We all roar. Savile laughing till his belly shakes throws a handful of mushrooms into the furnace of his mouth. Then, smearing a Titanic slice of bread with butter thick enough for a fly to drown in, he cuts a huge hunk of cheese, slaps it on top, and bites down, half of the slab disappearing in one gulp. The rest of us watch fascinated, but he urging, 'Eat, eat,' Buckhurst cuts into the cheese and Sedley munches his bread.

Savile hath buttered another slab of bread; and, pushing it upon Rochester, hectors, 'Now, an you eat not this, my lord, I vow I'll hold you here 'til you do,' so the youth crumbles off a small piece and pops it daintily into his mouth, whereat Savile clucks and shakes his head in disapproval. 'How can you so enjoy the pleasures of wine and women, then scorn the greater ones of the table? Know you not, my lord, that this is the Father to the Trinity?'

The wench then wendeth our way with more sack and a plate of pasties. Her greatest admirer, roaring with glee, generously refills everyone's tankard with more of the wine and commences to push a pasty on Rochester, insisting:

'Now, my lord, you must not stint on this: smell the steam arise from the small birds in their own sauce.'

Rochester crumbles off a bit of the pasty and commends it to its pleased sponsor, chewing and swallowing so slowly that the whole of Savile's hath disappeared in the meanwhile.

The wench returning to pick up the empty dish whereon reposed the mushrooms, Rochester beams meltingly up at her and says, in his sweetest tones: 'You do your family credit, Mrs Moll, in such a roistering mob as this.'

'My family, my lord?' She stares at him, her hand halfway to the plate.

Rochester reaches across the table, pulls our empty plates towards him, makes a stack of them on top of his, gathers our goblets together. 'Handling, with such address, so many rascals, such huge bills of fare. Have you a tray?'

'Ah ...' She looks about.

Rochester stands, snags an empty tray from a passing wench, and heaps it with the plates and goblets. 'Your father's cook surpasses any in London.'

She still gapes at the earl heaping up her tray for her. 'My father, my lord?'

'Is he not the owner?'

'Why, no, my lord. Who said so?'

Rochester looks rueful. 'I beg your pardon. It was a conclusion I drew, from your parts and address.'

The wench lingers though several diners about the room yell, whistle, and wave at her. Rochester draws forth a slight blush.

The wench glows, her milky bosom heaving with its invitingly exposed cleft. 'Well, you need not beg pardon for a mistake like that, my lord.'

He gazes up at her earnestly, then breaks into one of his dazzling smiles. She smiles back, her eyes fixed on his.

'Hey, Moll!' yells an irate voice.

Reluctantly she turns about. 'Keep your breeches on, now!'

Then she whirls back to our table, quickly gathers up another plate, leaning over Rochester as she does so and lightly grazing her arm with his. Her breasts hang down, half-exposed in the white shift, but he makes no attempt to grab for them, as Buckhurst would have.

In a soft voice he asks, 'Shall you need some help with the tray?'

Their eyes meet; speechless, reddening, she shakes her head, then picks up the tray and bustles off.

We eat awhile in silence; and the wench returning with two plates stacked high with pullet, Buckhurst then falls to grabbing and jesting, and the wench jesting back in a free-and-easy manner, giving kisses that are asked for and accepting of coins; she giggling with many a 'La, my lord,' and 'You wicked thing,' &c, till she wriggles off to another table.

Then applying himself to the pullet, my chum gives some good-natured advice: 'Forget your court manners, Rochester, with a wench: you made her uneasy.'

Rochester sits sipping and throwing hot looks across the room, behind Buckhurst's back: where the wench, taking of an order here, bringing a bottle there, keeps darting him glances and flushing.

Savile thrusts a pullet leg at his skinny young friend. 'Eat, eat.'

Rochester makes as if to pick up the proffered prize; but then the wench disappearing into the kitchen, he throws down his napkin and murmurs, 'Excuse me,' whereupon we see him make for the door in the other room.

'Now, what the devil is he about?' asks Shepherd, his mouth full of pullet. Buckhurst shrugs.

'Cut open the breastbone, my lord,' Savile urges me. 'There: see? They have stuffed it with almonds blanched, and the rice is seasoned with white wine: here, it wants more butter,' and he smears a great slab on my bed of rice.

Rochester returning presently, Savile exclaims, 'Now where the devil is our mistress Moll? We have a stream runs perilously dry –' and he peers woebegone into the empty tankard.

Rochester gliding into his place at the table, Sedley eyes him suspiciously.

'Here, now, my lord,' cries Savile, 'you must taste of this pullet.'

Rochester obediently hefting the drumstick, Sedley's merry little eyes twinkle. 'He has catched his own chicken.'

They lock eyes a minute. Rochester grins mischievously at him.

For a moment Buckhurst and I sit gawking, ignorant; and Savile is so absorbed in gutting his own lady with the legs up, he pays but little heed. Then all at once I burst out laughing and dig Buckhurst in the ribs.

'He used his court manners on a wench. Better advise him again.'

'Rochester,' cries Buckhurst, his pop-eyes wide with dismay, 'you haven't engaged her tonight, have you?'

'Who?' he asks innocently, setting down the pullet leg and wiping his fingers on the napkin.

Buckhurst applies to all of us, as if we be judges and he a pleading counsel: 'That should not have worked.'

Rochester sits back in his chair and oozes genial charm.

Anon the doxy returns, laden with orange cakes and jumbels, to be eyed sullenly by Buckhurst; and so elaborately doth she ignore Rochester, and he her, we know the truth of Sedley's suspicion.

'Mistress Moll,' crows Savile. 'you are our Ganymede in skirts. You bring us nectar and ambrosia – more nectar, if you please.'

She darts him a quick look and smiles quietly. 'Yes, sir.'

So subdued is she walking away that we know something hath shaken her.

'There's the look of a wench that hath been catched and tousled in a pantry,' observes Sedley. 'What say you, Rochester?'

He shrugs. 'I did not see, Sedley.'

'You did not see because you were busy doing. One of these days you will get your toe stomped and emerge as lame as Ashfield here.'

At this last pleasantry I sulk o'er my broken arm. The table rollicks with merriment at my expense.

'Give us a song,' urges Etherege, handing o'er a guitar to the Boy Genius.

'He can't play,' I put in.

Rochester cradles the instrument and runs his fingers o'er the strings, thrumming melodiously as a harpist would, not banging as I've a wont to do.

'Give us "Chloris, full of harmless thought",' says Buckingham.

In a sweet baritone, Rochester launches into a lyric he writ last May.

'As Chloris full of harmless thought
Beneath the willows lay,
Kind love a comely shepherd brought
To pass the time away.
She blushed to be encountered so
And chid the amorous swain,

But as she strove to rise and go,
He pulled her back again.
A sudden passion seized her heart
In spite of her disdain;
She found a pulse in every part,
And love in every vein.
"Ah, youth," quoth she, "What charms are these
That conquer and surprise?
Oh, let me – for unless you please,
I have no power to rise."
She faintly spoke, and trembling lay,
For fear he should comply,
For virgin's eyes their hearts betray
And give their tongues the lie.
Thus she, who princes had denied
With all their pompous train,
Was in the lucky minute tried
And yielded to the swain.'

He runs his fingers o'er the strings a minute more; then, seeing the attention of everyone in the room, colours and stops. At the ensuing applause he turns as red as his velvet jackanapes coat and thrusts the guitar back at Etherege.

'Tis plain who this Chloris is who once refused wealthy and important suitors and yielded to a comely indigent. I wonder if he ever found 'a pulse in every part' of her in some pastoral setting.

But I am vex't to the blood to discover, not only hath he learnt guitaring somewhere, but he also sings in a bewitching voice.

'Rochester,' I cry, 'I never knew you could play.'

He shrugs, 'Just a little something I learnt to stave off my boredom at sea.'

I could rend my periwig in frustration. Here I struggle at it these weeks, to no avail, whilst he 'picks it up' as if 'twere his sword or a woman.

But I refuse to yield to envy. I'd not be such a Boy Genius, in some pact with the Devil, to gain every accomplishment and lose my inner peace. I'd be poor dull me, with a semblance of contentment and control.

I then taking coach back to my lodgings, my man Edward greets me with the melancholy confidence that my wine is drunk up: the which I can scarce believe, but that he lays it all to that rogue of a señor, to whom in my charity I gave free access of my wine cellar, and who hath a thirst that would do credit to Tantalus. I give instructions that he may be released to his next gull.

For this 'little something' of guitaring, I hath found, is a dreadfully difficult business. E'en did I not struggle to cradle the instrument with this broken arm, my fingers hurt when I make shift to hold down the strings. That rogue of a señor would tell me to be patient, that my fingers will get calluses; but I suspect that my fingers are as slow to grow calluses as my brain to grow wits. The cittern which I paid for I will keep; it is very neat and pretty standing in the hall; and mayhap someone seeing it will assume I can play.

'My lord,' says little Jane, shyly accosting me. 'Did you meet with the Lord Rochester today?'

'Uncle Robert, now: remember?'

She runs to me and throws her arms about my neck. 'Uncle Robert,' she whispers at my ear; and the Devil take me, but my eyes tear up.

'Yes, Jane,' I pat her back. 'At the King's Arms.'

She disengages herself to whirl about the room, her arms clasped about her little waist.

'What said he? What did he?'

So now e'en my charity child hath caught the disease. He can put ideas in the minds of women too young to have 'em.

I mutter a reply, with as good a grace as possible, that he sang a song and made us merry. I am treated to the confidence that my Lord of Rochester showed her how to make shadow-puppets: that he is not an old man, like the rest of His Lordship's friends; but someone who would be just of an age with her when she grew up a little.

I stalk off to the library, to fling my wineless person into a chair and brood on him.

Here's a youth so brilliant of wit he hath the whole of the *beau monde* hanging at his elbow: a youth so gorgeously set out, by art and nature alike, he lays the women low like ninepins on a mere appearance. Visit his lodgings, and a man will see a library that would do credit to a bishop, plus volumes of all the moderns as well. Then put him into the Tower, and the cool elegance dissolves into fits of melancholy befitting a German, so that a man must wonder if the sickness hath been boiling about underneath all the while.

But his reason, being so powerful an energy, keeps his gigantic passions in check till now and again the volcano erupts, and a man is treated to a display of two lightnings singeing one another in a moonlit bank of clouds. 'Tis no marvel Rochester carries about him that air of supercharged magnetism that draweth the eye: he hath got going on in him a battle that would kill most men.

And such a contradictory coil are his impulses, though I have kept his company these nine months – nay, shared his bed and board – yet I am still perplexed to piece out his character. No one could contrive a brilliant phrase to sum him up, as Bucks once did the Duke of York and King: the one would be wise if he could and the other if he would. Rochester is both wise and unwise, often in the same breath. He forswears wine for weeks, then plunges into a debauch that hath his head cleaved in twain. He is the most notorious of all gallants for inconstancy yet loves one woman more passionately than the rest of us can conceive. So tender of sensibility, the little children flock to his knee; so gracious and friendly, the common folk talk to him in the streets or crowd his sea-cabin; so pitiless and bloodthirsty, he'd destroy all Holland in a savage campaign: he can be summed up only in superlatives: the best lover, fighter, poet, dandy, scholar.

And part of his fascination, I do believe, is that a man wonders what character will pop out next. the mystic reporting intuitions or the new philosopher testing all by reason? The easy, friendly confidant of the King or the rebellious child that insults him?

I breaking a message with the Lion and Unicorn sealed, do read that the King hath returned from Oxford and orders our removal thither. This he also announces at an audience in Wilton House, where he lodges, some three miles distant, in a home His Majesty's mother delighted in during the last reign: where everywhere's evident the symmetry of her favourite architect, Inigo Jones, he that also did the Queen's House, Greenwich, and the Great Banqueting Hall, Whitehall.

Rochester makes plans to remove with us, and I think on that butterfly bitch Mallet: what she feels, how she does. We've heard naught of her, save by second-hand reports, since the Life Guard set out to fetch her from Adderbury House.

Part IV

'Paid Down By A Covetous Parent For A Purchase'

Betty Mallet
June 1665–July 1666

Harriet: Shall I be paid down by a covetous parent for a purchase? I need no land;
no, I'll lay myself out all in love. It is decreed—
—George Etherege, heroine modelled after Betty, *The Man of Mode*

1

'While I Breathe and Think I Must Love Him'
June-July 1665

I know I must conceal my sentiments; I must smother hope; I must remember that he cannot care much for me. For when I say that I am of his kind, I do not mean that I have his force to influence, and his spell to attract; I mean only that I have certain tastes and feelings in common with him. I must then repeat continually that we are for ever sundered; – and yet while I breathe and think I must love him.
—Charlotte Brontë, *Jane Eyre*

Immured here in the country, crazed these weeks for news of my lord, I have dispatched a missive to Frances Fat-Front, weak trickle-stream of gossip, and asked her an hundred questions of everyone at court, the better to bury the chief concern 'neath the load of rubbish: 'How does Sir Charles Sedley? The Lord Buckhurst? Is my Lord of Buckingham still pursuing my lady Shrewsbury? Oh, yes, and that rascal Rochester, that adbucted me – is he still in the Tower?'

The rock in the wilderness, being struck by my wily rod, miraculously yields the living waters. One day at last I am answered:

Dear, Dear Elizabeth,
We make so merry here at Hampton Court, whither we have all fled against the plague. And we all laugh a thousand times over the tricks of my Lord of Rochester, who diverts us so extremely with his merriment and jests and his making so many women sigh for him. The King has missed him sorely and is much cheered to have him back gain in such spirits.

'In such spirits'! What is this? 'His making so many women sigh for him' – what, no sighing for me, who can sigh a tempest-full for him in a day?

Fear gnaws my stomach; then the worst comes:

247

But my lord is determined to be off to the wars, after adventures, and His Majesty regrets losing his merry companionship – and says, would he had enow gold to stay my lord's intents, but my lord has been hitting upon coming at a fortune, one way or another these months, and so must persevere—

Tears blind me from reading the further.

Making merry – courting women – these bespeak a want of love for me. Seeking a fortune – this would furnish his motive for wooing me at all.

I read the letter over and over, but still it says the same: no hint can I find of his grieving, yearning, refusing sustenance or turning pale – no hint of love for me.

Does he know I pled till Grandpa sent a message, advising the King to clemency? Does he know that for weeks I was in a delirium, ill with fear for him? Sometimes I fancied I could hear him call: I heard it so clearly, in his sweet voice – and waves of despair washed in over me, laid me violently low, hitting me in a blast of passion with the words, 'I'm never getting out of here! I'll die here. No one loves me – no one ever has – what's the use?'

Sometimes I'd sit by the cross-paned window in my chamber, my shoulder against the wall and chair rocked back at an angle, and feel his panic so clearly – 'I must get out of here, I must!' And I tried to send my love to him, but it couldn't get through. My soul floated with his in a black cloud of grief, shame, regret, fear, longing, hopelessness – some mingled with thoughts of me, but others with thoughts of unworthiness and death.

I know now he cannot love me. For if he loved me and were out of the Tower, would he not write?

Each day as I draw back my bed-hangings of rose velvet, my heart thuds with the hope that a letter may come. I haunt the alcove by the great oak door and peer from all the cross-paned windows; I jump at every message on the silver tray – but no crabbed scrawl, loopless and cramped together and standing straight like soldiers, under the imprimatur of 'Mrs Mallet'.

At first I think, being lately out of the Tower, he would have a few days to order his affairs. Then I think, e'en the fastest post must take a deal of time from Hampton Court to Enmore, Somerset, the length of a kingdom away.

But at last I grow uneasy; for there has been time, I think, to write and have a letter reach me.

Then do I itch to climb the oaken stairs, go up to my vargueno of

Toledo walnut and fold down its arms to a writing-desk, to dip pen in ink. The voice of passion whispers, *There is no immodesty, Betty; he would have married you – are you not almost his wife?* But then reason intervenes to remind me, *His closest relations believed not he meant to wed you.* And it warns, *Best wait – let him write first, lest by any unmaidenly eagerness you fright him off. Maids are to be pursued; the ones like Goditha Price that chase are heroines in lampoons.*

But what if he does not write within a few days? Or a few weeks? Shall I write then, to demand his intents and relieve this agony of waiting?

My heart whispers, *Yes*; it assures me nothing can be so painful as this wandering in a vacuum, wondering what he feels for me. But reason argues plainly, 'twould be far worse to write to a man whose passion is so dulled he cannot find time to put quill to paper.

Shall I chide him for not having writ first? Oh, that's brave: call the fly by throwing vinegar when he swims in the honeypot. Shall I write and make some feeble excuse – say I would inquire about Doll's health or his mother's?

Ha, that's more diverting yet.

No, there's no excuse will justify my repeating the indiscretion of writing first. I must wait – and trust that if he loved me enough to carry me off, he will think of reaching me by post.

But a painful voice of reason whispers, *Ah, did he love you, Betty? Or was he only attracted by your fortune, your nearness?* And – *You are in solitude, Betty, lodged in a great ancestral house almost at the western coast; he plays at Hampton Court, the most exquisite pleasure-palace of the kingdom, with all the most beautiful women in the land at his fingertips.*

Might he have less reason to think of you than you of him?

I tell myself the post has slowed, especially now the plague has settled about town and the roads are being sealed up. But still a cold fear gnaws at my innards more with each passing day.

I sit in my chamber, the window pushed out, my face to the high western wind, and look down the green hill into the lake and forest below: the Princess in the Tower, waiting for her Prince.

My grandpa and stepfather huddle o'er papers on the long banquet table; and though they grow silent at my approach, I hear muttered remarks, that the Lady Sandwich offers this or my Lord Ormond offers that. Grandpa extracts from me a promise I'll not marry without his consent, then huffs off to Bath, where he speaks of having 'great business – and all for you, my little hussy'. Fear gnaws in me as Mama, eyes bright, clasps me by the shoulders and promises they'll soon have me a husband.

So now what shall I do – my heart turning with despair at the growing suspicion he cannot love me – and my guardians about to present me with some husband? Shall I marry a man I cannot love or hold out for, without even the flimsiest excuse to make, and scarce a hope even to nourish myself upon?

2

'A Strenuous Effort To Bring Matters To A Head'

30 July 1665

Ormond's agent Nicholls, after the failure of Rochester's rape, made a strenuous effort to bring matters to a head. While Lord Hawley was away, he went down to the west to interview Elizabeth herself. He showed Sir John Warre a letter from Ormond's son, Lord John Butler, and then offered to show it to Elizabeth.

"Sir John Warre, when he saw the young lady so concerned to see my Lord's letter, begun to be very angry and told me he would not be circumvented by anyone, which I resented with as much anger and told him these expressions of his [were] not deserved from him for my plain and fair dealings. The young lady stood by all the while, and I believe she would have been concerned for me if she durst. She presently after drunk my Lord of Ormond's health, and my Lord John's, in a pretty big glass half full of claret, which I believe was more than ever she did in her life. Sir John and I became very good friends and he told me that they would be all for my Lord John, but if he had said they would be for themselves I would sooner have believed them."

—Graham Greene, *Lord Rochester's Monkey*

'Why, madam: here comes a rider.'

My woman and I've been ransacking my wardrobe, to see about its repairs. So the cold damp floor is heaped with silks and satins, dug from the old Flanders-cabinet with its gargoyles and masks.

Now my woman meanders, laced cap in hand, toward the great arched window, where she leans a knee on the cushioned seat below it and cries out her discovery.

'A rider?' I echo.

Dizzily I whirl down the angled oaken staircase, sharply turning left and right, hand atop the old-fashion banister joined with carven panels to the steps.

I trip and frolic towards the ancient Great Hall, hung with battle flags and Solomon Dividing the Child; with chain and mace and antlers and reverend ancestors; and I find, not too far from the massive fireplace, a man who is announced to me as Nicholls. He sits in state in our old crested and fluted arm-chair, with the brackets and velvet rose cushion, drawn up to the table with its bulbous old legs, and papers sealed and signed, spread all about him; and he says he represents the Duke of Ormond on behalf of Lord John Butler.

'Lord John Butler?' I cry. Lowering myself into a chair, tremulous excitement at my throat, I wonder if my friend has managed to help me somehow. 'How does my lord? What says he?'

Sir John Warre, my vulture of a stepfather, stands a few paces behind my chair and croaks, 'Here, now! We entertain no negotiations while Lord Hawley is away.'

'Bother that!' I wave a hand. 'There's naught of negotiation: I but ask a friend does.'

Nicholls, eyes shining and lips parted as if he shares my excitement, stares on me. Then, head down, he falls to shuffling his papers. A small, earnest man, he looks like a bald-headed squirrel rooting for a nut.

'Madam, I have a letter here he writ. It speaks many kind things of you. Would you hear it?'

'Indeed, yes!' I clap my hands like an infant, for with such trials as I've lately undergone, kind flatteries would be most welcome.

'No letters!' The Vulture, neck extended, strides a menacing pace toward me.

Peevishly I glare at him. 'What ails you, stepfather? What harm think you a letter can do me? Shall a djinn poof from it to fly me off on a carpet? Shall a perfume waft from it to spell me to a century's sleep?'

'No letters! You have promised your grandfather you would not marry without his consent.'

How he croaks, like a toad caught by the toe.

I lift my chin. 'What harm can it do for me to read some flatteries penned by a most noble and worthy gentleman?'

The Vulture trains on Mama a black and thunderous look. She's been standing off to the side, clasping and unclasping her hands like Lady Macbeth; but now she's inspired by the usual sheep prod: duty to her husband, activated by want of that duty in me.

'Betty, obey your stepfather. Mind what he says. If he says no letters, then no letters it is.'

I toss my head, making my fair curls tumble. 'This is a fine look-out,'

I grumble, 'when a woman so penned up cannot so much as entertain the shadow of a lover, in the cold kindnesses of inked characters!'

'Betty.' Mama shakes her head, looks as solemn and long-faced as one of the Old Testament hangings.

'Well, Jesu! You know how distract I've been of late, Mother! Now would you deny me the only diversion that's come my way?' Hands clasped before her, she looks hesitantly and shyly toward her thin-throated mate.

'No letters!' He shakes his head.

Then the miraculous occurs: the parting of the Red Sea must be nothing to it. For she thinks to raise a meek voice in opposition to his will.

'But, Sir John – my lord – can it do any harm? He's a worthy candidate.'

The Vulture shakes its head; she lowers her eyes to the floor.

It comes to me what such subservience must cost her, for I know her anxiety to have me wed to the Lord John. Then I grow angry, to think of these big, blustering hulks of men that would hector and growl and impose their will on the meek females, like bulls frighting cows with their great-throated bellows. God help such a one that seeks to fright silence into me! And to see my mama stand apart, hands clasped, eyes down, afore this long-beaked carrion-coveter!

Hotly I cry, 'Sir John, the worse be it for you, if you go so against your interest! But you know not what 'tis. You only thrill yourself with your hectorings and blusterings and forbiddings. The tilt of your head – like Jove's – see the world tremble! – Go fright a sheep: I am not much impressed.'

An astonished silence descends. My mama and stepfather stare at me as if I'd doused 'em with dirty laundry-water; Nicholls (poor man!) can scarce conceal his tremblings of delight.

Mama finds her voice at last: 'Betty, you amaze me. Go to your chamber this instant.'

'I'll go: but only because you ask it, Mama. He might ask all day for my departure ere I yielded it.'

My stepfather is one of those cold men whose fury rises silent but implacable behind a stony visage. He stares on me now with eyes like evil amulets.

'Young lady, you are not too old to be beaten.'

A momentary fear thrills me: but that this threat never having been made good before, I sense it as a bluff.

I stare him straight in the eye. 'I am also not too young to defend my mother.'

He shifts his eyes away. Bullies hate to be challenged!

'Betty –' My mother's voice is a whisper.

'Go to my chamber – I know, I know!' I turn to Nicholls. 'Sir, it appears that I must take my leave; but I wish you to convey my most hearty greetings to the Lord John Butler, who's one of the few true men ever come to court me.'

Then, standing, desiring to make some gesture of defiance and construct an exit like a tragedy queen's, I spy a goblet full of claret.

Grabbing it, I hoist it and cry, 'Here's a health to the Lord John, and the Duke of Ormond, too!'

And, tilting up the goblet, I gulp down its contents.

Slamming the goblet down on the table, my head spinning and cheeks burning, I note the gratifying amazement on the faces of Vulture and Mate.

'Young lady,' scowls the bird of prey, 'God send you a son as incorrigible as yourself in spirit!'

'Amen to that!' I cry.

And amen indeed: I can almost picture some dear little simulacrum of Lord Rochester, full of pranks and melting charms.

But the claret was very strong: never have I tasted a true, full-bodied wine, much less gulped a goblet full. Already my ears buzz, my stomach lurches, and my tongue thickens; and my cheeks are all a-heat.

Not daring trust my unmanageable tongue, I bob a pert curtsey to Nicholls. And as I sway from the room, I hear an argument commence 'twixt the two hectors of men, that collide like bulls with horns locked.

'Sir John, I beg you suffer me to show this letter –'

'No letters! Lord Hawley has given express instructions, no negotiations of any sort while he's away. He feared this very thing – that he might be circumvented –'

'Circumvented!' A crash sounds, as if a fist slammed the poor antique bones of the table. 'Sir John, I have not deserved this from you. Not after my plain and fair dealings.'

I meander back to the threshold (putting one hand on the door frame to hold myself up); and I am much delighted to hear the quarrel, which is the most diverting thing to have happened in this dull hall all the year. And 'twixt yelling at my stepfather, Nicholls throws me many winks and grimaces, till I wish to giggle at his silliness.

But when at last I totter up the stairs, the edges of all objects fuzzy and the steps oddly tilting, I determine to see in that mysterious letter. For I have curiosity and vanity enow, I am sure, to make ten maidens; and such a ninny as this Nicholls is, he will be easy to pump.

3

'St John'
31 July 1665

The young lady this morning came undressed into the parlour to take her leave of me: her mother would have her begone presently, but she would not, but stayed with me an hour at least, which time I improved to the utmost I could, assuring her of his [Lord John's] great affection and good disposition. I told her this morning that however the business were managed at Salisbury Lord John would come to see her. It was before her mother, for she watched me so close that I had not an opportunity otherwise. The mother said she would not see him. I asked her, Madam, I hope you will see him. She blushed and made no reply. Why, Betty, says her mother, you have promised your grandfather; at which she answered that without her grandfather's leave she would not, but spoke it in the manner of trouble and disconsolancy which I never saw. They have cunningly inveigled her to promise her grandfather that she will not marry without his consent.

Nicholls added that 'she has a great deal of wit, and affection for my Lord John'.

—Graham Greene, *Lord Rochester's Monkey*

St. John was a good man; but I began to feel ... he was cold. Literally, he lived only to aspire – after what was good and great, certainly.
—Charlotte Brontë, *Jane Eyre*

I've no time to pump my victim that night, as we sit to the grave ceremonial supper in the echoing vault, perched up on chairs along a table wrought in the age of giants. But he being a traveller, they must perforce put him up for the night as well as feed him, so I catch my chance as he's about to leave the following morning.

Donning my dressing gown, I skulk down to the grave antlered hall again, thence to the new-fashion parlour, where I find him stuffing papers into a saddlebag.

'Madam!' He starts as if in surprise, one hand still on a sheaf of papers. His brows go up toward the wisps of silver and brown threads peeking from beneath his cap; his eyes and mouth form three O's.

Then he stares at my imperiously extended hand and says, 'Should you disobey your stepfather, then?'

'I don't know. Should I? What would you say, Mr Nicholls?' I cock a mischievous eye on him, my hand still extended.

He breaks into a grin, ruffles through the papers in his saddlebag.

'Betty,' cries a voice from behind me, 'what do you here? You are not dressed.'

Mama stalks into the parlour just as Nicholls pulls a scrawled pair of papers from the bag.

'Only see, madam, how he loves you. That is all we ask.'

'Betty! What do you do?' Mama creeps up to grasp my arm. Ignoring her grip, I fall to perusing the scrawled characters.

'You must know the Lord John, madam, to understand how deeply his feelings would run, to make such professions. He is not one given to effusions of sentiment. He is not one to cry lightly his praises and flatteries of young ladies.'

I wave my hand. 'Let me read, sir.'

Mama stares o'er my shoulder, her hand still on my arm in a pretext of staying my purpose, but her eyes trained eagerly on what I read.

To His Grace the Duke of Ormond, Most Noble Lord Lieutenant of Ireland,
and my Honoured and Beloved Father,

It has come to my attention that marriage negotiations are being forwarded between Mrs Mallet and myself. Know, if my inclinations have any weight (as I am persuaded, with you, they must), that this is most retrograde to my desire; and I beg you, on my knees, that this match not be forwarded.

Know, I am obedient to you in all things and will submit – to any request but this. For honour demands a higher obedience from me. I have given the lady a promise that I will not sue for her, for she has an affection for another. And the lady's happiness being commensurate to my own, I would see her, if I could, settled with the man she loves – no matter how unworthy her choice or deep my grief.

I know that your grace tenders honour as dearly as your life and that you have been most studious to rear all your sons up to follow its dictates. Therefore I am sure Your Grace will understand this reluctant plea of

Your Most Obedient and Loving Son,
Ld. John Butler

My heart melts at the nobility of this man, his plain love for me and desire to sacrifice all to my happiness; then I feel Mama looking daggers at me, and I flush, knowing what part of the letter must have alerted her: 'promise' – 'affection for another' – 'no matter how unworthy her choice or deep my grief'.

'You can see how the Lord John loves you,' Nicholls presses.

My head spins. Here's Mama glaring on me, like a huntsman on a hound that let the partridge fly; here's a pang of pity and affection for the Lord John – but then, straight after, a rush of resentment and dislike. How priggish does this phrase appear – 'unworthy her choice' – and how cold-blooded does the Lord John seem to me suddenly, how full of honour but wanting in passion!

'Madam,' Nicholls presses, 'I can tell you have a deal of affection for the Lord John.'

'So I do,' I murmur, still turning the letter over in my head, re-reading the choicest phrases so as to get 'em out of book.

Mama stands at my side, her hand still on my arm, and I can feel her struggling with herself. Her modesty must be telling her, *I ought not while in nightdress entertain a strange man*; yet her partiality to Lord John must whisper that this man pleads her cause. Duty no doubt reminds her, she promised her father and husband not to negotiate on the sly; reason pleads that she ought not to refuse out of hand such an opportunity. Her heart no doubt warms with the Lord John's hints of affection, then chills with the further hints of my own. The struggle of reason and passion is all over her face, and I expect her to burst out in couplets any minute, all tragical indecision, like a heroine in a rhymed play.

'Madam, may His Lordship come to see you?'

I stare up, startled. 'Sir?'

My mama's talon tightens so it almost hurts.

'We in the family believe whatever has gone wrong betwixt you two might be mended. An interview or two – a bit of conversation – a little wooing –'

'No!' exclaims my mother. Then she makes a stop, stutters. 'That is – you must understand, Mr Nicholls, we have not consulted my father.'

'I cannot see the harm, madam. A bit of –'

'Mr Nicholls, we must not. My father left express instructions. All negotiations must go through him.' She then trains on me a bitter look. 'He, it seems, he has been made wary by young gentlemen that would court in their own persons.'

At this last I colour, especially to see how Mama sneers on me. And my fingers on the letter grow so limp, she grabs it and extends it

257

toward Nicholls, waves it till he, with a look of reluctance, takes it from her and folds it up again, for replacement in the bag.

Nicholls then stares on me a good minute and finally says, 'Madam, I hope you will see him!'

I glance at Mama, who urges gently, 'Why, Betty, you have promised your grandfather.'

So hemmed in with all these restrictions, so sick of being the goods toted from market to market with nary a say on my fate, suddenly angry that I cannot e'en hold conversation with a friend, I snap, 'You see how it is, sir. Without my grandfather's permission, I may not. I have no say: I'm but the prize sausage, vended in the market.'

'Betty!'

I hang my head. Mama and Nicholls exchange stiff farewells, to which I murmur a polite parting also – 'Good day to'ye, sir.' So he departs, and Mama stares on me so blackly I cringe from the thoughts that seem to stand out plainly on her brow: but still, no name of 'Lord Rochester' does she utter: the words being, I suppose, a black and evil curse to her.

But when she leaves me, my heart thuds anew to think that the post may have come, and I trip through the reverend draughty halls, past the visored frowns on this suit of armour and that, to the oakwood coffer that holds the silver tray. Then I go through my usual ceremony of magic: take in my breath, cross my fingers, and pray, 'Please, God'; then, my eyes opened again, I attack the pile – lawyers, merchants, the lady Sotherby from Shepton Manor – no crabbed scrawl.

My heart sinks to my slippered feet again; and a voice whispers, *Don't you know, now, Betty, that this will happen every day?*

But I refuse to believe it; and I know that tomorrow morning, I will go through the same ceremony, as if incantation and prayer alone could produce a paper on this silver circle.

Would it not be better, though, to take the Lord John Butler now, afore I'm left with Hinchingbrooke? And get to court by that means, so I could see my lord again?

I had determined to resist any coercion to marry, so long as my lord loved me. But what am I to do now?

4

"Twixt Lingering Hopes And Awful Fears'
1 August – 24 December 1665

Hard-hearted saint! since 'tis your will to be
So unrelenting pitiless to me,
Regardless of a love so many years
Preserved 'twixt lingering hopes and awful fears,
'Tis some relief, in my extreme distress,
My rival is below your power to bless.
                    —John Wilmot, Earl of Rochester

Ah! – shall I marry cold-bloodedly, like everyone else; take down my marital dose at night as best I can; and do without love, my life long?

I am grateful that the Lord John has writ he will not force me; but knowing the alternatives, I almost wish he would. For either I must remain a maiden prisoner here, at the western edge of Nowhere, or be left with a husband far worse.

And I would almost marry now, that I might come to court and see my lord just once – just see him, though for my life long I'd be forbidden ever to let him kiss my lips, though my body belonged to another man and I had no right to grant him e'en a trembling hand or cheek of it – still, to see him, to listen to his voice, that would be a great deal. It would almost be more than my senses could stand if at this moment it were granted me to watch him across a card table or ballroom, actually to watch his face rather than merely dream on it – even though the sweetness be mingled with such pain.

The temptation to honour would be dreadful, as strong as my feelings are; he would be certain to attempt me, if only for vanity's sake, to show the court how I loved him; and I owe more to a man so fine as the Lord Butler than adultery – indeed, I owe more to my own pride, which tells me by all rights I should have stopped loving this vain, fickle man some months ago.

Ah! – shall I shame myself and a fine husband by giving myself to a libertine who cannot love me?

259

No? Then shall I look upon him in common company without yielding to his soft persuasions that we meet alone?

Never! – Then shall I remain a nun in a cell here, my life long, dreaming on a face I can scarce recall?

No to that also? – Then what's to be done?

5

'Impotent As A Bird With Both Wings Broken'
25 December 1665

> My rest might have been blissful enough, only a sad heart broke it. It plained of its gaping wounds, its inward bleeding, its riven chords. It trembled for Mr Rochester and his doom: it bemoaned him with bitter pity; it demanded him with ceaseless longing: and, impotent as a bird with both wings broken, it still quivered its shattered pinions in vain attempts to seek him. Worn out with this torture of thought, I rose to my knees. Night was come, and her planets were risen: a safe, still night; too serene for the companionship of fear. We know that God is everywhere; but certainly we feel His presence most when His works are on the grandest scale spread before us; and it is in the unclouded night-sky, where His worlds wheel their silent course, that we read clearest His infinitude, His omnipresence. Looking up, I, with tear-dimmed eyes, saw the mighty Milky Way. Remembering what it was – what countless systems there swept space like a soft trace of light – I felt the might and strength of God. Sure was I of His efficiency to save what He had made: convinced I grew that neither earth should perish nor one of the souls it treasured.
> —Charlotte Brontë, *Jane Eyre*

The country folk say 'tis the season of magic, but all I see is the air glimmering on the snow without my casement; I see no animals kneeling nor cocks crowing, no angels bending low from their crystal spheres. And the cold creeps through the crevices, past the musty hangings of Old Testament torments, through the great velvet curtains of my bed, below the foxskins and wool blankets and velvet counterpane, into my lonely toes and joints. It freezes my cheek against the pillow, where the tears sting it, colder than death.

From below waft snatches of song; for the antique wood walls of Great House burst with the roistering cheer of company, all come to sit at cards, bob for apples, deck the halls, sing and drink and eat almond cakes and raise tankards to the burning of the ashen faggot that here in the West oft stands for the Yule Log.

261

I put my hair to rights, frowning into the glass, and wander weakly down the steps to the Great Hall. With wassail cup in hand, I stand in the oak-smelling hall and draw aside for pumping our neighbour the Lady Sotherby, whose son is at court.

'What's the news?' I beg, and must listen to an hundred dull tales.

'Why, my dear, the court is all loose amours. There's this new fellow – John Sheffield, Earl of Mulgrave – he's thick as thieves with the Lady Castlemaine. And it is all the talk that she will be brought to bed of the King's child any day now.'

'Loose amours, you say? Who else, madam?'

'Why, there's one Henry Savile woos the Duchess of York; and you know, my dear, Mrs Price is the Duke's whore. Such scandal! The landlords at Oxford complain that singing goes on all night long, and windows are broken open and whores brought in, and everyone pisses or shits in the fireplace. Then George Etherege and Lord Buckhurst (he that murdered a man and went naked on a balcony in Bow Street) fell into the River Cherwell with two whores as they dangled from a bridge,'

'What else?' I prod.

'Mrs Stewart, so the talk goes, is still the reigning belle. The King goes to her apartments daily, and his brother the Duke writes her billet-doux. And there's this: his wife the Duchess, beside walking publicly with that lewd Savile, has taken up with one Sidney, her Master of Horse.' Lady Sotherby shakes her head severely.'But no one's worse than that devil Rochester.'

Ah! That name at last. The blood rises and burns in my cheeks.

She continues. 'It is all the talk how has lain with enough women to people a nation. No one is more fickle in love, they say, nor as much given to drink. Strephon, they call him now: after the shepherd lad that's the lover in all the pastoral poems. Everyone waits for his latest lyric or lampoon. Everyone remarks on what a jolly rogue he is and how free from cares.'

I run my finger about the rim of my cup and hope to dear Jesus my face shows not what I feel as Mama, stalking up behind me, delivers the ill-formed infant of her opinions: 'That rogue! Someone should lock him in the Tower again and throw away the key. A woman cannot come in his company but she is ruin't – if not in body, then in mind.'

And here Mama glares on me so particularly, I blanch and look down.

'Well, 'tis so,' agrees the Lady Sotherby with a nod, her elegant snoot above the wassail. 'Of course, he's a great hero now. All's for-given him, since his valour against the Dutch –'

Mama's lips purse in disapproval; and the Lady Sotherby, seeing these grave airs, resorts to that feminine delight of needling.

'Why, Unton, certainly you must have heard!' And so she continues to lay out tales of my lord's courage, all as commended by Lord Sandwich, so that King Arthur must be nothing to him.

'Why, la – and only think, Unton, how ill-disposed my Lord Sandwich must have been to commend him, he being a rival with Hinchingbrooke for your Betty's hand – but then, I hear that the Lord Herbert is her suitor now.'

'My father mislikes all the offers so far,' puts in Mama. We look for a large enough sum to set up an estate for little Frank.'

Lady Sotherby cocks her head at this news and eyes me shrewdly. 'What say you to that, Betty?'

I shrug. 'I'd help Frank if I could.'

'Well, get Mr Jackson on your side.' She winks. 'Mr *William* Jackson.'

I smile wanly at this jest on His Majesty's favorite pseudonym, used when he wishes to travel incognito. 'Twas William Jackson that Lord Wilmot, later first Earl of Rochester, spirited out of the country after Worcester fight; and that same William Jackson, so-called servant to Lord Wilmot, who bent his head each time anyone asked him, Had he seen that tall fellow Charles Stuart?

I watch the company gulp wassail, sing with the virginals, and dance country dances, the great tables and chairs being pushed back: Joan Sanderson, the Rogero, and Sellenger's Round. I watch the games: hoodman blind and hot cockles and shoeing the mare; I help Frank roast chestnuts and bob for apples.

Then as the moon sinks, some misbegotten soul thinks to call for the dance 'A Health to Betty', and I must hear the words:

You loyal lovers that are distant
From your sweethearts many a mile,
Pray come help me at this instant
In mirth to spend away the while:
For my affection will not move
Though I love not where I love.

And, the tears threatening to spill forth, I wind up the stairs to my chamber and stand by the cold casement to stare at the frosty moon silvering the snowy bailey. I think of the old sad tune:

My love, what misliking in me do you find,
Sing all of a green willow;

263

That on such a sudden you alter your mind?
Sing willow, willow, willow.

Then another melody playing behind the first, and my heart beating
to a message I scarce dare hope for:

Over the mountains and under the caves
Over the fountains and under the waves,
Under waters that are deepest which Neptune still obey,
Over rocks that are steepest, love will find out his way.

6

'Thoughts Are Things'
December 1665 – January 1666

Truly, 'thoughts are things', and powerful things at that, when they are mixed with definiteness of purpose, persistence, and a burning desire for their translation into material objects.
—Napoleon Hill, *Think and Grow Rich*

Presentiments are strange things! and so are sympathies; and so are signs: and the three combined make one mystery to which humanity has not yet found the key. I never laughed at presentiments in my life; because I have had strange ones of my own.
—Charlotte Brontë, *Jane Eyre*

A surge of power sweeps over me. 'Love will find out a way.' Why must I believe I'm the helpless maiden? Why must I believe a man must carry me off or nothing will happen?

But a man has self-assurance, freedom of movement. Must I not wait for Grandpa to select a husband or the Lord John to propose some solution? Then I can react to their proposals – for have I not cunning enough to circumvent my guardians, aid some hero's plots?

Ah, but the Lord John did not offer me suggestions in that letter last July, as I'd hoped he would. He acted like one determined to let me direct my own fate.

Then what about my lord? Will he not offer to carry me off again? He's courageous and dashing.

Suddenly I put myself in his place. Suppose he does love me – if I were he, imprisoned and almost executed for such a prank, would I be likely to make another trial of it – especially when the lady were the length of a kingdom away?

No, indeed!

But men are different! They're not subject to fears and qualms.

But is that so? Could it be that men are like us, often affrighted – at times e'en shaking inside, just as much as we who openly burst into plaints or tears – but simply scorn to show their weakness?

This perception of the sex is so different that I ponder on it for days. At first I think it outrageous; but the more I contemplate, the more the idea grows in me. Men are human. Men can be afear'd. Yet they act anyway – why? Is it because of some innate difference given them at birth – or simply because they force themselves to banish weakness and act?

It is because they are different, I tell myself at first. They were born to act, we to react. But the longer I think, the more I wonder if this difference is not simply a will to be courageous; and the reason is, their great fear of appearing womanish. And so, their attitudes of one another – the expectations of all the females about them – so push them forward, the fear of not acting becomes greater than the fear of any consequences from bold deeds. And when they act, the hopeful results encourage them to act again.

Then I think on what keeps me from acting to control my fate. And I realize it is the assumption, as I'm a woman, I'm waiting for some man to make a move so's I can react to him.

But what if I had the self-confidence men naturally do and acted for myself? Am I not a deal wittier than most of the men about me; do I not often out-manoeuvre them as soon as they offer me a chance of reaction? Suppose I were a man, being marketed to rich wives yet feeling love for a lady across the kingdom?

Suddenly I'm aware, a man would never suffer such treatment; he would act till he brought about the wedding he desired: that, moreover, I'd have contempt for a man who sits as I do and mopes and waits for something to happen.

I don't have to be like this! I can do something!

The thought is terrifying yet delicious. It sweeps in on a surge of power. I can do one thing; then, if it fails, another: I can heap plot upon plot until at last one works. With my wit and skill at deceit, I can no doubt contrive plan after plan. It is only that I've not given myself permission to think what to do.

Then it comes to me, if I desire something badly enough, work for it earnestly enough, it will at last be mine.

The thought is staggering; for it means the only obstacle to marrying my lord arises from my own self-doubt.

But if he does not love me still?

Suddenly I dismiss that fear – for do I not have by instinct the wiles that attract men; have I not played with 'em since childhood – and watched their effects? Did I not attract him once?

But I'm not at court.

So why am I not manoeuvring to get there?

266

Sweet Jesu, that's it! Here I sit having spells of madness and melancholy because I'm not at court, yet I do not one thing to get myself there!

Suddenly my foolishness appears so large in my eyes I wish to laugh aloud.

But how to bring this plot about? The worst strategy would be direct frontal assault: once I ask my guardians' permission or plead the idea, they are sure to be on the alert for some nefarious purpose. And my being at court runs counter to their self-interest. 'Tis Mama's concern to keep me well watched; Grandpa's, to sell me to the highest bidder. What I wish is to be gay and entertain a lover privily, then choose him as a husband: the very last purpose either of 'em has.

So the castle's to be stormed by stealth.

I think, ticking off my options on my fingers.

There's no getting to court with their permission. So I must get there without – sneak off somehow.

Good: that's settled. Now how?

I cannot run off by myself. Even if I knew the precise roads to London, a maid alone on the roads is an invitation to ravishment.

What if I disguised myself as a boy in some of Frank's garments? There's something there. But I have no money to buy food and lodging. All my riches are on paper, controlled by my guardians.

If I watched and thought hard enough, I could probably manage to steal a small sum from the vulture-nest; but most of their moneys are kept with the London goldsmiths, to be put out at interest; and almost all of their finances are handled by draughts; so I wonder, with all my stealth, whether I could even come at a sum sufficient to keep me on the roads.

I must also consider my character. Strong as I am now in my new determination, I am no heroine in a tale but would grow a thousand times affrighted by each danger along the road.

No, I must cozen someone into carrying me off. But who?

Can I bribe or cajole some man-servant? No. What would he have to gain? And he'd have his whole livelihood to lose – not only his position, but hope of a character to secure another.

What about the men suing for me? Can I move one of 'em to circumvent Grandpa and carry me off? Then I can trick him and free myself once I'm in London – mayhap throw myself on the mercy of the King.

I run the current candidates through my head. Lord Herbert – I don't know him, so he'd be dangerous to trust. He might take a mind to ravish me or be difficult to shake off.

Sir Francis Popham – Jesu, not that fop, that empty rooster! He has no more daring bone than a chicken's. He'd never take the risk – nor do I know how serious his suit is. Mayhap he courts me because I'm the fashion, like man-tailored riding suits for ladies. No, the certainest thing he'd do would be to flourish my offer about court to ruin my reputation and raise his.

There's always the true man at issue – the one I know loves adventure and has daring – the one who attempted the abduction before. Him I would not even have to shake off afterward.

But should I make such a request of him, seeing as how he has so recently been freed from his last attempt – and I know not e'en what threats the King has laid upon him? Suppose my plea for elopement comes, and he's just received warning that the death penalty still hangs o'er his head if he misbehaves? Why, I warrant he's on probation now with His Majesty.

And should I throw him in a quandary, weighing honour to me against threat of the ax, by such a selfish appeal? And if he acted – which a man of his dash and courage would – suppose we fail and he's executed?

No, that's something I'll not risk!

And would he not have greater pride in me if I managed the business myself?

And I forget: I know not whether he still loves me.

No, I must work to attract him again first, be sure of his feelings: which means, I must get in his vicinity on my own.

So we come at last to the Lord John Butler. If ever I was in need of a friend, he said—

Quill in hand over paper, I muse. He's a man of honour – would harken to a lady's plea. And how much more so, the lady he loved?

I almost draw the characters of the greeting; then a thought stops me. Would a man of such honour carry a lady off from her guardians? I recall one of my thoughts during the journey to Adderbury House: Well! Here's one thing the Lord John would never have dared to do.

And suppose he did so compromise his conscience. For me, whom he loves. Then can I picture the scene – his yearning looks upon me, my stuttering thanks: 'Well, my gratitude, my lord, I've been able to use you, to get at the man I love and you despise. Oh! – sorry if you're shamed before your parents now and broken-hearted that I think you but a vehicle to use, a rug to tread on –'

No! I must never expose him to such degradation and heartache. I care for him too much.

Then who's left? Someone malleable – preferably stupid, so's I can move him now and shake him off after? Someone from whom I need not fear ravishment nor counter-moves? Someone I care for so little, I could laugh at his consternation and disgrace?

Why, how on earth could I not have thought of him before? And he the chief suitor of the moment!

Chuckling to myself, I dip quill in ink and put tip to paper.

To His Honorable Lordship,
The Most Worthy Lord Hinchingbrooke—

7

'A Mighty Sober Gentleman'
Sometime in February, 1666

The girl before this had tried to break away from her guardians, sending a servant to Lord Hinchingbrooke to suggest that the marriage should be arranged without consent of friends, but that young nobleman, 'a mighty sober gentleman' as Pepys described him, refused to listen to the proposal 'but in a way of honor'.
—Graham Greene, *Lord Rochester's Monkey*

My, my, what a furore the household's in! I am well pleased with myself, to have stirred up such a hornet's nest.

The Hinching-bloke, the goose, the dull cleaver that would seek to butcher me on the marriage block, has done what I might have expected: when the servant bearing Grandpa's latest brought him also my secret love-plaint, he showed it to his mama!

Dull sot! – who can think of no more to do with a future bride's pleas of passion! 'Let us run off now, without consent of friends, to London' – and he shows the offer to his mama!

I am well pleased with the storm this adventure has brewed up; for they are all convinced I think no more of my Lord Rochester. I am questioned, harangued; and what a nice face of deceit do I put upon my motives!

I squeeze out a tear, clutch a handkerchief.

'Grandpa, I'm ashamed of myself! Indeed I am. But you took so long at negotiating, I feared I'd never be married.'

Mama is incredulous. 'And you preferred the Lord Hinchingbrooke to the Lord John?'

'Yes! – I mean, I know not,' I whimper, snuffling, looking up at her, playing the weak and indecisive female. 'I wish to be married, to get to court – to dance at the balls and attend the plays! And I feared Lord John is so honorable, he'd ne'er consent.'

Mama stands amazed. 'You care not whom you marry?'

'No! Why should I?' I stare just as incredulous on her.

Mama looks on me, the astonishment writ large in her saucer-shaped mouth and eyes.

'Well, why should I care? A fashionable lady seldom sees her husband anyway. I'm a-weary of being the captive maiden here; I'm for the balls, the plays, the shops, the treats of the town!'

Mama looks on me so narrowly I must call up all my skills at acting.

'I had thought you determined to marry for – love.'

I wave my hand airily. 'A woman may set herself to love anyone. Have you not said so, Mama? Have you not said love begins after marriage?'

She looks uneasy but nods.

'Well, I like not this going behind our backs!' snaps the beak of the Vulture. 'It bespeaks some deceit of purpose.'

I snuffle into my handkerchief as if I be abashed.

'Aye, aye, there's something there.' Grandpa jabs at me with a knotty finger like a tree's. 'Why could you not wait for your grandpa, little hussy, and do the thing honorably? Eh?'

I pout on him prettily. ''Cause you were so long about it, Grandpa! I feared lest you keep desiring such bigger and bigger offers, everyone would give over.'

'Aye, she speaks truth, Lord Hawley,' interrupts my stepfather. 'In truth, have I not warned you of the same?'

They then set on one another like jousters.

'I seek the best offer, a pize on it! There's two or three dangling now; we can set 'em again one another and get 'em to go higher!'

'A bird in the hand is worth two in the bush. Already she grows older and less marriageable.'

'She's still of the proper age –'

'Barely! She'll be sixteen soon. And you are no closer to deciding than when you took her to London. This would be the thing, you promised us! And it is almost a year ago now.'

I pout. 'Y'have promised me a husband, and I would go to town.'

My grandpa looks in despair, knows not what to do with me.

'And don't forget Frank!' exclaims the Vulture, who is the most likely to forget Frank himself. 'Part of her marriage sum was to set him up.'

At this last the guilt winces deep in me, like the twist of a knife. Yet I cannot recant or withdraw my purpose now, so I only hang my head and look maidenly, as if grieved for my little brother. They know how I love him – and, though I wrong Frank, still I cannot resist using him, to play upon their knowledge of my feelings.

'He'll never have his portion –' I murmur, looking down '– if I'm not married.'

The tear that slips from my eye is real. There falls a silence of deeply moved glances.

'Who's the nearest to coming to terms?' barks the Vulture. 'Lord and Lady Sandwich?'

'Aye, but –' Grandpa shrugs.

'The Lord John Butler would sue if he could be convinced of Betty's feelings!' says Mama vehemently. She lays a hand on my shoulder. 'Betty, would you not prefer the Lord John?'

I shudder at the thought of that noble gentleman being used to forward my plots.

I look up and reply sweetly. 'Actually – no, Mama. For I wish to be a fashionable lady. And the best husband for such a one is a fool, that a woman may lead about and hector and cozen.'

She reacts as if stung. Then do I almost repent and confess, at the horror and disgust in her eye.

'Betty –' Her voice is solemn and shaken '– I am deeply distressed at what you say.'

I bite my lips and feel such a sting of shame I yearn to cry out, 'No, Mama! I plan on being a good and loving wife, not an adulteress: you'll see!'

But self-interest stops my mouth. I must make 'em all believe I have no thoughts of wedding my lord.

'Well, well, well.' Grandpa rubs his hands together. 'It appears we can all come to an agreement here –'

'Not I!' Mother lashes out. 'Father, she wishes to be married to someone contemptible, that she may live a scandalous life without regret!'

'Now, Unton. She said nothing of the sort.'

'She need not say it! I can tell what she thinks. She thinks of giving herself to – that villain!'

I look down at my hands. Then I hear Grandpa's bland voice.

'And if she does? Is that not the way of the world, daughter? How often does love come with marriage?'

An astonished silence descends.

That's not right!' she lashes out bitterly.

'Now, daughter.' Grandpa's voice is oily. 'Do not women – good women – often make marriages of convenience? Eh?'

His voice is sharp, ironic, nasty, The silence then descends like a pall of death. I can hear a short intake of breath from Mama beside me; and, though I look down, I can see her hands go toward her throat.

'That was not kind, Father,' she whispers.

Another silence falls – enough time for me to wish I'd hanged myself, for having wronged first Frank and then Mama. I'm selfish! I'll pay in the end!

No – I must be single-minded. Only determination will secure my dreams for me.

'Do what you all wish, then!' whispers Mama harshly. 'I'm a woman. I'm nothing!'

Her skirts sweep angrily on the floor at her departure. And I recognize where I imbibed the attitude which, had I let it, would have undone me.

8

'The Cruellest Month'
8 April 1666

April is the cruellest month,
Breeding lilacs out of the dead land ...
—T.S. Eliot, *The Waste Land*

It is one year ago today since I met him. I wonder, what will the next year bring?

The country folk say 'twill be one of portents: the three sixes signifying the beast of revelations, the comet warning us against the King's wickedness, the Dutch coming to punish him: that the black plague without is but a sign of wickedness within, as it was in antique Egypt, when an innocent people suffered from their Pharaoh's defiance of the Almighty: that this theory is proved in that the Pharaoh's heir was struck down and the King has none, that the pestilence and sword have arrived, and soon we'll have the fire.

All I know is, I feel a time of change upon me, as I did precisely a year ago today.

What will the change be? As yet nothing certain's come from my manoeuvrings. Is it possible I've built up my courage on false hopes?

All nature has burst forth in a cruel panoply of yellow and blue splendour. Flora has whispered to the rich green meadows and drawn forth the ears of buttercups and violets.

I traipse down the steep hill of the bailey and into the woods beyond, to pick wild roses by the stream. Then I lie on the tickly grass and watch the clouds drift by above the treetops. Like white-caps on the stream above, they keep breaking up and reassembling, always in different forms but always the same.

I am conscious today that a year has gone by – and that there may be other springs, a lifetime's worth – without him.

The sense of this day broods so in my heart. If he could be here now, we would splash each other like a pair of silly children, then lie side by side on the grass afterwards, talking and drying our cold feet as we baked together in the same drowsy sun. Our conversation would lull; we would hear the distant hum of the bees and twitter of the swallows;. all at once he would half sit up on an arm, bend down, and kiss me. I would put both hands up to his soft shirt to draw him close and long for him, like that time in the park—

Lying stomach down, I put my head into my hands and weep a good long while.

Oh, that I could melt into the warm spring earth and cease to exist! That I could be a clod of earth that bakes happily in the sun without the sense to feel this dreadful pain!

At last I snuffle away the tears. Then I plod back up the hill to Great House, its two storeys of reverend honey stone with lintels and pilasters of white, its two rows of windows like eyes, its grey roof peaked in front. I shove open the Titanic oaken door 'twixt the two white pilasters, to stand in the cool alcove and hear the Lady Sotherby's voice drift echoing in from the Great Hall:

'Oh! Unton, my dear, I think you may lay your fears to rest on that score. He's madly in love with a new creature at court, name of Anne Temple.'

This intelligence means nothing to me till, my hand on the banister, I hear Mama's reply. For she uses her 'Rochester' voice – that tone of mingled disgust, horror, and fear: 'Well, I don't know! He's such a monster of depravity, what's one "love" more or less, to him? He can be in "love", as he calls it, with some dozen or hundred at a time, I dare say.'

I stand still, scarce breathing for fear the noise will block out a word.

'Oh, but this is different, Unton, I dare swear! They say he is all respect to her – has not so much as laid a hand on her nor even offered to see her privily. This is the first one he's not treated like a doxy. So they say he has marriage on his mind, the first time, certain.'

I stiff my mouth in my fist to prevent a cry from issuing out.

'Well, he did not treat Betty with overmuch respect, that's certain! Hauling her off like a slave to a harem! And then one time, he lured her away from my side – she was not gone ten minutes, mind you – and I only just prevented him attacking her! Had I not timely come upon 'em, he would have kissed her.'

'Well, mayhap a good wife will mend him. It is sometimes so with these young rakes –'

'Not him! Pity the wife that lays awake o' nights awaiting *his* footstep.'

A lump rises into my throat, and I tear upstairs, to throw myself across my bed and weep.

But the tears won't even come any more. I've wept 'em dry; the only thing that's left is a dull vacuum, a listlessness beyond pain.

What shall I do? Perhaps write him?—

No, I will not stoop to so base a stain upon my honour – not after ten months of waiting to hear from him and enduring this dreadful silence instead. He knows very well, with his skills as a lover, 'tis the man's place to write first. The want of billet-doux indicates a want of interest, certain.

What a mess I am, for thinking to confess my love on a tear-stained page! But he always makes me lose control, as I did that time in the park, and forget every rule of virtue I've been taught.

And if 'twere immodesty then to show my love, what would it be now, when his silence signals his disinterest? He would but flourish the letter amongst his cronies, for a good laugh and triumph, as they sat over their tankards and bragged of their women. And I would lose even the pitiful consolation of honour.

Often I make shift to reach out and catch his feelings, but they are too jumbled to sort out: the need to prove himself and gain wealth, the desire to push himself and achieve greatness, the deep shame of being unworthy and sinful (no doubt a harpy-heritage) and a deep love-longing (which I suspect is mine, added to the mix). Then I feel a wall go up, with the thought, 'Someone is probing my defenses.'

I deceived myself to think that love meant the same thing to him it did to me. To him it is but pleasure; I was available, witty, beautiful, rich; I exercised a momentary attraction, no doubt based on the difficulty it took to court me. But now I am not around, and he has the most beautiful women in England at his fingertips. Why should he think of me?

I must try to stop these feelings for him. Mayhap eventually I can learn to love someone like the Lord Butler.

I will try to forget Him.

But even as I promise myself, a dim image of his face floats before me. It wavers in the air, beckoning and haunting. I cannot even recall his features any more, we have been so long apart; and yet why is it, I can recall Sedley's or the King's? My lord's face, the one I long to have firm in memory, is always melting in a haze, changing, shifting to something else.

Changing. An apt word for him.

Let me lie here, and let the waves of pain wash over me, one ripple upon the next: for I fear I will always love him, no matter how he makes me suffer; and even did I have a thousand lifetimes to suffer in.

9

'Fetches'

Third week of July, 1666

Harriet: My husband! Hast thou so little wit to think I spoke what I
meant when I overjoyed her in the country with a low
curtsey and a 'What you please, madam; I shall ever be
obedient'?

Busy: Nay, I know not, you have so many fetches [tricks].

Harriet: And this was one, to get her up to London. Nothing else, I
assure thee.

—George Etherege, *The Man of Mode*

'Sister,' whispers the loving voice.

I start from my daze o'er *The Romance of Arthur*. Frank's delicate
arms go about my waist. One hand still propping up the book, t'other
hugging his little person to me, I stare into the glass to see a beaming
mama in my doorway.

'Frank has somewhat to say to you,' urges the maternal stage-
director. 'Go on, now, Frank.'

'Thank you, sister.' His voice remains whispery.

'Why, for what, Frank?'

I stare quizzically in the glass at Mama's visage, hooped with smiles
as a barrel is with iron staves. Frank's skinny arms clasp me tighter, and
I pull his chicken-bone self against my bosom.

'Frank would express his thanks to you, Betty, for what you've done
for him.'

Fear chills my backbone and tightens my throat. 'Why, what's that,
Mama?'

'Well, we've settled on a marriage contract for you at last. And
there's plenty for a sum for little Frank – for improvements here on
the estate, too. And you, my dear, will soon see the town.'

A chill ripples through me.

Mama glides across the hard flagstones of the floor. I make a shift
not to shiver as her bony claws go to my bare shoulders.

277

Letting a moment of silence pass till I can gain a better control of my voice, I ask, 'May I know who my husband's to be?'

I wonder my voice can fool her. It sounds quavery and foreign. But she broadens her smile. Frank's stick-arms still clasp me, and I could swear he wishes to ask pardon rather than express gratitude.

'Of course, dear. It is whom you wished. The Lord Hinchingbrooke.'

In the silence that broods again, I battle down a rising anger.

She has stage-managed this announcement because secretly she understands my feelings. So she uses poor Frank as a prop, that I must seem unloving to him if I refuse her kind offer.

'He was the one you requested, recall,' she prods cannily. Her claws tickling my shoulder almost make me cringe.

'Yes, madam,' I say quietly.

'Well, that's settled, then!'

'Am I not to converse with him before my wedding day?' I ask, plaintively. I congratulate myself: the face in the glass shows a little-girl-obedient-sweetness.

'Why, I can't say.' Mama looks surprised.

I prod her. 'Recall, madam, we've said nothing to each other at all. We only conversed once briefly, in common company.'

'Well, there's something there.' Mama's brow-furrows deepen.

'I'm sure it would make the nuptial night rest easier on me, madam,' I say softly, 'if I did not go to a stranger.'

'Why, that's so, Betty.' She appears to ponder. 'We could ask him and his friends here.'

My blood chills. 'We *could* –'

'Well, but what?'

'But – aren't you a-weary of this old hall, Mama?'

'I? No. It's my home. Are *you?*'

''Deed, yes! The ghosts fright me as I walk the halls, and the grave ceremonial portraits stare at me with their beady eyes. Can't we travel somewhere to meet 'em – anywhere?'

Strategically I catch at my stomach and frown.

'Why, Betty, what is it?'

'Nothing. 'Tis nothing, Mama.

'It is so. I saw you wince! What is it?'

'Nothing – an upset of the digestion. I've had it these few weeks, off and on.'

'But you did not tell me!'

'Because 'twas nothing. I'm sure 'twill pass. Can we not meet Lady Sandwich somewhere, Mama?'

On a sudden my mother's eyes light up. 'I know what we can do,

Betty! We can meet 'em at Tunbridge. The court takes the waters there.'

So Frances writ me, Mama.

'And the waters would be just the thing for your belly-gripe!'

So I got it, Mama.

I smile at her oh so sweetly. 'You are the dearest mama,' I say, in my gentlest and happiest tones.

Part V

'Reminiscence And Legend'

Robert Blair, Earl of Ashfield
September 1665 – August 1666

Some of the best of Rochester's poetry was perhaps lived rather than written, and this kind of poetry, like the music of dead singers and the acting of dead players, can only be dimly guessed at by posterity. All that survives of it now is a mass of fragmentary reminiscence and legend.

—Vivian de Sola Pinto, *Enthusiast in Wit: Portrait of John Wilmot, Earl of Rochester, 1647–1680*

1

'Loose Amours'
26 September 1665 – 26 January 1666

... all the Court are in an uproare with their loose amours – the Duke of York being in love desperately with Mrs Stewart. Nay, that the Duchess herself is fallen in love with her new Maister of the Horse, one Harry Sidny, and another Harry Savill – so that God knows what will be the end of it.

... the King doth spend most of his time in feeling and kissing them naked all over their bodies in bed – and contents himself, without doing the other thing but as he finds himself inclined; but this lechery will never leave him.

—Samuel Pepys, *Diary*, 17 November 1665; 16 October 1665

From his prison the young Earl addressed a contrite petition to the King...

It was not likely that Charles would turn a deaf ear to such an appeal as this, and on 19 June an order was sent to the Lieutenant of the Tower authorizing him to discharge his prisoner on condition that he gave 'good & sufficient security' and promised 'to render himself to one of his Majesty's Principal Secretaries of State' on the first day of the next Michaelmas Term.

—Vivian de Sola Pinto, *Enthusiast in Wit*

And so we winter it in Oxford, cold city of Reason and yellow spires, the greater part of us taking up residence about the Carfax, where the four streets converge in the heart of the ancient city. We hath joyed ourselves in all measures possible, as playing with the fowl at Worcester College lake or the deer at Magdalen College park and groping titty in the pleasant airs and delicious walks of the Botanical Gardens founded by Lord Danby.

Some three days before Michaelmas, sitting to a chine of salmon and a good measure of Rhenish at the Trout Inn, Sedley shows me the plague bill for the week of September 12: of the 97 parishes within London walls, those dead of the plague are 1189; of the 16 parishes without the walls, 3070; of the 12 out parishes in Middlesex and Surrey, 2091; and of the 5 parishes in the City and Liberty of Westminster, 815. He saith that so thick and fast do the people perish, their corpses are piled high in the kennels; that, even did an hundred more carts creak through the narrow lanes of the town, and the men never sleep that piled 'em with burthens, still the air would be foul with the stench of decaying bloated carcasses, blown out with black buboes; but as it was, more and more men each day resigned the post or were cut down by death e'en in its very performance, to be shovelled into the common trenches where they themselves had laid so many to rest; that the sky was filled with smoke, stench, and the lamentations of the grieving and terrified arising from every chapel; that unscrupulous prophets had made their fortunes from the superstitious apprehensions of the vulgar, who packed their chapels and laid out their life savings for plague antidotes; that, e'en did anyone wish to escape the city now, the roads from London had been sealed up and citizens of towns outlying posted thereon with rifles to hinder the spread of the infection; and that this is damn'd fine Rhenish.

Two days before Michaelmas, the King saunters forth from his lodgings in St. Giles Fields to drink with us in the Mitre tavern near the Carfax. So many petitioners assaulted him, he saith, during his constitutional down Magdalen and Cornmarket streets hither, that he hath now decided to assume for this outing the pseudonymn of William Jackson, as he did fleeing the Roundheads after Worcester.

Of this ruse we all make a bad business, habit being so strong we 'Your Majesty' him half an hundred times, so that we all chuckle as we lift tankards at the long polished oakwood table. Well, our mistakes boot little. All of loyal England knows anyway of the servant William Jackson, whose hair was chopped off by Lord Wilmot, and who crouched each time someone at hearth or in kitchen bade him look out for that tall fellow, Charles Stuart.

Sitting across from the King, Rochester, his young face sombre and pale as a disc reflecting moonlight, says suddenly, 'It is almost Michaelmas, is it not?'

We all exchange startled glances.

'Faith, so 'tis,' says Sedley. 'Think you to go make some sacrifice to the gods? Or hear a service in Trinity Chapel? Come back and tell us if you do. I've a mind to sit here and drink the occasion through, myself.'

The laughter dying down, Rochester, frowning and tracing a pattern with his thumb on the tankard where drops of sweat bead, looks slantways down into his brew, then up at the King and says: 'I was to deliver myself up then, was I not?'

The King starts, then stares at Rochester. 'Why, faith, I suppose you were, my lord. But bruit it not about, and mayhap we'll all forget.'

We all laugh again.

'Your Majesty does not intend I should deliver myself up to his guards, then?'

'Oh, prisca fides, Rochester! Whatever for? That was but a ruse to get you out of the Tower. Now you tell me you would be back in again? Was't so salubrious and cheerful there? Faith, I've a mind to try it myself if it holds such charms for you.'

Amidst our guffaws I suddenly sober, for I see that Rochester appreciates not the joke. 'I was but keeping a promise made in honour, Your Majesty.' He gazes down into the tankard.

The King stares on him incredulously. 'Why, faith, my lord.' He reaches out a long arm and with his twiggy fingers grasps Rochester's forearm and squeezes it so the lad looks up. 'That was but a dodge to pacify Hawley.'

Rochester stares dubiously at the King, who removes his hand and continues, ''Twas a device, I tell you: to put him off 'til he forgot his anger. Time makes all men forget, and 'twere better he forget while you were out rather than in; for releasing you might then cause him to remember. I put him off with a shift of saying how dangerous was your confinement during the plague and we would re-confine you in cold weather. But you can see the whole business has died down now and your reputation for courage is now so high, no one, I think, would seek to reactivate that old charge.'

Rochester, watching the King closely, thumb and forefinger playing nervously with the handle on the tankard, says, 'I have done enough, then, to redeem myself in Your Majesty's eyes?'

'Odd's fish, Rochester! That was not the issue at all.' The King looks vexed now. 'You might have done nothing but pour in drink since you were back, and I would still have received you to my bosom. I might have liked it better if you had, for we've all got little enough from this Dutch War, despite what anyone can do; yet daily I take note of how pleasing your company is to me.'

Rochester flushes pink as he stares down into the tankard and murmurs, 'As Your Majesty's is to all who are blessed with his patronage.'

Shepherd, his mouth full of bread and cheese, saith, 'Well, pardon me, my lord, but why hang about the King if you thought you were to be confined again? Why not get out of his sight as fast as you could and lay low somewhere?'

Rochester, the lines of his mouth turned down grave on each side, his two eyebrows furrowed into a black line, says sombrely, 'That would be base and dishonourable.'

'A man of honour, too.' Buckhurst shakes his head and blows out his cheek. 'Plays he every role on the play-bill?'

'He shifts his characters,' says Savile through a mouthful of bread and cheese, 'as often as he shifts his garments.'

Rochester looks peeved with both of 'em. 'I do no shifting here. I have never acted other than honourably.'

Buckhurst rolls his eyes up toward the ceiling.

'Ask the women,' says Sedley, 'if that's so.'

Rochester's eyes twinkle. 'I have never lied to a woman.'

'No,' says Sedley, 'you make your cryptic and ironical comments, phrased so that they will misunderstand and lie to themselves.'

I ponder another likeness of Rochester to Raleigh, whom the first King James loosed from the Tower on a pull to get gold in the New World, and who kept his promise to return (though without gold) and yield himself up to be executed.

The King reaches over and yanks down the lad's broad-brimmed hat playfully. 'What say you we all give him a new name?'

'What about Strephon,' says Little Sid, 'after the shepherd in all the pastoral poems that gets the wench to lie down and open her legs?'

'Strephon you are dubbed, then. So, you've a new name, my lord, and need fear no prosecution of charge under the other.'

'So I'll say when the creditors call,' says the Boy Genius, to our laughter.

'Now,' says the King, 'let us be off to ride in Woodstock Park.'

The winter deepens. Castlemaine being confined against the birth of her latest takes to her in her isolation a new youth at court, John Sheffield, Earl of Mulgrave. The Duchess of York conceives a fancy for Savile, and they stroll arm and arm through the quadrangle like two amorous elephants with trunks entwined: Bucks fondles the Lady Shrewsbury but still cannot achieve the final prize.

The locals hit us up for gulls, as they always do. Here hath been this coxcomb that would show us Balliol College, and the other to trot us about Brasenose; this one that would get up his crumb by trundling us off to view the cloisters at Magdalen and New Colleges, and yet another appeared to show us University College, the which he takes an oath was founded by King Alfred; and a good hundred more would swear themselves experts to shepherd us about the Bodleian Library or the theatre going up beside it.

Then, the locals being done with us, the King must exhaust us with reminiscences of the government during the Civil Wars, and outings to view the earth mound and Oxford Castle near the river, or the statue of his mother and father in Canterbury Quadrangle.

Then, for an after-piece to all this boring business, we have Rochester to show us Wadham College at Holywell and Park streets, where he imbibed the new philosophy and was catched sneaking in his window at night in his twelfth year; we must needs visit Merton College. There we meet Robert Whitehall, a conniving-looking fellow that debauched Rochester in his tender years.

'Oh, my sweet dear one! How you've grown! But still the prettiest fellow that e'er I saw!'

Whitehall enfolds Rochester in a bear hug, slobbers kisses all over his mouth and cheeks; and then, pulling the youth close, mutters somewhat in his ear that makes him flush. 'What do you now, eh, my pet?'

'Still gives pleasure,' says Sedley.

I stand above the bridge southeast of town and hard by Christ Church meadow, where the Thames becomes the River Isis; and, throwing a small pebble into the still waters, I watch the ripples that spread outward as it sinks into rings ever widening. Time that seems scarce ever to move hath shuffled us all like cards. Now we are at sea and again in town; now we repair to the spire of Salisbury Cathedral beside the sweet-flowing Avon, and again to the turrets of Oxford beside the Thames. Then an arm is broke and then a heart; the sweltering heats of summer fade insensibly until we awake one day shivering with a cloak-whipping cold wind. Savile comes to joy us and Mulgrave to stalk about with his nose in the air, boasting of 'my Lady Castlemaine and I'; the Queen visits the Holy Well at Binsley, on a pull to cure her infertility; Buckhurst and I drink our way, from tavern to tavern, Iffley to Godstow, and e'en visit the coffee house opened by Jacob the Jew at the Angel Inn.

The plague begins, falters, and swells to a height, and all of us await its end like puppets, no better than the poor Sandwich, who bustles about his ship, the Dutch usually eluding him, then bustles home to a lady that looks out spouses for their lame daughter and ninny son, then pleads with a Parliament incensed, and, making a shift to ignore all, bustles back anon to sea.

The King, good as his word, honours Rochester with the gift of 750 pound for his courage at Bergen and Sole Bay; but 'tis little enough toward the ten thousand and more it wants to purchase his bride; and cash, anyway, runs through him like dirt through a worm. Nor will Rochester hear Mallet spoken of in his presence but shifts the topic: so who knows whether he still means to have her anyway?

I stare into the river. Time rolls, I drink to spend it, and who can see any design in't? 'Tis but the shadow of a dream; and we pass through it like flies that dance in the spring and die at the first winter's day.

2

'The Punchinello Sets Up For A Spark'
27 January 1666

Against his stars the coxcomb ever strives,
And to be something they forbid, contrives.
With a red nose, splay foot, and goggle eye,
A plowman's looby mien, face all awry,
With stinking breath, and every loathsome mark,
The Punchinello sets up for a spark.
With equal self-conceit, too, he bears arms,
But with that vile success his part performs
That he burlesques his trade, and what is best
In others, turns like Harlequin to jest.
So have I seen, at Smithfield's wondrous fair,
When all his brother monsters flourish there,
A lubbard elephant divert the town
With making legs, and shooting off a gun.
Go where he will, he never finds a friend;
Shame and derision all his steps attend.
Alike abroad, at home, i' th' camp and Court,
This Knight o' th' Burning Pestle makes us sport.
      —John Wilmot, Earl of Rochester, 'My Lord All-Pride', on the
                                              Earl of Mulgrave

As we remove to Hampton Court again, I having cheerfully agreed to
Barbara Castlemaine that I will be her conveyance, find myself in
company, the long three-days' journey thence, with a yapping brace of
lap dogs and a weeping chorus of 'Mama!', the which is uttered in
alternate chorus by Anne Palmer Fitzroy, not yet four years; Charles
Fitzroy, little short of three; Henry Fitzroy, almost two; and Charlotte
Fitzroy, but little wanting a year: the refrain to which chorus is, 'Hold
your tongue, you little bastard!' – whereupon Barbara, who looks ill
and by all rights should not even have left her lying-in, administers a
slap here and a box of the ear there.

 'Put a gag on that brat,' she warns the nurse, who dandles the latest,
'or I'll pinch him black and blue.'

I sit melancholy amidst the tumbling turmoil of royal infants and pup-dogs, across from the ugly gap-toothed nurse who gives lusty suck to George Fitzroy, born 28 December; and entertain the complaints of Barbara: how they have ruin't her figure and her health, how they will never close their whining mouths; and I feel the more melancholy yet to see how gravely the two eldest eye her at these outbursts, their little fingers in their mouths; and the third, Henry, clinging to her skirts, she shoves off: 'Can you not ever cease with the pawing and let me breathe?'

He beginning to whine and I fearing lest she will cuff him again, I take him on my knee; and the nurse, her ugly mottled breast still stuck in the youngest's mouth, advises the others: 'Come, children, and sit by me. Your mama is not well.'

'Christ, there's an understatement,' grumbles Barbara, leaning back into the coach cushions, her face white.

With so many small bladders, we must needs alight at every sign and meadow; and at each stop, a lap-dog runs away or a child must have a bite of cheese; and we must needs endure the pompous platitudes of the Lord Mulgrave, that follows us in his grand coach to make his devoirs to the lady.

'Chawmed, your ladyship, to have again this chance to meet up with you: may I be so bold as to kiss your lovely hand and offer again my services?'

And holding her hand, he bendeth sharply over it from the waist like some Prussian; and stalking off, his nose in the air, squires her away, her hand on his, whilst I am left with nurse and dogs and infants.

'One of the King's Bedchamber positions may soon fall open,' he informeth us grandly, through his nose, as I mope o'er a dinner of pasty and ale. 'Of course, His Majesty must choose carefully the candidate who is to assist at the levee behind the balustrade and sleep without the royal bedchamber a week at a time; and I flatter myself that His Majesty knows how loyal I am to serve him.' Drawing his self-complacency about him as if it be his cloak, he continues, popping some cheese into his mouth, 'Of course, I am but eighteen years of age; I do not expect it; doubtless His Majesty will choose some older man this time, already distinguished with several lesser honours: Lord Sandwich, for instance – but that his little indiscretion with breaking bulk has removed him from our midst and made him ambassador to Spain; then there's Henry Savile: he's closer our age, and in those delightful intimate gatherings, where His Majesty has been pleased to include me, I've sometimes seen Mr Savile – though not always – and he's already made Groom of the Bedchamber to the Duke of York – a convenience for his amours, eh? – ha, ha! – but he has no title; I am sure he does not expect it. You, of course, Lord Ashfield, might be chosen.'

And he nods graciously in my direction, his large nose still elevated and now growing red from the ale he drinks. Failing to get any response, he then repeats: 'I say, Lord Ashfield: you might be a candidate.'

I shrug. 'I doubt it. I'm not His Majesty's intimate.'

The children squalling and messing with the meal, the calm nurse gets pease-pottage out of this one's hair and orders another back to the table again.

Mulgrave elevates his nose a jot more. 'Indeed? But then, there are few, of course, that can make that boast. His Majesty, however, is most kind and gracious – at least I have found him to be so – His Majesty was pleased to make me many kind congratulations on my little endeavours with the fleet, where I served as a volunteer: of course I do not boast that I might have done all I could, the cavalry being my speciality – still, I flatter myself His Majesty has taken most kind note of what I've done.'

I huddle down miserably o'er my ale, drinking: whereupon, seeing he will get naught from me, the pompous ass begins to apply himself to Barbara, who in her wretchedness seizes happily upon any gallantry; and who, listening eagerly to how Mulgrave flatters her, agrees with him on flattering himself, which he doth with every breath, till I yearn for Sedley to be here to puncture him.

'Of course, a man cannot show his mettle at sea: I did not expect, to say truth, Lady Castlemaine, I would be fortunate enough to do as much as I did; I consider myself very well favoured by fortune to have been suffered to comport myself thus in His Majesty's cause; for 'til then my reputation had been with Venus rather than with Mars, ha-ha! – whose votary, let me be so bold as to say, Your Ladyship must always be; I am your slave, madam; you see how you draw me after; and let me say, Lady Castlemaine, mine has always been such a general heart, I had never believed any one woman would be so taking as to conquer it utterly – oh, I have been a hard-hearted wretch, I do confess it; it is pitiful what I have done; but, alas! A man cannot help it if he's of the inconstant humour; he cannot govern his taste as well as he can his sword, eh? – ha, ha.'

I summoning the wench and asking her for the reckoning, that I may be gone to walk the fields rather than listen, he turns his attention to me:

'What, done so soon, Lord Ashfield? Come, let us treat you to a

291

tankard or two of ale; have you seen Sir Charles Sedley's latest? – Hey, girl, another tankard for His Lordship here.'

Glumly I seat myself again and confess I have not indeed seen Sedley's latest. Nose still elevated, Mulgrave digs in his cloak. 'I had not expected you had; it is rather new yet and has not made the general rounds – not but that you, Lord Ashfield, are pleased to keep company with the wits: only, I have not seen you about of late at our little frolics. – Ah! Here we are.'

I have pressed upon me what looks to be a long pastoral dialogue, the dull sort of stuff I am surprised to see writ out under Sedley's name: but that a mere scanning of the first few lines showeth me the satire I might have expected cloaked under the pastoral prettifying:

> *Thirsis:* Strephon, O Strephon, once the jolliest lad
> That with shrill pipe did ever mountain glad;
> Whilome the foremost at our rural plays
> The pride and envy of our holidays:
> Why dost thou now sit musing all alone,
> Teaching the turtles yet a sadder moan?
> Swelled with thy tears, why does the neighbouring brook
> Bear to the ocean, what she never took?

I wince at the business of turtles and ocean, in its tone so clearly mocking; for 'tis plain who this 'Strephon' is, the best at piping (poetry) and jollity. And in Strephon's reply the plaints of love are even more greatly burlesqued:

> *Strephon:* Had killing mildews nipped my rising corn,
> My lambs been found all dead, as soon as born;
> Or raging plagues run swift through every hive,
> And left not one industrious bee alive;
> Had early winds, with an hoarse winter's sound
> Scattered my ripening fruit upon the ground:
> Unmoved, untouched, I could the loss sustain,
> And a few days expired, no more complain.

Amongst the other silly pastoral business, Strephon confesses the source of his grief:

> *Strephon:* Bright Galatea, in whose matchless face
> Sat rural innocence, with heavenly grace;
> In whose no less inimitable mind,

With equal light, even distant virtues shined;
Chaste without pride, and charming without art,
Honour the tyrant of her tender heart:
Fair goddess of these fields, who for our sports,
Though she might well become, neglected courts,
Beloved of all, and loving me alone,
Is from my sight, I fear, forever gone.

'Heavenly grace,' 'no less inimitable mind': these are phrases that ring of Rochester as much as the name Strephon doth. Sedley hath mimicked in this speech Rochester's parallelisms, antitheses, and complexities of expression; and then of course the woman described in her character and circumstance must be none other than Mallet, who neglects the court and is gone from his sight for ever and hath moreover a mind unusual for her sex, as well as an 'innocence' and artless charm, 'honour' and 'tender heart' and natural chastity to be found only where 'tis 'rural'.

Thirsis continues cordially enough to open to his friend the folly of such exclusive loving, so many other women being available; and the verse ends on a note not unfriendly, Strephon vowing, 'No dastard swain shall bear the prize away.'

But the implication is clear. Rochester must be hurting enough that one close to him seeks like Mercutio to gibe away the smart: 'He jests at scars that never felt a wound.'

As for my heart, it aches for him. 'Twould take a miracle to get his lady for him now. I know he's left off trying and will not suffer her name to be mentioned in his hearing. His frustrated desire for her, I know, hath helped change his character for the worse. I much wonder, this wild rake-hell, with his surliness and gibes and drink, could have popped out of the modest youth newly arrived from his Tour a year ago, his pale cheeks blushing prettily pink with each compliment, his manners politer than an ambassador's, his wit and charm pitched at giving pleasure to everyone he met.

And I somewhat doubt I must lay the change only to lost love. Some great melancholy hath come upon him as he lay in the Tower – as Clifford put it, 'Some bee in his bonnet, something driving him.'

Sometimes I sense an heroic frustration in Rochester, a despair and vexation that has nothing to do, I think, with losing his woman: rather like Prometheus in chains or Hercules in an infant's body, his strength dwindled to crushing snakes near his cradle.

Then, of course, this atmosphere hereabouts would encourage anyone's bent to whoring and drinking and cynicism and cruelty; so it seems, with that character as the fashion, he's determined to pitch upon it as a model, to show the world how he can hold more wine, ruin more women, play more tricks than anyone else: as if these were arts like handling horse or sword or guitar. Just as he put on the character that pleased his tutor on the Tour, so he puts on the character that will gain status at court.

And he having so much fancy, behold how wildly he plays our courtly game of gaining reputation by undoing someone else.

3

'Flattering Insinuations'
1 April 1666

Miss Temple was brown. . . . She had a good shape, fine teeth, languishing eyes, a fresh complexion, an agreeable smile, and a lively
air. Such was the outward form; but it would be difficult to describe
the rest; for she was simple and vain, credulous and suspicious,
coquettish and prudent, very self-sufficient and very silly. As soon as
[she] appeared at the duchess's court, all eyes were fixed upon
[her], and every one formed some design. . . . some with honorable,
and others with dishonest intentions . . . Two persons, very capable
to impart understanding, had the gift been communicable, under-
took at the same time to rob her of the little she really possessed:
these were Lord Rochester and Miss Hobart: the first began to
mislead her by reading to her all of his compositions, as if she alone
had been the proper judge of them . . . such flattering insinuations
so completely turned her head that it was a pity to see her.
—Anthony Hamilton, *Memoirs of Count Grammont*

'Oh, pshaw, Milawd! You flattew me, I'm sure.'

'Nay, who else but a lady of your parts could make a judgement on
these verses?'

I halt, surprised at this conversation overheard in the Great Stone
Galley at Whitehall, where Strephon talks to Anne Temple, new maid
of honour to the Duchess of York.

'Tis more than a month now that we've been settled back in town.
And the Duchess of York, being settled again at St James Palace across
the park from Whitehall, hath embarked on a campaign to stock her
court with beauties and wits: this new arrival being decidedly of the
first sort.

'Would you vouchsafe me to bring you some more of my compositions? They want a turn, I know not what.'

She flushes, looks down, fans herself. 'My lawd, you are vewy diffwunt fwom those other men. They saw me new at cawt and made
attack on my viwtue.'

Rochester puts on a pretence of outrage. 'Why aspire to your person when there are higher delights to be found in your mind?'

The highest delight of wits being to expose fools, I almost die from swallowed laughter; and the Great Stone Gallery being a major thoroughfare from the outer court to the King's riverside apartments, and a major spot for walks, gossip and dalliance, the beaux and belles on promenade there throw me odd looks. I stifle my merriment lest, despite being pulled back behind a grey stone outcropping of the wall, I be spied.

'You awe vewy diffwunt, my lawd.'

'Ah, can you have spied my intent?' he asks softly, giving her one of his sweet looks.

She whirling about suddenly, just as I peer from behind my post, sees us, flushes, and, bobbing a curtsey, and fanning, walks off through the entrance to the outer court, her head down, her fan blowing her dark curls.

When she's got out and gone, Rochester bursts out laughing, his devilish eyes twinkling.

'Rochester,' I say, 'is there no limit to your impudence?'

'Scarce any at all.' He leans an elbow on the grey stone ledge of the window looking out into the privy garden.

'Here's all these other men have been showering her with billet-doux, promises, invitations – making shift to steal a kiss –'

'And the quarry runs from 'em, does it not? The fox shunts when the hounds halloo.'

'But such a vain, silly prude as that.' I shake my head.

'All the more reason why she's not to be taken by a foolish onslaught, like a tower under siege.'

'Why bother to take her at all?'

Rochester with a killing smile touches the brim of his broad hat and nods. Two ladies going by giggle, flush, fan themselves, nod, and elbow one another. They disappearing through one of the painted hangings at the back of the gallery, where there's access to the riverside buildings, Strephon coolly replies, 'Is she not a prize that all men pitch for?'

''Tis vanity then,' I say.

'Three parts vanity, four parts challenge. I delight myself and divert myself in seeing what I'll do next, and how I can tease up the rare game without laughing.'

''Tis a day indeed for fooling. Your birthday too, is it not?'

'Aye. And so I give myself Saturnalian license to be the more foolish.'

Mulgrave going by, his nose in the air and full thighs rippling, stops to regard us with hauteur, his icy glance flicking up and down Rochester's slender and gorgeously clad form.

'Mulgrave,' I say, 'you should come with us tonight, to His Majesty's apartments: I'm sure we'll celebrate Rochester's birthday. And His Majesty has hinted Rochester is soon to be made Gentleman of the Bedchamber.'

He sneers down at us. 'I thank you, my lord; but I come from His Majesty, who says he cannot spare me from the war against the Dutch – alas, no one regrets more than I, that I will not make a party as usual at one of His Majesty's jolly little debauches, eh, ha-ha – but so it is when a man is known for his military prowess, eh? – it is like being known for his feats with the ladies – one's sword is always in demand – believe me, gentlemen, I would His Majesty could spare me – but, alas, he would have me be gone post-haste.'

'I can understand that, my lord,' says Rochester with a grave bow. 'Such parts as you possess will be a great asset to His Majesty in the North Sea. We will endeavour to console the ladies in your absence.'

'I thank you, my lord.' With a smug bow, he stalks off.

I explode with laughter. 'Rochester, one day he is going to start understanding you.'

With a dry look Rochester leans on the window. 'I doubt it: then he might have to take up the issue with my sword.'

4

'All Necessary Advances'
1 July 1666

Miss Hobart ... had already made all necessary advances to gain possession of her confidence and friendship; and Miss Temple, less suspicious of her than of Lord Rochester, made all imaginable returns. She was greedy of praise, and loved all manner of sweetmeats, as much as a child of nine or ten years old: her taste was gratified in both these respects. Miss Hobart having the superintendence of the duchess's baths, her apartment joined them, in which there was a closet stored with all sorts of sweetmeats and liquers: the closet suited Miss Temple's taste, as exactly as it gratified Miss Hobart's inclination, to have something that could allure her.

   Summer, being now returned, brought back with it the pleasures and diversions that are its inseparable attendants. One day when the ladies had been taking the air on horseback, Miss Temple, on her return from riding, alighted at Miss Hobart's, in order to recover her fatigue at the expense of the sweetmeats, which she knew were there at her service.

—Anthony Hamilton, *Memoirs of Count Grammont*

'Lord Ashfield! Lord Ashfield!'

   'Madam?'

   'Come hither – I must speak to someone – oh –'

   I strolling the halls of St James Palace, whither I have repaired to woo a lady, am ambushed by a fair creature, clad in naught but a dressing gown that she clutcheth about her, and hay-coloured curls all awry and lovely white breast panting.

   'Come to my closet – no, he awaits there – oh, God, what shall I do?'

   She with a hand on my arm pulls me one way, then another.

   'Madam, I'll be happy to help if I can.'

   'I know you will.' Her hazel eyes, brimming tears, stare trustfully up at me. 'All the court speaks of your good-nature. Here –'

   She pulls me toward a window overlooking St James Park. 'I'm Sarah Cooke. Upper-chamber-maid to the Duke and Duchess –'

Sarah Cooke! This would be the pretty maid-servant that is Strephon's latest conquest.

'I was determined to preserve my virtue, Lord Ashfield. But then *he* came along – Well! No woman can resist him.'

She buries her head in her hands. The gown falls open, to show a white expanse of belly with a patch of brown curly hair. I make shift not to look and pat her friendly on the shoulder.

'I mean Lord Rochester.' She comes to herself, pulls the gown closed, stares up red-eyed at me, the tears rolling down her rosy cheeks. 'I know he cannot marry me, Lord Ashfield! He's an earl. But he was so – but then he never actually said he loved me – and now –'

Still clutching the robe with one hand, she covers her weeping face with the other. I begin heartily to hate Rochester, friend or no.

We hang in the hedge a space whilst some ladies cross through the hall. Then, pulling me closer to the window, she saith, 'I was just now in the Duchess's baths, cleansing myself for him – no doubt he awaits me now. And I overheard a conversation – that makes me wonder whether he loves me. Does he love me, Lord Ashfield? Do you know?'

She stares pleading up at me. I run a finger around the inside of my holland-band.

'Madam, I begin to believe the one he loves is himself.'

She sighs, collapses against the window ledge, puts a hand on my arm and says, 'Let me tell you what I heard. I've a good memory, and I've got it pretty well word perfect.'

'If you wish, madam.'

'Mrs Hobart entered with Mrs Temple. You know of Mrs Hobart?'

'The somewhat mannish lady, mother to the maids of the Duchess?'

She nods. 'Well, the Duchess has been concerned for Mrs Temple's virtue, with the long conversations she's been holding with Lord Rochester. I thought him only getting her advice on his poetry – but now –'

Her voice trails off. I say sympathetically, 'You begin to have doubts?'

She nods, looks down at her twisting hands, the sides of her arms holding the gown fast against her.

'I drew closed the bath curtain and heard what they said. Mrs Hobart was feeding Mrs Temple sweetmeats from a cabinet and proceeded to warn her against all the men at court.'

'Her designs there are evident, madam.'

'Indeed, my lord! She coaxed Mrs Temple half naked, urging her to put off her sweaty riding habit and be at ease in her shift – praised her for her cleanliness by remarking on the filth of Mrs Jennings, who never bathes. I am much surprised she did not get her all naked into the bath where I was: I trembled each minute lest they should draw the curtain and spy me. But Mrs Temple was too greedy for the sweetmeats, I believe.'

It appeareth Rochester is not the only unscrupled conniver out to prey upon Temple.

Mrs Cooke draweth a long breath, her white breast heaving; rolls up her hazel eyes as if in thought, and then declaims a long speech, as if from memory: 'Mrs Hobart said, "Lord Rochester is, without contradiction, the most witty man in all England; but then he is likewise the most unprincipled, and devoid of even the least tincture of honour; he is dangerous to our sex alone; and that to such a degree that there is not a woman who gives ear to him three times but she irretrievably loses her reputation. No woman can escape him, for he has her in his writings, though his other attacks be ineffectual; and in the age we live in, the one is as bad as the other in the eye of the public. In the meantime nothing is more dangerous than the artful, insinuating manner with which he gains possession of the mind: he applauds your taste, submits to your sentiments, and at the very instant that he himself does not believe a single word of what he is saying, he makes you believe it all."'

At this last she bursts forth into fresh tears, covering her face with both hands, the gown falling open again a space to hint of her charms.

I pat her shoulder and make shift to say, soothingly, 'Now, madam. Remember the self-interested motive of the one who made this report.'

She glancing up, hazel eyes leaking tears, sobs, 'Yes, I know, my lord. But I had suspected – somehow I had never been sure of his love.'

'Was this all, then?'

'No.' She collects herself, wipes her cheek with a lovely white hand, and draws closed the gown again. 'Mrs Hobart said, "I dare lay a wager –"' She rolls up her eyes again and recites as if by rote – ' "that from the conversation you have had with him, you thought him one of the most honorable and sincerest men living; for my part I cannot imagine what he means by the assiduity he pays you: not but that your accomplishments are sufficient to excite the adoration and praise of the whole world; but had he even been so fortunate as to have gained your affections, he would not know what to do with the loveliest creature at court: for it is a long time since his debauches have brought him to order, with the assistance of the favours of all the common streetwalkers." Lord Ashfield! Can he be whoring all the while he enjoys me?'

I run a finger again round the inside of my holland-band. 'You had best ask him, madam.'

'Oh, I will!' She breaks forth into fresh sobs. 'To think – the while he made professions to me – he was going to streetwalkers and practising upon Mrs Temple –'

By God's beard, it grows hot in here: I sweat under my holland-band. And soon 'twill go even hotter for Rochester.

'Madam, you do not *know* this is true,' I point out.

She looks up at me again, her hazel eyes leaking tears. 'If it were not true about Mrs Temple, would Mrs Hobart have been so jealous and taken such pains to blacken him? She even produced an old lampoon of his upon Mrs Price and altered the meter and rhyme so the name was changed to "Temple".'

I resist the urge to chuckle. Sure, Rochester hath found an apt rival and is about to receive his deserts.

'At any rate, madam,' I say, patting her shoulder again, 'if he did have designs upon Mrs Temple, he is sure to be disappointed in 'em now.'

'Oh, she was in a fury! She was persuaded he made sly love to her face, only that he could the better laugh at her behind her back! The lampoon was truly frightful, Lord Ashfield: anatomised and took apart a woman's person in the most savage way possible. Lord Ashfield, what should I do?'

Those lovely hazel eyes upon me and the small red mouth parted, as if in trust, I offer, 'Madam, I cannot say: but that if I were you, I would ask the Lord Rochester to explain himself.'

'Oh, I shall, I shall!' She whirls about and, in tones of bitterness, says, 'I go to him now, and he will have explaining to do! Thank you, my lord, for listening.'

So she is off in a whirl of laces and silk; and I am off likewise on an errand of love.

But though comporting myself so as best to oblige, my mistress is in a humour to take snuff at all I say and do. I tender her no caresses, she complains; I make haste, she chides, to be done; but, faith, 'tis wearisome to drag the business out: when 'tis done 'tis done. I know not what she would have me do; I am sure I know how to find the cunny-hole, nor can she complain I want girth; yet she would hint of getting little joy from our amours: faith, let her examine her own carriage; she lies there bored and languid enough.

More and more dallying with these court ladies, I come to agree with Buckhurst's preference for whores, who know the tricks to please a man and are satisfied well enow by the bulge in a man's purse: no complaints from them! But these court doxies keep after a man to say he loves 'em, as if 'twere not obvious.

So we lie side by side under her feather counterpane, not touching, I watching the slow hand creep round the clock and considering when 'twould be polite to take my leave; and, still dripping from the mess of our encounter, I must needs entertain complaints: Why do I never make her verses but when she begs 'em? Why do I never hold her hand nor kiss her cheek? Faith, I've just given her my all; why must I proffer an anticlimactic hand?

In truth, 'tis that waning time when each of us would be better off with someone new. Yet 'tis devilish hard, when love cools as by its nature it must, how to bring it about to make an end. I have not the hardness of some around here, to jilt when I am wearied; and so I find myself ever keeping up appearances, pretending to love where it has faded. After this, methinks, 'tis to the whores, where the bargain's clearer.

I at last getting clear of her plaintive grasp, go strolling through the halls of St James again as the shadows of grey twilight deepen to night.

'Lord Ashfield! Lord Ashfield!'

I looking about see Mrs Cooke again, bearing down upon me with blooming cheeks and a beaming face, her breasts above the shift flushed as if with love, her fair hair flying and person modestly clothed in brown bodice and gown. 'Lord Ashfield, I was waiting to catch you! I had to tell you – I have done an injury to the sweetest, dearest man breathing!'

Good God, how has he managed to get out of such a spot as that? 'Tis plain he has; her eyes sparkle.

'Has the Lord Rochester managed to make excuse for himself, then?'

She puts a hand on my arm in the darkening shadows. 'Indeed he has! I have much abused him, Lord Ashfield: I, who claimed to love him. Well, I hope to make amends.'

'May I ask what he said, madam?'

She laughs, flushes, looks silly. 'He made me see how foolish 'twas to heed such a monster of self-interest and falseness as Hobart. When I asked whether he had an affection for Mrs Temple, he looked at me in that sweet, sly way he has, and said, 'Can you doubt it, since that oracle of sincerity has affirmed it? But then you know that I am not now capable of profiting by my perfidy, were I even to gain Miss Temple's compliance, since my debauches and the street-walkers have brought me to order.'

'Was this all, then?' I ask incredulously.

'Well, the substance – but, oh, you had to be there to appreciate it, my lord! – that soft, sly, humorous way he said it. He made me see the first charge could not possibly be true, since I knew by experience how the second was false. And this he conjoined with such sweet persuasions –' She sighs '– well, as is not proper to speak of.'

Now am I vexed at the very blood he hath got off so entirely.

'He's much concerned for his honour, Lord Ashfield, with such a monster as that Hobart blackening him. But I pled to be allowed to make amends for the wrong I'd done him, and he told me I might keep watch in the palace here, to inform him of their future plans and movements.'

'That was good of him, madam,' I say sardonically, 'to suffer you so to redeem yourself.'

She sighs, squeezes my arm. 'There! See what I've done? Discredited him before one of his friends. Indeed, I do have much to be sorry for!'

'Well, madam,' I reply, 'if you are satisfied, so am I.'

'Oh, I am, I am! It was only – Your Lordship would have had to be there, to see the way he *looked* and *spoke*.'

And this is the little lady who hath just heard, 'At the very instant that he himself does not believe a single word of what he is saying, he makes you believe it all.'

'But here comes his friend, Harry Killigrew,' she saith. 'I'll detain you no longer.'

With a squeeze to my arm, she floats off, like some lovely angel of joy.

'Lord Ashfield!' cries Lying Harry, bounding up. 'Come see what Rochester does.'

'I've had all of Rochester I care for today, thank you,' I grumble.

'Now, what ails you, my lord? Is he after that mistress of yours? Come thither; they are having the fiddles and dancing down the way.'

He grabs my arm and pulls me with him down the corridor.

'There's some jest afoot, certain! He looks on her impudently, as if he enjoys himself with coming close to vex her. And she keeps presenting her back and making breezes with her fan and saying the oddest things!'

Suffering myself to be pulled along the corridor, I grumble, 'Such as what?'

'That people may praise her beauty in public, but she knows they take her to pieces behind her back! When anyone commended her face or shape, she grew very angry and said, "Pshaw! It is very well known that I am a monster." Then the Duke of Bucks praising her brilliant eyes, she looks yet angrier and says, "Ha! All is not gold that glisters, and the compliments I receive in public signify nothing.'"

He pulling me down the hall, I hear the sound of fiddles and flutes; but before we can enter the scene of jollity, out from the room strides Rochester, gorgeously bedecked in brown velvet and laughing fit to burst.

'Rochester, hold up!' cries Killigrew. 'Said you anything to Temple?'

'Yes. That it were a marvel, she could look so charming after such a fatiguing day: to support a ride of three long hours, and Miss Hobart afterwards, shows a very strong constitution.'

He almost doubles over with laughing, his eyes sparkling wickedly.

Killigrew, arm still linked with mine, saith, 'Come along to the Dog and Partridge with us. We must hear what's afoot.'

'You go!' I drag my arm clean. 'I've a bellyfull of the fine jest.'

They both look saucer-eyed on me.

With a grim bow, I whirl on my heel and make off in the other direction. And not for the first time, I feel sickened at the cruelty and selfishness about court: where, it seems, everyone yearns to go, to be ruin't. Rochester's playfulness and dash this atmosphere seems to be turning into a nasty viciousness; and the ladies, it maketh them into tools to be used.

'Here's a plot,' I hear Rochester say, his voice drifting toward me, 'wants your fine touch, Killigrew.'

And so I make out of the red-and-white-brick-crenellated palace, and into the heat of a summer's night. What Killigrew will do to all this tangle, I can scarce imagine.

5

'Humor, Fire, [And] Wit
20 July 1666

Lord Rochester had a faithful spy. This was Miss Sarah. He was informed by this spy, that Miss Hobart's maid, being suspected of having listened to them in the closet, had been turned away; that she had taken another, whom in all probability she would not keep long, because, in the first place, she was ugly, and in the second, she eat the sweetmeats that were prepared for Miss Temple. Although this intelligence was not very material, Sarah was nevertheless praised for her punctuality and attention; and a few days afterwards, she brought him news of real importance.

Among all the compositions of a ludicrous and satirical kind, there never existed any that could be compared to those of Lord Rochester, either for humor, fire, or wit.

    —Anthony Hamilton, *Memoirs of Count Grammont*

'Stop, stop,' cried he, 'loveliest and most beloved of women, stop and hear me ... Can you then ... refuse me the smallest gratification, though, but yesterday, I almost suffered martyrdom for you?'

    —Fanny Burney, *Evelina*

Rochester bursts out laughing, tosses up the tankard to down half its contents, and breaks into spontaneous verse:
'We'll dance in the Elysian fields
Beneath the brow of Mars
And drink the elemental wine
From flagons framed of stars!'
The whole gang, sitting littered about the parlour of his Whitehall apartments, laughs and claps.

'Jesus, Rochester,' says Buckhurst, 'we've a mind to keep you pumped up with wine, the way it raises your fancy.'

'I've a mind to keep myself there, too.' He grins. 'It seems I dance across the clouds on it and kiss the moonbeams:
'And like a planet rowing to the skies,
We fall into the depth of Bacchus' eyes,

305

Where being drunk upon a lake we swim,
Till Venus calls us forth to love again.'

They laugh and applaud again. 'He groweth wilder and wilder these days,' observes Sedley, lifting the tankard. 'But I'd no notion 'twas wine to which we could lay the change.'

'Wine heightens the spirits,' rhapsodizes Rochester, 'warms the blood, puts a glow on the retchy world, makes the shit in the streets invisible.'

They all dissolve into laughter. But the business makes me shudder. Rochester, who always felt drink so bad for him, is drinking now more than any of us, and they encouraging him in it.

An urgent knock sounding at the door, the page bows, sets down the silver pitcher on a side table and goes to the antechamber, to see who's there.

'Let us lay a wager who 'tis,' says Shepherd drunkenly. 'Whom do we want in our jolly circle? Mulgrave?'

Now we laugh so hard we spray wine on our cravats.

'Let us pray our luck is not so bad as that,' says Sedley. 'Nay, I lay my life, 'tis some distressed female, who vows to kill herself an he not come.'

Rochester grins, his eyes dancing wickedly.

The page, reporting back to the room, says, 'My lord, a lady waits without and would have conference with you.'

'Nay, small wonder she'd not come amidst such a bunch as this,' says Bucks.

Rochester, draining the last drop of his tankard, then slings it down on the table, propels his prettily clad limbs upward; and, straightening his red satin waistcoat and pulling on his white silk sleeves, exits the room.

'Let us lay a wager who 'tis,' says Shepherd drunkenly.

'You're in a wagering humour today,' I snap.

He looks goggle-eyed upon me. 'What ails you, Lord Ashfield? You've become so morose at all our jollity. You're like the *momento mori*, the skeleton the Romans brought in to all their feasts.'

'He wants some more drink,' says Bucks.

'I *have* drink!'

'What he wants,' says Buckhurst, 'is a way to get rid of a mistress he's tired of.'

'Why not simply jilt her?' asks Sedley.

'No, he's too good-hearted for that.'

Shepherd adds, 'He must let her become heartily sick of him and do the jilting herself. And the way he's been acting lately, I wonder she has not done the business already.'

Before I can respond, Rochester bursts back into the room: laughing fit to burst, bending over, holding his sides. 'Killigrew! Killigrew! Here's our opportunity – quick! Are you drunk enough to be at the top of your fancy?'

Killigrew, grinning wickedly in his green and red velvets like some depraved elf, his monkey face with the lips turned up, tosses off more of his tankard. 'Now I am. What's afoot? Come.'

'Wait, wait!' laughs Rochester; and, bounding across the room, puts his mouth to Killigrew's ear and begins to whisper a long while.

Killigrew bursts out laughing. 'Good! Good!'

'Come now,' complains Sedley. 'Shall we not be in on the joke, too?'

''Twere richer a jest if you see it unfold,' explains Rochester. 'I'll tell you only this, to season your first course: that was my complaisant little informer at St James Palace. She's just got word that Mrs Temple and Mrs Hobart design to exchange clothes within the hour and go walking masked on the Mall, for the diversion of acting one another's characters.'

Sedley's eyes sparkle. 'And you've found a way to turn it to jest, have you? Let us in on the sweet whimsy of it.'

'Nay, nay, you're to be my audience! Come see. Killigrew –' Rochester elbows him. 'List here.' And Strephon whispers some more.

'Aye, aye! No need to give me further direction. I'll season it right properly.'

'Come on!' Rochester pulls on his arm.

Killigrew with another gulp goes tearing out the room in the wake of the Boy Genius. I sit there looking glum.

'Well, what ails him now? He's still the death's head at the feast,' complains Shepherd.

'Rochester would not be behaving this way if he were not drunk,' I say.

'Then all the more reason to keep him drunk! Come on.' Buckhurst hits me on the back; I take another gulp of my tankard, and all of us go careening out in a bunch to see what depraved deviltry Rochester and Killigrew can do.

This being not High Mall time but rather early in the afternoon, only a few ladies holding babes by the hands go strolling back and forth upon the gravelled path. We hang about in a listless clump, awaiting whatever great adventure shall be promised us. Rochester and Killigrew stand off to one side, whispering and elbowing one another like two boys at school about to pull a prank on the master.

Off in St James Park some nurses watch children at play, and along the rectangular silver expanse of the artificial lake laid out by Le Notre, some ducks bob. I stare at the wall of Whitehall Palace behind us, its many ugly chimneys sticking akimbo, hither and yon; and we hang about for a most boring part of an hour.

Then all at once Rochester and Killigrew, elbowing one another, make shushing noises and wink. And striding across the grass, from the direction of St James Palace, are two female figures, their cloaks pulled about 'em, curls covered with hoods, vizard masks over faces.

The broader one hath on a most delicate gown of pink silk and furbelows and lace, pinned with many amethyst jewel-drops – such as I have seen Temple wear – but the fabric straining tight across her bosom. The other, more slender, wears a green velvet that hangs on her.

Immediately Rochester with two bold strides is beside the one in the pink and seizes her arm impetuously so she gasps and jumps back.

'Madam!' he cries, loudly enough for his audience to hear. 'You have fled me almost these three weeks. And, sure, I know not why! But surmise what it is to have been starved of your inimitable conversation!'

And he shoots us a grave, ironic look from one of his dark eyes: a look that says, *Enjoy, but do you not dare to laugh.* So as best we can we hold the laughter in. But I feel Buckhurst and Shepherd shaking behind me; and I only, it seems, not diverted with the fine jest.

Now, it being clear to us this is Hobart he hath, both by the tightness of Temple's gown on her and the horror with which she finds herself pawed by her hated rival, she lets out a shriek and goes to wallop him with her fan. But he hath hold of one of her forearms and now grabs her wrist and says:

'Chaste as ever! But I'll not be put off a moment more. Ah! Loveliest of creatures – methinks I would cover your face with kisses.'

At this threat Hobart shrieks anew and begins to struggle. Rochester, having hold of one arm and one wrist, drags her from the Mall and begins to entertain her with importunities.

'Madam, you *will* stay and hear me! Too long my plaints have been denied; I have suffered martyrdom without knowing my sin. God wot, I have behaved honourably to you – unless some beast has buzzed in your ear lies about my honour.' He pulls her closer. 'But stop and hear me!'

All at once Hobart leaves off struggling – but, pulling her arm and wrist free from him, stands, cocking her head as if listening. I wager she suddenly realizes, if Rochester is to make plaint of love to anyone, to move her, better that it should not be Temple.

This lovely in the meanwhile hath been pitched upon by Killigrew, who grabs her arm as roughly as ever Rochester did Hobart's, and shouts in his low growly voice:

'Aha! There you are, Mrs Hobart, you conniving liar! And you'll not escape me, for I've been meaning to converse with you this long while about the injury you've done my friend Lord Rochester.'

Temple, not moving, begins to fan herself briskly with the free arm.

'You've blackened the honour of the noblest young man in England! You've spun a web of lies, altering a lampoon on Price and saying he wrote it on Mrs Temple. And we know your ruses, to get her all naked in the bath –'

In the meanwhile Rochester, courting Hobart, hath dropped to his knees before her and caught her by both hands.

As she struggles, he declaims, loudly and histrionically, 'No, I will not rise to my feet till you say you forgive me, loveliest of creatures! Tell me wherein my fault may be, that I may mend it!'

She pulls, struggles.

'No, I'll not let you go 'til you remove me from this hell of doubt!'

'– to feast your eyes upon her naked and work upon her with your lust,' says Killigrew. 'You are wagering that such an innocent lady cannot conceive that she is in more danger from *you* than from any man. So sly your advances, pretending only friendship, warning her against men, urging her to bathe, to strip to her shift – but that didn't bear fruit. What other pretext will you find to coax her out of her gown?'

With a gigantic effort Hobart pulls herself free, goes whirling about to see Mrs Temple, shuddering and shrieking, make about and take off flying across the green fields for St James.

'Wait! Wait!' Hobart cries, running after her, holding up skirts and almost tripping over them in her haste. But Temple flees in disarray.

Now Killigrew and Rochester fall laughing, fit to burst, into one another's arms, then shake hands. We all applaud mightily.

'Let's back in and drink in celebration!' cries Rochester, bounding off in a manner more befitting hind than man: like a bolt of lightning let loose, flashing sparks every which way.

We follow behind him more sedately, through the park, the palace wall, the tilt yard, across King Street and through the main gate into the bowels of the palace, where his apartments lie.

He's already back there, laughing fit to burst, ruffling with a hand the page's hair, tossing off a dram.

'Was it not great sport?' He claps his hands.

'You overplayed your part so, my lord,' says Shepherd, ''tis a wonder they did not spy the frolic in it.'

'There was no help for't, I was so vastly diverted with what I did.' Rochester holds up his goblet. 'More wine!'

The page nods, walks off with the silver pitcher. We all settle ourselves about in our wonted circle of chairs.

'Gad, I divert myself so, I know not what I'll do next!' crows Strephon.

'Well, my lord,' says Bucks, ''tis certain she'll be yielding to your arms now.'

'But beforehand,' says Strephon, 'let's conjecture what will tease the joke up higher.'

'You don't wish to possess her after all this you've done to have her?' I ask, incredulous.

'Of course I wish to possess her. But the games beforehand being so much more exhilarating to the blood, I play them out as long as possible, the way one plays out the height of passion and then is disappointed at the quick spending and aftermath.'

'Saw you the way Hobart looked,' giggles Killigrew, 'when his lordship courted her?'

'I knew that being pawed by me would be her greatest aversion,' chuckles Rochester.

The boy, returning with the pitcher, pours first in Rochester's tankard, then goes about to the rest of us. Rochester takes a great gulp of wine and says, 'But already the excitement has begun to fade. I want continual stimulation to pump up my blood.'

'Rochester, go not to war again!' cries Killigrew. 'We could be a team.'

Strephon shrugs, tosses off another draught. 'I've no urge to go to war just yet. But it is a way to court thrills. 'Tis been damned dull around here.'

'Liven your spirits by drinking!' exclaims Buckhurst.

They agree on this unhappy proposition; so I determine to call upon the Boy Genius on the morrow, to chide him about the dangers to his health.

6

'Heaven Did Not Allow Him An Opportunity Of Profiting'

21 July 1666

Rochester and Killigrew took leave of them before she recovered from her surprise; but as soon as she had regained the free use of her senses, she hasted back to St. James, without answering a single question the other put to her; and having locked herself up in her chamber, the first thing she did, was immediately to strip off Miss Hobart's clothes, lest she should be contaminated by them; for after what she had been told concerning her, she looked upon her as a monster, dreadful to the innocence of the fair sex.

Miss Hobart being desirous to come to an explanation, went back to call on Miss Temple herself, instead of sending back her clothes; and being desirous to give her some proof of friendship before they entered upon expostulations, she slipped softly into her chamber, when she was in the very act of changing her linen, and embraced her. Miss Temple finding herself in her arms before she had taken notice of her, everything that Killigrew had mentioned, appeared to her imagination: she fancied she saw in her looks all the eagerness of a satyr and disengaging herself with the highest indignation from her arms, she began to shriek and cry in the most terrible manner, calling both heaven and earth to her assistance.

This had been sufficient to have disgraced Miss Hobart at court, and to have totally ruined her reputation, had she not been supported by the duchess. Miss Temple, who continually reproached herself with injustice, with respect to Lord Rochester, and who, upon the faith of Killigrew's word, thought him the most honorable man in England, was only solicitous to find out some opportunity of easing her mind, by making some reparation for the rigour with which she had treated him: these favourable dispositions, in the hands of a man of his character, might have led to consequences of which she was unaware; but heaven did not allow him an opportunity of profiting by them.

—Anthony Hamilton, *Memoirs of Count Grammont*

The next day, being sombre with the headache, he is not flying quite so high in his fancy. I discover him in his Covent Garden lodgings and come to scold him about his drinking.

But he will scarce hear me, for calling the boy and asking him to fill the goblet again. All at once the boy, returned from one of his innumerable trips to the cellar, reports, 'My lord, the Lord John Butler is below and desires to know if he may walk up.'

Rochester tosses down a draught, where he sits behind the desk of his study, the shelves behind him filled with rich volumes, bound with green and red leather gilt. Then he pulls himself upright and says, 'Show the gentleman up.'

Butler enters – sober, stolid, with back straight and jaw clenched – altogether different from the youth I saw sporting with his sister Chesterfield. He looks like he is about to confront a creditor or swallow a noxious brew his nurse said would be good for him.

I stand to greet him, and a polite smile breaks across his face without reaching his eyes as he claps my shoulder, greets me in return, and bids me be seated.

Rochester pulls himself up behind the desk and a bit unsteadily reaches over, extends a hand. They shake hands and nod.

'My lord.'

'My lord.'

'Pray be seated, my lord,' says Rochester. 'Would you have some-what to drink?'

Butler's eyebrow goes up, this not yet being eleven of the clock, but then he says politely, 'Thank you, no. I cannot stay long.'

I have already seated myself; Rochester slings himself into the chair, one skinny leg over its arm; Butler lowers himself to perch, back straight, on the edge of the great chair just before the desk.

'What brings you here, my lord?'

Butler flushes, tugs at his plain neckcloth, looks down at the large square hands grasping the white plumed hat, turns it about. 'I scarce know how to begin, my lord. What I have to say is not easy.'

'Begin at the beginning, sir, and out. I promise 'twill not offend me, for I know you mean no harm.'

'Indeed, I do not.' Butler looks up, blue eyes serious, thin lips drawn in a line. 'It is this. Have you given up all pretensions to Mrs Mallet's hand?'

Silence descends. Rochester leans over, shifts his eyes away, hefts the silver goblet, twirls the stem of it betwixt his fingers, takes a sip.

'Sure you will not have some wine, my lord?'

'I thank you: no, my lord.'

Rochester sets the goblet down again, glances over, leans his head on a thumb and two fingers, and asks, 'Have you a sudden mind to pursue her more vigorously?'

Butler flushes, looks down, then up again. 'I – came to ask you that, my lord.'

'So we're in a stalemate, aren't we?' Rochester grins impudently and winks.

Butler laughs uneasily.

'We could sit here fencing half the afternoon on our intents, neither of us gaining anything on the business,' muses Rochester. 'For I believe both of us very interested, yet neither of us pursues the suit. Is that not odd?'

'Odd indeed, my lord. Especially – have you heard of the negotiations for her marriage contract with Hinchingbrooke?'

Rochester tilts up the goblet, drains it in a big gulp. 'I've heard it.'

'And –' Butler wets his lips '– you plan to do nothing?'

Rochester slams the goblet down on the desk, cocks his head again. 'Such as what?' His voice ever so slightly slurs. 'Take horse to the West Country and attempt another abduction? This time His Majesty might not be so gracious about suffering my head to remain on its shoulders. I've grown accustomed to my head – though 'tis often so muddled with drink, ill humour, and silliness.'

Butler looks frustrated: no doubt this sort of foolery suits him not so well as plain talk. His strong jaw clenched, he says slowly, 'I only mean, my lord, are you content to sit back and let her be married to Hinchingbrooke?'

'Content? Hell, no. But what can I do about it?'

'Your lordship has given up all pretensions of an honourable suit, then, negotiating with her guardians?'

'My poverty has given up my pretensions for me.' He waves the goblet in the air; the page strides briskly thither to provide a refill. 'There's no hope of my gaining her but in a pirate's or robber's way.'

'Do you love her, my lord?' asks Butler suddenly.

Rochester starts and pales, then makes of his face a mask; and, turning away, saith, 'I might ask you the same question, my lord. Else why would you be so concerned?'

Butler flushes bright pink. 'I feel it a shame that the lady be left with Hinchingbrooke.' His words are jerky. 'And His Majesty seems to care not any more whom she marries.'

'Aye, that's so, he's a wiffle-waffle king; put some self-interest of his in the balance, and see how fast it weighs one way or the other.'

'But I only mean, my lord,' says Butler, 'if you put yourself not

ROBERT BLAIR, EARL OF ASHFIELD

forward as a suitor – I was thinking – she being so close to a contract with Hinchingbrooke, it would be no dishonour for me to put myself forward in the last extremity of the moment, to rescue her.'

'Why wait for the last extremity?' asks Rochester with a shrug. 'Why ask me what I'll do? If I were in your place, I'd not come asking my rival's permission to press my suit. Not when you have all the accoutrements it takes to win her.'

'I do not, my lord. It seems the accoutrements are spread betwixt us. That is why I ask you what you do.'

'What do I have that you don't, with all your father's gold?'

Butler looks down but seems unwilling to speak.

All of a sudden Rochester says, 'Has the lady made any sort of confession to you – any confession of love?'

'She has. But not of love for me.'

Rochester sits back in the chair, seems sunk deep in thought. 'When was this?'

'The spring she was brought to the court, my lord, more than a year ago. And so I thought – the picture looking so changed these past months –' He shrugs and begins anew to twist his hat in his hands.

'The picture indeed looked changed,' says Rochester. 'What said she to the man you sent last summer to the West Country?'

'She told Nicholls many kind and flattering things. So kind, so flattering, I knew she could speak calmly of my virtues without any sort of feeling that would call forth a blush. So discouraging, I begged my father to have done.'

'The devil you say! It sounded not so discouraging the way it made the rounds.'

'No doubt. Nicholls was much encouraged; but his sense is all in figures, not in interpreting the carriage of young ladies.'

Rochester appears sunk deep in thought.

'So I ask you, my lord, if you still make shift to win her,' Butler persists. 'If not, I'll ask my father to reopen the suit. For I believe she'd be happier with me than with Hinchingbrooke.'

'No doubt, no doubt,' muses Rochester'. His goblet beside him sits suddenly unheeded.

'Then, my lord, I having been so frank – may I not have equal frankness from you?'

Rochester comes to himself, smiles, half stands and leans over to extend a hand.

'You may. I've not given up, Lord Butler. I'm pitching at one more chance to get the gold to win her.'

Butler having shaken the hand and released it, stands. 'Then I bid you good day, sir. And as long as you are in the field, my lord, you may apprehend no rivalry from me.' He goes to leave, then turns about suddenly. 'But I beg you, if you should give up your pretensions to her hand, to let me know.'

Rochester nods. 'I will.'

However, Butler having left, Rochester mutters, 'Foolish youth! I'd dance in hell before I'd help you to her.' He then turns to the boy. 'Tell Harry to order my wardrobe again and get to packing.' The boy nods, and walks from the room. Rochester scrabbles through his desk drawer, pulls out a sheet of writing-paper.

'Rochester, what do you do?' I ask.

'Write the King for another commission. I suddenly feel a yearning to be off at sea.'

7

'The Affair Came To A Head'
4 August 1666

> In August 1666 the affair came to a head with an interview between
> Lord Hinchingbrooke and Elizabeth at Tonbridge, where she was
> staying with her mother.
> —Graham Greene, *Lord Rochester's Monkey*

But ne'er was it an unluckier chance for his hopes that Rochester decided to be gone to sea. For his business with the lady, which hath sat dead centre above a year, taketh a sudden unexpected turn near Tunbridge.

Here the court hath posted; for the Queen, on a pull to conceive, taketh the waters each day by the instructions of old Dr Rowze in his pamphlet: three hundred ounces a dose by the first rays of the sun. And all of us drink, too, the scummy water with its iron savour being held so salubrious, till our bladders are fain to burst and we run for our relief: we gentlemen to the Pipe House, where, for half a crown's subscription, coffee, pens, ink, paper and pipes for tobacco may be had; and the ladies for their cot, where all but tobacco may be had for a like price.

The waters are called Queen Mary's Wells, for that they did cheer and revive the Queen Mother after her lying in with the present king; and much improved is the spot since Lord North early in the century came upon a spring scummy with minerals in a wild brake. For the old Lord Abergavenny, whose estate it was, did then cause much of the thicket and brake to be hacked away and the road improved, and wells to be sunk about the two main springs; then the spot paved and set about with wooden rails. Then the young Lord Muskerry (killed at Sole Bay, where Rochester was a hero), being then lord of Summer Hill some four and a half miles hence, made still other improvements.

So 'tis at this renewed pave I stand with Buckhurst, Shepherd, Sedley, and Savile; and near this hall, with the projection to shelter waters and dippers from showers.

'Why did we make out so early?' I complain, shuddering from the morning sun rays. 'No one else is here yet.'

They ignore me, for Buckhurst is busy complaining that his family teases him to visit Knole, the deer park and grand brick turrets of which are but a few miles hence at Seven Oaks.

'But I'll not be coaxed there again! For all my father does is scold at how much this costs and that and how much we all eat and how dearly our bringing-up costs him.'

''Tis a marvel he'd see you again, then.' Sedley sips from a long-handled dipper.

''Tis not he but my mother and sister Fanny. But I've told 'em I've a complaint requires a daily dose of the waters.'

A crowd then beginning to push in, both from the small path of the Lower Walk and the broad promenade of the Upper, they congratulate themselves on having forestalled it and, filling tall Venice glasses with the nasty brackish water, set themselves to promenade down the Upper Walk, bordered on two sides by elms like the walks of Hampton Court are by yews.

On the east side betwixt the shady elms and Lower Walk sit the marketwomen with their produce of cheeses hard and green, wild rock-roses tied up in bunches, pails of butter and loaves of bread in paper wrapped; their hares, poultry, and pheasants tied up by the legs; chines of bacon and pints of mum or beer; and sparrowgrass, dandelions and peas for salads; and the local thyme, which is strong and sweet, tied up in bundles. And mighty pretty too some of the cherry-cheeked Kentish lasses in their straw hats beribboned and neat shoes.

As Buckhurst and Shepherd joy themselves with chaffing the lasses and Savile with exclaiming o'er their wares, Sedley and I drift to the other side of the Walk, where we inspect the row of wooden booths there arrayed. Here mum is sold and there, claret and seed-cakes in honey dipped; here one may buy English laces and there, a bolt of the local wool. Here are rocks brightly coloured and put to a high polish, set in silver filigree to the shape of hearts; there, the large Venice glasses for taking the waters.

And everywhere is sold what no person of fashion would be without: that is, the Tunbridge Ware – the toys and gewgaws fashioned from beech, sycamore, or cherry tree: tea-chests, snuff boxes, punch bottles; fans, their sticks gleaming with patterns of holly; stick-babies dressed by seamstresses to the mode with straw hats of the Kentish fashion beribboned; pins for the bodice or for the sash.

Soon 'tis High Promenade time, about half past seven of the clock, and the Upper Walk is choked with strolling beaux and belles, sipping

317

of their Venice glasses, passing their time in dalliance and discourse. Savile making over to us, his arms laden with pheasant and thyme and honey-cakes, says, 'What's the stir over there?'

I, turning about, do perceive a mob assembled larger than usual about a knick-knack booth, and all of 'em seeming to watch something: some of 'em laughing and others with eyes goggled in appreciation; and all of 'em, I mark, being masculine. For what ladies do perceive the show but cast a glance on it and walk on, eyes averted and noses elevated; and those few remaining at the mob's edge tug at the arms of gentlemen.

Think I, here is some wonderful lewd game or naked courtesan. Buckhurst, mouth full of honey-cake, swigging on beer, cries, 'Let's see what mischief we can do there!'

All four of us laugh and, elbowing through the crunch, what do we see but the booth that vends the jewelled hearts; and stationed before it, a practised and stunning coquette, who hath known how to choose her stage to best advantage.

Prettily trussed in a blue moire with white laced undersleeves and a low pinner of point de Venise lace, her straw hat cocked at angle with ribbons to secure it above a cloud of wild, lush amber-honey ringlets, she is so beautiful as to startle the senses, with those winsome pouts and flirts about the rosebud mouth, those eyes that beckon and warn. Her cheeks bloom in a very high colour, and I harden my heart against her taking beauty as she cocks a head, crooks a finger, casts a flirting glance here and there, twists her fan now opened, now closed.

For 'tis that jilt Mallet.

She cocks a baby-pretty head and turns about, the better to show to advantage the slim waist and buxom white bosom, by the pinner all too modestly and tantalizingly concealed; raises a round white arm, snaps shut the fan, and, with brown eyes snapping, voice rising to a babyish cry and lowering to a sultry murmur, sports with the Duke of York at her elbow.

'Gad, who's that?' asks Savile, his mouth half-open and eyes wide. 'Has the King seen her?'

''Tis Elizabeth Mallet,' says Buckhurst.

We watch as she shoots the veiled battery of a look across the crowd to Prince Rupert, who gazes back in full until pulled off by the arm by his mistress, Mrs Hughes.

'Elizabeth Mallet,' breathes Savile, watching in a rapture. 'Faith, who else?'

The Duke of York, heedless how his mistress the Lady Denham

fumes nearby, protests with some silly comment at Mallet's garneted ear, his ugly head leaned down toward the white satin of her shoulder.

She tosses from out the corner of her brown eye a pert, seductive look and waves her fan closed so near his nose she almost catches it: whereat the crowd roars. She makes a pretence of looking astonished, then applies a pout so winsome it but invites. Then all at once she spies us.

'Sir Charles! Oh, Sir Charles!'

She flirts her fan; and, eyes sparkling, gathers up skirts to flounce through her throng of admirers to us. We all bow.

'And your bosom friends, too! Oh, how delightful! You are the very gentlemen to rescue me.'

She purrs, cocks her head at that angle, throws us each a mischievous look, and extends a soft white hand which the others look happy to kiss.

'From what, madam?' asks Sedley.

'The very dead dregs of boredom! My mama's somewhere nigh, and I feel her closing in like an ague on the eve of a ball. Can you not spirit me away for the day and show me the pleasures of the place?'

She tilts her head, and 'neath half-closed lashes bestows a mischievous, inviting look.

'Madam,' says Sedley, 'I'd be glad to oblige, but your mama's given notice she little approves a rescue from such a gang as ours.'

Her cheek pales, and her eyes grow bright as she trills a run of giddy laughter. 'Well, that's what's become of gallantry these days! Sunk like a raisin in a pottage –'

She restlessly scans the throng all about us; then all at once the colour drains entirely from her face. I look about to see what terror or mystery hath possessed her but see behind me no more than the back of some tall fellow in a dark periwig and brown velvets of a cut very simple. She stands pale, her lips parted, and I am sure scans him; he turns about and, seeing those gorgeous eyes bent full upon him, leers below his thin moustache. 'Tis Lord Herbert, and she makes a severe mouth at him and turns her attention back to us.

'Madam,' says Buckhurst, 'permit me to present our friend, Mr Harry Savile.'

'Madam.'

'Sir.'

At his bow she curtseys low, both skirts spread, eyes down, as if in the formal manner. Then she snaps up, her eyes dancing, as if formality were a great joke.

'Madam,' says Buckhurst, 'came you not here to be contracted to the Lord Hinchingbrooke?'

'So the rumour goes.' Her eyes dance devilishly.

Savile muttering elbows me. 'She'll make a cuckold of him before the stockings hit the sheets.'

Her attention wanders again to the crowd behind us, and Savile asks, 'Do you look for someone, madam?'

I am surprised to see her blush from the neck to the roots of her honey-coloured hair.

'Look for someone, sir?'

At that moment up rushes that scrawny bird of an old-fashion lady in a high gorget. In her basket is a load of Tunbridge-babies and other gewgaws.

'Betty! I turn my eyes from you in an instant, and you're gone –' She grasps the winsome lass by the arm; then, her eyes alighting on Sedley and Buckhurst, she blanches. 'Betty! Come away this instant, do you hear me?'

The little lady making no attempt to move, Sedley and Buckhurst bow low.

'Our honour to you, Lady Warre,' says Buckhurst.

'Madam,' says Sedley.

'Lady Warre.' I touch my hat.

She nods curtly. 'Good day.' Then she jerks the pretty little miss by the arm. 'Come away now; we've been here long enough.'

Mallet cocks a bold eye on Savile as if taking him in. 'And whom should I look for, sir: a poor simple country maid, unused to such elegant society as this?'

Savile chuckles at this irony and with a friendly look replies, 'The Lord John Butler, perhaps?'

'Oh, the Lord Butler!' She smiles. 'Is he here?'

Her mama tugs nervously on her arm. 'Betty. Come.'

'Or my Lord of Rochester, perhaps,' says Savile calmly, as if with an after-thought.

The lady turns as pale as death, then flushes red. The pious mama, clutching her offspring's arm, says, '*That* rogue! We'd as soon look for the plague! Well, if he's here, we shall make a quick business and be gone; if he's here, the women taking the waters will conceive *indeed.* That beast! That villain!'

I am vexed the little lady saith naught in his defence but stands, submissive and limp, at her mama's side.

'Come, Betty, and let's be gone.'

The little miss, suddenly lifeless, suffereth herself to be dragged a few paces by the arm but then whirls about and with brightly glittering eyes and an artful, brittle laugh, throws over her shoulder a sally: 'Well, Sir Charles! I hope you can set my mama's mind at rest! I hope the – rascal's not here!'

With a bow, his eyes sparkling, Sedley saith, 'No, madam. He's away at the wars.'

'Oh, good!' she cries in a hollow, bright voice. Vexed to the very blood at her callous, jilting ways, I stare at her retreating figure as it flounces down the Upper Walk and toward a waiting coach, the tall, angular woman pulling her along. 'Tis not enough she would jilt him: now she is thankful he does not breathe the common air about her.

I grumbling this observation to Buckhurst, he responds with his usual sally, 'Have you no sense at all?'

I looking about for Savile to take up my part notice suddenly that he is gone.

Part VI

'Fearful Hooks'

Betty Mallet
August-September 1666

Now Romeo is beloved and loves again,
Alike bewitched by the charm of looks.
But to his foe supposed he must complain,
And she steal love's sweet bait from fearful hooks.
Being held a foe, he may not have access
To breathe such vows as lovers use to swear;
And she as much in love, her means much less
To meet her new-beloved anywhere.
But passion lends them power, time means, to meet,
Tempering extremities with extreme sweet.
                    —William Shakespeare, *Romeo and Juliet*

1

'To Live An Unstained Wife To My Sweet Love' 4 August 1666

Juliet: O, bid me leap, rather than marry Paris,
From off the battlements of yonder tower;
Or walk in thievish ways
And I will do it without fear or doubt,
To live an unstained wife to my sweet love.
—William Shakespeare, *Romeo and Juliet*

A-Tunbridge! A-Tunbridge!

Balls on the bowling green at Mount Ephraim! Promenades of the beau monde on the Upper Walk!

Ah, let me but get there – and see. See – those hot, dark eyes ringed with thick screens of upturned black lashes, that willowy person with the delicious legs and the warmth so exuding from him.

And then – ah! Let me see how easy 'twill be to plot against all obstacles, get rid of Anne Temple somehow and my maternal shadow, too, and the dull cleaver that would seek to butcher me on the marriage block.

A-Tunbridge! A-Tunbridge! It seems, can I only get in his vicinity, all problems will be solved.

So what a sinking of heart do I experience, what a falling-down of my lifted-up hopes into the pit of my stomach, as I stand in the heat of the morning sun before the booth that vends the jewelled hearts, and pose my body just so, flirt my fan, tumble my curls, roll my eyes; attract as large a crowd of men as possible, that he may see my attractions and be drawn, too; and, scanning the crowd urgently for him – now right, now left, now up, now down – see only his friends, who being questioned closely, say, HE'S OFF AT THE WARS!

Off at the wars! How could I have believed he would be here? Have I not always known, in the secret depth of my being, 'twas I that loved, not he, 'twas I that sought, not he, and he would be ever running, not caring?

My eyes scald with hot tears that threaten to spill forth. And I bite my lips almost to bleeding. Please, God, let 'em not come out now.

All the high spirits that animated me to a lightning frazzle attracting the men now suddenly drain from me, leave me motionless, a wraith of myself. And, being found by Mama, I suffer myself to be led off in her claws.

What matter now? What matter? My fate with the cleaver is settled. I must submit and only hope for an early death.

As Mama shepherds me back to the coach, a claw sticking with its prickles in my soft upper arm, she hectors me.

'That will not do, Betty, that will not do! Good girls don't run off from their mamas so! They do not coquette it – and to see what men you were casting your eyes at! Oh, Lord!' She shakes my arm. 'Well, it is no easy thing being *your* guardian; and I warrant 'twill be well to see you married.'

The tears roll down my cheeks. She gives me another shake and harrumphs – in satisfaction, I suppose, believing that I weep for shame.

Behind me clatters a gewgaw gang of fops, yapping at my heels like the King's lap dogs. I had not heard 'em at first, but now their cries are plain. Not only have I wasted my efforts in vain; I've attracted a batch of dull blades and damp sparks, their craniums swelled with the notion of courting me.

'Madam, wait!'

'Madam, hold up!'

'Madam, may I wait upon you presently?'

A mincing, feathered little starveling hands my mama into the coach. With a claw she beckons from within. 'Betty. Come in, now.'

I stare dully at the clamouring mob. The coxcombs press for the honour of handing me in, like hens that quarrel over a succulent bug. How foolish 'tis of men to be drawn in by a few artful looks, a flicker or two of the fan and a calculated pout!

'Lord! What a clamour is here!' I snap. They fall silent.

Suddenly, like a whale parting the waves, or a great galleon sweeping aside the shallops, through the fop ocean there rolls a pomegranate of a man, a cavernous jolly smile below his pointy beard.

And bowing low, like an egg tipped on its side, he sweeps off the great plumed hat and says, 'Madam, I pray you suffer a hero of Sole Bay to pay his devoirs at the shrine of beauty.'

At first I stare on him dully. Then of a sudden a pang stabs my heart: a question makes hope rise to my throat.

Sole Bay. Was that not the battle in which my lord was such a hero?

'Betty. Come.' The claw beckons from within the coach.

'In a moment, Mama.'

I stare on the man as he straightens. His lips quirk, and his eyes shoot me a very particular look.

And is this not the man my lord's friends presented to me?

I bob a demure curtsey at him, hands clasped before me, legs barely dipping. 'Sir.'

'Madam! Madam!' cries the fop that handed my mother in, preening in his long red feathers like a cock of the walk. 'Methinks the sun smiles on us when we have your beaming rays.'

I dart him a look. 'Have a care, sir, lest they burn you up.'

Some of the others titter and elbow him.

'I say, madam,' presses the fat man, 'we wonder to see you here. We had not expected this – *none of us.*'

He puts such a stress on the last phrase, I peer at him. 'Aye, sir. And it took some doing, let me tell you.'

We exchange a long, meaningful look.

'Come in, Betty!' snaps Mama. 'You're not well.'

'Let me hand you in, then, madam.' He extends a gracious beef-steak of an arm.

I'm disappointed. It seems as if he must not be who I think, if he would so easily relinquish me. But then he says, 'You must take the waters, then, madam. They have the cure for all ills – dropsies, headaches (even of the megrim sort), problems of the digestion – and even of the spirits.'

'Aye, well, I know not if they can help *my* complaint.' I fix him with a particular look.

'Madam, what cannot be helped by the waters can oft be aided by a salubrious walk about the countryside. There are many pleasant pathways hereabouts, and I could recommend that you walk in some of them.'

'Oh?' I cock my head. 'Such as what, sir?'

'Oh, the High Rocks, about a mile and a quarter from here.'

'The High Rocks! I have heard of 'em, sir. What think you's the best time for walking?'

'Oh, about three of the clock. The sun's rather high at noon; it burns less at that hour, madam. But, then, too, there's a crevice, where one may take rest and refreshment – if the sun burns too nigh.'

We stare at one another a moment. He slams the door shut.

'Well.' I flirt my fan. 'I am mighty glad, sir, of your kind conversation.'

'And you, madam, live up to your reputation for wit.'

He quirks an eyebrow, sweeps off his hat to bow again.

Mama with a cane knocks the coach roof, and we're off.

She then proceeds to niggle and scold. 'I don't know what gets into you every time we get near the court! You are ever flouncing off and making mouths and behaving like the veriest coquette. It is all I can do to pull a rein on you. I dare swear, it makes me weary! You should be ashamed of yourself.'

I hang my head in pretended shame – but only to conceal the smile trembling at the corners of my lips. 'I'm sorry, Mama.'

'Well, you should be. Lord knows, 'twill be a load off my back to get you married, that you need not be watched any more.'

'Mama,' I say plaintively, 'may we go for a walk this afternoon?'

'A *walk?*' She stares aghast on me. 'When have you ever liked to *walk?*'

'That gentleman mentioned the High Rocks, Mama, and I would see 'em.'

'Well, you know not what you speak of!' She scratches her head. 'They're way out in the country, and a coach cannot even be got near there.'

I pout. 'We *never* see anything of the countryside here! We might as well not have come.'

'I know not what you say! Have we not just come from the Upper Walk? Have you not taken the waters?'

'Aye – but Mama, the country's so beautiful hereabout.'

'*What* country? Chalk downs and a few straggly flowers. Give me the green hills and meadows any day – which God knows why you sought to leave.'

I pout and let a sly tear creep down my cheek. 'I would see the High Rocks, Mama.'

'Well, I'm not going there with you!'

So vexed is she, I wonder whether her conscience tugs at her, to see my tear.

'And you certainly can't go alone,' she adds, her tone defensive.

I look down at the long, slender hands, pink-nailed, that smooth my skirt. 'Yes, Mama,' I say meekly. And I let a few more sobs escape my lips.

'Oh, for God's sake, Betty! Let's have no weeping. I told you I'm not going, and that's final. And your woman – why, she'd be no protection at all. This place is full of dangerous sparks.'

'Can we not find someone to go?' I whimper, eyes still downcast. 'Some man-servant, perhaps?'

'It is not fit you go out attended only by a man-servant.'

I snuffle and pluck my skirt. 'I would see the High Rocks,'

'Oh, for God's sake! Very well, very well. We'll let Lord Hinching-brooke convey you.'

'*Hinchingbrooke?*' I cry.

Then could I bite my tongue off, for it has been all my concern to act mildly and obediently toward this match, and I dare not give myself away now.

I see her eye me suspiciously. To cover my confusion, I add, 'Well, but, I mean – Mama! I stand much amazed you would let me go by myself, with a young gentleman.'

'Well, he seems safe enough. He's to be your husband soon, and – sure, he seems like he has not much gumption.'

So I'm to be delivered unto the cleaver. Well, so dull a blade is he, I'll find some way to divert his edge.

But indeed, I live now upon the very whipped cream of hope. For here I've exhausted my wit to get to Tunbridge to see my lord, who's not here; then exhausted my daring getting to the High Rocks, though I know not what will issue there. And what if I arrive there, take that long walk, and there's no jolly fat man with a message; or what if his message is not what I suspect, and he only seeks to attempt me himself?

But this, I find, is not my only problem; for now, taking coach, I have a cleaver to descend upon me, too.

As he goose-steps grandly, clicking heels, handing me with stiff cold fingers into the coach, he says little – but his eyes are narrowed to tiny flames that make me nervous. Then, sitting harpy-straight on the coach cushions, he sidles over to half an arm's length from me.

I scrunch harder into the white satin of the coach-side, as far from him as I can shove myself, and pretend to admire the countryside.

Birches straggle from rocky cliffs; wild thyme carpets the upland downs, its purple flowers blowing tangy-sweet on the wind. Here, though the earth be hard and barren, thrive blossoms determined to root and grow: the yellow trefoil and the modest pea; the wild-rock rose, its cheek blooming from out a crevice; and all making the air wild with mingled sweets.

All at once the cleaver chops up the space 'twixt us.

As I press myself into the far corner of the coach, he commences a jerky, flat speech in a passionate but firm tone.

'Now, madam. You see we are alone; and through the good graces of our friends have been able to bring about that end which both of us desire – but in the proper way.'

He sidles closer. I wish I were a flea, to compress myself smaller and slip betwixt the cracks.

Jesu! I'd thought the cleaver would offer me no familiarities nor advances. But my impulsive letter to him (writ for my own ends) must have fired up his cold blood.

'If you please, sir,' I say in a small voice, shuddering as I feel his cold side crowd against me. 'I am a maid, and somewhat unacquainted with men.'

'Aye,' he says gruffly. 'Well, that's all to the good. That's what a husband wishes.'

Now, though I shrink from him, his thick arm sidles down across my shoulders to make me cringe. How did I get myself into this coil? How will I get out of it?

That lump of lead across my shoulders makes my flesh cringe.

'My lord, if you please,' I murmur, my face turned away toward the window. 'It is not proper.'

'Aye, 'tis! Were we not put alone, to get acquainted? Are we not contracted?'

'It is not proper,' I squeak, sinking further down in my seat. The lump-of-lead arm comes down after, determined to pursue.

'It *is* proper! If it were not, your mother certainly would not have suffered us to be alone.'

'She said –' My voice is meek and small, my head turned away '– that she knew she could trust you not to make advances.'

'Very *well*!' he snaps gruffly and removes the arm. But still he sits so close to me, I cringe.

'A little further across the coach seat, if you please, my lord.'

'*Very well!*' He moves a fraction of an inch away, so he's almost touching but not quite. 'You'll have a way to go, madam, on your wedding night, if you're so skittish now beforehand.'

'It is not proper,' I say meekly, crunching against the coach wall.

The coach winds now through a forest, close-packed with tree trunks. On a sudden my blood chills, to think what a desolate spot I'm in, with this surprisingly forbidding man.

I turn to look at him, and his eyes gleam with flames of desire. Jesu, I had not thought it possible in him!

I grimace at him. He reaches forward to take my hand, and I shove the coach door open, cock my head, cry gaily as if on a frolic of hide-and-seek, 'Hinchingbrooke! Hinchingbrooke! All cocks hidden!'

And, scarce waiting for the footman's aid, I bounce from the coach. This sudden pretence of hide-and-seek surprises him. He stares at my retreating figure.

The High Rocks are said to be at the edge of this wood. I run panting to whither white daylight streams through the twisted trunks, and break into an open clearing. Far across it are the High Rocks.

A dark speck moves 'twixt the crevice in the rocks. I see it for a moment; then it vanishes within. So! There's my jelly-belly cupid, come as he hinted. So far all's well.

A crunching in the wood behind alerts me, so I frolic back into a thicket, calling, 'Hinchingbrooke! Hinchingbrooke! All cocks hidden!'

I frolic a good while through the wood, till I am certain the tail of this wild comet is fretful and exhausted; then 'tis across the green meadow intervening and past the solitary beech tree, up toward a multitude of jutting high cliffs.

Casting a look behind me, I see my pursuer has at last emerged from the forest, pulling down his neckcloth and looking every instant as if he wondered why he would ride this skittish colt. 'Madam,' he shouts, 'wait up.'

'Yoo-hoo,' I cry, and wave a fan at him across the meadow, 'catch me if you can.'

He lashes himself to a trot; I frolic into a crevice 'twixt two of the looming rocks and race down a gloomy passage, thence into another crevice. Anon I risk peeping out, still from my cave on the ground, and see he has begun to scale the tallest mountain of a rock, over the brow of which he disappears.

Well pleased with myself, I flit about to where Savile has hid himself behind the last long monolith of a cliff.

There before me, like a cupid – round and jolly-cheeked and set up for a Mayday frolic – there, like a moon-bellied son of Venus – is my suddenly dear messenger of love.

I bob a demure curtsey to him. He bows, one leg out stiff before him, one hand sweeping off the great hat.

A hallooing cries over the brow of the rocks above us, like a hound in full cry: 'Halllloooo, Mrs Mallet!'

I giggle wickedly, my fist to my mouth, to prevent a sound issuing forth.

Mr Savile, straightening up, his eyes dancing, says, 'By'r conscience, an echo! Even the disembodied voices follow you, lady!'

Now 'deed I 'most choke on my laughter; and, grinning back at him, say, 'This one keeps company with an even more tedious body, sir. So I advise you, to give me your message, before the two of 'em burst in upon us.'

He looks on me slyly. 'Message? Why, who said I had a message?'

Caught off guard, I feel my face fall. 'Do you not, then? Sooth, why did you draw me forth hither?'

His lips turn up broadly 'neath the small moustache. And his eyes sparkle, the large plumed hat on his head at a rakish angle. 'From whom do you look for a message, then?' he asks gently.

'Why, no one!' I snap, face turned aside, heat suddenly in my cheeks.

'No one? To draw you forth all this way, and in such inconvenient company? No one, with what plotting it must have taken you to arrive here? Or perhaps 'twas the hope of my company, eh?'

I look up, suddenly terrified. Now will I have another to fight off? But I see he only grins gently at me, in a pleasant, chaffing way.

My cheeks flush the more and I stare down. I feel my fingers working at the skirt-folds. 'You play with me, sir,' I accuse softly. 'If you were a gentleman, you'd state your purpose.'

'O-ho! But I am no gentleman; this is why I creep behind your mama's back to plead for a suitor she abhors.'

Now I look up keenly, hope in my eyes, and my hand goes to my throat.

He stares on me as if he would read every hint of my lineaments, and I know I give my feelings away; but, 'deed, I cannot help myself.

At last, because it seems he will not speak until I prod him, I say, 'Pray go on, sir. I – believe the suitor's intentions – are not so disagreeable to *me* as they are to my mother.'

His expression's now as softened as butter. I suffer myself one golden coin of hope.

'Only this, madam, have I to say –' He rests his broad ham of a hand on the hanger hilt. And I feel a twinge, so like a gesture is it to my lord's. 'I have a friend, Lord Rochester, who loves you well. I have watched him these long months as he drowned himself in drink, threw himself into one pleasure after another, sought to divert himself with silly roles and ruses – anything to block out the pain of losing you.'

My hand goes to my lips. 'I – I – believed such a mode of life indicated his utter want of regard for me.'

Savile shakes his head. 'Nay. Nay, 'twas just the opposite.'

'And – you are sure?'

He nods. 'Aye.'

'Then –' I pause a moment, but, having gone so far, determine to give myself wholly away '– why has he not writ me, these months and months? Why has he left me to see my store of hope grow smaller and smaller, 'til 'tis scarce a crumb that could keep a bird alive?'

Savile shakes his head. 'I know not, madam. Except – to answer from a supposition on his character – my lord is very proud and not given to expressing his feelings. And I am sure, would never think of writing, did he have the least suspicion his message would not be kindly answered.'

'When have I given him such a suspicion?'

Savile hesitates, then says, 'We got word at court, madam, last summer, that you had given many kind persuasions to the emissary of the Lord John Butler.'

'*That* little man!' I burst out indignantly. 'Why, I but sought to see in a letter my Lord Butler writ of me. Anyone of vanity would have done so, to gain the compliments on herself. Why, what said he?'

'That, madam, you had a deep affection for the Lord John.'

'Why, so I do. But I'd not wish to *marry* him!'

Savile's eyes glaze as if he's deep in thought. 'So,' he mutters. Suddenly he turns to me. 'Madam, I have a verse the Lord Rochester writ of you. Shall I show it you?'

''Deed, yes!' I cry. Then I cast my eyes down, twitch my skirt modestly. 'That is – I should be much obliged, sir.'

He grins, then fumbles through his pockets. 'Ah, here we are.' He produces a rolled length of paper, hands it to me.

With trembling fingers I open it, see not that familiar crabbed scrawl but a rounded copperplate.

'This is not his hand.' I turn about, lips parted.

'Nay, 'tis mine. I made a copy of the verse. It is one that has been circulated –'

'He did not tell you to give it me, then.'

'No, you would be the last person he'd have see it, madam, with his pride.'

My eyes eagerly scan the page. I step closer to the front of the crevice, where the soft golden rays of afternoon peep in, and I turn my back to my round-bellied cupid.

'Hallllooo, Mrs Mallet!' reverberates the voice along the brow of the cliff above, and I read:

Could I but make my wishes insolent
And force some image of a false content!
But they, like me, bashful and humble grown,
Hover at a distance about beauty's throne;
There worship and admire, and then they die,
Daring no more lay hold of her than I.

Something grips the pit of my stomach. I turn, lips parted, to eye Mr Savile. 'Are you sure, sir, this was writ for me?'

'Aye, madam.'

'Did he say so?'

'No need. Those closest to him knew.'

'But if he said not –' I make a stop, suddenly aware that Mr Savile has taken this charge totally upon himself, without any commission from my lord to say what he does; and possibly, all that he surmises is mere supposition. Lips parted, I continue, 'Sir, if you should guess wrongly in all this –' I do not finish, the possibility being too terrible to consider.

'No such possibility, madam. Rest assured.'

'But has he said aught of love for me?'

Savile cocks his head, the great hat on top like a huge saucer. 'Madam. You know him not well, if you believe he would go about making confessions of love, especially love that appears unreturned.'

'What about this – Anne Temple? Loves he not her?'

Savile guffaws. '*That* empty-headed little poppet! Now, whoever told you that?'

'Why, everyone in the country spoke of it! How he pursued her, how respectful he was.'

Savile laughs heartily, both hands grasping his huge egg of a belly. 'Ho, that's a good one! Him in love with Anne Temple? Why, he but toyed with her, diverting himself with silly stratagems to raise his reputation by getting her to yield. And then cared so little for her, once he brought her to complying, he stayed not about to make the assignation to enjoy her, but was off to war.'

'Off to war! And why?'

Savile gives me a level look. 'Because, madam – so it was told me by a mutual friend of ours – the Lord John Butler paid a call on him, carrying hints of your love; and our friend dropped every affair he had then in pursuit and took an immediate commission with the Navy, to assay once again to get the gold to please your guardians.'

My heart swells into my throat. Aye, have I not felt his love whenever he's been around? The only time I've doubted his feelings, it seems, is when he's been away. Then, when I seem to feel him low in spirits, I tell myself it must be over want of cash or the King's favour.

'Oh, Mr Savile!' I fly at him as if to embrace him – then suddenly blush.

He laughs genially, reaches forth a stubby hand and squeezes my upper arm. 'Aye, little lady. Fly at me if you wish. Right glad am I to see your affections – and will not misinterpret them.'

The tears start from my eyes, and I 'most crumple the sheet of paper in my hand. 'Thank you,' I whisper.

'But are you not going to read the rest of the verse?'

'Oh, yes!'

I scan it eagerly; and all the while, the hound bays above: 'Halll-loooo, Mrs Mallet! I say, come forth now!'

And how pertinent then is the next part of the verse:

Reason to worth bears a submissive spirit,
But fools can be familiar with merit.
Who but that blundering blockhead Phaeton
Could e'er have thought to drive about the sun?
Just such another durst make love to you
Whom not ambition led, but dullness drew.

Now I cannot but laugh; for e'en now, Phaeton blunders about, near the sun. The court's keenest satirist further anatomizes the cleaver that would hack a path to me:

No amorous thought could his dull heart incline,
But he would have a passion, for 'twas fine!
That, a new suit, and what he next must say
Runs in his idle head the livelong day.

'Tis true: the cleaver sits on its steel end, looking as if 'twould cut a joint but knows not how; it halloos above me, repeating, like Frances' parrot with its ten words of English: 'Mrs Mallet! Mrs Mallet!'

The verse continues despairing, in a tone to wrench my heart,

Hard-hearted saint,
Since 'tis your will to be
So unrelenting pitiless to me,
Regardless of a love so many years
Preserved 'twixt lingering hopes and awful fears
(Such fears in lovers' breasts high value claims,
And such, expiring martyrs feel in flames;
My hopes yourself contrived, with cruel care,
Through gentle smiles to lead me to despair),
'Tis some relief, in my extreme distress,
My rival is below your power to bless.

I sink trembling against the side of the rock; the clammy coolness is hard and rough against my warm arm.

Then another thought strikes me.

'Mr Savile,' I say suddenly, turning to him, 'how shall I rid myself of this cleaver that seeks to butcher me on the marriage block?'

He frowns. 'I know not, lady. How came you so close to being contracted to him anyway?'

''Twas the only way I could figure to put myself in my lord's vicinity. I moved this rock, then another, to push at my goal; and now, it seems I've pushed myself into a corner, and all the rocks about me – and know not quite how to get out of it. Though get out of it –' My voice is firm '– I shall! Now that I know he loves me, rest assured I'll marry no one else.'

He smiles gently.

'Hallooo, Mrs, Mallet!'

'But how shall I rid myself of *him*?' I roll eyes cleaverward.

Savile winks. 'Ne'er fear, lady. Play along with me.'

He takes my hand in his pudgy fingers, and we step forward, from the crevice – out of the dark and into the bright sunshine.

He holding my hand in his, we both stare upward at the brow of the rock, where the goosy cleaver stalks, some forty feet above, sweating and looking grim. Now he looks down aghast on us.

'What ho, there, my lord!' cries Savile cheerfully. 'Taking a day's outing, are you? Well, there's nothing like a walk in the fresh air, I always say.'

'Sir, who are you?' he squawks, like a gander caught by the webbed toe. 'With my affianced bride!'

'Why, nobody at all, air. Only a gallant that haunts about the rocks. She's your affianced bride, eh? I must say, I congratulate you on your taste.'

Enraged, the cold hulk clambers down the side of the rock, his feet slipping, his fingers grasping for holds and grabbing now a twig, now an out-pushed rock ledge.

'Well, this is a fine how-do!' he squawks, jumping down to the ground at last, several pebbles raining on his solemn head. 'So you brought me out here to meet your gallant, did you?'

I glance demurely on Savile, we still holding fingertips. Then I look down again, as if bashful. ''Deed, my lord, I know not what you mean. I simply happened to find this gentleman in the walks here – and he has a very pleasant wit.'

'Aye, so we can see! Well, come along, madam.' He huffs out his goosy chest, frowns 'neath his severe long beak. 'I must say, this looks not well in a future bride of mine; not well at all.'

Still holding Savile's fingertips, I look down and lower my lashes. 'Indeed, my lord, I know not what you mean. 'Twere hard if a lady cannot simply entertain a little pleasant conversation of an afternoon.'

'Aye, aye,' agrees Savile, still grasping my fingertips. ''Tis the way of the world, my lord. If you're to be married, you must learn that lovely, fashionable ladies are skittish horses; they balk at the curb and bit.'

'Come along, then, madam!'

I am astonished to see this cleaver step forward, a threatening look on his face. He grabs my arm, pulls me to him roughly, dislodges Savile with such violence that I gasp. I struggle and seek to pull away, but still his cold fingers grip my arm so hard it hurts.

Savile's eyebrows draw together and he whips out his sword, smiles pleasantly enough but says, with an edge in his voice, 'Have a care, sir, how you handle a lady in my presence. I've done a bit of battle with the Dutch, and I know how to use a blade to defend a lady's honour.'

Glaring, the cleaver steps backward and releases my arm, which I hold and rub. That one so cold should suddenly be so hot – and so rough, too! I shudder to think what a fate I'd meet in his nuptial bed.

But that will never be – never!

But now will there be swordplay over me?

No: the cleaver is too dull a blade for battle. He looks down, shifty-eyed, and mutters, 'I but claim my wife, sir. There's no need for violence.'

Coolly Savile says, 'There *is* a need for violence, sir, whenever I see a lady abused, wife or no; and I hear she's no wife of yours yet – nor may be.'

The menace in his tone causes the goose-neck to crane up. He stares first at Mr Savile, then at me. 'Madam!' he squawks, flutter-toned. 'Are you what you appear to be?'

I glare, still rubbing my arm. 'I'm chaste, sir, if that's what you mean. Indeed, there's only one of us, I think, that's not what he appears to be.'

Both of us glare cold hatred on one another.

'I think, madam, this is not overly a compliment to your modesty, that you shrink from the arms of him who's to be your husband yet are entreating most pleasantly this plumed and perfumed gallant here!'

'I think, sir, you have a most filthy mind, to think aught was going on. 'Deed, I'm surprised to find it keeps company with so stiff and rigid an exterior.'

'Madam, the liberty and vanity of your carriage displease me,' he orates pompously, his beak in the air.

'Sir, so much about you displeases *me*, I were hard pressed to recite all the particulars!'

'Well, madam.' He bows stiffly, clicking heels. 'Though you are so cold to me, I see that you are hot enough for someone else.'

'Indeed I am! And you might as well know now, sir, I'll never marry you: for I have an affection for another.'

'And I was on the verge of saying,' he lashes back, 'I'll never marry *you*! So vain, so frivolous, so coquettish, so light a female, so cold with your affianced husband and so warm with the first plumed scoundrel you see!'

'Then we are agreed at last, sir!'

He bows stiffly, clicks heels together. 'Madam – I leave you, to find an escort back with your gallant.'

He steps goose-legged and straight-backed through the meadow, as if he picked his way amidst cow turds.

I collapse laughing into the friendly Savile's arms. Then on a sudden I sober, the precious verse still clutched in my hand through all this travail.

'Oh, Jesu! What will he say when he returns to Tunbridge? Oh, dear! What a coil will I be in with Mama now!'

'Madam, have no fear. I'll escort you back; and 'twixt us we will contrive such a tale as will put him in the wrong. We'll put a face on it that you were roughly treated and frighted.'

'Aye.' I giggle wickedly. 'Let me tear a few laces and fill my cheeks with tears.'

He offers me his arm. 'Madam, allow me to say that I think you and the Lord Rochester are well suited.'

2

'The Liberty And Vanity Of Her Carriage'
4 August 1666

The business between my Lord Hinchingbrooke and Mrs Mallet is quite broke off, he attending her at Tunbridge, and she declaring her affections to be settled – and he not being fully pleased with the vanity and liberty of her carriage.

—Samuel Pepys, *Diary*

'Oh, God! Oh, God!' Mama stalks about, flutters her hands, squawks like a hen that has laid a square egg. 'I knew something bad would come of this. Betty, why did you insist on having him? Why could you not back me up in holding out for the Lord John Butler's suit?'

I stare down at the floor, my hands twisting, and e'en manage to draw forth a chaste tear. 'Oh, Mama, indeed you are in the right! Beshrew me, if ever I should think of not heeding your advice again.'

Beside me stands Savile, shaking his head sombrely; and so well does the devil read my mama's humour, he clucks, 'Well, madam. I am much surprised, you should suffer a beautiful and innocent young lady such as this out alone with a man of such questionable character.'

Mama's face contorts in agony. 'Oh, sir, it is not my usual practice, I assure you! I had thought him safe.'

I look down, my lips trembling, and with a histrionic gesture, flicker my long-fingered hand over the torn laces at the top of my bosom as if I sought to pull 'em up modestly.

'I am much surprised, madam: that is all I can say.' Savile shakes his head.

'But I had thought – him being her future husband – and of so cold and stolid a character –' Mama stops in confusion. 'Oh, Betty, Betty.' She kneels before me, clasps my hands in hers, till, 'deed, a pang of guilt stabs me – but not enough to repent and tell truth.

She looks up earnestly into my face though I keep staring down, trying to conceal my expression, so near am I to laughter. 'This is twice some man has inveigled to get you alone, stole you off from under my very nose – though Lord knows how you could be more closely watched.'

She forgets here, 'twas she petitioned the cleaver to come a-chopping of an afternoon beside me. But 'tis well. Savile and I need do very little on the plot, she does so much of it herself.

Savile shakes his head gravely, his hand on his hanger hilt. 'Madam, you've such a treasure there, I have small wonder so many gallants seek to possess it.'

She squeezes my hands till they 'most hurt. 'Betty, dear, are you well? Did he hurt you?'

I shake my head, looking down. 'No, Mama. This gentleman prevented him.'

'Thank God for that!' Still holding my hands, still kneeling, she looks solemnly over at Savile. 'Sir, I am much obliged to you.'

He shrugs, flourishes an ample hand. 'I were very happy to be there, madam. Fortunately, I always walk about the High Rocks at that time of the afternoon.'

She nods innocently. 'Yes, that's so. We heard you speak of it.'

Poor Mama! Her brain not being able to put cause to effect: not able to see, he only said so in order to draw me thither; and his figure portends as little of walking as my satin shoes might.

Still kneeling before me, still squeezing my hands, her face down and peering up to catch my expression, she gives my hands a shake. 'Betty, Betty, look me in the face that I may see you're well.'

I raise my head and make shift to smile through my tears.

'She's well, madam, I assure you. But I hope –' Savile lets his eyebrows come together in a frown '– I hope that you are not going to give her in marriage to such a ruffian as that.'

My mother bites her lips and, releasing my hands, stands up. Then she crosses her arms over her skinny ribcage and, pacing two steps to the right, stares off in thought.

'I have no wish to, but – Mr Savile, the contract's signed. I know not how to get out of it.'

'*Signed?*' Savile's mouth opens.

She nods. She turns to him. 'I never had any wish for this match for my daughter, sir. But I had not much voice in it. Everyone –' She gives me a steely look '– conspired against me, it seems.'

I blush and look down.

'What, this lady, too?' Savile's tone is incredulous.

'Yes, though the Lord knows why! She even writ him a letter, begging him to carry her off. Bewixt her manoeuvring and the stepped-up negotiations that resulted 'twixt his friends and my father, an offer was finally made for her, that my father and husband liked so well, they consented.'

Savile cocks an eye on me. 'Madam, I am much surprised you should move to marry a man I saw you shrinking from in such distaste.'

I look down, twitch my skirt. 'I – I suppose I know not my own mind, sir. I – had thought only that I wished to be married, and my guardians took such a long time of it, I – seized on the nearest fool and tried to push him. For –' I look up innocently at Savile '– I wish to be a fashionable lady, sir, and be at court and dance at the balls and see the plays; and Mama has always told me, a woman can learn to love her husband, no matter who he is.'

So innocently do I cant the proper text for daughters, Mama looks on me fondly. Savile plays his part as if he believed every word I uttered and shakes his head. 'Madam, you are very innocent, to suppose that all men can be so much alike.'

'Aye,' says Mama, arms still crossed about her skinny rib cage, 'that has always been her downfall. She knows not how innocent she is, and repeatedly gets herself in a deal of trouble; for she knows not the way of the world and yet knows not that she know it not; and so high are her spirits, so innocently wild and fetching her attractions, she throws 'em out on a lark, and then is much amazed she has the fish biting on her lure – and knows not then how to handle the dangerous situations she gets herself into. I shudder to think what 'twould be like if she were ever let loose, without me always to pull her out of the spots she gets herself into.'

Savile bows cordially, one hand still on the hanger hilt, one leg out before him. 'Madam, rest assured, her innocent sweetness will always find some protector.'

'Well, I wish I could believe *that*!'

On a sudden I brood on this latest in the conversation. For the next twist in the plot should be not only to unload my baggage of the cleaver, but to get to court; and with Mama so firm set against letting me about alone, how is that to be?

Casting my eyes down, twitching my skirt, I say meekly, 'Mama, how shall we ever get rid of my Lord Hinchingbrooke now?'

'I know not, I know not!' she snaps and paces the floor. 'By God, I've a mind to let you get out of it yourself, since you got into it!'

I snuffle, still looking down. ''Deed, I deserve no better.'

Savile shakes his head, crosses his arms over his large belly. 'I should not like, madam, to see so delicate and innocent a young girl as that

341

brought to a nuptial bed with the cold-hearted brute I saw mishandling her. She'd get rough treatment, sure.'

Mama shudders at this hint, clenches her arms tighter across her rib cage.

'And this is nothing to say how cruel his treatment might be in other ways. Why, though I but sought to rescue her, he fell upon me jealously with accusations that I were the lady's gallant – and drew her off so roughly, he hurt her arm. What such a one as that would be, given authority over her as a husband, I dread to think. He had about him the look, madam, of a gaoler.'

'Oh, God, oh, God!' Mama paces the floor; and, having pulled a handkerchief from her bosom, begins to rend it. 'What shall we do?' She whirls about. 'Sir, you see we are two women alone here. Would you advise us?'

'Madam, I'll try. I think your best course now would be to throw yourself upon His Majesty's mercy.'

'His Majesty?' Mother's mouth quirks, and her brows knit together.

'Aye. No one would persist in a suit His Majesty disliked. Especially milord Sandwich's family, who are in much need of royal favour now.'

'That's true, that's true,' she muses.

'Remember, madam: the Lord Sandwich is now out of favour, over the business of breaking bulk on the prize ships. And, I'm sure, seeks some means to get out of his ambassadorship to Spain and back with the fleet. Would he be likely to anger His Majesty, or suffer his wife and son to do so?'

'No, no,' she muses. She turns to him, her face sunny with smiles. 'Sir, what a wit you have! How glad I am we came upon you!'

'Tis all I can do now to stifle a laugh: for, though Mama sees his wit, she apparently thinks not what set of friends it would likely keep company with: that dear gang of rogues for whom I have such an affection. She continues, 'How should we address His Majesty, sir?'

'Madam, I have some friends that know him. And I'd be glad to speak a word or two.'

'Oh, would you?' She looks so pitifully happy that my heart cringes in guilt to see her: hands clasped together and twisted handkerchief hanging out betwixt.

''Twould be well if you writ also, madam: as evidence that I take not some impertinent commission upon myself.'

'Why, I can write, and you can carry the message!' she exclaims.

'Mama,' I say, my lips pouting, 'I feel so unworthy of you. You always have my best interests at heart, and I'm so naughty.'

She smiles benevolently, walks over to grasp my shoulders. 'There,

there, Betty. You're young.' She kisses the top of my head. 'But Mama knows what's best for you, and she'll help.'

''Deed I do not deserve it, Mama. I thank you from the bottom of my heart.' My voice squeaks babyishly.

She squeezes my shoulders in her two claws.

'It may be,' says Savile in that booming voice, 'we need not even manoeuvre too far with His Majesty. For this cold suitor of hers grew so hot seeing another man come upon her, that he orated his disinclination to have her at all.'

'Well, there's something there,' says Mama. 'But I daresay, he may well alter his opinion, once he gets back to his lodgings. That mother of his is always nosing into his business. And I daresay she'll put the advantages of the match to him again.'

At this diatribe against a bossy mama, it is all I can do not to burst out laughing. I bite my lips.

'And he is so led by her, he has so little wit of his own, she might reconvince him. For, sure, they've not nearly so much of an estate as Betty, and they're quite anxious to secure her.'

'Well, ne'er fear, madam. We'll outwit 'em.'

Mama, sweeping back skirts, settles herself on the stick-chair before the desk to write out the letter to His Majesty.

I stand with my eyes meekly on the floor, not daring to meet Savile's gaze lest I burst out laughing or roll my eyes and Mama suspect the frolic.

'There, sir!' Mama turns about, smiling. 'I said to His Majesty, I should be much obliged if he should help to break this contract with the Lord Hinchingbrooke; for we have found him to be other than we supposed; and I being a woman alone, am wanting advice and would appreciate some from him.'

Savile clears his throat, looks thoughtfully at the ceiling.

'Well, is there something I've left out, sir?'

'Well, madam, I was only thinking, you might add a part that you should be much grateful to His Majesty, if he could suggest some means to get your daughter married with as much dispatch as possible to a suitable young man.'

Her brow furrows, and her lips purse.

Savile continues quickly, 'For it seems, madam, that you are much oppressed by the men in your family. And if they've tried to force such a husband as this on your little one, it may be they will do so again – and perhaps at some time when you have not the ammunition to do battle with them again, as you do with my humble aid.'

'Why, that's so.' She ponders, lips parted.

'But, madam, if you seek His Majesty's help, it seems you have such cannon as your menfolk must succumb to.'

'Yes, yes,' she muses. 'Why, I remember, sir –' She jerks her head about to look on him '– I remember, when they would have pushed this man on Betty, that I knew better than that she should really like it: how I tried to plead the Lord John Butler's cause, and they would hear nothing of it, for I was a mere woman.'

'Just so, madam.' Savile nods. 'It is the way of the world, I am afraid. Women must look to protectors. And so I advise you: why not seek out the first man in the realm?'

'But would he help me, I wonder?'

Savile nods. 'I think he would, if your cause were made plain to him. He has a tender heart. And – I will see what I can do to have my friends work upon it.'

Mama looks sombrely upon him. 'Sir, I know not how to thank you for your goodness toward me.'

Poor Mama! How easily she is played upon; how little she sees what a net closes about her! Savile shrugs, looks down modestly. 'I do very little, madam.'

'Well, *I* think it very much.' Mama rolls up the letter, pours the wax on it and stamps it with her seal-ring. 'Here you are then, sir.' Turning about in her chair, she holds out the scroll. 'I'd be much obliged if you could get this to His Majesty as soon as possible. And tell him that I put myself in his hands, for whatever course he shall suggest.'

Savile bows low.

3

'A Sprightly Mind'
4 August – 1 September 1666

Her lively looks a sprightly mind disclose,
Quick as her eyes, and as unfixed as those:
Favours to none, to all she smiles extends:
Oft she rejects, but never once offends.
                    —Alexander Pope, *The Rape of the Lock*

Well, here is such drama as would have diverted an hundred naughty
and frolicsome maids. For barely has Mama bid adieu to her melon-
bellied Saviour – barely has the curtain rung down on the tragic-
pastoral of *Innocence in Bondage* – than we have the after-piece to the
play, an Italian farce of *Mamas Furens*.

A thunderous knock presents us with Lady Sandwich, all puffed hair
and consternation.

'Lady Warre, I must say, I am most severely distressed!'

So now I know where the goose got his grave honkings. 'I am most
displeased' – 'I am most distressed' – as if their reaction lays upon us
an obligation to care about it.

Mama regards her blandly. 'Come in, my lady. So are we. It is right
kind of you to call with your apologies.'

'Apologies? Your sly baggage of a daughter insulted upon my poor
shy son!'

'Poor shy son? He almost ripped my daughter to pieces! Cast an eye
on her laces, if you please.'

She does – dubiously. 'He would not do a thing like that.'

'No, not before his mama! But he did it; that's plain.'

The Lady Sandwich regards me with a mother goose's sharp eye.
'Well, that's yet to be proven.'

Mama draws herself up threateningly, crosses her broomstick arms
o'er her rib cage. 'Have a care, madam, how you insinuate upon the
virtue of my daughter. That is not the issue here.'

'Isn't it? I think it the very issue!' The Mother Goose's finger waves in Mama's face. 'Did she not inveigle my son into taking her off to tryst with her gallant?'

'Her gallant?' Mama's eyes widen; then she laughs harshly. 'A man she met but this afternoon and exchanged some three or four polite words with? Why, that's absurd! He but happened to be walking about the rocks – and a good thing he was, too.'

'And a very suspicious thing, wouldn't you say? Especially considering his reputation?' The Mother Goose's eyes narrow like slits on a castle wall.

'*What* reputation?'

Oh, Jesu. Now Mama will find out whose friend he is.

'Why, Unton, surely you must know! He's a lewd fellow: the Duchess of York has been his whore. But yet he's been given a place about the Duke, to put an agreeable face on their meetings.'

'I care not who's been his whore!' Mama waves her hand grandly. 'That's his business. Tis plain, he's a gentleman respects innocence – as your son does not.'

To think of Mama defending adultery! But then, her task now is to confound the goose family, not maintain her usual antique opinions.

Mother Goose pounces upon the bug of this insinuation about her hatchling. '*My son* is the gravest and most proper young man to show his face at court, that's certain! And I'm surprised to hear your free speech, Unton Warre, indeed I am. Have you not told me a thousand times you shared my disgust with the lewdness of this age? But then, your candidate for her hand is no better than he should be.'

'*My candidate?*' Mother opens her mouth like a frog catching dragonflies.

'If you think the Lord John Butler is perfectly chaste, you're mistaken.'

This accusation, I would think, would only serve to recommend him as a husband. Why race a spirited horse with a jockey that's never ridden?

Mama's humour does not permit her to think of such a retort: she only says, 'Leave the Lord John out of this! He's not at issue here. But perhaps he should be: for the only reason she's not married to him today is his high and noble sentiments, his niceness about appearing to force her. We pass over the obvious contrast, here, to one who appeared such a bully when –'

'I will not stand here to hear my son insulted!'

'Well, you see where the door is,' offers Mother blandly.

'Your daughter concerted beforehand for a meeting with her gallant, then made my son the booby!'

Indeed, that took no making save his own.

'Her gallant!' Mama laughs harshly. 'Jemima Sandwich! Agreeable gentleman though he is, Betty can do better than *that*.'

Indeed, she knows not how true she speaks.

'She certainly can, if she persists in wantoning with her eyes and gestures as she does! I must say, she has never looked modest to *me*.'

Savagely Mama snarls, 'She has natural beauty and grace, if *that* is what you mean! Indeed, her innocence appears in the very arts she uses – for she never sees the effects of what she doesa till some ruffian seizes her!'

'Well, such "seizings" occur remarkably often, if you ask me!'

Why do people say 'if you ask me' when 'tis the last thing their adversaries would do?

The goosy honks continue: 'I think it admirable, for all you try to watch her so closely, these mysterious capturings and seizings will occur – and she look so innocent! But at least we have the evidence of *one* letter, to show how innocent she is!'

'That is beside the point –'

'I think it is not. I think you have an artful baggage on your hands there, the veriest coquette; and if she is still chaste –'

'If!'

''Tis only that you have locked her up so close, or she has not met the properest bargain yet to make her whore.'

Mama sputters, but it will never be given to know what she would have replied. For another knock sounds on the door.

'Jesu!' cries Mama, incensed. 'What do people think we keep here, a shop? Betty, see who 'tis' – for no servants are in evidence, being sneaked off to enjoy the day.

I bob a curtsey and flounce across the sitting room; and as I throw open the door, the mamas still collide in the centre of the chamber like elephants in a rutting fit.

'Don't think you've heard the last of this, Unton Warre! We'll appeal to His Majesty.'

I stare up at the second-tallest gentleman I've ever seen, one hand with its long, swarthy, slender fingers on the door: his limbs equally long and slender like my lord's and his periwig dark and negligently curled, but his face long and swarthy and lined with age and his dark brown eyes alight with cynical mischief.

'Well, who is it?' snaps Mama, scratching her head. 'Have him state his business or begone.'

I make a shift to squeak out a question to him; and, this failing, turn about to cast pleading eyes on Mama and croak: 'Oh, Mama –'

'Well, what is it, girl? Don't stand there gaping!'

But I cannot help myself. All I have wit to do is sink to a very low curtsey, holding out my skirts, bowing my head.

'Madam,' booms his low, hearty voice from the hall, 'it is Mr William Jackson. I'd be very pleased if you'd grant me entry. I believe I can help you.'

'Well, then, come in! Betty, why don't you ask him in? Why do you – oh, my God.'

For Mr Jackson has sauntered into full view now. As he stands in the room, eyes dancing and lips curved toward the long age creases on either side of his nose, the maternal combatants follow my posture (their quarrel forgotten) so we look like three collapsed gowns on a seamstress's floor.

'Come, now, ladies,' he says in that pleasant, merry voice. 'This is no way to treat humble Mr Jackson.'

His fingers are long and limber and hot as they twine through mine to raise me.

I stare up at him, and he grasps my hand hard, then squeezes it afore he releases me, his eyes trained so intently on me I grow hot in the cheeks and look down.

The *mamas furens* have arisen from their old joints, too.

'Your Majesty,' wails my mother, 'why did you not have yourself announced properly, so we could have known you?'

'Because, madam, His Majesty would have inspired such a scene as this one. It is my humour to play plain Mr Jackson today while I am on holiday.'

He grins impudently on me, with an expression so like my lord's, I pout, head cocked and lower lip thrust out; then I toss my curls and flash a wicked smile, make my eyes sparkle and dance.

Mama frowns on me (levity being, according to her antique code, improper carriage toward a king) and complains:

'I but thought you were sent by Mr Savile! I but thought you a friend of the King's.'

'I try to be, madam. And though I sometimes behave against his better judgment, no one is closer to Charles Stuart than I.'

This sort of fooling is so very like my lord's discourse, I burst into a delighted run of laughter, pealing up and down my voice scale from low throatiness to a high squeak. Mr Jackson treats me to a mock bow, a nod of the head – then a wink – a gesture so like my lord's, I feel my face grow soft as a pease-pottage with longing.

Mama frowns on me so hard now, one would think I were two years of age with my hand in the sugar bowl. 'Betty, leave us.'

I pout on His Majesty like a little girl silently pleading with her papa. 'Madam, let her stay,' he says. 'What we discuss concerns her nearly.'

Mama curtseys low, skirts spread, head down (no doubt to conceal her chagrin: for she's ever sending me off when arguments or negotiations grow interesting).

'I have heard there has been a disagreement between this young lady and her contracted husband.'

'Your Majesty,' Mother Goose begins, but he holds up a brown, twiggy hand to silence her. 'The particulars do not interest me. Suffice it to say, I assume the contract is void.'

'Your Majesty,' flutters Mother Goose, curtseying three times rapidly like a bowing mandarin, 'they have put their hands to a seal, pledging all manner of things.'

'Come now, madam,' says the King. 'We'll find a way to make it worth your while, we promise you.'

She bites her lip.

'I promise you,' the King says firmly.

Still she makes no reply, for the King's great on promising yet slow on delivering.

'Lady Warre,' His Majesty then says in a brisk tone (she curtseys), 'I have considered what to do about the last part of your appeal.'

'The last part, sire?' Mama looks on him quizzically.

'About the finding out a proper husband for your daughter; and I have considered, the best way's to offer her a place at court.'

My heart leaps to my throat and stands in my joyous eyes. Mama turns paler than a fish in Billingsgate Market.

'I – thank Your Majesty –' she gasps, as if her gills swallowed the alien and poisonous air '– but – but – I think we will take her back to Somerset – if Your Majesty please.'

The King, his voice pleasant but his mouth in a firm line and eyes hard with warning, replies, 'It does *not* please me, madam.'

Mama is in despair, knows not what to say. She clasps and unclasps her hands like Lady Macbeth with the dread spot when she sees where her own contrivance has led her.

Now, though good girls are to be seen and not heard when their characters are being itemized and futures being settled, I cannot resist putting an oar into the turbulent waters. 'Mama, let me go to court! I'll be good, I'll be careful – I promise you!'

I throw myself to her feet and clasp her hands in entreaty, my eyes pleading upward in a most becoming tragical gesture.

She shakes off my hand and mutters, in clipped tones, 'Betty, I'm ashamed of you. Get to your feet at once, and leave us.'

Still on my knees, I turn to His Majesty. My voice as sweet-little-girlish as I can make it, I force a tear into my eye and lift my delicate white hands. I have practised gestures oft enough in the glass to know how appealing I can look, especially when I thrust out my lip and toss my curls this way.

'Your Majesty, I beg you to intercede for me.'

He strides the two spaces betwixt us and lifts me up by the fingers. His hand, hot and moist, clasps mine so hard that his rings cut ino it, but I restrain myself from wincing. His Majesty looks on me intensely, as if to say, *Ne'er fear, little lady: I'll help you and my young friend.*

He then raises me up, stares a few instants more into my face, which I make as pleading as I know how, and releases my hand, to say to Mama: 'I will command you if I must, madam, but I would prefer to leave the matter an invitation.'

Mama wrings her hands in anguish. 'Your Majesty, she is very young and innocent.'

'I will take her under my especial protection.'

This promise only makes my mama wring her hands the more. 'Your Majesty, she – has coquettish graces that are but natural to her. Then she marvels at their results and knows not how to handle herself – I beg Your Majesty not to subject her to the manners of the court! They would fright her, certain.'

The King looks on me, then back on Mama. 'She seems not very frighted, madam. And I have said I'll make her my special concern.'

Mama bites her lips. My eyes dance and sparkle with the thrill of knowing I'm so close to my lord at last and we have such a powerful ally.

'I thank Your Majesty,' I murmur.

We exchange a conspiratorial look.

'Well, I see which way the wind blows!' says Mother Goose curtly. She scissors her gloves hard 'twixt her fingers, in a brisk gesture for leaving.

'We will expect your daughter at court within the next few weeks, then, madam,' says the King.

'Well – oh, I don't know, Your Majesty! – I must write to my husband and father.'

'Good,' says the King genially. 'I will write to them as well, to lay out my commands.'

I grin wickedly at this suddenly regal Mr Jackson. 'Your Majesty plays himself now.'

'It is sometimes to my advantage to do so.'

I look with pert demureness on his cynical smile.

'Tis then a contest to see whether Mr Jackson or Mother Goose can take an imperial leave first.

But turning about near the door, as if with an afterthought, my tall and lean saviour says, 'I presume you come to the ball on Mount Ephraim tonight, Lady Warre.'

Mother's eyes are two wary flames. She hems, haws (it being her usual concern to keep me on the dull inside) and at last says, shifting her gaze to the floor: 'I had not thought much on it, Your Majesty. I'm a-weary – and – 'tis well above a mile away.'

'I will send my coach for you, then,' he says pleasantly. 'About seven of the clock.'

Mama curtseys low, her skirts swept out on the floor and her head down.

'Oh, hurrah! The ball!' I clap my hands in glee, for I've wheedled her on this subject afore and got no more than a 'We'll see' – and every daughter knows what *that* means.

And so I get to see Mount Ephraim after all, where the newest and most fashionable lodging-houses perch on a high seat about a half mile from the wells: where the Castle tavern and bowling green are and the assembly room and coffee houses, as well as the many rambling structures, gabled and scattered amid the trees, where are lodged the King and Queen and Prince Rupert. For, we arriving in Tunbridge so late after the court, were able to find rooms only in antique Rusthall (a mile from the wells); and the goose family nested in Southborough (two and a half miles distant and equally antique).

I am in Mama's ill graces the rest of the day. She speaks little to me, but to say I have behaved badly and she is ashamed: that my airs before the King were shocking and I go about briskly digging the hole that will swallow me up.

But she conveys me to the ball nonetheless (in the royal coach, my dears!); and I frolic there with gay abandon, where torches flare in the darkening sky, whipping to the breath of the summer winds; and I with more partners than anyone could have wit to dispose of, even all my dear one's friends such as Sir Charles Sedley, my Lord Buckhurst, and the good Mr Savile, who winks on me so drolly I burst out laughing as we hop and skip to the measure, our fingers curled together.

Then the music makes a sudden stop, and the company bows. The King appears, leading on his arm the poor Queen, with whom he leads off the courante; and a bransle following which he dances with the Lady Castlemaine, and I am thrilled to be presented with the arm of that most handsome of Stuarts, Prince Rupert.

The Prince has been a secret romantic hero of mine since I was nourished on girlhood tales of his mother's tragical flight from Bohemia, having reigned there only a winter, and his family's exile in Vienna and the Netherlands; then the Prince's confinement as a prisoner of war (where his gaoler's daughter very suitably fell in love with him) and his gallant heroism in the great Civil Wars of the last age, where he was the finest general to help out his uncle, the late martyred King.

'Tis amazing. I know the Prince is of middle age, older e'en than His Majesty, whom I deem an old man; but His Highness appears so the dashing hero to me, I smile happily up into his swarthy oval face with the aquiline nose and believe him as handsome (almost!) as my lord. The soft guttural burr of his speech, with its traces of his German beginnings, makes him seem only more romantic.

I think he might e'en have bid for my hand for another dance. But as the music fades, I am astonished to see the King lead the Lady Castlemaine back to the crowd, past where Frances bats her eyelashes at him, and wheel back to lope up to us and bow. 'If you please, cousin.'

The Prince makes a grave leg and replies, in that low, gutteral, charming tone, 'Anything Your Majesty pleases is pleasing to me.'

I blush from my bosom up and curtsey low. As the King raises me with his fingertips, I cast a glance across the crowd at Mama, who looks nigh to a falling-fit and flutters attendance on herself with a Tunbridge Ware fan. I suppose she believes the King will somehow ravish me before the amazed eyes of his courtiers.

But I glow all over, like another torch, to mark how everyone in the court stares at us – whispers, nudges, murmurs behind fans. I'm dancing with the King! And everyone sees me!

For a while we're absorbed in running and gliding to the triple time of the song. I yearn to ask him if he can be sure of the success of our plot, but I'm too awed to speak. At last he says, however, 'It might be to your interest to know, I've writ a most persuasive message to your stepfather and grandfather this afternoon.'

In the darkening shadows of twilight we exchange a conspiratorial look, our feet gliding, our hands clasped and held high. I toss my head prettily.

'Your Majesty is most kind.'

'I look to my interest – and the interests of my friends.'

He puts such a stress on that last word, looks into my eyes so intently, my heart swells to think of the one he so obviously means here! I break into my most special smile and bob my head at him.

'Worry not about your guardians,' he adds. 'I've taken special care to appeal to their avarice.'

And so he has: for, being arrived back at Great House, where the redwoods, firs and beech mump at me from below the bailey, and the rooks hang above 'em to caw at the lake, I find Grandpa smacking his lips in covetous glee.

The King's message has ridden post to him, to arrive a day before us; and though my stepfather advises 'em all to have a care, that a bird in the hand is worth two in the bush and he believes I cunningly un-cleavered myself somehow, Grandpa announces this twist is as pat as may be. It seems he has been dangling after another cold fish in the brook and wants no Hinching-goose paddling around to fright it away.

And he waves His Majesty's letter, with hints of 'your daughter can do better for her family than the Lord Hinchingbrooke, Lord Hawley, if you send her to court to sell herself and leave the final negotiations to me'.

'Aye, there's the way now!' He chortles, rubs his hands in glee to think of an amour with his beloved guineas. 'Now we've got His Majesty on our side, eh? There's the way!'

'Well,' snaps Mother, 'you're mad, Father, if you think of letting her loose at court, with *her* airs!'

''Tis her airs will seal the business for us, daughter: have you understood nothing?' He pinches my cheek. 'Well, we've been going about the selling of our girl the wrong way: haven't we, little hussy?'

I giggle and purr, linking my arm through his. 'Oh, Grandpa, you have always smoked me. Even when I tried concealment, you've tracked the fox to its very den.'

'Aye, aye, mum to all else, mum's the word now, but your old grandpa knows!' He lays a finger aside his nostril. Then he grins and tweaks my cheek again. 'Grandpa knows his naughty little hussy! She'll present us with something better than we old men could bargain for, eh?'

'Father,' cries Mama, outraged, 'you know not what you say. You know not how the King looked upon her and how she played with him –'

He shrugs blandly. 'And if he did, eh? Don't the King find good matches for his leavings?'

'Father!' Mother shrieks in horror.

'Mother!' I shriek at the same time.

There follow an hundred sermons from Mama on the necessity of preserving virtue, to which I cry, 'Oh, Mama, for pity's sake, I have some sense after all!', and with a flurry of silks and satins from

Bridgewater and seamstresses to sew 'em, with a renewed lie that I'll marry no one without Grandpa's consent, and a rain of falsehoods on how I'd wed someone vastly rich and enjoy the pleasures of the town, I throw off the traces and am bundled with my trunks, hutches, pounding heart and new maid, to get the coach to London.

Oh flame of love, burn high for me, that your message may be writ in earth and sky!

Part VII

'Fire From Heaven'

Robert Blair, Earl of Ashfield
2–6 September 1666

And fire came down from God out of heaven and devoured them.
—*Revelation* 20:9

In the book of Revelation, 666 is the number of the beast, whose attributes included the ability to bring down fire from heaven. Sixteen sixty-six had long been heralded by visionaries and hellfire preachers as the year when God's punishment would be meted out to sinful London. Debauchery of the court of Charles II added to the puritan certainty of divine retribution, and prophecies of doom and gloom, many suppressed by the King's surveyor of the press, forecast 'great drought and barrenness, conflagrations or Great Destruction by Fire'.

—Neil Hanson, *The Great Fire of London in that
Apocalyptic Year, 1666*

1

'And The Fourth Angel Poured Out His Vial'
2 September, 1666

And the fourth angel poured out his vial upon the sun; and power
was given unto him to scorch men with fire.

—*Revelation* 16:8

Leaving Whitehall chapel about eleven this morning, we meet with a
passionate clerk of the Navy Office, who blurts out in manner but half
articulate the intelligence that there is a great fire in the city. It does
sound mighty bad, even beyond the last that burnt down the shops on
London Bridge; for above 300 houses hath been burnt down since
sometime last night, and not a coxcomb doing aught to hinder it:
everyone, I doubt not, hoping 'twill go away if they avert their eyes; or
what is more like, not caring how it ruins all else, so My Own Dear Self
be temporarily unthreatened. This blaze, however, appeareth different from the usual in the city, for it refuses to go out of itself. It hath
burned already upwards of ten hours and only increases in proportion
as it finds new matter to feed upon.

The news is, Farriner that doth all the baking for the Navy and some
for the palace is said to be the cause, the fire having started at his shop
in Pudding Lane, hard by London Bridge. 'Tis no marvel, for the
arrant blockhead hath before this incident mixed up orders and
scraped sugar into turkey-pies for salt. I take an oath he hath forgot to
quench his hearth before retiring. And those that are reckless with fire
tempt fate.

The main problem is, the houses in the path of the ongoing blaze
ought to be pulled down that its forward progress may be halted; but
that no coxcomb would be taxed with the responsibility of pulling
down a house, lest he be charged with the replacing thereof. Those
that lie in the imminent path of the conflagration would rather
sacrifice all than do aught to halt it; so we have a mass of huddled,
frantic human stupidity: this one bestirring himself to jump in the
Thames with his own bundle of goods, and that one rescuing his best

357

coverlet and bolster pillow from the flames, but all things going to wrack for that no one will do aught for the general good.

The news-bearing Navy office man, one Mr Pepys, hath at least discovered sufficient sense to bustle down to Whitehall; and his tale being told, we take him whither the King and Duke still abide in their closet in the inner chapel. Then we busy ourselves in gossip on the business: how 'twas inevitable, with such a dry summer as we've had, and the city being composed in the main of materials so combustible, as overhanging timber houses in narrow alleyways; how in the most crowded warrens and dens of Whitefriars there are the soap boilers, dyers, brewers, and lime burners to practise their trade foul and smoking; and how elsewhere even among the Quality there are large blazes that those wanting reason or caution are heedless of screening or damping, so that they encourage a general destruction, like unto the black plague.

I returning to my lodgings am ambushed by little Jane, who would hear of the fire; and so intent looks she, with such a frown on her lovely forehead, I ask, 'Jane, think you of your mother?'

She bites her lips and shakes her head, one foot over the other.

'No reason for fear – your mother will have had time to flee, and the fire is nowhere near here.'

I bid her eat with the tutor tonight as Uncle has a lady visitor.

I conclude the day's business by supping with Sarah Cooke, the little maid-servant Strephon got the best of some months before: a pretty little creature and good-natured, too, but by no means a wit.

And Strephon, I see, hath not left her with the remnants of very much virtue; for I thinking but to begin a conversation on love, do find myself in the midst thereof, growing exceeding free in dallying with her, and she not unfree to take it: first with the kissing of her mouth and stroking of her breasts in the parlour; and anon she breathing hard and so letting me do all I list, I wax yet the bolder and propose a shift of our quarters, to which she right gladly makes assent.

So here is a pleasure mighty welcome though unlooked for. We strip in the bedchamber and fall together merrily enough, I ramming and swiving away with a lusty will, and she humping and sighing; and I so potent, as to make her die. A hymn, to love! – apt conclusion to a hot night, full of fire.

Then, our flames momentarily damped, we trussing ourselves again, she opens to me her desire to see this dreadful blaze she hath heard of; so finishing off the bottle of claret that did raise our own fire, we proceed from my lodgings (she pressing my arm most sweetly in a way these women hath to joy a man) and engaging a pair of chairmen that wait before the columns of St Paul's Chapel, are conveyed from Covent Garden to Somerset Stairs, where we take water and so eastward-ho.

Everyone being occupied in the passions raised by the fire, we are spared the usual gibes of the vulgar rogues that make free with their tongues against the Quality on the water. In times less urgent the vile rascals hath even jeered the Queen that she hath produced none of His Majesty's offspring; but tonight we are the lesser show, everyone floating in barges to watch the inferno boom and crackle, or throwing into the Thames chairs, candlesticks, and themselves.

Sarah leaning against me clasps my hand, her eyes round: for it is indeed an awesome sight to watch from the safety of our place on the water as the shoreline is consumed by flames.

The wind being very high drives showers of sparks thick as snow-flakes to the west: whereat I grow not a little concerned, for whatever hath been done for the quenching, it hath been but poor. The fire flames out against the black sky like a devil's inferno and makes a great roaring like unto the howling of a thousand of the damned; and so booming and bellowing as it swells and eats up the dry timber of one cot or shed after another along the waterfront. The smoke billows skyward in great choking grey blasts; and fire flakes drift everywhere on the high winds, like sparks shot off from a demon's forge.

Sarah crying out hides her face in my cloak: 'tis like a premonition of hell.

'Look!' she crieth at once, pointing shoreward.

I strain my eyes through the dark all about us, but see naught unless it be the billowing orange-red furnace that licks the black from the sky in great draughts – that, and the panicked dark figures of the tiny men silhouetted against it, running hither and thither, with boxes and sacks. The din is terrific, so that I can scarce think: the fire with its crackling, whipping, and roaring as it makes its gigantic meal of timber, one building after the next: then exploding like the blast of Bergen cannon as the flames lick at another storehouse of combustible chemicals – the whoosh and crash as roofs collapse, and the shrieks everywhere: children lost from their parents in the darkness, and screaming devils trapped beneath a burnt wall.

'Madam, what?' I yell over the thunderous blaze.

She points yet more urgently, at which my eyes follow her finger. A warehouse hath suddenly ignited, five buildings further to the west.

Then I think I know what she would mean: that this devil's wind driving the sparks westward will prove a great calamity; but then she suddenly cries:

'Fireballs! Jesus help us, we are invaded!'

I peer the more urgently through the flames; for we having but recently fired Brandeis, and destroying 160 merchantmen at anchor in the harbour thereof, have anticipated how the Hollanders might wreak their vengeance. No Dutchmen, however, see I, nor any of their ships: but only our own panicked and surging citizenry; no fireballs being thrown, but only pitiful bundles, and those into the Thames.

I open it to her full and plain how the wind is the agent throws the fire; she, however, but buries her head in my cloak, sobs – her sense so utterly gone she neglects e'en to beat out the sparks that alight on her, so that it falls to me to beat 'em off both of us.

Why the devil must women be so unreasonable? Some amongst 'em have their share of wit and sparkle, *à la* Mallet; but never once have I met one with a truly solid head on her shoulders.

The waterman impresses me not overmuch with his parts, neither: for he enlightens me then with his considered opinion, 'tis not the Dutch that fire the city but the old Republican fanatics: that they have arisen en masse (though we cannot see 'em) to lead a new Revolution: September 3rd being the anniversary of Cromwell's great victories at Dunbar in '50 and Worcester in '51, beside of his death in '58, they have chosen this day to fire the city, and the government will topple on the morrow. He then argues it to me full and plain, all the best fortune-tellers had long ago predicted London would be burnt in the year of the treble sixes; that e'en had his parson not preached upon the signs made so plain these twenty months past in the book of nature, they were writ across the sky for all to see, in pestilence, fire, and sword. Next I doubt not we will all look toward Tower Hill, to see Moses holding up his staff o'er the city; and Cromwell bearing up his weary arms for him; and a fiery horseman galloping above all, tossing out his vial.

Disgusted with the both of 'em, and their galloping unreason, I ask to be taken back to Somerset stairs. I am a little loathe to leave the fire and its compelling spectacle: destruction on a scale so massive hath a fascination, or we would not so love tragic heroes: yet I see plainly the waterman prepares to open to me the meat of all the sermons he hath heard since the plague, or mayhap e'en the Christmas Comet: this, along with being singed by approaching too near the blaze, is enough for me to bid adieu to the excitements of excess and decide for bed.

Little Sarah remaineth so frighted, I cuddle her beneath my cloak as we float onwards to Westminster; the fire behind us looks like a great orange bow, lengthening itself westward along the waterfront. Flames and a bow: I am reminded of Cupid, a proper emblem for this wicked town.

Then I hear a terrific boom, which causeth Sarah in my arms to quake, and another gigantic jet of flame shoots upward toward the black sky banked in drifting billows of grey. Another warehouse hath ignited, this one undoubtedly containing a dangerous chemical. A shower of sparks hits me, which I beat off: but feeling more with every instant as if I've moved backwards in time to Bergen.

All about us in the dark water float parcels and sticks of furniture: here a jointed stool, there a harpsichon or table of fine cherry-tree: the poor devils along the waterfront having tossed 'em out as if to the wheel of fortune, probably wanting either the fare or opportunity to secure a waterman.

As we row smart to the oars back toward Somerset stairs, I look behind. A good half of London Bridge is burning, and the grim heads of the traitors, spiked above Southwark gate, watch the flames impassively: standing sentinel o'er the pitiful spectacle of human waste and suffering, like some *memento mori* of mortality.

2

'The Number Of The Beast'
4 September 1666

Here is wisdom. Let him that hath understanding count the number of the beast: for it is the number of a man; and his number is Six hundred threescore and six.

—*Revelation* 13:18

There were great churches and guildhalls, cavernous warehouses; and in the narrow lanes running down to the river, crowded together so densely that most lay in almost perpetual darkness, were stores and cellars, docks and wharves, ships' chandlers and rope makers, workshops and manufacturers, containing every material and every trade on which the city thrived.

Among a thousand 'wares and commodities stowed and vended in those parts' were oil, pitch, turpentine, brimstone, saltpeter, gunpowder, cordage, resin, wax, butter, cheese, brandy, sugar, honey, hops, tobacco, tallow, rope, hemp, flax, cotton, silk, wool, furs, skins and hides, and the wharves where coal, timber and wood were unloaded.

—Neil Hanson, *The Great Fire of London in that Apocalyptic Year, 1666*

Dining with Bucks today, who hath much of business in his life of late: being gone to sea in June, and leaving vexed when offered no command; and in the same month, lying with the Lady Shrewsbury and her husband in the same summer house, enjoying the favours of the first almost before the eyes of the second (and a handsome woman she is, too, though foreign and flighty); he shows us his new picture-box, which is most diverting, and we dine on a dish of anchovies, a delicate fine pig, and a good dish of neats' feet and mustard, with a most excellent fine Rhenish, all very neat and handsomely done up on silver dishes and with forks, too; and his boy playing airs all the while on the lute.

Here we have more news of the dreadful fire: Sedley reporting, that ninny of a Lord Mayor, Bludworth, hath done no more to check it than a bawd would to preserve a maidenhead; but hastened about crying 'Lord, Lord,' and wiping his face with a handkerchief and all was wringing of hands and nothing much to the purpose; that he hath ceased even that pretence some six-and-thirty hours ago and got him home, saying, there was nothing he could do. That the fire hath burnt down all of Fish Street and St Magnus Church, and the streets swelled with carts removing of goods from one house to another, so there was scarce any walking; and the goods being removed to Canning Street, it hath caught fire too, they now removing such stuff as can be saved to Lombard Street and further; but that the fire hath swollen exceeding great from the warehouses along the river packed as they were with combustibles of oil, wines, brandy, and chemicals; and then the houses so thick in Thames Street, and they full of pitch and tar.

Bucks then relates how one of his footmen, being gone to Tower Hill some time yesterday on a pull to view the spectacle, reports there hath been much suffering amongst the poorer people, those wont to dwell in their little houses by the river; and that they now huddle en masse on the hill with their pitiful bundles and dull eyes, with no will to do aught more than await whatever new blows fortune may deal.

Buckhurst relates that Shepherd having an uncle in Canning Street, they have removed his possessions to Dorset House; but that with no little trouble, the streets being so full of horses and men burthened, and the sick being carried on litters; and that St Paul's Cathedral swarmeth with people that hath carried thither their bundles, books, and armloads, knowing not where else to go.

I then relate my own news, how the booming devil's furnace being viewed from the river did whip and roar skyward unlike any natural flame ever seen of me; and that before my very eyes it grew, now a church steeple alighting with the fire flakes and being consumed in a torrent of red; and then a house and another all one fire and flaming at once, the long bow of the blaze lengthening a mile and more even as I watched, and the clamour of its roar filling the skies. I then ask, is nothing being done at all?

Bucks relates then that the King and Duke hath set up fire posts, the which are commanded by various peers of sense and courage, who hath taken on themselves the responsibility of pulling down houses; and that there are some hopes of stopping the blaze about Botolph's Wharf in the east and the Three Cranes in the west. I then surprise all of the company, myself included, by venturing the remark that I would assist in doing what I can.

Sedley stares at me incredulously o'er his glass of Rhenish whilst a liveried lackey removes the plate. 'Faith, why bestir yourself? 'Tis certain to be much hard work with little reward. You may even get burnt or robbed.'

I stare about the white-and-gilt-wainscoted dining room of Bucks' Wallingford House. 'Nevertheless, I recall how my conscience stung me when we all fled the plague last year to debauch at a distance 'til the infection spent itself amongst the unfortunate. This time I'd assist 'em in what I can.'

Sedley shrugs. 'A conscience is an uncomfortable piece of equipment for a man to carry about; but if you have one, I suppose 'tis like an empty stomach and must be satisfied.'

'Jesus,' says Buckhurst, feeding his fat cheeks with some plums from the gilded bowl nearby, 'recall how the Earl of Craven did during the plague? – going about through the vilest dens of dirt and infection – cleansing the ill, feeding the sick, offering physic.'

'And I hated myself,' is my grim-lipped response, 'for being cowardly and not doing't along with him.'

Buckhurst shrugs with a look noncommittal; but after so many years, I know him: he hath conscience enough to be stung, too.

Sedley, of course, responds, 'Faith, 'tis of no discredit to a man that he prefers his own skin to that of some lousy beggar.'

A dispute then arises, I reminding Sedley that Craven emerged from his mission of mercy as whole as before – and that, at any rate, this sort of crisis hath not such danger to't.

Sedley shrugs, sipping the Rhenish. 'I suppose if you must do penance for your fortune by tending the poor, 'tis better to be seized by virtuous resolutions in the midst of a fire than during a plague.'

''Tis settled, then,' booms out a good-natured Savile, popping a handful of plums into his cavernous mouth. 'Come, my lord: I'll venture; let us seek out the Lord Craven at his fire post.'

'Savile,' rallies Little Sid with small black eyes dancing 'neath the huge periwig, 'faith: how can you so bestir yourself, who have not seen your toes these ten year, any more than a great-bellied woman, the week before her lying-in? What will you do with that hogshead, that noble orb of pleasures past you carry before you, as she doth for nine months the proof of her indulgence?'

He laughs and slaps it. 'Why, as I'm mightily attached to it, I'll take it along when I offer my services. I tell thee frankly, my lords, I've been distressed of late at my poor capacity for wine; I had yesterday not above two hogsheads; and what better way than fire to raise a man's thirst to a generous pitch?'

This is the way he hath, of disclaiming modestly his good nature through the exercise of wit. And so we toss off our glasses together;

and, taking leave of the others and issuing our thanks to Bucks for his hospitality, we go hence to seek out Craven – and I greatly comforted for my part to be doing someone good besides a tavern-keeper.

3

'Rich Men, Weep'
3 September 1666

For the sun is no sooner risen with a burning heat, but it withereth
the grass, and the flower thereof falleth, and the grace of the
fashion of it perisheth: so also shall the rich man fade away in his
ways.

Go to, now, rich men, weep and howl for your miseries that shall
come upon you.

—*James* 1:11, 5:1

Now did I have a mind to be superstitious, I lay my life I'd look
skyward for the opened heavens and the Judgment Seat, o'er which
bendeth the ireful brow of a God of vengeance wrapped in a pillar of
flame; for this is the nearest hell a man may approach and yet live, and
all the world in a passion as fiery: some standing dazed and others
running mad, and goods of every sort choking the narrow streets –
carted, carried, heaped in kennels, buried in gardens and consigned
to the waves; borne from house to house on weary arms as the flame
roars down another street and roofs collapse with a whoosh; and over
all, the towering arc of fire, higher and higher heavenward, the night
sky horrid with its bloody glow, as if the sun consumed itself and by its
dying blasts made permanent day.

All the night and morning too in Tower Street, I did what I could 'til
the great flame corning on with infinite fury into that narrow street
from both sides met in the middle and swallowed all; and I to Tower
Hill then, shouldering through the screaming throngs and burthened
carts, to mill with the disordered mob thereon and watch the world
below all wrapped in flame: houses, churches, and shops burnt down,
and chimneys wrapped in spirals of flames; roofs with a smash collapsing into crypts below, and cellars of wine and oil booming out to
flare brimstone; and the Tower looming over all; brooding, antique,
wordless behind its cool, silent curtain. The yellow walls gleam red

beneath the glowing sky, and flakes of flame are borne on the westering wind like snow alit by moonshine.

The world below the curtain writhes in smoke and fire, from Pie Corner and Newgate Market far in the northwest to Trinity House hard by us in the south: fire all along the water from the Custom House and westward, even beyond Salisbury Court and Blackfriars Stairs, and northward into the very heart of the city, block upon block, eating into the shops of the rich merchants on Lombard Street and their dwellings hard by; burning down Fleet Street and the Old Bailey: St Paul's burnt down, and utterly gone to wrack, the whole height of its ruined Gothic spire and long nave collapsed into the crypt of St Faith's below, and the windows did shatter and buckle with the heat, and the stone melt in the inferno that boomed all about: so the man tells me that stands dazed beside me and shows me the scorched sleeve he got when the jet of flame spurted thence to whither he carted his wares from Goldsmith's Row.

Walking through Aldgate then and into Goodman's Fields without the eastern wall, I do perceive to my sorrow how the people flock together there thick as thieves in Alsatia, and all with their pitiful bundles and no roofs over their heads, not anything of sustenance nor anywhere to get it, the markets having all burnt down and bakeries and cook-shops too consumed by the great flame. And there in a corner of the field I do perceive to my great disgust a fanatic exhorting the multitude, how the fire is a judgment brought from God against the wickedness and licentiousness of the court.

Here it is my fortune to meet with Etherege, and a sorry sight he is, too, with his plume burnt down and fine tassels soiled grey with ash; and both of us with arms and legs so aching and throats so parched, we take a resolution to go for a draught and a joint of mutton at the Bear in Southwark.

But it is hard going down Water Mark Lane, where the flames licking all over in the next block to our right, the acrid smoke maketh our eyes to smart, and we must needs cover our mouths with handkerchiefs; and then the narrow street besides so jammed with carts, porters, horses, and people distracted, 'tis like the Exodus of the Jews from Egypt, all noise and clamour, shrieking and wailing and choking beside from the thick grey air.

Here is a woman with a lap dog tucked beneath her arm and a man with a gittern and nothing else; and here a wasted old man lolling on a mattress borne by two younger, so that I thought of Aeneas bearing his father from the flaming ruins of Troy; and all of 'em bound for Goodman's Fields: as, Etherege tells me, those by the northern wall hath taken to Moorfields or Smithfields, having nowhere else of safety to lay their heads: pray God the weather still continue mild for them.

Over our pints and joint we exchange our solemn news: I relate how in Tower Street the people did fling their goods into the kennels and went about distracted, some of 'em to cart 'em off in armloads, and others to dig holes for the burying of 'em in gardens; how Mr Howells (Turner to the Navy Board) having flung out a quantity of tools, we dug and spaded with 'em as best we might or used 'em for the grappling and pulling down of houses; and how Sir William Batten I did help to dig a pit in his garden for the burying of his fine wines, 'til the flame roaring down into the street with the blast of the fiery furnace, we were forced to abandon all but hastened then to the foot of Tower Hill, where some of us helped the Duke of York to blow up with gunpowder the houses in the imminent path of the flames, and there stop them from feeding and spreading the more; but that we were sorely encumbered by the surging masses of the vulgar, who screamed and pled with us to forebear, and fell to their knees terrified as a blast rocked the ground of the narrow street and the timber that used to be their houses toppled all about; how a woman had even gone so far as to lay violent hands on her King's brother as he sat his horse, and we had had much ado to subdue her; and how a fanatic in a loincloth bore on his head a bowl of fire, running nigh onto a charge of powder lit, and we were put to laying violent hands on him to pull him back, and got for our pains a verse from Leviticus: that 'there went out fire from the Lord, and devoured them, and they died before the Lord'; and how then the booms and blasts as the powder exploded like a thousand cannon rocking the streets and people to their feet, and how the people, falling, uttered their lamentations. And over all, I told of the great crackling roar as the bloody flame washed over the blue of the sky; and the smoke so thick a man's lungs sting with it; and then the boom of another house blown up, and the dead pigeons falling to the street all about for that they would not leave the eaves of the houses wherein they had all their lives dwelt, any more than would the people that pulled on us and shrieked.

Etherege relates to me then the pigeons he did see, having remained in the last minute in the houses about Pie Corner: how they fell to the street with their wings singed; that all of Cheapside was burnt before his eyes, and he doing perilous little with the pitiful hand-squirts to halt it; but that it was good to see of what industrious parts the King had shown himself today, who was there for several hours helping with the hand-squirts and engine; took his turn at holding and pumping; and like any common beggar knelt down in the soggy ash to dig at buildings or grapple with hooks; and cried to urge on the vulgar, scattering coins amidst 'em; and his brother the Duke riding up to do the same.

But that notwithstanding, the fire continued within the northern wall unchecked; that the 'Change was burnt to ashes, its grand colonnade and all the statues with it but that of Sir Thomas Gresham, and from one of its chimneys he took out a poor cat from a hole, with the hair burnt off its body but still alive; and being taken out, it bolted away yowling like one possessed, and with no more sense nor judgement than its two-footed relatives.

And the saddest of all sights, I do believe, is the rich merchants that flock to Lincoln's Inn Fields: men who being accustomed to the finest of wines and jointed furniture, of family portraits and china and Japan screens and hangings of heavy velvet tasselled, of silver soup tureens and golden salt-cellars, find themselves today levelled with the lowest of the vulgar that huddled in sheds beside the river: nay, worse: for a brawny-backed porter or carman has the strength to save his goods and get up his crumb carting for others: they have but stood in Cornhill or Threadneedle Street helplessly to watch the orange flame lick toward their life's possessions in their neat fine mansions stored; or watched the whirling orange furnace burgeon into the shops that are their livelihood: Lombard Street, Goldsmith's and Silversmith's Row, the 'Change. Though the treasures of their shops hath been carried under guard to the Tower, they have no homes now, and a weary time ahead, starting over. Two of the poor devils sit dazed, hard across at a table from us; but so turns the wheel of fortune without notice: the high are made low and the low high, and nary a man can do aught.

We buy them a pipe of claret, and they being gentlemen, I offer 'em lodgings at my place in Covent Garden: whereat they thank me heartily, having no other place to lodge but the open fields; and so with a note I commend 'em to Edward and send 'em thither to get what rest they can.

Etherege and I take water then (the bridge being burnt up) to walk about the ruins of St Magnus Church, near the Bridge-Foot, where all is grey ash smoldering underfoot, still so hot a man can scarce walk; and here and there and everywhere a piece of stained glass so melted and buckled with the heat 'tis like parchment; the very stones scorched.

All at once we look up to see a hackney-coach bearing down upon us in this hell of ash and mud. The driver drawing rein before us asks, 'How now? I'm conveying these folk from the country to the city.'

'You'd best convey 'em back,' says Etherege, 'at least for a time. A dreadful fire has burnt the city, and mobs rampage, thieving and killing.'

The driver, being the servile sort, knows not what to do. 'I was told to convey them to an inn-yard in Fleet Street.'

'You fool,' I say, hand on the near horse's bridle, 'have you no ears? There's no inn any more nor Fleet Street neither.'

'Yes, sir. But I was told –'

All at once the coach curtains part, and a feminine hand, dainty and long, with well-kempt nails, is shown.

'Driver,' a firm voice says. 'Convey us back to the inn-yard in St Albans.'

He leans down. 'Begging your pardon, miss, but –'

'NOW.'

The driver and I gawk at one another, never having heard so firm a female command before; though I reckon the Duchess of Ormond sounded thus, during the late troubles, defying Cromwell from the castle battlements.

The driver runs his conflicting orders through the imperfect engine of his brain; and then all at once beneath the hellish booming red in the night sky, there issues a clamour of voices confused; and across the fields of burnt grey ash where once stood Clothworker's Hall there comes running a terrific mob, men and women alike, and all armed with sticks and stones.

As the coach is spied, a greater clamour goes up, the sticks waving.

I draw sword. 'Obey the lady!' Still holding the horse's rein, I lead the team about so it faces whence it came. 'Do as she says, fool, NOW – or face the consequences.' He still seeming stupified, I hit the horse's flank with my hand. It starts, and the others with it, and the coachman still gaping. Anon, shaken from his daze, he sees the mob and slaps the reins.

But now, having been deprived of the spoils of the coach, the mob reverses direction, surging toward us again. I break out into a sweat and grip my hanger hilt; but it seems they have found other prey: before 'em, like a cony ahead of hounds, a poor devil who cries and runs, his pockets bulging.

Now a heavy rock thuds against his shoulder and again a smaller one off his head, 'til a great stone catching him on the temple, he falls into a pile of scorched grey stones screaming, and the blood trickling in a long line from the gash on his head, the pack are upon him with their sticks, screaming, 'Papist dog!'

And an hundred sticks and more raised and beating him to a bloody pulp, as he shrieks above the roar of the flame that licks the sky above; and they beating still in a furious mob, some his feet and others his hands and body, 'til the blood gushes from his mouth and his arm cracks open to run red blood and sticks out white bone.

'Jesus God,' cries Etherege; and the both of us running thither as fast as may be, shout above the clamour to stop in the name of the King, and make a shift to pull off a man or two, but so fast as we pull another takes his place, and all of them beating still like men mad. I slash out with my hanger, but it is yanked from my hands, trampled, and snapped in five pieces, then thrown in the scorching rubble.

Nor does Etherege fare any better, getting a cracked skull for his pains: he sits stunned a moment amid the scorching ash 'til a flame flaring up from a live coal, he cries out and jumps up; and neither of us having any pistol wherewith to stop the dreadful slaughter, it is over in a moment's time: the man lying his bruised head to one side and his body torn to shreds, the whole chest caved in purple and red, with a white rib sticking up through the green waistcoat, concave in a pool of pink guts.

And now the mob tearing through his pockets throw out a watch, a miniature, a purse, and silver stuff one thing after another, as a spoon, a salt-cellar, a candlestick; and paying so little heed to these valuables, 'tis plain their main motive was not robbery.

Then a wave of nausea hits my stomach, what with the claret and mutton and the sick sight of the man, blood welling from his wounds and shattered bones here and there in the smouldering ash that filters grey onto the bloody pools as they dig. I turn about and spew, my stomach wrenching.

'Here now!' cries an exultant voice. 'Fireballs!'

And, my stomach spent and wrung, I turn about in time to see 'em pull from the poor devil's pocket a round bundle, wrapped in parchment, which when torn open proveth to be a pouch of old jewels.

Some of the mob, now come to their senses, pause, not to regret that they have murdered an innocent man, but to scoop up his valuables, yelping a little as the flames lick out to scorch their fingers, and quarrelling over this and that jewel.

Etherege and I pick ourselves up, too sick to do aught but stare at one another, then at the bloody mass of tissue that an instant before was a fellow human creature.

Gentle George then opens it to me, a mob very like this one earlier in the day would have attacked the Portuguese ambassador, but that the Duke of York was there with firearms to drive 'em off; that the unreasoning vulgar have been seized with the conceit that either Papists or Dutchmen have fired the city; that rumours fly wild, it being said a force of some 50 thousand hath landed at the Steelyard and go about the city throwing fireballs and putting the citizenry (women and children as well) to the sword; and that of consequence, the filthy, smouldering rubble swarms with violent mobs, some of 'em an hundred and upwards; that on the sight of a Dutch jacket or sound of a French lisp will tear a man to pieces: more, that they have demolished with sticks and stones and broke open the windows of every shop known to be owned by some man of foreign birth; and where he had not the presence of mind to escape, torn him limb from limb; and some of these his old customers that hath bought his bread or pies these years. That the Duke had committees out searching the streets for men of foreign blood, that they might be taken into gaol for safe-keeping, lest they be killed in the violent confusion.

So this debacle affords another spectacle of the degradation of the human beast. What a passion is lit in man, and so low the reason that may damp its furnace. We walk to the rubble of the Old Swan (I still sick to the very blood), there to take up water to Westminster again; but waiting above an hour and paying treble the usual rate, and sharing our barge with such a heap of virginals, silver, and heads sculpted of Galileo or Cicero, we can scarce float, our lighter riding almost with its prow in the water, and the waterman transported with glee at the fire, to tell us in delight how much profit he hath made this day.

Man is, as Rochester says, his own worst curse; and man in the mass is even more revolting than man *solus*.

4

'The Flames Burst Upon Cheapside' 5 September 1666

> As the sun rose, the flames burst upon Cheapside. No street in London had played a greater role in the city's history. Now in the space of a few hours it was utterly destroyed.
> —Neil Hanson, *The Great Fire of London in that Apocalyptic Year, 1666*

Awaking this morning to a strange sound, I lie within the hot, dark cloister of my bed hangings and much wonder what is the eerie apprehension that hath brought me to awareness.

Then I feel the knowledge steal on me of what 'tis: the sound of quiet. The wind no longer beats howling against the casement; and I can hear no more the horrid terrible roar of the blast that hath assaulted my ears the two days of exhausting labour before.

Making William to dress me with haste, I leg it down the stairs, whither several gentlemen hath made up pallets on the white-and-black-checked floor, and where I am accosted by the tutor, who asks me if I know the whereabouts of little Jane.

I stand amazed, for it is not like her to rise without greeting the both of us. Then one of the gentlemen unwrapping himself from his blankets, asks, 'Would this be a pretty fair-haired child, slender, about twelve year of age?'

'Yes, my ward!' Anxiety thuds in my chest like one of the Lord Craven's drums.

'She feared for her brother, who was apprenticed to a French baker; and was gone to the city to seek him.'

'She *what?* Her *brother?*'

'Edmund Seward, she said his name was. She left early this morning to seek him.'

'*Where*, for God's sake?'

'Somewhere in Cheapside, she thought. She bade us tell you when you were arisen.'

Anger rises to my throat, and I grasp the fellow's shoulder. 'And you let her go?'

'My lord, please! She took a footman – Edward, I think his name was.'

Edward? That blockhead-headed ninny? Some help he will be!

Throat constricted by fear, and not even stopping for a morning draught at Locket's, I make the best horse to be saddled and bid John gather the other men to follow behind to the city.

The wind has died as suddenly as it came, the air being foetid, still, and heavy with the smell of ash and death. My heart in my very throat for fear, I ride in a wasteland of smouldering grey ash, scorched stone, and gutted timber; the horse's hoofs descend with a splat onto wet mud, and its legs step gingerly o'er chunks of buckled lead and burnt stone.

'Jane!' I call. And the footman huffing after echoes me. 'Jane!'

We make our way to Cheapside.

Here, I tell myself, dazed, is where St Bride's used to stand; that pit of smoking timber used to be someone's wine cellar; and this buckled fragment of glass, by the location of't, must once have been part of St Paul's: for mark, amid the still-hot ash and molten lead, amid the pile of exploded stone, there stands its gutted, roofless shell; and within, only the effigy of Dean Donne, wrapped in his chiselled shroud; and all about 'em, a level mile from the river to the burnt-down wall, nothing but a grey field of ashes: as if some divine blast of wind and fire had levelled the city and passed on: nay, as if no city had ever stood here but a desert of rock and wood parched by preternatural heat: as if the Roman legion had passed over, and this were Carthage, and Cato the Censor had commanded that naught be left to mark the presence of a civilization on this spot.

'Jane! Jane!'

We ride past St Paul's. With great sadness I direct my horse o'er the grey wasteland and scorched stone of what was once Cheapside, all of the picturesque taverns of which hath become this ash beneath my beast's hoofs: the Mermaid, where old Shakespeare was wont to talk with Ben Jonson; the Boar, where Falstaff frolicked.

'Jane! Jane!'

In the far distance I see another mob, armed with sticks. Oh, no. Oh, Jane.

'Here we are, my lord!' Edward saunters up behind the other men. 'She couldn't find her brother, though.'

'You fool! She could have been attacked and killed.'

I fling myself off the horse and race to catch her up in my arms, swinging her off the ground and holding her to my breast. 'Jane, oh, Jane – never leave like that again.'

'Well, the devil you say, milord – I was aiming to get a nice reward for not suffering her to go alone.'

'You absolute and utter fool!' I cling to Jane, who buries her head in my neck.

She says softly, 'My brother – I was afear'd – the men staying with us talked of mobs.'

'And so how do you think *I* felt when you put yourself in danger?'

'I was with her,' Edward says, puffing out his chest.

'Yes, you, you arsewipe: what a consolation!'

Edward, looking a little deflated, says, 'I told her not to go. I said you'd have her beaten.'

'You total and utter – if anyone's to be beaten, it will be you! And I've a mind to do it now.'

I hoist Jane up onto the horse and tell the men to walk back with it slowly, as there's no sidesaddle.

Jane looks down on me with eyes of cornflower blue, filmy with tears, and says, 'My lord – Uncle – I thought you wouldn't care.'

I bite my lip. 'Oh, my dear heart, my little girl. Prithee, Jane, never, *never* leave without telling me. An you feel the need to go on a quest again, open the matter to me instead of striking off alone.'

I draw a deep breath and swipe at my eyes. Why hath this child the power to make me unman myself? I take her little white hand and kiss it. 'Tomorrow you'll tell me of your brother, and I'll put out the word to search for him.'

As I watch Jane ride off, surrounded by footmen, I entertain visions of hanging Edward upside down over an open latrine.

Then my whole person relaxes in a great sigh of relief; and, as I'm in the part of the city that's burnt, I determine to seek out Craven and see what's to be done.

The fire has done its worst all the way along the river, from the Tower to the Temple, where the Duke at both places hath halted it by blowing up houses, against the protests of the unreasoning vulgar; it hath burnt west as far as Newgate, there releasing all the felons, who hath joined the violent mobs; north as far as Moorgate, even leaping the wall into the Liberties. It hath utterly eradicated every shop in Goldsmith's and Silversmith's Row, and though the smiths had the sense to cart off their wares to the Tower for safekeeping, structures of infinite beauty are for ever gone to the windborne blaze; it hath burnt down the markets, the 'Change, and virtually every home or church of beauty.

Dorset House is gone at last, and the post office burnt up almost from the beginning; the Wardrobe is consumed, and the Guildhall, and Fishmonger's Hall. The fire even blazed so far west as the Holborn; and Craven tells me it is still flaming pretty badly at Cripplegate: whither I then walk, to do what office I can with the hand-squirts.

One poor devil that works the engine and hand-squirts with me, and dazed to a glassy-eyed disbelief with sorrow, opens it to me he hath lost every priceless portrait and silver piece in his fine home on Threadneedle Street; for when the fire flamed thither, a cart could not be had for rent, but for an hundred and fifty pound in ready cash; and he had but fifty in his purse, the rest having been banked or newly spent. He saith moreover that bound hither to do what service he could, he was questioned closely by a mob of ruffians armed with sticks and stones, who surged through the rubble looking for Dutchmen or Papists; and who, bye the bye, hath robbed him of the last fifty he had into the bargain. Him too I direct to my lodgings in Covent Garden, where above a dozen of gentlemen now lie in the chambers and halls: whereat he thanks me.

'Tis like walking on the bed of hell to go anywhere in town: ashes and coals still smoulder everywhere underfoot, and live flames lick suddenly out from cellars or beneath fallen timbers. A man may stand in Cornhill street and see to the Thames, the entire city levelled, and all of wet mud and scorched ash, so I know not how we will ever clean up the mess, much less build again upon't; nor know I what the homeless hordes, numbering in their thousands, will do in the meanwhile. The Duke says the King will make a plea to all the kingdom for charity, and collections will be taken up. I hope the spirit of beneficence touches the hearts of all, else these poor wretches will ne'er survive, and winter coming on, too.

Leaving Cripplegate about two of the clock to get some dinner, I see how the sky above doth shine again with its lustre of a natural blue, undimmed by fire or smoke. The Duke's use of gunpowder hath removed from the path of the blaze its sustenance; and the wind having so eerily and suddenly died down, no fire flakes drift any more westward on its breath.

Riding through Smithfield on my journey westward to Westminster, I do perceive how the open space is jammed with crowds of homeless people; a mob of 'em in one spot are praying their thanksgiving to the God that hath ceased his breath o'er the city and left 'em alive. The fire hath been grievous enough, but humanity is a far worse curse to itself. Mad, capricious, a prey to the nearest sensation; slow to reason but ready to be ignited on the merest whim; ravaging, looting, murdering, credulous; piling wood on the flames of human suffering and turning a natural inferno into a tragedy of human waste; then kneeling in the fields, heads bowed, to take comfort in the knowledge that 'tis all the will of God.

Part VIII

'Her First Appearance Upon The Busy Stage Of Life'

Betty Mallet

September-December 1666

... a young female, educated in the most secluded retirement, makes, at the age of seventeen, her first appearance upon the great and busy stage of life; with a virtuous mind, a cultivated understanding, and a feeling heart, her ignorance of the forms, and inexperience in the manners of the world, occasion all the little incidents which these volumes record.

—Fanny Burney, Preface to *Evelina* (1778)

1

'The Mind Of A Young Girl Thrust Into London Society'

9 September 1666

... the real virtue of the novel lies in Burney's capturing the mind of
a young girl thrust into London society; she stated herself that her
aim was not to show the world what it actually *is*, but what it *appears*
to a young girl of seventeen.

—Martin S. Day, *English Literature, 1660–1830*, on
Fanny Burney's novel *Evelina* (1778)

Oh, God. Oh, God. Can I really be here at last?

I stand amazed, beyond belief, in the white cobbled square before
the palace gates and the Banqueting House whilst my new woman
Susan issues orders about the unloading of my trunks. I'm put to
lodge in Scotland Yard – not amidst the maids of honour at the river.
Ah, well. The important thing's I'm to be lodged *somewhere*.

Into my withdrawing room I pad, to seat myself at a secretary of
cherry tree, then scrabble for paper and ink and quill, and write to Mr
Savile:

> Dear Sir,
> You can see by the conveyance of this paper to you, that our plot
> has succeeded so far, and I am at last got to court, chiefly on the
> contrivance that I will help my guardians to select a man of
> means as my husband; and I have promised not to marry without
> their consent. So I am in a pickle unless I choose or wed pretty
> soon. I am frank with you, sir, as you have been with me; for I
> believe you my friend, as well as his.
>
> Now, sir, I request whatever direction or intelligence you can
> give me of how to proceed next. For truly, I see not what my way
> is now, he being away at sea, nor even know how much of our plot
> you have let him into. I could wish, sir, for a conference with you
> on these matters; for I remain, sir,

> Your Most Obedient Partner in Crime,
> Elizabeth Mallet

Susan is then entreated to find out Mr Harry Savile. She's gone above two hours; and in the interim, I have time to watch the shadows lengthen into cold evening and believe myself alone in this place.

But at last she returns, and I break open the red wax of the reply:

> Madam,
> Right glad am I you have slipped off your chains and joined us here. As for my lord, he keeps as close-mouthed with me as he does with you.

At this hint my heart sinks. Have I done all this scheming for naught? No! I'll force the issue somehow: will him to be mine, now I've gone so far. I read on.

> But for revealing his true feelings, he does little. I dispatched him a long manuscript shortly after our antics at Tunbridge, to tell him pretty frankly the plot you and I had hatched and the purposes at which it aimed. He writ back but little, saying, he were very glad such a beautiful and worthy lady as yourself were not to be served with that hollow musk-melon that when thumped, echoed the last halloo.

Here I cannot but laugh, to recall how the musk-melon bounced on the brow of the cliff, hallooing with its cry of 'Mrs Mallet'.

Mr Savile's letter continues:

> But of report of his feelings, I could find none. He remained very guarded and general, and said, that he hoped you would still be at court when he was done with his business at sea; for it would be very pleasant to converse with you again and he recalled you as a most witty and deserving lady, a very good, sweet, innocent person; and he wished you all the best, as anyone must, to hear that you were to be served such a matrimonial dinner and then be joyed at your change in menu.

My heart drops. This argument sounds not like that of a lover rejoicing at a reunion with his sweetheart. Could Mr Savile have been in the wrong?

The next part of the letter answers my question.

Madam, I believe I was in the right in reading his affections. But there is something within him that makes him chary of opening his feelings to anyone. Perhaps he feels that this crowd here would jeer him. But no matter how lightly he mentions coming to court again, be assured he will begin moving in that direction now he knows you're here. And be assured, once you're with him again, the encouragements that your carriage and looks will give him will open him up.

I remain, madam, your friend and confidante,

Harry Savile

I bite my lips o'er this last. Yea, sooth, will my looks and carriage give him encouragements! And now I wonder what sort of encouragements he looks for.

For it seems I keep deceiving myself and having to scold myself into reason again. Here I have been all frenzied-up to get to court, that he and I might be married at last; and so set was I with my hackney on that path, I forgot what was at the end of my trip to Adderbury, when his relations could find no hint of a marriage: and, indeed, every evidence that he but played one of his antic games.

And what can I expect, when he shall come hither, but that he shall do the same? Yea, sooth, I can well believe that he will call on me, converse with me, and get from me what can be gotten. I know well what his games with maidens are.

I sit by the window as it greys with thick mists of chilly twilight. As I clutch the bleak letter in my hands and bite my lips, I feel the hot tears scald my cheeks.

Did I manoeuvre to get to court only to be ignored or ruin't?

Oh, God help me. Whom shall I find as a protector strong enough to aid me now?

Suddenly, as if in answer to my prayer, a knock sounds at my door. And Susan bears in to me a message, which listlessly I open. Then my eyes dart to the signature: 'Charles R.'

The King has writ me! Why, I just now asked for an ally, and here he is! Oh, thank you, God.

Eagerly I read:

Madam,

It has been brought to my attention that you have at last been brought to our environs here and settled in. We would like to welcome you to the best of our ability and therefore (and also to discuss a few small particulars) most heartily plead and request your presence at a small supper-party to be given tomorrow night in our private apartments at the river's edge. This will serve as your invitation and conveyance.

This is to let you know, I am no tardy host in welcoming you but believed your journey would so fatigue you, that the first day were better spent in rest.

Charles R.

The King will help me! I knew he would!

The 'few small particulars': that would be my marriage. Oh, how wonderful that His Majesty loves my lord so well, his fatherly protection extends to me, too!

2

'My Hopes Were Dead'
10 September 1666

A Christmas frost had come at midsummer; a white December storm had whirled over June. My hopes were dead – struck with a subtle doom, such as in one night, fell on all the first-born in the land of Egypt. I looked on my cherished wishes, yesterday so blooming and glowing: they lay stark, chill, livid corpses that could never revive.

—Charlotte Brontë, *Jane Eyre*

Awakening in the grey dawn, shuddering, burrowing down beneath the coverlets, I long for warmth in a way that I did not in the country. And through the day the chill lodges in my heart.

A liveried page knocks me up later in the day, to confirm the invitation and issue orders about the great event. I've been sitting with my hair up in curl-papers, exulting with Susan as we paw through my gowns, rings, and ear-bobs. I am astonished when the page announces the supper-time to be eleven of the clock.

Eleven of the clock? Lord! I must eat a supper to hold me till supper!

Well, I can see I must learn new habits here. It seems the greater part of the day begins at night.

For being arisen at my usual hour this morning, a little after the sun, I could hear no one stirring till almost the noon hour; could see no one traipsing the brick court below till well after ten of the clock – and then, folk in livery or plain garb, white folded papers clenched in their hands or borne on silver trays.

I begin to suspect, as late as these folk send messages, they must not even dine till two of the clock.

Shaking my head, I make a fist and knock my brow, to drive out the country humours. What's more, my first day in this exciting town, now I've the freedom I've fought for, how do I spend it? Hunched up in my four small rooms.

I feel afear'd to step out anywhere: not even think to step out, for being unused to the notion that I can flit whither the whim takes me. In Somerset there isn't anywhere to go, and in town Mama never suffers me to go anywhere – at least not without herself in tow.

I venture forth not even for food, but send Susan twice: to buy sugared buns at a bake shop near Charing Cross; and then later, to order a dinner at one of the taverns there and have it sent over by runner. For I know not whether 'tis proper for young ladies to frequent taverns with their maids. What an absurdity! I'm more a prisoner now than e'er I was with my mama.

When at last 'tis time to make ready for the great event, we having so long picked over the proper adornments, I make a quick business of dressing, Susan helping me into a tight pink satin with a low décolletage and placing a garnet instead of a pinner at the cleft of my bosom. For we have deliberated whether that modest piece of gauze worn in the country should be draped about my shoulders and bosom, and we've decided to err on the side of daring fashion rather than rural dullness.

And over my carefully coiffed curls, brushed and curled into ringlets around Susan's finger, gathered up in garnet pins in a cascade at each cheek and a long coil behind, we've slipped a gold net embroidered with garnets of a likeness to the dangling ear-bobs. On my finger is slipped a tiger's-eye ring; on my feet, pink satin pumps, fashioned from the same cloth as the gown by busy Somerset fingers.

And then we construct me a face – a pretty London face: a high colour wash on the cheeks, a beauty patch to the left of my rosebud mouth, black soot-base applied with a brush to lengthen my lashes.

Oh, how Mama would scold to see my painted face! How she grumbled, indeed, to see the paint-pots new bought at Bridgwater go into my valises! But she'd say naught except, 'Well, I hope you use discretion in the amount of this stuff you put on your face.'

But discretion, dear Mama, is o'ershadowed by fashion!

Then the pink lips are painted pinker with a brush from the colour-pot so they glow of a sameness with my gown.

I stare delighted at the apparition in the glass: the daring and fashionable young lady with sultry eyelashes and rosy lips and two white balls upthrust above the tight pink bodice.

At half past ten of the clock, the page comes to escort me to the supper. Refusing his arm, I follow him through the dark, lifting up skirts and hobbling on the cobbles in my new shoes, meandering through a maze of alleys where buildings meet at angles.

Anon a fresh-water smell, stinking sweet with refuse, announces the river, and we break into a square where fruit trees hang with bird cages and candles. This is the Aviary Court, where lodge Frances and the other maids of honour.

We pass into a broader plain brick court, the river gurgling and slapping and running moon-stained to the left and buildings rising on the other three sides.

The page guides me into the greatest building, across the square from the river, where a beefeater with a pike nods us through a tall door. In the chamber within, the one piece of furniture – a green canopy and chair of state – increases my timidity.

Following the page, I mince, my spirits cowed and stomach trembling, through a threshold at the far left, to find myself in the royal bedchamber. The bed of state, hung with scarlet silk, is shoved against a window and marked off with a balustrade. The walls are heavily pictured; and a doorway off to the distant left leads, I suppose, to the fabled closet, where none but the King's intimates may enter.

But my eyes pop and my knees turn to butter when I see, before the balustrade, a tiny table laid with two plates and sets of silver.

I stare at the page. I am sure my amazement and fear must be writ all over my face.

'Two places?'

He's too well-bred to show his surprise at my consternation. He makes a leg, one foot thrust out straight, and says, 'Madam, I will tell His Majesty you are here.'

As he disappears my head reels so that I clench the gilt back of one of the chairs. Two places! The bedchamber! Oh, Jesu! Why did I not understand?

The table dances before me, its white tapers leaping flame in a silver candelabra.

No, no. Get a grip of yourself, Betty. Why, of course he wishes to speak to you alone. Would he parade your private concerns before the court?

Get a grip, now. His Majesty loves Frances. He has no designs on you.

A rustle startles me so I look up; and in the light of the wax candles in sconces, I see entering from the portal within a tall, lanky man with a curled dark periwig and – oh, Lord preserve me! – a dressing gown – a scarlet robe, ermine-trimmed, belted negligently at the waist and falling to his knees to show his hose and slippers.

Oh, dear God! What implies this state of undress?

Hoping I let not my fear show on my face, silly and countrified as 'tis, I (still gripping the chair with one hand) curtsey low, my pink skirts spread out before me, my eyes cast down into the cleft of a bosom which I realize with dismay is too far exposed.

'Come, come, no formality here,' says a husky voice. 'His Majesty is out tonight.'

The hand that grasps my skirt is suddenly captured by a moist warm claw that tugs me upward.

As if attached to a string, puppet-like, my gaze travels to the heights where his head is perched: first to the cynically smiling full lips, then the tiny moustache, at last the bulbous nose and the narrowed, greedy brown eyes.

What is it they gleam with – lust?

I jerk my fingers away and my gaze, too; and, staring at the candelabra, I murmur, 'I think Your Majesty cannot be out for me. I am a simple country maid and cannot forget I'm in the presence of my monarch.'

'Come, come,' chafes the pleasantly intimate, humorous voice. 'We'll help fix that before the end of the evening. Perhaps a little wine?'

He snaps his fingers. I stare transfixed down at the table, where a carven silver pitcher is thrust before me, a bubbling gold liquid tumbling out of it and into the tall Venice glass on the right.

Jesu, what next?

Meekly I murmur, staring at the molten gold that froths from the pitcher into the glass, 'I am not used to strong drink, Your Majesty.'

The voice toward my left, still haughty and intimate and bemused, replies, 'This is not strong at all, only a very fine champagne.'

Champagne? Jesu, I've never tasted it.

But then, there'll be much tonight, I fear, that I've never tasted.

Now, stop that, Betty!

With a splash the liquid foams into the other glass; and then the voice, whose origin I still dare not confront with my eyes, says curtly but pleasantly, 'Leave us.'

Footsteps echo ever fainter, followed by the click of a closing door. My stomach thrums with hollow fear.

'Now. Shall we sit?'

Bleakly I nod but still stare at the candle flame. I'm shaken, though, to see the skeletal claw with the rings beside mine on the gilt frame of the chair. I pull back, stunned – partially by his closeness, partially by the knowledge that the King of England is pulling out my chair for me.

'Come. Sit now,' he says pleasantly, 'little lady.'

Obediently, I sweep out satin skirts and into the chair, which he pushes up for me. And with one long, graceful motion of lanky legs, he falls into the other chair, to lean himself negligently in it, one leg thrust out, another arm over its back, his face watching me with a bemused smile and dancing, tender eyes: his whole carriage so like my lord's, I almost faint for combined wistfulness and apprehension.

'Well, now. Here we are. Do I detect a note of uneasiness?'

I stare down at the gold-engraved plate, my long white hands plucking at the pink satin of my skirts.

How many times has my fancy painted for me an elegant Whitehall supper at which I would sparkle? And now I can but pluck my skirt, curse my silent tongue and burning cheeks, and play the veriest gawky innocent.

I am disgusted with myself. Till now I've prided myself on the role played before the King: witty, coquettish, appealing.

And, oh, dreadful thought! What if Mama is i' th' right: what if I throw out signals that men catch the wrong way and get myself into scrapes from which I can no wise extricate myself?

I see he waits for a reply. I stare at the bubbling liquid in the glass and twirl the stem absently.

'Take a sip, my dear,' says that husky voice, 'and you'll feel better.'

My cheeks hot, I lift the glass to my lips. The crystal's frosted, etched fine as a spider web, and the liquid's sweet, heady, with bubbles that dance in my mouth and nose and expand, fruity, many-layered, with a kick 'twixt my ears, and trill down my gullet.

''Tis very good, sire,' I murmur.

'Of course 'tis. If 'twere not, Chiffinch and some others would have to answer for it.'

Chiffinch – is that not his private valet, that is said to sneak the women up the back stairs, under cloak of night? Jesu, am I one of 'em?

'Now, little lady –'

My hand still lies on the table, the stem of the glass 'twixt thumb and forefinger; and all at once, my round plump fingers are captured in his bony, swarthy ones. Oh, how then do I recall a thousand of Mama's sermons, all of which I thought antique!

He speaks again. 'Can you guess why I've brought you here, little maid?'

His hand feels alien.

'I – know not, sire, save – it be on account of my marriage.' There's a silence, but thank God he withdraws his hand and says pleasantly, 'Well, we will speak on that anon, if you like. Let us eat somewhat first.'

The door has opened again, and the page has borne in a silver tray, dome-covered. Balancing his burden betwixt us, he lifts off the top, to release a cloud of steam. A plump bird, baked to honey-brownness, sits on a bed of parsley and mushrooms. With a nod of the King, the page sets the bird down and commences to carve.

In the meanwhile, two other liveried boys bring in a silver-handled canister, three-bowled, from which they dip for us buttered peas, toasted almonds, and spirals of orange-peel and persimmon.

The three boys leaving with a bow, and I falling to, picking up the meat with my fingers and munching it, notice that His Majesty uses the knife and fork!

Blushing, I set down the meat, wipe my hands on a napkin, and pick up the utensils, to imitate him. I've heard of these new-fashion forks but never used one before.

His Majesty, having sampled some of the meat, puts down the fork, picks up the meat with his fingers and says, 'These forks are still very new, and I haven't got the hang of 'em yet.'

My heart warms, he works so well at putting me at my ease. Gingerly I pick up the meat again and give him a shy smile.

'There, that's better,' he says. 'No need to be afear'd of this ugly old Rowley here: he won't eat you up, my dear.'

I giggle and pat my lips with the napkin.

There follows quite a general conversation, for which I'm grateful. He tries me first upon the topic of state affairs and the condition of the Treasury and the Navy and kings and courts of Europe; but seeing my ignorance, he soon drops that strategy and tries me on a domestic topic.

'What think you of the fire?'

I look at him blankly. 'Fire? What fire, Your Majesty?'

His dark brows arch up with surprise so that he stops, a piece of breast 'twixt thumb and forefinger.

'You have not heard?'

I shake my head. 'No, sire.'

'There was a great fire, directly before you arrived here. It burnt up nigh onto everything in the city.'

'The Royal Exchange, too?' I cry.

He nods. 'E'en that.'

Startled, I digest this intelligence, hands in my lap. All the shopping excursions I've planned, vanished in a poof of smoke!

'There's been much suffering amongst the poorer people,' the King continues, his brows knitted, 'and those of the middle rank have fared little better. I'm proclaiming a general emergency throughout the kingdom and asking for what charity people can spare.'

Now I am ashamed, thinking of my selfishness about the shops. 'Oh, write to my guardians!' I lean forward. 'They'll contribute something handsome.'

He nods gravely. 'Aye – 'tis not a bad idea, for me to have sent out under my seal a special plea to all the larger landowners in the realm.'

I nod.

'But you've not drunk much of your champagne,' he says, one of his eyebrows up.

'Oh, so I haven't!'

Smiling, I tilt up to my lips the frosted glass etched with grapes and cupids, to let the kicky, bubbling gold tumble down my throat.

'Mmmm, 'tis good!' I cry with a giggle.

He smiles indulgently.

'Now let us hear about you, madam.' He pats his lips with his napkin.

I am a little discomfited here. But indeed, I feel more at ease than I did before – perhaps because his attentions have dwindled to kindliness. Or perhaps indeed this liquid is too strong to bear much drinking of; for I stand outside myself, to watch my giddy talk.

'Well, sire! Let me see. I suppose there's not much to say but that I'm a chick who's been long in the shell and just ventured out into the great world – and too timid, indeed, to see aught of it.' I giggle, my hand to my mouth. 'Can Your Majesty guess how I spent the day?'

Smiling, he shakes his head, scoops his peas up into the spoon.

'Why –' I lean over confidentially '– I sat in my chambers the whole day, for being afear'd of going out anywhere, lest I seem loose walking out without my mama. Is that not absurd?'

'It is indeed, madam.'

'Tell me, sire – that is, if you will, please – is it proper for a young lady to go hereabouts unattended – I mean, with her maid only?'

'Aye, anywhere in Westminster. There are places in the city, though, which I'd not recommend you to set foot without male escort – especially now that the area has been reduced to rubble, and gangs of cutthroats roam it.'

I shudder. 'No, that sounds not too nice.'

'But you've not told me about all your lovers.'

I hear my brittle laugh. 'Jesu, what lovers should a woman have when she's so shut up by her mama, Newgate must be nothing to it?'

He laughs. 'Come, let's hear of your suitors.'

I shrug my shoulders, toss him a roguish look, lowering my sooty eyelashes. 'Oh, my Lord Hinchingbrooke would have had me; the

Lord John Butler might not have me; my Lord Rochester would have forced me; Sir Francis Popham would kiss my breech to have me.'

The King bursts out laughing, his eyes twinkling. Still giggling, I look down, my cheeks flushed.

'And who else do you think would have you, my pretty maid?'

'Well, sire –' I look up and prepare to make a pert answer but then suddenly see those brown eyes piercing into mine. Fear rises in my stomach and throbs in my throat. I clench the napkin in my lap.

All at once he leans over, and his arm goes round the back of my chair.

'I –' Oh, Jesu, my tongue, my wit, help me out now! 'I – think I know not, sir, but – if I did, I would tell you, that no one who would have had me has had me yet.'

The King's eyes narrow and glint at me. 'Not yet, eh?'

He reaches out a long, bony hand and seizes my plump white one that rests on the table. What should I do now? Reprove my monarch and draw my hand back? No, I cannot do that. He is my king, after all!

I look down and away, my cheeks flushed, and murmur, 'Not until I'm wed, sir.'

'Do you intend to put off all lovers until after your marriage: is that it, fair cruelty?'

Still looking away, I murmur, 'Yes, sire. And the only lover I take will be my husband.'

I think he's going to reply but that a bustle at the door announces the page; and His Majesty drops my hand, which quickly I settle into my lap, and leans back again, pulling the arm from behind my chair.

Oh, this is a fine pickle I've got myself into! Never would I have eaten supper alone in a gentleman's bedchamber, but it seems in my foolish innocence I did not regard the King as a man – only an office that was going to welcome me officially and prate of my marriage.

The page draws away the gold-etched plates that have held the pullet and peas, we having devoured the bird down to its bones; and his smaller assistant puts before us a yellow crème, whipped with sugar and garnished with sugared sliced almonds. The third boy replenishes our glasses, at which I know not whether to be grateful or sorry, the liquid being so delicious yet so strong. And I note, there's another wine glass not even been touched yet.

The King digs his spoon into the lemon crème, so I follow suit. Casually, betwixt bites, he says, 'That's an unfashionable attitude, pretty lady.'

I shrug, stare down at the whipped lemon crème, and at last reply, 'It appears, sire, that though I wished to be fashionable, and came here believing I was fashionable, and passed for fashionable in Somerset, I've so far been much surprised at the ways my manners have fallen short of fashion.'

'Should you not mend them, then?'

'Insofar as my conscience will suffer me, sire. But even small changes in manners take some getting used to.'

I look ruefully down at my too-exposed bosom and wish a thousandth time for the pinner I've always worn. I continue, 'But changes in conscience may not be in order at all. For my conscience grew up with me, as my heart and limbs did, and I know not whether I'd cut it out, simply to pass for a great lady.'

'Well said. But it may be —' He shoots me an arch look, his black brows going up 'neath the periwig, his full red lips curved, 'you'll want no such a surgical operation, for it may be that property will fade insensibly from contact with different manners here.'

I shake my head. 'I think not, sire.'

'Then you will be mightily different from the other maids from the country.'

Something gives me courage to stare him straight in the eye and say, 'I doubt not I will, sire.'

He leans back in the chair, one arm over its back, the other hand thrumming the table with its fingers.

'Have you a candidate for marriage in mind?'

I flush and look down at my empty dessert dish, my hands in my lap. 'I —'

What to say now? This is the place where I've been thinking to insert a plea for aid in marrying my lord, but I know not any more whether my lord would marry me; and to confess my love, it seems, would put me at a double disadvantage. For the King, being so close to my lord, might confess it to him, either to make him laugh or take advantage of me; and I've begun to suspect, if I'm to get aught out of this King, I must needs play him carefully. Though he may have forwarded the match 'twixt my lord and me before, his attitude now might be to have me for himself and frustrate the attempts of anyone else. And, God knows, perhaps if I confessed the fatal name, some means would be found to keep my lord at sea indefinitely.

So I pluck the tablecloth hanging o'er my lap, look down, and murmur, 'I — my guardians have sent me here, Your Majesty, to make that choice.'

'Very well, pretty maid. I'll press you no more on that subject. But what about on another?'

I've had my hand in my lap to prevent his capturing it on the table top; but on a sudden, I feel that hot, bony claw fall down to grasp my fingers. This is worse, considering the demesnes where his fingers now move!

Gingerly I lift our entwined hands to the table top. I shoot him a frantic looks but dare not withdraw his hand where he presses it, and his rings bore into my flesh.

His eyes holding mine, he says genially, 'This makes you uncomfortable, does it not?'

I nod feebly and stare down. 'Aye, sire.'

'Has no swain ever got your hand like this before, pretty maid?'

'I –' I look down, then over at him soberly. 'Yes, sire. Once.'

'And did he do this?'

Suddenly the King turns my hand over and kisses the palm. I shudder in fear to feel his moist lips and tongue run over my skin. My heart is in my throat with terror, for I can think of nothing but what he is said to do to Frances.

'Yes, sire – but –'

Hearing my squeaky voice, I grow angry. Why am I suffering him such impertinence? He will not force me – and, sure, I'm a freeborn citizen of England and have a right not to be handled so.

I jerk my hand away and say, 'But he was devilish bold.'

The King chuckles with a sip of his goblet. 'I would have been more surprised if he had not been.'

'Your Majesty and I differ there,' I reply pertly, 'for in men's boldness there is much to surprise *me.*' And I sit forward in my chair.

He chuckles again. 'Then I fear you're destined to be much surprised at court.'

'Surprised, perhaps, Your Majesty,' I reply firmly, 'but not taken by surprise.'

He laughs. 'A boast requires a trial.'

All at once his mouth is so close I can smell the sour wine. Heart pounding, I pop up my fan.

'My, but it's grown too warm for *me,*' I observe pointedly, making a furious breeze.

I fear at first he will be angry; but he's gentleman enough to know what unfair advantage he has tried to take of me. He sits back and smiles slyly.

'And yet I have heard that you were not above a kiss.'

Worse and worse! Now will I discover that my lord has been boasting of my favours?

I train a severe look on the King (where has my spirit come from?)

and say, 'It were no gentleman, Your Majesty, that would have said so of me; and no gentleman that would have repeated it.'

'No gentleman indeed,' he agrees, 'but a raving mama, who writ to me and recommended a certain young suitor of yours be locked up – at which I was forced awhile to oblige her.' I feel my face grow hot, and he adds, 'But I am justly reproved. It is not the kissing that frights you, then, but the man?'

I colour still more deeply.

'Let me show you what a pleasant experience 'tis – there's no harm in it.'

'There's a great deal of harm in it, Your Majesty, especially unattended as we are,' I return soberly.

'Not if I give you my oath only to kiss.' The King shoots me a droll look. 'I can keep to the promise. I am no hot, groping youth.'

Now I blush to the roots of my hair, so particular a look does he give me. 'Your Majesty, I find this discourse most abashing; and I would consider it a special favour if you would not vex me with it the more.'

He leans back and snaps his fingers – but with his hand still on my chair back – and so quickly does the head page appear, I know he's been lurking just without the door and overhearing all.

Oh, dear! Trouble piles upon trouble. Now I will have a reputation all over the court.

And what is this thick brown liquid being poured into the silver goblet?

'What's this?' I ask suspiciously.

'Only a little brandywine, my dear.'

Brandywine! That's stuff's supposed to be as strong as Devil's brew. Sure he means not to drink me insensible and then ravish me?

No, a king must have honour, after all.

'Drink, drink,' he urges, the boy bowing and leaving. Knowing not what else to do in the face of a command from my monarch, I lift the goblet to my lips and moisten 'em with a drop of the fiery substance.

'Let us discuss your abashment a moment,' says the King, tossing down so much of the brew that I gape at him. 'Is it not constraint, brought on by a strangeness betwixt us? Would not a little more familiarity make you easier in my company?'

I stare down into the demoniac dancing fire of the liquid and shrug.

'For I *do* plan to get to know you much better, my dear,' he says ominously.

Oh, what to say now? Where is the tongue that wagged me free of difficulties but a few moments before?

'Just one kiss,' he says.

What shall I do now? Must I kiss him, let him fondle me? For he is stronger than I and can force whatever caress he will. I cannot slap the face or stomp the foot of my King; and after all, do I not live in his house?

Now, for the first time, do I consider what some pretty serving-maid must feel, to serve in some lecher's home – to be chased up and down cold corridors by the Lord Buckhurst.

All at once I feel his hot breath on my cheek. I turn my head away as far as I can, to remove my lips from the vicinity of his searching mouth, and feel something hot and moist slide across my cheek.

'Come, that's no good,' he murmurs huskily.

His bony claws grasp my arms, and he's turning me toward him. I still keep my head turned away; but he's half risen from his chair; and hovering over me, grasping my arms, he plants his hot, wet mouth on the corner of my lips.

'Kiss me,' he murmurs.

I still hold my head rigidly to the side, so he slides his mouth around to my lips and covers 'em. The slimy cavern of his mouth makes me almost faint, but I keep my lips clenched against his probing tongue and hold my body rigid as a poker.

Releasing me, he says curtly, 'tis plain you're much wanting in the instruction you feel so loath to take.'

This summation angers me. That he should have the arrogance to assume I'm cold, simply because I have no taste for him!

I yearn to wipe my violated mouth but dare not, so simply stare back frigidly at him, the wetness and bad taste clinging to my lips, a shudder of disgust and fear going down my frame.

'Then Your Majesty should wish little to do with me, I think,' is my curt reply, 'seeing as there are others so much abler.'

'Not at all.' He smiles – as he thinks – pleasantly. 'I've a great mind to try challenges. And we can't let you go so cold to your poor husband, can we?'

I yearn to say, I could never be cold with *him.*

'Well, come, come. All such trials – both yours and mine – are over for the evening. Ask one of the boys to convey you back.'

My heart leaps at this suggestion of my release. Thank God he has not the stomach to ravish a woman's stiff, unyielding body!

But my heart plummets down again when he says, 'Don't think, however, that the issue's closed. I didn't work so hard to get you here because I owe your grandpa a favour, you know.'

I stand so quickly the chair falls down behind me, and he laughs. 'Frighted, I see, my poor little country rose! Well, we'll give you some time to think on the first lesson and absorb it before we proceed to the second.'

I curtsey low, spreading my skirts out, looking down. Then, eyes still on the floor, I back as quickly as I can toward the door, find the knob with my hand, and propel myself backwards out, to the sound of his hearty laughter.

3

'I Looked At My Love'
11–25 September 1666

I looked at my love: that feeling which was my master's – which he had created; it shivered in my heart, like a suffering child in a cold cradle; sickness and anguish had seized it; it could not seek Mr Rochester's arms – it could not derive warmth from his breast.
—Charlotte Brontë, *Jane Eyre*

The lady of the West is at Court without any suitors, nor is like to have any.
—Letter, 10 September 1666, from Sir George Carteret to Lord Sandwich

Another grey morning – and another – rolling into my bleak life – and I'm forced to re-examine my position; and, sunk lower in spirits than ever, to realize, not only am I foiled of my dearest dreams but I am endangered as I never was in Somerset.

For I'm without confidantes or protectors, in peril of being ravished by a lewd old man from whose power there's no appeal.

Should I confide in Mr Savile? No. What can he do? And I cannot but remember his polite but cool reception of my first plea. Nor can I blame him. Is it his responsibility to protect all the women in love with the infamous Lord Rochester?

How can I pretend to be anything more? Can I assume the posture of affianced bride when he takes not even the trouble to communicate with me, offers no sign that he rushes to my side after a seventeen-months' absence?

This disinterest gnaws on me worse than anything else. I think I could keep my spirits up to fend off this old lecher if only I knew my lord were hastening to be with me, yearning for me as I for him; if only he were writing me dear little billet-doux.

His Majesty invites me to no more tête-à-tête suppers, thank God – not that I hope the chicken hawk has forgot the hatchling. No, he but plays me out like a game fish, gives me time (as he said) 'twixt lessons.

I venture forth with Susan in a chair, for buying of scents and laces and other gewgaws at the New Exchange in the Strand; and though I quake with every glance cast on me, no one offers to attack or reprove me for showing myself unattended. So soon I think nothing of stepping into the shops and cook-shops and inns up and down the Strand and Charing Cross – nor *even* (in a gay flight of abandon) taking chair over to Covent Garden and popping in to Will's for a dish of coffee. But all this adventuring I do markedly without the enthusiasm I'd expected; and I must confess, the hollered compliments on my charms make me quake.

But I encounter a new friend, Frances Jennings, at the great Gallery separating the outer demesnes of Whitehall, where anyone of quality may enter, from the inner chambers, where one must be known or have written conveyance.

I'm strolling there of an afternoon, to take the fashionable promenade, a laced cap on my head and white knotted stole about my shoulders against the chill, when I hear raucous laughter.

By one of the windows hacked from stone and overlooking the privy garden stands a beauty of the type called a *sparkler*: fair, bright, full of nervous, flitty movements like a lightning bug's.

'Oh, lud, oh, lud, I thought I should die for laughing!'

Going by, I cast her a shy smile, for she's caught my eye upon her; and in her frank manner, she cries out, 'Why, lud, who's this? Some new beauty, I vow. Come over here, my dear –' and waves me with a friendly hand, her face like a long white melon, smile-cracked in the bottom half, her fair curls bouncing, her leg thrust in, then out, and her wand-like form turned right, then left.

Picking up skirts, I obligingly waddle over (feeling like a duck beside her with my slower movements and round body). As I nod she thrusts out a hand and says, 'Jennings' the name. And what's yours?'

Gingerly, not quite knowing what to do, I take her hand, which she pumps; and with a giggle return, 'Elizabeth Mallet, madam. I'm pleased to –'

'Mallet!' she breaks in, brown eyes snapping 'neath the arched amber brows. 'O-ho, so you're the one. Mallet. You're quite famous here, you know,'

She drops my hand and winks – leans against the wall, arms crossed, like a gracefully swayed willow.

I start at this suggestion but then reply pertly, 'Famous but not infamous, I hope.'

'Oh, both, I assure you, dear!' She pops open a fan and makes her bright curls fly upward in the breeze. 'Why, when my Lord of Rochester abducted you, we could all talk of nothing else for days!'

''Twas quite an experience for me, also.'

'Mallet, permit me to present Elizabeth Hamilton –' A plump sparrow with chestnut curls, small bright eyes, and a sober, down-turned mouth bobs a curtsey on the right '– and our beloved Price –' A lady shaped like a bulb on top of the King's sundial, her face screwed into a grimace, bobs at me from the left.

Price then speaks in a harsh, gravelly voice. 'I congratulate you, madam, on surviving a fate worse than death.'

I look at her blankly. 'Why, whatever mean you, madam?'

Jennings bursts into a ripple of laughter. 'Oh, Mallet! Pay her no mind. She and the Lord Rochester have diverted us all so much, these months and months, more than the bear and the dogs would a crowd of 'prentices at Hockley in the Hole. Why, he has writ lampoons on her; and she has fumed and spread rumours about him; and they've given one another such looks at all the assemblies! Why, she simply believes you were carried off by the Devil himself and set awhile in the den of hell, that's all!'

I burst out laughing, my hand over my lips.

Jennings arches one fair eyebrow up and one down. 'Now that you're here, we can all satisfy our curiosity on one point. 'Did he –' She leaves the question hanging, her brown eyes sparkling with mischief in her narrow face.

I look at her pertly. 'No, more's the pity. He sent me off with chaperones and was captured and put in the Tower directly after.'

Jennings and Price laugh as I pout, lip thrust out.

'Maybe not such a pity,' says Hamilton in a prim, severe, careful voice. 'If he'd truly got you alone, my dear, you might have been very sorry indeed.'

I gawk at her, and the madcap Jennings bursts in, 'Oh, Mallet, pay her no mind! She's ever with her "watch-out-for-it's" and "you'll-be-sorry-for-it's". We know you wouldn't have done anything. I was only hoping there might have been a few juicy details – but, say! – 'tis well you were not alone with him.'

'He would not have ravished me –'

'Ravish! No, I'm sure, not: that's not his style. There's no one he'd ever *need* ravish. No, he smiles so sweetly, and talks so affectionately, as if the best of friends – and then he kisses a hand – and then a lip – and WHAM!'

Jennings laughs so mightily at her own jest I cannot but join in, though her two companions look sourly upon her.

400

'I thank you for your advice, madam,' I say, still chortling; and then some madness seizes me – only, I think, to know I have such an audience as Jennings, for I add, 'I'll take care when his whammer's out.'

Then indeed both of us laugh so hard, holding our sides, we turn red. And Mrs Hamilton draws herself up to the firm regality of her height, crosses her arms, and says, 'Well!'

Jennings, though, falls cackling into my arms. 'Oh, Mallet, I dare swear you'll be priceless about here! Where do you lodge?'

'Off Scotland Yard.'

'I'm in St James, with the Duchess of York's train,' she says, just as if the whole kingdom knew naught of the fabled Mrs Jennings. 'Price is over there, too – and my mother and little sister Sarah. Hamilton lodges at her uncle Ormond's at Whitehall.'

I burst out, 'Oh, her uncle Ormond's! You are kin to the Lord John Butler, then.'

Now she treats me with another look of disapproval. 'Yes, madam. I am his cousin.'

And very unlike him, too, you snipped-nose primrose.

'Well,' I say in chilly tones, 'I only mean, the Lord John has been a friend to me when I've been in distress.'

'There has been talk of you in the family, madam.' She holds her plump body rigid, *à la* harpy.

Fortunately Jennings thinks to break into the awkward conversation with a change of topic. 'Oh, Mallet! Price and I were just discussing what a lark 'twould be to disguise ourselves as wenches and go down to the city and view the ruins of the dreadful fire. Would you care to come along?'

'What?' I shriek. 'But His Majesty has said it is very dangerous down there.'

This response draws two different replies. Elizabeth Hamilton's eyebrows go up, and she says, '*His Majesty!*', whilst Jennings tries to defend herself:

'Aye, but of course 'tis, Mallet! That's the great sport. But a few years back, Price and I disguised ourselves as orange wenches and went down to the city to ply our trade in the theatre and fell into a thousand adventures and were almost caught by Mr Brounker and put into his stable. Oh, 'twas quite an adventure! The tame life here can be nothing to it.' She waves an expansive hand.

'No, thank you.' I shudder. 'I've been too much protected all my life to delight in such a frolic.'

401

'Well, we'll teach you better manners here.' Jennings grins, elfin-mischievous.

'How came you in conversation with His Majesty?' thrusts in Hamilton, with an eye for what she believes the main point.

I flush. 'He – he – asked me to supper to welcome me to me court, madam.'

All three of 'em exchange glances.

'So that's what it means,' Price mutters.

'What what means?'

They are silent.

'What *what* means? Jennings?'

She shrugs her shoulders, casts her eyes away. 'Nothing. Something we heard.'

'Well, tell me what 'tis!'

'Well, 'twas one of those fifth-hand things. Somebody heard some-body say that there was a very beautiful and wealthy young heiress, lately come up from the West, to dwell at court. And it was said, she'll soon be game for all the gallants here. And someone else said that he thought not there'd be any that would dare to court *her.*'

I get a hollow feeling at the pit of my stomach. 'And?'

Jennings shrugs. 'That's all.'

I stare at all three of 'em: Hamilton's primly elevated nose, Jen-nings' calculating scrutiny, and Price's evil smirk-glare.

'You think I'm brought up here to be his whore, but that's not so! And no matter *who* thinks it,' I add pointedly.

Jennings shrugs, arms crossed. 'Very well. We believe you.' But I can tell they do not.

'Jesu,' I cry, 'is my reputation here ruin't already, and I've done nothing?'

'No, no, Mallet! 'Tis not so.' Impulsively Jennings throws her arms about me, clasps me in a brief hug. 'We didn't know; that's all. There now. Unruffle your feathers. Why, His Majesty has a go at every new young beauty here.'

'Aye,' confirms the gravel-voice of Price. 'He tried Jennings awhile.'

'What did you do?' I ask, mouth a little open.

'Why, simply refused to meet him alone anywhere.'

'You can *do* this?'

'Why, of course. Simply turn down his invitations.'

'I had not thought I could –'

'Oh, Jesu!' exclaims Jennings. 'Why, your innocence is going to get you in more trouble than all the wordly-wiseness of any great lady of the town.'

Oh, dear. Where have I heard that before? From a mama whose ravings I never heeded.

'Mrs Jennings, I hope you will be my confidante, for it seems I want instruction.'

'Why, I'll be happy to!'

She's then for the city, so we say our good-byes but promise to meet anon. And, waving a gay hand and picking up her skirts, she flounces chattering down the gallery, Price lumbering in her wake like an overfed bear.

Hamilton stands primly, hands folded before her, and bobs a small curtsey, straight-backed, before whirling off in the other direction.

So here's a friend I've made; and, it seems, an enemy. There are so many things to be careful of here!

Then, strolling back to my apartments in Scotland Yard, knocking up Susan and being admitted, I am astonished to find a message that gives me cause for delight and alarm.

4

'Who Sees Her Must Love'
25–30 September 1666

The nymph that undoes me is fair and unkind,
No less than a wonder by Nature designed;
She's the grief of my heart, the joy of my eye,
And the cause of a flame that can never die.

Her mouth, from whence wit still obliging flows,
Has the beautiful blush and the smell of the rose;
Love and destiny both attend on her will,
She wounds with a look, with a frown she can kill.

The desperate lover can hope no redress
Where beauty and rigour are both in excess;
In Silvia they meet, so unhappy am I,
Who sees her must love and who loves her must die.
—George Etherege, 'Silvia' (first published in 1672)

Her Majesty sponsors a treat in my honour, to welcome me to Whitehall!

Now, this twist is curious indeed: I've been at Whitehall above ten days, and only now does Her Majesty think to welcome me? Who, I wonder, has prompted her to notice my presence at all? The cat that lurks round the corner and twitches its tail at the approach of the mouse?

But the mouse presents itself, nonetheless, on the day and time given, in the Queen's red-wainscoted Presence Chamber, just behind the Great Stone Gallery.

The Queen – poor squat dark nun of a creature – sits bashfully smiling and remote on a gilt chair beneath a red state canopy; and after a warm but halting greeting in English, her hand extended for me to kiss, suffers the whole of the treat to be directed by two officious persons: the merry and red-faced Lady Bridget Sanderson, mother to the maids of honour; and a large, rough-voiced Mrs Hobart, mother to the maids of the Duchess of York. This latter worthy welcomes me with great heartiness, even kissing me, squeezing my bare white arms, and praising my beauty with a frank generosity very unusual to our sex.

Then a parade commences of so many notables my head reels: all the famous names I have heard these five years, with faces at last to put to 'em. Here is the Lady Anna-Maria Shrewsbury, gypsy-dark and handsome with her wild snapdragon eyes, holding out a long, slim hand; and here's a background player to her, their arms linked together as though great friends: a placid-faced old woman, who bobs a serene head and says, 'Mary Villiers Buckingham, dear.'

My eyes pop at this tableau of whore and wife. Does this poor old dustmop of a duchess not know, pretend not to know, or renounce all pride to please a beloved husband? The Duke stands behind 'em both, resplendent in his white and gold velvet and red and white sash, and smiles with brazen geniality. Jesu! If this is the court manners, give me the country any day.

A parade of others known to me follows: a flirting, simpering Frances Fat-Front, who blinks as usual to clear her head of the wisps ('But I am so happy, now, dear, indeed I am; we shall have such frolics together, I know'); the Duchess of Ormond, pressing my hand and urging me not to be a stranger, and her husband the Duke seconding the invitation; then most of their delightful noble children in a pack – Emilie Ossory extending me an invitation to come the next day and see her babies. Castlemaine traipses up, looking blowzy and out of humour, so that I am much surprised how her beauty has been taken down – and do I see a patch of white lead meant to hide a wrinkle? And Sir Francis Popham is here to wave his laced handkerchief and lisp an hundred times, 'La, Mrs Mallet, our western flower,' and to stick at my side like an humblebee to a stamen, buzzing his impertinences at my ear.

At last, after a steady stream of some hundred and fifty notables – including all my Lords this and that of the Bedchamber or Stole or Wardrobe, and my Lord Stewards, and Mr Price the court physician, and Mr That from the Royal Academy, and Chancellor Clarendon and his swollen spawn the Duchess of York, and scores of names and faces I pray Jesus I will never need to keep track of – the crush dies down a bit, collies clumping together, and the fiddles and trumpets playing Lully's tunes as a background.

The wizened smiling monkey of a queen sits like a backdrop in her own Presence Chamber whilst Castlemaine traipses about, hectoring in a raucous voice the quivering houseboys, and Frances Fat-Front lisps, rolls eyes, shrugs shoulders, and gathers a crowd at the treat-table.

Is this the polite manner, for a wife to welcome her husband's whores? My head buzzes, my face aches from smiling, and I wonder where my friends the Lord John and Mr Savile can be. All seems hollow and false about me, and I keep sidling away from the rooster that would cockle-doo his love-plaints.

All at once I tread on the heel of some tall man.

'Oh! Your pardon, sir.'

He turns about, his eyes narrowed to a wicked twinkle above the moustache. Ugh! How like the King he looks.

'We meet again, madam. I trust, not for the last time.'

I flush. 'Sir, I do not know you.'

His eyes narrow to glinting. 'And yet you smiled on me in Tunbridge.'

My face grows hotter. 'Sir, I think I did not.'

He leans down, leering over large white teeth, his blue plume tickling my nose. 'And yet you did.'

I cast a wild eye about the chamber but see no protector: only Jennings making wry faces, her head at a pert angle. Sir Francis stands beside me, silent and gaping above his chicken-neck, and takes snuff 'twixt a twiggy forefinger and thumb.

The impertinent leering villain runs a practised eye from my forehead to my feet, as if I were a filly at auction. 'Lord Herbert, madam.'

'And should I know that name, sir?'

His grin widens. 'If you do not, madam, your grandfather will be making it known to you.'

'Your pardon, sir,' lisps a voice on my left. 'We must speak with an old friend here.'

I gladly take the extended arm of George Etherege and smile up into the kind blue-grey eyes 'twixt the sandy periwig and bony cheeks.

Elbowing my tormentors aside, my rescuer conveys me to his circle, with whom I have a long, laughing conversation. Sedley and I divert ourselves by satirising everyone else in the chamber, libelling their garb and naming what birds they would be and why; Etherege bounds off to secure for me a silver cup of something red and strong and sweet, which I sip as I tease Buckhurst on his war feats; then Sedley rallies Buckhurst for his silly, silent countenance and urges him, 'Drink, man –'

All at once a flourish at the door causes me to look up.

I blush all the way from my neck up to the roots of my hair. For the Lord John Butler enters, tall and muscular, with his grave, handsome, cleft-jawed face and curled fair periwig, his dark blue jacket draped with a red and white sash.

Hat under arm, he stalks toward me, his other arm swinging, to bow stiffly and say curtly, 'Madam, I am glad to see you well and among us.'

So grim is his frown on me, I cry, 'Lord John! What is't? Are you angry with me?'

'Madam, I could never be angry with you,' he says abruptly.

I pluck his sleeve and say, 'Can you not unbend a little, then, sir?'

His brow unclenches then, and his eyes go soft.

Oh, no! Have I made a mistake in urging him to treat me more friendly?

Quickly I remove my long white fingers from his arm. 'I – mean – that is, I'm glad to see you well, sir.' I stare down at the white-and-black-checked floor.

What gaze do I feel boring into me? A glance from the corner of my eye detects the prim-faced, fat-cheeked Hamilton glaring on me, her hands crossed before her skirts and her back in a harpy-straight carriage. Other eyes regard me from above fluttering fans or lifted goblets, and hasn't the conversation lowered to a buzz above the fiddles?

Lord John and I stand together in an agony of abashment, knowing not whether 'tis worse to speak or part.

'Madam, I –'

He makes a stop, fumbles with the hat 'neath his arm, moves it up and then down his side, looks at the floor, then at the musicians.

'Madam – I – I hope you have been well.'

'Oh, yes, thank you very much,' I lie in a squeak.

'You look rather pale.' Then he adds in a consternation, 'I mean – that is – not to say –'

''Tis the indoor life here,' I babble quickly. 'In Somerset I was much more wont to step outside for walks and rides.'

Jesu, what an inane conversation this is! Neither of us saying what we mean—

'If –' He pauses.

I look up curiously from where I've regarded the interesting chessboard of a floor.

'If what, sir?'

'That is – I mean – I only meant to say –'

Poor Lord John! I recall him from our early conversations as quite a man of parts; but these days he always seems in such a foolish flutter about me.

'I – that is – there are places, madam, where you may want coach and conveyance or escort, and I'd only have you know, that – if you should discover a need, that is – I'd be happy to furnish you escort of any kind, or simply a coach.'

'Why, thank you, Lord John. That's most kind of you.' Another pause threatening, I babble idiotically, 'I've been trying to visit the shops, but I hear many of them have been burnt up.'

'Yes, madam. There's some few in Westminster to see, however.'

We're about to seize upon the silly topic of the shops in order to cover up why he really offered his family's coach, when George Etherege insolently interrupts our conversation.

'Madam, we were wondering if you heard what a great hero my Lord of Rochester has recently been at the battle on the Downs.'

My face goes hot, and Lord John's turns pale.

'No, sir,' I squeak, then look down at the floor.

Etherege is himself interrupted by Lord Ashfield, the lazily drawling, sandy-periwigged young beau that's so shy and well-looked. His clear, candid green eyes sparkle above the upturned nose and boyish grin; he slouches indolently, ignoring the female glances turned toward his broad shoulders and rounded thighs.

'The battle must have been a fearful thing, madam: five thousand of our men killed and three thousand taken prisoner.'

My heart thuds in my stomach. Why had I never considered how he risks his life? Why think I of him as invincible, as some young god of battle, charmed and relentless?

'Almost all of our officers killed, and everyone else – that is, almost everyone – turned coward under fire. 'Twas June, and the guns so loud, they were like thunder e'en from the gravel pit hard by St James Park. Hundreds of us stood there listening.'

I moisten my lips and lean forward. 'And?'

He is determined to relate everything about the bloody and drawn-out battle against the Dutch but what I would hear, and does so until I could scream; how can he ramble so: he is more meandering than the dull goose that picks bugs in the pasture.

A lady shuffling by in taffeta moire, with blue overskirts and a yellow petticoat, squeezes his arm and lifts her lips to his ear, to whisper and stick in her tongue. I'm much scandalised at such bold behaviour, but Ashfield nods vaguely and absent-mindedly rubs his ear, then continues the tedious narration.

'For God's sake, my lord!' bursts in an exasperated Etherege. 'Tell of Rochester!'

'I'm getting to that! Hold your peace.'

The prowling lady, who has flaming hair and no doubt a temperament rightly fitted to it, fumes and hangs at Ashfield's elbow, but he seems utterly unaware of her. He is too intent on his long, dull tale.

But at last he cracks the nut and picks out the meat.

'The point is, madam, no one in the fleet showed courage comparable to Rochester's. Madam, Sir Edward Spragge found himself commanding shipsful of cowards. One captain in particular avoiding engagement whenever possible, Sir Edward wrote him out a direct order commanding attack but could get no one to deliver it. Almost all of the volunteers on his ship had already been killed, and the fire was so heavy, everyone else clung to the deck and refused even so much as to put his head up to man a gun, much less go rollicking in a small boat through the thick of the fray. But immediately Rochester heard of the problem, he came cheerfully to volunteer his services.'

Past the ball in my throat, I whisper, 'Was he hurt?'

'Amazingly enough, no, madam, though 'twere a miracle.'

I let out the breath I've been holding.

Ashfield continues, 'When he returned to the *Lion*, a great cheer went up from the deck, no one having anticipated ever to see him again, much less unwounded.'

Etherege inserts, 'He's been a great hero and led the boarding of the ships.'

Why does he such things? 'Tis enough to acquit one's self bravely under fire; a man need not venture his life so daringly on each encounter that all onlookers marvel. Does he try to prove something – and if so, to whom? Sure he knows that such extreme gallantry is not necessary to prove his reputation? His friend Buckingham, though no coward, ne'er risks his life when he can squirm gracefully out of a battle or duel; nor do I note many of the other wits even going to war, though Buckhurst is said to have gone once and done nothing.

Eyes glazed with tears, I murmur weakly, ''Tis indeed courageous.'

Ashfield puts in, ''Twas a battle, madam, that blew many men's reputations for courage. The valour of my Lord Rochester stood very much in contrast to the cowardice of all the others.'

I make a senseless noise in reply.

But truly my heart beats so hard, partially simply to hear the dear name again (for in Somerset 'tis a blasphemy ne'er to be spoken); partially to fear for his life; partially to hope that his friends try to distract me from other suitors; till with forced casualness I ask, 'When think you he'll be here again?'

Ashfield shrugs, his oval face split with a grin. 'Madam, I cannot say. A friend of his, one Harry Savile, is gone to the fleet to fetch him, though.'

So that's where my jelly-bellied cupid's gone!

Sedley winks a small black eye at me. 'I wager 'twill not be long – ho!'

As best I can, I conceal my glowing joy, and a stiff voice says suddenly, 'Madam, I'll leave you now.'

Poor Lord John, whom I'd forgot, and who's been swallowing the bitter pills of his rival's gallantry, bows with one leg thrust out and, whirling about, stalks off.

Poor Lord John! Indeed I'm sorry for him, but what can I do?

I've barely digested the happy news when another flourish draws my eye to the door.

In strides a tall, skinny, swarthy figure with red ermine-trimmed robes, one shoulder emblazoned with a round seal of the garter, one hand grasping a long gold walking stick, both feet surrounded by yapping little dogs.

I flush and curtsey.

His Majesty nodding politely on all sides lopes o'er to the isolated queen perching in her chair, hands clasped in lap, eyes staring meekly about. And I'm touched when he kisses her cheek. He's not a bad man, just a slave to his vices; and I'm half ready to believe that his attack on me was compounded of the wine he'd drunk and the amazement of being refused. Everyone bows in rows and clumps as he passes and waves a negligent hand.

And, Lord! He makes his way to *me*!

One of the puppies has been yapping at my feet, and without thinking, I've picked it up and clasped it to my bosom to stroke its little neck.

The King, striding up with gold cane and spaniels, observes, 'Well, there's a pleasant place to be.'

I look down at the black and white fur ball clasped to my bosom.

'Enjoying yourself, I hope, pretty maid?'

I nod, stare down. 'Yes, sire.'

'You see I can be a gentleman when I wish.'

I nod, still looking down. 'Yes, sire, of course.'

The King flourishes an impatient bejewelled hand, and I hear the rustling of cloaks and murmurs of 'Your Majesty' as my friends abandon me for the four walls.

The King steps closer and murmurs in a husky voice, 'I would like to apologise for my carriage to you at our last meeting.'

I gawk up at him. Apologise? The King apologise? Sure I'm hearing things!

'Your Majesty is in your own house in your own kingdom,' I murmur. 'For what should there be need of apology?'

'Nevertheless, pretty maid, I've a mind to. This soiree is one part;

410

the other I deliver in my own person. I'd like to entertain you at another supper, to have a chance to make amends.'

Now indeed do I regard the checks on the floor again and feel a heat in my cheeks as I stammer, 'Your Majesty – I – think not.'

'What's this? Afear'd?'

His voice is low and chuckling; he moves so close, I can smell his sour breath. Oh, for the arm of Etherege now!

But he's melted into a corner. I throw him a frantic glance, and he leans impassively against the wall, his brow furrowed and arms crossed as he watches me with the King.

'I – I have been taught by my mama, sire, a woman should not receive a gentleman alone, and I have seen nothing to disprove my fears on that subject.'

'But yet, you did meet me alone once.'

The puppy is warm and fuzzy and comforting against my bare breast: I clasp it tighter, partially for support, partially for concealment of my upthrust white mounds.

'I – did not know many things.'

'Such as?'

My eyes on the chessboard 'neath our feet, I say miserably, 'That we were to be alone. That I were allowed to refuse my monarch – or would have cause to.'

'Well, pretty maid, that many have not found *cause* to is so. Nor do I think you will, for ever. What say you to being a countess?'

I look up, eyes sparkling in delight, lips parted. 'Oh, Your Majesty!' Eagerly I scan the swarthy face with the small, merry eyes, bulbous nose, and little moustache; then suddenly I realise he refers not to my taking the honour by marriage. I blush and look down.

'Ah, there's a near hit!' he chuckles, moving closer. 'What say you to being the Countess of Derbyshire? It could be arranged – if I had reason to be grateful –'

Eyes still cast down, cheeks still hot, I murmur, 'I – no thank you, sire. I thought – you spoke of my marriage.'

I can sense his vexation.

'Becoming a countess by marriage,' he snaps, 'requires putting up with an earl. Becoming a countess by other means entails freedom, a living, and the security of the court and no impediments.'

Eyes down, I murmur, 'It is the impediments I wish, Your Majesty – of an honest marriage.'

I can feel all the eyes in the room on us, and I'm flushed with the triumph. And the fear. The King is beside me – the King – I don't know what to do—

411

'You wish a cover, an appearance of honesty, is that it? In case our embraces bear fruit?'

My face goes hot with shame. 'I wish – an honest marriage, Your Majesty.'

'Well, I catch your drift,' he says pleasantly. 'There are many who feel your way. We'll see what can be done.'

I look up keenly, my eyes sparkling. 'If Your Majesty does, indeed, catch my meaning, I'm grateful to Your Majesty.'

But does he understand? Will he back off and help me wed my lord, or does he plan to foist on me some marriageable lackey like that wretched Lord Herbert?

His Majesty smiles down on me pleasantly enough, the corners of his mouth turned up in the creases that run from his nose, but in his eyes there's determined lust.

5

'Too Inexperienced And Ignorant'
Early October, 1666

I am too inexperienced and ignorant to conduct myself with propriety in this town, where everything is new to me, and many things are unaccountable and perplexing.

—Fanny Burney, *Evelina*

I'm afear'd to go out any more as twilight falls. For the shadows lengthening in long grey fingers, as I step into the corridor without my apartments, the King's often lurking there. He sneaks up behind to envelop me like a great pseudopod: 'Well, pretty maid'; or, 'Well met, sweet child. Where go you?'

And he grasps my soft white hand in a bony claw and plants wet kisses o'er the knuckles. He pulls me tight against him and violates my forehead or cheek with his hot, moist mouth and his steely fingers dig into my back and hurt. I turn away; and, were I not pulling off from him so hard, I shouldn't like to think what part of him I'd be pressing against. 'Tis all I can do to summon up the strength to push him off and keep a space 'twixt us.

He asks me to no more private suppers – knowing, I s'pose, that I would refuse. But I quake, coldly, to think of that ugly face, dark almost as a blackamoor's; that long, bulbous nose; those wickedly glinting eyes hovering over me i' th' secret murkiness of night corridors, where a candle makes one small circle of light far down the hall, or a torch shoved in a wall recess glimmers demonically several doors away.

And I begin to fear what he meant by his promise that he'll advance my marriage with someone malleable, someone dependent on him for a living, so he can have me as a plaything.

Oh, God, what shall I do now?

Getting a letter from my mother, asking me how I do at court, makes me feel no better. For I cannot tell her of this ball of lead deep in my stomach and the fear making my head crazy. And her letter is so breezy, gay:

> ... Betty, dear, I know how happy you must be and how little time you must have for writing; but do let me know of some of your pleasures, that I may share 'em. Have you discovered any eligible young men yet? Be sure to send your grandpa word so he can, as he says, 'Smell 'em out'. There is one Lord Herbert writes to us. Have you met him yet? He is heir to the Earl of Pembroke's estates, dear, including Wilton House near Salisbury. Your grandpa writes him to say, perhaps some means of introduction could be arranged betwixt you two. I've heard he's a comely young man as well as wealthy. Well, this is all for now, dear. Tell me of your pleasures and gaiety, and let us know whether the funds run low at the goldsmith's, dear ...

Oh! Oh! What an agony is it then, to know how I'm trusted at home – how I abused that trust simply by getting here – how Mama ruminates o'er my joys and I have nothing but sorrows; how one day succeeds another like a blank slate on which are writ Confusion, Desolation, and Ruin.

I dare not e'en think of my lord any more. Savile has been gone perhaps over a month now, and I know not e'en whether he was pleading my cause. Why, he may only have missed his friend (as who would not, with such a sweet one?); and, thinking to entreat him back, is equally glad to stay, so pleasing 'tis in his company.

And everybody around here lets me alone, as if I had the plague. My lord's friends, so warm to me at the treat, seem pretty afear'd to be familiar with me any more. As we meet at assemblies, nod to one another at the cockpit presentation of Beaumont's *Wit without Money*, cross paths at a ball at St James or a harpsichon playing at my Lady Castlemaine's, they will bow pleasantly, say 'Madam' or 'My lady', but remain remote and then back off as quickly as ever they came on before.

And I have no one, no one, with whom to share my feelings. The women keep off from me and regard me with arch contempt, eyebrows up, fans over noses and mouths, with flutterings and murmurings as I pass.

Only two female friends have I, and neither of 'em confidantes. Emilie Ossory invites me for her cow-eyed banalities on babies, and I dry her tears when her husband's thrown in the Tower three days. It seems he issued a challenge to the Duke of Bucks who, during a debate in the Lords over the Cattle Bill, rose in his droll, thoughtless way to comment that whoever is against the Bill is there led to it by an Irish interest or an Irish understanding: which is to say, he's a fool.

Jennings acts the gay, knockabout companion. We adventure to the New Exchange in the Strand, for raiding the shopkeepers of their ribbons and laced smocks; their scented soaps, apricot paste, and Martial gloves; and their little silver bells to hang from the new Japan fans of ivory depainted with mournful nightingales and ladies putting swords to their guts.

And we make a stop at fashionable inns, where we giggle o'er the fare and our heaped-up boxes. At the Rose in Russell street, Jennings like a talking gazetteer enlightens me on the environs: the pictures on the walls; the fine ordinary dish of base roast beef, marrow bones, and cheese; the King's House theatre nearby; the good proprietor Mr Long, whose gently teasing merriment and benevolence draw the patronage of the wits; the wench at the bar, who's the sort men look for here. And my madcap comrade will not rest but she must throw a nutmeg into the muscadine wine she has insisted on ordering; and so we get a fit of the giggles, in which I'm sure the drink played no small part.

And then we're for her apartments at St James, to titter and collapse and satirize those absent. It is her humour to congratulate me on Sir Francis Popham, who struts about saying how like he is to have me. She rallies me on the conquest, asks how Hinchingbrooke and the King will bear the pain of losing me. And to each protest I make, she protests in turn, '*D'autres! D'autres! Tell it to everyone else!*' or, 'Confess, Mallet, you love him; 'twas his wit'; or, ''Twas his handsome slash'ed doublet'; &c &c.

Jennings teaches me anew that one mustn't reveal true feelings. One must make a joke of the King's attentions, no matter how they frighten; of those of Sir Francis, no matter how they annoy.

Jennings draws forth some Rhenish. I sip; she splashes more into my goblet; and then, on th' alert for some way to instruct me (or perhaps best me) – not to mention considerably loosened up by Rhenish – she begins to regale my countrified and innocent ears with explicit facts about men and women. She may be virtuous, but she seems to have picked up a deal of fascinating knowledge somewhere.

Both of us are incomparably delighted with the conversation: she to tell, I to know. I pump; she explains. She tells me about tongue kisses (I shudder at my secret knowledge of their nastiness), and she relates all the kinds of gropings that go on around here: how men will try to get a hand down the front of your bodice to fondle your tits; how, that fortress bridged, they slip a hand up beneath your gown and up your thigh to stroke your thing; how, their breeches being untrussed, they stick out in front when aroused (how odd it must look); how large they swell up to be, as big as a banana and a little pink thing on the end like a cherry that squirts; &c &c.

All of this wicked discourse is incomparably fascinating: I have long been curious about men, what they look like and do, but have never had anyone to put my questions to. My mama only acted horrified when I asked her anything and said my questions would be answered with marriage; and so I had to satisfy my curiosity by piecing together what I heard and saw through keyholes with the woodcuts in some of my stepfather's books and the frank manners of horses and dogs.

Jennings cannot tell all, of course; but she can tell so much, I am astonished. With no qualms she admits to having been to bed with her lover, Jermyn, both of 'em all naked; and she insists, this is not only what Frances does with the King each morning before breakfast, but that all lovers at court do so (save a few like that prude Elizabeth Hamilton); and that one must simply refuse granting the final favour in order to be held chaste and honourable.

I am sure my eyes must be standing out like two grapes. How shall I ever control such dangerous fondlings? 'Tis hard enough for me to say 'no' to him when he's fully clad.

'Jesu,' I say, 'what a place this is for love!'

'Lud, yes, indeed!' she cries brightly, having mistaken my irony for straightforward observation. 'As good a place as Fountainbleu. Here is the King that loves Lady Castlemaine and Frances Stewart; the Duke of York, that loved Hamilton awhile, and the Lady Chesterfield too 'til she died, but now he's quit loving Price and loves the Lady Denham; then there is the Duke of Richmond, that is the greatest catch, who loves Hamilton but is rival to the Comte de Grammont. I love Jermyn, as everyone knows, and he loves me, and we will be married some day, which puts Talbot not a little out of countenance, for he's always loved me to distraction; but Castlemaine loves not only my lords Mulgrave and Sotherby now, but Jermyn as well, which vexes me not a little: I think she keeps him in gold and out of marriage –'

She must see the odd expression on my face, for she stops her bright babble.

'Mallet, you're not laughing.'

I run my finger o'er the goblet. 'I can't see much to laugh at. It all sounds very sad.'

'Sad? Lud, no! Love is gaiety, love is frolicks.'

'I have not found it to be so. Nor do I think we've been speaking of love just now.'

She sighs. '*La trieste hiérrite,*' she murmurs, repeating the pseudonym the Comte de Grammont is said to have given me: 'the melancholy heiress'.

'But here,' she says. 'Listen! Mama and Sarah have returned; I must play the virtuous lady.'

An older woman, wrinkled and glum, with hard blue eyes, pokes her bonneted head through the threshold from another chamber. 'Frances, mind you watch the drink.'

Jennings casts her head down and says, in a shy voice I cannot recognize, 'Yes, Mama.'

A little girl with blonde curls and a ready smile pokes her head round also. I think she will speak, but the grim-faced old woman grasps her hand and says, 'Come, Sarah – mind your manners.'

I stare at Jennings, still looking down, and at the smaller version of herself, looking down also, and both of their spirits quelled.

'Hello again, Mrs Jennings!' I cry, and hoist a goblet to her.

She makes a face at me and draws off Miss Sarah.

Well, there's the thunderstorm that has doused our fire; so I take polite leave of Jennings, leaving her amidst the parcels, and tell her I'll send Susan for mine by and by.

What a strange change of humour in Jennings: any modest child, scolded by Mama, would look down in shame, but Jennings looked absolutely quenched, squelched – and, now I think on't, afear'd – nay, terrified. How very odd! For what can such an old woman do to her?

6

'My Own Punisher'
10 October – 14 November 1666

'Be honest, then, my love, and speak without reserve; – does not the country, after so much gaiety, so much variety, does it not appear insipid and tiresome?'

'No, indeed! I love it more than ever, and more than ever do I wish I had never, never quitted it.'

'Oh, my child! that I had not permitted the journey! My judgment always opposed it, but my resolution was not proof against persuasion.'

'I blush indeed,' cried I, 'to recollect my earnestness; but I have been my own punisher.' ...

'... you fancied Lord Orville was without Fault ...you supposed his character accorded with his appearance: guileless yourself, how could you prepare against the duplicity of another? Your disappointment has but been proportioned to your expectations, and you have chiefly owed its severity to the innocence which hid its approach.'

—Fanny Burney, *Evelina*

What am I doing in this place? I don't belong here! These people are so hard and cruel, for all their glitter.

What am I doing here? I think, day after day, as the rains pour from the skies in drenching, soul-devastating torrents, and I brave the drenched court, cloak billowing and smock stuck to me, to hear a Fast Day Sermon for the Cessation of the Fire or see a performance of Etherege's *Love in a Tub*.

What am I doing here? I think at the afternoon soirees, where there are little seed-cakes and the new-fashion tea (a strong beverage that makes my heart flutter and is said by some to be medicinal, by others to be dangerous); where the King will pull his chair close to mine and murmur low in my ear and his knee will press into my skirts, and everyone will stand about us in a ring, muttering and chattering. How I'm thrilled they see me talking to the King! And at the same time, there's a low beating of panic with the pulse in my stomach: what shall I do? What shall I do?

What am I doing here, where the greatest triumphs are mixed with such pain?

The day I ride the Ring in Hyde Park, where everyone's coaches pass in parade 'twixt the narrow wooden rails, I've a great thrill. I've borrowed Lord Ormond's coach for the Tour, for one cannot ride a hackney there, and one *must* go there, to have one's hair and gown and bosom admired. The rules are: no stopping; one must keep circling the Ring, round and round, 'til the King pulls out and leaves by the opening in the rails. But His Majesty may stop the promenade at any time, if he sees passing across from him someone he wishes to engage in conversation.

And, what d'ye think? The day I ride the Ring, basking in the devoirs yelled from coaches going t'other direction (''Fore God, she's handsome, I vow!' 'Hey, beauty!'), His Majesty stops for some three quarters of an hour to talk with me. He does it, I am sure, as a sop to vanity; for fashionable folk crane their necks from coaches to see who 'tis he's engaged. Eyebrows go up, with gawkings and peerings through eyeglasses – leanings from coach windows lap dogs clasped under chins and low murmurs. And I'm ecstatic with vanity that the King's talking to me and everyone sees it, and he makes the whole world stop – for me!

But then, leaving a ball at St James, he catches me in another dark corridor and presses against me and forces open my mouth with his tongue. Oh, how I yearn to slap him! But he's my monarch; I cannot.

As best as possible, I wrest apart from him and say, 'Your Majesty, I beg you' – then – I dare to do't – I wipe my mouth with the back of my hand in front of him. He says nothing, only smirks down at me, pats his lips with a handkerchief, sticks it back into his sleeve, gives me a mock salute, hand against high plum'd hat, and whirls off.

Oh, God, that my lord would only be here! But, no. Why do I even think of that? He cares nothing for me, despite what Savile says, or he would have at least writ by now. I've dug my own grave and must perforce fall into it, with this old lecher.

What am I doing here? I think as I sup on champagne and lobsters at Wallingford House. The world's suddenly so cruel, and all this elegant company so complaisant in discussing its barbarities.

The House of Commons, says one supper guest, is stirred up over Papist plots. They've found two fishing knives in someone's house and suspect these will be used to overthrow the government.

Yes, says the King, they badger me to banish all priests and Jesuits.

The town runs mad, too, says another, with sailors mutinied from the ships. Their families are starving for that they've had no pay these months. The Dutch beat us at sea, says someone else; our merchant-men are all out and not like to return; we've seized the grand sum of one prize, a French flagship that sailed up to our fleet by mistake; the Prince and Lord Albermarle are much in disgrace for their inept stratagems. Those that return at all from the fleet are like to have their reputations blown.

As I sink into despair o'er this last, my stomach twitching already from sympathy for the Papists and starving seamen, someone else asks, Have we heard some hundred thousand persons were left homeless in the fire? And some thirteen thousand dwellings are gone, and four and six weeks later blazes are still leaping out of cellars when people turn up boards? Well, God continue these rains, to extinguish the last of the blaze.

Then I stare bleakly down the table at our host, the Duke of Bucks, who regales the elegant company with his cruel wit: does mimicry of Jermyn, with his spidery body and spindly legs; of the lecher Price, fat and choleric; the pig-eyed, blinking Mrs Blague, with her white eye-lashes and ruddy skin, and her vacant swain Brisacier, who speaks no better than he sings.

The whole table laughs fit to burst; I sit, eyes down, fingers plucking at the gold plate; and a little page goes about with incense, perfuming the air, whilst five footmen hover about to refill champagne glasses, remove or deliver plates, and present silver fingerbowls with rose-water and a rose floating in each. And my waist hurts from being pinched in with tight laces, and my head aches with the multitude of pearl-pins. And my heart hurts for these people who have feelings yet are made sport of.

I steal a look up and note, Lord Ashfield is not laughing neither but applying himself to the wine; and next to me Mr Etherege, a polite smile on his face, lifts his glass to me in salute – whereupon I do likewise. I ask him about his history.

'A rich vintner's grandson, madam, and son to a Cavalier captain, who was once Purveyor to Queen Henrietta Maria, and whose early death made his grandsire's charity a benevolent blessing, when he took on the expense of seven orphans and a distressed mother.'

I smile. He continues, 'He was comfortable enough and left me some parcels of land in Kent, sufficient for a gentleman if he watches his extravagances.'

'I enjoyed your play. Have you another in the works?'

'I would, but for what my Lord of Rochester calls my crying sin, idleness.'

I laugh delightedly at the dear name. He smiles cordially.

The discourse then turns to foolish husbands, on which topic the Duke proves most eloquent. He laughs at Sir Charles Denham an old man with a young wife: 'The staple of comedy, the old cuckold: one who will have his young bride and then rage that she gives him horns! Jealousy is droll enough over a mistress, but a wife? She's an old shoe grown dull with use, a daily dish of curds, a surfeit-water to be consumed after a banquet elsewhere!'

All these remarks he accompanies by gestures and grimaces so droll, the company laughs, His Majesty the loudest of all. And footmen carry in ortorlans, some wonderful fat birds brought from Bordeaux especially for the King to eat; and behind a screen a brace of fiddles and bass viols and flutes warble low the grandest tunes of Lully.

Like Ashfield and Etherege, I'm not laughing. I give silent thanks that the gentle Duchess of Bucks has left the table a while; and I watch the great glass above the dining table: faces dance in't like depraved phantasms in the low glimmer of candlelight.

'What think ye of this rain?' the Duke continues. 'I wish the Lord would make up his mind whether to destroy us by pestilence, fire, or another flood; He's looking as reckless a ruler as our King.'

When His Majesty laughs, the crowd joins suit.

The supper breaking up, a footman presents Etherege with a basket of broken breads. I wonder whether he feeds the poor, but at my inquiring look, he says, 'For the birds.'

A kindred lover of animals! I say, 'Oh, may I have some, too?'

Etherege and I share a conspiratorial look as he fetches a napkin, fills it with crumbs, and presents it to me with a flourish. 'We share a vice, I see.' He adds, 'I've been admiring the blue stitchery on your stomacher and shoes – very nice: have you some pearls to set off the white?' This is his way of complimenting people – humorous and kind, without a trace of malice.

Slowly, as I traipse from this supper to t'other play or consort, I am aware what a pyramid of hierarchy there is at court, structured with extreme niceness and exactitude, on the basis of handsomeness, wit, and cruelty. The King, of course, is the lover at the top of the heap; but also at the pinnacle stand those with the hardest hearts and prettiest persons, as my lord and Frances: both, it seems, have gained much status, not only by making many conquests but by using their victims hardly in public, that the court may enjoy their suffering. At the next rank comes Jennings, who fell from the pinnacle by avowing her 'love' for Jermyn; men like Sidney and the Duke of Monmouth for handsomeness; the wits for their conquests and powers of repartee. Then there is the third rank of those that are liked for their sense and agreeableness, as my lords Ashfield and Butler are, but not particularly emulated.

All of the others provide handy victims: the wits lampoon 'em, and the lovers play upon their gullibility. The more gulls one has ruin't, the higher his own status: so everyone is constantly at work probing the defences of everyone else. The only ones that seem to escape are those like Etherege and Ashfield, who admit and laugh at their follies: this seems to earn 'em a certain left-handed respect. 'Tis hard to lampoon someone for his notice of fashion when he has already tagged himself Sir Fopling Flutter; or to rally someone successfully o'er his phlegm when he is ever laughing over't himself. Then too Etherege has creative genius and a deal of good nature, both of which make him liked; and Lord Ashfield is the model of the handsome, well-dressed, complaisant gentleman: 'twould be hard indeed to dislike him. The ones that are truly made a prey are those that are ignorant of their follies, as the chicken-necked Brisacier, whom the Duke of Bucks is ever prevailing on to sing; or his inamorata, Mrs Blague, who, despite her piggy eyes and face and form, will be eager for love; or those that are enraged by lampoons, such as Chesterfield, Price, Denham, or Hobart.

And where do I fall on the pyramid?

I seem to be included in all the invitations, even the most elegant and private ones that the lesser folk would kill for; but I doubt, given my ignorance and countrified manners, I'm sought for myself. No – everyone must suspect I'm to be the King's new bedwarmer: for everyone treats me with a sneaking contempt varnished o'er with respect.

Shopkeepers on the Strand send me presents: small porcelain eggs, opening on a hinge and lined inside with rose velvet for sticking in of pins; gold hairpins with pearl handles; exotic scents – and always with a note: Will I ask His Majesty about this? Will I recommend these gloves, simply by wearing 'em? And could I perchance drop the shopkeeper's name?

There's only one soul in this court I feel akin to though I almost never see her: the Queen.

Sometimes I sit by my window and stare out at the bleak, red-bricked court; and I feel so sorry for that tiny dark nun, cloistered away in her apartments, bowing only at the few great balls, keeping to her intimates amongst the ladies-in-waiting and doing her embroidery.

Then one day I meet another woman of virtue in this stews.

Being returned from a visit to Emilie Ossory, I see the door to the apartments beside mine ajar; and my curiosity being what it is, I peep within.

There, amid a welter of hutches and trunks, is a small but regal maiden, her auburn curls tight and her carriage erect, firmness lining her mouth and glinting in her pale blue eyes. With a wave of a long, delicate hand, she hectors some footmen, who dance about rearranging the hutches.

I invite her for tea and cakes, for which I dispatch Susan to a teashop in Charing Cross; and as we begin to talk, I see the lady has sense; so mayhap, despite her air of grave modesty, she will make a companion.

She gives her name as Emilia O'Hara and her age as two-and-twenty; then, spine erect and finger daintily curled over teacup, she asks me of my history.

'Oh, I fly from a most unnatural family: a pack of cannibals that would live off my flesh.'

'No!' she cries, astonished. 'How so?'

I see that she watches me with a sparkle in her light blue eye, as if appreciative of my wild airs, like an indulgent mama with a giddy infant, so I begin to perform for her, the way Jennings always does for me.

'Oh, the usual way –' I flip my fan '– with the marriage market their Afric cauldron.'

She laughs merrily, chooses a cake from the plate passed by Susan, and smiles, large pale eyes sparkling.

'It sounds as if you've led a busy life.'

'Oh! This is nothing. Then the vexations of my mama's lectures, read to me from cock crow to matins: "Mistress, you behave not like a modest country gentlewoman! Flighty colt, we'll break you to the gag-rein and rope you up with bridle and bit! We'll marry you off so a grave man can tame your paces; but first hear this Bible reading, then tend to your embroidery!"'

Emilia laughs, then smiles – a bit condescendingly. 'I have a much duller history, I fear. My nature is too calm for such turmoils.'

'Poor Emilia!' I cry, with a roguish look. 'The waterfall beats the pond: plunge into a little turbulence, and see what it does for the blood.'

She smiles. 'Turbulent, I will never be.'

I lick the fingers that have plunged into the sweet cake. 'So – your history?'

She sets down the teacup and, still smiling pleasantly, says, 'I am the eldest daughter of a small Yorkshire landowner of Irish descent, Harry O'Hara. He and my mother are the dearest, most humorous people ever adored by a countryside; they brew a great quantity of bad ale on which they carouse merrily every night and are so lovable they can refuse nobody anything.'

I laugh; she continues, 'I also have a giddy sister, twelve year of age, who lives by the court gossip and believes herself a great poet; she is in love with my Lord Rochester by repute, and she has made me promise I must write her each day and tell all, especially of the most notable sparks.'

I blush at the dear name. 'A humorous family indeed!'

'Yes,' says Emilia, lifting a dainty hand with long nails o'er the tea-cup, 'but though they suit not my discreet nature, so dear are they I must love 'em, nonetheless.'

'That, at any rate, is a welcome salt to a humorous meal. How came you to court?'

'My father helped the King with horses and money during the late troubles; and as a favour, His Majesty agreed to grant me apartments here, till I could find a husband suited to my humour.'

So cold is this phrase, I cry, 'You mean not to fall in love?'

She smiles faintly. 'I doubt I am capable of it.'

'Emilia, you have glands, after all.'

'Elizabeth, you are something shocking.'

'So my mama tells me.' As I trill a run of bubbly laughter, she smiles and chuckles.

'Well,' I say, 'I think we make good comrades; you'll tame my paces, and I'll lighten yours.'

'How long have you been at court?' she asks, with another dainty sip.

'Since right after the dreadful fire.'

'I'm amazed you got here,' she says. 'My coach was turned back. We were saved from a mob by a most brave gentleman.' She sips. 'Have you found anyone else congenial here?'

I shake my head soberly. 'Not many.' I yearn to say, There's someone that my mind, heart, and whole being move in tune with – but where is he now?

Then there comes a night that makes my heart pound for days afterward.

7

'I Would Adventure For Such Merchandise'
15 November 1666

Romeo: Oh, speak again, bright angel!
I am no pilot: yet, wert thou as far
As that vast ocean washed with farthest sea,
I would adventure for such merchandise.
　　　　　　　—William Shakespeare, *Romeo and Juliet*

'Tis at the Queen's Birthday Ball, in the Great Banqueting House.
There the Rubens fresco spreads across the ceiling, its figures muscular and robed like Michelangelo angels, their heroic postures
garbed red and blue and amber before a thunderous sky. The white
chamber fills, the ladies glittering with diamonds and the men draped
in braids and sashes, their slashed doublets and waistcoats of silk and
velvet; and all above us, the three-quarter loft burgeons with throngs
of the envious and curious: petty officials, merchants and their wives,
all dressed to a fineness of satin and velvet and goggling at those of us
that set the fashion.

Three pages in livery have let down the great chandelier, and they
light the candles of white wax; now a thousand fires ascend into the
heavens. Seven pillars stand against each wall; and dividing them,
seven windows black with the sky of a winter's night.

The hall fills up and the loft too. Frances makes what she supposes a
grand entrance in black and white lace with a scallop like some
antique fanatic, her head and shoulders dressed with too many diamonds for taste; the Duke of York appears in cloth of silver, and the
Duke of Buckingham in a vest sparkling with jewels; Jennings, nudging
me, whispers he laid out above a thousand pounds on it. I gape at the
splendour everywhere – the most glorious, she says, since the cor-
onation: every man having laid out at least an hundred pounds on his
vest alone.

Now Castlemaine makes an entrance, the hundreds of diamonds
glittering from her, and sweeps to a seat in a gilt chair beside mine,

with much ado to pat my hand and call me 'dear', that all the world may see how little jealous she is; then at last, when the Great Banqueting House is full, the trumpets aloft in the gallery set up a blast, to which the strings answer; and the King and Queen enter from a door beside the rose canopy, her hand on his arm.

The poor little creature wears no diamonds at all but looks very happy to be escorted by her husband on her birthday. Honest vanity forces me to compare myself with her; and I must confess, never have I looked more beautiful, in the new pink satin with laced undersleeves, my head dressed in pearls. My bosom has always been one of my best features, plump and white; and it shows extremely well above the white pinner, secured with a pearl broach.

The King in a rich vest of silk and silver trimming leads off with the bransle, his queen on his arm; and with him by set arrangement fourteen others of the highest rank, as all the dukes and their wives and ambassadors; and then the general dancing begins: a courante, and now and again a French dance or two, one called the New Dance with much bowing and whirling – but none of your country rounds or trenchmores, sir!

I am pleased with the show I make and the eyes of the wistful in the loft upon me; but then, on a sudden I think – all those men! What if some stranger should ask me to dance? Or what if I should sit here in plain view and no one ask me to dance at all?

I suffer a qualm of shyness and decide, whate'er my fate, I cannot suffer it so exposed to the public view; and with a squeeze to Castlemaine's fingers, interknit with mine, I murmur an apology and abandon my chair, to slip backward into the crowd.

Castlemaine turns to her left and begins the most shocking conversation: 'Stewart may be a raw girl, but the bitch has cunning. She has got the fool dangling his pr—k at her but will not suffer him to stick it in. 'Twere not for that Portuguese porridge, the bitch would be queen now.'

Chuckles run through the throng, and I blush, not daring to look round to see whether anyone enjoys my maidenly discomfiture.

'And this is what I get for bearing his brats, losing my figure.' Castlemaine fingers the diamonds glittering at her throat.

Her confidante, red curls dripping from a feather secured with jewels, answers, 'Well, you know he was urged to the Portuguese marriage for reasons of state. And you were married to Roger,' she adds, a circumstance which indeed Castlemaine oft forgets.

I crunch against one of the columns, lest someone ask me to dance. Oh! Sirs! Sometimes I can rally and coquette it to a wonder; at other times I'm too timid to speak. I'm dazzled at the candles catching light from all the jewels – proud at being on the floor instead of in the loft – yet bewildered and terrified, too.

The gawkers in the loft elbow one another, point at Frances or Castlemaine – and some e'en at me.

Oh, God, here comes His Majesty towards me. 'Madam, may I have the honour of this bransle?'

I nod, extend my fingers.

We are immersed then in the hopping measure, His Majesty looking down with greedy eyes that devour me; I glancing up and then timidly down, one hand engaged in holding my skirts. He speaks nothing – only possesses me with those glittering, lecherous eyes. Then, the dance winding down, I stand helplessly beside His Majesty, not knowing whether I'm released or not, and my fear mingled with delighted pride at the stares of loft and court.

I gaze upward at the loft, at the burghers and their wives dressed in what they believe the height of fashion. One bullet-boobied woman sports a ridiculous pink plume; I stare fascinated at it as it nods with the sagacious motions of her head.

The measure has still not struck up for the next dance, nor has His Majesty led me back to my wonted spot. But with his head turned, he converses with someone in the crush behind him.

'It was a rough go, then, was it?'

Whoever 'tis speaks in such a murmur, I can scarce hear him. But I catch a few words: 'Beg Your Majesty's favour for the pride and privilege you show this evening.'

'Well,' His Majesty returns, 'it won't be the first time you've done it to me. Here, then, take her; but not for forever, mind.'

What's this? A man bold enough to claim me as a partner from the King?

This surprise makes me curious; I take a step backward and crane my neck to the right; His Majesty at the same instant grabs my small white hand and draws it over beyond him. I turn with its motion to the spot that had been at my back before. And as His Majesty places my hand in another's, I shriek, 'Oh, my God,' and stagger backward.

His Majesty seizes my arm to hold me up. 'Some wine, ho! Or a physician!' he shouts.

Someone thrusts a goblet beneath my lips. I feebly beat it off. 'Let me be!'

'Not ill, I hope, my lady,' says a melodious, caressing voice.

The floor rights itself. I shake off the helping hands and stare upward.

Though I have yearned for him desperately these eighteen months, I have forgot how beautiful he is. The face so blurred in my memory is nothing to the wonder before me now: though I dimly recalled dark almond eyes, delicate features, manly grace, yet I forgot how they were all arranged; and most of all, I forgot the vital spirits that illuminated all – and that would have attracted attention e'en in a man much less handsome. He glows all over with animal spirits. His eyes look black under the dim gleam of candlelight and set out by the ebony of his velvet suit and negligently curled periwig. He wears the finest point de Venise lace at his cuffs and cravat; a fine etched silver garniture around his vest and cape; silver buckles on his shoes; and one perfect diamond, gorgeously irradiating light, to secure his white plume to his broad-brimmed black hat. As usual, he outshines everyone else with their tawdry tassels and colours; he's like a comet in a winter sky.

I feel my blush deepen as he beams on me thus.

And, oh! How ashamed of myself I am then, for my womanly weakness! He's seen the love all over my face; he's seen my confusion and falling-fit.

But indeed 'twas not fair for him to come upon me so – he must have been at court for hours, as delicately as he's dressed, and smelling so of lavender and lemon! And no thought of writing to me – only that 'twould be a good joke to creep up and fright me out of my wits.

Now I'm angry with him – look at him grin – he wished me to make a display before the whole court, that all might admire the potency of his charms!

I make a shift to glare at him. 'My lord, you do give a body a start, the way you go popping in and out of her life without warning! I would say your legerdemain is quite breathtaking.'

He grins impudently and extends an arm. 'Would you like to see what 'tis like on the floor, my lady?'

I bow my head in acquiescence, then think to glance over at His Majesty, who nods, lips pursed, and mutters, 'Go to,' the corners of his mouth turned down and eyes cold on us.

My lord breezily ignores his monarch's reaction. Then, as we step forward, our eyes upon one another, I feel His Majesty fade into the backdrop. The nearer we draw, ignoring every other figure about us, the more I realize how desperately I yearn to fall into his arms. And then I become conscious anew of the peril I'm in, to be at court without guardians and feeling such passion for a man of no modest reputation. I must be careful, lest I be ruin't: then, I know, he will never marry me.

As he holds out an arm, his dark eyes fixing mine, I feel that we have danced thus before, though I cannot say where or when. I reach out a hand to rest it on his arm, then look away, under pressure of what I feel to touch him again after so long. My hand on his velveted forearm, I think there is no other part to my body, and no other sensation in the Banqueting House than this thrilling contact. I can barely hear the music struck up for the courante.

As I stare up into his tender gaze, all I can think is how I long to kiss him; but I manage to gather up my pink skirts with a free hand and pace a few steps with him, to halt beneath a stormy blue-and-gold panel of cherubs, the steps of the courante leaping and gliding all about us.

He's but a hair's breadth away, and he smells so good.

Trumpets crash, echoing betwixt the pillars, beneath the red-and-gold glory of the frescoed ceiling; and all about us the dancers whirl, leaping and gliding, posing and dancing.

He dances with an unusual flair; and I wonder, what is there this prodigy cannot do? 'Twould be sufficient were he a clever conversationalist and poet yet half-hearted warrior; or a skillful dancer, dresser, and swordsman yet mediocre poet; or even brilliant of parts and ordinary of face and person. But then, to possess all these virtues in abundance and have learning besides; then to display all his accomplishments so naturally, looking always so unaffected and casual: 'Tis no wonder everyone delights in him: he is indeed the ornament of the court; and to be so deeply in love with him is no disgrace.

I get enough of a grip on my passion to control my blushes. Fortunately, I am a skillful actress, and ere long I can glide through the courante with him, smiling comfortably into his eyes, as if he were a pleasant acquaintance, and as if the light touch of his fingertips on mine did not make me giddy with desire.

Actually to see him again! To delight in that angelic voice! How could I not have known he was just behind me?

I wonder whether to talk or be silent, whether to look at him or at the floor. It seems I dare not look at him, that my face give away my feelings; yet not looking's worse, as long as I've waited, so I keep staring upward.

He does not speak, yet the devil's eyes glint at me as if he invites me to make some sally, so at last I offer: 'The town says great things of your bravery, my lord, during the Dutch wars.'

'Then I must thank the town,' he says smoothly, 'for being so kind to me in my absence.'

The kettledrums in the loft thump, and the trumpets blare. We glide and turn.

I yearn to ask him, has his mother writ about our encounter at Adderbury House? And what was that trip about, anyway, and what was to come of it, and what will come of it now? But I hold my peace. Certes, he means to court me – does he not? Did he not walk presto into the ball and claim my hand for a dance?

'The town says great things of you, also, I see,' he says drily. His lips curved in a mischievous grin, he nods his head toward the loft, which is a-buzz, with its pink plume nodding.

'Oh, they! They've something to say about everyone tonight.'

'About every partner of the King's: that's certain.'

'What have you heard about me and the King?' I ask, suspicious. We go through a turn.

'Nothing,' he says smoothly. 'What should I have heard?'

Now, this is fine; he's pumping me instead of the other way.

'Well – but – I only meant, my dancing, my –' Suddenly I look up at him pertly. 'Why, nothing, my lord. You've been at sea.'

'You are determined to torment me,' he accuses.

We take another turn.

'But I will bear it like a gallant gentleman; and not call you out, as I would a man, to a meeting with seconds. 'Beware, though, I may call you out to something else.' He grins.

'I can defend myself, my lord, against any blade.'

The grin broadens. 'By heaven, I've sadly wanted your pert, taking ways, mistress minx.'

My heart leaps in my breast and fires an inferno in my face. Oh, God, how I love this man!

The music having died down, we're surrounded by all his friends, clapping him on the back, asking him how he does, saying how he's been missed. I feel myself farther and farther pushed to the periphery and almost wish I loved a man less fashionable.

I stand out the next dance at the edge of the circle, exchanging intimate glances with him whenever I may; then – oh, woe! Here comes Sir Francis strutting up to claim me.

I cannot tell him nay, as I've been seen dancing; so with a pitiful look o'er my shoulder at my lord, I'm conveyed off; and my lord left to converse with his gang, and apparently not noticing my glances of dismay.

However, I've one friend that notices – the Lord John Butler. And he rescues me for the next courante.

But, oh, where has my lord got to now? This is scarce the meeting of

two lovers separated for two years with a deal of trials and torments. My
heart aches. He still dances with no one – simply converses with his
laughing friends, who loose a great volley of guffaws that float above
the music across the chamber.

Savile patters up, fat-legged, with a couple of goblets, to thrust one
in my lord's hand. In the meanwhile, the courante being done, the
Lord Butler conveys me back with him for pleasantries with his family.
But I must confess myself inattentive to Lord Arran's pleasantries on
stag hunting or Emilie's on baby-nurture. I cast many a yearning,
nervous glance across the thronged white chamber. Why does he
behave thus? Did he simply ask for one dance in order to keep me
dangling in order to raise his reputation and fire my yearning?

The infamous Castlemaine slumps yet in her gilt chair, to the right
of the Lord John's clan, and she keeps up her coarse speech.

'See that one there, Anne? Over there?'

'No –'

'In the black and silver. Gawd, he knows more ways to go than a dog
has fleas.'

Oh, no. She's pointing with her fan in my lord's direction. He's
nothing but a piece of meat to her.

I sidle closer to the Duchess of Ormond, so as not to have to hear. I
wonder: is Castlemaine recommending him by private experience or
only by reputation? Oh, why did I think love could blossom in this
court?

But at least my lord has not asked someone else to dance. He seems
very immersed in joshing with his cronies – hitting Buckhurst's arm,
embracing the Duke of Bucks, letting loose a sally that draws roars of
merriment, leaning forward to gesticulate with his goblet and speak
with his face all animated. Oh, that I might be across the room! I
cannot bear that he should ever say a wonderful thing again and I not
hear it.

I keep attempting to converse with the Lady Ormond but casting
unhappy glances across the chamber, and the Lord John keeps casting
unhappy glances at me. And Mrs Pink-Plume above ogles all, like the
eye of God.

'Madam,' at last comes the Lord John's soft Irish lilt, 'would you
have me convey you thither?' I nod, holding my throat, blinking back
tears. 'I pray you, do.'

Abashed at how my yearning stands out all over my face, I meet the
Lord John's extended arm with my my fingers; and so, with one arm
behind his back, he promenades me gravely to my lord's circle, which
parts in a friendly enough manner to receive me.

431

'Ah, there's our little lady!' cries the jovial, barrel-bellied Savile, his lips splitting below the pin-thin moustache. 'We were just speaking of fashion, lovely lady, so you've come in time to lend us a hand.'

'We were considering,' says Sedley, with his small, merry eyes, 'whether gewgaws bought off the Strand are superior to those found in the New Exchange and whether this sort of frippery here –' Sedley reaches out his pudgy fingers and flips the dainty, fine-spun lace of my lord's cravat '– this sort of super-fine stuff ought to be truly in fashion for the masses.'

My lord rolls his eyes toward the heroic ceiling. 'Such stuff as you folk here can think to converse on! Gad, I've come from a spot of space – not too many miles distant, as the universe is measured – in which men are getting their guts griped by holes made by twelve pounds of steel! And all the news here is what piece of frippery is to be tied round a man's neck.'

'I notice, sir,' says Sedley, 'that your piece of frippery is also well tied – and ever properly fripped.'

'Well, 'twere a scandal if a man knew not what garb to put on his person on each occasion.' My lord shrugs. 'That's but part and parcel of a man's living apparatus, not the *raison d'être* of his conversation, or the ruling passion of his waking hours, I should think.'

'Well, there are some around here, sir, that have no great military exploits to speak of – and can boast of nothing more strenuous than a day in the selection of a cravat or the turning of a pair of hose so the embroidery faces out neatly above the ankle.'

Etherege seems absorbed in staring into his goblet.

'For which reason,' says my lord, 'give me the honest seamen every day.'

'Pay him no heed,' roars out Savile. 'Whatever group my lord's with, he chafes. And the "honest seamen", as he calls them, were not really admitted to his bosom companionship. I know not why he loves 'em so, now he's away from 'em.'

'Human nature is so,' observes my lord. 'We sigh for what we have not; and, having it, we no longer sigh for it; and so we devalue it straight.'

Oh, dear. Does this maxim refer to me, too? I stare down at the floor.

'But, say, we draw off too much of your time!' Sedley claps his arm. 'What say you to another turn on the dance floor, that all the court may admire your charms and your beautiful suit?'

'Do you ask me to dance, Sedley?' my lord inquires drolly.

'No, man. You must have the brains of a wooden puppet, to view this beautiful lady standing here unattended so long. By God, if she were casting those blushes toward *me,* I'd be leaving quickly, you can bet on it.'

'Mayhap I like not to make my moves with this whole crowd of gawkers and laughers,' my lord shoots back peevishly.

'We promise to gawk, but not to laugh. Certainly, what's to laugh at, with such success? Go on, man.' Sedley shoves him toward me.

I look down, blushing with shame that Sedley should have to force him to dance with me.

'Indeed, my lord,' I murmur, 'you need not –'

'Oh, but I must.' I feel a warm thrill in my hand as he takes it in his. 'Is it not the reason I am here?'

I look up keenly at him; his smile down on me is earnest. Do I see some unguarded love in those dark eyes?

Then they change, and a veil drops over them.

'The reason I am here' – does he mean because he loves me? Is that why he returned from sea?

No, surely he means the ball: he came here to dance.

There's only time for a few more dances before His Majesty arises, and the Queen with him, to signal the end of the ball. As they troop out, hand in hand, nodding, desperation seizes my heart. Here's the ball breaking up, and will I not be able to see him now?

By ones, twos, and larger crowds, the fashionable sally through the lintelled doorway. A good many of them as they go by catch my lord's arm, squeeze it, extending him a hearty welcome.

I feel stupid standing hopeful and immobile beside him, with the crowds surging past us like a great sea; but he makes no move either. I know were I a modest lady, I'd think to curtsey and move off; but I just stand with him and he with me, till the crowd thins. I stare up and drink in those dark eyes, that white skin, those boat-shaped red lips. I can't believe I'm seeing the real man, after trying so long to conjure him up in dreams!

He stares back down at me.

People mill past us – a red satin gown, a yellow moire sweep by – Oh, God – must we part so soon? What will he do? Is he as uncertain as I? What thinks he – to bid me a polite farewell, as any gentleman would? Am I no more than someone he can laugh with?

I put a plea on my face.

He says, 'Would you care to go off awhile, have some conversation?'

'Yes, indeed,' I murmur, my eyes on his.

I know how I tell him my love with my eyes, but I don't care. I don't even care that he may have responded out of politeness to my plain invitation, writ all over my face. At least I can be with him a little longer; and even more, he's done the asking. There's even a chance he loves me but is uncertain how to proceed, after all we've been through, without encouragement.

But who cares what his motives are? What's important is being with him.

He smiles in that charming way, letting the warmth of his eyes show his caring (the way he does with everyone), and politely offers me his arm. All a-tremble at the thought of touching him again, I look down, to disguise my expression whilst I put my hand on his arm.

I feel a soft pressure; and when I look up, he's smiling, with his other hand gently squeezing my fingertips.

He quickly lets me go as people brush past, but when we're out in the cold alone, past the crunch of cloak-donners and chatterers at the bottom of the stairs, he clasps my hand again, this time not just to squeeze but to wrap his fingers about. I intertwine my fingers through his but dare not look at him.

Every so often as we walk, we'll come upon someone, and then he'll remove his hand, to leave us in the conventional pose whilst he calls, 'Sedley! Hold up! We'll walk with you a way'; or 'Good evening, madam: isn't it a fine, brisk night?' I'm sure he'd have no one spy us in a familiar pose whilst I am aching to have all the world see me as his lady, with a hand clasp or arm about the waist. I know not why he withholds his affection in public. I like to think 'tis his respect for me in a place quick to cry scandal. But I fear 'tis either shame for his feelings – or, worse, a want of affection.

But I'm hopeless; every time he thinks to reach up for my hand again, I squeeze his fingers eagerly.

We walk with Sedley a way, I joining in the chit-chat and wishing my lord would clasp again the hand resting on his arm. I feel a warmth of approval emanating from Sedley: a circumstance, I think, which can do me no harm.

As Sedley bids adieu and toddles down King Street, no doubt to get drunk or seek female companionship, my lord heads me in the direction of the palace gate and into the red brick court. He hasn't told me where he's taking me. But he seems purposeful, as if he knows the way well, even in the dark and without a link.

The suspicion grows, he's taking me to his apartments. Where else? 'Tis too cold to talk outside; and if he meant to take me to a tavern or inn, we would have gone down King Street with Sedley.

Of course, you ninny. Where else would he take you but his

apartments? Would you wish him to take you to some public place where he couldn't kiss you?

He's going to kiss me: I know it. I can almost hear him thinking about it. I could hear him thinking about it when he said 'conversation'.

His hand clasps mine again. We walk a while in silence, our feet crunching the snow patches. We've never been so silent together before or so serious. 'Tis as if we can feel the undone kiss hovering in the air.

With a pang of guilt, I recall how I promised Mama never to meet a man alone. And such a man! – What if I pled the reluctance I should be feeling and said I'd go to some public place? He'd go without a murmur, I know. That's part of his well-bred manners. Ah! – but he knows I won't say it. I'll pretend I don't know where we're going; he'll pretend there's nothing scandalous or disrespectful about taking me there; we'll both pretend we don't know what the other is thinking.

I don't even have any real scruples. I long to kiss him so badly, I take care not to spoil my chances by asking whither we go and, possibly, activating his honour.

We go into a low brick building, step inside the door and into a hallway, where the bitterness of the air warms to a chill. How odd, I think, as he pushes open the door: we're still so silent: no 'La, sir, where go we?' – no coy demurrals or witty byplay. There's such a bond betwixt us as makes convention absurd.

He pushes the door open. No servant's in evidence, but two candles burn in wall-sconces within.

I walk before him into the soft golden light and hear the door click closed. Then I turn and look up at him.

He stares down at me. I stare back up; and there, behind the door, beneath the candle glow, he bends his head down and catches my right upper arm 'twixt his thumb and fingers.

Oh, God, his head is coming down!

Eagerly I hold up my face and close my eyes.

Now, I'd expected to be kissed: 'deed, I'd have felt him block-headed or downright ill-bred had he returned me to my quarters in my pristine condition, But I'd thought we'd go through the usual polite tête-à-têtes first.

His other hand catches my left arm; and by the time my eyes are closed and my hands grasping his elbows, his lips are grazing mine.

I've imagined half a million times what it would be like to kiss him; but I find, none of my imaginings were accurate at all. I'd pictured scenes in which he crushed me to him and lightning bolts coursed through my thrilled frame; I'd pictured anxiety as our noses collided or fear as his lips ground into my teeth – but never this slow-stealing, dizzying honey, this warmth so pleasant I cannot get enough. He understates the kiss: grazes my lips, brushing softly. I make a short noise of desire and lean up.

Then he breaks off, to slide both arms around my back and hug me to his breast, close, till I dissolve into desire, cling against him like an ivy against a tree. I have fallen into an ocean of the sweetest imaginable sensation: lavender and wine, honey and velvet and puppy fur.

'Oh, God,' I mutter, the tears in my eyes.

'What's that?' he murmurs.

I turn up my head; he takes the message and bends down. 'Tis difficult, with him above a foot taller: I stand on tiptoe, hold my neck up as high as I can. Still he kisses so gently, nuzzling but barely making contact, teasing my lips with light feather brushes. I move my mouth back greedily and press him close.

His lips are warm and sweet and soft, like rose petals.

All at once the tip of his tongue gently touches the top of my lips, then the center, lightly exploring. I strain against him harder and open my mouth.

Almost simultaneously, he opens his, and we go into a very deep, urgent tongue kiss. Oh, God. 'Tis a fearful rouser of passion: I feel he's deep inside my body already, his tongue and mine intimate as two bodies in a bed, naked and moving together. My hand tightens at his back; and my pulse beats, hot and demanding, betwixt my legs.

I put both arms about his waist and yearn against him. For a long time we stand there, he embracing and kissing me and not seeking to do aught else, till my knees would fain unhinge. It is very moving to stand near to him thus, with that merest suggestion of growing pressure down there that the merest innocence might not take note of; and the longer he kisses, the weaker I feel. He is so gentle: he holds me to him and rubs my back, so bit by bit as we draw nigher it is not fearful at all but very thrilling to feel how I have moved him.

Jesu, but he can kiss. I flick my tongue back eagerly over his: a long kiss, with our lips pressing hard and our tongues loving softly.

He rubs up and down my back till I get a warm glow all over; then his hand slips down to the small of my back, to press me fiercely into him, till we melt together through all of our clothing. I sigh with the wave of pleasure that floats through me; a current of feeling shoots straight from the back to the front.

Finally, he stops the kiss. I sigh deeply and bury my head against his chest and hope he doesn't feel the tears spilling out against his jacket.

'Get over here,' he murmurs, 'where we can be comfortable.'

Holding an arm about my shoulders, squeezing me to his side, he draws me into the dimness of his sitting room.

Moved away from the wall and toward the fire is a settle, with cushions covered in red-figured white satin; thither he guides me by the hand. He sits, then draws me onto one of his knees. My arm goes with eerie familiarity about his neck.

What am I doing in this posture, in a man's apartments, alone?

Why does this whole scene feel so proper, as if he's my husband, come home from a long absence?

He kisses me more firmly now, and my mouth opens gladly to meet his. We kiss a good long while, and as he draws me into him closer, I am very aware that, sitting across one of his knees thus, my upper thigh is pressing into that part of him of which I should not be thinking. And I seem to feel more and more of it press into me.

All at once his hand sidles over to my breast.

No, I think; but I do not get quite enough breath to say the word.

I should say no right now. But it feels so good. Gently the palm runs back and forth where the pap is concealed beneath the satin. I lean into him, my hand tightening about his neck, and make a little noise of desire as he slowly rubs, back and forth, until the spot 'twixt my legs grows uncomfortably wet and hot. I twist toward him, and more wetness unaccountably gushes from me.

Suddenly he drops his hand down from the hardened pap and onto my hip bone. A twinge of excitement thrills from his palm and through my belly.

Now his hand creeps over toward the front of my skirt, to hitch up the satin. Weakly I murmur, 'No.'

With the hand that had been clasping his waist, I reach about to pull his palm back over to just under my breast. But I feel a great pang below.

Slowly his hand steals upward to the breast again. I wonder if I should forbid that, but it feels too good. Back and forth he rubs again, till the pap pops out and almost hurts. Then he draws his hand up to slip it beneath my pinner and bodice.

His hand explores beneath the bodice, till two fingers find the pleasure-sensitive pap and stroke it gently. I gasp, clinging to his neck.

'Mmmm!' I cry. 'You shouldn't.'

He pulls his hand out. With his free arm he presses me closer into him, where I sit across the one knee. My hand slips down his side, to the corner of his hip. Jesu, I never knew desire could be so powerful. I leave off clutching his hip and grab his arm.

He slips a deft hand up under my skirts and trails it across my naked thigh.

This is just what I said 'No' to a moment before; but somehow I cannot find the will any more to speak, except in a soft moan. The hand trails to my inner thigh and across the little bird's nest, so that two fingers settle gently in the middle there. Now this indeed I should be forbidding; 'tis very wicked; but 'tis such a relief: I've been literally hurting there from desire.

Slowly the two fingers rub in the center of the cave there – rub the button of flesh gently, slowly up and down, till the desire rises higher and higher in me, and I think I'll faint.

'Oh, God, we must stop this!' I cry.

I am limp with an agony of desire, yet each new motion of his fingers spirals me upward, floating, to an ever higher peak. I clutch his neck and grow rigid, quivering. My God, how shall I ever summon up the will to stop him now?

I leave off clutching his hip and grab his arm.

'Why?' he murmurs.

''Tis dreadful; 'tis wicked.'

''Tis only a little pleasure. Don't you enjoy it?'

I push against his arm, but I haven't much push. My God, how can he keep up such dexterous movements?

A terrible tremor washes through me, bearing me like a breaker, higher; I hang on a peak, quivering.

'Oh, God, oh, God,' I moan.

All at once he removes the fingers: at which I feel a terrific pang. Has he taken it upon himself to stop, like a man of honour?

No.

His hand pushes up the pink gown so that it rides clear up to the top of my thigh; then I feel some movements and look down just in time to see him unfastening his breeches.

'Ye gods! No!' I cry.

I reach down to stay his hand.

'You don't desire to?' He looks at me intensely. 'Have I read your body wrong?'

What a devil he is.

'You know very well you haven't. It's just – I mustn't, that's all – I can't.'

'Very well. We'll go the other way, then.'

'The other way?'

He's unbuttoned the top button of his breeches, and there does seem to be a strain there, though I really can't see anything.

He takes my hand, slides it over to the front of him.

'What do you do?' I ask suspiciously.

'Nothing that will impugn your chastity, sweet one. Help me out a little, and I'll help you.'

I've no idea what he speaks of, but if he promises to keep my chastity safe, 'tis well.

He moves my hand a little farther till it rests on the front of his breeches. 'Tis very exciting to feel the bulge there, and then he trails his hand teasingly up my inner thigh, across the quivering flesh.

As he draws his fingertips in chilly lines across my lower belly, I turn in anguish, to feel the light, ruffling touch creep across the hairs, then around the fringes of the hot little cave. I turn closer to him, in agonies; and as his fingers begin to rub up and down along the outer side of the lips, then nestle farther inside, ever so gently, I shudder with excitement and catch him closer.

'I don't know how much more of this I can take!' I cry. 'We'd better stop now.'

'Perhaps we'd better not,' he says, 'the way we're both feeling. Here, rub on me whenever you feel like it and just do what you feel like doing. I promise I'll leave you intact.'

He goes to work again; I squeal and stiffen into his side and leg. Oh, this is too much to bear! I know not how we'll ever keep up without finishing the business.

Left to do what fancy can suggest in the face of inexperience, I keep rubbing across him; and – did he not tell me to do what I list? – I stealthily undo a button so I can reach inside and feel his warm skin, where 'tis swollen, and stroke that. He sighs and pulls me toward him, begins rubbing all the harder. God, I can't take it, I can't take it.

By now I not only shudder all over with desire; my whole body has climbed to a rigid peak; I sit collapsed in his arms, trembling and shuddering. I arch my body toward him and wonder why he would proceed with such exquisite torture. In the fierceness of my sensations, I've left off rubbing him and am clinging to his jacket with both hands. I shudder some more; my whole body hangs floating on a peak, where I hang with it, trembling and unhappy.

All at once I get a strange, thrilling, sucking sensation below where he rubs; and to my great abashment, a terrific explosion, like a cannon blast. I shudder all over; waves of spasms jolt me downward, plateau to plateau, making my body jerk uncontrollably, forcing animal cries from my lips. I try to control my reactions, knowing not what they are nor how he might be disgusted by 'em; but I cannot.

'Oh, God, Oh, God,' I gasp. 'Oh – I'm sorry.'

What's the matter with me, that I moan and jerk?

'Oh, God – stop; it hurts now,' I cry.

But he does not; he keeps on rubbing till I am almost in pain; and then a greater cannon blast explodes, spreading through my belly, deeper inside.

When the jerking has ceased a few moments and I am utterly spent in an anguished relief, he stops the movements; then, with a gentle thumb, he rubs the tears off my cheeks.

I can barely look at him, I am so abashed at my jerking and moaning and weeping; but he seems pleased rather than disgusted.

'Oh, what a relief it was,' I say. 'What was that?'

'What was that?' He stares at me in frank amaze. 'You don't know? You mean you've never felt it before?'

'Why, no. How can you think I'd be in such a posture with a man?'

'I don't mean a man, but have you never done so to yourself?'

'To myself?' I gawk at him. 'Why, no. How would I know what to do?'

He bursts out laughing.

'I'm not near so diverting as you think I am, sir.'

'I know; I know. Help me a little, will you?'

'Of course. What can I do?' I feel very warm and close to him, like a best friend rather than a maid in danger; and I'm eager to help him after the relief he's shown me.

He unbuttons the last two fasteners on his breeches. Now I'm caught 'twixt conflicting desires: to look away in timid shyness and look toward in curious fascination. I satisfy myself by glancing first at the fireplace, then at what he uncovers – just long enough to see if what Jennings has said is true – and – it is.

I fear I'll make him shy with my glance, but he seems utterly unperturbed. 'Come back and kiss me, and I'll show you,' he says.

I go eagerly into his mouth, and he gently guides my hand down on him to rub, till in a very short while a trickly fluid spills out on my hand.

'Have I hurt you?' I cry, breaking away to check for a wound.

But I see only white liquid, not red. He laughs.

'No, my sweet innocent. We've only spilt a little sperm. Here.'

Removing a handkerchief from his vest pocket, he wipes my hand. Very soon he shrivels to a smallness. How strange the human anatomy is!

But then I blush all over, to think of what I've done with him, and I bury my head in his shoulder.

'We've been very wicked! We mustn't do so again.'

I feel him shift; he must be buttoning up his breeches. He pulls me close into him so that I sit wholly across both knees, my head gathered to his breast. He holds me to him and strokes my shoulders like a papa with a little girl. 'Oh, we mustn't, must we? I'll remind you of that the next time we're alone, and see what you say.'

Laughing, I pinch his ribs. Then I sober.

'But – I – assure you, I don't go round doing this with just anyone.'

'I know it.'

'I've never done this before.'

'I feel sure you haven't.'

A silence then falls. I cuddle close to him in the orange crackling glow of fire light and feel so good, but why will he not say 'I love you?'

His arm cuddles me closer, so my head rests against his neck; and it occurs to me, this is the only way he knows how to say 'I love you'. There's something in him that forbids the words from coming out. Yet I ache to tell him I love him and trade with him memories of this agonizing separation.

'Tell me about your year,' I prod him.

'There's not much to tell. A deal of drinking and piracy.'

'And whoring?' I pinch his ribs again.

'Yes, whoring, too: there's no way to deny it.'

'No, sir. Not as well as you've learnt this business you seem so good at.'

He laughs ruefully.

Timidly I say, 'I had thought – that is –'

'Yes?'

'I had thought – people could not spend together without there being the final enjoyment.'

'And now you know. Oh, there are infinite numbers of ways to put bodies together to receive pleasure.'

'And I s'pose you've done this with other women.'

'Oh, yes, millions of times,' he replies breezily.

I'm aggravated – I know not why – for, sure, he couldn't have suddenly invented so thrilling a thing to do to me on the spot without having practised it many times before.

I try to pump him, but of his feelings or experiences he'll say little, only make jokes.

All too soon he says, 'Come on. We'd better walk you back to your apartments before anyone spies you're gone and talks about you.'

So he conveys me back through the snow to Scotland Yard, clasping my hand all the way, and leaving me at my door with a squeeze to the fingers and a grin.

441

I peer up at him; and a woebegone expression, I am sure, must be writ all over my face.

'I'll call on you,' he says softly.

Has he been reading my thoughts? I look up at him timidly.

'Well – I wondered – that is – what we did was very wicked –'

What I try to say is, *Have you lost all respect for me now, the way I misbehaved on our very first evening together?*

He bursts out laughing. 'My sweet little innocent! You know nothing of wickedness.' He reaches out to touch my cheek gently. 'I'll be in contact with you. Truly.'

And then he is gone, into the snow-bitten darkness.

8

'Why The Importance Given To Virginity In Women?'

16 November 1666

Why can men confess indiscretions, even boast about them, but if a woman is honest about the same actions, they, and other women, will regard her with less respect? Why the importance given to virginity in women, but not in men?
—Laurel Elizabeth Keyes, *The Mystery of Sex: A Book about Love*

Awakening late and groggy, I remember all my bliss; and behind the chilly darkness of the bed hangings think to hug it soft and warm to my bosom.

But then dismay hits the pit of my stomach. In the thrill of the reunion, I have forgot the most important thing: he has made no mention of marriage or even of love. Ooo, yes! In the heat of passion, I took his kisses and caresses for love. I took his settling of my head against his neck, his warm sighs, as some sort of declaration that reticence would not suffer him to make. But now, i'th' first light of dawn, how foolish do all my presumptions seem!

Of course he would not say he loves me, for he does not. Of course he would not mention marriage; why should he, when it should be evident to him he can get me the other way?

Oh, what a mess have I got myself into! Why could I not have been stranger with him?

Well, 'tis too late to put the milk back into the bucket. He's done all but the final thing; and must it not follow, as night to day? Yea, sooth will he call upon me: why should he leave such an easy citadel unconquered?

Whilst I fret in fear, a familiar cramp gripes my gut, followed by a warm, sticky gush, to announce my old adversary, the flowers. Oh, this is fine: this is all I wanted, to put me in a worse humour. Now I must resign myself to lie abed all day with megrim and cramp like a mailed fist squeezing and the nasty rag shoved 'twixt my legs. There will be too much gushing to go anywhere today, without bleeding on the floor like a slaughtered sheep.

But I find I'm not to be left alone in my sufferings; for two kind female friends call on me in my dishabille. A little after noon, Emilia waits upon me, with Elizabeth Hamilton in tow: and, I find, for no good purpose.

As they sit shaking heads and clucking, hens confederate to the plot, I advise disagreeably, 'Very well, cluck no more, but out with it.'

They exchange glances across my great bed, for one of 'em sits on each side, like sisters.

'Betty,' Elizabeth Hamilton begins, 'it is not as if we would interfere –'

This of course is the phrase that infallibly precedes interference; God knows how oft I've heard it from an older female tongue in Enmore.

'Don't say how you will not do,' I snap impatiently, pounding the bolster-pillow behind my back, 'but do and be done with it.

They exchange glances again, but Hamilton seems to have lost her nerve, so Emilia takes up the banner. 'Betty, we saw what intimate looks you and the Lord Rochester gave one another yesternight at the ball; and we are bound to tell you – as friends – how we fear for you.'

By God this makes me angry: 'intimate looks'? What implies she therewith? And what friendly office is this she would pretend to, sneering at me from the pinnacle of her reproachless purity?

'I know not what you mean by "intimate",' I snap, a twinge cramping my poor, disgusted gut, 'but you cannot say he was so bold the whole time as to touch me except by way of the dance.'

'We only meant –' Hamilton pauses delicately; and I know she wishes to say, the touching's been in other ways in other places. She tries another tack: 'We wondered if you were aware how warm were the looks passing betwixt you – and how bad his reputation is. There has been talk already.'

Now I feel my cheeks on fire with shame, e'en though 'tis so unfair. 'Whoever talked is a vicious old fury. I have done nothing wrong – only kissed and toyed a bit.'

'You have let him kiss you?' Emilia almost falls from the bed in speechless amaze.

I flush the more. 'And why not, when he has been my lover almost these two years and gone to the Tower for trying to marry me? He has never been aught but honourable to me; in fact –' I get an inspiration

'– I'm sure not many men would have been so gentlemanly to me, as we were in his apartments.'

Now I feel they will suffer a falling-fit.

'Oh, Betty,' blurts out Hamilton,'you haven't so far forgot yourself as to go to his apartments?'

'Where else could we be private awhile,' I demand, 'an the snow all over the ground? Must we stand freezing an hour in the Privy Garden because we would kiss and have our arms about one another? And his restraint has proved his honour to me.' I studiously omit references to the work of his hands.

'No, indeed – only his guile.' Hamilton smiles – as she thinks – so earnestly.

I am vexed at how they poke their priggish noses in the air.

'I am sure he could have done more an he wished: he kisses as if he wrote the book, and I grew so moved my loins were on fire.'

Now indeed they pull such grave faces as would have gratified my mama, and they strive to make me promise I will leave off fondling with him.

'Why should I? From what I've heard, no one else at court is too nice for a little kissing and toying.'

'Then everyone else puts herself in great peril.' Emilia crosses her dainty arms and shoots me a look of blue fire.

Under the coverlet I settle back, chilly and cramping and altogether vexed.

'Stuff! Wait till you find someone worth kissing, Emilia; your harp will play a less angelic tune.'

Emilia pokes her priggish nose in the air: 'I scare think I will be tempted.' I am about to pitch into her for a bodiless wonder; then on a sudden I notice how silent Hamilton has been during the latter part of this exchange, so I attack her instead.

'Hamilton, what think you of Emilia's iron-coated honour? Are you too nice to enjoy a kiss?'

She evades the issue: 'We speak not of what I may do with some man less dangerous.'

I give her a wicked look. 'Who has kissed you? Grammont?'

She tries a great shove to get the discourse from the particular to the general. 'If a woman suffers these things, she must be either of a very prudent carriage indeed, or assured of honour in the man to whom she suffers 'em. If you had told me you had dallied with my cousin John, I had never been concerned; he would never debauch a woman of virtue. But Rochester only cultivates the pretence of honour whilst he is busy engaging the lady's affections. He slowly insinuates himself into her heart, gradually takes possession of her mind – and all the while does more and more.'

I glare vexed upon her. 'What does Grammont do? From what I hear, he is not exactly a virgin.'

'Whatever Grammont does,' she returns loftily, 'he has not done't to me. I would certainly never go to his apartments alone.'

I regard her with a dry look that shows how little I credit this dodge. 'What have you done outside his apartments?'

She flushes a little. 'I am sure I have not felt the sensations you did.'

'But you have done enough: I see't on your face. Therefore read me no more lectures on virtue.' And I huddle down 'neath the coverlet, so frigid cold as 'tis today, my bones tremble.

'Very well,' she returns loftily, ''tis your own affair what you do. I only sought to warn you out of friendship what peril you put yourself in, with the most dangerous man at court.'

Now, 'tis a poor strategy to needle anyone in her time of the month. I snap, 'Agreed: Rochester is more dangerous than Grammont, for his lordship is much prettier and has a deal more wit and address. I can imagine Grammont would be infinitely easier to resist: why, he is older even than Etherege. How many times have you kissed with him?'

She elevates her nose yet the higher. 'I can see, Betty, that you are either in a wretched mood or that I presume on the liberties of friendship by giving advice where it is not appreciated. Pray forgive me.' She stands, nods, and sweeps from my closet, so extreme nice and proper, she might have been Lady Charity with her basket spurned by the poor of Whitefriars. I burst out laughing, but then I see with what pity and horror Emila eyes me.

I sigh and settle down under the chilly bedclothes. 'Emilia, make no mouths o'er the artichoke pie till you've tasted it.'

'I have not kissed anyone, nor do I intend to,' she replies, folding her long, delicate hands primly in her lap. 'Nor will I continue to give unsolicited advice.'

I give her a roguish look. 'However –'

'I cannot see a fellow member of our sex put herself in jeopardy without being concerned,' she continues. 'The male sex is able to keep us in line, and play upon us, because they keep us stirred up to a constant rivalry amongst ourselves. By God it makes me angry, to see women mistrusting one another and playing along with their natural enemies.'

I gawk, very surprised. I have never heard a woman speak in this vein before, to actually admit the backbiting we do, much less regret it; but I requite her honesty with mine.

WHY THE IMPORTANCE GIVEN TO VIRGINITY IN WOMEN?'

'Why, that is the way women are, Emilia. 'Tis the nature of the beast: geese honk, horses whinny, and women compete.'

'It doesn't have to be that way,' she says passionately. 'The men are true friends to one another, are they not?'

I think on how his friends have befriended me and furthered our cause.

Emilia continues, 'And yet name any two women in court who will trust one another: you cannot. Even in plays and poetry it is assumed that women cannot be friends to one another. Where is the female equivalent of Damon and Pythias?' She elevates her nose triumphantly, with a delicate gesture of the hand.

I retort, 'It is natural for women to be harpies to one another. We must compete for all the men.'

She shoots me a rueful look of her sparkling blue eyes. 'Only because they subordinate us by law and custom.' She straightens yet more her rigorous carriage. 'The men all band together, make the laws, contrive plots against our virtue, write verses that they circulate and sometimes correct for one another, jilt us, hand us on to someone else, or let us wait about to be noticed. They are in control.'

'Of course they are: they are the men.'

We both look at one another, vexed.

'What is so reasonable about that?' she demands. 'Why should women not be equally in control?'

'Women?' I stare at her incredulous, then burst out laughing.

Now Emilia is very vexed with me. 'What is so diverting about that?'

'I cannot see myself swaggering about in breeches, waving a sword, and brawling with you in a tavern over a man. 'Tis too outrageous.' And I plump the coverlet about me, my laced sleeves jiggling prettily.

She glares irritated on my kittenish mouth. 'You know very well I speak not of wearing breeches or waving a sword. I but say, why should they have all the advantages? Why should they be the ones to sit in Parliament and make the laws that keep the other half of the human race in bondage?'

I look in shock at her; then I bite my lips to keep from laughing and lean over to my corner cupboard, take a sip of chocolate, and retort: 'I have seen very little bondage here. It looks to me as if we are both very prettily dressed, I in my lovely nightshift, you in your elegant gown.'

Emilia is indignant. 'Prettily dressed! So are the Circassian slaves, in their harems! 'Tis bondage nonetheless.'

I sip. 'We are as free as the men to move about as we please.'

'Oh, we are?' She crosses her arms. 'Then let us take a chair into the heart of town tonight and walk about the Bridge-Foot.'

447

'Now you're being silly. You know we could not do that.'

'But the men could.'

'Of course: what woman would force a man?'

'Now you get my drift.'

I eye her aghast. 'This is the maddest conversation I've ever been involved in!'

'Only because you've been taught to accept certain customs without ever exposing 'em to the light of reason.' Her blue eyes glint triumphantly. 'So: we are as free as the men are.'

'Yes,' I protest, 'not to walk about within city walls, but to do all else. We can go to the plays and balls, buy what we wish in the shops; our apartments here are just as good as theirs.'

'What about our social freedoms? Are they as good?'

'Social freedoms?' I set down my cup.

'Tell me what men you know of that are locked in their chambers and forced into marriages.'

I grow a little uncomfortable. 'I am sure that guardians can apply pressure to them, too. An older son, for example, could be disinherited –'

'Whereas a woman could never hope to inherit, did she have any brother at all: were she twenty and he five, the estate would be his. Think you your father would have left you his lands if he'd had a son?'

I think on how uncomfortable I've grown each time this thought has occurred to me; and how bitterly jealous I grew at Frank's Christening party, when all the neighbourhood praised my mother for at last producing a son.

But to defend my position, I say, 'Women need no power of their own. The men take care of 'em; they cherish 'em for their beauty, their airs.'

'Marry 'em for their dowries, which they dissipate on wine, women, and cards.' She raises an imperious eyebrow at me.

'Not always!'

'An they wished, what's to stop 'em?' Her red eyebrow arches yet higher. 'Men are protected by law; women, by the goodwill of men.'

I shrug. 'What's the matter with that, as long as all are protected?'

'All are *not* protected. You know very well of men that have married and taken advantage of women.'

'The law is not so infallible a protector of rights, neither,' I argue. 'You would do better to talk of the difference made 'twixt peer and beggar than 'twixt man and woman.'

She picks up her own cup and saucer then, to hold 'em daintily in her two hands. 'I do not deny the inequities of privilege, in rank as well as sex. Your lover abducted you and lay three weeks in the Tower. A less privileged man had rotted in gauntlets at Newgate, then hanged.'

I hop into the space she has just left in her argument. 'As far as I can see, you have just made a cause for my side. We women are the privileged creatures like the peers; we are doted on, gifted with presents and verses. All we have to do is sit here, to wait for the shower of pleas and scents and gloves to descend; we are in control; we can say 'em yea or nay.'

Emilia gives me an ironic look o'er the cup, which she then sets daintily and deliberately on the saucer, her eyebrow up.

'As for me, I prefer not to twirp happily in my little cage and be hand-fed my crumb. Suppose we took a notion to desire a man who took no heed of us?'

I look at her roguishly. 'There are arts to use, to get him to notice.'

'All of this artful business disgusts me!' She sits straight and firm o'er her China cup. 'Why cannot men and women be honest with one another?'

'They can, if they wish,' I argue. 'Castlemaine picks the men she'd have and summons 'em in.'

'Only because she has unusual power, force of personality, and beauty. The ordinary woman must wait around for a lover and hope he calls, while the ordinary man may do the calling.'

Poor Emilia: I see what bothers her now. Generously I try to raise her spirits a little. 'Emilia, you have not been here very long, and you are very pretty. You'll have a lover soon.'

She gives me another glinting blue look. 'You have misinterpreted everything I've said, and I think you have done't willfully. But do me this favour: consider me a friend, a true one. And for God's sake, think what you do before you go to Rochester's apartments alone again. You trust yourself to the hands of someone that does our sex great injury.'

I shrug. 'I admit he uses his victims cruelly. But then, who around here does not?'

'A good many people: the Duke of Ormond's sons, for instance.'

I am vexed at her triumphant smile. 'But now you speak of men who do not work for status. To get status, one must be cruel. It is a game everyone plays, to stay at the top of this slippery pyramid at court.'

The eyebrow is yet higher o'er the ironic glint of pale blue. 'Whatever you call it, beware lest he play't on you.'

'He would not: he loves me.'

She gives me a pitying look.

'He does! He has tried to marry me this year and more. He feels differently about me than he ever has about anyone else: I know't.'

She does not reply.

'I do!'

All at once I realise how defensive I sound.

Her eyebrow up, she snaps crisply, 'Do you also know of all the other women he's enjoyed "this year and more"?'

I shrug. 'He was only after a quick thrill or two. Men are like that.'

The eyebrow arches further up. 'Oh, now you will say we cannot expect constancy of 'em.'

This is indeed what I'd meant, but I'm clever enow to turn the argument topsy-turvy: 'Nor can they of us, from what I've seen around here.'

'And yet the men are suffered to fall into bed with whoever will have 'em; and the women, if they yield, must sulk about in vizards that hide their faces, or become social outcasts.'

'I suppose you're in the right, but –' I get an inspiration. 'Men are different.'

Her eyes sparkle yet the more with that glint of merriment. 'You're telling me that women are less intense in their passions and so are better able to exert control?'

I hesitate, for in comparing myself to Lords Ashfield and Butler, I know how untrue 'tis. 'That is not what I mean.'

'What do you mean, then?' She eyes me regally o'er the cup and saucer. 'Price is lampooned for being man-hungry; who makes sport of my Lord of Rochester or Sir Charles Sedley for their appetites? Sir John Denham is rallied as a cuckold for suffering his wife to wander; who would think of lampooning the Duchess of Buckingham for the same? She is expected to accept her husband's infidelities as natural.'

'The Duchess of Buckingham is unusually forebearing,' I protest.

'Then let us consider how this social game affects you.' She sips of her chocolate and then replaces it, with dainty deliberation, into the saucer. 'From what you've hinted and I've been able to infer, you are in love with someone and would like nothing better than to share his bed. Yet you dare not yield: you would lose all your status at court, all his respect, all hopes of ever marrying him. You must stifle all your natural longings lest you be, as the word goes, 'ruin't.' Yet he is given free rein to indulge his, not only with the woman he "loves" (whatever that means), but e'en with any common woman he may pick up in the pit or on the street. E'en more, the greater the number of women he ruins, the higher his reputation soars. Where is the justice in all this?'

'The way you put it,' I admit, 'it does sound unjust.'

'You bet it is.' She gives me a cool, glinting look of irony. 'Here we must needs listen to Elizabeth Hamilton puff her cousin John as the man of honour, for lying only with women already corrupted; yet how do they become thus? Less scrupulous males, like your lover, play upon their natural longings and vanities until they yield: so what really goes on is that men with fewer scruples supply a herd of concubines for everyone else of their own sex. It is a game they all play together, and we are the pawns.'

I look at her in surprise. Though I had of course recognised the sexes were engaged in a warfare, I'd never seen it presented in quite this light before.

She continues, her eyes blazing, 'And now back to your cause, Betty. The situation forces you into a kind of contest. Your lover is supposed to try things that you are supposed to resent, no matter how you may wish 'em. This seems to me a relation inimical to the notion of love, which is supposed to be founded on mutual trust. In a situation of true love, you would both of you be agreeing to enjoy, or not to enjoy – depending on the balance of pleasure or pain to be got together from the encounter. You would not be engaged in mean power plays.'

I am surprised at how clearly Emilia has voiced some of my own feelings during the last part of this tirade. But of course I dare not tell her, lest I give her the triumph of being i' th' right – which she would doubtless find ways to flaunt at me in the future. So I try to explain.

'I felt that kind of trusting closeness with him very clearly, Emilia. Not only whilst we joked and talked, but e'en more when he ceased his advances that way.'

Her eyes glint merrily. 'Had you not told him to cease?'

'But he could tell how hot I was. He knew, if he pressed, I would yield more than I wished.'

'He is too clever for that. He also knew, if he pressed forward too early, you would grow wary of him.' Her eyes glint at me beneath the imperial raised eyebrow. 'Instead he chose to play the man of honour, that you might be lulled into a false security and trust him. This way he will get you to yield more favours more quickly.'

'Emilia,' and I eye her plaintively, 'what can he do to please you? Had he behaved t'other way, you had grutched at that, too.'

I am surprised she yields the point, and that gracefully. 'You're in the right, of course. I am so angry over the wrongs he has done our sex, I could not believe an honourable motive of him even were't demonstrated infallibly. Whereas you – well, your passion blinds you to his faults. Then, too, he is determined to please you, to secure your affections: he will naturally suppress the more unpleasant sides of his nature 'til he is sure of you.'

I gloat happily in my warm bed. 'Whate'er the unpleasant sides of his nature may be, the agreeable sides will dwarf 'em, I assure thee.'

She shakes her head. 'I hope for your sake you're in the right. But before you decide to marry him, take a good look at the Duchess of Buckingham, and decide whether it is worth it to be in her shoes.'

I stare open-mouthed at Emilia. 'The Duchess of Buckingham? That poor, spiritless old woman who makes friends with her husband's whore? Why, Emilia: how could you possibly think I would stand for such stuff?'

'If you are in love with your husband,' she counters, 'you may do a deal of things to please him, no matter how you feel.'

'Not I! And at any rate, that would be the surest way to earn his contempt: 'twould be bad policy.'

'Very well, I am pleased to find you so reasonable.' Emilia draws on her gloves as if preparing to take her leave. 'But take heed what his model and idol does, and be prepared to cope with the same connubial treatment.'

'His model and idol?' I stare at her. 'The Duke? Why, they're only friends!'

The eyebrow is up again. 'Very intimate ones, wouldn't you say? The Duke lampoons someone; your lover is quick to follow suit. The Duke contrives a cruel plot against someone; your lover takes part, then contrives one of his own.'

'But all the courtiers do these things!' I protest. 'And why should someone with my lord's fancy imitate anyone? Why, everyone takes their cues from *him*.'

She shrugs. 'I cannot tell you why he does; I only know what I have heard and observed. He and the Duke are inseparable: did you not see 'em at the ball, huddling together like an old satyr and his apprentice?'

'Emilia –' My voice takes on a warning tone.

'Very well, that was nasty: I apologise. But if you must keep company with him, do me the favour of being wary. '

'I am.' Then I look at her roguishly. 'If you are going to have a lover, you had best be wary, too.'

'I plan to be.' She gives me an arch look. 'Women do not have law and custom on their sides, so they must look out for themselves. But still I will never suffer myself to be courted by a man I cannot trust.'

I look at her pertly. 'No man can be trusted.'

'If that is true, then this is a sad world, and I will never marry.' She stands up and gathers her cloak.

'It *is* a sad world,' I admit, 'and we must live in't, married or no. He is no different from any other man; he tries to take advantage, but he can be manipulated, given the proper approach.'

Cloak in hand, she looks at me as if in pity, but then says, 'Very well, if you will look at it that way, let me give you a few hints. You've not been manipulating him carefully enough.'

Emilia has shown herself so clever in this discussion, I decide to get her aid if I can in this delicate situation.

'What would you do?'

She slips on her cloak. 'I would not see him alone, especially in his apartments. You yourself admitted how weak your will was: think you, he will exercise restraint forever?'

I brood o'er the coverlet. 'I suppose not.'

'No, I suppose not, indeed. After this, have him only to your apartments, and receive him in the company of one of us.'

I pout. 'I could scarce feel comfortable kissing him with someone looking on.'

She eyes me shrewdly. 'That is precisely the point.'

I pout yet the more. 'If you had felt it, you would not be so stoical about giving it up.'

She puts the hood o'er her head. 'If you *must* kiss him, give me a signal, and I'll turn my back. Of course, you need not take my advice at all: ride post to your ruin if you like. But remember: the higher your honour, the more like he will be to marry you sooner. 'Twere me, I would lend him nothing but my hand.'

I know very well that Emilia may be jealous, that she resents my having a lover to give me delicious kisses; yet I must also admit she has voiced some of my deepest fears.

I say, agreeing with her, 'I will get you to sit with me, Emilia.'

She leaves me then, to my cramp and mess and book; but I muse a good long while on her character. Though appearing with an enemy of mine, on an apparently malicious motive, she proves to be a friend; and, though so new at court, sager in some of the ways of the world than Jennings. On the merest acquaintance she has approached me as frankly as a sister, refused to be intimidated by my ill humour, and seemed to have my best interests at heart. In some respects, she is prudish enough to make me shudder; yet in others, she is shockingly bold. Here she swears she will not kiss a man, advises me to cease any familiarities with my lord; then in the same breath she regrets she cannot go bed-hopping like the wits. She seems very innocent of some ways of the world, urging that women be friends and the sexes be honest with one another; yet she offers some shrewd criticisms on social inequities, and I note she does not urge me to be honest with my lord: *au contraire*, she gives me new hints on how to manipulate him.

She is a most interesting female, a strange blend of humours; and I will enjoy studying her further. I will be even more diverted to see what kind of men attack her; how she combats 'em; and what will be the issue: for I think she will play the game in odd and diverting ways. And I can use all her help, to land the big fish in the pond afore my mama or the King intervene.

9

'Our Sweetest Songs Are Those That Tell Of Saddest Thought'

Late November, 1666

We look before and after,
And pine for what is not:
Our sincerest laughter
With some pain is fraught;
Our sweetest songs are those that tell of saddest thought.
—Percy Bysshe Shelley, 'To a Skylark'

Here in this chill court, with no one to succour me but he whom all say I must be most wary of, I spend my days sitting in the grey mornings and twilights and the long afternoons, reading signs and fears into everything.

First, there are the days that he neither calls nor writes. On these days I convince myself that all my dreams have been but fantasies: he has not loved me nor never will: he's only playing with me and is off chasing some handier skirt at the moment. Then on the days that he writes, I'm immediately thrilled: the whole world is turned topsy-turvy. I dance about in an ecstasy of delight and think, *He loves me! He loves me! He writ.*

Then straightforward I fall to examining what he writ and always find it too cold. The salutation says 'Madam' instead of something tender. He signs still 'Rochester' instead of 'Your Lover' or 'John'. Then 'twixt the salutation and closing, each word I mull over and, methinks, find too distant. For he never writes of love; he dispenses brief notes to ask me, will I meet him at La-Frond's to dine? Or at the Chapel for the services? Or may he convey me to the shops, or will I come out for a walk? Never 'I love you', no dear little posies of the heart to hold within me and sigh to, like a nosegay, that the sweet odour may seep through my being.

And I had thought the lovers hereabouts rhymed to their mistresses; so, chiding him with the want of verses, I get some, but all of 'em with a whimsical, witty turn, none of 'em so tremulously full of passion as I would wish: as if he keeps a part of himself closed off from me in fear somehow, as if he feels (what an absurdity) that I might do him hurt.

But sure 'tis my fancy to believe he would think so. What hurt would I ever do him, who have loved him devotedly almost these two years, broken every rule of modesty I've ever been taught for his sake?

No, 'tis only he loves me too little. And this holding back, I fear, is but a want of deep affection. He simply cannot love as I do, and there's an end on't; and I suppose I must ever be satisfied with whatever crumbs he will grant me as long as he will. If I would have him, I must pay this price, and 'tis worth it.

So he sends me this verse: a whimsical satire on the late rebellion:

To this moment a rebel, I throw down my arms,
Great Love! at first sight of Olinda's bright charms.
Made proud and secure by such forces as these,
You may now be a tyrant as soon as you please.
When innocence, beauty, and wit do conspire
To betray, and engage, and inflame my desire,
Why should I decline what I cannot avoid,
And let pleasing hope by base fear be destroyed?
Her innocence cannot contrive to undo me;
Her beauty's inclined, or why should it pursue me?
And wit has to pleasure been ever a friend;
Then what room for despair, since delight is love's end?
There can be no danger in sweetness and youth
Where love is secured by good nature and truth.
On her beauty I'll gaze, and of pleasure complain,
While every kind look adds a link to my chain.
'Tis more to maintain than it was to surprise,
But her wit leads in triumph the slave of her eyes.
I beheld with the loss of my freedom before,
But hearing, forever must serve and adore.
Too bright is my goddess, her temple too weak.
Retire, divine image! I feel my heart break.
Help, Love! I dissolve in a rapture of charms
At the thought of those joys I should meet in her arms.

'Tis a light-hearted Ovidian epistle, rather than a lyric breathing fire and tenderness. My lord conceits himself a Cromwell, who has here-tofore rebelled against King Cupid, but on meeting my forces has surrendered at the first engagement; he then leads a three-pronged offensive on my vanity, to celebrate my innocence, beauty, and wit.

The substance is wit *à la mode*, but 'tis not very passionate or intimate. I even ask him, wherefore the last couplet, the future tense of 'those joys I should meet in her arms', when he's already been there? For I even suspect he's passed off on me some old thing writ for someone else.

Oh, he insists, this is one he writ the spring we first met, but he'll endeavour at a fresh one. So next I'm treated with:

My dear mistress has a heart
Soft as those kind looks she gave me
When, with love's resistless art
And her eyes, she did enslave me.
But her constancy's so weak—
She's so wild, and apt to wander—
That my jealous heart would break
Should we live one day asunder.
Melting joys about her move,
Killing pleasures, wounding blisses.
She can dress her eyes in love,
And her lips can arm with kisses.
Angels listen when she speaks;
She's my delight, all mankind's wonder;
But my jealous heart would break
Should we live one day asunder.

First I melt in delight at the sweetness here, but soon I puzzle o'er the hints of jealousy. What have I e'er done to make him doubt my love? I, who misbehave with him and have put off a king and two marriage matches for his sake? Is he resorting to conventional conceits, like his mention of 'base fear' in the other poem?

Then I recall the poem Savile gave me on the sly, and I retrieve it:

Hard-hearted saint since 'tis your will to be
So unrelenting pitiless to me,
Regardless of a love so many years
Preserved 'twixt lingering hopes and awful fears
(Such fears in lovers' breasts high value claims,
And such, expiring martyrs feel in flames;
My hopes yourself contrived, with cruel care,
Through gentle smiles to lead me to despair),

'Tis some relief, in my extreme distress,
My rival is below your power to bless.

But, sure, he cannot still feel such doubt, after the favours I've let him enjoy! He also shows me another verse he writ long ago, after first we met:

'Twas a dispute 'twixt heaven and earth
Which had produced the nobler birth.
For heaven appeared Cynthia, with all her train,
Till you came forth,
More glorious and more worth
Than she with all those trembling imps of light
With which this envious queen of night
Had proudly decked her conquered self in vain.
I must have perished in that first surprise,
Had I beheld your eyes.
Love, like Apollo when he would inspire
Some holy breast, laid all his glories by;
Else the god, clothed in his heavenly fire,
Would have possessed too powerfully,
And making of his priest a sacrifice,
Had so returned unhallowed to the skies.

This is indeed a reverent, fiery Pindaric ode; I am said to surpass the beauty of the moon goddess; and love, if he suffered its motions to possess him too powerfully, would be like the god Apollo entering at full force the breast of a Delphic priestess – it would kill.

Yet I cannot but note, here's another excuse for holding back his passion. It seems he tries to tell me something in code, but what? Why is he so afear'd to let go and love me – he, who is said to be the greatest lover at court?

Part IX

'That Thing Called Woman'

Robert Blair, Earl of Ashfield
18–20 November 1666

Trust not that thing called woman: she is worse
Than all ingredients crammed into a curse.
> —John Wilmot, Earl of Rochester

1

'Not Only Beating, But Battering'
18 November 1666

A child's life prior to modern times was uniformly bleak. Virtually every child-rearing tract from antiquity to the 18th century recommended the beating of children. We found no examples from this period in which a child wasn't beaten, and hundreds of instances of not only beating, but battering, beginning in infancy.
—Lloyd DeMause, 'Our Forebears Made Childhood a Nightmare',
Psychology Today, VIII, 11 April 1975

Rochester and I, walking out of the palace gate this afternoon by the Banqueting House, see Castlemaine alighting from a coach, with her little half-witted son Charles. The footman holds the door open; Castlemaine steps down and pulls the child down after her by the arm, but not being old enough to have perfect balance yet, and indeed being pulled out before he gets a fair stance on his feet, he trips and falls to the cobblestones on his hands and knees.

His eyes open wide in pain and surprise, and he cries out; but just as I expect his mother to gather him up, and by kisses and caresses soothe the hurt she hath accidentally caused, I am dismayed, instead, to see her jerk him up by the arm to a standing position; scream, in a rage, 'You damned clumsy fool!'; and then, still grasping him with one hand, begin to whack him on the back of the skirts with the other, so hard, the blows echo all over the open court.

The footman still holds the coach door open and looks up to the sky, as if impervious to the cruel scene before him; but what, indeed, as a servant of the lady, can he do to halt it? I note that Stewart and her maid, coming out of the palace gate before Rochester and me, glance at the display, then avert their eyes and walk on to where they take a chair by the little posts nearby: what indeed can they do either? For the child being Castlemaine's, she may do with him what she list.

I hasten my steps to escape the dreadful scene as soon as possible; for my tender heart is wrenched, to hear the little boy utter such fierce, sharp sobs, and to see her still continue whacking away with the utmost vigour.

All at once I am astonished to see Rochester, who has no business at all in this matter, stride rapidly o'er to 'em and grab her wrist, just as her arm was poised to administer the next blow. He glares on her coldly; she eyes him with astonishment, as do I, for this is the first time I have ever heard of a mortal interceding at a child's chastisement, unless't be another parent of the child, as the soft-hearted Lady Ossory, who cannot bear that her babes should cry an instant and will stay her husband's arm after the first few blows.

Castlemaine glowers on him. 'Keep out of this, Rochester. It is no affair of yours.'

She glares him a warning and attempts to wrest away, but he grips her wrist tightly and replies, ''Tis everyone's affair, but that the world is chiefly composed of fools and cowards.'

At this last, I am ashamed to the blood, for I recognize myself in the latter character. 'Tis true, I felt how wrong and cruel the business was, but had wanted the moral courage or social aplomb to intrude myself into a situation where I felt I had no authority. To me, 'twas of greater importance to observe the rules of social intercourse than it was to relieve the misery of an ill-used child.

Now Castlemaine, seeing herself bested in this battle, lets go the child: who, still weeping lustily, rubs his breech with a hand, as if very sore there; and looks up at his mother with fearful, uncomprehending eyes. Castlemaine begins to struggle in Rochester's grasp; but seeing that she has released the child, he does likewise to her: at which the boy, sensing a protector in this man who has made him poppets and paper boats, prudently steps behind him and grabs hold of his breeches leg, still watching his mother with large, fearful eyes; but Castlemaine has a new object of rage now and cries, in a fury:

'What in the devil gives you any rights over this child? This is but another trick to get leverage over someone and make me look like a damned fool in public.'

Rochester eyes her with that cold contempt he always uses on some fool he is about to slice with his wit. With one hand atop the child's head, he responds, arrogantly: 'You look like what you are, madam, give or take an inch of paint; and you are of your own making. I myself have always thought it fantastical, to see a great bully beat a small, helpless child, and no one save the extraordinary few summon up the bowels or wit to prevent it.'

Castlemaine, flushing, abandons herself to the humours of her furious temper, shrieking and shaking of fist.

'You Goddamned son of a whore! You'll be sorry that you ever meddled with me! I'll to the King, and have him on your arse faster even than I was on his little bastard's.'

I cringe at the coarseness of her language before the child; and Rochester, with the same expression of contempt, replies, 'His majesty will scarce support your attacks on his son, madam.'

'Attacks?' screams Castlemaine. 'Rochester, you fool, you arrogant goddamned son of a whore, the stupid little bastard needed a lesson! Attack? Why, I didn't even use a rod.'

'Spare me the airing of your maternal sanctities, madam,' he replies coldly. 'It wants none of your weapons to hurt, given the strength of your blows and the injuries which I've no small suspicion your womanly tenderness has previously inflicted on his helpless form – shall we lift his skirts and make experiment?'

This was something I would not have thought of; but Rochester, smiling at the little boy to encourage him, kneels to his level, and turning him about, gently hoists up his skirts.

Castlemaine, shrieking, lunges at her challenger and cries, 'Get your hands off my son!' She manages to jerk his hand away, but not before there hath been momentarily disclosed a blue-black field, interlaced with cuts.

Now, this is no more than one would expect, on a child with a severe guardian; but Rochester, standing, throws her a look of such contempt and disgust she flushes yet the more.

'I see you are a mistress of many engines, madam: a virtuoso of cane and lash alike. Think not think that your handiwork will escape the King's attention, for I'll report this entire incident to him.'

She lifts her head contemptuously, her eyes flashing fire like Hera's. 'Do as you will, and I'll do the same. But have no illusion, Rochester, he has the ballocks to interfere: he'll offer no more than a meek protest, easily silenced. He knows what trouble I can make; and he has long ago acquiesced to the principle that, as their mother, I have the right to do as I wish.'

'Then he has not seen their wounds.'

She continues to flash contempt back at him. 'He has seen their wounds, as you call 'em. Protest to him if you wish, and let us see who has the greater power.'

'I am not of the humour to challenge your power, madam, only your barbarity, which is so marvellous in a creature that would call itself rational, as to leave me mute with wonder.'

'Thou arrant devil!'

'Thou true mother!'

At this she grabs the luckless child by the hand and huffs toward her apartments, towing him along behind.

Then tonight, after supper in the King's closet, we play with some pups newly born to one of His Majesty's spaniel bitches, and Rochester makes a clever proposal.

'Your Majesty, suppose I were to hoist up this puppy, then stand with it, drop it to the floor, and begin beating it when it yelped.'

The King's eyes widen. 'Odd's fish, Rochester: what new prank is this?'

Rochester hoists up the puppy in both hands and gets to his feet. 'I am about to do't. Will Your Majesty prevent me?'

The King immediately starts halfway from his chair, throwing a look of alarm across the golden plate still littered with lark and gravy; but then, sizing up the situation aright, he laughs and winks.

'Very well, my jester –' He sits back, eyes sparkling, fingertips placed judiciously together '– what frolic or riddle have you to divert us now?'

Rochester stands beside a large, round vase with Japan scenes etched in green and gold. 'A not-so-diverting piece of nonsense: I beg Your Majesty play along and see its justice. Would Your Majesty prevent me?'

The King chuckles, tapping his fingers together against one another. 'You know I would, just as as I know you wouldn't.'

'Your Majesty loves your dogs?' Rochester presses, securing the point of dispute.

The King winks at me across the round walnut-tree table, the silver candelabra glistening 'twixt us. 'Mark you, Ashfield: this comedy will end with some diverting analogy on natures canine and human. Yes, Rochester: I love my dogs: as anyone in the palace must know, observing my retinue and stepping into its remnants.'

I chuckle.

'Your Majesty loves your dogs and would act to protect 'em from a bully.' Rochester pauses dramatically. 'Do you love your children as much as your dogs, Your Majesty?'

Now at last the King sees whither the conversation is going; and the analogy, which he once believed would be diverting, proves uncomfortable.

He looks away, picks up his golden goblet, and sips.

'Rochester, I know what you are about to say and why you are about to plead the child's cause. I command you to forebear.'

Rochester sinks into the black velvet sleeping-chair in the alcove nearby and, still holding the puppy, he peruses the King's face.

'Can she really be so frightful to Your Majesty as she is to a little boy whose wits she has turned for fear? What rod can she apply to her superior?'

The King frowns, darting him a look over the goblet. 'I have commanded you to forebear.'

Rochester cannot ignore this; but I know he must be thinking, like me, that it is a cowardly answer. I see him working very hard to keep down his furious temper; he looks away, as if to scan the Venus and Mars inset above the fireplace of black marble, and all the while absent-mindedly stroking the puppy's head; then all at once he gains control of himself so far as to look back on the King with a beaming, winning smile – I suppose, to solicit the King's approval, for Rochester's smile never fails to melt hearts. Then I find out where he inherited the trick, for His Majesty, smiling back, observes, 'You always put me in mind of your father when you do that.'

Rochester continues to smile. 'You put me in mind of him, too, Your Majesty.'

'Tis an innocuous enough remark, and Rochester continues to beam innocently; but the King flushes, his face contorted with anger, and barks:

'You are the most insolent young scapegrace it has ever been my displeasure to meet. Leave us until I give you permission to appear in my sight again.'

Rochester still smiles. 'Very well: I most humbly beg Your Majesty's pardon; for I see that I have intruded upon Your Majesty's pleasures by broaching a most unpleasant subject. 'Twas inexcusable, and very bad breeding on my part; but as Your Majesty is well aware, I was badly brought up; and often ignore, to the discomfort of those about me, the social amenities whereby the more polished gentlemen of the world are governed. Perhaps, had I been so fortunate as to enjoy more converse with the affable, well-bred gentlemen of the world, such as my father and Your Majesty, I would learn to come agreeably into company with blood and screams, by averting my eyes to what is distasteful. But wanting the usual good breeding that God has approved for men in my class, I fear I must be eternally damned to make myself disagreeable. Again, my sincerest apologies.'

The King turns trembling and white-faced to me. 'Ashfield, escort him thither before he talks himself into the Tower again.'

So I drag the foolish youth out by the arm, past the many ticking clocks and down the stairs into the Great Bedchamber, thence through the Presence Chamber and into the court, and I cry, 'Rochester, in God's name, why did you deliberately provoke him?'

Rochester's face is shrouded in darkness, but his voice is taut with rage. 'It is a sorry monarch who recognizes not his responsibilities as a man.'

'You are too hard –'

'Scattering his seed where he may, ignoring the pitiful fruits of his enjoyments!'

Huddling against the cold, Rochester strides with his long legs o'er the bricks and westward toward the Gallery.

'This is a pretty speech, but for aught we know, you yourself have fathered half a dozen babes, all the way from Italy to Oxford.'

'And you think I am not haunted by the thought?' He halts a moment in a small court just east of that of the maids of honour, the moon casting silver on his pale, earnest face. 'If ever I found one, and it were not being properly cherished by the mother, I'd have it away in an instant.' He whirls on his heel and, cape swirling, stalks off into the night.

But I've not heard the end of this frolic.

2

'Good Parenting'
19 November 1666

Good parenting is something that has been achieved only after
centuries as generation after generation of parents tried to overcome the abuse of their own childhood by reaching out to their
children on more mature levels of relating.
—Lloyd DeMause, 'Our Forebears Made Childhood a Nightmare',
Psychology Today, VIII, 11 April 1975

Today, meeting with Buckhurst and Shepherd at the great half-crown
ordinary at the King's Head, near Charing Cross, we have a most
excellent neat dinner, though Killigrew coming in at the end makes a
stir amidst the diners with his lewd jests. He hath no discretion and
seemeth to have learnt naught from his being recently banished from
Court for his scurrilous saying on Castlemaine, how she was a
lecherous little girl when young and used to rub her thing with her
fingers or against a form, and that now she must be rubbed with
something else.

Fleeing the frolics of Killigrew, I've then a month's mind to go
about to the New Exchange on the Strand, where, as Buckhurst
informs me, there's a new wench, mighty pretty, selling of gloves and
laces on the second storey of the colonnade. But taking coach thence,
and climbing the stairs thereto, I am forestalled of offering up my
homage, Sedley having preceded me, and the wench crying to him,
'Nay, well, of all rogues, commend me to you, sir, for the greatest,'
with such a coy and mincing air, I give o'er the fortress already lost.

Sedley hurrying me away, though with little enough cause, as I've no
mind to compete with one of his wit, we hang about in the street
listening to the news being cried up and fall into a lazy discourse. He
asks me if I have seen Holler's new print of the city, with a pretty
representation of the part which is burnt, the which I hath not; and I,
stamping my feet against the cold, which is very bitter, and considering
how to take my leave, open to him what little news I have: which is

Rochester's capricious conduct of yesterday, which hath earned him (like Killigrew's loose tongue of October) Castlemaine's wrath and a temporary banishment from the court.

Sedley acts little surprised. 'I'faith, this is no marvel. Rochester has always carried himself to children with such a defiance of ordinary sense that his error becomes cunning.'

I laugh, hugging myself against the cold. 'This is indeed the hall-mark of his wit: the leap beyond logic which seems, on the conclusion of't, eminently logical.'

We both of us hang in the hedge a space to watch a pretty lady and her maid pass through the great lintels 'twixt the colonnade, after which Sedley continues:

''Tis part of his erratic brilliance that he can get into children's heads the way he can into women's. Indeed, I put him to dine with my daughter the very day he returned, at Chatelin's, that he might get into her head for me: else I had lost all hopes of control.'

I laugh. 'With your Kate, I had long given up such hopes, Sedley, and meekly handed over the breeches. Ne'er stir, if I were her father, I would be utterly her creature now. What was her recent freak?'

A little girl approaching with a basket of China oranges, we each buy, and Sedley, peeling his, replies, 'She embarked on a ten-days' extravaganza of such wanton follies, a Nostradamus could not have predicted where she would conclude. At first we were treated to a fit of the sullens: you know her way, Ashfield, Hoity Toity Miss Touch Me Not. I assumed the very mantle of Job and ignored it the whole day, for Rochester had previously advised patience in lieu of correction. But leniency, contrary to his assurances, only worsened the light in which I stood: emboldened, she exaggerated the humour; a Princess Royal of Spain cannot have been nicer. She would have her meals sent up on a tray, lest she come about the filthy beasts that abided with her; she would languish all day in a dressing gown, none of her attire being fit for her delicate tastes; she would call me *Papá*.'

I laugh heartily, and Sedley, with eyes twinkling 'neath his mountain of a periwig, tosses off an orange peel, then continues, 'Endurance having proved so useless, I tried retreat: I closeted myself with a whore for three days, hoping the freak would pass in the interim. And so it had: she was now in the hoyden's airs; she would appear, without warning, to dance and sing as I tried to read. It was by now full and plain to any man of sense, she was determined to jolt me from my forebearance: determined I should notice what she did, were't necessary to crack a brandy bottle over my head and dance on a rope above the chandelier. So I advised her, as she was a reasonable creature, to deal plainly with what was in the wrong or give over communicating altogether.'

'And did this suffice, then?'

Sedley waves off a boy that hawks the *London Gazette*. 'With Kate? No, mere reason has never been sufficient to move her; she but retorted I must know what vexed her if anyone did.'

'If you had known,' I laugh, 'you had not been in this trouble.'

'Precisely, and so angry remarks were exchanged on the difficulties or impossibilities of mind-reading: at the conclusion of which, she pushed disrespect too far and called me a damned whoremaster.' Sedley pops a section of orange into his mouth.

'Good God!'

'There could be only one issue to this: she had forced me to the point of beating her; and I confess, I was angry enough to do a thorough job.'

'And did this bring her around at last?' I query.

Sedley throws me an ironic look. 'Yes, around to the sullens again; for when I was done, she screamed she hated me to the bottom of her heart and would never speak word to me again. This was no idle threat: for the next morning, when we all arose, she was as good as her word: dramatically silent, with her nose in the air, directing all messages meant for me to some intermediary; and then only when pressed for a response. And this went on four days: I tell thee, Ashfield , the blushing virgins at court did not more anxiously await the sight of Rochester than I.'

I laugh. 'And he actually mended matters?'

Sedley nods.

'But how?'

A vendor of broadsides then disturbing us, we take a resolution to be gone from the cold and distraction of the place and back to Whitehall; so Sedley, climbing into my coach before me, answers:

'Faith, who knows how he does anything? I have seen him with her some several times; he carries himself to her in startling ways that seem to gain her confidence – treats her as a child where I would demand more adult manners; then, this concluded, turns about and treats her more like an adult when I would approach her as a child; and just as I think his carriage the maddest, she opens up to him like a flower.'

Thinking how his manners enraptured little Jane, I settle myself into the coach cushions. 'What did he this time?'

The whip cracking, we make the brief distance to the Strand.

'First he had her to dine, to air her feelings, as he always does.'

Sedley throws the remnants of his orange into the stinking kennel as we turn onto the Strand.

'What did she say?'

'Apparently she must have complained about her mother and me, but I cannot say, for he would not tell me much.'

I am astonished. 'Why not?'

We jog past Bedford House and toward St-Martin-in-the-Fields.

Sedley gives me a dry look of his small, merry eyes. 'She had sworn him to secrecy, and he is more respectful of her confidences than I would be of his.'

I laugh. 'Then what?'

'He brought her back, considerably calmer, and bade me apologize to her.'

I am aghast. '*You* apologize to *her*? Whatever for?'

'Resorting to violence, as Rochester calls it; and then she had to apologize for being sullen, wild, and disrespectful. And we had to kiss before him and promise to air our feelings plainly to one another, instead of engaging in the subtleties of flank and counter attack.'

I am astounded. 'And it worked?'

'Yes, to an extent.' We jog past the cookshops and taverns of Charing Cross now. 'Not that Kate is a perfect child – but we talk to one another more plainly now rather than resorting to manoeuvres. We still quarrel, but he has taught us to read one another's signals more clearly now.'

I shake my head. 'How does Rochester do't?'

Sedley shrugs. 'The same way he debauches women and charms the King: by entering into the feelings of others. It is his theory that a father should always get inside a child's head, sympathize with its feelings and draw it out, rather than punishing it into obedience.'

I muse o'er this odd notion as we jog past the first buildings of the palace. 'This is all very well, but it seems to me 'twould only work with all unusually docile child or an unusually brisk father. In the Lady Katherine's case, there is a real danger of her taking complete control.'

'Do I not know the danger better than you?' Sedley gives me a dry look that makes me laugh heartily. 'I am far from comfortable with the situation: not only have I had to re-think every impulse, I am daily conscious how far I voyage off the charted boundaries of child-rearing. There's not a manual but recommends beating on the first motions of disobedience. But the orthodox method didn't work at all: the more I beat, the more I was forced to beat anew, to gain more compliance, and even then, the most I got was sullen acquiescence: her rage was smouldering yet and would always erupt later. Rochester convinced me, did I aim to control with force such an ungovernable temper, I must be prepared to beat her once and twice in every day until her spirit utterly broke; and so I gave over, for though she's a demon, I love the girl, and it was an agony to me even to have these scenes twice and thrice a month when she grew so provoking I knew not what else to do.'

I look glumly out at the buildings about the coach as we draw up to the palace gate. 'I think I will never have children; I know, I could never do't.'

'Cheer up: perhaps all your children will be as languid as you and want the spirits to be bad.' Sedley jostles me playfully with an arm. 'And if all else fails, you can enlist the footman's aid.'

'I would be afear'd lest he hit too hard.'

Sedley shakes his head and gives me a droll look. 'You're hopeless: best marry a strong-minded woman.'

'If I marry at all – which is doubtful.'

'How now, what faltering of courage is this!' The coach door opening, Sedley, taking up his cane, urges, 'Come, you must be wedlocked: never did I more anxiously await an event as the birth of children to you and to Rochester. I yearn to see him father some hellion of a son who will laugh in his face at his sympathizings and grow sufferable only under repeated exposures to the lash.'

I climb out after him, the footman holding my arm.

'And what amiable curse have you for my future?'

He gives me a droll look where he stands before the palace gate. 'That you have a scholarly son who corrects your Latin and a rough, cruel one who pulls wings off flies and laughs at your tender heart; then a soft, yielding daughter who takes her nature from yours and is sure to be brought to bed directly she turns sixteen.'

'Enough!' I cry. 'Now I know that I will never marry.'

Nor is this an idle threat, for how many successful marriages have been made in our class? Here is Bucks, who wed in the usual fashion, cold-bloodedly; he then comes to love Shrewsbury's wife, and their boldness hath caused such a scandal, the husband's friends hath charged him he should issue a challenge. Here is the King, married to a poor, quiet Portuguese reared in a convent, being as polite to her as possible in public but frankly seeking his enjoyments elsewhere. Then we have Sedley, married on a mere whim in youth, to secure him a mad daughter and madder wife, and his house always in such an uproar he can scarce support entering it.

And finally we have a man truly loves his wife, Sir John Denham, and he going mad himself to watch how she openly cuckolds him with the Duke of York: since June last, she hath gone boldly up the front stairs to his apartments, having insisted she would not be relegated to the back stairs like poor Price.

With these unhappy examples and others before me, I have now taken a resolution not to marry at all. For if I love my wife, I must be concerned lest she play me false; and if I do not, she will make my home unquiet. Then when we have children, I must either suffer 'em to be indulged and run wild out of tenderness, or study to keep what the fanatics call 'a due distance', and discourage their familiarities, with at least a mien of sternness, if not repeated chastisements.

No, let my title die afore I be forced into unhappiness or brutality. There's no happy marriage to be got in this court: not, at any rate, in the set of the fashionable.

3

'The Stress On Repression Rather Than Encouragement'
19 November 1666

> The doctrine of Original Sin strongly encouraged the stress on repression rather than encouragement as the core of educational theory.... 'If thou smite him with the rod, thou shalt deliver his soul from Hell,' was a quotation from the Bible that Protestants took very seriously indeed.... Many late sixteenth-and seventeenth-century mothers were both caring and repressive at the same time, for the simple reason that the two went together.
>
> —Lawrence Stone, *The Family, Sex, and Marriage in England, 1500–1800*

Tonight, at the fiddles and treats in Castlemaine's music room, I am surprised to see Rochester. The hostess so elaborately ignores him, 'tis plain she feels his presence; and the King hits his arm, calls him 'bold fellow', laughs aloud at his sallies. 'Twere hard to countenance those two had quarrelled a mere twenty-four hours before; but then, this would not be the first time a monarch had showered a favourite with cuffs and kisses.

Some three score sit at cards; but Stewart, who plays little by reason of her dullness, leans her boobies on the crimson velvet covering of a black table, to squeal and clap her plump hands at Bucks' card-castles. The King then excuses himself from Rochester and legs it to whither his jackal guards the carcass for him, leaving Rochester, who hath not the taste for high play, momentarily alone. I wonder where Mallet can be tonight, much surprised one of his passion would let her alone or one of her vanity would miss such an opportunity to make her little mouths and flaunt her conquest in public. And I wonder too what goes on 'twixt Strephon and the King on that battlefield. His Majesty hath seemed to ignore her this week past, and mayhap scouts other territory; for Bucks asking him earlier what new was to do, the King replies, he hath resolved to resort to a new bawd: a husband in want.

Taking a goblet from the little black houseboy who circulates with his tray, I stride up to embrace Rochester and offer my congratulations: 'This is the shortest banishment anyone has ever suffered, unless it be Castlemaine. The King indeed loves you.'

He shoots me from the corner of his eye a dark ironic look. 'My person less than my tricks. I attached a comical verse on dogs to the tail of the spaniel that whelped and released her into his levee.'

I laugh as I toss down a great gulp of hippocras. 'What'd you say?'

He answers, 'Some such silly stuff as this:

If I had a pup who set up for a wit
And when he came to sup gave his monarch a fit,
I'd warn him, "Be wary whose hand you just bit,
Or like the mad earl you'll be sorry for it.
Your jester begs pardon with doggerel he's writ
And sent in by me, whose appeal is more fit."
Silly stuff indeed, but it worked.'

'I can see how that must have charmed someone of his humour.'

'Mere buffoonery.' Rochester shrugs, stares off into the distance, a glaze over his near-black eyes. The Devil take me if he doth not look melancholy tonight, despite being reinstated to the royal favour.

All at once Castlemaine shrieks with rage and throws down her hand. He observes, drily, 'There goes another thousand pounds out of the Irish treasury and another inch of flesh off Charles' back. God bless thee, woman! And bestow upon thee another friendly snake, to enjoy thy fall. Heavenly bliss be thine forever after, with a forked tongue that will doubly tease up thy c—t.'

I laugh but then quickly sober up.

'Rochester,' I say, 'you really ought to try to make it up with her. Recall what just happened to Killigrew; she can be a powerful enemy.'

He tosses down another draught and gestures to the houseboy, who plods over with the tray. 'Were't so, I would not be here now, to rail at the image behind her false face.' He exchanges the empty goblet for a full one. 'No, she has become a mere vizard of herself these few months past. The King besots himself on Stewart and pays little heed to what she does.'

I glance nervously about, but no one seems to hear Rochester's speech. Those playing basset chatter or study their cards; gossip-groups murmur about the walls; the King stares delighted on his bauble, who rolls her eyes and giggles.

I shift subject: 'I heard from Sedley this afternoon how skilfully you handled the Lady Katherine.'

Throwing me a look o' er the raised goblet, Rochester replies, still in that cutting, brisk tone, 'For a witty man, Sedley can be very stupid: if he treated his daughter as he does his mistress, he would have no trouble with her at all.'

Surprised and diverted, as always with him, I query, sipping, 'Treat his daughter as his mistress? How should he do that?'

'Lay aside his damned book and listen to her, as sincerely as if he had designs to debauch her; take her out to dine or see a play: not to pit-hop and collect gossip, as a wild dog does burrs, but to whisper in her ear and act as if he enjoyed her company. He gives more kisses and treats to any whore at Black Bess's; and she but misbehaves because he seldom notices her otherwise: he is not even home very often. And you know how mad her mother is. The little girl's but hungry for attention – preferably, at her age, of the masculine kind. It thrills her beyond measure when I offer my arm, assist her from coaches and through doors, pour some watered wine into her flute-glass, and take note of her pretty gown. It makes her feel very much the grown-up lady, and so she acts one. If Sedley takes no heed, she'll become whore to the first oaf with sufficient wit or cash to provide these little attentions.'

'Rochester,' I laugh, 'you amaze me, the way you dart in and out of people's minds. Have you told Sedley this?'

Rochester broods. 'Yes, but 'tis scarce to his advantage to credit what I say – then his conscience might urge him to spend less time with his whore and bottle.'

Hearing the bitter tone in Strephon's voice, I wonder what preys on him.

'Until this business came up about the children, I never knew you could be tender-hearted like me.'

'Usually I am not,' he says, tossing down another draught. 'I only remember very clearly how it feels to be on the wrong end of a lash or cane.'

'Who does not?' I shrug.

'Many people: for look how many children are beaten.'

We both set our empty goblets on the returning houseboy's tray and exchange 'em for new; this last batch is a claret, with legs enough to kick a bull betwixt the eyes.

'I suppose 'tis necessary sometimes,' I muse.

He shoots me a dry, ironic look o'er the raised goblet. 'Why?'

I shrug. 'Oh, for dull scholars such as me.'

'Was your recall sharpened when your schoolmaster grinned and fingered the birch? Or did you suddenly forget all you knew? Did he apply only a few taps to the incorrigibly lazy? No, I thought not: he laid on stripes as if he were superintending Bridewell.'

I laugh. 'I've had thoughts similar to this myself. So you would countenance the rod only in punishment of mischief?'

'Never believe it. When you've drunk too much, need Edward take a cane to you before you know it? Or has the duty already been performed by your aching head?'

I laugh again, fully suspecting he but plays with me as is capricious wont. 'Rochester, you know very well they are not adults.'

'Agreed: they are more loving and fragile.' He gulps the heady brew. 'You I could wallop with a cane and injure very little. A small son of mine, if I gratified my ill humour on his body, would suffer more intensely – and not the least from the lapse of love I'd shown.'

This is a unique way to look at it. 'Children must be taught and guided,' I probe, more to see his reaction than to argue.

'I never said they did not. To say truth, they are guided too little; for they are regarded either as cunning toys, to pet or break at will, or as little beasts barely to be foreborn.'

This last being my usual view of 'em, I query, curious, 'How do you see 'em?'

'In each is a little person determined by nature that tries to unfold itself, as chicks do from eggs.'

Fascinated, I ask, 'How would you bring out the chick?'

'It more or less brings itself out,' he explains calmly. 'That's nature's way.'

The spendthrift Arran having apparently gone through all his cash, I see him tap the funds of his brother Richard, who grumbling produces a purse, his wife frowning behind him.

'Then why have parents?' I demand.

'Properly, to protect and nurture the little creature while 'tis still but fragile and encourage the incipient movements of its nature.'

'What do you with upper servants that beat the children in the kitchen?'

'None have dared, so far as I know.'

'Don't you take a rod to your page?'

'I would never take advantage of my size and strength to inflict pain on a little person.'

'This is indeed flying in the face of custom,' I marvel. 'The world would say you are a lax employer and will be a very truant father.'

'The world is half-mad and half-witted,' he retorts.

We raise our goblets in mutual salute.

The drink-infused clamour in the chamber grows, 'til my head threatens to ache; the King and Bucks roar together at some jest, Stewart giggling 'twixt 'em, and Grammont raking his winnings from a card game towards him. Price cries out 'A mischief on all Frenchmen!' 'Ods Bobs!' cries Denham, rearranging his cards; and the fiddles play yet louder.

'Where will you send your sons to school?' I ask.

'I will not. There's no lesson can't be learnt at home, and I will make it very clear to anyone concerned with my children they must use their wits rather than their strong right arms.'

Laughing, I suggest, 'You will have some difficulty getting nurses and tutors.'

'Never doubt it,' he returns drily. 'People seem to love a chance to give a good whipping.'

'I think your idea's better,' I confide at last. 'My grandma would forbid me my pony a day or two, and the nurse would slap my tail hard with a hand.'

He gives me a severe look. 'No one is going to slap any child of mine.'

I begin to laugh.

'What?' He regards me, outraged. 'Would you whack that way on one of yours?'

I consider. 'Probably not, but I'd think 'twas only my folly. Now I find you are foolish, too – 'tis good to have company for a change.'

'Common sense is never foolish,' he retorts, 'but being such a rare commodity, it does well to find itself hospitably treated by two gentlemen about town.'

I laugh at him again; and indeed I have been laughing the rest of the night since, over this prodigious fantastical friend of mine, who has ill-used half the women in town and is as gentle as my grandma in managing a child. I think the human beast must be even more full of foolish contradictions in real life than his pasteboard shadows on the stage.

4

'Salvation From The Hands Of The Devil'
20 November 1666

One reason for [the] particular emphasis in Puritan circles on the
education of children, and their salvation from the hands of the
Devil, is that it was only by mass conversion of the younger generation that they could hope to create or perpetuate the godly
society to which they aspired.... The second reason for the severity
accorded to children at this time is the rapid spread of knowledge of
the Bible, and Protestant treatment of the book as an authoritative
source on all subjects. The Apocrypha and Proverbs contain some
extremely harsh instructions about how to bring up children....
The advice is to keep psychological distance. No hint of tenderness
is to be permitted, since this would undermine authority and
destroy deference.
—Lawrence Stone, *The Family, Sex and Marriage in England,*
1500–1800

Today being a Fast Day, we must needs torment ourselves again, to
hear for two hours how we caused the plague and how fortunate we
are to have escaped our just desserts; and how, being on probation, we
are like to incur another disaster unless we cease our sacrilegious
fooling. I sit there the whole time feeling mighty vexed that some
impertinent fool would read his betters such lectures. I wish I knew
why the King saw fit to command us to this rack: I think by the life he
leads he must believe no more than I in Christian superstition, so I am
sure it must be the effects of policy: he would have the city and country
folk see a little piety in us. I yearned to leave off this tedious business
today and sneak off for a quiet bottle; but knowing how His Majesty
would scold, and how the ale-houses be closed anyway during the
sermon, off to the services it is, as if I be but seven year of age.

Everyone is there at the Chapel Royal, in various stages of boredom
and agony; Savile shifts about uneasily, as if anticipating the goose and
bottle already at the end of so many 'Amen's; the King sits behind the
elaborate carved screen of his side pew behind the altar, that we may

not see the glazed church-look of his eye; the Duke of York ogles Lady Denham, who ogles him back; Sir John frets beside her; Etherege keeps craning his neck about to see who's here, what they wear, and who and who's together; Mallet and Rochester giggle, poke one another, and look as if they would fain be gone somewhere to kiss; &c &c.

Afterward, galloping out post-haste down the long gallery and about its corner, I stand about looking for someone to lament with about the great loss of time; and am just about to leave, for a bottle and dinner, when a lovely flame-haired lady comes storming up, her eyes blazing blue fire, and cries to Elizabeth Hamilton standing nearby:

'Well, that Rochester is certainly the worst man breathing!'

Hamilton looks arch over her ivory fan sticks. 'You'll get no argument from me there.'

'He has stepped right out of the chapel uttering the most incomparable blasphemies,' rants the lady, her long black lashes batting furiously over eyes of the palest blue. 'Nay, he did not e'en step out first; he still had a foot in the House of God when he began airing his wicked, atheistical views.'

Hamilton fans herself and with a hard look replies, 'That does not surprise me in the least. I think we have definite evidence of God's gracious mercy that no thunderbolt has got him yet.'

'Then I wish God would be a little less merciful. And that little hoyden Elizabeth!' The lady crosses her arms with a delicate but firm gesture, her jaw set in determination. 'Why, she stood there the whole time trying not to laugh. Is she an atheist, too?'

'I hope not, but I cannot say.'

The lady raises her nose fastidiously. 'If she is not, he will make one of her soon.'

Hamilton leans a little forward, pops up the fan, and with a malicious look whispers, 'With her gaiety and coquettishness, that is not all I expect him to make of her.'

They both exchange knowing looks and laugh heartily, each behind her fan. Women can be so damned savage to one another; at least we will quarrel fairly, in the open; give one another a nick or two with a blade, and then be friends again. This female backbiting has always made me so melancholy.

'I have tried to be a friend to her,' orates the tempestuous lady with brilliant smile and eyes snapping, 'but her response is to put on airs before me, then laugh when her diabolical companion makes a game of my beliefs.'

'He has caught her in his toils indeed.' Hamilton shakes her head. 'I knew't by the way she carried on t'other day.'

This at least will be a pleasant hint I can drop to Rochester; I prick up my ears, to see what more I can hear to help my friend. The lady pops her fan closed and with an arch look replies, 'She scarce sounded modest to me. I believe he has done more to her than she will allow.'

Hamilton then darting a glance to me and spying my presence pops up her fan and mutters, 'Hush, see where his friend Lord Ashfield listens now.'

The lady whirls about, eyes flaring, and crosses her arms.

'You are his friend?'

Suddenly very glum at the thought I will be called upon to participate in an argument, I shift about uneasily but admit, 'I try to be, madam.'

Hamilton leans over to the other woman's ear. 'Earl of Ashfield, the Lord Buckhurst's best friend since school.'

This titbit digested, the lady looks me up and down with those cool diamond-bright blue eyes as if I be a beetle under a microscope – at which I fidg.

'Do you, my lord, share Lord Rochester's atheistical views?'

I run a finger around 'neath my holland-band and wish I had a mug of something bracing in t'other hand. 'I share his views; but I am no atheist, nor I think is he.'

'Well, he certainly talks like one!' she snaps.

I shrug. 'Yes, I suppose he does.'

She looks at me in surprise: I think she must have been expecting another answer there, though I know not what it could in reason be, for Rochester disputes against religion as violently as any atheist ever could.

She hath still trained on me the piercing blue beam of those sharp, all-knowing eyes. 'Do you go about blaspheming God to His followers, my lord, and mocking their belief?'

'I think much of religion is a mockery, and I often laugh over't.'

The lady raises a cinammon-coloured eyebrow, crosses her arms more tightly, and glares.

'Well, what about a good argument now?'

'With you, madam?' I am surprised. 'Why should I wish to argue with you?'

'The Lord Rochester did.' Her eyes flare at me.

'I am not Rochester. I despise arguments; and if you are so vehement in your belief as this, pray enjoy't with all my blessings; you'll get no mockery from me.'

She looks at me in surprise again. Then she offers up: 'Well, your lordship certainly differs from the Lord Rochester in this respect.'

'Yes, but I have less cause to hate religion than he.'

She had uncrossed her arms and turned to go away, holding up her deep blue skirt with two dainty hands, and a fan dangling from one arm; but this last remark stops her. She turns about, her eyes wide with surprise. 'Less cause? What mean you, my lord?'

'My grandmother only dragged me to church and got me bored. His mother whipped him raw every Sunday forcing Scriptures and theology down his throat.'

The lady seems very surprised. 'I had not known this; I had always assumed his mother must be some whore or baggage.'

'Would that she had been,' I return with an earnest smile. ''Twould've contributed greatly to his peace and happiness. The Duke of Bucks tells me he was not even suffered to cough during the services; if he so much as scratched an arm, she would glare and pinch him, and then march him home afterwards to a vigorous session with the rod. His Grace says he never saw Rochester on a Monday but that he seemed in pain at the slightest attempt to walk or sit; is't not natural, madam, that a man so brought up should be violently predisposed against the cause for which he suffered such pain?'

The lady looks very impressed by this intelligence, and, her humour considerably altering, says, 'Yes, indeed: though I still cannot condone his blasphemies.'

'There are aspects of his behaviour that I cannot condone either, madam,' I reply earnestly, as I see her gaze on me pensive and receptive, 'but in many ways he is a fine man.'

Her eyebrow goes up, but only a little, and an ironic curve appears at the edge of her rosebud lips. 'Oh? And what ways are these, my lord?'

'He is a very loyal friend to those that do not betray his trust,' I explain. 'He has a mind so deep, and a command of language so keen, as to earn my highest admiration, and' – I look sheepish here – 'you will believe I jest, madams, but truly, he is very kind to horses, dogs, and children.'

Here she laughs heartily, holding her sides for merriment – as indeed I thought she would. But 'tis very true.

'He is not perfect,' I press on earnestly, 'but he is my friend, and I love him. And truly, madam, in such a world as we inhabit, is't not better to love one another?'

'Yes, it is,' she agrees, and then looks on me very thoughtfully, as if she would pierce to the fibre of my being, to know the full core of silliness therein; and then she startles me by asking, 'Where have we met before?'

'Madam?'

'Your voice is familiar to me.'

I shrug. 'I've been hereabouts.'

She rumples her broad white forehead with a frown. Then she surprises me again by asking, 'What think you on the topic of female education?'

I start. 'Female education? Why, I've never thought much on't at all.'

The lady speaks vehemently now and wags her finger in my face. 'Do you not think it monstrous, my lord – nay, unreasonable – that half the human race is denied the educational opportunities the other half enjoys?'

I consider. 'Why, I suppose it is. But I wonder, madam, at your use of the word "opportunities". I would have gladly given up my place in Westminster School to any little girl that desired it.'

Now, though she had looked so vehement before, she starts, then bursts out laughing, to conclude by giving me an ironic look, her eyes sparkling. I grin, whereat she sobers, gets that vehement look on her face, and says, pointing at me with her fan: 'Will your lordship give your daughters the same education you give your sons?'

I wonder what all this can mean, but I answer, 'I am very little like to have either if my present prejudices against marriage remain, madam.'

She presses, 'But if you did marry, my lord, and have children – what sort of education would you give 'em?'

'Faith, I don't know,' I respond helplessly. 'Probably whatever sort they wished: I am very malleable.'

She bursts out laughing again, then with a coquettish look of those big blue eyes, taps me with her fan and rallies me a little. 'What if your son never wished to learn to read, my lord? You would indulge him in his ambition of being a great booby?'

I grin. 'I would see to't his mother and the tutor made him learn.'

Now the lady laughs in earnest; her eyes sparkle like two lovely bubbling streams. I grin, for I always enjoy making a parade of my silliness before an appreciative audience; and this audience is delightful indeed: a true woman of spirit and fire.

I add, 'I have a ward, madam, named Jane, but she and the tutor decide what to study, now she has her letters and numbers – I leave it to them. I believe she has geography and history and literature and French, I know not what else.'

Her eyebrow up, the lady says, 'She should have Latin.'

I shrug, 'I had no joy of it myself, madam, but she is welcome to't, if she wishes.'

'She chooses what she studies?'

'Yes, to some measure, in conference with the tutor and me. He believes in building on her interests.'

The lady looks thoughtful. 'Interesting.' Then she sobers, inspects her fan, and asks me, 'What is your opinion, my lord, on the subjugation of the female in this country?'

This at least I do have an opinion on. 'I feel very sorry for 'em, madam.'

She looks surprised, questions me, 'And why is that?'

'Everyone plots against 'em, uses 'em, casts 'em off.'

The lady regards me all over in her pensive gaze. 'Do you never do so, my lord?'

'I am not innocent, by any means,' I explain, 'but I only enjoy where I am certain the lady will get equal pleasure from the encounter. I would not ruin a virgin, nor jilt a lady that believed she loved me, no matter how sick I got of her. It is a great weakness in me.'

The lady smiles, her lips curving wide. 'Or, a great strength. Do you believe, my lord, men should be equal with women?'

'Equal?' I ask, surprised. 'In what way?'

'In all ways.' Her eyes snap. 'In their legal and social rights – as inheriting property, moving about freely, sitting in Parliament –'

'It is a rather startling idea,' I admit.

Her eyebrow goes up. 'Startling? How so? Do you not know, my lord, women that are capable, men that are incompetent?'

'Oh, yes,' I agree heartily. 'I only meant, 'twould be a startling change in the world. But there is no reason why't should not be thus: I would have no objections to't. I almost never go to the lords anyway. There is endless talk and no action.'

'Oh,' cries the lady with wistful eyes, 'how I wish I could get in there!'

'You are welcome to my seat, madam, if you wish,' I offer cordially, 'but I doubt you could coax 'em into admitting you.'

'Yes,' she sighs, 'I doubt it, too.'

''Tis a pity.' I grin. 'I'm sure you could stir 'em up famously.'

She laughs. Then, smiling, she extends a dainty white hand, which I clasp a moment. 'Lord Ashfield, I have enjoyed this conversation. I am Emilia O'Hara; my apartments are hard by Elizabeth Mallet's in Scotland Yard, and I hope to see you again. Fame has not reported wrong of your lordship: you are one of the best-natured men alive, and, I find, one of the most reasonable.' Her brow rumples. 'I wish I could recall where I heard your voice.'

'No doubt hereabouts, madam.'

She curtseys; I bow and express my gratitude, tell her I have enjoyed the conversation also: at which she marches off, holding her skirts with both hands purposefully, and looking in considerably better humour than when she marched hither. What, I wonder, ailed the woman at first? I suppose Rochester merely stirred her up: he is famous for lighting a fire under the female beast, one way or t'other.

Part X

'A Tongue To Tempt The Angels'

Betty Mallet

November-December 1666

Oh, he has a tongue, they say, would tempt the angels to a second fall.
(The heroine's mama commenting on the hero, Dorimant, modelled after Rochester)

—George Etherege, *The Man of Mode* (1676)

1

'Sir Walter Raleigh's School Of Atheism'
20 November 1666

Of Sir Walter Rawleys school of Atheisme by the waye . . . and of his
diligence vsed to get yong gentlemen of this schoole, where in both
Moyses, & our Savior, the olde, and the new Testamente are iested
at . . .

— Robert Parsons *Responsio ad Edictum Elizabethan*

Today, the King having proclaimed a fast day for the cessation of the
plague, all of us prepare to go to the Chapel Royal; and I am not a
little surprised to get a brief note from my lord, asking if he can take
me to services and then to La-frond's after. Of course I answer in the
affirmative, but when he appears at my apartments, looking very
handsome in a brown velvet suit, gold garnitured, I cannot forebear
rallying him: ''Tis a miracle indeed will inspire such a heathen to
attend services.'

'No miracle. His majesty dispatched 'round orders, we were all to
make a showing of piety, for the edification of the vulgar; and I am his
pensioner.'

This last comment comes in so sardonic and cutting a tone, I sense
some hidden resentment, but think better of probing and scurry to get
my cloak.

The parson outdoes himself in gravities and nonsense; my lord and
I alternate 'twixt falling into a stupor at the dullest parts, then giggling
at the most ridiculous. I am afear'd we did not behave any better than
a pair of naughty children; but then, none of the other courtiers look
very thrilled at the entertainment neither. Mr Savile fidgs about in a
perfect torment, so that I cannot resist poking my lord and whispering, 'Fast days are not for him.' We giggle o'er this sally, our eyes
linked in merry intimacy; and then, at long last, the two-hours' agony
is over.

My lord quips, as we escape, 'Any God with parts enough to create a

487

universe must be wonderfully diverted by such nonsensical worship as this.'

We walk beneath the lacy pendants of the fan-vaulted ceiling, 'twixt the glossy walnut-tree pews.

I laugh.

We arrive now, the crowd scurrying before and behind us, at the giant baptismal font of oak tree beside the door.

'There's scarce any limit to human folly!' exclaims my lord. 'That a man will pay, to support in luxury a gang of collared cutthroats, to tell him to believe what he cannot believe in!'

All at once a voice behind us rings out crisply, 'I wonder that your lordship would have the gall to step inside a church.'

We turn about, startled. At the chapel door stands Emilia, in a smart indigo gown with a lace scallop, and looking very offended on my lord. I am so surprised at her rudeness in interrupting us, I know not what to say, but my lord is very quick to retort, haughtily, 'The greater gall, madam, is yours, who not only pretend to know the unknowable, but even defy your own greybeard of a God, who laid down a stricture against the judging of a fellow mortal by another. Your own Saviour would have preferred the company of his penitent whore.'

Emilia goes pop-eyed in amaze but at last manages to sputter, indignantly, 'How dare your lordship use that word to me!'

'What word? Whore?' Now my lord puts on a pretence of surprise himself. 'Why, that is a holy word.'

'Holy word?' She stares at him. 'How can it be?'

By now we are out of the chapel proper and into the gallery of oak panelling and hangings without. We have also collected a delighted audience, no doubt eager to hear the fanciful leaps of my lord's wit, especially after having been bored so long by his philosophical antipodes.

'It is not,' my lord smiles calmly, 'unless one believe that the Scriptures have divine sanction. Is that your belief, madam?'

Emilia begins to stammer. 'Why, yes, but that need not mean –'

'Then you must believe the words therein are holy – especially a word so often used as this one, "whore". Do you deny it is often used, madam? If so, I'll be glad to cite you half a score verses or so to support my thesis.'

I have never seen Emilia so at a loss for words; how I wish I'd had my lord with me when she argued about the men and women! She seeks to recover her ground, but in her voice there is a decidedly defensive air: 'But for you to call the Magdalene our Lord's penitent whore! 'Tis blasphemous.'

My lord smiles arrogantly. 'Was she not penitent?'

'Yes,' snaps Emilia impatiently, 'of course.'

'What did she repent of?'

My lord knows very well that a woman abashed at the word 'whore' will not be able to answer such a question. She looks down angrily, blushing, but makes no reply.

'Well?'

At last Emilia looks up, eyes blazing. 'But the way your lordship speaks of it, you imply Our Lord used her body.'

This last is a rather quaint expression. My lord's eyes harden at it.

'I cannot vouchsafe any evidence, madam, one way or the other. But I am sure, did Jesus indeed enjoy her, 'twas in the spirit of love which he lived and preached, and which his modern text-hawkers have long forgot.'

Titillated giggles go through those watching at this naughty turn in the debate; but Emilia, who is little diverted, cries in horror; 'You cannot imply, my lord, that Jesus had a woman!'

'Why not? Have you any evidence to indicate that He confined Himself to boys?'

At this, the audience about us bursts into rollicking laughter, and Emilia turns several shades redder. And even though I am horrified at what my lord says, and eager not to offend Emilia by laughing, still his wit is so clever, I cannot resist the chuckle I've been holding in.

'If you do,' he continues sweetly, 'I'll not be averse to hearing and weighing it. For in this age of reason, it is the duty of man to prefer sense over nonsense, the evidence before his eyes, rather than the marvellous impossibilities of the invisible, superstition being the rotten timber of ages past, and man striving to shake off the accumulated illogic of centuries which familiarity and custom alone support, and which you yourself have been known to attack, madam, in the cause of reason, and for the sake of advancement in your species.'

Now I turn away, to choke with laughter; someone has enlightened my lord on all of Emilia's grave humours: her pride in reason, her attack on male privilege. He has not only bested her on her own ground, but he has uttered the word 'species' with such a twinkle in his eye, it cannot mean mankind in general.

Now Emilia is so furious she could spit venom; but though it kills her, she controls herself and makes a valiant attempt to set up for reason before all of us.

'Reason,' she orates with a rigid calmness, 'may be defined as a consensus –'

'I do not accept that, nor do you.'

She continues, tight-lipped, '– what all men of reason believe must be true; therefore we know there is a God.'

'I do not accept that proof of God,' smiles my lord sweetly. 'And by that same logic, you are a fool: a consensus of reasonable men in this society says you have an inferior female wit.'

There's a great explosion of laughter at this, and Emilia loses her temper at last. 'I do not accept that!'

'Then you are the greater fool: for in arguing a defence of the consensus you would attack, you prove the consensus accurate on the state of your wit.'

The laughter grows louder; Emilia, who knows she wants the wit to answer my lord, whirls on me.

'Do you hear how your lover disparages your wit?'

'It is not hers I disparage,' cuts in my lord, 'but yours. You are the one contradicting yourself.'

Now Emilia is screaming. 'You have just said that all women are fools!'

My lord eyes her with bemused detachment. 'I have just said your logic proves you a fool, and your carriage does little to abate my former opinion.'

Emilia gets a grip on herself, for she always tries to set up for reason, and so must exercise it. With a shaking voice that bespeaks how hard is the struggle to put on that mien of calmness, she replies, 'Jesus died a virgin: everyone knows that. It is unreason for you to distort the truth, for the sake of disputation, by these clever tricks.'

My lord crosses his arms. '"Jesus died a virgin": very well, I have been made mindful of your thesis, and I now await the proofs which you are to provide in support thereof.'

Emilia is at a loss, for this is where her argument of consensus was to go, and so she must fall back on the crutch of all clergymen: 'There are some things that simply must be accepted on faith.'

A glimmer of merriment flickers through my lord's eyes. 'Which things are these?'

Emilia flushes. 'Your lordship knows very well what they are.'

'No, faith, I am at a loss, and you must tell me. Am I to believe that maids swell up with children? Or is it sufficient for me to believe that corpses jump out of their shrouds, to fright women in gardens and ascend on the thin air?'

Emilia grips the sticks of her fan as if she wishes they were his neck. He smiles sweetly and continues.

'Galileo was punished for not believing the earth was the centre of the universe; will I be punished likewise? For to say truth, I have looked through telescopes and studied rhetoric, and I can no longer return to my state of virgin innocence, which you call faith.'

Emilia regards him bitterly. 'Does your lordship have faith in nothing?'

'Nothing at all,' he returns serenely, 'except the power of my will and reason; and the way they are wont to play the devil with me, very little faith e'en in them.'

Emilia glares at him.

'I now await the proofs, either logical or sensory, that Jesus died a virgin.'

Emilia haughtily elevates her turned-up nose. 'Well, I certainly cannot provide any sensory proofs.'

'I congratulate you, madam, on a very logical proem: your cause looks well already. No, you cannot provide any sensory proofs: first of all, there are no physical marks of innocence on a man, as there are on a woman; to prove his unblemished state, one would have to be with him, eyes open and observing, for every second of his life. And such a watch by one man would be impossible: soon he must sleep, and then our Jesus might go out and have himself a good frolic, like an erring wife, and be back in time to smile sweetly for breakfast.'

There are great explosions of laughter, and even though I disapprove of what my lord says, I cannot resist giggling myself at the absurdity of a slyly frolicking Jesus.

'No,' he continues briskly, 'innocence cannot be proved by any sensory means, although its absence might be proved, by a slightly less rigourous watch, which would catch him in the act. But this is a difficult enough feat, even for modern husbands with live lovers; I doubt we could do't, madam, with a man who has been dead for seventeen hundred years, and whose very bones have been carted off by Papist fanatics and auctioned off to the gullible.'

Now the explosions are great indeed, and 'tis all I can do not to laugh aloud. Though I suppose my lord's wit would seem to some very blasphemous, yet 'tis also very clever and logical; and I am sure God, being such a merry Being, must be laughing, too. He would scarce support trafficking and cony-catching with His son's bones.

But I can see, Emilia is not at all diverted: not only is she being walloped in an argument, she is too grave and sanctified to enjoy this sort of foolery. So in pity of her, I restrain my merriment as best I can.

But trying to remain logical, she says stiffly, 'Then I will appeal to the pure force of reason to support my arguments,'

'Good,' applauds my lord, dark eyes twinkling. 'The pure force of reason, could we ever attain it, would indeed be an indomitable

491

weapon against superstition and canting. What has the pure force of reason to say on behalf of Jesus' honour?'

I can see Emilia twisting her hands as she glares on my lord, her pale blue eyes flashing. 'With the kind of life he lived, no one could believe he yielded to lust.'

'Faith, I am disappointed,' retorts my lord, enjoying himself immensely. 'I see that man has still more than a little way to go before his reason is so pure and indomitable as you lately gave me cause to hope.'

Emilia gawks at him. 'Your lordship does not believe that Jesus lived a virtuous life?'

'I do not believe in much,' returns my lord in a quieter tone, 'but I have a cautious confidence he probably did, from the evidence that has been recorded of his deeds.'

Emilia crosses her arms, her blue eyes flashing triumphantly. 'Well, then.'

'What has the one to do with the other?' demands my lord. 'Can a man not be a lover of his kind, a skilled teacher and healer, and enjoy embracing women? Faith, I should think his emphasis on love would tell his true predilections.'

'Jesus preached against fornication!' Her voice is a shrill shriek.

'Where?' he demands calmly.

'There are passages a-plenty against fornication in the Bible. You cannot deny't.'

'Yes, but when did Jesus preach against it? Consider: we talk not of what some Old Testament fanatic believed, upon growing his thousandth white hair. We dispute on what Jesus said.'

'St Paul set up the Christian doctrine,' huffs Emilia, 'and he said virginity was the preferable state.'

'Yes, from his own enthusiastic misapprehension, in changing his Master's doctrines to please himself, as his spiritual descendents are now so prone on doing; and not a one of 'em with any notion what their Master spoke of. Least of all would He have condemned anyone for loving another or enjoying life.'

'I do not have the Bible before me,' she returns heatedly, 'but I know Jesus preached against sin.' All at once her blue eyes flash, as if she had an inspiration. 'Did he not tell the Magdalene, "Go, and sin no more"?'

My lord shrugs. 'What she did and what he did were probably two different things; even I am not a whore.'

Emilia draws herself up to the full height of her five feet and two inches and crosses her arms regally. 'I will go immediately to my apartments and comb my Bible until I find a condemnation of what your lordship accuses him of.'

My lord nods, his eyes twinkling. 'Good: for that will contribute a little toward making your point – but not much. For many men will advise conduct in an ideal sense as virtuous for others, which they would never dream to bind themselves to attaining. I plan to advise my sons to lead a different sort of life than mine'. At this mention of 'my sons', my heart so dances I almost escape hearing his conclusion: ''Twould be to their advantage to do so.'

I dare not look at my lord, to see whether he looks at me; and Emilia at last gives over, for she knows she cannot outwit him, and she spies a chance to get out of her predicament with a gibe.

'With that last statement, I heartily concur. Betty, I leave you now to the company of the man who has no faith and no respect. 'Twere me, I'd think twice about keeping company with an atheist.'

She whirls away.

My lord shouts after her as her straight-backed, dark-garbed form treads down the gallery, 'Best hasten off, madam: the bolt that punishes me may get you, too.'

She turns a corner and huffs out of sight.

My lord's audience, responding with scattered chuckles and applause, then disperses gradually, all of 'em no doubt making for dinner appointments elsewhere; but as we exit into a small courtyard past the hangings of Adam and Eve, I, holding his arm, ask timidly: 'My lord, are you truly an atheist?'

He gives me so sweet a smile then, I know not which is dearer, his face or the pressure of his arm 'neath my finger.

'No; but then, neither do I think that Jesus and the Magdalene were lovers.'

My mouth and eyes are round. 'Then why argue so intemperately?'

'Because I have no infallible proof they were not.'

He walks me gently into another court to the east of the Presence Chamber. 'And that tormenting Amazon would speak of *pure reason* and *infallible proofs* and *consensus,* to argue a kind of illogic that has caused great pain in the world. Who knows whether Jesus had one woman or ten or none? Who cares? Least of all would He: that was not the point of His teaching.'

'Y'are, sir, a strange contradiction,' I muse. 'Are you a Christian?'

'Not as the word is presently used.'

'But you do believe in a God?'

We walk through a small and very narrow passageway by the Presence Chamber; and seeing in what a private place we are, he breaks stride a moment, halts, and with the sweetest of smiles settles my cloak a little closer to my neck on both sides with his hands, more like a father with an infant than one lover to another, 'til I yearn to murmur and lean against him.

'As some kind of vast force,' he returns softly, 'completely remote from man and utterly unmoved by anything we poor creatures might have to say about It.'

I look up into his eyes, 'Does it bother you if I am a Christian?'

'Does it bother you if I am not?'

A little surprised, I answer honestly, 'No, not particularly. I think we share the same hatred of dulless and hypocrisy.'

'Then our faiths can coexist peacefully. But do you believe in this miracle stuff?'

All I can think of is what a miracle 'tis to look on him thus and have a gloved hand over his where it holds my hood at the neck. But I answer, 'I never think of't much; I suppose a God powerful enough to have created the universe could part the Red Sea if he wished.'

His eyes are brooding, pensive. 'But you are not sure.'

'No, how could I be?'

I gently rub a finger across his hand a moment, for it has just given a soft caress to my cheek where I have put it nigh.

'If you doubt,' he asks, in a voice curious rather than censorious, 'how can you believe?'

I smile up at him again, my eyes shining. 'Because I do not doubt I have a Father in heaven will forgive me my little follies as my own father did.'

His eyes grow bitter and seem to stare beyond me. 'That were a comfortable doctrine indeed, could one believe it.'

A snowflake drifting past catches on my lips, and another on my eyelid.

'You mock me, my lord,' I accuse in a small voice.

'No, indeed.' He looks down on me now again and smiles. 'I am glad you are happy in your belief. Would I had it, but I cannot accept in my heart what my reason rejects.'

I give him a soft look. 'Then I will believe for both of us; and I cannot but believe, a God who sees into people's hearts will judge yours well.'

Now he looks at me softly too; then on an impulse he reaches down, with his hands still over the hood at my neck and ears, and gives my lips a little peck – not a very long one, for voices drift to us echoing across the court beyond; and looking a little abashed, we both take up our journey again down the passageway and into the Court, I holding his arm again, my lips still warm and sweet from the small kiss.

'What do you believe, my lord, happens after death?' I ask softly.

The snow swirls around us now cold and bitter on the icy bricks of the deserted court. He stares down as he walks. 'Annihilation,' he murmurs.

I do not reply, but I know I would hate to believe I'd never meet him again after this life.

2

'What May Be Your Stint?'
Late November 1666

Dorimant:	You were talking of play, madam. Pray, what may be your stint?*
Harriet:	A little harmless discourse in public walks; or at most an appointment in a box, bare-faced, at the playhouse: you are for masks and private meetings, where women engage for all they are worth, I hear.
Dorimant:	I have been used to deep play, but I can make one at small game when I like my gamester well.
Harriet:	And be so unconcerned you'll ha' not pleasure in't.
Dorimant:	Where there is a considerable sum to be won, the hope of drawing people in makes every trifle considerable.

—The Hero and Heroine in George Etherege,
The Man of Mode (1676)

stint: amount a player is willing to yield before withdrawing from a game

My lord keeps inviting me to his apartments, no doubt planning to wheedle out the final favour; and I am sorely tempted but always conclude by exerting my reason and replying, I have thought better about coming to his lodgings alone but will see him for a walk or a ride, a play or consort, &c &c.

I am surprised at how difficult it is, faced with the immediacy of new kissing and fondling, to carry out my resolutions. Each time I dispatch his little page back with the reply, I spend the whole day feeling as full of self-renunciation as a nun at a fast; and dozens of times I almost send Susan post-haste with a recantation. However, I miserably hold the line, leaving us with such paltry intimacies as the tiny buss in the courtyard after services. So anon I'm treated to a scolding poem, in couplets, on how I defy my destiny in restraining love with honour:

All things submit themselves to your command,
Fair Celia, when it does not love withstand:

The power it borrows from your eyes alone
All but the god must yield to, who has none.

Hyperbole follows, lest I become too vexed by his sauciness:

Were he not blind, such are the charms you have,
He'd quit his godhead to become your slave,
Be proud to act a mortal hero's part,
And throw himself, for fame, on his own dart.

I am then reminded that the universe was created from harmony and 'mutual love': that even the mute, insensible objects in nature will know enough to kiss and coy:

See gentle brooks, how quietly they glide,
Kissing the rugged banks on either side.
While in their crystal streams at once they show
And with them feed, the flowers which they bestow.
Though rudely thronged by a too-near embrace,
In gentle murmurs they keep on their pace
To their loved sea, for ev'n streams have desires:
Cool as they are, they feel Love's powerful fires,
And with such passion that if any force
Stop or molest them in their amorous course,
They swell with rage, break down and ravage o'er
The banks they kissed, the flowers they fed before.

Here is a clear enough meaning: I have imposed too rigid a control on our passions; and in damming up their flow, I am like to cause a violent flood, either in his rage or in our mutual desire. With a little more intimacy, however, the stream would glide 'quietly' betwixt its banks, 'feed' our love, and never attempt at a 'too-near embrace.' A scolding then follows:

Submit, then, Celia, ere you be reduced,
For rebels, vanquished once, are vilely used,
And such are you whene'er you dare obey
Another passion, and your love betray.

So I rebel against my very nature in not fondling, and there's even a vague threat, though followed by more praise:

497

You are Love's citadel: by you he reigns
And his proud empire o'er the world maintains.
He trusts you with his stratagems and arms:
His frowns, his smiles, and all his conquering charms.

Lest I forget the main argument, however, he concludes on a warning note:

But if you're fond of baubles, be, and starve;
Your geegaw reputation still preserve;
Live upon modesty and empty fame,
Forgoing sense for a fantastic name.

I see that he will not take 'no' for an answer, after such hints of my passion as he has got; if he cannot contrive to caress me into compliance, he will dispute me thither. The references to 'Love' do not impress me much, for I know what the courtiers mean by it, especially in context with kissing streams and swellings; and the bold rascal hints he knows I 'starve' myself along with him.

But I have decided to let him suffer a little: despite his clever discourse of floods and banks, a man so jaded as he will soon grow weary of mere play and seek to relieve me of more than the 'fantastic name' of modesty. But if I keep an edge to his appetite through abstinence, I may tease a marriage out of him sooner.

As I grow stranger and harder to him, he then begins to gift me with remembrances: one lovely little puff of pink fuzz, impregnated with the sweetest scent, to be laid in my linen-drawer or set upon my toilet table, for the application of powders and ointments; and a watch-ring that shows the hours and seasons set round with emeralds and diamonds.

This last indeed makes my eyes pop, and I believe 'tis the first thing that makes me believe he's serious.

I cry, 'My lord! Can you afford such a beautiful thing?'

He grins. 'Probably not. But have no fear: the kind shopkeeper will never see much of his money on't anyway.'

We both laugh.

'Well!' I say possessively, holding my hand up and flicking it round, so the light shines off the gems. 'He better not come here to repossess it.'

My lord looks at me drolly. 'What about *my* payment, though?'

'What?' I stare at him.

'Do I receive no payment for this bauble I've brought you?'

He gazes on me with melting earnestness and exudes that incredible physical presence at me from his eyes.

I blush.

For the scene takes place in my apartments, where I've enlisted Emilia to sit with a grave tome, to keep our endearments modest. And though she huddle by the window, her eyes ostensibly on the page, and my lord and I repose on two chairs, drawn together in the centre of the sitting room with their backs to her, still, many sour looks have passed betwixt her and my lord, and I believe she misses nothing.

I stare at her, and with a grim look she shrugs her shoulders and turns about sideways in the window-seat, her back to us. I lean forward, putting my hand to my lord's cheek, and gently touch my lips to his. He leans into my lips for a sweet kiss that ends with our tongue tips touching. His cheek is soft as silk, and his lips are sweet as warm honey.

'Mmmmm,' he murmurs, gazing upon me with those melting dark eyes, the lashes a little lowered for a sultry effect. 'It's been too long, my lady.' His voice is low and thrilling, melodious and soft.

He reaches out to capture my hand that touched his cheek, and he nibbles the knuckles, all the while staring me in the eyes, and murmurs: 'Let's to another private meeting again.'

I shake my head, blushing, and stare down, though I do not withdraw my hand. 'I can't, my lord.'

'But I have promised. You do not believe my honour?' he says, very low.

'I – do not believe I should put either of us to the temptation, my lord.'

'I swear –'

I look up at him drolly. 'You often swear.'

'But ne'er was I so faithful in my oaths as this.'

'Sceptics such as you,' I retort, 'have no faith.'

'We have the faith of our mistress; and to that religion, I promise I'll be constant.'

'Constant?' My eyebrows go up. 'That's a word I thought was not in your vocabulary.'

'Ne'ertheless, in my promises to you, soft maid, I'll be constant; and in my thoughts of you also.'

I blush happily and look down. This is the closest to a declaration of love he's come. I wait, but still he does not say the words.

He squeezes my fingers. I look up at him.

'Come to my apartments tonight,' he murmurs. 'I swear you won't regret it.'

I shake my head and look down, blushing. 'No, my lord.'

BETTY MALLET

Oh, how many tormenting interviews are there like that!

After he takes his leave, leaning down to kiss me quickly at the door, I flaunt the watch-ring to Emilia and draw her out, so cordially to receive her compliments on this prize stallion my rope has snared. Now she has seen for herself what I meant about his wit, charm and address, she must be on fire with jealousy. And she, poor dear, has no lover at all!

She points her priggish nose into the air. 'He's very charming and witty, I grant you. But I still would not have him courting me.'

I look at her pertly, my arms crossed. 'And why not, I pray, Mrs Grave Airs?'

She looks up calmly from her book. 'I would not be wooed by a man so dangerous I must see him in the presence of another woman, a man who boasts that he believes in nothing and will seek, in every way, by the cleverest devices, to ruin me –'

I break in, 'Any man with spirit, any man worth having, will seek to go as far as he can! Would you take a country parson for a husband, to respect your honour beforehand, then skulk ashamed to your bed after, to read you a Bible verse and ask you what to do?'

She blushes – then laughs. I am surprised at the contradiction: she is a deal more modest than your giddy humble servant here, but not too nice to enjoy what abashes her.

'Fie, Elizabeth!' she laughs. 'There you go again, with your wicked, wagging tongue.'

I flounce over to the pier glass, adjust my ribbon, turn about to admire th' effects. This seems to divert her, I know not why, or mayhap she still enjoys the remark on the bed, for she looks on me merrily.

I prod her a little where she sits, her feet on the rose jointed stool with tassels, and the vase near her of pink China-stuff with a griffin on top.

'You cannot say you would marry some dull stump of a man, who would entertain you with his gravities of an evening, wear a nightcap to bed o'his shaven pate, and give you loud wet kisses.'

She laughs. 'Fie, Elizabeth! You are too shocking.'

I adjust my curls in the glass, but I can see her across the sitting room by the window hung in rose curtains. Still laughing and blushing, she protests, 'If I had as little sense as you opine, I would not be at court; I would long ago have wed with the local bumpkin, the squire's son, to sit over my embroidery all day while he goes hallooing down hills after the hounds.'

Surprised, I look at her in the glass and laugh. So she has some wit, after all!

500

'No,' she continues, 'I simply would not have quite so thrilling, quite so enchanting a lover.'

I prod her, for I feel she must only be jealous. 'And why not?' Whirling about, I flounce over to plop on the dear damasked chair still warm from him. 'If we must marry, why not a man who has the skill to love madly and deliciously in bed, leave a gorgeous verse on the breakfast table and sparkle with a lightning fancy all afternoon?'

Silence.

I cross my arms. 'Well?'

She replies, '*Imprimis*, I have heard no talk of marriage yet.' I redden, but before I can protest, she raises a dainty hand and continues. 'But let us say you snare him. When a man so prides himself on his lovemaking abilities, think you he will be constant?'

Once again she has voiced one of my deepest fears. But of course I'm angry with her for speaking so – never mind that I drew it out of her; she ought to have lied and admired him, if she would truly (as she says) be friends.

She even continues, 'Think you that such a man will become a quiet, faithful husband? What attracts you will attract many others as well. And from what I know of him, I think he will not stick at the pursuit of anyone who gives him hints, be he married or no.' She pauses a moment, her large pale eyes pensive. 'If you would be his wife, to enjoy such ecstasies of lovemaking as you think he'll provide, you must accept the notion you will not enjoy 'em alone. You must be prepared to abandon all honour, to fawn and wait for a crumb, like the Duchess of Buckingham. 'Twere me, I'd have a different sort of marriage.'

So: Emilia is just like every other woman, despite her fine professions of friendship. Her only thought is to triumph over me. She cannot best me in beauty or wit, so she will flaunt her ponderous virtue and reason. She cannot snare a thrilling lover, so she must needs pretend to prefer the kind she will attract.

Arms still crossed, I glare at her – then flounce up to stride across to the window and stare at the frozen pane. The snow flurries in little gusts without, to land upon the icy bricks of the Yard and stick there in fragile crystals.

'I congratulate you, madam,' I throw her a bitter look past the curtains of rose. 'You have indeed writ me a tragedy of the age: love against honour, passion against reason. At the end of the fifth act, you will come onto the stage, clear away the bodies of the wasted lovers, and pronounce a prudent maxim on their folly.'

Emilia sounds rather tired now. 'I was not trying to be spiteful. I was only trying to open a part of his character to you. I would have you forewarned, before you leap into the waters, how rough they are like to be.'

'I thank you, madam,' I murmur. 'But I do not care. I don't care what happens – so long as he's mine.'

3

'A Lent For A Mistress'
Late November – early December 1666

Harriet: To men who have fared in this town like you, 'twould be a great mortification to live on hope. Could you keep a Lent for a mistress?

Dorimant: In expectation of a happy Easter and, though time be precious, think forty days well lost to gain your favour.
—Sir George Etherege, *The Man of Mode*

'With your permission, Mrs O'Hara.'

My lord glares upon her, and reluctantly she turns her back to us – though I can tell she tries to peek.

He draws an arm slyly over the back of my chair, behind my neck; and with his lips close to my ear, he murmurs, 'This is hell's own torment!'

And then he gently caresses my earlobe with his mouth. I shudder.

He runs a finger up and down my neck, and looks into my eyes as if he burns to kiss me; but he does not, and I think has a more powerful effect on me this way than if he had covered my face with kisses all day. Then he clasps my hand with his free one and raises it a moment to his lips, still holding me with his gaze.

'Come to my apartments tonight.'

I sigh. 'No, my lord.'

He bends close and proceeds to work on my neck with his mouth, kissing and licking and nibbling his way to the earlobe, which he then takes betwixt his teeth and so gently plays with 'til I am wild with desire. I sigh deeply and clench his head to me, with an arm about his neck. Then he disengages himself, to clasp my hand and look on me with melting sorrow.

'You deny us both much relief and pleasure.'

'No, my lord,' I say, my voice quavering.

But I tell him to wait upon me again, on the morrow at three of the clock.

And then I find out his diabolical cleverness. Having glimpsed a weakness in me, he is determined to work upon it: when he comes to make his addresses, he brings his friend Ashfield.

'What's this?' I cry. 'Do you too have a guardian of your virtue? You need not be so careful, my lord, unless you fear encountering Castlemaine in the Yard; for I'll not attack you.'

He grins. 'What's to fear if you did? No, Lord Ashfield is here to converse with your lovely friend. I told him what a fair flower was blooming in the window alone, and he came to offer it homage, lest it fade for want of attention.'

Emilia's eyebrows come together, and she falls upon my lord with a vengeance.

'I am grateful, Lord Rochester, for your pity, but it has always been my opinion that women are competent to do for themselves. I have a book here, and I *do* understand the words in't; you need not fear I will languish for want of male companionship.'

She lifts a regal nose, her hands clasped daintily o'er the grave tome in her lap, and sits on the window-seat as if enthroned beside the great griffin vase. Her very eyes snap an imperious blue challenge at him, and I fear lest we'll have a famous tournament, for she has just thrown out the gauntlet to a man never averse at taking it up.

His eyes gone narrow, he opens his mouth, but Ashfield interrupts, to fix all with a comical speech.

'Mrs O'Hara, I would be the last man to assume some woman were languishing for want of my competence: Rochester's cook is a more capable manager than I. But I am bored and in want of diversion, and I recalled how pleasant our conversation was, Fast Day last. Will you entertain another discourse?'

I am surprised at how quickly her temper mends. She smiles warmly. 'I see no harm in't.'

And then I see that the Lord Ashfield has his orders, for he asks, 'Will you walk apart in the gallery, where we can be private?'

Now, the gallery is at the other side of the palace. I cross my arms and shoot my lord a pert look. 'Aha! I thought so: a plot.'

My lord stares on me as if surprised. 'Why, women are the very devils for suspicion.'

'And men the greater devils, to make 'em always suspect.'

Emilia has got his game, however. 'I'll walk elsewhere, my lord, if they'll do the same. Otherwise, we'll all stay where we are.'

My lord shoots poor Ashfield a black look, and he cowers but shrugs his shoulders helplessly.

Emilia smiles brightly and pats the window-seat beside her. 'Come over here, my lord, and let us make the best of our confinement.'

Ashfield strides across the sitting room, makes a hesitant stop, colours, then grasps a damasked rose-and-white chair, to drag it toward the window and plop down into it. I lead a woebegone my lord to the two stiff chairs again.

And so my frustrating courtship proceeds.

I wonder what's become of the old black and bulbous-nosed hound that panted on my path so closely. Why, I had expected a fine confrontation 'twixt him and my lord and trembled to think what might have happen'd. But instead – nothing. Not a sign nor word nor letter from His Majesty, as if he'd been no more than my host these months.

But I trust him not and wonder what he plots. And I tremble, too, with every message brought in to me, lest it bring a note from Mama in Enmore, saying Grandpa has smelt up a new suitor or announcing her arrival here to chaperone me in this dangerous place or escort me to some wedlock. 'Tis certain they'll not suffer me to remain here much longer without they begin prodding about husbands. They're at the point of delicate hints now, and soon 'twill be open remarks, and then ultimatums.

And God knows what will happen when they find out with whom I'm keeping company. 'Tis certain there are no secrets in this court. If the tongues were wagging, as Hamilton and Emilia say, merely to see the looks my lord and I exchanged at the ball, surely his coming in and out of my apartments, his dispatching notes and gifts to me, my blushing every time I look at him, our appearance together at various consorts and plays, shops and eating-houses, all these cannot go unremarked.

And what is remarked in town cannot take that long to travel into the country. For all I know, Grandpa may have planted spies about, including that wretched Lord Herbert, who's ever leering at me. Or, if nothing else, the silly young Lord Sotherby, whose mama's estate is near mine, is so thick with Castlemaine that he sees all and no doubt will tell all, too. And what goes to my Lady Sotherby goes to Mama. And if 'tis about me, 'twill go all the sooner.

So I wonder how much time I have and grow very nervous as the days and hours lapse one by one and I'm still no closer to a wedding.

4

'A Nightmare From Which We Have Only Recently Begun To Awaken'

Early December 1666

For most people in our society, infants and children are small people to whom we should try to offer aid and comfort whenever possible. This attitude is new. A search of historical sources shows that until the last century children were instead offered beatings and whippings, with instruments usually associated with torture chambers. In fact, the history of childhood is a nightmare from which we have only recently begun to awaken.
—Lloyd DeMause, 'Our Forebears Made Childhood a Nightmare', *Psychology Today*, VIII, 11 April 1975

And then I saw, what the perturbation of my mind had prevented my sooner noticing, that he had led me, though I know not how, into another of the dark alleys, instead of the place whither I meant to go.

'Good God!' I cried. 'Where am I?'

'Where,' answered he, 'we shall be least observed.'
—Fanny Burney, *Evelina* (1778)

What a day! First I dress and visit Emilie Ossory at the Duke of Ormond's: she is a true friend, so sweet and stupid she can be counted on to celebrate my triumphs wholeheartedly. But today all is in confusion: she is weeping, and her children are weeping, and her husband – who is the only mortal can ever soothe her – is nowhere to be seen.

At last I get her to wipe her tears with one of my handkerchiefs, and I caress and soothe the babies, who I think must only have been distressed to see their mama weep, and then I say, 'There, now. What's the matter, Emilie?' And then with a good deal of sobbing and clenching of the handkerchief, she opens it to me that her husband has whipped their eldest boy.

'Is that all?' I laugh. 'I had thought someone had been killed, at least. Now, blow your nose, Emilie.'

Dutifully she does, but then protests, 'You didn't hear it; 'twas dreadful how long and hard he struck, and he always uses that horrible rod. My poor baby cried and cried.'

I pat her shoulder where she sits on a chair beside me. 'I am sure he did. But, Emilie, knowing your husband, I can't believe he would've done't without cause.'

In her usual soft-witted way she misses the point. 'Wait till it happens to *your* baby some day. You'll feel different.'

All at once I see poor Lord Ossory standing dismally in the threshold of the sitting room. I suppose, knowing he has caused her distress, he is ashamed to approach her: he is always so tender of her feelings. She still sobs with her head in her hand and does not see him.

'Emilie.' And I pull a little on her hand. 'Your husband is here; pray tell him you forgive him.'

'No! I vill never obey him in this.'

I try not to smile at the silly spectacle she makes, red-eyed and weeping, her distressed babies clinging to her and her voice reverting in her distraction to the heavy guttural intonations of her Dutch birth.

'Emilie, y'are being unreasonable: you treat him as if he's an ugly giant, and you know how he loves all of you.'

With tear-stain'd eyes she looks at him. 'How could you hurt our baby so!'

Poor Lord Ossory looks more and more wretched. 'Did you think I enjoyed it? I only did what I had to.'

'You didn't have to do it so thoroughly!'

Poor Lord Ossory, the marks of distress all over his serious and craggy countenance, replies, 'What would you have me do? You know I warned him what would happen if I caught him lying; would you have me appear inconsistent?'

I pat Emilie's shoulder. 'He's in the right, Emilie: a child must understand what the rules are and know they'll be followed. Here – blow again.'

She shakes her head, but, wiping a stray tear away from an eye, she then picks up the nearest sobbing little girl to offer soft sounds of consolation.

Ossory's face assumes now that grave, responsible air. 'Lying is a very serious defect of character, my dear. You know we cannot tolerate it.'

'You are too strict! You are always vipping one of them.'

He looks at her helplessly, then turns to me. 'Mrs Mallet, I know not what to say rightly to apologize for your witnessing this family crisis, but I hope you cannot think I do this sort of thing as a custom for the sheer joy of't.'

'No, of course not! Everyone knows how your lordship loves your children.'

'He is too strict! He doesn't always have to vip 'em, or vip 'em so hard.'

I turn to her, surrounded by her cuddling entourage of babies. 'What would you have him do, Emilie?'

'I don't know. That's his business – he's the head of the household.'

What a ninny this is! Ossory and I exchange a smile over her foolish flaxen head.

I tug her arm. 'Emilie, you wish your children to have good characters, I know.'

She resorts to the only argument she knows. 'You cannot understand how I feel. You're not a mother.'

'But I will be, and I can understand what he did.'

She hugs a little girl to her bosom. 'Wait until you are sitting in the next room, listening to the cuts and the cries, and they go on and on.'

Ossory explains, 'Emilie was reared less strictly than I, and though she has been an obedient wife in every other respect, she cannot understand that the father must see to the children's correction.'

Now this is a common and sensible enough remark, but all at once a terrific thought floats through my head.

Lord Ossory sees the change of expression on my face, and as he strides across the floor of polished oakwood to take up in his arms a blubbering little girl, he offers earnestly: 'Mrs Mallet, I hope you'll not believe I've been brutal; but if you do, I have no apologies for doing only what I felt was necessary.'

He jiggles the little girl on an arm until her sobs become shorter as she clutches his neck with an arm.

'No, no,' I assure him, turning about to regard him keenly with my arm on the chair back. 'Lord Ossory, are you rearing your children as your parents did you?'

'I try to, madam.' His face assumes that lofty expression so common to't. 'I believe they did a good job with us. And of course, it is natural to fall into imitating in our later lives the patterns we observed earlier. I find myself reacting in domestic situations pretty nearly the way my own father did – to Emilie's distress, as she was reared gently.'

What a dreadful presentiment am I getting now.

At her husband Emilie stares, her tear-stained eyes wide in horror over a silken head of another little girl. 'Do you mean that Father, who is such a dear, good-natured man, took one of those ugly rods to you?'

The little girl in Ossory's arms squirming, he sets her down to run, finger in mouth, to Mama's chair. 'Not himself: he used to enlist a footman's aid.'

'Oh, that is vorse!' she blurts out. 'They would strike even more mercilessly.'

'Then there is the added humiliation of being beaten by an inferior,' Ossory adds. 'Hence I force myself to take on the task, though it pains me.'

That is just like the Lord Ossory to exhibit such a proud spirit and think of his son's possible humiliation.

I tell my butter-brained friend, 'Emilie, don't you see how he thinks of your babies, even when he has to whip 'em? He tries to assuage their pride.'

'Assuage their pride!' She snuffles contemptuously into the lace handkerchief. 'By cutting up their poor little bodies.'

'You know I never hit long enough to draw much blood.'

'You hit a great deal longer than you should. And you hit so hard –' She breaks down into snuffling again, and I am sure part of her agony is in disagreeing with her husband, whom she always delights to obey.

'Boys must be beaten thus,' he seeks to explain. 'But you know I never hit the girls with all my strength.'

She shoots him a bitter look through the tears. 'It is wrong. You have so much strength for a man, and they are so small.' She then turns to me. 'Betty, even he feels miserable the whole day after, watching them unable to sit down.'

'I admit I hate to see't, dear.' Now he has come to stand beside her and pat her shoulder. 'But what else is to be done?'

'You might reach a sort of compromise,' I suggest, 'and agree to whip 'em with something else. When I was little, my mother got after me with a little stinging rod; it welted but drew no blood. I've sworn no worse than that will be applied to my own children.'

Emilie shoots her husband a bitter glance. 'You had best choose your husband carefully, then; for you'll have nothing to say about the matter.'

A cold shiver goes up me again; Ossory sees it and gives me a keen look. I return, as gaily as possible: ''Whoever I marry, I'll have something to say about everything, or you don't know me.'

But I feel miserable the rest of the day, trying to imagine how I will feel to hear my lord applying a cane or birch to our children e'en half as vigorously as his mother did to him. What must I do – vacillate 'twixt sobbing in the next room as Emilie does and then running in to stay his arm and provoke a scene? He is such a perfectionist in his dress, his verse; and so demanding of his tailors and footmen; I fear he will come down far too hard on our children for their ordinary infantile follies.

I am perishing to ask him his views on the correction of children but dare not. I dread to hear his answer and provoke a disagreement before the proper time comes. I recall how my father and mother used to argue about this and that and grow very heated anticipating problems that never came to pass.

When he calls for me tonight to escort me to a consort at St James Palace, I decide to pump him as subtly as I can without arousing his suspicions. As we juggle together in the sedan chair, bumping pleasantly against one another in its close confines, he clasping my hand, I open the topic gradually. 'I visited Emilie Ossory today.'

'I wonder you could suffer such a nit-witted goose.'

'Who, Emilie?' I laugh,

'Her head is lighter than a feather pillow.'

Now I must needs laugh at the truth of this; but then I sober, for my cause looks ill already.

'What think you of her husband?' I probe.

'Tis too dark to see his face as he makes evasive reply. 'It is usually difficult to think of him otherwise than with the highest respect.'

'He said his father brought up the whole family that way, and he was trying to do the same.'

I am making a mess of trying to get to the point at hand; I am so conscious of how I skirt toward the topic of matrimony that I blush all over, lest he think I'll try to tease out a marriage proposal. Indeed, he gives me a very sharp look; I can see't as a shaft of moonlight strikes through the sedan curtains, which he'd opened a bit to peer from.

'I am glad both you and Ossory have such joy of his family.'

Now, what did that mean? I stumble on. 'There was not much joy there today: he had to whip one of his babies, and everyone was miserable.'

'I am sure the baby felt even worse.'

We laugh; my lord has such a comical way of looking at everything.

'The child had told a lie,' I explain. 'Of course you know, my lord, how noble Ossory is: he could not stand for't.'

Though my lord's face is hidden in darkness, his voice has an edge of dry satire to't. 'I have heard of the noble Ossory's leniency before: Sedley is always rhapsodizing on't.'

I probe. 'You speak, my lord, as if you do not approve of't.'

'I cannot find it in my heart to do so. His system of correction produces too many young liars. Here we are.'

The sedan chair jolting down with a thud, my lord helps me from our curtained sanctuary and pays one of the men. Then 'tis too late to resume the discourse, for we're before the red-and-white brick front of St James, and Sedley's toddled up to clap my lord's arm.

'What ho! I see you're in such company again as will make us all pant with jealousy tonight –'

And the evening's launched with the usual crowds and pleasantries, to forestall private conversation.

But I scarce hear the consort for such a sick feeling in my stomach at the confirmation of my worst fears. Here Ossory whips his children 'til they cannot sit for a day, which is a measure of the limit of strictness before it shades into cruelty, and my lord believes he is so lenient, the children must grow up with bad characters.

Then I find, going to the Duke of York's supper afterward, we are seated next to the Hamiltons and Ormond's family – on the supposition, I believe, that the arrangement will please me; and also, I am happy to note, on the tacit recognition that my lord belongs with me rather than with Sedley and crew. Emilie and her husband look so cheerful I feel 'tis safe to ask 'em o'er the fricassee of beef whether the crisis with the children be solved.

'Yes, thanks to your inspired suggestion.' She beams. 'He has agreed to use a riding crop after this.'

My lord, giving me an innocent look and putting down his napkin, asks, 'You have suggested they use their children as horses? That is a stroke of economy.'

The whole table bursts into laughter.

'No,' I giggle into my napkin, 'only that they whip 'em with something besides those birch rods that leave the marks and draw blood.'

'Excuse me. I had thought that riding crops were used only for horses.' My lord smiles genially and tilts up a Venice glass of claret. All of us seated about gape at him, not certain what he can mean, but conscious how particular his voice was.

'Of course they usually are,' Emilie explains at last, the candelabra near her making a halo about her sweet face in the darkness. 'But both of us were too tender to endure the way the pain lingered after those dreadful rods.'

'Such tenderness speaks well of your love for your children. Being so tender you have, I know, tried all other means of correction and found them wanting.'

What is my lord about? The whole table grows silent with surprise,

511

James Hamilton smiling and poking his solemn-faced sister Elizabeth, as if to say, *Let's see what diversion the court jester has in mind now.*

'Other means?' queries Ossory.

My lord's face is so shadowed in the darkness I can but barely see him set the glass down again. 'Ashfield's grandmother, for example, usually forebade him his pony for a while.'

'Oh,' cries Emilie, 'that sounds a good idea!'

What in the name of Jesus is my lord's game? Is he at the court diversion of exposing a fool, trying to draw Emilie out that she may exhibit her folly? But although she is not very brisk, I cannot think maternal tenderness so bad a trait.

Ossory replies dubiously, 'Our children's ponies are at Kilkenny.'

All at once the Lord John Butler, who has been silent as a stone during the whole supper, cuts in: 'As an acknowledged expert in this matter, Lord Rochester, what do you suggest as an appropriate measure for lying?'

Now we all begin to skate on very thin ice at such a double entendre, but my lord's reply must wait until a liveried footman has removed his plate. Then at last he replies, coolly, 'That would depend on the motive for the lie. We never punish those dissemblers that please us, only the ones that tell unkind truths.'

This is so subtle a remark I see the Lord Butler wondering if he has got the full meaning of't; he gives my lord a sharp look, but his face is still shadowed: on the surface of't there is nothing to resent; he has but told a social truth. Does my lord, as a satirist, class himself with the dissemblers that tell unkind truths and then tell Lord Butler the unkind truth that he dissembles every day to be civil in society? Or does my lord class himself with the agreeable dissemblers, who need not be punished?

Of course, every bit of this has gone over Emilie's head. She explains, 'My husband punished our son for lying, and I know that children must be punished for that, but it seems very hard to beat them so severely. What would you have done, Lord Rochester?'

'What did the child lie about?'

I wonder that none of the rest of us thought to inquire into the circumstances, but I suppose they must make a difference.

'He had broken a very valuable vase –' Emilie leans over that the footman may remove her plate '– and he kept saying he did not do't.'

'Of course, you ascertained first of all that he had done so.'

'Yes, two of the servants saw him.'

'And you next investigated, to be certain that the servants were not merely putting the blame on a helpless child.'

Emilie's mouth drops open; she looks at her husband.

Already I am astounded at my lord's perception, but Ossory at least had the sense to consider this option.

'Yes –' Now he leans over too as the plate is removed '– the boy at last admitted the truth, and I could tell by the look on his face that he was lying,'

'If you could tell't by the look on his face,' replies my lord with imperturbable cool, 'there is still hope of his redemption. You will know he is three-quarters or more a rogue when nature teaches him to lie consummately to protect himself. You were in the right to recognize the situation was serious.'

My lord's logic turns so fast here I cannot quite make it out, but he seems to be on Ossory's side. I suppose all adults must realize the seriousness of lying in children (e'en though no doubt we all did it).

'Not that it is always so,' my lord continues genially. 'As I pointed out to the gallant Lord Butler, ethics depend largely on circumstance. My friend Killigrew lies inveterately for sport but does no hurt thereby, for no one will believe him; he lies as a jester tumbles, to divert his friends. But, of course, your child's lie had different motives.'

'Yes, of course,' returns Ossory gravely. 'He knew I would scarce be entertained by his telling a falsehood.'

My lord smiles. 'Nor did he lie to spare your feelings, as I might do with a lady a little along in years, who asked me how old she looked.'

We all laugh.

'No,' agrees Ossory, 'I had already warned him he would be whipped if he lied. This is what distressed me the most and what I cannot make out: he had no motive at all.'

The footman moves on down the table, clearing off plates, and two others move about replenishing wine. 'With such a powerful inducement to tell the truth,' my lord points out, 'it is difficult to understand why he preferred falsehood.' He pauses whilst his glass is replenished, then adds, almost as if 'twere an afterthought, 'Unless, of course, he was playing at odds.'

'Playing at odds?' Ossory frowns.

'If I am playing ombre,' my lord returns cryptically, 'and I know that half my fortune is riding on the next trick, and no trump cards have already been played, I will probably lead with the highest trump I have, rather than with a queen of another suit. I already know that I'm in a bad spot and like to suffer something unpleasant, but where there's still a chance to get out of it, wit and nature alike combine to tell me to take that chance.'

Ossory leans over as a footman puts before him a plate of lemon crème. 'You think my son was lying because he was afear'd not to?'

'How does it appear to *you*?'

Startled, the Lord Ossory muses, 'I suppose it does make sense – but still, he should not have lied.'

'Agreed,' returns my lord, 'and knowing the calibre of your children as I do, I am sure it was not his wish to lie – and that he would gratefully accept all proper support you could give to induce him not to do so the next time.'

'He didn't look so grateful to me,' observes Ossory ruefully. 'He hasn't spoken to me the rest of the day.'

'Mayhap his idea of proper support differs from yours,' suggests my lord. 'He is only a child, you know, and cannot understand the world as larger people do. Also, as a living being he seeks to feel pleasure and avoid pain.'

'What do you get at, my lord?'

'I only make an observation on human nature.' My lord leans over as the dessert is put before him. 'I am sure he would have felt pleasure at telling you the truth, and this is why I say he will be grateful to have an opportunity to do so the next time, should you extend it to him.'

'I already did!' cries Ossory, perplexed.

'Yes, I know. But he is only a child; perhaps he did not understand that you would not have whipped him for breaking the vase.'

Silence.

All this time I have been gawking at my lord in the dimness; I have never heard him speak thus, to lead people so cleverly around to his point of view; at every twist of the argument, rather than criticizing, he builds up the other person's vanity or gives him a graceful out.

It is very obvious by the look on Lord Ossory's face that he would indeed have whipped the child for breaking the vase; and that he now understands what my lord meant by playing at odds; also that he now sees the situation from the child's point of view for the first time – as indeed do I. I had never thought beyond the fact that the child had lied and so must be whipped.

At last Ossory observes, uneasily, 'If he had told the truth, the issue would have been more complex, for then I would have had to devise some punishment for breaking the vase.'

It is obvious that he pumps my lord to find out what he would have offered as punishment. My lord replies with another clever lead: 'Yes, of course. Children cannot be suffered maliciously and willfully to damage property.'

We all gawk at him again in surprise. At last Emilie swallows her mouthful of lemon crème and blurts out, 'Our son would not do such a thing wilfully!'

'It was an accident, you mean.'

'Yes, of course!'

'I am glad to hear't. This means your husband's problem would have been solved, for of course people should not be punished for what they cannot help.'

Now we gawk at him again, for though this observation is so plain, none of us have thought to apply it to children; the usual courtesies that are extended to adults are not suffered 'em, lest they take advantage and grow up vicious.

Ossory replies, uneasily, 'But shouldn't children be taught the value of property?'

'That would not be a bad idea,' agrees my lord. 'Can you think of any tactic that would teach that particular lesson?'

This is a clever stroke: a lesson somehow related to the offence. Emilie, though usually so stupid, actually arrives at one.

'We could have told him what it cost.'

'That's a very good idea,' my lord responds, 'especially if you put it in his terms, such as how many ponies it is worth – and most especially, if you kneel to his level and speak gently to him: for little people take fright at large persons yelling down at them. Or, still speaking kindly at his level, ask him how it happened and how it might be prevented the next time. That places the child's offence in a sphere he can understand.'

Another clever lead. Ossory picks up on it.

'You think he does not understand why I whipped him?'

'How does it appear to you?'

'I thought he would understand,' observes Ossory helplessly. 'I explained why I was doing't before I began. He knew he had lied.'

'Yes, of course.' My lord sips more claret. 'But children are not always as reasonable as you or I. He probably felt so trapped by the whole situation, he was too full of resentment to hear what you said. And now, of course, he feels even worse; he blames himself for failing the father he loves.'

My lord has lost all of us by now.

'How can he feel miserable,' demands Ossory, 'for something he wilfully does?'

'You do not understand the destructive impulse. You have not got drunk so often as I.' At this understatement we laugh indeed. 'He has had sufficient time to calm down now,' my lord continues, 'and I know that when you go in to kiss him tonight and explain that you understand his feelings, he will be very grateful.'

Ossory looks as if he would know what it is he should explain; my lord senses as much and finishes calmly, 'If he sees that you are sorry for what happened betwixt you, that you understand why he lied and think none the less of him for't, he will be comforted to know that you love him and that you realize you have done him an injustice. Of course, to retain his trust you must prove to him that you will not inflict pain on him again.'

At the latter part of this discourse, with the words 'injustice' and 'not inflict pain on him', Ossory looks uncertain, but he gracefully expresses his gratitude to my lord for his help. He cannot be so grateful as I, for I suddenly understand the purport of his remarks on Ossory's system of correction, and I am aware what a wonderful father I've chosen for my children. He seems to see into their minds as clearly as he does into everyone else's; and the solutions he arrives at are so clear and plain, I am abashed to think on how little they are perceived by anyone else.

I would not whip my children so severely as Lord Ossory does his; but in the same situation, I would have reacted the same way, without even pausing to think why the child must be lying. My lord's method not only removes the grievous necessity of inflicting pain; it considers the motive for the lie and enlists the child in understanding what happened, what it means, and how to prevent it – and thereby prevents some future whippings.

I scarcely hear the conversation afterwards, I am so absorbed with his notion of human creatures seeking pleasure and avoiding pain. It is Hobbes' theory, but I wonder no one else ever thinks to apply it to children.

When he escorts me back to my apartments, I am still so deep in thought, I acquiesce without thinking to his suggestion that we walk. But anon as we have cut away from the Mall and through the formal array of trees flanking it, then through the luscious, tree-hung solitude and past the little arbour across from the Horse Guard Yard, I begin to suspect he takes not the most direct route available.

I look at him pertly. 'Do we not go in the wrong direction?'

'A little walk in the crisp air is very salutary.' This he has the effrontery to say when we are shivering with the bitterness of the wind.

'Only to a designing lover.'

He continues to walk through the line of trees stretching back at an acute angle into the bowels of the park. I tug on the arm I have been holding and firmly turn him about.

As I begin marching him t'other way again, he observes drolly, 'I must have the King lecture you on the benefits of exercise.'

'Such exercise as you have in mind, my lord, he would be certain to support the benefits of.'

'You have nothing to fear from me,' he says in a voice of the sweetest innocence.

I wonder if he'll wheedle again to get into my apartments, Emilia being absent; and as I summon the will to deny him upon this projected confrontation, I see that we are got back to the little arbour again, which means we've strolled too far in t'other direction again – which of course he did naught to prevent, the devil. I turn him firmly about and lead him from the trees onto the open close-cropped grass of the park opposite the Horse Guard Yard.

All at once he halts.

The moon breaks from the clouds; he looks down with such tenderness on his face, I cannot help giving him a very soft look in return. He is so handsome, and I desire him so.

I still have hold of his arm; he turns to me, catching my hand as he does so, and gathers me into his arms. My heart pounds like all the bells of Westminster; I had not anticipated he would attempt aught out here in the public and the cold; and before I can think of what my better resolutions would have advised, my lips are melting into his warm ones, and he holds me close to his breast. I put both arms about his waist and yearn into him, pressing all of him against me; and I now feel the tip of his tongue on mine, for our lips have begun to nestle into one another very hard now.

All at once we hear a noise, start, and pull away. A group of courtiers returning from St James walks off the Mall toward us, laughing. I blush all over, to think how they might have seen me betray my modesty with the most notorious man at court; my mother, I am sure, would faint on the spot to know I've forgot myself so far as to go about handing out kisses the way I do – and such kisses as he has taught me! – not to mention the wicked play that first unguarded night. And now how forward and immodest I've become: it was he who embraced chastely and I that pressed him close, his lower part against mine, until I unfairly aroused his passion and felt against me what I longed to feel and what made me weak.

Did they see me? If they did, how ruin't is my reputation? Too late I recall a maxim quoted on my lord's character: 'a woman seen three times in his company is considered already ruined'. And that's only for women that converse with him!

Why, oh why can't I learn to control myself around him? I always

517

grant him favours which we both of us know very well he ought not to enjoy and then I feel guilty afterwards, and God knows what he thinks of me or says of me in private to his friends. And now I'm the one to blame indeed, pressing him close at the small of the back, pressing into him, and arousing a natural reaction.

The laughter echoes away (is it laughter at me?), and he reaches out to pull me to him again.

'Come here,' he says softly, with an endearing smile on his face.

I blush and look away and disengage myself.

He guesses my feelings and says, gently, 'Sweet and beautiful! They didn't see anything. And even if they had, what was there to see?'

I blush, still unable to look at him. 'A good deal more than there should have been.'

'We were barely doing anything at all.'

At last I look at him. He wears an innocent expression on his face, but then he has got every muscle in it under his command.

'Come into the arbour, then,' he urges with a sweet smile, 'where no one can see.'

'Oh, no!' I cry, horrified. 'That's worse.'

He laughs. Then he gives me a very soft look. 'I'd only have you in my arms again.'

I hesitate, which is a mistake. He sees the way I look into his eyes; he takes me gently by the gloved hand and draws me into the shaded dark nook. Still gazing up at him, I whisper, 'We shouldn't.'

'"Shouldn't" makes it all the more delicious.'

'I' faith, my lord!' I cry. 'You are to blame!'

It is very dark in here. I feel a snowflake fall suddenly on my eyelid, and he must be cold, too, for as he takes my other hand and pulls me into his embrace, I feel him shiver.

He pulls his cloak about me; I feel very warm and snug and safe somehow, leaning against his breast, and not like a maid in danger at all. I long to draw my arms about him, to feel his sweet body again; but I dare not risk the temptation; nor does he offer to move them there for me, but he rubs my back and kisses my hair softly all over where it peeks out from under the hood, until I look up again, and he takes the cue to capture my lips.

We have a long, long kiss, with our mouths open and our tongues loving one another more softly than before, until I can stand restraint no longer: I draw my arms about him under the cloak, and we move near enough to brush against one another again. His back feels very cold, and I have the urge to rub it all over and warm him, as I would with an infant that has played too long in the snow. 'You feel cold,' I whisper. And I slyly rub his back, as if I did it for health's sake.

He stops kissing and catches me to his breast with a little murmur until I almost lose my breath, I yearn for him so. I am so ashamed of myself: I tell him no and then press against him, and I can tell by standing against him how much he feels.

He rubs up and down my back, too, 'til I get a warm glow all over; then his hand slips down to the small of my back, to press me fiercely into him, so we burn together e'en through all our clothing. I sigh with the wave of pleasure that floats through me; then all at once his hand slips down to the soft part of me, my tail, and I find 'tis sensitive to pleasure as well as pain: a little current of feeling shoots through me straight from the back to the front where he presses against me in both places; but when he begins to rub there, the sensations grow unbearable, and with a pang I move his hand back up to my waist again.

He continues to rub my back 'til I yearn for him to rub my tail again. We cling a little closer, and the snow begins to fall more thickly: it is almost as if we defy the winter to do its worst. I think no more about how abashed I was before the other courtiers; and when he moves his hand down to rub my tail again, I sigh, helplessly, and press closer, my arms about his waist: almost in tears from the height of the sensation that keeps drifting higher from one plateau to the next.

Slyly I move my hand down on him too, the better to press him in very close. He fetches his breath and shudders. I cling to him the harder and press him into me, sighing.

'Oooo, God,' I cry. He always gets me so tingly-wet down there, every time we go into a close embrace. I long to rub his backside, too, but I don't quite dare.

Then he puts me from him a little and kisses at my snow-flecked eyelids, more chastely than passionately, and I cling to him miserably, with both hands at his waist.

He goes to rub my bum again, more tenderly and slowly; and when I whimper and catch him close, he murmurs, 'All on fire yet – but I cannot do aught for you out here: let's back to your apartments.'

'No,' I whimper.

'I only aim to take your heat down like before,' he persists.

'No,' I cry, clinging to him and wondering why I cannot seem to feel him any more.

Still holding me with one arm, he slips t'other down the front of me. As he rubs, I shudder and grow rigid; but 'tis a perfect torment, so muted are the sensations through the velvet.

'Lift your skirts,' he murmurs.

Needless to say, I've forgot the cold, forgot e'en every vestige of modesty in the anguish of my desire. Pressing against him with one shoulder, I hitch up my skirts to the thigh so his hand can go under. He barely touches me at all there before wave on wave of keen pleasure shakes me; every nerve i' th' opening dish seems super-sensitized. I climb to a peak, then clutch him, waiting – ah! There's the little fall, the catch, the tremor, and then I'm shuddering and falling, plateau to plateau.

'Ooo, God,' I murmur, 'that's enough! that's enough!' But still he keeps it up to the point of pain. And once again, deeper sensations arise in my belly past the pain point, and I explode in his arms. Then we're clinging close, our arms about one another, my skirt down again.

'You always keep on when I cry halt!' I accuse.

He kisses the top of my head. 'This is because I obey your body, madam, and not your words.'

Then am I seized with a dread remorse. 'You must promise never to do this thing to me again!'

He smiles into my hair and holds me to him tenderly. 'I will promise anything to please you, especially since you know we will fall into it again at the first kind opportunity.'

'This is dreadful' I cry. 'Can I not e'en walk with you any more?'

'I suppose not, if you're determined to struggle against nature. For my part, I can't think why you choose to put us on this rack.'

'You know't very well!'

'No, faith. Your body told me very clearly that you feel the way I do –'

I break in quickly. 'What I feel does not necessarily dictate what I do.'

'That's an uncomfortable philosophy.'

I groan at his diabolical ways and tug his arm. 'Come, take me back.'

We begin to walk again, his arm about my shoulders and mine about his waist.

'Come to my apartments –'

'– said the fox to the goose.'

'I swear not to go inside you. Come, give us time for some proper play.'

'Proper's a new word for it!' I pinch his ribs.

'This clutching through clothes in the woods doesn't give me leave to show you what I can do,' he frets.

'I know very well what you can do. If you can get this far in five minutes in the woods, God help me at your apartments.'

So I manage to get to my bed still a virgin; but as I dismiss him at my door, with a smile and a little peck, I close the door and lean against it weakly, and Susan, who answered my knock, regards me closely. How long can I ward him off, feeling the way I do? And what must I do to get him to marry me? 'Tis plain he's marked me down for an easy pigeon to shoot, so unattended and warm as I am, and love or no, he means to get me the easy way. I must enlist Emilia to play mama more often and accompany me on all occasions.

Part XI

'Neurotic Symptoms'

Robert Blair, Earl of Ashfield
December 1666

[M]en ... who devote their lives to unrestricted sexual satisfaction do not attain happiness, and very often suffer from severe neurotic conflicts or symptoms.

—Erich Fromm. *The Art of Loving*

1

'Is The Name Of Love So Frightful?'
Early December, 1666

Dorimant:	Is the name of love so frightful that you dare not stand it?
Harriet:	'Twill do little execution out of your mouth on me, I'm sure.
Dorimant:	It has been fatal—
Harriet:	To some easy women, but we are not all born to one destiny. I was informed you use to laugh at love and not make it.
Dorimant:	The time has been, but now I must speak—
Harriet:	If it be on that idle subject, I will put on my serious look, turn my head carelessly from you, drop my lip, let my eyelids fall and hang half o'er my eyes – thus, while you buzz a speech of an hour long in my ear, and I answer never a word. Why do you not begin?
Dorimant:	That the company may take notice how passionately I make advances of love, and how disdainfully you receive 'em!

—George Etherege, *The Man of Mode*

Strephon and I going to call on the ladies again, he impresses on me the necessity of drawing off Mrs O'Hara somewhere; but how a woman of her humour is to be cozen'd is more than I can know, especially by a man of mine; and I much wonder why in this business he doth not make his Damon of Sedley or Savile, who are wily enow to do his bidding.

'But what shall I do?' I ask him helplessly.

He shuffles through some papers on his writing desk. 'Do? Why, take her to one of your haunts, or to the gallery, or to the Devil, where she belongs.'

'But if she will not go?'

'Damn you for a vanishing apparition,' he mutters but seems to address the papers he shuffles. Anon he looks up, putting on a mien of resigned patience, as a kindly schoolmaster might do with a dull child. 'Tell her you grow faint in the heat of the sitting room or you would have her see your coach. Tell her you've a man wishes to set up a grammar school for girls and would speak to her at your lodgings about the curriculum. Dispatch a note 'round to Killigrew; he'll don a beard and gown and oblige.'

'I could never pull it off,' I protest desperately.

Strephon eyes me dismally. 'No, probably not.'

'Why do you not enlist Sedley in this business?'

He shuffles the papers anew. 'Sedley she loathes for his neglect of his wife.'

'Why not Buckhurst?'

'Buckhurst she cannot abide for his whoring and coarse humour.' Strephon continues to shuffle and mutter to himself. 'And Savile for engaging the Duchess in adultery.'

'Then I suppose that lets out Killigrew,' I muse.

'Is there any doubt?' demands Rochester. He looks up at me ruefully. 'Endure your destiny, Ashfield. You're the only human creature in breeches the bitch can suffer.'

'She's not a bitch,' I protest, secretly basking in the delight of knowing she likes me.

'At last,' he sighs, pulling out a paper.

'Is that a verse you've writ for your mistress?' I ask; and he nodding, I beg leave to read it, which he grants:

Love bade me hope, and I obeyed;
Phyllis continued still unkind.
'Then may you e'en despair,' he said;
'In vain I strive to change her mind.
'Honour's got in and keeps her heart;
Durst he but venture once abroad,
In my own right I'd take your part
And show myself the mightier god.
'This huffing Honour domineers
In breasts alone where he has place,
But if true generous Love appears,
The hector dares not show his face.'

Let me still languish and complain,
Be most inhumanly denied.
I have some pleasure in my pain;
She can have none with all her pride.

I fall a sacrifice to Love,
She lives a wretch for Honour's sake;
Whose tyrant does most cruel prove,
The difference is not hard to make.
Consider real honour, then:
You'll find hers cannot be the same.
'Tis noble confidence in men;
In women, mean mistrustful shame.

He is the only man who can court with gibes and not risk a slapping.

'Rochester,' I say, 'what is all this business with love and honour anyway? Why not simply marry her, as you've been hankering to do almost these two years?'

'Ashfield,' he complains, 'you are as ignorant of the world as if you had spent your four-and-twenty years in a cave with a beard and considered calculations of the substance and accidents of the soul.'

Sulking, I hand the paper back to him.

'Come on. Or are you going to refuse to help me?'

'I'm coming, I'm coming!'

Anon we are received anew into Mallet's pretty pink parlour; the verse is offered, the wench hands 'round the wine, I enter into a refined discussion with Mrs O'Hara whether the French or English be better playwrights, and Mallet and Rochester enter into a closer discourse, too private for the hearing, during which she attacks him with her usual battery of pouts and frowns and mischiefs. And thus we sit a good twenty minutes until, getting many a pregnant look from Strephon, I ask the lady who has fallen to my lot whether she will whisper a moment. Smiling faintly, she nods, her eyes on me searching; whereat I inform her of my plight.

'Madam, I have been given explicit instructions to draw you off; but you are so brisk, I despair of ever doing so without your aid: to which I now appeal.'

Her eyes dance merrily. 'So that's it! Lord Ashfield, I'd fain oblige, but I too have my orders. She dare not trust herself alone with him so much as to walk across a courtyard.'

'Then she knows him not,' I argue earnestly.

Mrs O'Hara regards me with pale eyes sparkling. 'She knows him all too well. She told me not two hours ago how dangerous he is.'

I wheedle. 'Madam, I feel sure he would but attempt a few modest endearments to seal the bargain and make him more certain of how to proceed.'

527

'From what I have heard, he has enjoyed enough certainties to proceed farther than he should.'

'You wrong him, madam,' I reply desperately; 'indeed you do. He has the utmost of respect for Mrs Mallet.'

She laughs heartily. 'You read his character, Lord Ashfield, too much through the prism of your own good nature.'

'He has been pining to marry her –'

'And he said this to you?' She regards me with her eyebrow up.

I run a finger under my tight holland-band. 'Well, not in so many words.'

'No, I thought not.'

'But you must understand Rochester! And anyway, no man goes about telling another how much he is in love. Especially a man with such a reputation as Rochester.'

She shrugs. 'Well, it boots not. I'd not believe whate'er he said, for he's lied so much he no longer knows truth from falsehood himself.'

I give it over as hopeless, for if she's determined to doubt Rochester, there's naught I can say to convince her otherwise, especially as his reputation stands in the town.

She ponders. 'It almost comes to me where I heard your voice before, my lord. But it was more commanding.'

I shrug. 'Then it was probably not mine.'

We stare bemused at the courting couple, who play with one another. She cries in her baby-voice, throws him one of those looks that would kill, then pouts with her lip thrust out. He gives her a pleading look into which he concentrates the full power of his animal charm, lowers his lids, draws an arm o'er the back of her chair and murmurs, 'I swear –'

I have seen him pull this look from his arsenal before; it makes 'em drop the plate or tankard they carry in the tavern or fumble with their pearls in the drawing room; and to say truth, Mallet is far from impervious to its effect: she flushes, then glances away; then, with a demure gaze from the corner of her eye, which turns to a pout, then a wild stare of inviting mischief, she says, 'Tempt me no more, demon, for I am resolved.'

He leans back in his chair and smiles ruefully. 'Oh, now you are Christ in the desert.'

'Yes, indeed: not even my pride will make me fall.'

'What about forty days of hunger?'

She smiles with demure eyes and out-thrust lip. 'Oh, I've had fifteen years of't and can bear it very well.'

The air betwixt 'em is supercharged with sparks, as if in a summer storm. But it vexes me to the blood to hear so many metaphors and postures and nothing to the purpose. I snap, 'Why do they gaze and flirt and kill and not get to the plain purpose? I confess it wearies me to watch 'em.'

Mrs O'Hara hath been eyeing 'em with a regal contempt which bespeaks the same opinion, and now she agrees heartily. 'I loathe this sort of artfulness; it has always gone against my grain.'

'It is one of the reasons I have never trusted Mrs Mallet above half,' I explain.

'Nor the Lord Rochester neither,' she agrees, her eyes on me large and smiling.

'If a man think to proceed by an inviting look, the next instant he is slammed down by a frown.'

'Nor can a woman trust a man who puts on a look of love as he does a periwig.'

'I know not why a man would pursue such a woman,' I complain. ''Tis like to scurry about in a thunderstorm and get his skin drenched to the blood and beg to be struck by lightning when he might be in front of the fire with a good book. But yet, she cannot go anywhere without the men follow in droves to be spurned. I cannot make it out.'

'You say true, my lord.' She nods soberly, then her eyes round on mine. 'And I confess, Lord Ashfield, it makes me glad to hear a man of sense who would not be drawn in by such a shallow creature. Though she's my friend, I confess it annoys me to see her flouncing and fluttering and the men idiots enough to tag along.'

'And when all's said and done, what have they to show for their trouble but a deal of frustration and uncertainty? If she blow hot, next she blow cold; I've watched Rochester squirm with it this year and more, as she changes her affections like her petticoats; and I confess it doth make me doubt his sense, to see how he will not give over, but must out with the net again and dance the hills the thousandth time after the butterfly.'

'I have told her that this artful business disgusts me,' confides Mrs O'Hara, leaning over to whisper lower, 'but she was too shallow to know what I meant. Indeed, your lordship is the first person I've ever been able to talk with thus.'

My heart warms. 'And he is no better,' I protest, taking up a derogation of poor Rochester because I know 'twill please her. 'He must make her verses, throw her killing looks and metaphors of compliments convoluted by scolding. Why says he not plainly, 'Madam, let us be married or leave off this fooling: it hath dragged itself out almost

these two years to no purpose. I confess I think he enjoys the stratagems more than he will the possession.'

She nods soberly. 'He is not so sincere a man as your lordship.'

'What's this?' Rochester yells to us. 'Here we have asked you above a
score of times whether you will not go with us to Chatelin's, and you
buzz together like two old maiden ladies over your quilting.'

Both of us blush and jump up, and I help my fellow chaperone into
her cloak.

2

'Afraid To Let Others Get Emotionally Close'
Mid-December, 1666

> People who are promiscuous often have never been able to have a
> close relationship. They may be afraid to let others get emotionally
> close to them because of their fear of rejection, or they may simply
> be incapable of a deep, loving commitment.
> —Dr Joyce Brothers, *Houston Post*, 17 November 1982

Legging it across King Street to the park side of the palace, Rochester
and I settle in the cockpit, which hath been converted to a theatre,
and suffer D'Avenant's silly adaptation of *Macbeth*. The audience about
me seems mightily pleased, save the Boy Genius and his echo Etherege, who cocks ear at the paragon's right to learn what must be
damned next.

Rochester leans back in his chair so it tips on its two hinder legs and
balances himself with a foot propped up on the chair before him.

'This is the silliest thing that ever I saw! Anon an engine will come
forth from the sky carrying ghosts playing fiddles.'

Etherege giggles.

'That a man should have to watch such stuff as this,' proclaims
Rochester, 'in the guise of a reverence for art! Nay, that such silly stuff
is encouraged and applauded by the vile rout in the theatres! And the
King can have no better sense than to bring it here.'

A gentleman before us turns about and glares on Rochester. 'If you
please, my lord.'

'I do please, sir. I please to speak my mind: have you a mind to deny
me?'

The man turns round again.

'There's one who's not been to the theatres,' muses Strephon, 'for
he knows not play-going manners. Or perhaps he's sat in the boxes
with all the pretty, mild ladies that keep their ears cocked and their
mouths shut.'

Now, this observation is an insult of sorts; for all the bold men of fashion sit not in the boxes with the virtuous ladies but in the pit, to yell their opinions of the performance and woo any doxies bold enough to venture there masked. Moreover, the slur was spoken audibly enough for the man to hear; but he acts as if he's not of a mind to challenge the blade of the war hero.

Then a soft Irish lilt behind us says, 'My lord.'

Rochester and I both turn about, knowing not which worthy is meant by the title, and espy the Lord John Butler.

His eyes blue as turquoise lakes, Butler ventures, 'My lord, I believe the play no credit to art either, and I've something preying on my mind and would have conversation with you.'

Rochester, half-turned round in his chair, and with an arm slung o'er the back of it, nods cordially. 'Speak, sir.'

Butler casts a few nervous glances around. On his right sits Lord Arran, and all about are eager listeners.

'My lord, I know not if you'd converse here amongst this public.'

Rochester shrugs. 'Why not? 'Twill be more diverting than the play.'

Butler tugs at his holland-band. Every time, the man seems out of countenance when speaking to Rochester.

'Well, my lord. It is this, then, to come plainly to the point' – for poor Butler knows no other way to come – 'Have you put aside your plans for marrying Mrs Mallet?'

Rochester's two black brows go down toward the long bridge of his nose. He rocks the chair down. 'May I ask, sir – your being no confidant of mine – why you would make it your business to ask so?'

'Well, I –' Butler sits up straighter; his jaw sets in a hard line. 'The lady's happiness is very dear to me, my lord.'

'I see.' Rochester's face is imperturbable.

'So may I ask whether you've a mind to marry her still?'

Rochester stares at him a moment, then answers him once again with a question. 'And if I do not, what then?'

'Why, then I'll consider the field open, sir, for my pursuit.'

'And if I do?'

'Then I will continue to hold back.'

Rochester stares, his face impassive. 'It seems to me, Lord Butler, you move against your self-interest. If I loved the lady, I'd pursue her no matter who else were courting her. So I see not why my intents make a difference with you.'

'That may be so, sir. I cannot answer for your motives nor your putative actions. But I feel bound in honour by the promise I gave you, some months past.'

Rochester shrugs. 'If that's what's bothering you, you may consider yourself absolved from it. I neither sought nor approved such a promise – in fact, you'll recall, was surprised that you made it.'

'It is not my honour to you that I consider mainly – though I thank you, sir, for releasing me. No, it is the honour of the promise I made to the lady, that I would not force a suit of marriage on her while she had a chance of wedding with the man she loved.'

Rochester appears in deep thought. At last he replies, 'And are you willing to affirm that she told you that she loved me?'

Butler nods.

'She did not make general allusions nor talk vaguely about gentlemen but named me specifically?'

Butler nods; then, his brow furrowed, says, 'But surely, my lord, she must have told you herself.'

'I'm not saying she did not. I only ask what she said to you.'

Butler scratches his head, and I suppose it must appear to the man that he's nowhere closer to his end than when he began this conversation. For, sure, no one can manipulate talk better than Rochester.

'Well, then, my lord, may I ask whether you've a mind to marry the lady?'

'I've a mind to let the lady do what she wishes, sir,' says Rochester. 'I claim no ownership of her, nor would I even were I her husband. She is a rational creature free to make her own choices; and if you've a mind to woo her and she's a mind to accept your addresses, there's not much I can do to prevent either.'

'Sir –' Lord Butler's mouth is tight '– you deliberately persist in misunderstanding me.' He pauses and moistens his lips. 'But I say to you, sir –' He pauses again as if at a loss for specific phrasing '– I – I would not take it kindly, if I were to find any gentleman trifling with her affections and attempting to do her dishonour.'

Rochester shrugs. 'Nor would I.'

'I only think it best to warn you, sir.'

Rochester's brows come together again. 'Warn me? You need not warn me. If you've a challenge of some sort, my lord, issue it straight, and we can choose our seconds.'

I groan and slump down into my chair.

'It was not my intent to issue a challenge, sir – though if you will press me to the point, I have no qualms about accepting one.'

They both stare at one another like gamecocks looking for the first strike.

'Look here, my lords,' bursts in a conciliatory Etherege. 'Let's not do anything rash! I think neither of you wishes to fight, but you're both about to push one another into it. Come on, now. Is that true?'

They both look at Etherege, then at one another.

'I've no particular wish to fight the gentleman, but neither do I shrink from any offer he might make,' says Rochester.

'Well, we are in agreement there, my lord,' says Butler.

I breathe more easily.

'My lord,' says Rochester, 'you seem under some misapprehension that you need protect Mrs Mallet from me. But you may ask the lady herself whether I have in any way degraded her or forced her submit to any advances that were disagreeable to her.'

'You speak well, my lord; but we both know very well what we each mean. I do not accuse you of forcing disagreeable advances on Mrs Mallet or attempting to ravish her. I only thought –' Butler's voice trails off.

'That I had taken or was about to take her honour: a conclusion you have likely drawn, from seeing us in close conversation and weighing my reputation into the balance: an imputation that is as unfair to her as it is to me; and which, I pray, you will deny to all the nosy tale-bearers whose tongues are wagging over the juicy details they them-selves have invented. The truth is much duller – and stranger, I admit, given my usual games with women. What we enjoy is one another's company; and each time she expresses fear about the dangers with which her female friends have filled her ears, I remind her that I have promised not to attempt her honour; and, yes, it is a promise I intend to keep, for I'd have her trust me; and, no, despite my reputation, I have never lied to a woman about my intents.'

This is a terrific speech, but it sounds sincere and convincing, and Butler has not much to say it, except, 'Then why have the banns not been posted?'

'Has it occurred to you, my lord, that the announcement of any banns betwixt us would bring all her friends up from the country so fast, it would make our heads swim? Has it occurred to you that those same friends had me thrown in the Tower once before for only looking as if I were going to marry the lady; that the King has forbade me to take any action that might make them sound the alarm again; and that the King is not someone whom favours can be got out of but by long wheedling? I see by your face that none of these things have occurred to you.'

'Are you saying this is why –'

'I'm not saying anything. I'm putting part of the case to you. Has it also occurred to you that the lady and I've spent very little time together and that we may not be sure of one another's feelings yet?'

'You meant, my lord, you are not sure of *your* feelings.'

'I neither said that nor meant it. I merely put to you all the aspects of the case. Now, let me put another aspect to you, my lord. You know that I've kept lodgings near Covent Garden, do you not?'

Butler nods.

'Has it never occurred to you why I spend most of my time now in my palace apartments?'

Butler shrugs.

'It is because Whitehall affords sanctuary from any duns that may care to seize me for non-payment of debt. So the palace is a little less dangerous than my home right now.'

Butler murmurs, 'I – had no idea –'

'No, I suppose you didn't. That's hardly the state of monetary affairs in which a man can support a wife, wouldn't you say?'

'But Mrs Mallet's fortune –'

'Entailed, on the consent of her guardians.' Rochester shrugs. 'If I do wed the lady, it's not something on which I'm counting. I doubt we'll be able to secure it.'

'And so you are saying you cannot wed without more money and the King's consent?'

'I'm saying I would be a fool to consider it.'

'Then that's what you're waiting for?'

'I only open to you all the facts of the case, my lord. There are a good many reasons why it would be imprudent for me to marry right now. I'm letting you see some of the angles, that you may judge for yourself. There can be many reasons a man can love and honour a lady and not marry her quickly.'

'I had no idea –'

'No doubt, with your wealthy father and your maintenance assured and everyone's friends approving of you and no debts. You know not what a precarious existence I live. Nor do most people.'

Butler's eyes flick over Rochester's gorgeous gold silk waistcoat, embroidered finely with gold thread.

'Yes, I dress well,' says Rochester. 'That's part of the reason I'm living precariously.'

'Surely your creditors would not seize you, my lord, being an intimate of the King?'

'Probably not, but my intimacy with him remains ever perilous, depending on how well I perform to please him; and sometimes my pride gets in the way of my monkey's and juggler's tricks, and I lash out at him. Or, pursuing interests of his own, he ignores the petitions I make him. Not the least precarious part of my existence is my relationship with Charles Stuart.'

'I see now why you cannot post banns, my lord,' murmurs Butler.

'I remind you, my lord: the banns must be read three Sundays in a row. At the first hint that skinny old hag would burn up the roads to get hither from Somerset before we could be wed, and snatch the lady from me, and I'd be no better than before: nay, worse, I'd be back in the Tower. No, if and when we do wed, it will have to be an elopement.'

'You would dishonourably go against her guardians' wishes?'

'Lord Butler, your notions of honour frustrate me. First you say it is a dishonour not to wed the lady; then you say it is a dishonour to wed her secretly. These are contradictory, for how am I to wed the lady any other way at all whilst her mother disapproves of me, which is like to continue 'til Judgment Day?'

Etherege bursts out laughing, and Butler grins slightly.

'Now, if you've a mind to challenge me on the basis of all this, I've a sword and no doubt can supply some second or the other. And if you've a mind to court the lady, I'm no Turk, to claim that I own her heart or soul. I've but opened to you some of the consequences, sir, of which I believe you previously ignorant.'

Butler nods. 'Yes, my lord. I see. But –' He has been about to lean back in his chair, then sits up suddenly '– what if the lady's guardians in the meanwhile should force some suit on her? For she was to come to court to select a husband.'

Rochester nods. 'I've thought of that. I suppose we'll have to deal with the problem when it comes.'

Part XII

'The Core Of Her Nature'

Betty Mallet

Mid-late December, 1666

Woman cannot find life meaningful without love. It is the core of her nature. She will endure privation and suffering, and display amazing fortitude if she feels she is loved. Men ... must be admired to sustain their pride.

—Laurel Elizabeth Keyes, *The Mystery of Sex: A Book about Love*

1

'Woman's Whole Existence'
17 December 1666

Man's love is to man a thing apart: 'tis woman's whole existence.
—Lord Byron, *Don Juan*

By my window again looking out on life, the green velvet gown draped in folds about the chair-legs and a ribbon of like stuff drawing back my curls, I am interrupted in my dreamy musings by a knock at the door. Lord, who can that be?

Susan returns promptly with the answer. 'Madam, my Lord of Rochester waits without and desires to know if he may walk in.'

Jesu, what a question! Were it two o' clock of a morning and I with my head in curl-papers, he might walk in. 'Of course, of course.'

Susan bobs a straight-legged curtsey and returns to usher in the prize, who seems in an impudent humour today. His dark eyes sparkle wickedly, and his cheeks are rosy with the cold as he rubs his hands together.

'Come,' he says. 'We're going on an excursion.'

I look at him pertly. 'An excursion, sir? Why, where?'

'Well, first down to the Yard below, where you're going to get your face brushed with snow.'

I squeal.

'And then to a tavern 'round Charing Cross, where we can take something to warm ourselves up after we've got ourselves good and cold.'

'Well, I don't mind the tavern part, but I'll pass on getting cold.'

'Now, there's the speech of someone who's been brought up by herself, with no elder brothers to teach her what snow's for! Come: 'twill be a delightful experience for you.'

I nod toward my woman. 'Susan, my cloak.'

But when she brings it, he will not suffer her to put it about me but takes it himself, settles it on my shoulders, pulls up the hood and does the fastener, then grins at me and holds out his hand.

'Take Dada's hand, now.'

How dear of him! I'd just been thinking he behaved to me like a father, and once again his thoughts have flowed beside mine.

How good 'tis to have him walk hand in hand with me and not seem to care who sees us. And he chatters like a happy magpie, jesting about a dreadful butchery of Shakespeare that he saw i' th' cockpit yester-night and vowing how he wished Sedley had been there to help him damn it.

'Where is Sedley, my lord? I've not seen him lately.'

'Oh, in Paris for the Holy Season. He's to be back next month sometime. But here: you must meet your fate.'

I squeal as he reaches down to scoop up a handful of snow and brush it on my cheek.

'No fair, no fair!' Breaking away from him, I stoop to ball a globule of snow as best I can and pitch it his direction. Of course, he jumps out of the way, and it misses him entirely.

'No fair!' I cry as a tremendous glop of snow hits me in the face.

'Very well, I'll stand here and suffer you to hit me, like an agreeable gentleman facing another with pistols.'

And he's as good as his word, so I fashion a great glob of snow and fire it at him, but so weakly does it strike, it barely brushes his cloak.

'My turn,' he says, and stoops down, and straightway a tremendous, well-packed glop hits me in the neck.

'This is not fair!' I cry. 'You're much bigger and more skilful than I.'

'Come, lie down in the snow then, and I'll show you how to make an angel.'

'An angel? I don't know that I'd lie down for that –'

'Come on.'

At his coaxing I lie on my back as he does and imitate the downward motion of his arms.

'Now I'm all cold,' I pout, my lower lip out. I sit up with the imprint of the angel behind me.

'Here.' He's already leapt up and holds out a hand, which gladly I take. He pulls me up and then brushes my cloak all over.

'You're not very adventuresome.'

'I s'pose I had a different childhood from you.'

'No doubt,' he says, with a dry undercurrent in his voice.

'Did your elder brothers play too rough with you?'

'They were much larger but took care not to hurt me.'

More than he can say for the she-viper that bore him.

'Now,' he says, 'are you ready for the second part of your treat?'

'Only you can contrive such treats – but yes, indeed.'

'Take Dada's hand, then.'

Gleefully I put my small gloved hand into his. He grins at me and crunches my fingers as we stroll through the network of courts over to the palace gate, where I complain, shaking out one of my shoes: 'Oh, my feet hurt! These nasty little pumps weren't made for walking so.'

He shakes his head. 'How you women can contrive to wear such stuff that binds you in everywhere, I'll never know.'

'Well, I didn't make up the fashion – I only follow it,' I pout.

So as usual, to spare my feet, he takes to ordering the chair, which we ride the short distance down the Strand to Charing Cross.

We get out at the sign of the Boar, a lovely little tavern where warm, steamy smells of beef and hog mingle with the crackle of the fire.

A rose-cheeked serving maid, with hair like sausagey dark curlicues straggling 'neath her cap, says, 'What would you please, sir?'

'Two dinners and some mulled ale.'

'Ye gods, no!' I cry. 'I can't eat a whole dinner – I had something a short while ago.'

'Are you sure?'

I nod.

'A beef pasty, then. We'll both nibble on't.'

'My lord, if you've not eaten, please feel free to have what you wish before me.'

He shakes his head. 'I'm not really hungry. If you'd wished the dinner, I would have joined you.'

So what a good time we have, just drinking the ale, which is warm and mulled with ginger, a little pippin apple floating in't – all spicy and hot and delicious.

'Mmmm, this is delicious,' I cry.

'Of course 'tis. You didn't think I'd bring you somewhere with cold ale, after such a dousing as you'd just got?' He adds, 'I knew you'd like it.'

And he crumbles off bits of the pie with his fingers and feeds 'em to me; and somehow it makes me feel warm and safe that he plays father to me so much today – so secure, I feel somehow he is my father, so loving and powerful that nothing can ever hurt me. He says, gently, 'I enjoy watching you enjoy your meals.'

I swing my legs like a little girl; for, 'deed, I'm short enough to be his child.

'Now, tell me what you've done these days,' he commands.

I shrug, for what I've done is pine by the windows waiting for him to write or call upon me. But admitting as much scarce seems good policy.

'Oh, nothing. What have you done?'

'Been fitted for some new suits, been to a few wretched plays and consorts.'

I wonder if he can feel me thinking I'm jealous of each entertainment he attends without me and I wonder why he puts me on such a rack of waiting, fearing, and then despairing to know he's been somewhere I could have joined him. Then quickly I block my thoughts, for he gives me another of those odd looks, as if once again he knows what goes through my mind.

Presently, sipping the warm ale in the booth before the crackling fire, he begins to talk to me of some of his dreams, and I fall into a spell, listening and admiring.

'This sort of existence that I lead is pitiful, meaningless. Why are we put here, to dress and preen before one another, and jump in snowbanks and drink mulled ale? Is there no more meaning to life than this?'

I shrug. 'I don't know, my lord. I've never given it much thought.'

Today, I pride myself, I'm remembering propriety and adding the 'my lord'.

'Well, I have, 'til it's nigh to make me mad! I look all about me, and what do I see? Men pursuing an aimless existence, like pigs or dogs. We wallow in our pleasures and fall dead asleep and then awake the next day, to repeat the cycle. Must there not be another purpose to existence than this?'

I shake my head. 'I don't know.'

'I've been turning it 'round and around,' he muses, 'and I've decided, if there were a God, He cannot take much of an interest in man's fate. He must've created this pitiful creature that we are and left him to torment himself and his fellow and wander in a maze and lose himself in thorny brakes and rambling woods.'

I shake my head. 'That I don't believe, my lord. I believe that God watches over us.'

His eyes grow dark and intense. 'But what evidence have you for such a belief?'

'There are moments, sometimes, when I feel a deep peace – what the Scriptures call "the peace that passeth understanding". It comes over me sometimes, and especially about this time of year, the Holy Season, I feel very close somehow to something divine. Do you not feel so?'

He shrugs and stares. 'Not really. I feel an elevation, an exultation sometimes – in my cups or quips or someone's bed. But peace, I've never felt.'

542

Now I feel so very, very sorry for him, I know not what to say. For peace is the greatest gift of the Holy Spirit, I believe; and if he has not felt it, small wonder he cannot have faith as he should. I link my arm through his, and he turns about with a smile.

'You'll feel it some day,' I whisper.

He shrugs. 'Perhaps.' Then abruptly he changes the subject. 'What are you doing Christmas Day?'

I blush and look down. 'I – have no plans, my lord.' Then I look up roguishly. 'I s'pose I've been waiting for you to ask me that question.'

He laughs. 'Well, I've smuggled Doll in from Adderbury, and she's taken up residence in my Covent Garden lodgings.'

'Covent Garden lodgings? I didn't know you had any.'

'Yes, the palace apartments were lent me only, by his gracious majesty the King, when I complained my pension was not being paid. At any rate, Doll longs to cook you a Christmas goose with mulberries and all the trimmings, so I've been sent over on commission to ask you.'

I laugh, but then sober at the thought that he must use Doll as a front and cannot admit he wishes to spend Christmas with me.

'You may tell Doll that I accept most readily. Is Gill here, too?'

'No, she's recently wed to a young farmer in Adderbury, Joseph. They seem well suited.' He drains the last of his tankard and then slams down some silver on the table and, standing, holds out his hand to me again, which gladly I take.

'How are your feet? Can you walk now?'

I nod, for though I'd rather ride, I know he loves to go by foot.

And so we meander down Charing Cross and the Strand, smell the tempting odours wafting from the bake shops and press our noses against the pane to see the marchpane candy and gingerbread and iced cakes. And I enjoy being seen with him and watching him call out hearty greetings to the people in the street.

After a leisurely stroll back in the jostling crowds, we halt at my door so's I can knock up Susan. Still clasping my hand, he squeezes it and murmurs, 'May I come in with you awhile?'

I look up suspiciously but yearningly. 'I think it not a good idea, my lord.'

'If I absolutely swear not to misbehave?'

I hesitate.

'I'd only have my arms about you. I swear, I won't even kiss you.'

Temptation overturns reason, and I nod. 'Very well, my lord.'

So as Susan answers, we walk in together.

'We're going to be in the sitting room awhile, Susan. We'll call if we need you.'

She bobs a curtsey. 'Yes, madam.' And like a discreet servant, she takes the hint to disappear into her room on the right.

He sweeps me into his arms for a long, sweet, luscious kis, 'til my heart warms and that treacherous spot 'twixt my thighs tingles. But he more or less obeys his vow, for he's more tender than passionate.

When he breaks from me, he still clasps my hand. 'Come on. Let's sit by the fire.'

So we cuddle on a settle just across the room from the warm blaze, my head against his shoulder and arm about his waist, his arm about me and pulling me closer, both sets of legs stretched out on a stool.

For a long while we don't even speak. I revel in the tender closeness and watch the fire lick the log and feel how much in love with him I am.

And I yearn for him so, with our two lower parts so close, I can think of nothing but what I feel down there.

Why won't he say the words?

But he does not, so custom forbids my saying 'em first, though I yearn 'til I ache with longing to say, 'I love you.'

2

'Only The Person Who Has Faith In Himself'
25 December 1666

Only the person who has faith in himself is able to be faithful to others, because only he can be sure that he will be the same at a future time as he is today and, therefore, that he will feel and act as he now expects to.

—Erich Fromm, *The Art of Loving*

Mistletoe and holly and warm kisses sweetened with mulled wine before a fire crackling with a smoky smell; warm arms to hold me fast, like an ocean of delight: this will be my happy Christmas.

Awakening in the dark of pre-dawn, the bed hangings still closed, I thrill with excitement. This is the most wonderful of Holy Seasons, for I'm to be with him.

And I'm barely awake before there's a knocking at my outer door, to the amazement of Susan.

'Madam,' she says, plucking back the heavy folds of velvet so a chill draft flows in, and clutching her dressing gown to her throat, 'my Lord of Rochester is here.'

I blink in astonishment, my head sticking out with curl-papers still attached.

And then Susan shrieks.

Startled, I pull the covers to my chin; but the bed hangings are yanked back, and there he stands, impudently grinning.

'Oh, my lord, you did give me such a start!' I cry. 'I had not bade you walk in yet.'

'Ne'ertheless, I did. And took my bidding from my own heart and impudence.' He grins.

'Oh, sir,' I cry, 'you have caught me at such a disadvantage!' And I make shift to cover my head, which sticks out a thousand way with crinkly tails of fuzz, like so many caterpillars from a rotten apple.

He laughs heartily. 'So this is what husbands are faced with! Faith, if many men knew it beforehand, they'd never take the plunge.'

I blush fiery red and stare down, at the first mention he's ever made of 'husband'.

'Come: Doll's ready to receive you.'

'Well, I scarce look ready to go!'

'Make yourself ready, then. I'll hang about and help you. '

'Ooooo, no,' I reply pertly. 'I can tell by your look, you've a mind to peek. Susan, escort my lord to the sitting room.' I cock an eye at him. 'Must I tell her to lock the door, or will you behave as a gentleman should?'

'Gentlemen are always catching peekings. But, nay, you need not lock the door. I'll respect your modesty.'

I s'pose modesty is silly at this point, given the places he's touched me; but he never has truly seen me yet; and what's more, he shouldn't have done what he has. So I'm a little shy, especially before Susan, who gawks frankly at him as if she believed him most indiscreet. I wonder sometimes what goes through her head, for she must have glimpsed a deal of scandalous familiarity 'twixt my lord and me over these past weeks.

So I have shiny sausagey curls brushed smooth 'round Susan's fingers and gathered up behind with a pink bow; and I'm trussed into another pink satin, the white scallop of my shift pulled up above the bodice in a modest lacy trim; and then Susan must lace me tight and pull.

'Ye gods!' I groan, hanging on to the bedpost as she pulls. These dinners and suppers and drinkings will have to cease, or I'll look a beached whale.

So just as the sun rises above the palace walls, making a red-gold haze i' th' smoky air, I'm walking with my lord to the palace gate and shuddering, hugging my cloak to me, against the bitterness.

'Why must we be up so early?' I demand. 'I thought you courtiers were not early risers.'

'Neither are my creditors.'

I look at him inquiringly.

'Just a joke of mine. But i'faith, at dawn of a Christmas I'm less likely to meet anyone standing outside my lodgings and waving a bill.'

'Oh, my lord, if you're in such straits, I have plenty –'

'No more of that,' he cuts me off. 'I'm not in any straits at all. The King's friendship protects me. And I doubt anyone will be out trying to collect on Christmas Day.'

Indeed, the streets are so quiet one would believe 'em under a spell: all is echoing mist and emptiness, like a city of ghosts. But a lone chair does wait before the palace gate, and we engage it for Covent Garden, though I don't see the trip. For, the curtains being pulled, i' th' darkness of the little sedan chair he pulls me to him hard for a long, sweet tongue kiss, one hand gently massaging my breast.

I sigh and move his hand down to my waist, then pull out of his mouth to murmur, 'My lord, didn't you promise to be good?'

'This is not so very bad. And it's been a long time since we've been able to enjoy any intimacies.'

Well, that's true enough, given my programme of starving out a declaration from him.

'Come here,' he murmurs.

I go back into his mouth again for a dizzying, warm play of the tongues; and his palm strokes across my breast, where the cape falls open, so that the pap pops out hard into the satin.

My arm tightens about his waist, and he slides his hand down to rest it in my lap and gently stroke there. I can't feel much through the heavy satin, but his touch is feathery, and with the insistent rhythms high 'twixt my upper thighs, the crevice below sharpens, twinges with a hard yearning.

The chair sets down with a jolt, and we hastily pull apart, brush and straighten our clothing. I pull the cloak o'er the blush on my bosom and feel all on fire with yearning, and the sun barely up. At this rate how will I e'er survive the day?

I give him a warning look and murmur, just as the door's thrown open, 'You'd better keep your promise and behave, my lord.'

He grins mischievously.

His house is a fashionable white three storey and attic, with stairs up to a lintelled door. Beyond the alcove, its floor checked white and black, rises a new-fashion stairway, its banister a rail rather than carven close-wood; and to the right stretch three rooms.

His first activity is to show me 'round the house, so we enter the first doorway on the right. Here's a front chamber crammed wall to wall with bookcases, their glazed doors showing books of fine leather bound behind 'em, and many of the spines stamped with foreign tongues; but no other furnishings, save a few chairs drawn up along the walls. The second chamber's a small wainscoted dining room, with carven cabinets of black walnut tree and a table of the like, a chandelier and a large looking glass. The third's a white-painted and gilt parlour done in gold carvings, and the chairs and stools of white wood trimmed with blue figured velvet – but I am surprised to see the settle, in a mode usual with him, drawn out of position and placed before the white marble fireplace, in defiance of the fashion that sets furniture about the walls. The kitchen's at the end of the hall and six steps down, being at the ground storey and above the wine cellar.

My heart pounds as he takes my elbow in the dark, lonely passageway and his arm touches me. And then we are got into a brilliantly lit clutter. Before us on a table of stout oak are scattered dishes, pots, pans, tubs, wooden spoons, a rolling pin and mortar and pestle, all in various stages of gooey unwash; and a grater with pungent pieces of ginger clinging to't. Behind that are a brick oven whence issues the delightful aroma of roasting goose; a hearth where a girl turns a small bird; and a floury apparition, girded in apron and wielding a cleaver, and by whom I'm straightway seized.

'Well, bless our very souls, if it ain't the little ladyship!' The apparition gives me a hug that would do credit to a bear.

'Doll!' I squeal.

'Law, law, many's the time I've asked his lordship to have the little ladyship here! And here you are. Shall I send up the punch directly?'

'Yes, for 'tis Christmas, after all. Come – I'll show you the rest of the house.'

As I follow him up the dark stairs, he reaches a hand out to grasp mine and guide me, and I tingle all over.

We emerge in the dimly shadowed hallway again, to pass the three rooms and climb the banistered stairs.

He shows me first the great bedchamber. 'This is where I sleep – when I'm here,' he amends. 'Would you care to come over with me and try out the bed?'

'Oooo, you! – Never missing a chance.'

'I try to live up to my reputation. Here, you can see out on the balcony –' He motions me to a set of wide double doors that open out onto a balcony. We stand in the crisp cold and look down at Covent Garden, almost deserted on this fair, bitter early Christmas morning: the piazza far ahead and the other rent-houses scattered about, with the chapel of St Paul's off to the side, white-columned like most of Inigo Jones' creations.

'Step toward your left.'

Obediently I do, and see another set of doors off the balcony.

'This leads into another bedchamber.'

He pushes the doors, and we walk into a dainty room trimmed in different shades of pink and rose.

I blush all the way up to the roots of my hair to see laced bed hangings and a lady's toilet table, with a large dressing-room area, and the whole done up in the shades I oft wear.

I cannot look him in the face. Does he know what conclusions I draw? Does he bring me here so I will draw them?

'A second bedchamber,' he says pointedly, 'which has not been used yet.'

I blush too hard to look at him but just nod and stare down.

'Come,' he says breezily and pulls me down the hall to open a third door across the way and show a chamber deck't in green. 'Doll's been sleeping here, but it could be for guests – or – for a nursery.'

Still I dare not look at him.

'The lesser servants sleep above, in the attic. And this is all of my lodgings: not very large but commodious enough, considering I'm but one and stay here but rarely.'

We descend the staircase.

'My lord,' I ask, 'why do you keep this establishment – if, as you say, you spend most of your time in the palace?'

He shrugs. 'I suppose I think it fit for a man in my station. And there are some times, like today, when I'd entertain. Then, too, there are people here I'd not wish to turn out.'

'Like Doll?'

IIc nods. 'Like Doll – though she oft goes to Adderbury.'

'I notice you had a deal of books in your first room, my lord.'

'Yes, I used to have a study in the old house I rented. But I sold the desk.'

I dare not ask him why: I know the reason must be money.

'For a while I used the second upstairs bedchamber as a study, but I've recently redecorated.'

Now my heart leaps into my throat and I yearn to ask him why, but dare not. Why will he tease me and never say the plain thing?

'Here,' he says, for I've been craning neck at the book room, so he obligingly shows me the gold-stamped volumes, bound in red or green: Latin, French, Italian, English; modern philosophers and lyric poets; sceptics and divines; comedians and tragedians; satirists and historians; mathematicians and natural philosophers.

'My lord,' I cry, handling a Cicero, 'you must be very learned.'

He shrugs. 'Not really. It's the common gentleman's education. And I have but little Greek.'

'Yes, but I don't see such a library in most gentlemen's homes.'

He shrugs. 'Perhaps not. But I've a fondness for study, even though I don't do it as often as I should any more.'

I run my fingers lightly o'er the philosophers: Hobbes, Bacon, Pico della Mirandola.

'Who are your favourites?' I ask.

'Lucretius and Ovid for the ancients; Waller and Marvell for the moderns; and Falstaff in Shakespeare.'

I shake my head in wonderment. 'I like the King Arthur stories and modern poets. And the tragedies in Shakespeare.'

'Let's go sit by the fire 'til dinner's ready,' he suggests.

Hand in hand we stroll into the sitting room, decked out in the rich green pointy hands of holly, with its blood-red berries.

And as we sit before the fire and he draws me close into the hollow of his arm, i' th' dimness of the room I feel somehow secure, protected against prying eyes, the sheltering shadows lit only by the cheery orange glow of the warm, crackling fire.

We move close into one another's arms and work our lips and tongues as if we'd crawl into one another through sheer force of desire. Our hands gently explore one another's clothed bodies.

'Mmmmm,' he sighs, pulling out of my mouth to catch me close to the side of his cheek. He shifts a little in my arms in response to the sly rubbing I do. By now his hand has found its way underneath my skirts, so I can feel more keenly the gentle stroking that was so muted before through the satin. I catch my breath sharply as the teasing fingers probe a particularly sensitive spot and nudge me up higher.

'Oh, this is wicked!' I cry. 'And we do't' – my protest comes out in gasps – 'every time we are alone.'

I'm so ashamed at how we can't keep our hands off one another.

'It is – ahhhhh,' I cry, for I'm trembling and collapsing in his arms again.

And I rub him hard through his breeches 'til he trembles and sighs himself.

He kisses one of my hands and says, 'Let me be off a bit to clean myself; I'll be back presently.'

So in the few moments he's gone, I'm left to half-lie, half-sit, flushed and dishevelled and gooey on the seat and curse myself again for a wanton.

When he returns with a little handkerchief to daub the tear stains under my eyes and wipe me clean below, I plead, 'Let us not do this thing again – it makes me so ashamed.'

He nods. 'Very well, sweetness. At least for today, anyway. Come into my arms and let's cuddle.'

Scarcely without knowing what I say, I cry, 'I desire you so, and it's – and I have so little control, and I get so ashamed.'

Then I make a stop and blush all over and regret what I've said, for 'tis scarce modest.

His arm tightens about me. He strokes my back. 'I know, my sweet.

No reason for shame. Your body prepares to receive me, and mine, to enter you; it is natural, for our bodies have no understanding of human conventions. I think none the less of you for your responsiveness: indeed, I am glad of it and would not have you cold to me. I desire you, too.'

'Shall we – can we –' I hesitate and bite my lips.

I've just been on the verge of saying, 'Shall we never be married, so I can truly give myself to you and without shame – be able to sleep beside you with our warm nakedness pressed together and be able to feel you inside me?' But I stop myself just in time.

'Shall we what, my sweet angel?'

He feels so warm, with my head leaning against his shoulder.

'Nothing, my lord.'

A moment of silence descends.

At last he says, and his voice sounds peculiar, as if he's jerking his words out – I've never heard him falter so – 'You know, I – I love ...'

I stop my breath and hold it.

'– being here with you like this.'

My heart plummets to my feet again.

Both arms round his waist, I hug him tight. 'I – love more than just that, my lord.'

His arm tightens about me. 'I think you know what I mean,' he murmurs.

I hold him so close, 'tis a wonder he can breathe; and I decide he's so near the edge, I must push him over now.

'No, my lord,' I murmur. 'Why don't you tell me?'

His lips caress the top of my head. 'You know how I feel.'

I shake my head hard, moving it vigorously against his arm and breast. 'No, my lord.' My voice is small. 'I do not.'

'What, can there be any doubt?'

His voice is teasing; his hand lifts my chin so I can see the love writ all over his face.

'There can be,' I say softly, 'if the words have not been said.'

Gazing at me, he moistens his lips. 'I – you know what my affections are for you.'

Damn! Why can he not say the words?

Staring him straight in the face, I capture his hand with mine and squeeze it. 'What particular word do those affections include, my lord?'

He draws our hands down to press his lips on my fingers. His eyes dark and intense, he asks plaintively, 'Must I spell it out for you?'

I nod. 'Yes, my lord.'

He leans over 'til his lips are at my ear and whispers, 'My sweet little Sab, I love you: can you doubt it?'

I squeal and hug him close. 'Oh, my lord, I love you, too – so much! I thought you'd never say it.' Then I make a surprised stop. 'Sab?'

He laughs. ''Sweet and Beautiful.' It's a name I've called you in my head – lo, these many, many months.'

'Oh, I like it. You must call me "Sab" often. And I shall call you –' I look down. 'May I – call you "John"?'

This is horridly familiar; I've heard no one but his elder sister-in-law use it of him, nor are ladies wont to address their husbands by Christian names, like servants. But I decide, if Castlemaine can bark out 'Charles' at the King, I'm not going to keep on saying 'my lord' – not in private, anyway. And he smiles as if touched.

'I'm in your hands for naming me what you will, pretty Sab.'

'Oh, how good it is to get that barrier broken down!' I cry.

'What? You thought I did not love you, little silly?'

'I could not know – I – some of your carriage has been so contradictory.'

'Well, I'm a contradictory man, I suppose. Sometimes I have difficulty knowing my own mind.'

'How long have you loved me?' I tease.

He shrugs. 'I cannot say.'

I pout.

He stares at me, then forces forth a little more intelligence, knowing how greedy I am for't. 'A very long time now.'

'Before you went off to war that first time?'

'Oh, before that. You think I would have carried you off and not loved you?'

'I didn't know, I didn't know!'

'Well, I admit I didn't either, at that point. I didn't know what I did. It seems that only a long while afterward, when I looked back and scrutinized my actions, I saw I'd been loving you a good long while and not knowing it.'

'When was this, that you realized?'

'I think it was when I was off at sea. So many of my friends needled me that I went to get the gold to win you, and I think they were in the right, though I wouldn't admit as much to myself. Oh, I had any number of motives I gave myself for going off. And any number of times since then, I've told myself I've forgotten you. I've tried to forget you, God knows.'

'But you could not?' I squeak.

He shakes his head.

'Oh, I'm glad!' I hug him closer, lay my cheek against his shoulder. 'But' – I am amazed at my courage – 'can we not do anything about it now?'

'Do anything?' He gives me a blank, then guarded, look.

Suddenly I cannot meet his gaze. I watch my fingers, plucking at his shirt.

'I mean – you say you love me, and I say I love you –'

I cannot finish the sentence, for 'tis evident how it should be finished.

He's grown distant from me suddenly; I can feel a wall go up. I put my arms tighter about him, but that doesn't bring him back.

'I'm – not in a position to do anything definite right now,' he says. 'I pray you grant me sufferance.'

Crushed, I nod. 'Very well, my lord. But –'

'But what?'

'Nothing.'

I had wished to say, I fear lest my guardians apply pressure on me to marry someone else; all I manage to get out is, 'My guardians –'

He nods. 'I know they will not have me. My affairs are in much disarray now. I beg you, grant me sufferance.'

I nod. 'Yes, my lord.'

I notice I'm using 'my lord' again: we've gone back to formality. 'Tis almost as if the sweet confession had never been; and I'm uneasy to see, the rest of the afternoon's polite.

For Doll announcing the dinner and a footman and page waiting upon us, he simply entertains me like a gracious host; and after a brief general conversation in the sitting room again, he sitting beside me but barely touching me, he escorts me back to the palace.

'Tis as if I've drawn from him more than he wished to have drawn, and he retreats inside himself. I can scarcely digest the thrill of hearing he loves me for marking how quickly he draws back after making the admission. This man is so hard to get to: he has got a Great Wall of China 'twixt himself and the rest of the world and two thousand mandarins scouting the top.

So he leaves me at my apartments 'twixt three and four of the clock of an afternoon. Indeed, we've spent some eight hours together; but still I yearn to be with him 'til the advance of night makes me too sleepy to hold my head up any more. Why seeks he to be rid of me so soon? Has he another engagement? Have I pushed him too hard, and will he grow distant now?

I try to put my fears aside and bounce exultantly over to Emilia's, to bang on her door.

And, being admitted by her woman, I cry, 'Emilia! Emilia! He said he loved me, he said he loved me!'

I dance all about her sitting room and hug myself hard, so she stares up in surprise from her grave tome, and e'en the shepherdesses mincing above her mantel seem to draw back in amaze.

'Oh, what a happy Christmas this is! He loves me!' I whirl like a top about her sedate environs.

She stares at me in stark surprise. 'He's said he loves you? Well, I hope he has. Do you mean it's taken him all this time?'

Suddenly I realize what a foolish admission I've made.

'Oh – well –' I make a confused stop.

She watches me, one of her eyebrows up. 'Betty, you haven't been alone with him, have you?'

'Well –' I regard the floor and blush.

'Oh, Betty! Not when I've warned you.'

'Well, he came in the other day and was so sweet – and just had his arms round me by the fire.'

'Well, I warrant that won't last long.' Her eyebrow's still up, and her tone is railing. 'I see by your blushes he did more than that today.'

'But he never – forces me.'

'No, of course not.'

'And – he does not – press me for the final favour.'

She shakes her head. 'Oh, Betty. What am I to do with you?'

I pout. 'Well, Jennings says, by the court manners, that a lady in love may do what she wishes as long as she does not grant the final favour.'

'And how far away from it do you think you are? Did he touch you again like you were describing before?'

Blushing, I nod.

'Oh, Betty. How can you think he has any respect for you now?'

'I don't know,' I say miserably, plopping onto a walnut stick-chair, my skirts furling about me. 'I only know I love him so much.' I look up, my lip quivering. 'And he did say he loved me, Emilia – he did!'

'I believe you. And I believe he does love you.' Then she purses her lips. 'But still no talk of marriage?'

I shake my head.

'That doesn't look well, Betty. You know it doesn't.'

'I know,' I squeak softly and look down. 'He – he said his affairs were in disarray, though.'

'So he did mention marriage?'

'Well – I'm afraid –' Now I blush harder '– 'twas actually I that mentioned it.'

'Oh, Betty!' she moans. 'Your case looks worse than ever.'

I look up, lip trembling and tears in my eyes. 'Does it e'en so?' I – I had thought – since he said he loved me –'

'I warrant you forced that out of him, too.'

Head down, plucking my skirt, I feel the tears roll down my cheeks. 'I s'pose I did.'

'Oh, Betty. There, now, dear.' She slams down her tome and strides across the room to pat my shoulder, then hug me. 'I'm sorry to rail at you so. But indeed, you're never going to get yourself married this way.' She shakes me by the shoulders. 'Betty, look at me.' I do, through the tears. 'You must never receive him alone again, do you hear?'

I nod. 'Yes, Emilia.'

'Now, I'm sure we can mend the damage some. Are you to see him again?'

I nod. 'Yes, tomorrow, for St Stephen's Day.'

'Well, tell him you mustn't see him alone and that he must make arrangements with my Lord of Ashfield and me to be with you.'

I nod. 'Yes.'

'What were you to do?'

'Simply to go to his lodgings and have some punch and cakes and such.'

'Well, tell him you've thought better about going unless my Lord of Ashfield and I can come too.'

I nod. 'Yes, Emilia.'

And not 'til I'm back in my own quarters do I begin to wonder about something: why does she insist so firmly that both she and Ashfield must be there? She alone would do the business. Might she have a motive of her own in offering to be my duenna? Might this not be her only way to get close to Ashfield, who's notoriously shy and self-effacing about women of virtue, for all his handsome face and pleasing manners?

Well, no matter. She's i' th' right about the main issue: I've set myself back rather than forward in my hopes. And so this Christmas, which began so beautifully, which had my heart thrilling with his declaration, grieves me with gnawing fears, now that I've forced from him what he would not say.

3

'Serious Emotional Deprivation'
26 December 1666

Strange as it may seem, some people arrange their lives so they'll be rejected because they don't want to know what they missed in childhood. If they were never really loved by their parents, they may repeat those patterns of rejection without being consciously aware of what they're doing. Almost everyone has some memories of pain during childhood years and most people suffered some emotional deprivation, or didn't get as much love as they wanted or needed. But when there was a serious emotional deprivation, the person is apt to look for lovers whose behavior is like the less-than-satisfactory parent. When this kind of person finds someone who is able to really love him or her, the person will interfere and destroy the love because it's too great a contrast to what was known in childhood.
—Dr Joyce Brothers, *The Houston Post*, 24 August 1982

Christmas-time, gaiest festival and sport of the whole year: mummers in masques and Harlequin faces; wassailers in Loxley Wood saluting every tree with the spiritous bowl, 'til Mama, with lips pursed, orders the coach out to glean the forest for their tipsy remnants; the Yule Log crackling in the great carven fireplace, bringing peace for the New Year and warmth to those carolling about it; Packington's Pound, Joan Sanderson, and other country dances – the tangle, with hands all joined weaving in and out 'til we fall laughing on our haunches; kissing dances and kissing mistletoes; holly and pungent rosemary and ivy with its leaves like hearts; and meat and drink to fill Goliath – tarts of cherry, strawberry or wild pear preserved; Spanish or French crème, trifle and posset; sugary Twelfth-Night cakes with the almond hid inside; mulled wine, spiced wine, and syllabub in flute glasses, or frumenty for the little ones; currant cakes, chestnuts pulled glowing from the hearth with a yelp and marchpane to make small eyes pop, carved into little horses, pigs, oranges, apples, or bunches of cherries; hoodman blind, snapdragon. And the whole of Great House scented with good things, with the rosemary and pine boughs of the Great Hall or the warm bakery smell of the yawning kitchen. These are my memories, but with my dear one beside me at last, the Holy Season is more magical than ever.

Somehow his very presence – the sweet nearness of his warm arm, his silkily seductive voice – melts my heart with such joy as dispels fear. We celebrate with Ashfield and Emilia, even play silly games like snapdragon and burn our fingers plucking the hot raisins from the fire; eat of Doll's sugared currant cakes and call her up to take bows on the warm spiced punch.

And yet – and yet – does he not seem relieved not to face me alone? Does he not laugh overmuch with Ashfield, avoid my eyes, forebear e'en to touch my hand?

'Tis true, we all giggle, sing songs, munch – and the guzzling we do would warm the heart of Bacchus; and we tease and rail at one another and complain how every underling we ever knew has accosted us today with a Christmas box, after the fashion of begging silver for the year's services. My lord grabs a lute to bewitch us with the sweetest baritone and string-plucking ever heard; we rasp along, half in tune. But are there not perplexing undercurrents to the merriment?

By nightfall we've downed enough of Doll's punch to bring all of our strangest humours out. Ashfield, reclined back in a sleeping-chair and lazy from good cheer, recalls the wonderful Christmas baking his grandma did: the mince pies, plum pudding flamed with brandy wine, currant buns and wild blueberry tarts. My lord and I sit listening on a settle with damasked cushions, I very conscious of his arm drawn up behind my neck and wishing he'd sling it across my shoulders; Emilia sitting proper as always, knees together and dainty hands folded in her lap in a chair of white and blue figured damask nearby. Ashfield done, she unbends to tell us of her jolly mother and father that keep open house the twelve days of Christmas for all the neighbourhood, and with so much wine flowing, by noon her papa is drunk and looking like a frolicsome leprechaun; and her mother, who will not rest but insists that everyone must eat to bursting; and the lutes and fiddles playing four-and-twenty hours of the day, with plays, games, treats, and no one's cup suffered to be half empty e'en; and the little yapping dogs of her spoilt sister Kitty, that her parents make a pet of, encouraging her dreadful verse and stuffing her round body with yet another tart.

I then recall how Grandpa used to joy himself in the Christmas celebration, which was his one great act of rebellion against 'that damned usurper Cromwell', who had forbade it: how he was accustomed to thunder out great, daring toasts o'er the wassail, of 'A health to the King, across the seas,' and congratulate himself as though he did it in Parliament House, rather than almost at the west coast, where no one could hear nor care.

My lord has been so silent during our narrations, I am about to probe him for his Christmas memories, that I may hug more sweet intelligence to my heart; but I stop myself just in time.

Why, he must have had no Christmas celebrations; for his house was headed by a Cromwell. All the fanatics are bitterly set against what they believe a pagan holiday: 'Heathen's Feasting Day', they call it.

My lord's gaze is so deliberately guarded, I think on how to break in and shift subjects; but Emilia, who is talking, will not hear me. She leans over sideways in her chair, hands still daintily clasped, and talks a merry chatter to the grinning Ashfield, his long body collapsed in a tangle of bent arms and legs.

'How I miss the Yule log this year! But there's none to be had in town, especially after the dreadful fire. Nor are the fireplaces large enough – you must all come next year to my home in Yorkshire.' She turns about to include us in a polite nod and sweep of her head, though she'd taken little note of us before. 'My household delights in company – oh!' And her eyebrow goes up as she purses her lip looking on the dangerous male beside me. 'And my little sister will be so transported at the sight of the Lord Rochester, she'll faint on the spot. She makes me write of everything he does, 'til I am sick to death of the subject.'

'If you write of everything he does,' I put in, 'I hope she's at least fifteen.'

My lord cocks a mischievous eye at me.

'Twelve,' sighs Emilia, her little finger crooked o'er her punch cup, 'and a great trial to us all. She yearns to come to court and bother him in her own person; then we would indeed have no peace. My father says, she would fain come with her own coach and band of men and carry him away to Uxbridge.'

Now we all laugh indeed, I especially with a secret delight to know how famous is our love story o'er the kingdom.

'Twelve,' muses Ashfield. 'She's of an age with my ward.' He grins. 'She's in love with Rochester, too.'

My lord sips from the cup in his left hand. 'When did Mrs Kitty have occasion to be smitten by my charms?'

'She has not seen your lordship: she loves you from afar, by reputation.'

I regard him seductively from the top of my eye. ''Tis the easiest conquest he ever made.'

'And 'twould be the most troublesome,' shudders Emilia, 'if she was ever got to town to torment him. She teases my father to bring her hither, but he knows better; and now I'm at court, I hear nothing by every post but that I must prove the loving sister and invite her.'

'Emilia, why do you not?' I cry. 'Think what a thrill 'twould be.'

Emilia shakes her head, lips purs'd and eyebrow up o'er a large and ironic eye of pale blue. 'You know her not: she is all giddiness and humours, would run us mad in an hour – and make the Lord Rochester so miserable he'd wish to hang himself.'

My lord laughs; and, his eyes sparkling 'neath their screen of thick black lashes, urges, 'I've a hand in managing young ladies: pray suffer her to come. I'll play the gallant to her.'

Emilia groans at the thought. 'You have not met her, my lord, or you'd not be so complying. She has hounded me these two weeks to sit beside you at table and grab a crumb to enclose in my next.'

Ashfield, who was engaged in sipping of his cup, spews wassail from the energy of his laughter, while the rest of us titter as Emilia shakes her head, cradling her cup daintily in her hand. He says, 'This is a young lady that must meet my Miss Jane. She's another such.'

Emilia rolls her eyes. 'If my mother and father were not saints, they had long been disgusted with her freaks; but, no, they will encourage her: buy her treats, soothe up her silly airs.'

'They sound like sensible folk,' smiles my lord.

Emilia is aghast. 'What, to indulge their silly child?'

'What better way to make her feel loved and happy?'

My heart throbs anew to know what a perfect father I've chosen for my children.

'Again,' insists Emilia in those firm imperial tones, 'your lordship has not met Kitty.'

'We can remedy that: bring her to town. Shall I write to extend the invitation?'

Emilia rolls her eyes. 'Oh, good God. That would be the end.'

'Mrs O'Hara,' laughs Ashfield, 'beware Rochester with that gleam in his eye that would portend some new diversion.'

'He would not be so diverted as he thinks,' retorts Emilia crisply, her mouth turned down; but then she stops to shoot Ashfield a very broad smile before she laments, 'I wish my father would not make such a pet of her and soothe up her horrid freaks.'

'She will grow out of 'em,' insists my lord, 'and then she'll be the better person, for remembering how her father loved her.'

I give my lord a tender look. 'Was your father like that?'

He starts. '*My* father?'

I give him a sad look. 'I suppose, as you lived at Ditchley Park and he with the court overseas, you did not see him often.'

'I never met him.'

We all look aghast on him as he sips steadily of his cup.

Emilia cries, 'What, never even once?'

He shakes his head.

'How old were you, Rochester, when he died?' asks Ashfield.

'Almost eleven.'

'Of course,' I break in quickly, watching his impassive face, 'Cromwell had set a very high price on your father's head; 'twould've been extreme folly for him to come into the country.'

My lord shrugs. 'He used to come in spying all the time. Once he stayed a quarter of a year in Oxford.'

A horrified silence falls. Then Ashfield is stupid enough to burst out: 'And he avoided seeing you in Paris, too, didn't he? I recall Bucks saying –' Ashfield then flushes bright red at his mistake.

A deep silence falls.

My lord slings himself up from the settle, ambles over to ladle himself another dose of wassail-punch and holds the cup up, in mock salute: 'A health, to marriage,' he says grimly, staring at me with his mouth tight.

I swallow hard. Another silence descends, during which the hard lump in my throat near chokes me. His gaze on mine is all savage irony, with not a trace of love. So this is my payback for forcing his hand.

'Not all marriages are bad, my lord,' objects Emilia.

'No doubt, no doubt,' he says bitterly. 'And there may be somewhere such a bird as a phoenix.'

I see that Emilia is about to engage with him, but I cannot bear argument on such a topic: the glacial hardness in his gaze has opened my heart already like a wound.

'Let's play another game,' I break in, my voice falsely gay through the quiver in't. 'One person begin a line of verse, and the next add a couplet; then another line and a couplet, and so on.'

Ashfield groans. 'The mob is always doing that; but I confess I can't, Mrs Mallet: I have no invention.'

My lord takes a few steps towards his former seat, halts, pauses, then cuts abruptly to his right, to head purposefully for a lone chair away from the group. My heart sears in me like a great pain.

'Oh, come, my lord,' chides Emilia, tapping Ashfield with her fan. 'Surely you can comply, for the sake of the Christmas spirit?'

'Well –' His square face splits into a helpless little-boy grin.

My lord looks suddenly over to meet my gaze, and I wonder if he reads the pain on my face. His lip tightens, and his eyebrows come together; with a set of his jaw, he whirls about again and strides back across the room, to collapse beside me.

Thank you, I think, my eyes smarting with tears. He glances at me and smiles faintly, then looks away and tosses off a gulp of wassail.

'Oh, very well, madam,' drawls Ashfield, running his finger 'neath his holland-band and colouring foolishly, looking first at her and then away. Emilia clasps her hands on her knees and begins. 'The holly that hangs above the door.' Then she nods toward Ashfield.

He groans and tugs at his holland-band and, at last, grinning sheepishly, supplies, 'Is certainly not on the floor.'

Now we all laugh at the wonderful absence of his wit.

'The little leaves prickle and stick,' I say next.

Now we all look expectantly at my lord, slumped beside me; all at once he bursts out laughing and throws a droll look at Ashfield.

Emilia and I sit stupidly staring whilst the men both chortle at one another. Then all at once I recall some of Castlemaine's franker conversations, and I squeal, then put a hand to my mouth and blush and giggle fit to burst, to think what rhymes with 'stick'. Emilia, who has always been such a terrible grave prude, is even worse drunk; she arises majestically, her eyebrow up and lip down, to parade across the chamber and pretend to look for another currant cake.

'Remember, Rochester, you rhyme in different company here,' protests a guffawing Ashfield, as my lord throws him a wicked look that says very clearly he's invented some priceless filthy line.

'Beware to touch them lest they prick,' says my lord at last.

Emilia parades back to sit straight in her chair, cake daintily in hand. 'The berries are the shade of blood.'

We all look to Ashfield; desperately, he supplies, 'They're certainly not the shade of mud.'

We shriek with delight; he grins, his green eyes sparkling above the little blub nose.

'A drop of blood drawn from the heart,' I add.

My lord sips and tosses out effortlessly, 'For maids to draw that men may smart.'

I pout at him, but he will not look at me.

Emilia casts an imperial blue eye about the sitting room; and, glimpsing the ivy wreathed about the fireplace, says, 'The ivy trailing to the floor.'

We all look at Ashfield. Desperately, he thinks. At last he replies, 'Is certainly not above the door.'

We laugh.

'He writes the same line over and over,' complains my lord, shaking his head.

''Tis but economy,' grins Ashfield, unperturbed. 'Why spend all my words at once?'

Our laughter at last abates enow so that I may supply, 'The evergreen hearts wind through the room.'

My lord tosses off a dram. 'Engulfed in its devouring womb.'

Emilia's eyebrow goes up, and she snaps, 'I know not why we must be filthy to divert ourselves.'

He glares on her, his brows knit together. 'What find you filthy about the parts Nature gave you? But then your sort would cut off –'

'Please, I pray you,' I beg. 'Let us have no quarrels today. Emilia? Your turn.'

She nods reluctantly, then casts her large pale eyes about the chamber for more inspiration. We've already made use of the holly that drips in sharp bloody clusters from the harpy's portrait, as well as the green hearts of ivy that trail across the icy marble of the mantel. Her eyes drop a moment to the soft-glowing embers of the fire within the marble, then to the floor nearby, where the pungent rosemary boughs are scattered.

'Rosemary branches are at our feet,' she then announces.

Ashfield hesitates and thinks, his brow furrowed.

'You may have to lash Pegasus a bit further on his ascent to Parnassus,' my lord advises. 'I doubt if you can use your ready-made line there.'

'Pox on you, Rochester – ah, I've got it.' He grins proudly. 'My, but rosemary does smell sweet.'

Trying to hide my giggles behind my hand, I add, 'A savoury odour warmed by the fire.'

My lord sips. 'Emblem of memory and pungent desire.'

Emilia lifts her imperial eyebrow o'er us. 'Desire! I might have known he'd get to that.'

I look at him wickedly. 'Somehow, I felt it coming, too.'

Then, realizing the hidden meaning of what I've said, I squeal and cover my mouth.

We all roar laughing now, except Emilia, who turns away; I can tell she is very vexed with me and will lecture me all the next morning. She lifts a regal nose and eyebrow o'er my frolics as I sit, hand to abashed mouth, giggling and blushing, and toss now and again a demure look, then a wild one, at my lord. He smiles with tender merriment on me and draws an arm up over the seat back.

Nose lifted, Emilia intones, 'Mistletoe is the plant of love.'

I scarcely hear what she says for feeling the sun warm my cold life again as my lord looks kisses, dark-eyed and intense, all over my face. He's lowered the wall; he loves me again – but why? His affection is like God's grace: both unexpected and undeserved, as easily granted as withdrawn.

No matter. My heart swells like a star so that I yearn to hug silly, handsome Ashfield as he sips, grins his lazy smile, and leans back in the sleeping-chair, cudgelling his brains for the next verse. 'Let's see – ah. It always hangs up above.'

My lord explodes with chortling glee and slaps his thigh. So relieved at his merriment and warmth, I giggle for happiness and bask in love, a liquid bubble that marks us off from the world and draws us close. Emilia glares – such a grave drunk! – and Ashfield grins sheepishly as my lord chortles, 'Better and better: soon Waller will indeed have something to fear from you.'

Still giggling with my overflowing joy, I recite, 'The berries like plump white moons do rest.'

Grinning, my lord runs an exquisitely gentle finger over my ribbon. 'But colder than my lady's breast.'

Emilia's eyebrow goes up, and her mouth pops open with indignation. 'I will not sit here and watch you be so insolently familiar with a friend of mine – my lord!' She spits out the last two words, her lips sneering.

His black brows come together. 'You see the door, madam; but if you'd avoid insolent familiarity, best leap out of your own skin.'

Here we go now. It seems impossible to get these two together without a quarrel: they began by disliking one another and before long will be at cuffs. I beg 'em once more, for honour of the Prince of Peace, to have done.

Grudgingly they agree, and I instruct my hot warrior, 'You must finish the verse now, with a triplet.

'I will indeed. You must be kind and make me blest.'

I gape at him, without knowing what this little advance can mean, but then I see he holds a mistletoe twig o'er me. I squeal and flush and cover my lips with a hand.

'Come, madam,' smiles Ashfield. 'You must pay up. Remember the poem by Herrick: no lady can refuse to kiss under the mistletoe bough.'

I sit there, abashed and torn, one part of me delighted I've the excuse to kiss him again; another part mortified to do't before witnesses, especially Emilia, who so puts up her nose at me; but the greatest part thrilled he loves me enough at last to show affection publicly.

I cast a dismal glance toward Emilia and hope, though she has no bodily feelings at all, she will understand I can kiss more happily without witnesses. She seems to understand the message.

'Come on, Lord Ashfield.' And she stands. 'Let us see if any more snow has fallen.'

He looks at her so melancholy where he lounges, half tipsy. 'What, go out in this weather without I am pushed? I have just got warm.'

'And I have just got a signal. Come, to look out the window at least.' She flashes him a broad smile and strolls over, holding out her hand.

'Very well,' he groans, ever affable, and pushes the chair up three notches 'til 'tis straight, his leg still over the side. 'But I have just got comfortable here, and I warn you, madam –' He gives her one of his comical looks '– I am so drunk, I may fall down.'

They laugh heartily together; and he, grasping Emilia's hand as if 'twere a rope thrown to a drowning sailor, manages to hoist himself up, though almost pulling her down in his lap instead. Emilia – give her her due – frowns not nor scolds on his 'insolent familiarity', I suppose knowing 'tis but his tipsiness – and e'en laughs along with him.

Now they stand at the dark pane pretending to watch the snow fall against it, and they tell the designs of the snowflakes that strike one by one pattering at the glass, then melting together. My lord and I lean together, and our lips meet.

Now, a mistletoe kiss is supposed to be a mere token; but we kiss once, twice, and then I put my hand to his neck and lean greedily toward him again. He draws an arm 'round my shoulder; and as our lips press, he brings out his tongue to bid mine hello.

All at once I consider how Emilia may have peeked over and been scandalized to mark how our mouths were open; and, blushing mightily, I cry, 'No, not here –' and with a hand to his breast, push gently away from him.

'Why not?' he murmurs, his voice sweet.

I look away blushing. ''Tis scarce decent.'

'Decency is a matter of degree,' he coaxes softly.

Now Emilia, whom we had forgot, but who has scarce forgot us, can bear the dispute no longer. 'Betty, you see how far he is to be trusted!'

We both turn about, surprised, to the window behind us, where she stands straight and regal, her arms crossed; Ashfield, half-stupefied by the wassail, stares too. Her eyes flash at me. 'For God's sake, whatever it is he would have you do, forebear complying.'

'It is scarcely anything at all,' begins my accused ravisher.

'I cannot believe it,' Emilia rants on, 'not here in the same room with us: has your lordship no restraint at all?'

'What's to do?' asks Ashfield.

Emilia whirls enraged toward him. 'He tried something.'

Ashfield grins genially. 'He is always trying something: that's why he ends up succeeding so often. I thought you knew.'

I try to distract my lord's black glare from Emilia by whispering to him and pulling on his hand. Ashfield must be attempting a like office, for he says apologetically, 'Mrs O'Hara, pardon us: we are all more than fairly drunk.'

'I notice one man in the room, though,' she says crisply, 'has no difficulty behaving like a gentleman.'

My lord glowers. 'With you, madam, I could be equally restrained.'

Here we go indeed.

'Rochester,' scolds Ashfield, 'what mad demon of drink possesses you sometimes?'

'It was Emilia's fault,' I lash out. 'She would poke her priggish nose i' the air.'

Now she and I glare on one another: she with an imperial hauteur, I like a diminutive faerie whose leaf-bed has been rumpled.

'Priggish nose?' Her eyebrow goes up. 'I have a pretty good idea where his hands were going.'

I gape at her, and my lord cuts in, 'Then your imagination is more heated than mine: I did not think to move 'em anywhere. But then, your sort –'

'*My* sort!'

'Madam, your brain is full of worms and eggs, and ever busily projecting outward what you do not do. I advise physic: Ashfield, take the lady upstairs. And give her a good –'

Now I gasp along with Emilia.

'Rochester,' says Ashfield, 'I am sorry we want a Yule log: there's a superstition that their burning dissipates hostilities. Why do we not throw you on the fire instead? You have just annoyed everyone in the room, and to get rid of you must relieve the tension; not to mention, you are overheated enough e'en to take the chill out of my liver.'

This is said with such a comical lazy drawl, my lord cannot but smile. Ashfield, though wanting my dear one's wit, has a droll buffoonery of his own that is very engaging: he can scold people so whimsically, he gets the point across without making anyone angry, usually because he gets a sly dig in at himself as well.

'Come, now, madam,' he says soothingly to the ruffled termagant beside him. 'My friend is very drunk and will be very sorry on the morrow.'

But Emilia decides we must be gone now; she has had enough and would leave, nor would she leave me in the company of such a depraved man, especially when I have drunk too much to be in full mastery of my reason. Ashfield sends for his coach, to convey us back to Whitehall, but says he will stay awhile with my lord – who lets go of me so readily, I suspect they are going to get drunker and then go out after some women. This is a very vexatious thought to have, when I am just as fired up as he but cannot go out to get a man. 'Twould be so much happier if we could only go out and get one another.

This I tell to Emilia in the coach, and she almost faints: she scolds me all the way back to Whitehall and reminds me more of Mama with every instant; she says that she can see no wit in my lord at all, but his obscenity and want of breeding are so startling, they pass in his set for cleverness; that Lord Ashfield has more true wit and is more hand-some beside, not to mention more dependable; that I had utterly overvalued my lord out of an intoxication o'er his physical charms, but he does not deserve me, and I am far too good for him; that I have a much better mind than to love such a rat such as he, with no mind at all; that it was a defect in the English educational system that women with parts were kept down by not allowing them learning, that any drunken ladykiller with a little Latin and French might impress 'em, as long as a dashing manner went with it; and that to hang about him is to court my ruin, especially if I will encourage his advances that way, to defend 'em before his very eyes and squeal at every naughty turn in the conversation. I *have* got a brain, she tells me, for she has seen evidence of't; and so I'd better make use of't now.

So I retire miserable and ashamed. All my inhibitions seem to dis-appear when I drink: thinking back on some of the loose things I laughed over or said, I know my lord may think me light. But 'tis hard to know how to behave: I love him, and I cannot let him think I do not desire him; he said he was glad for evidence of it; then, too, he seemed to unbend only when I did.

Oh, sir! Y'are such a puzzle: you pull so far from me and then move in so close, play my father and then freeze me with a look. You say you love me, but only when I wrench the words from you – then bitterly denounce marriage on the same night you look it into my eyes. And no matter how deliriously happy you make me, I'm always aching with pain beneath.

Why? Oh, why?

I go to bed with an aching heart. Oh, if only we could be married: all my problems would be over.

Part XIII

'Good-Nature'

Robert Blair, Earl of Ashfield
28–31 December 1666

Good-nature is that benevolent and amiable temper of mind, which disposes us to feel the misfortunes and enjoy the happiness of others; and, consequently, pushes us on to promote the latter, and prevent the former; and that without any abstract contemplation on the beauty of virtue, and without the allurements or terrors of religion.

—Henry Fielding, 'An Essay on the Knowledge and Characters of Men'

1

'Such An Ideot, Such A Trembler'
28 December 1666

... in the company of women of reputation, I never saw such an ideot, such a trembler.

—Oliver Goldsmith, *She Stoops to Conquer*

Today promises to be so melancholy and lonely: all of my friends are engaged. Buckhurst and his clan hath repaired into the country, to celebrate at Knole the usual frolics of Yule Logs and wassailing; Sedley is in Paris, to imbibe the fashions and catch at the women. Rochester is so engaged with Mallet, he can think of no other human creature, but hangs at her skirts as a boy doth at his Mama's, and if spoken to will not hear for looking into her eyes; so he's a Lost Man, as Bucks says, 'til he's been married at least a good month. I toy with asking Savile to supper, but then I realize I have no humour for such ribald foolery; and I find myself wishing I could coax Mallet and Rochester away from their proposed supper tonight – not for the delights of their company, which they would provide in conclave on the settle, finding excuses to smooth one another's gear, whispering and giggling secrets, and exchanging looks as if they fain would be gone somewhere to kiss – but for that they would bring with 'em Mrs O'Hara, whose conversation I'd fain enjoy tonight.

I send a note round to the Boy Genius to ask his advice on this business, but he is gone the whole day – no doubt sitting with his head in her lap whilst she drops daisies onto his face and pouts and frowns. I e'en take a coach to the King's House theatre, but the reward of my search is only Bucks, who hath seen the Phantom Strephon at the New Exchange, a-buying her another gewgaw, and talking of the boat ride and dinner they were to have this day.

I grumble at her consumption of his time: 'twas bad enough we could not get him o'evenings; then it became that he must be always escorting her hither and thither by day; and now, after he sits half the night with her playing some insipid game of Kiss and Coo, she will begin to hold levees, and we cannot even reach him by mail.

'Let the disease be cured by time,' philosophizes Bucks. 'Its throes are so violent they cannot endure more than three month's cohabitation. Once he's made her a wife, he'll be happy enough to 'scape her follies: the pouts, flirts, and glances, relentlessly repeated, will annoy where once they charmed; trying to engage her mind, he'll find nothing there; and when he's swived her thrice a day some quarter of the year, he'll know her body well enough to be sick of that, too.'

'I'd not have him so sick as that,' I mutter. 'But still, 'twould be pleasant to have a piece of him again.'

'Trust me.' Bucks grins cynically. 'There's no physic for love like marriage. And howe'er cleverly he thinks he 'scapes the hook, he dangles and gasps on it e'en now.'

I decide not to ask the advice of Bucks, whom I cannot trust, and who would draw false conclusions if I confided I mulled o'er a way to ask a lady to supper; so 'tis home again to brooding, considering who there is to ask to make her invitation honourable, yet who will be kind enough not to interrupt our conversation or engage a piece of her attention. Rochester is the only one I can trust for this detachment: he so despises her and so engrosses himself with someone else.

All at once a daring notion presents itself: why not ask her to come alone?

But no, that is mad. A woman with her high honour would not dream of coming to my lodgings unattended; she might even be so insulted at the invitation as to refuse ever seeing me again; and that I cannot risk. I have come to enjoy her conversation too much.

And yet, I would so like to enjoy her company tonight. She hath such an arresting combination of sense and shrewdness; she wants the usual vexatious frivolities of her sex and the cynical hardness of mine; and withall is so charming to look upon, with those big friendly pale eyes, those dainty gestures, that soft little hand.

I sigh, brooding at my desk o'er a Venice glass of Rhenish. Why is't men and women must manipulate coyly o'er their cant of honour? Why can I not simply state my ideas honestly?

Well, why not? She hath always seemed to enjoy my forthrightness before. If I word the invitation in the right fashion, she should not be afear'd; after all, is she not a woman of reason?

Hesitantly, I dip quill in ink and begin:

Madam,

I have been brooding this whole day, wishing to invite you to supper at my place, but yet fearing to do so, lest you mistake my meaning. Mrs Mallet and the Lord Rochester are already engaged; and so many others out of town, or uncongenial (fancy a supper, madam, witnessing the freaks of Mr Killigrew); I cannot think of anyone to invite along with you to satisfy the demands of honour; and I fear mightily to invite you alone, lest you take snuffe at my boldness and I lose your friendship altogether. Therefore I lay the cause upon you, madam, what I am to do; for you may know of some discreet female to bring to serve as your protection. I would e'en be very obliged to your faith in me if you would trust me so far as to come alone – though I hasten to add I am not so bold as to expect you would so trust one of my sex. If you do come, we will sup with my ward little Jane and her tutor Mr Rivers; they do retire early, however.

Pray lay your commands upon me what I am to do, that I may confirm to the cook, who grows resty at my delays, how many she is to serve. I send this invitation far too late, from worrying myself o'er it all day; you have every right to refuse it; and I now sit here anxious that you will, madam, who am your

Humble Servant,

R. Ashfield

I read it o'er: as a letter to a lady, 'tis not much; and I am grateful Rochester cannot see't, to dissolve into laughter at my timidities. But I somehow doubt that abduction is the approach to appeal to Mrs O'Hara, and the Devil's in't; of course, my purpose is different; she is but a companion.

So I sit in the chill of my library, sweating and drinking; wondering if she read the letter now or is within to receive it and if 'tis enough time for her to make answer – a damned plaguey ridiculous way for a man to act over a supper. I've never been so concerned thinking whether Buckhurst might be engaged; and can I not see her again when we may meet by chance in the gallery or engage with Mallet and Rochester another night?

In what is truly not so long a space of time the boy returns with a reply in a bold hand:

My Lord,

I am pleas'd to accept without reservations or fears of any sort your invitation to supper; for I believe you so much the man of honour, I would never seek to find a companion to restrain you. For in your humour there is so much of restraint, anyone must be moved by your respect of the strictest proprieties. I am most willing to make trial of your intentions again tonight, my lord, and am most pleas'd to meet Miss Jane and her tutor. I will take chair to your lodgings about nine, if that is convenient, remaining, sir, 'til then and after

Your Humble Servant,
Emilia O'Hara.

So my heart throbs with pride that she hath such trust in me, after such suspicions that she holdeth about others of my sex; and I take twenty vows to myself to avoid even the appearance of any underhanded purpose; and I issue orders at last to Mrs Marshall the cookmaid, who hath hung in the hedge railing this whole day that I take no resolution; and I even surprise William by having him issue orders for bathing.

Hence we pass an agreeable evening after all.

I am much delighted with the way she and little Jane take to one another; for soon after she arrives, the footman announcing dinner, she and I repairing both ends of the table, he then announces, Miss Jane Seward and Thomas Rivers, M.A.; and polite presentations are made all around, with bows and curtseys.

The maid-servants have made our Jane especially lovely tonight, with her blonde curls hanging on two sides and trussed up with white ribbons, and the shift pulled up above her stomacher and showing puffed sleeves with white lace at the wrists. As she grows, her cornflower-blue eyes tilt up in a promise of unusual beauty above the sweet, shy smile.

She sits gracefully, Mr Rivers pulling out her chair for her, and sweeps her sun-coloured silk overskirt around the chair. As the tutor seats himself opposite Jane, she lifts the cover of the soup tureen and releases a savoury cloud of steam. 'Mmm! Mrs Marshall's mushroom and onion soup. We're in for a treat, Mrs O'Hara.'

Two footmen ladle out the soup, put bowls in front of us, and hand around the hot fresh bread and butter; a third fills the glasses with Rhenish, well watered for Miss Jane.

Over the soup, Mrs O'Hara addresses herself to Mr Rivers:
'*Scirit Latine ea?*'
He replies. '*Non scirit, sed gallicum habet.*'
'*Amabile dictu!*' she exclaims.
I suspect she's testing his understanding of Latin, and he must have

passed the test, for she is smiling. He must see my blank face, for he enlightens me, 'Mrs O'Hara expressed surprise that Miss Jane has not Latin but only French. Would you enjoy Latin, Miss Jane?'

She smiles politely and shrugs.

Mrs O'Hara says, 'If you have Latin, the whole world is open to you – and such a world! Not only converse with all the learned men of the day, but the wonderful fables of Ovid's *Metamorphoses*, and the tragic love story of Dido and Aeneas – so affecting, and all in such beautiful language!'

Little Jane, being shy, smiles, ducks her head, and studies her soup bowl.

'Jane,' I say gently, 'you and Mr Rivers will discuss it tomorrow, and let me know what you think.'

'*Oui, monsieur,*' she says, looking up with a shy smile.

I grin. '*That* I can understand.' She laughs.

Mr Rivers asks, 'My lord – forgive me for asking, but did you not attend Westminster school?'

'For a short time, Mr Rivers. Being terrorized didn't manage to knock much Latin into my skull.'

He frowns. 'Small wonder.'

'Miss Jane,' asks Mrs O'Hara, 'how came Lord Ashfield to be your guardian?'

She says, soberly, 'Because he is the kindest and sweetest man in the world.'

I feel my face grow hot as Mrs O'Hara smiles on me appraisingly. I look away and apply the goblet to my lips as she asks, 'Did a relation die?'

Jane shakes her head. 'I am a guttersnipe.'

Mrs O'Hara's eyes grow wide; then the hint of a smile plays across her face.

Now I almost spray my wine. 'Jane! Never use that word about yourself! Where'd you hear it?

'Sir Charles Sedley.'

'If he called you that to your face, I promise to thrash him.'

She laughs merrily at the thought. 'Never you, Uncle Robert!' Mrs O'Hara smiles on both of us. 'No, I heard him say it as Edward led me off that first day.'

'You don't miss much: I'll have to be careful what you hear from now on.'

She giggles.

'Jane,' asks Mrs O'Hara, still prying for information 'did he adopt you from a poor family?'

'He bought me for fifty pound from me mam. She was an East End whore.'

Mrs O'Hara's mouth is open at this frank truth, narrated in a voice suddenly redolent of the Bow Bells. I have never heard the child speak thus; she sounds like Buckhurst's new mistress, Mrs Nell Gwyn; and there's such an honest charm to it I cannot but smile. Mrs O'Hara, I note, is smiling too, her eyes a-twinkle.

'Why did he buy you, do you think?' she probes, with a merry smile to her eyes, as if she would enjoy more.

'Not to be his whore, as Edward first said.'

Here's another reason to string Edward up by his toes over a snake pit.

'He did, did he?' I shake my head. 'No wonder you were so frighted. Mind you heed nothing Edward says.'

'He's all right. He tells me stories.'

'Including some, no doubt, that are not for your ears. Mr Rivers and I will speak with him on the morrow.'

But now Jane continues, her voice earnest, 'My Lord of Rochester says I was very fortunate, to have caught the attention of the kindest man in the world; that few men of fashion would have paid fifty pound to relieve a child of her misery and make her a lady. And that I should never forget what I owe Uncle – as if I could!'

Suddenly she is up from her chair and has put her little arms about my neck. I pat her back and feel the tears glaze my eyes; but Mrs O'Hara looks very softly upon the tableau.

'It's all right Jane,' I say softly. 'I was right lonesome before you came.'

She settles herself in her chair again, picks up a spoonful of soup and says, 'My uncle Robert is *that* brave: he rode out searching for me when I went missing during the fire. I was looking for my brother. Show her how you called, Uncle.'

Obediently I shout in a strong voice, 'Jane! Jane!'

She giggles. 'That's so! And Edward and I heard.' She sobers. 'A mob came after, so Uncle saved me just in time.'

'It was not so heroical as all that,' I begin – then make a stop, as Mrs O'Hara is giving me a very peculiar look. All at once she says 'Oh!' and pales.

'Madam?' I ask. 'Are you ill?'

'No – I just remembered something.' She looks away from me and asks Jane, 'Did you ever find your brother?'

Jane nods. 'Yes, madam. Uncle rented him a shop and set him up as a baker. These are his breads – the best in London! That's the motto over his shop. Mrs Marshall says we'll have his iced cakes tonight, too. He bakes for all the Quality now.'

Embarrassed at this puffery of myself, I stare down and spoon up the soup. When I look up, Mrs O'Hara is staring at me as if I were scummy water under the King's microscope, about to yield some world crawling with the fascinating and hitherto unknown.

After the supper Mr Rivers takes Jane to her chamber, and I invite Mrs O'Hara into the sitting room. We can talk on all manner of subjects; she is one of the few folk I can talk modern literature with comfortably, only Buckhurst and Rochester having a comparable knowledge of't, and the one always contriving to mortify me with his assumption of superiority whilst the other does't unawares by his brilliance. She, however, is pleasantly disputatious without being unduly vehement, deep, or witty – and indeed takes as much delightful care with my pride as I do with her delicacy. She opts for Donne and Milton and I, for Suckling and Lovelace.

Then, suddenly, she says, 'I like little Jane.'

'And she you, madam, I could tell. She is usually shy with strangers; I've never heard her so sprightly and confiding.'

'She has your lordship's good nature and colouring and modest manners.'

I think I see what she gets at. 'She is not my natural daughter, madam, though she could not be dearer to me if she were.'

We grow a little quiet; but it is not an uncomfortable silence, only a pleasant sense of being together: such as I have never felt with anyone else before, male or female. We sit before the fire, sipping brandy (both tricks taught me by Strephon, who says women are impressed by brandy and that a settle before the fire is very agreeable).

She tells me of her relations: how everyone loves her father on sight and her mother can deny naught to nobody; how dearly they love one another and how the servants rule 'em both, they are so gentle: how, from the age of some five upwards, Mrs O'Hara herself was forced to take all in hand and hector and set things to right, and defend her father when her mother's relations niggled at him, and her mother when her father's relations made demands: else the one had heard for hours how spineless he was, and the other be required some thrice a day to take coach five miles to bring a soup or marmelotte.

I laugh heartily and confess to her, that picture sounds like the one I've got from others of my parents, who drowned when I was very young.

'Who reared you?' she asks, no doubt from politeness.

'My grandmother,' I explain, replenishing her glass from the decanter, 'and she, I suspect, was even more tender.'

Mrs O'Hara laughs. 'What did she do when you were bad?'

'Once or twice she set out to beat me with her hand, but scarcely hard enough to feel, and when I began to cry from fear, she cried, too.'

Mrs O'Hara laughs, her lovely tapering hand o'er her mouth, eyes sparkling at me. I grin and finish, 'So she struck upon scolding me and taking away a privilege.'

Now those large, thoughtful blue eyes hold mine. 'Was that sufficient, do you think?'

'For me it was, but I have always been of an easy humour. For wilder children it might not suffice.'

She shudders. 'I wish you could see what such leniency has made of Kitty! She is a perfect wildcat.'

'This would be the little girl that loves Rochester?' I rally her a bit. 'No wonder you believe her lost, madam.'

She laughs heartily, then sobers. 'Truly, I should not be laughing. I fear she will contrive to undo herself some day, as giddy as she is, and as much as my parents grin at her follies.'

'Rearing children is a hard business,' I agree. 'When Jane went missing during the fire, I was frantic.'

'Tell me how your parents died, my lord.'

Now I grow melancholy. 'I cannot recall't very well. They drowned when I was about six years: they were going on holiday to France and left me in the care of my grandmother.'

She has been looking at me very closely. She suddenly offers up, in gentle tones,

'You must feel their want keenly.'

I look at her: she stares at me so intently with those big blue eyes; I wonder why. She has the oddest look on her face – I feel odd, too, just looking at her, like little birds fluttering all about in my gut.

I am so busy staring at her gorgeous pale eyes and her sweet encouraging smile, I scarce know what to say, but one part of me manages to make the comment required of the moment: 'Yes, I do.'

She makes no answer, and I wonder why, for I have never seen her at a loss for words before.

All at once I get the strangest feeling that she'd have me kiss her.

I have never kissed a completely modest woman before; the closest I've come is Frances Stewart, who hath but the technicality of innocence, and so I'm not even certain I am in the right about the signal I am getting. My past mistresses have given out signals so much plainer, that what I take here for an amatory encouragement may be only friendly interest; and if I make a sudden lunge toward her, I may well get slapped or at the very least spoil our pleasant friendship. Yet I am conscious at the same time that I do wish to kiss her; and that she looks on my face with those big, breathless blue eyes as if she knows what is on my mind and seeks to encourage me.

I try to think what Rochester would do in this situation; and I recall him advise, when in doubt, to move in slowly. So trying to look casual (but not, I fear, succeeding very well), I slowly drape an arm over the back of the settle. And the whole time I almost faint from fear, for every instant I expect to hear her snap, tone outraged and eyes flaring, "What do you do, my lord?' But she does not. But then, mayhap she does not realize why I have left my arm there: mayhap she believes I am but stretching – a woman as modest as she.

Now I wonder what to do next to test her ability to take a kiss, without so committing myself that I must be slapped if I have misread the situation. So I look at her dismally, hoping she will give me some plainer signal, such as putting a hand to my cravat or closing her eyes, such gestures as I see Mallet always bestowing upon her swain – but this lady does nothing, only looks at me with those big blue eyes and smiles.

What would Rochester do? I cudgel my brain and try to think, but I am not Rochester and so do not think as he would; not to mention, 'tis difficult to think at all, with those big blue eyes fixing mine.

I could ask her permission, but no one's done that since the Revolution. And what if modesty requires she refuse verbally what she might have accepted silently? And what makes me think I could get the words past the boulder in my throat, anyway?

Perhaps if I lean toward her, just a fraction—

All at once I recall how adamant she was in her letter about my high restraint, my not offending the strictest proprieties; and, recalling the proprieties Grandma taught are due women of honour, I feel my courage fail. I am suddenly certain the letter was phrased thus to warn me off any such attempt as I am prepared to make. Is she not horrified, as she hath often shown, by the familiarities Mallet suffers Rochester, which I am certain are but tame gestures of affection? And they are avowed lovers; this is a very proper lady, much less wayward and free than Mallet: a lady, moreover, with whom I have no understanding. She has but tried to show friendliness and would be horrified and disappointed if I misused her trust.

Disappointed myself now, but relieved too that I scanned the situation anew before jeopardizing our trust, I gulp brandy to gain somewhat of my composure; and on a desperate shift to pick up the conversation we have dropped, begin to chatter inanely about my youth. But my arm feels like a lump of lead on the back of the settle, and I am vexed with myself to feel inside a sort of sinking and dismalness.

'Tis almighty folly – incomprehensible – for a man of my experience to be fretting over the want of a mere kiss: can I not get kisses in plenty whene'er I desire? And why, at any rate, do I e'en think of kissing someone when the kiss will lead nowhere? Do I not secretly gloat to myself over the silliness of Rochester, who dallies and coos by the hour, getting nowhere, instead of seeking honest relief?

But something hath made us awkward now; the early easy familiarity is gone. I wonder, so brisk is she, if she hath not smoked my intents and become abashed by 'em; and so vexed am I with myself that the man-woman business almost intruded to spoil such a pleasant friendship, I take a vow to be more on my guard in the future.

But I sleep very ill this night and determine, if this restlessness keep up, I must act somehow – though I know not what to do.

2

'I'll Be Hanged If A Modest Man Can Ever Counterfeit Impudence'
31 December 1666

An impudent fellow may counterfeit modesty, but I'll be hanged if a modest man can ever counterfeit impudence.
—Oliver Goldsmith, *She Stoops to Conquer*

The more time passes, the more doth the business with Mrs O'Hara prey on me, though I know not what preys on me, nor why; I think it was the plaguey business of the unresolved kiss: a man hates to leave these things hanging, like a picture on the wall that's crooked 'til it's made straight. I wish now to the very blood I'd had the courage, when the opportunity presented itself, to test my fate. For then I would have known – what, i' faith, *would* I have known?

At least I would not be skulking o'er this bottle in my withdrawing room, considering her every look and remark, and turning it about in my unhappy skull to view it at every angle for a meaning. Had I made the attempt, I'd know whether she would have kissed or no – though God only knows why I sit here a-mulling over such a silly thing.

Hadn't she a notion what I'd a mind to do? Now that I think on't, her gaze on mine looked to be very steady and encouraging. But then, she's always been friends with me, trusted mine honour – why should she not give me a friendly look?

I take my doubts to the Master: not, of course, naming names or circumstances; and after a brisk stroll on a hard, clear day across the piazza, catch him at his rental house, having his boots pulled on for an afternoon ride with that succubus that consumes all his energies.

'Rochester,' I begin. 'Suppose there's this woman, very modest, and a man had a mind to kiss her – how would he know whether he should make trial?'

He gives me an odd look; and for a moment I'd almost swear to God, he made shift not to laugh; but he returns, very seriously, his man Harry pulling at his boot: 'She'll let him know; and when she does, his part is to act.'

'But how,' I persist, 'should she let him know?'

Rochester hangs in the hedge to commend Harry, who could not do better an his fingers were all lopped off by the Inquisition; then, lounging arrogantly back across the green counterpane of the great bed, Venice glass in hand, replies: 'Ashfield, if at the age of four-and-twenty years at court, you've not yet learnt to read a woman's face and gestures, best apply to no one but Madame Ross.'

I sulk. 'Of course I can read gestures, Rochester; but what if the gestures are not so plain?'

Harry now struggling with the other boot, Rochester bursts into a volley of ill-natured laughter. 'Wilt thou ever be poaching my wine of a morning and not doing my service? A phoenix that burns itself up every thousand year is not more slow about its business than thou art.'

Harry looks up, grinning impudently. 'Aye, your lordship is hot for this riding, methinks.'

'Rogue!' scolds Rochester. 'Whence came that rascally tongue?'

'Nay, I know not, sir, unless it be from the example of my betters.'

The two of 'em laugh heartily whilst I sit, glumly.

Anon Rochester recalls himself from the usual game of exchanging raillery with his help and addresses himself to my problem. 'Watch for what her eyes and body tell you.' He sips, the fine filigree of lace tumbling about his sleeve, holds out the glass to me, but I shake my head. 'Move in, put your arm about her shoulders and see what she does. I thought I had told you all this before.'

'You did,' I reply desperately, 'and I did't, but still I wasn't sure.'

He stands, glass still in hand, and kicks the boot against the floor; then, Harry bustling to lay hands on the rich red velvet coat, quizzes, 'How did she react?'

I shrug. 'That's just it: she didn't react at all; she but continued to watch me, as if to see what I'd do, and I didn't know myself.'

He laughs fit to burst; never did I loathe him more, with his God-damned clean cuffs and pretty face and twinkling dark eyes and, above all, those insolent Goddamned nineteen years.

''Tis not so diverting,' I snap as Harry holds the coat to his back. 'I'd be bold, too, with signals so clear as what you get.'

He looks up, surprised, one arm behind him to shift into the coat. 'What signals are these?'

'When your lady saw the mistletoe, she put a hand to your waistcoat, closed her eyes, and put up her lips. Now, if I'd a signal like that, faith, I'd act, too.'

He shifts the Venice glass to his other hand that Harry may assist with t'other arm.

'You cannot think,' he counters, 'I got so kind a reception the first time. I swept her by surprise into my arms.'

'You swept her by surprise? And she didn't slap you?'

'I knew she'd like it. Other times, I've kissed when they told me "no".'

I groan. 'How could you dare?'

'I knew they didn't mean it.'

I groan again. 'This is impossible.'

He comes to pat my arm where I hath flung myself desperately into a little velvet jointed chair.

'Here.' He presses upon me the glass, from which I take a hearty swig. 'Heed what they say with their eyes, not with their words. Did she endeavour to stop you?'

'No,' I admit, 'but she didn't do anything to encourage me, neither.'

Now his comic muse gets the better of him again. 'If you mean she didn't lie down before you and spread her legs, you cannot in reason expect from Mrs O'Hara the sort of encouragements you and Buckhurst get at Black Bess's.'

'I am glad all this is such a joke for you,' I snap.

He makes a shift to sober himself. 'Ashfield,' he asks in a friendly way, 'how came you to kiss the first time?'

I think. 'A dairymaid in a loft.'

'It was the same with me,' he says. 'Someone older who knew what to do. If you'd dally with someone innocent, you must be bold.'

As Harry brings him the wide plumed hat, he advises, 'You must be prepared to break down her false reserve; you must be ready to ignore her soft pleas of "no" when her body leans against yours and her eyes are asking you to force her a little.'

'I refuse to force anyone.'

'They *want* you to force 'em; you bonehead – you must force 'em a little, for with the cant they've been fed of honour, they believe you expect a refusal. But they are even more disappointed if you don't: they hold it more against a man than anything else if he will not compel 'em to do what they've a mind to and help 'em excuse it to themselves.'

I can see how useless it was to come to Rochester for advice; though he may have the face to force a woman, I know I could never do't.

'I wonder you don't have the law on you,' is my parting shot.

Then, at the card party tonight, in the King's Privy Chamber, the most confusing business is brought to pass of all, so that I much wonder if this creature female, so mysterious as she is, can e'en lay claim to being of our same species.

I wander in when the games are already in full swing; I am like Rochester in not caring much for dropping hundreds of guineas on a handful of pasteboard when it can be livelier spent on wines and dinners. He and Mallet are there, as always, when there is a crowd to appreciate their wit: they both hold court at one end of the chamber, with Bucks and a score of lesser creatures laughing and listening; they sharpen one another like two knives – no matter what one says, t'other tops it, and then they emerge from the match glowing and invigorated. If I were called upon to be brisk in public thus, I'd fall on my face; I am like Etherege, in that it takes me a while to think of anything witty; then I go home mayhap to write it down – and, unlike him, get no credit for't.

I languish about, wonder what to do now I am here, and wish heartily that Buckhurst were back from the country. Ossory sits in a corner speaking to his wife, but so earnestly involved, I fear 'tis some private conversation that should not be disturbed. Some of the maids of honour are here, but all seem engaged in dalliances or sit to cards, as doth Mrs O'Hara, who seemeth not to espy my entrance: she frowns and purses lips over her hand, and her cheeks are rosy with a high colour. The King even plays with Grammont and the Hamiltons – a match which means he'll be e'en poorer on the morrow. No one has ever caught Grammont cheating, but 'tis prodigious odd he never loses much, that he supports himself at court utterly on his winnings and seldom e'en goes to the Jews. A few years ago he gifted His Majesty with that magnificent glass coach, whereat our monarch was mightily taken; but I believe 'tis the dearest coach anyone ever got.

I suppose my only recourse is to amble over and become part of Strephon's audience, tho' I am not in the humour for dramatical performances; and thither, first catching a footman with a tray of goblets, I prepare to go; but that I hear a voice call, 'Oh, Lord Ashfield!' I look about, to see Sir John Denham's wife. I wonder where her lover the Duke of York is; or, e'en more, her old jealous husband, that dogs her closer than her own shadow and makes Chesterfield's paroxysms look tame.

Despite such considerations, though, 'tis tempting to hark to a beautiful lady, and Lady Denham is one of the most gorgeous. She hath Temple's dark colouring but with a white skin; e'en more, she hath something in her cranium besides air. She is very lovely tonight, in a pale pink gown that showeth her plump white arms to great advantage.

I walk over to her; with a smile direct into my eyes, she touches my am. 'Are you free a moment?'

I acquiesce; but then she begins to drag me from the chamber. With a nervous eye cast about the throng here assembled, who (it seems) all eye me covertly and snicker behind their cards, I say, hesitantly, 'Is your husband about, madam?'

'No.' She smiles boldly at me. 'I have given him the slip; he looks for me with some friends in Greenwich. Come.'

Knowing not what else to do, I comply, goblet still in hand. 'Leave that here,' she orders briskly, and lets go my arm an instant, the better to seize the goblet and consign it to the passing tray of a footman. With a melancholy look, I watch it disappear among a throng of laughers, waving plume and fan; and with a look almost as melancholy, I mark how many glances follow our progress. Now this will be all over court, and I hope to God it will not end with a blade in my bowels.

Still towing me by the arm, she drags me purposefully through the outer Presence Chamber and thence into the cold, brisk night air toward the Privy Stairs by the river. She walks half a pace ahead of me, and I note how perfectly her shiny black curls are dressed, with the pink ribbon around 'em, and I have the fleeting desire to reach up and touch one.

All at once I notice she has dragged me to the water closet.

Now, I have been at court these four years, and I happen to know this water closet has been used for kind relief of more than one sort.

I look at her in surprise; for of the two purposes, there is only one for which she would need my aid.

'My lady,' I say, 'what is this?'

She replies, 'It is certainly not a water party, and I'm not about to push you through.'

She drags me from the small wood gallery and into the water closet; helplessly I hook the door. I suppose Rochester could be completely composed in such a situation as this, but I am about to faint from combined surprise and apprehension. I am the sort of man who needs to work up to these things; if I am taken unawares or apprehensive of discovery, I often go limp. Lady Denham is not the only woman about court who takes situations into her own hands, and this sort of woman has never failed to fright me. They all seem to believe that, like Rochester and Bucks, we are ready to stand to in a moment of the least provocation; that, indeed, we would be delighted at an opportunity to do so, particularly with a handsome woman.

She puts her arms about my waist and presses close against me, so that her whole body melts into mine; I put my arms around her and go into her mouth.

I can tell even from the first kiss that she is the most passionate woman I have had in a long while: she really seems to desire it, and her eagerness does much to dispel my lingering reluctance and apprehension. Her tongue works very urgently in my mouth; I work mine back, and before I know't, nature very willingly takes her course, without any apprehensions getting in the way. In a situation like this there is no time for long preliminaries: I fondle her breasts a moment, draw up her skirt about her thighs to caress her there; almost immediately she has me untrussed with one fumbling hand.

Now comes the problem: I have never tried to perform standing up before. I try to smunch down, she to climb up; and it wants a little adjusting and giggling (which I pray God no one strolls by to hear), before we manage to fit ourselves together; and then, as we hit against the wall, I am sure the bumping sounds as loud as the Lord Craven's drums; a curious swan even drifts around below and peers up at this strange cousin of his, the rational animal, in the throes of passion.

It does not take very long (nor can it) before we are smoothing one another's clothing again, and I feel a keen sense of regret: I suddenly realize I would like to know this woman and embrace her in my arms awhile and have her a better way.

After we have adjusted our clothing, I take her into my arms and murmur into her soft ear: 'What brought on this sudden fit of passion?'

She embraces me, murmurs, ''Twas not sudden: I kept sending you ocular messages – which you never got. The Lady Castlemaine told me I should seize the bit in my teeth, and so I did.'

I laugh. 'That sounds like her advice. I'm glad you took it; but I must admit, you surprised me.'

She nuzzles into my ear, puts her arms about my neck, and gives me a sop to vanity. 'You and Monmouth and Rochester are the three best-favoured men at court: let one of you walk through a consort or theatre in your velvets and plumes, and we all get sensations. But you seem not to know't the way they do: you never act on't.'

I reply, 'You flatter me outrageously: I am no lover.'

She kisses my ear. 'Only because you do not choose to be. You are, to say truth, the most desirable of the three. Monmouth is stupid;

Rochester, too clever. But you're sweet – mmmm, sweet.' She kisses my lips a few times.

Then regretfully we leave our trysting-place – no Bower of Blisse, i'faith, with the bitter wind wafting up through its seat above the river. She goes first; I follow shortly after. We have agreed to meet again when we can, but 'twill not be easy, with a jealous husband watching her, and the next King of England as her lover.

I cannot but be vain about the compliment to my charms; some of't must be true if she felt moved to assault me that way, having a lover already. As I pass the pier glass of black horn in the Presence Chamber, I cast a sly glance into its reflection. 'Tis plain I have not the insipid baby-prettiness of Monmouth, nor the spirits that draw eyes to Rochester's gorgeous face and person; but yet, my features are very well, better by far than Buckhurst's or Sedley's, and my person taller and more slender than theirs. The Devil take me if, keeping company so long with Rochester, I hath not underrated my own charms.

But coming again into the fair company assembled at cards, I wonder if something may not show on my face, for I see several people shoot me devilish grins. Bucks throws me a knowing look, Rochester a wink, Mallet a mischievous smile. Mrs O'Hara no longer sits to cards but stands to watch over the shoulder of Elizabeth Hamilton; and, regarding me with those ironic brilliant blue eyes, steps over to say, 'I see you stepped out for a breath of air, my lord.'

I adjust my neckcloth, wonder if I am blushing, sweep my hat nervously beneath an arm. 'Ah – yes.'

She looks at me still, a merry sparkle in her eyes: they are the largest, most striking blue I have ever seen, pale like watered silk and fringed with large black lashes.

She nudges my arm with a fan and adds, with a dry smile, 'Or to relieve a lady in distress.'

I look on her all melancholy; she bursts out laughing.

I grin sheepishly. I never know how to take Mrs O'Hara: one minute she seems so modest, I fear to take her arm; the next, she seems as gay almost as Mallet or Jennings. With her complexity of humours, she is certainly the most fascinating woman a man could ever meet – though, as Strephon never fails to inform me, I am sure she could be a tormenting one as well.

Part XIV

'The Threat'ning Danger'

Betty Mallet

27 December 1666 – 15 January 1667

As Amoret with Phyllis sat
One evening on the plain
And saw the charming Strephon wait
To tell the nymph his pain,
The threat'ning danger to remove,
She whispered in her ear,
'Ah, Phyllis, if you would not love,
This shepherd do not hear!
None ever had so strange an art,
His passion to convey
Into a list'ning virgin's heart,
And steal her soul away.
Fly, fly betimes, for fear you give
Occasion for your fate.'
'In vain,' said she; 'in vain I strive!
Alas, 'tis now too late.'
—Song by Sir Car Sroope, included in Etherege's *The Man of Mode*

1

'Anything Rather Than Be Married To A Man I Do Not Care For'

7 January 1667

Busy: What will you do, madam?
Harriet: Be carried back and mewed in the country again – run
          away here – anything rather than be married to a man I do
          not care for.
                                —George Etherege, *The Man of Mode*

Awakening in the grey pre-dawn, I blink, woollen-eyed, but I sigh 'neath the counterpane of velvet and thick wool woven. The chill of my hands and feet would portend a fire burnt low.

All at once something falls with a thud on my stomach. I shriek: is't a rat?

The heavy bed-hangings part, to let in grey light and a blast of chill air. On my chest is a black-and-white pup that licks my nose and makes me laugh.

I stare open-mouthed up at the tall, slender figure slouched in the aperture of the curtains and still garbed in the red waistcoat, gold garniture, and white puffed sleeves of our engagement the night before.

'Why, my lord!' I cry. 'Have you not been in bed yet?'

'Read my message,' he instructs.

'Message?' I stare at the squirming furball. Ah, but see: there's a letter tied to its tail.

My heart warming to think how he cares to be up so early to treat me, I fold open the letter, squinting in the murk.

''Tis too dim!' I cry. He snaps his fingers, and Susan appears with a candle in a holder, which he takes from her and, bending into my bed hangings, holds above the letter so I can read:

My Lady,
Being unable to crawl into your bed,
I send my faithful cur instead.
Not all I would, he'll do;
But let him wait on you,
And whate'er you may find wanting in my suit,
Be assured his kiss and love will do't.
Your humble servant,
John.

My heart expands and glows.

I gaze up at him through the dimness and respond with a special smile, to let him know I understand the quirk in his character forbids him telling feelings; and that I appreciate the wit and affection that sent the pup to do't.

Giggling as the messenger licks my nose, I drink in the signature, 'John'. He gives me permission, again, to use his Christian name; for I've not dared to since the day I pled it of him and earned such a cold response.

'But why such a nice present?' I ask.

With a wave of the hand, he dismisses Susan. She curtseys, straight-legged, but looks at me hesitantly. I nod. 'Yes, Susan, you may leave us now.' I suppose 'tis scandalous, but who cares? I've broken almost all the rules anyway; what's one more? 'Twas bad enough I left her orders to admit my Lord of Rochester at once, any time he calls.

With disgraceful and endearing familiarity, my lord seats himself on the bed. My lord? – No! I must not call him so any more: he's granted license for a nearer title.

He grins and leans his upper body over my legs, his arm making a tripod with the mattress on t'other side. 'I see you've not got yourself up as a Hottentot last eve.'

I burst out laughing and put a hand to my uncurled tangle of hair. 'No. We came in too late.' I look at him impertinently. 'You, I see, sir, have not been abed at all.'

Grinning, colouring slightly, he glances down at his suit. 'I cast myself upon the humours and fortunes of the town.'

I dare not ask what this admission meant: I know it means he's been with some whore.

'But why the gift, sir?'

''Tis New Year's, after all.'

So it is. I had not dared ask myself if he would procure me a New

Year's gift, and I yearned to buy him one yet feared to be thought forward.

'What are you doing today?' I ask shyly and hopefully.

'Sleeping most of the day, most likely.'

'Oh,' I nod and look down. 'Yes, of course.' I rub the pup's neck. 'He's sweet: how came you by him?'

'One of the King's dogs whelped. Being a royal bitch, she should have been called Castlemaine.'

I burst out laughing. 'But, see,' I cry, turning the plump-bellied sweeting on its back for an inspection. 'Your experience has failed you for once, sir. We've to do with a she here, not a he.'

He laughs. 'Well, I robbed the litter early, and for once in my life, had not an eye cocked upon gender.'

My face falls. 'You robbed it? And the King doesn't know? I'll have to give her back?' I thrust out my lower lip in a pout.

'No, indeed. I've been promised to take my pick when I would, and I decided to make my seizure a few days before the New Year.'

'I'm glad you did.' I snuggle the puppy under my chin.

'Sometimes a fantastical whim will seize me, and I must do a mad thing simply because 'tis mad. And so I decided, before I should go to bed, you should be up – with my substitute sleeping beside you.'

I giggle. 'Thank ye, my –' I start to say the formal honorific, then cut it off and look at him. We both laugh.

'Your squib, your firecracker,' he says. 'Take care, now.' Capturing one of my hands in his, he squeezes the fingers and stands.

'What? You're leaving?' I pout.

Still grasping my hand, he leans over and brushes his lips against my forehead. 'Yes, I came only to bring your puppy. I'm for sleep now.'

Sleep? If he must sleep, why can he not do so with his head in my lap? Why, for that matter, must he sneak off and filch from me all those hours that hang so heavy in my solitude?

Oh! That we were married now – that every hour, minute, second of his life would belong to me! We would never be apart.

He looks down into my eyes. I know he must be reading the desire on my face. Why did he kiss me as if I were his sister?

After staring a few instants, he leans down and grazes his lips against mine. Then he squeezes my hand again. 'Take care, now. Sleep well.'

He squeezes the hand once more, draws the curtain. Why did he desire me so little? I s'pose 'tis what happens to men after they couple with a whore. Oh, that we were married, that he would not have to resort to such filthy vessels of lust!

I sigh and cuddle down 'twixt the cold sheets, one arm about the pup, and soon we drift off to slumber together.

Later that morning I cuddle her to my breast as I peer out of the frosty pane, sipping chocolate and watching a gentleman cross the courtyard below in a new-fashion vest (long-waisted, black with white trim: a mode the King tries to encourage, lest we be too dependent on French fashion).

A large snowflake splats against the glass, then melts downward in a long, slow drip; another, being smaller and falling next to it, tries to trickle down its own path, meandering, but keeps being drawn by magnetism into the larger one: it fights and struggles a few moments, then the two of 'em leap together, and it is absorbed.

I sigh and wonder what I can get sweet John as a New Year's gift, now custom suffers me to make a small return on the scents, watch-ring, verses, and puppy with which he has stormed the citadel of me.

Emilia arrives this morning almost before the messages e'en, to apologize for her carriage last night; she says drink always brings out the argumentative side of her (as what does not?); that she has never liked John, for the wrongs he has done our sex; and when she understood he would be vexed with her for playing the prude, she could not forebear it, to needle him. She says also that she hopes Lord Ashfield does not believe her such a dreadful prig; but I say, 'What matter? He's a good-natured sort who cheerfully enjoys the rest of humanity for what 'tis, without censuring its little humorous quirks.'

'I know,' she insists. 'He is one of the best-natured men I've ever known – he and my father. I mean – I would not have him believe me some cold, insufferable prude.'

She colours, looks away, and then leans down to hold out a long, slim hand to the pup-dog, who trots over, tongue out and smiling, from her dishes of water and chicken with sardines.

Only half-listening, for wondering if 'twould be proper to give a jewel to a lover, I say, 'Who cares?'

She replies, still looking away, 'I value his opinion.'

He signed himself 'John' for the first time today. That's something. But then, he only followed my lead of asking to call him by his Christian name. When, I wonder, will he call me 'Elizabeth'? Or 'Betty'?

On a sudden I become 'ware of what I've heard. 'Ashfield's opi-nion?' Then I shriek. 'Emilia!'

She colours yet the more. 'Oh, Elizabeth' – and she throws me an impatient look – 'why must you believe everyone in love simply because you are?'

'So,' I return, with a roguish look and lift of the chocolate cup, 'now I know why you are afear'd of playing the prude. You would be caught under the mistletoe yourself.'

Susan has appeared to hand her the chocolate cup and grate chocolate over it; and, like all good servants, pretends to hear naught whilst she drinks in every word.

With a flush Emilia glances at her, then retorts, 'That is not at all what I meant. Come now – you have sense, when you choose to exercise it: did the Lord Ashfield and I behave like a pair of lovers?'

I have to admit they did not. But then, she and Ashfield could *be* lovers and not behave it nor know it neither, as humorous as they both are, he so languid and she so reasonable.

'You're the one to be concerned over,' she points out. 'You're the one who's getting everything, it seems, except a marriage.'

Indeed, 'tis true. My John and I grow closer by the day, and still I've heard no more of a wedding than a presbyter would of the Mass.

And so we drift through the sweet Holy Season, taking strolls down Charing Cross and through St James Park; making appearances at consorts and suppers, where we dazzle admiring throngs with our byplay of wit, and all the world encircles us and listens and laughs. I buy him some silk shirts with Venetian lace: at which he commends my taste, perhaps not suspecting I have observed his fine gear as closely as I have, nor got the name of his favourite shopman from Mr Etherege. We eat apple tarts at a shop on the Strand and bob for apples with Ashfield and Emilia. Ashfield and I crack heads over the bucket and laugh ourselves silly; we collapse on the seat of the settle together and point at one another and rally like old friends.

On the eve of January 6 we eat Mrs Doll's Twelfth Night cake with Ashfield and Emilia, and the almond falls to my lot, so everyone must do what I say all evening. My first command is that Ashfield must kiss Emilia, and both of 'em stare on one another, as dreadfully abashed as if they had been children urged to kiss slobbering Uncle Joe they've just met.

John laughs so hard he is like to split the seams of his new shirt. 'Come on, man,' he cajoles merrily, 'or never ask me another thing, when the plum of opportunity so kindly ripened –'

'Rochester,' he breaks in, with a fury unusual to him, 'an you stop not your mouth –'

'– lies rotting to be thrown to the resty hogs that gobble time.'

Ashfield slings himself out of his chair, his face flushed bright pink, and stalks over to Emilia, who sits hands claspt and head demurely down, her cheeks as pink as his. Then he reaches over and brushes his lips quickly in her direction – I think, grazing a curl or ear.

''Slife,' says John, 'what pallid ardour – must I show you how?'

With a mischievous look on his face, John arises, to perform the helpful office of friendship: at which Emilia shrieks, putting both hands before her. 'Don't you dare!'

I pull him down by the sleeve, and she cries to me, her eyes flashing, 'Elizabeth, I demand you cease these antics.'

But the antics continue. I make the mistake of thinking a dispute would be diverting, so I say, 'Now Emilia and my Lord of Rochester must discuss religion.'

Ashfield looks woefully on me.

But they are happy enough to collide, she needling him on his atheism and he citing Scripture against the upstart and pretending women that put themselves on a footing with men: '"Let your women keep silence in the church: for it is not permitted unto them to speak: but they are commanded to be under obedience, as saith the law." Look it up in First Corinithians.'

'Yes, but that speaks of church leadership. I only say –'

He smiles sweetly. 'Find me a verse on female equality, and I'll bless you for it.'

'You speak as if I had the Bible at my fingertips.'

'What, claim to be a Christian and not know your Bible?' With a droll look he tosses off a draught and continues, 'Proverbs: "A foolish woman is clamourous: she is simple and knoweth nothing."'

Emilia is the very genius of rage, to see how this heathen bests her in his knowledge of the Bible; but knowing not how to controvert him, she tries to shift the grounds of the argument.

'Well, of all the effrontery, for a man of your lordship's life to quote the Bible!'

'Would you not hear the words of your favourite, St Paul?' drawls my impudent lover, his eyelids drooping, to let down a screen of black lashes. '"Let the woman learn in silence, with all subjection. But I suffer not a woman to teach, nor to usurp authority over the man, but to be in silence. For Adam was first formed, then Eve. And Adam was not deceived, but the woman being deceived was in the transgression." Therefore curb your tongue, foolish woman, as your Scripture tells you, lest you suffer another Fall.'

Emilia flies into a temper.

'Well, I've heard the Devil can cite Scripture for his own purpose; now I know 'tis true! Does your lordship have the effrontery to quote the Bible to me, with the kind of life you lead?'

Seeing that she will ride her hackney down this particular road, John halts it with a shrug.

'Why not? I make no claim of being a Christian. But you do, and so I remind you of what you are supposed to believe. What? By the sour look on your face, I see your imminent recantation: faith, I am delighted to have made another convert to reasonable religion.'

Emilia, being unable to answer John, turns savagely on me. 'Do you hear what your lover believes? Woe to the woman he might ever marry: he'd keep her in utter subjection.'

John smiles sweetly. 'I? No such thing. Have I not told you I pay no heed to such superstitious canting?'

Throughout this exchange, I giggle 'most fit to burst; Ashfield looks so amazed he appears to have lost his tongue – he is as silent as Paul wished the women to be, and merely gapes like a good little huswife, learning in silence.

So with such communal frolic spend we the Season through Twelfth Night, but there are also sweet times alone. Some nights I'm not as good as I ought to be and admit him to my sitting room, and he undoes my hooks and laces, and the gown falls below my breasts, which he so plays with that the paps harden to hurting in the orange firelight; and I pull out his shirt to stroke the warm skin of his breast and abdomen (ah! so silky and smooth and dear it feels); and we grow so miserably hot with that and kissing, I can scarce fetch my breath and keep him – most of the time – restricted to explorations above the waist. Ah! – How provoking 'tis, how frustrating-sweet!

But the charmed season soon passes. On January 15 I get a dreadful letter. Then do I see how I've been casting to the winds golden grains of time that run steadily out.

2

'Many a Man does not Intend to Marry'
15 January 1667

> Many a man does not intend to marry when he is young. But,
> something he says is misunderstood and he finds that the girl is
> expecting him to marry her. He resists for a time.... Actually he is
> looking for a mama and the girl is looking for a father.
> —Laurel Elizabeth Keyes, *The Mystery of Sex: A Book about Love*

'Madam.'

Susan enters the sitting room, the silver tray bearing a message. I sit at the window, my hair done up in a velvet ribbon to a likeness with my yellow gown.

'Yes, Susan?' I turn round about.

'Madam, the post is come in, and you've this from your relations.'

The post – my relations – oh, God – a presentiment seizes me, and I'm almost frighted to read what 'tis. I stare at the folded paper sealed with red wax, and moisten my lips. The silver tray is cold against my fingers.

Letter grasped in hand, I nod. 'You may leave me now, Susan.'

She bobs a curtsey and (reluctantly, it seems) retreats to her chamber, but casting many a glance behind her. I wonder why she's such a mind to see what I've been writ from home. I s'pose her life has so little drama to't, she lives my doings vicariously.

With trembling fingers I break the seal and open to my mother's hand:

> Betty,
>   We are very worried about you here. It is not that you do not write enough: God knows, I'd not reproach you with that, for I know you're busy, though more letters would be welcome ...

A pang of guilt stabs here.

... But we're uneasy at some reports we've heard, that you are not keeping modest company: in short, that you have been seen, and often, in the company of that rascal Rochester: that, more, you seem to encourage his advances & look very lovingly upon him in company. *This must stop*, and to endeavour it shall do so, I am packing my trunks and hutches for a present journey into town, to give you the kind of supervision which God knows I never wanted you to leave off having.

The only good that's come of this, Betty, is at least *some people* that overruled me have seen the errors of their ways. I do not blame you, child; he's a notorious deceiver; I am sure, wormed his way into your affections and company; and I know you're well, Betty, for I trust you & know you still keep your innocence as well as your promise to Grandpa, not to marry without his consent. But indeed, that court is such a pest-hole, you cannot be too soon out of it.

My heart sinks into my stomach, thence into my shoes. I clutch the paper and feel the tears start forth. Oh, my God. What shall I do now? My lord unwilling to wed, my mama on the way soon. Nay, as the post travels less than 10 mile a day, she may be on her way already! Why did she write first? Why did she not simply surprise me?

The last of the letter answers my question.

I write, Betty, that you may make preparation for my arrival, be ready in your mind and your belongings for a trip out of that place as soon as we can convince His Majesty; & until then, I will stay with you. I also write, that you may know I give my commands, you are not to see the Lord Rochester again, except in such common company as you cannot avoid, at the larger parties & so on. I do not mean that you must be rude to him, Betty: but a lady knows how to put a cool politeness in her voice, a firmness in her denial, so that even a rake (in gentle company) will know not to press. This I ask you to do, dear, & am sure you will be obedient as ever; for know, Betty dear, your grandpa and I trust you.

'Til the roads clear somewhat of ice, there's no travelling for a gentlewoman; but I dispatch this by present post & hope to follow, as soon as circumstances permit, who am

Your Loving Mother,
Unton Warre

Oh, God, oh, God, what am I to do now?

Clutching the letter in both hands, tears streaming down my cheeks, I look down to the brick court below and see the small, rotund figure of Sir Charles Sedley strolling below, his periwig curling in huge cylinders past his shoulders, his legs strutting, his hand swinging a walking stick.

I pound furiously on the pane and yell, 'Sir Charles!' He does not see me; I pound again. Startled, he looks up. I make motions to him; he stares up at me. I point to him and mouth, 'Stay there.' He nods.

Whirling about, I yell, 'Susan, my cloak!'

Her eyes first wide, then veiled, she bobs a curtsey and flounces over to the peg where my cloak and mantle hang.

'Hurry, hurry!' I cry, donning my gloves.

She cannot quickly enough tie the string 'neath my chin; then I'm off in a flurry. 'Oh!' I cry, heading back to my window perch, where I seize up the letter, and then tear out the door, into the hallway, and down the spiral staircase to the ground storey and without, where Sir Charles waits in the Yard.

'Good day, madam,' he says. 'You look most distressed. May I be of service?'

'Oh, Sir Charles, thank God you're here! You must help me; I –'

Suddenly I make a stop and bite my lip.

'Oh – oh – forgive me, sir. I – know not what possessed me. It's just – I'm so in want of a friend – and – I saw you. 'Twas as if –'

He nods gallantly, puts a friendly, pudgy hand to my arm. 'There, there, now, little madam, have a care how you ruffle yourself. Whatever 'tis, I'll do what I can to help you: be assured. Should we be standing here? Shouldn't we go somewhere to sit out of the cold?'

I nod. 'Yes – if you please. Yes – that would be good.'

'Let us make for the Strand, then. We can take some tea or coffee, and you can tell me what's about.' He extends his arm and smiles, the corners of his mouth arching up toward the prominent cheekbones. 'You can also tell me the news, for you're the first gentle soul I've seen since I've returned.'

'Oh, yes!' I respond, half-heartedly. 'How was your trip?'

'The French are still French,' he reports blandly. 'Meaning: I'm only too glad to be back again. But come, 'tis you we're to speak of.'

He ushers me into a coach that he has waiting at the palace gate. A coach! He must be richer than my lord.

'Tis but a few moments' joggling to a little tea-shop on the Strand. We sip deep of the medicinal concoction and munch hot-cross buns, dusted with sugar.

'Now,' he says, his mouth full of bun, 'tell me what I may do for you.'

I look down at my steaming tea. Tears sting my cheeks. and the fragrant jasmine cloud heating my nostrils does little to cheer me.

'Read this, sir.' I hand him the letter.

He laughs over't a moment, then frowns. I know not what he can find diverting in such a tragedy: perhaps my mama's antique humours. But his face is entirely sober as he takes in the last of the letter and hands it me.

'It looks as if your cause is grave, madam. What will you do?'

I shake my head and stare down. The Chinaware cup of blue and white figures swims before my liquid eyes. 'I know not, sir.'

'You must show this to the Lord Rochester, of course.'

I look up keenly. 'Would that be wise, d'ye think? I mean –' I stare down and pluck at my skirt. 'I mean – he's in no hurry to be married, I've found.'

'No, I've noticed that also.' Sedley's face is pensive as he crumbles off a piece of bun. Our sudden intimacy has caused me to take note of his features: with those small black eyes and high cheek ridges, he looks a dough-man into which a cunning baker has plumped two raisins.

'Do you know why that is?' he asks suddenly.

I shrug, look down. 'I s'pose he docsn't love me enough.'

Sedley brushes his hands briskly together, hefts the teacup and sips. 'Many men have married more quickly with less love, lady.'

'Then what do you see? How does it appear to you?'

I hear myself using my lord's language. I have been with him so much now we seem two halves of the same being.

Sedley shrugs, sets the teacup down. 'I think he's simply marriage-shy, for some reason or t'other. I think he wants a good shove to get him over the brink.'

'Well, I've been shoving and shoving!' My voice ascends to a little-girl wail. 'And I s'pose I don't have enough strength, for I can shove him only so far, and then he balks like a mule and steps backward.'

'Well, mayhap you've not been doing the right sort of shoving.'

'I've done't the only way I know how – almost said the plain question to him.'

Sedley laughs. 'Ho! I'll wager that got a reaction from him.'

''Deed, it did – one I didn't like.'

Sedley shakes his head. 'Well, he loves you right well, never fear; but I believe him well capable of dancing the coranto about the business for some few years before he bows to the inevitable yoke.'

'The inevitable?' I ask hopefully. 'You think 'tis so?'

'Why, everyone that watches him but he knows 'tis so. And even one part of him knows it. He simply will not put his foot on the fatal slide down to the hell he knows gapes for him.'

Seeing my melancholy look at his figures, Sir Charles laughs. 'No, 'tis only our court talk on marriage, little lady, not what he thinks life would be with you. But he knows he must marry, to get heirs; and he knows you must marry, to suit your guardians; and he knows he would not see you the wife of another man; and he knows you both love one another. What he does not know is how he can bring himself to do the final thing.'

'But I don't understand,' I wail. ''Tis so illogical.'

'It's been a long time since I thought Rochester was logical.' Sedley sips blandly.

'But I always thought he was! So brilliant of mind –'

'Ho, he can talk a neat argument when he wishes. But his affairs are always in a muddle. He can be quite logical about everything except himself. Like most of us.' He grins. 'I can find out his faults pretty clearly, arrange his life for him. 'Tis my own problems that remain the mystery to me.'

I laugh. Suddenly I feel so close to Sir Charles.

'What shall we do, then?' I ask plaintively. I lean forward and rest both of my arms on the table. 'I mean – will you help me?'

'I'd like to.' He stares off pensively, then slaps the table. 'By God, I will. Why shouldn't I? 'Tis an office of friendship to him, to get him to take down the medicine that he knows is his proper dose.'

'I know not if I like being named a dose,' I mutter.

'Well, 'tis only more marriage talk. I mean only, 'tis a rare joke on a friend, to shove his neck into the noose.'

I'm determined I'll not resent Sir Charles's terms for my life's goal. If I'd have his help, I mustn't reproach his figures.

'Also,' he continues, 'I can't think of a better wife for him, lady, than you; for 'tis plain you love him dearly. You may even do him some good and tame down his rascally way of life. Nay, why not? I'll help you.'

'Oh, good!' I clasp my fingers together eagerly. 'What shall we do, Sir Charles?'

'Well, I'll have a talk with him.'

'Oh, pray be careful! If you push him the wrong way, he's like to balk and run.'

'Nay, I know how to push him. I may be able to get His Majesty to help me, also.'

I bite my lips. 'I wonder –'

Sedley's eyebrow goes up so he reminds me of Emilia. 'Yes, you wonder what part His Majesty will play in all of this. Well, so do we all. He's not been attempting you of late, has he?'

I shake my head. 'Not since my lord returned from sea.'

'Well, I like not that. 'Tis right strange. Usually, when he has his mind set on a woman, he'll not give her up easily. He's begun to look at Buckhurst's new mistress –'

'What, Nell Gwyn the actress?' I cry.

'Aye. So perhaps he's been diverted from you. More likely, I think he plans to take the two of you down like a brace of pigeons some day: a matched set, diminutive and golden-curled and witty.'

I gasp and put my hand to my throat. He laughs. 'No worry: our monarch is no ravisher. But I wonder mightily why he leans so lazily back and lets Rochester do the pursuit and wooing. I think I'll sound him out on the topic of the marriage, too.'

Wetting my lips, I put my hand atop my friend's. 'Be careful, Sir Charles,' I whisper.

He nods. 'Aye. I will.'

Part XV

'A Man Who Didn't Want To Love'

Robert Blair, Earl of Ashfield
7–19 January 1667

I knew a man once who loved, and didn't want to love, and this duality made him behave very badly.
> —Merle Shain, *Some Men are More Perfect than Others*

1

'Solicting His Affairs'
7 January 1667

Dorimant:	Call a footman.
Handy:	None of 'em are come yet.
Dorimant:	Dogs! Will they ever lie snoring abed till noon?
Handy:	'Tis all one, sir; if they're up, you indulge 'em so they're ever poaching after whores all the morning.
Lady Townley:	Pray, where's your friend Mr Dorimant?
Medley:	Soliciting his affairs; he's a man of great employment – has more mistresses now depending than the most eminent lawyer in England has causes.

—George Etherege, The Man of Mode

The morning messages bring word from Buckhurst, who hath scarce waited for Twelfth Night to leg it back from his rustic holiday of family cheer. His mistress Pretty Witty Nelly, he writes, wants his immediate attention; but he hopes to see me at play-time at the Duke's House.

Putting myself in the barber's hands and then in William's, I send word across the piazza, to Rochester, asking if he will dine at Long's; but the boy returns with the notice that his lordship is still gone, not having returned from the night before.

Here's a morsel of gossip, for I know he was bound for his lady's apartments, and not even Rochester could think of so many ways to kiss he must be at it all night. If she hath granted him the possession of her person, she hath made the most famous tactical error since Antony engaged by sea.

Deciding to eat alone, I take a coach; but no sooner have we trotted about the piazza than I spy the wakeful swain, alighting from a sedan chair, his last night's garb setting on him awry.

'What, just back from your lady's?' I yell out.

Startled, he looks about; I tap the coach top with my cane, and Andrew pulls the horses to a halt.

With one hand Rochester knocks at the door and with t'other, he motions me over. With nothing better to do, I open the coach door, Jack hopping down to assist me out.

'Wait for me,' I tell 'em.

But the proposed tale proveth nothing so intriguing; as I approach he leans over to me confide: 'No, but sitting with her long enough, and I was in no fit shape to go home unf—ked.'

So he's been at it again. 'You will f—k yourself out before you reach your majority,' I warn him.

The groom-porter finally sees fit to open the door, whereat Rochester scolds him, 'You lazy dog, were you half so brisk as you show yourself at my kegs, we had been in five minutes ago.'

The fellow grins, showing split yellow teeth. 'Aye, or half so brisk as your lordship at the women.'

Rochester chuckles and hits his arm lightly with a fist as we stroll in.

'Rochester' – I tug his sleeve – 'come with me to Long's, to dine.'

He is aghast. 'What, in my dirty linen and shirt?'

'I'll wait.'

'A bowl or two of something would not be amiss,' he answers; then, to a footman, 'You, sirrah: send some water up.'

'If your lordship please,' says the man, 'I've already carried some up.'

'Only a few days in my service, and you know my humours. What think you of a master who uses water as others do perfumes?'

The man, who is gawky and horse-faced and lean, stammers and stares at the floor. 'I – I know not, your lordship.'

'Tis plain this one, not being in Rochester's service long, expects a bullying rather than a jest.

'What, no opinion of your master? Though he keeps such silly hours and scours his mouth with herbs and sticks and cloth?'

The man looks down, says nothing.

'Go to! Tell me a jest you have heard below stairs.'

'Well – Mrs Doll said she's a mind to tempt your appetite. And one of the men said,' and the man looks up uncertainly, 'she served you not the dish you liked best; whereon she clouted his ear.'

Rochester bursts out laughing. The man grins.

'Here's for your pains –' Rochester tosses the man a coin. 'Tell everyone Mrs Doll may suffer 'em to play truant: I'll be gone until the morrow.'

The fellow shyly nods, darting a glance up and grinning. 'Yes, your lordship. I thank your lordship.'

'Get yourself a draught or a woman,' Rochester advises, hitting his arm.

We stroll across the entranceway of white and black marble che-quered, past the pretty pier glass, sticks, and table of silver and up the stairs to his bedchamber.

'Send Harry in to me,' he orders a maid-servant in the upper hall. She bobs a curtsey. 'Yes, my lord.'

'I hope you did not eat up all the tarts. Mrs Doll will scold –'

'Oh, my lord! Oh, why, your lordship knows I hate those gummucky things as has the walnuts –' The woman makes a face, her cheeks turning pinker.

'She eats up all the tarts,' Rochester informs me, 'and goes about all day with walnuts on her breath.'

'Oh, your lordship! You know I never – how you do worry a body so! Why, what will this gentleman think?'

She turns laughing and blushing to me, her chestnut curls tumbling about a round pink face, 'Oh, sir, 'tis a wonder we can get our work done, his lordship keeps us laughing so with his foolery! He'll come down in the kitchen and sit and carry on the whole night.'

'And she'll wait 'til no one's looking and then eat the tarts.'

'Oh, your lordship!'

They laugh, but I'm uncomfortable. I know not that 'tis proper, the familiar way Rochester carries on with his help.

We stride through his pretty dressing room of green and white and into the bedchamber where reposes the great bed, that, could it talk, might make its fortune in the 'Change telling what it had seen. He gropes 'neath the apparatus of green velvet hangings and coverlet for the chamber pot: being more cleanly than some of us, who take the easier shift of using the fireplace.

'Did you sleep any?' I ask, seating myself on a chair near the French window.

'Not very much. I broke in a new virgin but lately come to Bess's and took my leave just as the dirty dawn seeped through the sky.'

I mark with irritation how neatly he hits the target though at a distance, as though even in this minor art he must be perfect, but take comfort from the evidence I'm definitely larger than he.

He throws himself down into another chair and massages his eyelids as if utterly spent. Then he pulls the neckcloth off, and kicks off his satin pumps.

'I've never known Bess to take on a virgin before,' I muse. 'Was she frighted?'

'Weren't you?' he counters. 'Isn't everyone?'

He pulls the large billowing shirt over his head.

'How do you bust a virgin in such a place?' I query. 'Did you manage to quell all her fears? Or did you have to force her?'

The thought of forcing such a girl would chill my blood, but I know 'tis regularly done.

He throws the shirt at the bed, where it lands atop the periwig already there tossed; and, flinging himself up with an effort, stows the chamber pot beneath the bed again and makes for the basin of water.

'Forcing, the way you mean it, is the worst of all ways. No, Bess asked me to do her a favour, free of charge. It seems the girl had requested that her first time be special. She was shy at first but wanted only a bit of courting and caressing to become very passionate and willing.'

I watch him strip, then go about his tedious morning ritual of washing.

'How –' I hesitate, considering what to ask. 'How did the girl decide on this – course of life?'

I shrug. 'That's the one thing you never ask. The one thing I did ask, before I began, was whether I had her free and willing consent or whether she was being imprisoned or forced in some way.'

'Not at Bess's,' I protest.

'So I thought, but one never knows. She said she was sure and had asked Bess to choose a good lover for her first. Afterward she thanked me for being gentle and giving her pleasure.'

The social situation seems so fantastical, I cannot use my imagination to picture myself in it. I ask, 'How long did it take?'

He laughs, wiping his face with a towel. 'Why so many questions?'

I tap my cane against my foot. 'I may actually marry some day –'

'– and face that formidable beast, which of all others has most terrified you: a maid.' He grins. 'Be not so perplexed, Ashfield: just remember you must be gentle and slow. Raise her heat first, and then take your cue from her body.'

I shudder as he turns to the basin again. 'I will never be able to do't. Do they not bleed and scream and weep?'

He laughs. 'Not if you stretch 'em first and take care to get 'em highly aroused.'

I stare goggle-eyed. 'Stretch 'em?'

Having washed all over, he gropes for the towel again. 'With your fingers – you know, make the passageway larger to dispel the greater part of the pain.'

No, I don't know.

'I will never be able to do't,' I groan, and take a silent vow anew never to be married. 'I have heard such tales of tears and blood –'

'Obviously, from some oaf who just stuck it in, without the proper preliminaries.'

''Twas Mulgrave.'

'He's the type, ne'er stir: the more blood, the more glory, and all the better if he can hang out a sheet all bespattered with it the next day like some damned Italian.'

Rochester collapses on the bed and massages his eyes. 'Where is that damned Harry?'

'I could never have done't,' I lament, 'not to some poor little miss, the victim of some wretched social system –'

'She enjoyed't.'

'I could never have done't –'

'Ashfield,' he breaks in, fresh linen in hand, 'were you not well-looked, you would never get anything at all. You have scruples against streetwalkers, against virgins, against most servants, against ladies at court that look too nice or not nice enough. You'd never so much as show a verse you'd made, did the lady not invite you to her boudoir first.'

'I'm brave enough with the right sort, did you know all,' I protest; then pride requires a small boast. 'Not a week ago I grabbed a handy bit of enjoyment in the infamous water closet.'

'Who hasn't?'

But now Harry is pleased to make his tardy entrance, to be greeted with a volley of gibes.

'Where hast thou been, dining with the Cham of Tartary? A thief walks not more slowly to the gallows than thou dost to my bidding.'

'May't please your lordship, I was below –'

'– and all the furies of hell confound thee there! Fetch fresh linen and the brown with the gold garniture.'

Stumbling cheerily o'er to the hutch, Harry says, 'Your lordship would have laughed so, at what they all said in the kitchen. A man was come with another bill –'

'Aye, a matter for laughing indeed! How turned you him away?'

'As your lordship said: that they were to apply to the King, who was in arrears with your pension. But Mrs Doll threatened him so, with a ladle, he took to his heels running.' Harry chortles at the remembrance, his red hound's face stuck out with prickles of unshaven beard.

'Would she'd take a course with you.' Rochester turns to me. 'What's o'clock?'

'Just one. Is it your day to serve the King in the Great Banqueting House?'

'No, but I've promised to be at St James at half past two.' He scowls at Harry's slow progress with the hutch.

'Rochester, how can you be always at it thus?' I demand. 'I'm glad to the very blood I'm not the tutor had charge of you on your Tour.'

He chuckles. 'There's more than one grey hair the good man owes to me.'

'I wonder you never got a knife in your ribs. I know that all of 'em on the continent have husbands and brothers that take unkindly to such goings-on.'

'Latins are not as cordial as the English about sharing their c—t,' he agrees. 'I was fortunate: I was beaten a few times, but that's all.'

I shudder. 'That would be enough to turn me off such adventures.'

'To say truth, it was a spice to the meat.' By now, Harry has produced fresh linen, which Rochester dons. 'But, then, we all enjoy differently. Take Buckhurst.'

Interested, I probe, 'Yes?'

He steps into the breeches Harry holds out for him, then adjusts their fit. 'He cannot enjoy himself with aught but some trull or whore, and he craves 'em constantly. I warrant he had a cold mother and got his love from the servant girls.'

'Rochester, you're amazing!' I cry. 'To speak plainly, Lady Dorset is a very refined woman; she never saw her children but to have 'em in the parlour fully clad to pat their heads and send 'em forth again.'

'It shows. Were she more like the Duchess of Ormond, he'd have turned out more like St John Butler.'

Harry, having retrieved the silk-and-lace shirt from the counterpane, slips the garment o'er his master's head.

'What say you,' I ask mischievously, 'of a man who pursues every manner of woman, even whilst he courts a special lady?'

'What, you'd have me expose my craziness to you? No such thing: figure't out yourself.'

I watch Harry at his usual clumsy art of tying on the neckcloth.

'How can you juggle so many women?'

He answers, as Harry slips on the jackanapes coat, 'How can you eat a variety of foods? Each satisfies a different taste.'

I shake my head.

Harry having buckled on the sword, Rochester grabs up his cape and nods at me. 'Come on.'

We descend the stairs, where another maid-servant lingers in the entranceway, a pretty little fair thing, and pretends to dust the banister but casts a timid, longing glance up at us.

Rochester in passing favours her with a dazzling smile, halts to touch her cheek.

'Will you be in tonight, my lord?' she asks, her voice plaintive and eyes pleading.

'Sweet, I think not. Wait not up for me.'

He chucks her beneath the chin quickly, as one might do with a favourite dog, and she turns about to watch him as we pass through the entranceway. There's a servant doomed to be put away as soon as there's a Lady Rochester.

The groom-porter opening the door for us, I observe, 'Rochester, all of your women are going to be your undoing some day.'

'No doubt, no doubt. I must learn to sleep as my pintle plays.'

We hop down the stairs and cross the cobbles to the coach. 'You'll both have some rest next week,' I remind him. 'Isn't that your time to lie in the King's bedchamber again?'

'Yes, but who can lie easy on that damned pallet with the damned clocks chiming all night long and the dogs licking his face? I've had many a whore that was more soporific.'

Jack opens the coach door, and we settle within. 'At least you can seize the time to remind him of your annuity.'

'That, and some other things.' He stares thoughtfully into the distance.

'Such as Mrs Mallet?'

He gives me a sharp look. 'What would he have to say of her?'

The coach starts up, and I run my finger beneath my holland-band. 'Oh, such as granting you permission to marry.'

He settles back into the coach cushions and crosses one ankle over a thigh. 'Or asking his leave on when *your* banns can be posted.'

'*Me?*' I start.

'You are so cordial as to arrange my affairs: I can scarce do less, out of friendship for you.'

I hit his arm.

We take a private room at Long's, I to eat and he to drink, and the pictures on the wall to stare down at him for his unhealthy habits.

Anon he leaves for St James Palace and I, for the Duke's House, Lincoln's Inn Fields.

There, at the edge of the old Lisle's tennis court and hard against Portugal Row, I am pleased with the opportunity of handing out of her coach Mrs O'Hara, who hath arrived in a hackney. We stand about without the playhouse, enjoying a delightful brisk debate on the Ancients and Moderns, 'til I would fain repair with her to a box and forget poor Buckhurst, who no doubt awaits me in the pit after so many days without the comforts of my friendship.

She quotes a line or two of Latin, on a shift to support her side of the Ancients: which I strain to follow and lose. It must be the push and shove of the great crowd about us, the coaches letting off the fashionable before the Causeway, and the sauntering topers filing past from the Grange Inn; but a voice cries out at my back, with another explanation for my ignorance, 'Madam, he has forgot whatever Latin he ever knew.'

I turn about to see Shepherd and embrace him, though at the moment I'd prefer to cuff him. And though 'tis usually a dangerous practice with him, having no other alternative, I present him to the lady.

'Where got you your Latin, madam?' he asks politely. We stand apart to make way for the Duchess of Ormond and two of her sons.

'I studied with a tutor, my lord. Women are as capable as men to learn Latin: I was out of Lilly's by my ninth birthday.'

'Lord Ashfield never got out of it in his life: he cannot even conjugate *agricola*.'

Mrs O'Hara gives him an ironic look with those lovely pale blue eyes. 'Decline, you mean, sir.'

Now 'tis Shepherd's turn to blush red, and I have the luxury of laughing at him for a change.

'Lord Ashfield,' he scolds, 'you should not keep company with a woman such as this: she will make you look a bigger blockhead than ever.'

I am about to open my mouth to invite him to return to Knole when Mrs O'Hara speaks up, with an imperious lift of her head at him: 'There are more virtues than the knowledge of Latin, sir.'

Now I feel warmer than ever toward Mrs O'Hara, and I am about to make a compliment to her, could I but think of one, but Buckhurst appears. Tongue-tied, as usual in the presence of a virtuous woman, he bows, then embraces me. He pulls on my arm.

Feeling like Mallet led off by her mama, I bow in Mrs O's direction and watch her speak a word to Elizabeth Hamilton, newly alit from a coach.

'Where were you last night?' He pulls my sleeve and me with it into the reconverted tennis court. 'We came in late to the Twelfth Night card party in the King's privy chamber, but you weren't there.'

'I was at Rochester's. His lady came over with Mrs O'Hara.'

He eyes me shrewdly as we mingle with the crowd pushing in.

Shepherd says, 'According to the talk at the card party, you've been seeing much of her of late, my lord.'

Feeling myself flush from the baseless imputation here, I shrug. 'She's Mallet's friend. Mallet calls her the duenna.'

A man behind us shoves, then asks our pardon.

'Jesus, she has the character of one,' observes Buckhurst.

'If ever an effective shield were to be put up against Rochester's attacks,' adds Shepherd, ''tis she.'

I laugh, we milling through the entranceway. 'What, have either of you attempted her?'

Buckhurst rolls a protuberant eye at me.

'She's scarce our sort,' says Shepherd. 'But some have been working on her. She'll talk to a man, but only to argue him into her views. Once Sir Charles Sedley tried to kiss her, and she stomped his foot.'

I laugh heartily. 'There's a timely warning: I might have made the same attempt before long.'

We are in the theatre now. Buckhurst stares at me incredulously as we each flip half a crown to the doorkeeper.

'What? You?'

Shepherd flips his coin to the doorkeeper. 'The languid lover?'

Jostling through the crowd, we make our way into the pit. Buckhurst shakes his head. 'What courage!''

Augments Shepherd, 'The woman has airs about her that would put off Brounker or the Duke of York.'

I cast a glance upward toward the boxes – where, however, she hath not yet appeared. 'She is modest, but I've never noticed such forbidding airs about her. Once or twice, when we were alone, I got the suspicion she might have taken a kiss, but I don't know.'

'No, you don't know, indeed,' Buckhurst agrees. 'Nor do I. Busby had a hopeless job when he sought to beat anything into these noggins of ours.'

'You're probably i' th' right,' I agree. 'Rochester has almost given up on me for my dullness with women.'

'Stick with the Lady Denham,' he advises. 'There's ample angling there.'

He pulls me down to the places his boy hath saved us and, dismissing the lad with a smile and tossed angel, is rewarded for this unnecessary kindness by a broad grin and bow.

I cry, dismayed. 'What – has that made the rounds already?'

'You thought it would not? The two of you, as I heard it, going out together, and then the way you returned –'

'How did we return?' I ask, feeling increasingly melancholy.

Shepherd guffaws. 'She looked satisfied; and you, apprehensive. Knowing the characters of both of you, everyone guessed the purpose of your errand.'

I groan. 'Someday I will learn from Rochester how to control my face.'

He smugly pulls off his gloves. 'That is not the only lesson you could learn from him, I'm sure.'

'Nor you neither.' I dig his ribs; then, my eyes on the curtain, fall to sighing.

'What, in love?' asks Buckhurst kindly.

'No, we barely exchanged two words; but she's a handsome lady, and I hate to think of her married to that jealous old man. He was yelling at her some few days ago in the Great Stone Gallery, and I wondered whether I might be to blame for any of't.'

'The way I heard the tale of your amours,' Shepherd says, 'you were to blame for very little, my lord; you almost got ravished.'

I look at him drolly. 'Who told, the swan?'

Now we all laugh; they know very well what I speak of.

'The King had a very diverting story to tell last night, of how she yanked you from the chamber; he and the Duke of Bucks were laughing over't,' says Shepherd.

Buckhurst smiles. 'They said you looked like a boy being taken out to be whipped.'

I grin. ''Twas a deal pleasanter than that, I assure you.'

The music starting up, the crowd hoots and applauds: the rogues in the high slanted galleries fall to roaring and pounding their staffs, practising their catcalls and bussing their doxies; the gentle folk in the boxes below lean curled heads together to murmur, clap mincingly, ogle Stewart in the royal box gilt with the figure of Apollo. The pit about me roisters, shoves, pushes. Etherege grabs my shoulder from behind and, well in his drink, hoists himself up to stand on the bench at back of us and yell, hands cupp'd over mouth, a couplet from his comedy, *Love in a Tub*:

'And, gallants, as for you, talk loud i' th' pit!
Divert yourselves and friends with your own wit.'

Lounging grandly beside him, Bucks yells over the applause, 'For in the play will you find none of it!'

The crowd roars and applauds; Bucks acknowledges the homage with a few smiles and haughty nods. Then a brave push sends Etherege tumbling down among us, his coat flying; with irritation I push him from my lap.

Now he shouts from behind me: 'Gad, the hornpipe!'

A taking, pert lass hath minced onto the stage, the breeches tight across the two round apples of her little bum. I settle back; the crowd bellows approval, claps hands, pounds staffs and canes. Buckhurst sports with the orange wench, calls her 'sweetheart', refuses to give her sixpence unless't be sweetened by a kiss, &c. 'Twas this trade his mistress Nelly Gwyn plied before Charles Hart, the actor, discovering her many delights, put her on stage.

Two benches before us a ruffian smites another across the back with a cudgel, then stands guffawing at his own fine jest, called by the vulgar of the city *dumfounding*. The victim of this prank leaps forward with a shout to throttle him. Anon fists flying and bargains being issued as to what part of whom should be kissed, the guards start up to halt the fray. Further to the left in Fop Corner, a lady masked hath dared venture down here amongst us – sure sign of readiness for an intrigue – and a gentleman on each side tries raillery with her.

Along the edge of the stage the wax candles are lit and in the white haze the girl dances harder, her titties jiggling, her breeches pulled up tight in front into her groove. I lay my life, this part alone is worth my half a crown.

The orange wench hangs over me, the musk of her dangling boobs making my breeches tight, a pert smile on her blub-nosed face as she, rolling an orange across those two half-ripe fruits she beareth before her, purrs, 'China orange, m'lord?'

I shake my head, swallowing.

So cramped is this makeshift building (but lately a tennis court), the bodies here crammed make a stench and heat even of this cold, and I hear plainly in the nearest box, thrust out over us, how the box-keeper pleads with Ormond's son Arran, who is ever behind-hand, 'Please, sir, pay me now.'

The orange wench leans over me, towards Buckhurst. 'Now, my lord, I'd wager you'll have another.' Her skirt hitches up with the strain, and the sweat stands out in my armpits.

'That I would, Moll – and I don't mind if an orange comes with it.'

'Get along with your lordship now!' she cries above the cheers and applause, throwing her hands out in pretty appeal to the delighted audience.

The boxkeeper's pleas grow louder. 'Set it down,' says Arran, with an irritated wave of the hand. The man bows and disappears, with another four shillings to go on tick.

But now the hornpipe being done, the curtain opens upon the dullness of D'Avenant's *Macbeth*, which I care not for but have seen some half a score times, on this social errand or t'other.

617

'Is Mrs Nelly so important,' I complain, 'that you have time for me only at this wretched play?'

'He's just stolen her from Charles Hart,' says Shepherd.

Buckhurst grins. 'She said I'm her Charles the Second.'

I groan. 'You had better not play rustic at Knole too often, or there will be another Charles the Second. She has been supping with some of us in the King's company, and he's taken quite a fancy to her.'

'I have Rochester watching her for me.'

'You had better watch Rochester, too.'

'Everybody had better watch Rochester,' he philosophizes. ''Tis part of the price a man pays for his friendship. And Rochester had better watch the King.'

I digest this morsel, all through the silly spectacle of the witches in the Second Act as they divine only brief glory and death for the hero.

All at once Sedley sidles into place beside me and reaches over my belly to tug on Buckhurst's arm.

'Where've you been,' Buckhurst asks, 'to come so late?'

'To the palace. Have you heard about the Lady Denham?'

I tear my eyes from the swirling mist and death's heads on the stage. 'What about the Lady Denham?' I ask.

'She's dead.'

2

'Some Consequence Yet Hanging In The Stars'
7 January 1667, presently

Romeo: ... my mind misgives
Some consequence yet hanging in the stars ...
　　　　　　—William Shakespeare, *Romeo and Juliet*

The four witches wind in and out the mist, singing their hellish song; two, screeching, climb upon the machine which bore 'em down, to point where two death's heads, painted on the flats, merge with the image of a third yet indistinct. Thunder rumbles, and a blast of trumps echoes from the upper regions as the witches dance an ungainly and grim galliard.

Thy wife shall, shunning dangers, dangers find,
And fatal be ...

The noise of the pit clangs hollow against my ears.

'Ashfield.' Buckhurst shakes my arm. 'Are you going to be sick?'

I shake my head, though butterflies play in my gut and I feel all in a tremor, for a man is not to be affected by these things, much less show it.

'The case for poisoning seems strong,' Sedley rattles on blithely.

'Then there's two, counting the Lady Chesterfield.' Buckhurst shakes his fat chops. 'Hang me if ever I marry, especially a woman I love.'

I stand shakily, the bright images on stage gone suddenly dim.

'Ashfield,' cries Buckhurst, still seated on the bench. 'What ails you?'

Scarce caring what conclusions they will draw, I excuse myself and press past Sedley's knees. The witches exit flying; Macduff's family troops back to its chariot, digesting the prophecy of doom that hath befallen two cases parallel to himself; and, the second act concluding, the scene men draw over the flats whilst the musicians above begin to

619

play the interlude. Striding numbly out through the narrow aisle 'twixt the raucous benches, I brush shoulders with the poor doorkeeper, who warns:

'Sir Charles, you're only suffer'd an act's looking in; if you stay the third, I must have after-money.'

'The devil you say! I hath been here but these five minutes –'

I take chair to my lodgings, where I lie down, the curtains drawn about my great bed, and feel sick all over. Even though I knew not the lady well, we shared the most intimate embrace possible for a man and woman, and she was a lovely lady. Eventually, we might have had a real love; but now she is dead. I lie there tormenting myself with the notion that somehow my part in this business may have brought about the crisis. Denham may have endured a lover as important as the Duke but been determined not to suffer *two* men. Could there be any doubt he knew about me? Word of our amour had apparently got all over court.

I hear the wind beating against the cold pane, and I think of her beautiful sweet face and would fain weep – she was so young to die.

All at once the damned page raps at my door, whereupon I must needs wipe my eyes and ask him in. He tells me that Mrs O'Hara is below and would walk up.

The surprise of this last is almost enough to make me forget the other. Mrs O'Hara coming here unattended and unbid? The longer I know the woman, the more she astonishes me; I have heard Mallet tell Rochester she would never come to his lodgings unbid, and indeed compromises herself, so she saith, with the bravado of frolicking about unattended as she doth, receiving him in private here and there; and here is the lady that Mallet calls duenna and prude, the lady that Mallet abashes with her rattling tongue, calmly doing what Mallet would not think of with a husband almost contracted.

Knowing my bedchamber is scarce the place to receive such a modest lady (be she daring or no), I tell the page to show her into the withdrawing room and offer her some wine. Then I make shift to compose myself and straighten my clothing, hoping to Christ I look not as if I've been weeping. I much wonder what her errand might be, to draw her from the playhouse thus suddenly; no doubt she hath heard from someone in the boxes that Mallet and Rochester hath fallen out, and she would have me help her make 'em friends again: the tale hath been told, no doubt, how he swives his way across town, a habit not conducive to peace with one's lady.

When I walk into the withdrawing room, Mrs O'Hara stands to greet me, a gesture a little surprising; and then, looking me over with those large pale blue eyes, comes to the plain matter with a directness most unlike the usual coyness of females, that would be forced to say what they've a mind to say:

'I saw you leave the playhouse, my lord. Heard you about the Lady Denham?'

Now I am surprised indeed: of all the errands she could have had, this is one I would not have thought of. I wonder what her game is; and I nod quickly, hoping my eyes give nothing away.

She standeth very straight and brisk, like Rochester's cook-maid about to hector the help, her little hands clasped before her. 'I thought you might wish to talk of it, my lord.'

I can do naught but stare at her. With a hint of a lovely smile, she explains: 'I had a feeling you could not confide in any of your so-called friends, my lords: they scarce seem the type who would understand the affections of a feeling man.'

I nod, still silent, watching her; the smile broadens, and her eyes crinkle at the edges.

'If you would not talk, my lord, say so. But I am very conscious, were I in your lordship's place, I'd need a friend in whom to confide.'

I still know not what to say to her. There's not another woman at court would react thus; I feel I tread on alien ground and cannot get my bearings so much as to put one foot before another. A modest woman comes not to a man's lodgings, unless in great emergency; ordinarily I would assume, herc's a lady in want of a tumble; yet this is a woman who wears her impenetrable virtue about her like a suit of armour, so that everyone at court comments on her assured and honourable bearing; yet she marches boldly to my lodgings, without a thought, it seems, of how I might interpret her carriage. Then too there is the incredible purpose of her errand. If she believed me a potential lover, she would never compromise her position so far as to appear to pursue me; she would hang coyly back on all occasions and manoeuvre me (as Mallet doth Rochester) into making moves of my own: never would she acknowledge I might be moved by the death of a woman I had just swived; she would ignore the whole business or make coy comments as she did t'other night. On the other hand, were I of no interest to her, she would not have taken the trouble to be here at all and left a play she'd already paid four shillings to see.

I cannot make it out. But then, the most incredible part of the whole business is, she has guessed the situation aright. I am in desperate want of someone to talk to, and a man cannot speak of such things to his friends. But can I confide in her? I have never been able to understand her nor to make out her shifting humours. What can her motives be?

621

I stammer, 'You have guessed my humour, madam. But – I know not what I would say, nor how I would say't.'

She seats herself on the settle, smiles, and taps the cushion beside her with her dainty white hand. Feeling like a little boy with his mama, I go obediently over and sit down.

She looks at me keenly. 'Did you love her, my lord?'

I shake my head. 'No, madam: I had no dealings with her, except for that night.'

She peruses me with those keen blue eyes. 'But that would be enough, for a man of feeling, to experience pain over her death. I am sure you must feel dreadful just now, my lord.'

I nod.

She touches my arm with her light fingertips. 'Why don't you lie down here, my lord, and I'll get a cool rag to bathe your face, and some wine.'

Reluctantly, I object, "Tis scarce proper, madam, for me to lie down in your presence.'

'Oh, fie! Lie down at once; I know 'twill make you feel better, my lord.'

She stands up, pushes me gently back on the settle, rearranges the pillow 'neath my head, then calls for the boy – in a far more purposeful tone than ever I have – to tell him to bring wine and a wet cloth at once, and be quick about it. She hath that air of regal authority about her that causes him to obey instantly, without ever asking my view of the business. But indeed he can see I am her captive already: am I not lying down as she bade me?

Standing above me, her hands laced, she smiles sympathetically. 'How wretched it must make your lordship feel, to know a woman so intimately, then discover she has died.'

This prodding gets an admission out of me.

'I cannot but think, madam, it is partly my fault.'

'I thought your lordship would be feeling that way,' she breaks in. 'You're not the kind of man who can shrug things off lightly.'

The page enters with the rag, which she applies to my head, and the goblet, which she applies to my lips; but anon she leaves me to sip by myself and dismisses the goggle-eyed boy with a curt smile.

'But examine the case reasonably.' Her smile broadens; she fusses with the pillow 'neath my head, then stands hands laced again. 'What else could your lordship have done? First choice: you could have refused to leave the chamber with her. But your lordship would not so insult a lady: you are too honourable and good-natured; if she requests your services, you will provide 'em.'

Now I feel better already – nay, almost comfortable – and cannot forebear grinning. 'The service was done good-naturedly, but not honourably, I fear.'

She bursts out laughing, slides the cloth about on my forehead a bit. 'Very well: let us continue a reasonable examination of your lordship's alternatives. Having left with her on some unknown errand, as in honour your lordship was bound to do, you then discover her purpose. Here again you have two choices: to perform or no. Suppose you had refused to comply?'

I consider a moment. 'I would not be much of a man, would I?'

'No, indeed,' she agrees heartily. 'Your lordship would have been laughed out of the court as a fearful prig; no man nor woman neither would abide you, except perhaps the Lord Hinchingbrooke, and he is scarce congenial company.'

We laugh. She continues, 'I believe your lordship behaved the only way a man of honour could.'

I am surprised. 'Man of honour'? How so? I enjoyed another man's wife.'

She shakes her head. 'Your lordship responded to the desires of a woman who obviously felt in need of you; and by the happy look on her face, 'twas obvious you made her feel desired. I am sure that the Lady Denham had a miserable time of 't, with a jealous old keeper of a husband and an oaf of a lover. Your lordship gave her a little happiness before her death, and apparently did it gallantly. You neither played the prig, my lord, and refus'd; nor the rake, and exploited her afterward.'

I smile at her. 'I must have you around more often, madam: you raise my spirits to a wonder.'

Softly, she continues, 'Your lordship was reasonable enough not to go after a woman with a jealous husband but reasonable enough not to refuse a good offer when it came your way. You were honourable enough not to disturb her tranquillity by making an amourous attack yet honourable enough to comply gallantly when asked. I would have your lordship know, I admire you very much; I think you the noblest gentleman at court, and I will defy anyone to argue against me.'

I am stunned and happy. 'Madam, you are most kind, so perversely to misinterpret my silly behaviour thus.'

'Fie!' She crosses her arms and looks at me firmly. 'Your lordship is the only man at court who has both reason and honour. You merely cannot see yourself as others do.'

I sigh, snuggling happily down into the pillow. 'You have made me feel a deal better, madam, and I cannot but admire you for having the courage to come hither this way, to raise my spirits.'

She dismisses the notion with a contemptuous wave of her hand. 'Courage? What courage? How should I care what fools think of what I do? I knew your lordship would not misinterpret my motives. 'Twould not have been reasonable to sit at that play knowing your lordship needed comfort and not come here to deliver it. Are we not friends?'

I smile at her happily. 'We are indeed, madam.'

She pulls a chair up beside me, and we talk a long while more: I feel warmer and more comfortable by the minute. I had not realized what a gap I had in my life, 'til I saw how she could fill it. I have never been able to talk to anyone thus: I am always in the position of an adversary with my friends or the women I woo; but with her I feel there are no barriers. She is a very unusual woman in an age of coy jiltflirts, and I count it a very fortunate day when Rochester dragged me in to sit with her.

All at once she says softly, looking down, 'Do you know when I first heard your voice, my lord?' She glances up; and, no doubt seeing blankness on my face, says, her voice stronger, 'When you rescued me from a mob.'

'*Me?*'

'Yes, indeed. When the city was burnt.'

Cudgelling my brain, I recall the hired coach, the commands given by the lady with the firm voice and pretty hand.

'That was *you!*' I am amazed – then happy, that she should have seen me in my one heroic moment. 'Why, madam – it was but little –'

Then, as I silently thank Dame Fortune, the door cracks open. 'Mrs O'Hara's here!' cries Jane, joyfully. She scampers into the withdrawing room, then cries, 'What's to do with Uncle?'

'A small indigestion, my dear; he'll be fine presently.'

She shakes her head and says, like a small parson, 'Too much wine.' Then she grasps Mrs O'Hara's hand. 'Come, come, you must see my translations! I've done some real sentences from Terence and Cicero!'

'Have you truly? Already?'

'Mr Rivers found some easy sentences – ' She pulls on the hand of Mrs O, who scans me in concern.

'Go on, madam. She has been chattering about you ever since you left. I will rest here. Have her call my coach for you when you are ready to leave.'

'*Arma virumque cano!*' sings out Jane, tugging on Mrs O's hand. 'Know you what that is?'

'"Of arms and the man I sing": the opening of the *Aeneid.*'

'I told Mr Rivers you recommended it, but he said we could only do sentences for now, and he told me the story –'

But after she leaves, I grow melancholy again, thinking on the Lady Denham. I no longer feel personally responsible, the reasonable way Mrs O'Hara hath allayed my anxieties; but I cannot shake off a sense of foreboding at the way love always ends up in this court.

It seems to me, the only way to love a woman properly is with a man's whole being; yet those that give themselves over to such a passion always come to a tragical end. Here are Sir John Denham and the Lord Chesterfield, madly in love with their wives, great jokes that turn tragic. Here is everyone else, pursuing a round of pleasures and calling their business love: the sort of play that hath made of my life a wasteland.

Small wonder that Rochester balks at marriage. And even greater wonder, some fortnight hence, when I see who hath become its advocate.

3

'This Livelong Minute'
18–19 January 1667

If all the world and love were young,
And truth in every shepherd's tongue,
These pretty pleasures might me move
To live with thee and be thy love.
But Time drives flocks from field to fold
When rivers rage and rocks grow cold,
and Philomel becometh dumb;
The rest complain of cares to come.

—Sir Walter Raleigh

All my past Life is mine no more;
The flying hours are gone,
Like transitory dreams given o'er
Whose images are kept in store
By memory alone.
Whatever is to come is not:
How can it then be mine?
The present moment's all my lot,
And that, as fast as it is got,
Phyllis, is wholly thine.
Then talk not of inconstancy,
False hearts, and broken vows;
If I, by miracle, can be
This livelong minute true to thee,
'Tis all that heaven allows.

—John Wilmot, Earl of Rochester

For I find Sedley very hot on the topic when next the gang assembles to tope a few at the Bear, Bridge-Foot.

Some of 'em are dicing. Savile in a gold velvet jackanapes coat and scarlet cloak lets fly the dice, rattling o'er the wooden table, and they both spin to a halt showing six. A great roar goeth up.

Savile winks and tosses off a tankard. 'Ho, beat that if you can, my lords.'

Bucks shakes his head. 'Well, I'll try. Best two out of three.' He reaches out a stubby hand.

Sedley, leaning his meaty jowls on his pudgy fingers, gives Rochester a droll, penetrating look where the lad slumps, seemingly deep in thought, one arm thrown over the back of his chair.

'Methinks Rochester would not venture on a roll.'

Strephon glances at him sharply. 'What is't now, Sedley? Some new witticism on my life, I vow. Well, out with it.'

Sedley's little black eyes twinkle. 'I mean, your lordship' – he drawls out the word with mock solemnity – 'has become mighty cautious of late.'

Rochester leans a pale cheek on his hand so his near-black eyes cock at an angle at his friend. 'And what is this I'm cautious of?'

'Faith, that's what I'd know.' Sedley tosses off a bumper, smacks his lips, holds up the tankard. 'Landlord! Hey, good sir – another here!'

The man behind the bar nods briskly and catches at one of the women rushing by, her hands full of clasped tankards.

Sedley turns round to Rochester again. 'Nay, that's what I'd know when the prize you went to the Tower to steal is now within your grasp and you make no move to secure it as yours.'

Bucks exchanges a look with Savile and me, then says in a loud, haughty voice, 'Well, let's see what we have here –' He rubs his two hands together, the dice betwixt 'em. 'This way we magnetize it with some of our luck.'

'Better not get it near me lest it magnetize with some of mine,' says Rochester morosely.

Savile grinneth, fat-cheeked and moustachioed, upon the Boy Genius. 'My lord, we still await your reply.'

Rochester snaps, 'And are like to do so 'til Doomsday.'

'Come, come! What, i' th' sullens here?' chides Sedley. 'You've a beautiful young lady madly in love with you. And tho' you'd like as best you could to hide your affections from us, we know you've taken mightily to her as well. So what stops you from making all legal?'

Bucks throws a two and three and curses. Savile reaches for the dice.

'I haven't noticed you, Sedley, marrying every woman you've a mind to.' Rochester slumps back and glowers.

'Nay, one wife's enough for me. How could I take another e'en if I weren't surfeited with the business of marriage?'

'You are surfeited, yet you push me headlong into the jaws of the beast from which you are ever running.'

'Nay, 'tis not the same beast, by far. You've a real prize on your hands, Rochester, and 'tis mere folly to dally 'til 'tis lost you.'

Strephon shrugs, leans back, picks up his tankard and sips. 'I've no sign it's lost to me.'

'Cat's eyes!' cries Bucks. Savile curses and hands over the dice.

The red-cheeked wench puts another tankard before Sedley. 'That'll be fourpence, sir.'

He drops some coins into her hand.

'Why, thank you, sir.' She gawks at her treasure, and he reaches about to pat her rump, whereat she giggles and moves away. Savile and Bucks keep the game going, throwing high, then low; exclaiming and cursing, but not bothering to keep score.

Then at last, recalling himself from the distraction, Sedley argues, 'Oho! You believe she'll dally about these next few decades and wait 'til you've a mind to be married. Well, let me tell you this, Rochester: I've been hearing talk.'

'Talk? What talk?'

'That her guardians have got a whiff of your attentions to her. I think that little slip of a maid she keeps about her is peeling eyes wide and telling tales.' Sedley sips, apparently imperturbable, smoothing down his thick laced neckcloth with one pudgy hand to keep the ruffles away from the tankard. Then he gives Rochester a penetrating look. 'Now, close-mouthed as you are, only you know what the maid could have seen.'

Rochester colours and looks down.

'But the talk is, the mother is mightily on the alert, and dashing hither from the West Country as soon as ever the roads thaw a bit – which, mark you, they already do.'

Rochester shrugs. 'Mere talk.'

'Not mere talk, neither: I've heard the lady's been writ a letter, a maternal epistle, promising just that thing.'

'Who told you this?' Rochester's eyes are dark and narrow.

Sedley shrugs. 'I have sources. sir.'

'She has not spoken to me of this.'

Sedley leans back in the chair, drums with two fat fingers on the table top. 'Well, why should she? You've shown no readiness to be married. Why should she think that pleading this cause to you should move you e'en more? 'Twould only humiliate her.'

Rochester's eyes narrow. 'Are you and she in some sort of plot?'

Sedley holds out his hands in entreaty. 'Sir, would I betray my own sex and become compatriot with the natural enemy? And play cony-catcher against my nearest friend?'

Rochester grins sardonically, cocks his broad hat down over his eye. 'Aye, you would, and make a great joke over't afterward, too.'

The table rollicks with laughter.

'Come now, Rochester. Why don't you admit you've a mind to have her – marry her quick, afore the "skinny old witch", as you call your adversary, locks the lady up again? Think how you'll feel then.'

Rochester broods. 'Damn, but I hadn't looked for this yet.'

'Yet?' Sedley rolls his eyes. 'You're scarcely the picture of haste, sir. You've been dallying with her – how many months at court now?'

Rochester shrugs. 'The time seems to slip through my fingers.'

'Aye, well you may say that, with the fix you're about to be in, sir.'

Rochester's fingers trace patterns on the table top. 'If only you knew, Sedley, half of the problems that confront me.'

'Well, spit 'em out. Let's hear some of 'em.'

Rochester shakes his head. 'It's not so simple.'

'Well, I tell you what is simple enough. It will be damned simple when the mother gets here and locks the lady up again and forces someone like Herbert on her.'

'Herbert?' Rochester looks up.

'Aye, that's the current choice. I've seen the little snip of a maid whispering to him, too, and taking coin from him.'

Rochester glowers. 'I like not this.'

'No, I thought you would not. And even though 'tis not considered the part of a friend to push a comrade into the jaws of matrimony, still, where your case is concerned, the alternative's far worse.'

Rochester stares down at his tankard, drums it with his long, slender fingers.

'Now, come let us hear all your objections to matrimony, sir,' says Sedley.

'Well, to begin, I know not whether she'll have me.'

'Tsh! Tsh! If this is the sort of paper dragons we must fight, we've no problems at all. Come now, sir' – Sedley leans forward, a wry smile across his chops – 'are you going to entertain us with all your fears of success in courtship now?'

Rochester grins, shakes his head. 'No.'

'I'll be hanged on Tyburn tomorrow if she will not have you. Now, what are some of the others?'

'Cash, for one. My annuity's much in arrears.'

'Well, that's no problem that I can see.' Sedley shrugs. 'No one's denying you credit, I presume.'

Rochester frowns, shakes his head. 'No, but –'

'And no one's going to arrest you as a friend of His Majesty. Has someone threatened it?'

Rochester shakes his head. 'No, but –'

'But what?'

'Well, there are other considerations.' Rochester nervously turns the goblet around in his hand.

'Such as?'

'Well, there's the King.'

'And what about him?'

'I –' Rochester looks up, his eyes thoughtful, then smouldering. 'To say truth, Sedley, I have many qualms and fears and doubts on the score of the King's reactions; and there's a tangle here I cannot quite sort out, nor do I know I'd care to.'

Sedley bites his lip, looks down at the tankard.

'So. Have you thought to press the King at all on the subject?'

Rochester slumps back in the chair, drums on the table top. 'I – pressed him about it last week, but could not get much of a satisfactory answer.'

'So you think he will have you confined again, for attempting to marry the lady out of hand?'

'I don't know, I don't know. Nor will the damn'd King say.' Rochester tosses off a bumper. 'He's playing some sly game of his own there.' He slowly and penetratingly scans the faces about the table. 'I'd be much obliged if you gentlemen could help me find out what 'tis.'

An uneasy silence descends.

'Well,' Sedley saith at length, 'so the King is the only real block in your way, is he?'

Rochester shrugs. 'I suppose so.'

'Why do we not pursue him, then, at the card party tomorrow night? We'll all back you up and help you.'

Rochester shrugs. 'I suppose 'tis the best thing to do.'

So the luckless swain sails ever on through the rapids toward the port of marriage, with less and less tide, it seems, to hold him back, but now ever onward, on the top of the flow.

At the card party in the King's Privy Chamber, His Majesty in a white-and-gold-brocaded suit, his yellow plume nodding over his swarthy face with the nose like a ninepin, we huddle en masse around the royal chair; and Sedley, shoving Rochester forward like a mama with a coy infant about to do a recitation, says: 'Rochester has a thing or two to bring up with Your Majesty.'

The King looks up through the heavy piled feathers, one black eyebrow cock'd. 'Send them to me, Rochester. I'll tell 'em to issue notes against your coming pension but that you're not to be disturbed.'

Rochester shakes his head. ''Tis not that, Your Majesty.'

'What, then?' the King drawls easily, shuffling the cards with his skeletal fingers.

'I –' Rochester makes a stop, moistens his lips. 'I wondered – if Your Majesty still had a mind to see me married.'

The King pauses a moment in his shuffling – but only a moment – and begins briskly to deal the cards. 'I've no mind one way or the other that way, Rochester,' he says smoothly. 'Suppose you tell me what *your* mind is.'

Rochester looks unhappily about the circle of our faces; Sedley pokes him from behind.

'Your Majesty, I scarce know what my own mind is, but my friends seem to have made it up for me.'

'Mine did the same,' says the King, 'when I came to be married.'

The toadies at the table laugh uproariously.

'Well said, Your Majesty!'

'Well said!'

The King's eyes twinkle. 'Your friends have a worthy candidate in mind, I assume,' he says drily, arranging the cards in his hand.

Rochester nods.

'Well, I know not that you need my blessing.'

'I do, Your Majesty, if I'd avoid a nuptial night alone in the Tower.'

'Oho,' says the King, his brows arching up and eyes shifting toward Rochester, ''tis that one, is it? Well, I cannot pretend to be much surprised.' He looks down at his cards, rearranges them, frowns, and waves a hand at Rochester. 'As you please. I'll not say you nay.'

'Your Majesty will not enforce the law against abductions?'

'Oh, *prisca fides*, Rochester. If the two of you go off together of a morning, accomplish the thing, and then consummate it –' the King looks drily at Rochester '– which I'm sure you'll not be slow in doing ' – the table titters again – 'the law against abductions cannot apply. The husband cannot be arrested once the thing has been done.'

Rochester wets his lips. 'I may also hope for some promise of additional support from Your Majesty?'

The King negligently waves his hand. 'Yes, I'll take on Hawley if that's what's bothering you.'

'I thank Your Majesty. More tangible support would be welcome as well.'

The King sighs. 'Back to the same old topic, I see.'

He grimaces o'er his cards, throws one down on the pile before him, and Grammont takes the trick. 'But I suppose we could find some post or other for the new Lady Rochester. We will also see about getting a trickle of gold to come your way from your pension and a post for you in the Bedchamber.'

Rochester bows. 'I thank Your Majesty.'

Sedley breaks in, 'Your Majesty, the mother is on her way to town, and they must needs marry quickly, without the banns.'

'That can be arranged.'

Rochester bows again. 'I thank Your Majesty.'

'You've done an almighty lot of thanking me,' says the King drily. 'I haven't heard you so sweetly compliant in the thirteen years I've known you.'

The table tittering again, Rochester flushes hot, opens his mouth, then shuts it again. At last he says, in measured tones, 'I was not sure what plans Your Majesty had for the lady.'

They both stare at one another – a long, uncomfortable, calculating look on each side, 'til the silence about the table hangs ominous.

At last the King turns back to the cards. 'Who leads?' he says cheerfully, then gives Rochester a penetrating sidelong look.

Part XVI

'Give Me My Romeo'

Betty Mallet
25–29 January 1667

Juliet: Gallop apace, you fiery-footed steeds,
... Hood my unmann'd blood, bating in my cheeks,
With thy black mantle; till strange love, grown bold,
Think true love acted simple modesty.
... Give me my Romeo; and when he shall die,
Take him and cut him out in little stars,
And he will make the face of heaven so fine
That all the world will be in love with night
And pay no worship to the garish sun.
          —William Shakespeare, *Romeo and Juliet*

1

'Sir Walter Enjoying His Damsel One Night'
25 January 1667

Sir Walter enjoying his damsel one night,
He tickled and pleas'd her to so great delight,
That she could not contain t'wards the end of the matter,
But in rapture cried out,
O, sweet Sir Walter! Oh, switter swatter!

—Henry Purcell

When he finally asks for my hand, he makes of the proposal a joke.

No passionate vows – no declarations of love – but, in the midst of a mad towsing and tumbling across my bed – my petticoats flying, our bodies pressing hard – amidst giggles and kisses and shrieks, gropes and rubbings, he says:

'Well, I suppose you'll have to marry me – since it's plain you're not going to have me any other way.' My heart stops.

In the golden glow of candlelight, I stare up at his grinning face, hovering above mine, and my fingers dig into his shirtsleeve. We've stopped in tableau, his leg slung o'er my thigh, my skirts hiked up.

My voice trembles as I say, 'Do you mean it?'

'Think you I say what I don't mean?'

'Every moment you breathe.'

To my tone – kittenish, coy, railing – he makes a quiet and serious reply. 'Not this moment.'

'So.' I follow his early lead and speak lightly, *à la mode*, rather than opening true feelings. 'Are you to make of me not only an honest woman but a countess?'

'Aye. And no doubt, within a week thereafter, a penitent.'

I snuggle into his arms. 'And what am I to repent, sir? Becoming both countess and wife to the man I adore?'

He laughs. 'How can the world bear the contradiction, that a countess should be in love with her husband? You must never fright and amaze the crowd by any demonstration of affection to me.'

'I shall be very grave and polite – and not kiss you immoderately in the public view, and hold your arm only when I am beside you.'

He booms out with a great laugh and flops down beside me to hug me to him. 'Good! I'd not have my wife be too immoderately fond before others. Only a few kisses now and then, of course, to make Sedley and Buckingham grind their teeth over the bed that they're not in.'

'And,' I say coyly, 'don't think that I'll praise you before others too much, for your taste in wines and garb; your gentle, expert touch; your wit; and your surprising sufferance of my freedom.'

'Nay, why that? There's so many other things to praise me for.'

I pinch his ribs.

'But you,' he says, 'must not quarrel with me when I lie not in your lap all day and hum you love tunes; for I think we're loving one another best when we each love our own souls and freedoms first. And the same for you –' He grins, and his eyes crinkle '– my lady. I swear, I'll ne'er ask you where you're going –'

'Or where I've been,' I break in, laughing.

'Nor what you've done there. For my trust in you will be heart to heart and not a bond to be laid down by lawyers.'

My heart warms and swells at this rarity: a marriage contract arranged not by articles and clauses but by trust and affection.

'So we have agreed. Now let us seal it.'

He leans over me for a sweet kiss. A different bargain, oh careful mother, than thou wouldst have made with thy lawyers!

He breaks away with a wicked laugh. 'So, we're married now.' His hand slides down my thigh.

I catch it and smile pertly. 'Or so you'd like me to believe.'

'But have we not made our bond and contracted?'

'We have, but there's the legal seal to be set upon it yet.'

'The legality's here,' he protests in a voice oh-so-innocent, 'if the bond is.'

'Aye, so gentlemen say, to women who end up being deceived.'

I've heard that a contract and consummation will stand up in court, but why put an uncertainty to the test?

'Very well,' he says with an air of mock resignation. 'What would your honour have me do? Decide: I'm in your hands.'

I pout at him. 'Only to make it legal.'

'Tell me where.'

'St Pancras, on the morrow.'

'On the morrow, wench! I must needs get a licence first. '

I pout the more. 'Are you not intimate with the King?'

'Very well. I will see if we can waive the license. I will tell him I was abducted – borne away by a will stronger than mine.'

We laugh.

I grin pertly up at him. 'Did you not first abduct me?'

'I taught you a lesson that you should give it back to me. But now, what say we seal our bargain?'

His hands work deftly at my hooks; I push him off a little. 'This is too hot for me –'

'I think not, sweet maid.'

He pulls me nigh him, nestles into my neck, and eases me into him, his hand against my rump. I sigh and press against his delicious hardness, and we kiss a long while, our mouths open, and his hand swirling my pap n'eath the opened bodice.

'Nay, no more,' I protest weakly.

He pulls me tight against him, and we continue to kiss hotly. My skirt has ridden up my thighs, and as his fingers trail along the flesh, it quivers. I press against him and sigh.

His hand keeps pushing me at the rump, close into him. It has been a long while since I've suffered any touching below the waist. But now my hands go round him as if I'd melt my body into him. His other hand behind me fumbles with my laces.

'No,' I say. But still I feel him fumble. 'No,' I say again.

He pulls me close then and starts working the skirt further up. I pretend to ignore the ploy 'til 'tis on the edge of disaster; then I feel him shift about.

Oh, God. He's undoing the buttons of his breeches. With a hand to his hip, I hold him off.

'No,' I whisper, putting a firmness in my eyes and voice. 'Not 'til after.'

He sighs and pulls me to him again. 'Well, I know not whether 'twill be tomorrow. But I tell you this, wench: 'twill be soon.'

I burst out laughing.

'And in the interim look for a new woman.'

I stare wide-eyed at him. 'A new woman? Why?'

'This one's been betraying you to your relations.'

My face flushes hotly. 'Oh God! What's she said?'

He shrugs. 'Ask her. I only know she's been taking coin from Herbert, writing to your friends in Somerset. '

'Oh, God! But why?'

Bitterly I recall all my little kindnesses to Susan: the gifts of money and gowns, the afternoons and evenings off.

'Probably, because she's doing the job she's paid to do.'

'John,' I whisper, looking up sombrely, 'let's not be too long about it.'

'We won't. I'll let you know soon. Truly.'

2

'At Once The Wife Of A Man You Adore – And A Countess!'

29 January 1667

'You may well be frightened, my dear,' said she, ironically; 'for really there is something mighty terrific in becoming, at once, the wife of the man you adore – and a countess!'

—Fanny Burney, *Evelina*

The coach bounces me hard within the road ruts, bounces in and out of the kennel carrying the street refuse, and I am dazed, disbelieving, all the world around me a white fuzz.

That other coach ride flashes on me – oh, seemingly centuries ago! – when I believed he was carrying me off to be married and my journey ended in such despair.

But this time my dreams have come true.

I glance slyly over at him, where he sits on the coach seat beside me. He's withdrawn and quiet, slumps in the corner, his chin rested upon his hand as if I carried him off to be executed.

But was't not *he* that asked for *my* hand? Did I not ask him if he was sure?

One part of me almost longs to ask him, 'My lord, are you sure you'd marry me?' But I dare not, for fear he'll say, relief in his eyes, 'No, I'm not sure: let's hold this off.' I dare not risk such a danger, now that I've brought him so far; for as I lean my head out the window, I can feel the air less sharp; and I see the snow turn to slush and the ice melted to black, slippery goo.

I wonder whose coach this is, then think how beautiful he looks, clothed in white from his satin pumps to his plumed hat, and his ferrandin cloak and jackanapes coat edged in curlicues of gold braid. I stare at the gold repeated in the delicate embroidery of his pumps and gloves, in the tassel caught just below the knee at his breeches band.

That black periwig makes his eyes so dark against his pale face. Such a contrast he is, of light and dark.

Pensively I stare down at my ivory satin gown and pumps.

All purity are we, for a fresh beginning.

We joggle down Fleet Street, through the grey heaps of rubble from the fire and over the nasty, brackish stream in the Fleet Ditch, thence 'twixt city walls at Ludgate, with its mythic statues of King Lud and good Queen Bess. Up Ludgate Hill and about St. Paul's Churchyard, we see the sad remains of St Paul's, a great shell of roofless stone and molten lead, the Inigo Jones portico of columns bravely supporting gaunt triangles and flying buttresses with no innards.

Then we make left behind St Paul's and cross the intersection of Cheapside, where the taverns were, and Paternoster Row, whither the booksellers and stationers have moved since the fire, to joggle left again toward Aldersgate.

A string of churches do a lucrative business in irregular marriages, and two of 'em – Covent Garden and St James, Duke's Place – are close to Whitehall. But were Mama to thunder into Westminster and hear of our elopement, those would be the places she'd look. She'd never think of St Pancras.

The coach suddenly jostles to a halt, and my lord springs from his side afore the footman can help.

I, however, await the ceremony of the door being opened and steps folded down and liveried arm proffered. Then I meander round the back of the coach, to join my lord. His face is strained as he darts a look at me and pulls on his gloves. His whole carriage screams, 'I would not go through with this, now we've come to the point.'

I smile weakly, hold out my hand as if all were well; and arm and arm into the chapel we go.

As the parson here will marry any couple during the canonical hour (that is, the hours before noon), there's a spousal pair ahead of us, having hands joined whilst the busy officiator pronounces the final vows over 'em. They smile at one another – and the man heart-whole, it seems, more than this shaky swain I have with me.

He's contrived to shake off my hand already, so we walk up the aisle without touching; and at the inquiring look of the parson, who has a long black vestment with a short white top, my lord says, in a quiet and strained voice: 'The Earl of Rochester. I dispatched a note round to you from His Majesty.'

The man immediately brightens. 'Oh, yes, my lord, yes. I've the note – and I thank you very much for the handsome sum. All will be in order, I'm sure.'

This busy marriage-maker already has the prayer book open and must only thumb back a few pages to begin re-reading the service at tongue-tripping speed. Methinks this victory is hollow. For he rushes through – his eye no doubt on the next couple, whom I've heard rustling and murmuring behind us; and my lord mutters his replies, as if a schoolmaster quizzed him on some puzzling translation.

I work to put a meaning in the experience by smiling, saying my responses passionately as I gaze upon his face; but he will not look at me: only stares grimly, straight ahead, as if at his doom.

Jesu, this parson must run 'em through like lambs to slaughter. For we're barely done when the next couple steps up behind us and says, 'Johnson. We're appointed for three quarters past eleven.'

'Ah, yes.' The handy husband-maker consults his watch, drawn out from beneath his robes. 'Early. Well, step up.'

And so we slink off, more like from a judgment at court than a wedding.

'Well, let's back to my lodgings now,' he says abruptly, and stalks before me out of the church, not even holding my arm. I feel ready to burst into tears. Is this the dream I've waited for for so long?

Was't wrong of me to ask Sir Charles to compel him? No, surely not. I know he loves me. 'Tis the yoke that frights him, but 'twill grow easier with time.

If he didn't love me, why did he marry me?

He climbs once again into the coach, leaving me to the graces of the footman on t'other side. We huddle in our separate corners for the journey back through the fire-ravaged streets.

The vendors' cries go up: '*London Gazette*! Strawberries, fresh strawberries!' The coach wheels jar into ruts and spray mud up onto passers-by. With much shouting and fist-shaking, we lock wheels with a brewer's cart.

I'm almost in tears. A dozen times I verge upon saying to him, 'Well, will you not at least put your arm about me?' But I will not so shamefully beg for love.

So we ride in silence and at last pull into Covent Garden piazza. Abutting the square ahead and to our left are the colonnades, where fruits are sold and bills stuck up for plays and nostrums; at the side of this square behind us is Inigo Jones' four-columned chapel; and at its right, across the piazza from us, the walled gardens of Bedford House, which fronts the Strand.

We jog half the piazza's length and then left through the first colonnade and into James Street, to my lord's.

'Tis a more sedate street than the one that boasts Long's ordinary and Will's coffee house – but still, Mama would faint that I live in the dreaded Covent Garden. The whores of Long Acre Street are not two blocks to our right; the infamous Cock Tavern of Bow Street (Oxford Kate's, where Sir Charles and Lord Buckhurst did their naked sermonizing) is on the other side of the piazza; and this is not to mention the theatres. Bridge's Street, Drury Lane, is but a few blocks hence; and Lincoln's Inn Fields, but three long blocks or so past Drury Lane. So, for miles about the formal piazza, all is laid out for the pleasure of the fashionable.

We halt in James Street, before a familiar new-fashion four-storey house. This time my lord does walk round the coach to stand beside the footman opening the door and put out his hand for me to take. Has he resigned himself to his fate – or does he know that the help watch from the house?

The coach – whoever it belongs to – then starts up and joggles off. We step up the stairs, he holding my hand and helping me. But at the top of the stairs he drops my hand again and bangs with the new-fashion knocker.

A red-faced groom-porter, a snaggle-toothed and grinning fellow I've not met, opens the door. 'Welcome home, my lord.' Abruptly my new husband gestures toward me. 'This is your lady.'

'Most pleased, most happy to meet you, my lady.' The wizened figure bows so low he looks hump-backed.

I stand, uncertain; my lord reaches out to capture my elbow and gives me a gentle push before him, inside. He then releases me as we stand on the black-and-white-checked floor of the alcove.

He looks on me uncertainly. 'Well? What would you do? Have somewhat to eat? We can get Doll to –'

I stare up at him and shake my head. He looks down into my pleading eyes, and for the first time today he breaks into a grin.

Then he turns round to the groom-porter and a handful of footmen that lounge back in the hall. 'Mind you see that we're not disturbed.'

They smile and nod. 'Aye, my lord.'

One of 'em says, 'Mrs Doll may be that vexed, my lord: she had a wedding breakfast –'

'Well, we'll make it a wedding dinner. My lady would see her new quarters – and they require much exploration.' He grins outrageously, so I blush, look down and bite my lips before the strange men – who, thank God, have the charity to smother their merriment into indulgent smiles.

Where have I got my boldness? How can I think of desiring him when 'tis barely noon? But want him I do – very much.

We walk slowly up the stairs together; and, with his hand on my elbow, he pushes open the door to his bedchamber, the one done in green, and ushers me in gently.

With a soft voice, I murmur, 'I have no woman to undress me.'

For Susan has just been dismissed, with coin to secure her journey back to Bridgwater.

'I'll be your woman.' He smiles and undoes the ties of my mantle, his fingers gently rustling against my throat.

Suddenly I'm 'ware of how much light there is in the room, and I blush as he pulls off the cloak. Then a knock on the door startles me.

As he opens the door, I hear a female voice murmur, 'Is there anything you'd have, my lord?'

'Yes, privacy. See that you keep everyone away from the upstairs hall for the next hour or two.'

'Aye, my lord.'

As he closes the door again and turns the key in it, I've a queer feeling of how unlike the usual marriage ceremony ours is. Had we been wedded the usual way, we'd have first signed contracts drawn up by our friends and their lawyers and set a seal to how much dowry I would bring him and precisely what lands would go to him and how. Then the banns would be read some three Sundays in a row, and we'd have had a ceremony at Westminster Abbey with all the world watching, then a whole day full of dining and puppetry and plays and music; and finally, clear into the night, the ritual of putting the bride to bed whilst, laughing and blushing, I'd been conveyed 'twixt the sheets by my ladies and he'd been brought in by his men, to climb in with me; and everyone would have made the customary raillery and bawdy jokes as we sat abed together in our night clothes. Then the men and maids would have stood, backs to the foot of the great bed, and thrown the socks over their shoulders for good luck, and the men would have kissed me, and the women, him.

But this strange solitude and silence – I know not whether I like it. 'Tis an odd feeling, his simply joining himself to me rather than two estates and families making a social congress under the eyes of the world.

Slowly, gently, he takes me into his arms and kisses me – a few soft nibblings first, with his lips together – and then, as I strain toward him and open my mouth, a more passionate encounter, our tongues working. He embraces me and murmurs, 'Turn about.'

I do, and he works down the hooks on my back. I feel the gown gape open and, suddenly shy, I put my hands up to catch the garment afore it falls down. I feel gentle fingers unlace my busk in back, then massage my shoulders from behind.

He murmurs, 'Would you be more comfortable removing your garments yourself and slipping into bed to wait for me?'

I nod. He squeezes my shoulders, then steps through the French doors onto the balcony and into the room next door.

Hurriedly, I let the gown fall to the floor, pull off the tight busk, slip my petticoat down, kick off my shoes; and, sitting naked on the side of the bed, pull off my garters and long white stockings – all in a matter of seconds. Then I whip beneath the covers and proceed to wait a long age for him.

At last he returns through the French doors, closes 'em; and, smiling, begins to divest himself of his gear. He throws his broad plumed hat at the chair, pulls at his cuffs, tosses the jacket atop the hat, kicks off his shoes, pulls the billowing white shirt over the top of his head – and the periwig falls off with it.

I giggle, to see him the first time unwigged. For he has long, luxuriant, dark hair – almost black – and wearing a periwig's a mere affectation in him, his own hair is so beautiful. Not like my old grandpa, whose pate is bald.

He sits down on the edge of the bed, to pull off his hose; and I muse, giggling, 'I'd always wondered whether gentlemen's hair was short beneath their periwigs.'

He turns half toward me and grins. 'For most it is, but I'm too vain to have my locks cut.'

'Also,' I say pertly, 'you are frequently required to appear socially in dishabille.'

We laugh, and I feel more comfortable.

I sit up, sheet clasped to breast, admiring the long white slope of his back. As he stands to pull his breeches off, he turns slightly toward me, and I notice what a beautiful breast he has: lean, hairless, white, lightly muscled. Just the way I thought 'twould look from the times I've reached under his shirt to caress him.

But then, as he fumbles with his breeches buttons, I turn away, shy.

A movement of the mattress indicates he's here beside me, 'Afear'd?' he asks softly.

I turn back toward him. 'A bit.'

'We'll go slowly and stop whenever you're uncomfortable.'

'I don't care to stop, my lor –'

We laugh. 'My lady,' he says sweetly.

He takes my hand and pulls me into his arms. Ah! How good it feels, with his warm, naked flesh against mine. I press him closer, and he plants feather-like kisses on my face, my neck. When his mouth encircles my sensitive breast-knob, I tense, but he uses his teeth and mouth so gently, I am soon moaning, the heat striking down to my molten core, my legs thrashing helplessly as he laughs and holds me off from him whilst he plays on my body like a lutanist upon strings.

'Are you ready?' he asks with a chuckle.

'Yes, yes!'

Then his hand drifts down, caressing, to the part of me that is wet and swollen with desire. I gasp as his fingers move into the little cave and to the pleasure-button. His fingers work skilfully, and he teases me slowly, to raise me higher and higher to the point of tension.

'Very well,' he murmurs.

But still he won't: he but leans on one elbow; and, pulling away to do so, he slips his fingers down farther, then gently inserts two of 'em inside me. I'm surprised at how fast they come smack up against the wall of my maidenhood.

And as I sigh and grip his back with one hand, he carefully and slowly moves his fingers about till they proceed a little farther in.

Part of my desire has been eclipsed by curiosity; but then his thumb rubs me higher up, at that swollen button of flesh.

'Oh,' I cry, and grab him and arch towards him.

Still the two fingers gently work, pressing further and further inside me. 'What do you do?' I ask, wondering why he has not come to me yet.

'Enlarge the opening somewhat, so there'll be very little pain.'

How dear of him!

Anon he removes his fingers; and, sliding his hand to my hip, pulls me in towards him; and, still leaning on an elbow, looks down and asks, 'Are you ready?'

'Yes, yes!'

For I've been ready the greater portion of this hour: I feel the moment must be here at last; and if 'tis not, I may somehow find out the knowledge to do to him what my mother had always feared he'd do to me.

'Let me know the moment it hurts,' he instructs in a serious tone.

I'm grateful for his care but also frustrated by it: he behaves like a dancing-master demonstrating the steps in the right way more than a lover transported by passion. He seems preoccupied with what he's doing and how to do't properly – detached from the whole experience: not like I, who am quaking with passion.

'Come on,' I urge softly. 'I know't must hurt a little.'

This is, thank God, all the hint he needs to go inside me. Now I am indeed moved: I think, more by the thought that we had finally got here than the actual sensation, for as yet he is in but a little way – and hard against the wall of my virginity, tight as a drum. He moves carefully, lest he give me pain – now to the right, now to the left: the friction takes me to a higher peak, but still he has not broken down that wall. He presses against it a little, but very gently; I can feel't push back at him; and I am conscious, if he remains thus careful of giving me pain, we will never break it down.

'I'll push a bit,' he murmurs, with a kiss at my ear, 'and you pull me in. But mind you let me know when it begins to hurt.'

I nod.

So we work together – he gently pushing and I pulling – our movements coming together – and I'm so frustrated with him hanging in between there, that I grasp him about the small of the back and pull tightly; there's a little pang, a tear, and he's all the way in.

Ah! What a relief 'tis, to feel him filling up my naked, empty pain.

'Ahhh,' I cry, at the warm keenness of feeling him all inside. I clasp him tighter at the small of the back; and he gently, leaning on his arms, begins to pump within me. I feel all tender yearning, not fierce as before, but very comfortable and sweet.

This sport is different from the other, softer and deeper and not at all frantic. I never come close to that painful tension but only feel dissolved into a gentle love.

But 'tis over all too soon: after a few moments, I cannot feel him any more within me.

He rolls over to his side, then on his back – throws an arm up over his forehead as if in deep thought. Timidly I lean into him.

He glances over toward me with a smile and gathers me into his arms. And as I cuddle into him, my legs drawn up, he slips a hand down 'twixt my thighs. Still quite stimulated, I quiver with delight; and as I lie there, my cheek on his shoulder, he begins slowly, then more rapidly, to rub in my little dish so that I clutch at him and cry.

Within a few moments I have ascended to that height and fallen, collapsing and shuddering down.

Then we lie quietly, I pulled up at his side, and rubbing my hand over his breast.

We lying there a short while longer, he says abruptly, 'I'm hungry. Aren't you?'

'I suppose.' I haven't thought about food much: I've been so absorbed in these new sensations: this widening and slime below, this utter warmth of the belly and relaxing of the body all over. My whole being seems subtly different, altered: not only my flesh but some inner part of me, jumping and changing and adjusting to take on his contours.

'Doll's waiting a meal for us: let's go down and see what she has.'

He whips his side of the covers back and sits up on the edge of the bed, his back to me. All at once I cry, 'Oh, my lord!'

I've fallen into formality again at my surprise. He turns about quizzically. 'What is't?' I bite my lips. What has surprised me is that now, taking a clear view of him from behind in the daylight – from down his lower back to where he sits – I'd seen a white network of old scars: some fine and jagged, others broad.

Quickly I flush and cover my confusion by inventing a small lie which is actually no lie at all. 'I – I know not how we can face the servants after we've been up here so.'

He grins. 'Well, they're well-bred enough not to abash you, my lady. Come.'

He stands; I avert my eyes again – partially from modesty, partially from shame at my recent reaction to his body. But in the name of God, what kind of beatings must he have got as a child, that the scars are still visible on him?

By now he's got his breeches on; and, grinning, he carries my gown in a heap to me. 'Would you get into this complicated gear again, or shall I go next door to find your dressing gown?'

For my belongings have been packed and borne, over the last few days, into the pretty pink bedchamber.

I give him a pert look. 'Think you we can convince the servants we've been up here inspecting my quarters?'

'I doubt it, not as loud as you've been moaning.'

I flush and giggle.

'Well, go get my dressing gown. I'll be more comfortable.'

Pulling his shirt over his head, he unlocks the door and strides through the hall, to return in a few moments with my lace-trimmed silk gown.

The breakfast is a true delight, sitting in the formal dining room, giggling, teasing with calling one another My Lord and Lady. He holds my hand at table, rallies with the footmen that, grinning, step in and out with buns and butter and strawberry marmelotte, cold meats and cheeses, warm mulled ale and strawberry tarts; and I feel the shell round him dissolve as if 'twere never there.

'Mmmm!' I cry, savouring the rich saltiness of the creamy cheese. 'Gloucester, my favourite! And Cheshire!'

He smiles indulgently on me: I enjoy the textures and tastes of food, as he does not; however, I note he's eating more today, especially the rare roast beef. I crumble off a bit of buttered bread and slip it into his mouth. 'Taste this: it's hot and fresh.'

He laughs. 'You and Mr Savile are in another plot, I see, to manage me for my own good.'

At last I sigh and rub my mouth and hands with the napkin. 'I am stuffed like the Christmas goose!'

He captures my hand and kisses the knuckles.

'Come, let's to bed again.'

We repair to relieve ourselves, then off with the gear and into bed again.

God, he's beautiful naked. As he lies beside me, relaxed now, I lean on an elbow and run a finger over his bosom and recall the myth of Adonis, the beautiful youth that Venus espied sleeping naked and fell in love with. I always fancied he looked just so, white and slender and long-limbed, with the face of an angel out of some church window, and hair long and dark and soft as midnight.

I wonder if this gorgeous husband of mine knows the way women look at him from behind. He has the sort of form that should be dressed in tights, as they did in Queen Elizabeth's day. He would have done well back then, with his figure and wit, his sense of drama and gallantry, his verse and heroism – and a queen on the throne to boot.

I play with the threads of his hair, which are glossy and satiny and smell of lavender. Then I run my finger down his chest and belly and whisper, 'You don't mind when I do things to you, do you?'

3

'Where Love And Peace And Truth Does Flow'
29 January 1667, presently

When, wearied with a world of woe,
To thy safe bosom I retire
Where love and peace and truth does flow,
May I contented there expire
Lest, once more wandering from that heaven,
I fall on some base heart unblest,
Faithless to thee, false, unforgiven,
And lose my everlasting rest.

—John Wilmot, Earl of Rochester

'Mmmmm,' he murmurs, and nestles my head against his neck. 'I am yours, my lady: do with my flesh as you will.'

I take his earlobe 'twixt my teeth and nibble till I feel him stir; then, running my tongue down his neck, I slide my hand down his thigh, to below his belly, where I let my hand wander and explore and tease and caress. Anon I run my lips and tongue behind his ear, down his neck, and over his chest, to play with his breast as he does with mine, and caress it with my tongue and teeth.

As I tease him by withdrawing my hand, to rub across his belly and kiss all over the quivering flesh there, he says 'Oh, my God'; and with a moan, he curls his fingers in my hair.

'Let yourself go,' I yearn to tell him; but there's no need. He seizes a handful of my hair and draws my mouth to his; and as both of us tease one another with busy fingers, I fall into a fit of something that can only be described as pure lust. The heat is terrible: he works on me with one finger inside and the rest outside, till I burst with terrible tender prickles of hot pleasure-pain.

'Oh, please please please,' I cry, and grab his hips.

Now he loses control, and he takes me, hard. As he pounds within me, I go wild now too, for there comes from deep within me a surge, the like of which I've never felt before. 'Oh, God, oh, God,' I cry.

The harder he pounds into me, the deeper the wave crests.

Then it halts, retreats – and leaves me clawing his back in frustration. 'Oh, my God,' I scream. 'No. Oh, oh, yes.'

For here it comes again.

I become like a wild woman, squirming and writhing against him, crying out, thursting, clutching his back. He throws me sideways and plunges into me harder, higher; and, just as he slides a finger down, the waves break, so that his touch jolts the sensation with a higher crash of pure pleasure. I break into a long shuddering wave with a lightning bolt darting in and out of it, and he and I ride it down together.

When it is over, I am gasping, the tears in my eyes. 'Oh, dear,' I say. 'What will the servants think of me?'

He bursts out laughing.

'Was I very loud?' I ask.

'Don't worry about it,' he says. 'Are you sore?'

I nod. 'But it feels good, too.'

'I was determined to use you carefully and gently.' He seems vexed with himself.

'I'm glad you didn't. I'd rather you lose control.'

'I told myself I'd initiate you carefully, then wait a good twenty-four hours before entering you again. Now see what I've done.'

'Oh, John,' I say, touched, 'the hurt is almost nothing – not one tenth of what the pleasure was.'

But still he frets. 'It is not as if I am some oaf: I know better.'

I run my fingers through the fine dark silk of his hair. 'Will you stop railing at yourself? The fault is mine anyway. I deliberately set out to tease up your desire.'

'My mother warned me once,' he says, 'with the sort of life I led, I'd end up using my wife like a whore.'

My heart chills. There is something so foreboding in this remark – yet I can't figure out what.

I say, 'I know not what that means, but I hope you'll not hold back with me.'

He sighs and presses my ear close to his heart. Then he says, very low, 'I don't know how it is, but I have such trust in you.'

I sense this as a greater intimacy, a greater compliment, than 'I love you'. I hug him tighter.

He chuckles. 'Your mother, when she arrives, will hop like a toad on a grate.'

'And yours will think I am with child.'

'Well –' He shrugs his thin shoulders '– it is not unknown at court.

Who knows? If we'd waited too many more months, the prophecy might have come true.'

I shriek and pinch his ribs. 'You think a great deal of my virtue, sir!'

'I do –' With a cocky smile he grabs my wrist '– but I think more of nature.'

I jerk free. 'I was determined to preserve my virtue –'

'That may be,' he counters, 'but that you did was owing to my restraint.'

'What!' I shriek.

'Ne'er doubt it. Had I been the rogue your mother believes, I could have taken your maidenhead half a dozen times.'

'By ravishing me, perhaps –'

'No,' he says calmly, 'by arousing your desire and then refusing to satisfy it, save one way. And if you doubt my skill in doing this, madam, I offer you a demonstration tomorrow morning.'

I sit up on an elbow and stare astonished at him.

He continues, 'I have done it many times to women I had no feelings for. How think you I got my reputation? But you I never intended to make my prey.'

This indeed puts everything in a different light.

'You,' he said, 'I always intended to leave intact, from the time that first night when you told me it was important to you.'

'That night you asked for my hand –'

'I was rallying you, and you know it. If I had wished to have your head on my girdle along with all the other fair ones dangling there, I could have made sure of it the first night.'

'I said no –'

He bursts out laughing.

'How long do you think that would have lasted? If I had paid assiduous court with my tongue and fingers but left you hanging? And pulled you down beside me, or under me, whilst you were mad with desire?'

I stare, eyes round, at him.

'I knew I could take you if I wished. I knew precisely when I could have done it, and how. Instead I relieved your pain and gave you pleasure. But I could have stretched you out on the settle and taken you. We were about two inches from it.'

I am astonished. 'All this time I thought –'

'I know what you thought, and I kept telling you that you were in the wrong. It's your fault for not believing me.'

'All those times you sought to get me alone in your apartments –'

'As I said: to take down our heat, to feel the pleasure of one

651

another's unclad bodies. We could have had an Eden's worth of pleasure and still left you intact. You doubt I could do that, too? Faith, here are two demonstrations to provide: which would you like first?'

I am amazed. 'And you would have restrained yourself?'

'Not for the rest of our lives, but for some several months it would have been no problem. The only problem was the way *you* kept restraining us.'

I groan.

He stresses his point: 'We could have been enjoying all that pleasure these last two months, instead of stewing miserably in our heat.'

'And then,' I say pertly, 'no doubt you'd have been so satisfied, you'd have been in no hurry to marry at all!'

'I didn't marry you to enjoy you,' he says. 'I married you because your mama was about to appear in a puff of smoke, like Beelzebub, and carry you off to some hell with some smirking fop or honourable sot.'

'You married me for pity?' My heart stops.

'I married you for the same reason I left you your maidenhead: for love,' he says simply. 'Why won't you believe that?'

'Oh, John!' I cry, my heart melting. 'I'm sorry I had so little faith in you.'

I snuggle down happily into his shoulder.

As we drift into sleep, our limbs tangled up together, he murmurs, 'Sab.'

'Mmmm?'

'You need not feel you must sleep here.'

'What?' I am broad awake now.

'I had the other chamber made up for you so you could be private when you wished.'

'Why, so I thought,' I say, 'but I planned to read there, dress there, primp there, perhaps rest of an afternoon there – not sleep there. Why should I wish to sleep there when I can sleep with you at last?'

He sighs and pulls me closer, my head against his shoulder.

I ask, 'You'd not have me leave, would you?'

'No. If you go, I will yearn for you very much.'

'Then let's hear no talk of it.'

The shadows darken, and the day at last ends.

January 29. The date burns in my brain: the consummation of my desires at last. The day of my most perfect and pure happiness.

Indeed, with almost a presentiment I recall how the gods in Greek tragedy envied perfect mortal bliss. But whatever the issue, this brief winter's day would be enough to live a lifetime on.

—End of Volume I

Dear Mother!
Forgive me for what I have done. I could not resist love. In agreement with him I wish to be buried by his side.... I am happier in
death than in life.
Your Mary
                    —Note written by Baroness Mary Vetsera, 29 January 1889,
                          before her death in a suicide pact with Crown Prince
                                          Rudolf of Austria at Mayerling

Afterword by the Author

> A love story, eclipsing more placid affections, may have lain hidden
> between these two young, witty and unhappy people.
> —Graham Greene, *Lord Rochester's Monkey*

Background

When I first read these words in Graham Greene's biography, I picked
up a pen and began writing. Though I was working on a PhD in
Restoration literature, I almost couldn't finish my dissertation. I'd find
myself in the library, jotting down scenes on index cards, unable to
stop the flow of Betty Mallet's dialogue and feelings in my head.

It was easy for me to write about Lord Rochester. Since the age of
fifteen, I had been scribbling novels about a tall, slender, dark-eyed,
and pale hero who was irresistible to women and addicted to alcohol.
At the age of eighteen I had written a volume of poems to this ima-
ginary hero, whom I called 'The Phantom Lover'; I could close my
eyes and see him clearly, and I could hear his speech: witty, literate,
intelligent. I assumed that my subconscious had fixated on a literary
archetype: some combination of Heathcliff, Don Juan, and the Scarlet
Pimpernel. But during my freshman year in college, I scribbled a
question on a page of class notes: 'Why am I seeking dark eyes?'

I remember the first day I heard his name.

I was sitting in a graduate English seminar at the University of
Houston, the text of a Restoration drama book spread open before
me. We were about to begin discussion of *The Man of Mode* by Sir
George Etherege.

The play had transported me into a glittering world where I felt at
home: the world of the hero Dorimant, with his ready wit, his easy
charm. 'He has a tongue, they say,' admitted one character, 'that
could tempt the angels to a second fall.' Captivated, I had watched
Dorimant seduce a virgin, fire gibes at adversaries, advise lesser mor-
tals on their dress, read people's tastes and feelings, charm even his

enemies, and deliver delicate speeches to the heroine, an heiress named Harriet.

This world of 1676 seemed far more real to me than the world of 1974. I slipped happily into a milieu of silks and satins and lutes and witty conversations. This was the first place I'd felt at home in my entire life.

Especially did I find it easy to slip into Harriet's feelings. As I read I became Harriet, with her wildness and innocence, her pouting rose-bud lips and adoration for the dashing rogue Dorimant.

The professor said that *The Man of Mode* had been the hit of 1676, perhaps because the characters were based on real people. They were the social leaders, much like our movie stars today. Most of the attention focused on the hero Dorimant because he was the foremost leader of fashionable society and everyone recognized him at once.

The room wavered like a mirage. The professor was saying the name of the man who'd served as the model for the hero Dorimant: 'Lord Rochester.'

The world was no longer grey but Technicolor.

I sucked in my breath and closed my eyes. I got a vivid impression. A pale oval face, sensuous full lips, nose like the Apollo Belvedere's, chocolate brown almond eyes – heavy-lidded, drooping with thick black lashes, a bold, frank stare – a mischievous and sultry quirk to the bow-shaped mouth.

I heard a voice that murmured seductively, with a throaty catch on emphatic words. A voice that lulled and soothed, like a hypnotist's.

'That Dorimant's a bastard,' said one of the seminar members.

My eyelids popped open. All about the rectangle of the table, heads nodded in agreement. I swung around in my chair.

'What are you talking about?'

'Look at the way he uses women, seducing and leaving them.'

'That just proves his appeal,' I argued.

'I'm amazed that Harriet would want him,' said someone else. 'He won't be faithful to her, any more than he has been to anyone else.'

'So? She didn't expect him to.'

'Then she was pretty weak.'

I grew vehement. 'He was a wit. That was what they did, to gain status.'

By now all of the other students had pounced on me. Ironically, they condemned Dorimant by the feminist standards I myself espoused, and I defended him.

'No!' I argued. 'You can't evaluate the Restoration by twentieth-century standards –'

For twenty minutes I proceeded to defend Dorimant/Rochester as the professor looked on bemused. I left the room wondering what had happened.

Afterwards I grew obsessed with *The Man of Mode*. I read it again and again in my leisure hours. To me, Dorimant was the most wonderful lover who had ever lived. Everyone in the play admired him – except for the few characters who argued against him, but they too succumbed, in the end, to his charm.

Yes, it would be enough, I felt, to be loved by such a man – no matter what the price.

While I felt these strange emotions, I could not analyze them consciously. They floated past like a stream of thoughts, like logs going down a river. I observed them but never thought to ask why they were there.

Then one spring day in 1975, with a sense of rising and inexplicable excitement, I opened a book titled *Lord Rochester's Monkey, being the Life of John Wilmot, Earl of Rochester, 1647–1680*.

I had been driven to order the book, wildly impatient for it to arrive. Each time I'd heard Rochester's name in a graduate English seminar, my heart had been flooded with tenderness; my mind, with an image of satin, plumes, dark eyes, mischievous smile and gentle voice, boldness and softness, sensitivity and swashbuckle, utter masculine grace.

I clawed open the corrugated brown cardboard wrapping and came face to face with the jacket.

It was a portrait of Lord Rochester, by Huysmans. A round face with sleepy, heavy eyelids stared back at me: Lord Rochester, his hand crowning a monkey with a laurel wreath.

I thought, *That doesn't look like him! His features were much more beautiful; he was more slender, with much more sparkle.*

I skimmed through the pages. The book fell open to the portrait by Lely, and I sucked in my breath.

There he was – the man I'd visualized when I'd first heard his name – complete with brooding dark eyes and willowy grace, with a magnetism that jumped off the page, over three hundred years of distance.

The casual red satin drapery, the white puffed sleeves dripping lace suggested an easy elegance that was at once the height of fashion and the equivalent of seduction. Dorimant, captured on canvas: the man no woman could resist.

I flipped some more pages and came face to face with a plump blonde woman, her lips curved in a coquettish pout, her eyes haunted with sadness, her delicate hand holding a rose.

It was a portrait of his wife, Betty.

I slammed the book shut. *Oh, no, how dreadful that this portrait had been the only one preserved; this was the one that made her look so fat and ugly. She was much prettier.*

I skimmed through the book and found quoted one of Rochester's letters: he was 'in a great fright' lest her portrait 'be like' her: it was so 'puffed-up.'

There, I knew it. This explanation should have been quoted beneath the picture.

I didn't observe my feelings consciously because they made no sense. But I pored over the book, visualizing each scene, identifying with Betty, evaluating author Graham Greene's interpretations. Sometimes I chuckled, 'Yes, she really pulled a fast one that time!'; other times I thought peevishly, *No, she didn't feel that way at all.* The portraits of the children drew forth love; the miniature of his mother, equally intense rage and hatred.

The biography was a dual book club selection, paired with *The Complete Poems of John Wilmot, Earl of Rochester.* I opened the poems next – ran my fingers over each page, loving the verses with my touch. Each word sank into my head and lodged there. Many lines I memorized on first reading.

He wrote this to her, I'd think. *This one, too.*

Her voice sang in my head: pert, kittenish, demure. His lilted a low melody in response.

I jumped from biography to poems and back again. Suddenly a line in the Greene book hit me like a lightning bolt:

'A love story, eclipsing more placid affections, may have lain hidden between these two young, witty and unhappy people.'

Yes, I thought. *Oh, yes—*

I grabbed a pen and began writing that story. I felt Betty's feelings so intensely, they were more a part of my reality than Houston, Texas, where I lived.

Sensitive novelists can access, in certain cases, the personalities and events of times past. Best-selling British novelist Elizabeth Chadwick does so regularly, she says, using the akashic records of past events to augment her research. Isabel Allende claims to have written about accurate facts she can not have known while she writes in an altered state.

My method was empathizing with Betty. I used self-hypnosis: relaxed my body, closed my eyes, and directed my mind to enter a scene, which I narrated onto a cassette tape. Most of the dialogue, as well as Betty's thoughts, I derived from this method. To fill in other details, I

657

consulted microfiche, articles, books, and Internet sources. I also visited England in 1976 and 1980 and experienced an affinity with the places Betty had visited.

In at least once instance, I may have experienced the phenomenon of remote viewing. I felt myself hovering over the ship in which Rochester, at sea, made his pact with Montague and Wyndham, then felt myself drawn into the scene, which I saw as if from outside.

Like Isabelle Allende, I also wrote about facts I could not have known. I sent Lord John Butler from Ireland to London in the spring of 1666; then, researching the Battle of Bergen in the Earl of Sandwich's navy log, I came across a reference to that very trip. I sent Sir Charles Sedley to Paris during the Christmas season of 1666 even though I kept wanting to write him into court scenes because of his wit. A few years later, reading Pinto's biography of Sedley, I came across a comment that he had applied to go to Paris then and had very likely gone.

Now, Sedley is a minor poet, known to graduate students of literature and even to some English majors. Perhaps I had read an account of his movements and then forgotten. But Lord Butler I had never heard of till I had begun researching the novel. How could I have read, then forgotten, the movements of the youngest son of the Duke of Ormond?

The answer, as Chadwick and Allende might say, is that attunement to a person, place, or event draws on sources beyond the conscious. Allende says that books happen not in her head but in her belly.

The Fictional Characters

Early on, I decided that Betty's voice would not be enough. I noted that my favourite author at the time, Susan Howatch, used multiple first person narrators, so I invented Lord Ashfield to be where Betty could not. His voice I cultivated by reading for thirty minutes in Pepys' diary before beginning to write. Of course, Ashfield needed a female interest so there could be a contrasting pair of lovers, as in Shakespeare. Emilia's look and gestures are based on those of a senior in high school I admired as a sophomore. Her personality was inspired by the women's movement, raging in the late 1970s, and by the respect paid reason during the period. She seemed a good foil for both Rochester and Betty, as well as a feasible mate for the reticent, easy Ashfield. Her parents are based on my parents, and Kitty is a portrait of me in my harebrained teenage years.

Rochester's Stereotype Revised

You can glimpse Lord Rochester in novels such as *Forever Amber*, where he plays the witty rake and libertine. Yet to me this stereotype is the most superficial part of him.

In fact, biographers despair of capturing on paper all the complexities and contradictions of his character: libertine vs tender husband and father, religious sceptic vs mystic with the deathbed conversion. I am aware that I am presenting in some ways yet another – and admittedly prejudiced – point of view: still, during my years of research on this book, I was in a special position to know many sides of him – including, I think, one or two that no one else has seen.

Bunny Paine-Clemes, Ph.D.

Extract from *Absent from Thee: A Restoration Tragedy*, Part 2, Acts III–V

Chapter 1 'To Thy Safe Bosom I Retire'

February 2, 1667

> When, wearied with a world of woe,
> To thy safe bosom I retire
> Where love and peace and truth does flow,
> May I contented there expire ...
> —John Wilmot, Earl of Rochester, 'Absent from Thee,
> I languish Still'

Nestled close in bed, in one another's arms, we drift in that twilight world 'twixt sleep and waking. After four days of marriage, we have already a sleeping-posture; he on his back, me nestled against his side, his arm about me. I revel in this warm closeness, in this Paradise bounded by closed bed curtains. Often I dreamt of it, the two terrible years we were parted because my guardians would not have him and he was thrown into the Tower for abducting me.

A hard knock raps on the door.

We struggle awake through the veils of sleep. John says, 'Be gone.'

'My lord,' says a man's voice.

'Is the roof in flames? Are the Dutch in Covent Garden? Or have you—perish the thought—forgot your orders or made some wager what I'd do if we were disturbed?'

I giggle. We are at war with the Dutch, but they'd scarce advance to the Duke of Bedford's red brick rental houses about Covent Garden Piazza. Despite John's ill humour, the man persists.

'My lord—my lady—my Lady Warre desires that you will walk down.'

Oh, God. This is worse than the Dutch: it's my mother.

John says, 'Bid her to the withdrawing-room: we'll attend presently.'

'Can she separate us?' I ask.

'No. By English law, you belong to me now, not to her.'

Thinking that my friend Emilia O'Hara would say I belong to myself, I fumble for a dressing-gown to cover my nakedness.

I shrug into my dressing-grown, which he assists me into; then he dons his own of red silk. In dishabille thus, he makes me hungry to toy with him. His robe loose, the silky black cloud of his hair loose to his shoulders, he looks like the angel Gabriel. This Gabriel, though, besides a pretty oval face, has dark almond eyes, curving black lashes, a long fine nose like a Greek statue's, and luscious red lips. I grasp both sides of his gown and stretch up, head tilted, so he leans down for a quick hug and kiss. His warm lips send a tingle through me.

Hand in hand we walk down the stairs together, to meet our doom.

As we stroll in, he releases my hand—I suppose out of deference to Mama, as she once came upon us about to kiss and yanked me away.

She stands and scrolls over both of us with her eyes. She looks a severe and angry bird with her narrowed eyes, needle nose, and tight mouth. Tall and thin, like the Pitchfork of Judgment about to scoop us into the Bad Place, she takes note of our undress. She still wears a heavy red velvet travelling cloak and gloves, as though she would not grace this palace of sin any longer than she must.

'Lady Warre,' says my lord with a polite bow. 'We were most pleased to learn of your imminent arrival.'

She glares at this remark: which, of course, thanks her for warning us so we could be married on the sly, before she came to prevent us. But then he adds, 'You are most welcome to our home.'

She looks from me to him and back again. Her mouth a grim line, she gazes from my tousled honey hair down the line of my ruffled loose dressing gown. I flush and look down, my hands working with the pink ribbons in the laces.

'Betty, prepare yourself to come with me.' Her tones are as rigid as her tight, straight posture.

'No!' My arm goes round his waist. 'He's my husband.' I lean my head against the lower part of his breast. Protectively he throws an arm round my shoulder.

Her hands clench and unclench at her sides. She stares at me and says icily, 'You promised your grandfather you would not marry without his consent.'

I hang my head, but my lord says, in his melodious voice, 'A promise made under duress.'

She pulls on her gloves and says, in tones measured but angry, 'We will have this annulled.'

I cry out and hug my lord's side to mine.

He asks in a voice smooth and congenial, 'On what grounds,

661

madam? Go to the register at St. Pancras, and you will find the wedding recorded. Or perhaps you've a mind to quarrel with his majesty, who authorized the match in writing?'

She presses her lips tight, then says, 'I would speak with my daughter alone.'

He looks inquiringly down at me. I nod.

When we are seated alone in the withdrawing-room, she throws off her cloak and pulls off her gloves. Fixing me in a firm stare, she says, 'Betty, if you support me, we can work to have this marriage annulled.'

'No!' My hand flits to my cheek. 'Please, Mother, I love him. I always have. You know that.'

Now I expect she will attack and scold. I brace myself for the onslaught. *He has no estate; he chases women; he keeps company with the King's merry gang, the wits, who abuse all decency and morality; and at whose folly the king winks.*

But she is silent. Some sort of struggle wrinkles her face, a conflict of love and honour, passion and reason. The hand in her red velvet lap unclenches. All at once she stares at me, as if absorbing me, a peculiar look on her face—a wary look, then a gentle smile, 'Betty,' she says, '— are you happy in your marriage bed?'

This is the last thing I expected her to say: she, who always niggled and scolded about modesty, about keeping my virtue. For she asks now if I am happy with my virtue lost.

I feel my face flare bright red. I look down and nod.

When I look up, she is smiling. 'Come with me to the shops. We'll get you some fine wedding linen: chemises and smocks and nightgowns.'

I look uncertain on her.

'I will not carry you away and lock you up. I would buy you some bridal gifts.' She pauses, says ruefully. 'He is in the right, you know; under English law, I have no power over you—especially with the King's consent. She smiles. 'Unless perhaps the marriage is still unconsummated?'

'Why, Mother, how can you –'

Then I see her sly smile: she is rallying me. I throw myself into her arms. Her soft dark brown curls brush against my face.

My lord, however, is not so trustful. When called to return, he says to me softly, 'Will she not carry you away?'

I shake my head.

'You have more trust in her than I.'

'She seems changed—she asked me if my marriage bed was happy.'

'Ne'ertheless, go with her in the company of some of our footmen.

Say they will carry the bundles. I'll dispatch a note round to Ashfield for his coach.'

Soon I'm washed and clad in laced smock, white stomacher embroidered pink, white hose with pink garters, white silk shoes, silver skirt, and rose-coloured velvet overskirt.

Mama and I plunder the shops of Westminster, and she happily chooses linen for me: silk nightgowns with laced necks and sleeves, shifts of fine cotton thread, dressing gowns of amber and red velvet, detachable puffed sleeves, and ribbons to thread in them. She says to the shopkeepers, 'My daughter's newly wed—and now a countess.' They pretend to be impressed in their intent to show that a countess should have the best.

The odours mingle in the streets: here a smell of roasting venison from the Bull's Head, there a whiff of fresh excrements and stale urine from an alley; and, as the jostling crowd passes, such a stink of stale bodies that my eyes water. I mince about in the filthy snow, with slushy ice grey from coal soot, my heavy boots on over the silk shoes. Snowflakes drift down in the sharp air, and we catch our cloaks about us.

At Locket's we dine on beef sizzling with claret and capers, along with rolls that we sop into a dish of crème. As Mother sips her claret, she says, *All she ever wished was for me to be happy. And she can see I am.*

She says, 'I would have chosen a different husband for you. But I see this is the one that will make you happy, so I am content.' She repeats, 'You look very happy.'

'I am, Mother. So much—I love him so.'

'And happy in your bed,' she says.

This is a surprising emphasis from her. I blush and look down. Then I look up. 'As I would be with no one else.'

She smiles and seems satisfied.

When she returns me with boxes and footmen to our rental house in Covent Garden, my lord looks easier. He is now washed and prettified, in his curled brown periwig, small jacket with the amber ribbons over a billowing silk shirt with laced sleeves, gold velvet knee breeches, and point de Venise cravat; and he seems determined to play the role of genial host. 'Lady Warre,' he says, 'of course you will stay for supper?'

She agrees, and Doll sends up a lovely supper: chicken roasted golden and steaming with onions, an herb pie with parsnips and carrots in cream, and an orange pudding. As Mama eats and sips a glass of Rhenish and he exerts his powers to charm her, she relaxes in his presence.

She says, 'All I ever wished was for Betty to be happy, but I fear my father and husband will have something else to say.'

'No doubt, madam: but I have asked my mother to engage 'em, and if they can stand up to her, they are rare men indeed.'

My mother looks dubious, but I explain, 'She outwitted Cromwell and managed to keep her Lee estates, from her first husband and secure more land as well. She balanced the Stuart interests against the Roundhead ones and got favours from both parties.'

My mother looks surprised, not being one to challenge male authority herself.

She says, 'What shall I tell my father and husband?'

'That your goal was achieved and your daughter is happily married,' says John.

She pulls a face. I tease her with another suggestion. 'That love is better than money.'

'Oh, Lord.' She rolls her eyes, knowing how that declaration would be received in Somerset.

'That you were in the right,' says my lord mischievously, 'and your daughter was not to be trusted alone with the scoundrels at court.'

I burst out laughing. Mother smiles. 'I think that will do't.'

He signals the footman to bring in the brandywine, and my spaniel pads in, tongue out and smiling.

'Well, hello,' says Mother, extending a hand, 'Who's this?'

'Samantha,' I answer.

'After your first dog.'

Samantha licks the extended hand.

Mother scratches a long black-and-white ear. 'How came you by her?'

'A New Year's gift from my lord. From his majesty's latest litter.'

'She's a little darling.' Samantha busily washes Mother's hand.

'If we leave the door unlocked,' I say, 'she pushes it open and jumps on the bed and licks our faces.'

'Inconvenient at times,' says John, a mischievous twinkle in his eyes, napkin patting his full lips.

Mother and I both blush and giggle.

'What does she eat?' asks Mother.

'A mash of what we have. Her favourite is chicken and herrings.'

'Hold out a piece of chicken,' says John, 'and she'll beg.'

Mother pulls a piece off the bird and holds it above the dog's head. 'Samantha! Here!'

She sits up on her hind legs and emits a high-pitched bark. When my mother lowers the prize, Samantha jumps up, grabs it, and runs away to enjoy it.

'She's good-natured,' says John, 'but will growl if you approach when she's at her chicken. Like most of us, she's not keen to have her pleasures interrupted.'

We all laugh. Mother seems charmed by John.

After she leaves, I say, 'My mother's change of character was a greater surprise than if I'd heard you'd become a parson.'

'We have both done her wrong,' says John. 'But you, who knew her so well: why did you not grasp her motive earlier?'

'Because she worked so hard to separate us.'

'She thought you'd not be happy with me,' says John. 'That was her motive.'

'But now she sees I am.' I smile, and he leans down for a sweet kiss.

'But, John,' I say, as we ascend the stairs for our chamber, 'think you we'll get the estate?'

He shrugs. 'I never expected it; but if my mother involves herself, I'm sure Lord Hawley will have more than met his match.'

His mother the harpy? A formidable creature indeed: I recall our skirmishes at his manor house at Adderbury after the abduction.

As we reach the top of the stairs, I indulge myself in the fantasy of Grandpa doing battle with the harpy. Indeed, I could almost feel sorry for him, but that he himself has scant interest, it appears, in me, save for the money he thought he would earn selling me on the marriage market.

Glossary of Some Late Seventeenth-Century Words and Expressions

Angel: a coin worth a considerable amount of money
Baggage: a light female
Ballocks: testicles
Bear at Bridge-Foot: a popular place for food and drink at the foot of London Bridge in Southwark
Busby: severe master at Westminster school, notorious for sadistic beatings
Busk: slang term for stomacher, the tight straight front of a corset drawn over a gown and laced at the back
Cause: for contemporary 'case' as a legal term
Chaffing: teasing
Cod: testicles (i.e., what was in the codpiece in the Renaissance)
Colly: close friend, bosom buddy
Coy: a verb meaning 'caress,' as in 'kissing and coying'
Doxy: light woman
Fidg: fidget
Fit of the mother: hysterical fit
Flowers: menstrual period
Friendily: an adverb in the Restoration
Get out of book: memorize
Gorget: a collar falling from the chin to the shoulders, like a wimple (for antique ladies)
Gull: victim of a con man
Hang in the hedge: wait
Hardly: in a hard or very cold way, as 'to use someone hardly'
Herrbone: cosmetic used to dress hair
Holland band: tight neck-band securing cravat
Hottentot: African with hair sticking out in frizzles, with bows
Husband: one meaning: one who 'husbands' or cares for resources
India-men: Dutch ships loaded with rich plunder from the Indies
Jackanapes coat: worn by men in the mid-1660s, a tiny jacket covering

667

just the sides of the breast and leaving the abdomen open to show the white shirt

Joy: used as both a verb and a noun in the Restoration, as in 'little like to joy me'

Knock up: knock on a door to rouse someone within

Link: a torch or lantern carried by a boy at night, to light the streets

Make shift: try

Mamas Furens: 'Furious Mamas,' Betty is viewing the scene a drama like *Hercules Furens*, 'Hercules in a Fury.'

Man-tailored riding coat: fashionable riding habit for women

Mistress: a woman one loves (no sexual connotations), also a woman in general (usually shortened to 'Mrs')

Monteer: fashionable hat with women's writing habit

Month's Mind to: eager to

Mrs: a title for all women past puberty, married or not (like contemporary Ms.)

Nadie me tergit: Latin for 'Nobody dares touch me.'

Ordinary: tavern that serves a meal, as in 'the great half-crown ordinary,' which would have been expensive, at half a crown

Poofing: Betty's coinage: the devil in old plays would appear, 'poof!' in a cloud of smoke

Present runner: like a pizza delivery man, running out to bring the food at once

Presently: immediately

Resty: restive

Servant: a woman's suitor (who seeks, in courtly love fashion, to "serve" her)

Shago: rough, heavy textile

Spark: lover on the make

Swire: have sex with, slang like f—ck

Twenty-five hundred a year: Betty's fortune – 'pounds' were usually omitted from such sums.

With full mouth to the business: eager or ready to act

Worcester fight: the fateful battle that lost the Civil War for the Cavaliers and sent Prince Charles (the future Charles II) fleeing for his life, with the help of Lord Wilmot, who was later created First Earl of Rochester

Your Negative: Betty's right to say no to any marriage match proposed by her guardians

Well-looked: good-looking

A Bibliography of Works Consulted

Andrews, Allen. *The Royal Whore: Barbara Villiers, Countess of Castlemaine.* London: Hutchinson, 1971.

Bell, Walter George. *The Great fire of London in 1666.* London: Bodley Head, 1923.

———. *The Great Plague in London in 1665. With Fort Illustrations comprising Contemporaray prints, Plans and Drawings.* London: The Bodley Head. Rev. ed., 1951,

British Museum. *Jewellery through 7,000 Years.* British Museum Publications, 1976.

Bruun, Bertel. *The Hamlyn Guide to Birds of Britain and Europe.* London: Hamlyn, 1970.

Bryant, Arthur. *King Charles II.* London: Longman's, 1931.

Carte, Thomas. *The Life of James, Duke of Ormond.* Oxford: University Press, 1851. 3 vols. Originally published 1735-1736. Google Books, n.d. 22 June 2011 *<http://books.google.com/books?id=dzHOAAAAMAAJ &printsec=frontcover#>*

Cecil, C.D. "Raillery in Restoration Comedy." *Huntington Library Quarterly* 29 (1966); 147-59.

Chancellor, E. *The Annals of Covent Garden and its Neighbourhood.* London: Hutchinson, 1930.

De Mause, Lloyd. "Our Forebears made Childhood a Nightmare." *Psychology Today* 8 911 April 1975) Revised and augmented in "The History of Child abuse." 21 June 21 2011. *<http://primal-page.com/ph-abuse.htm>*

———. "As Published in the Huffington Post: Historical History of Child Rearing." 2010. 21 June 2011 *<http://www.lloyddemause.com/ Lloyd_DeMause_on_Psychohistory/Home.html>*

Etherege, George. *Letters of Sir George Etherege.* Ed. Frederick Bracher. University of California Press: Berkeley, 1974.

———. *The Poems of Sir George Etherege.* Ed.James Thorp. Princeton, NJ: Princeton University Press, 1963.

Evelyn, John. *The Diary of John Evelyn.* Ed. E.S. de Beer. 6 vols. Oxford, Clarendon Press, 1955.

Fraser, Antonia. *Royal Charles.* NY: Knopf, 1979.

Gilmour, John, and Max Walters. *Wild Flowers: Botanising in Britain.* 5th ed. London: Collins, 1973.

Greene, Graham. *Lord Rochester's Monkey: Being the Life of John Wilmot, Second Earl of Rochester.* A Studio Book. NY: Viking, 1974.

Griffin, Dustin H. *Satires against Man: The Poems of Rochester.* Berkeley: University of California Press, 1973.

Hamilton, Anthony. *The Memoirs of Count Grammont.* Philadelphia: David Mckay, n.d.

Hanson, Neil. *The Great Fire of London in that Apocalyptic Year, 1666.* Hoboken, NY: John Wiley and Sons, 2001.

Harris, Brice. *Charles Sackville: 6th Earl of Dorset: Patron and Poet of the Restoration.* University of Illinois Studies in Language and Literature, 26. Urbana: University of Illinois Press, 1940.

Harris, F.R. *The Life of Edward Montague, K.G. First Earl of Sandwich (1625-1672).* 2 vols. London: John Murray, 1912. 22 June 2011 <*http://www.archive.org/stream/cu31924092739410/cu31924092739410_djvu.txt*>

Hayman, John. "Raillery in Restoration Satire." *Huntington Library Quarterly* 31 (1968): 107–122.

The History of Furniture. Introduction by Sir Francis Watson. NY: William Morrow, 1976.

Holly, Hanford James, ed. *A Restoration Reader.* NY: Kennicott, 1954.

Huseboe, Arthur R. *Sir George Etherege.* Twayne's English Author's Series, 336. Boston: Twayne, 1987.

Johnson, James William. *A Profane Wit: The Life of John Wilmot, Earl of Rochester.* Rochester, NY: University of Rochester Press, 2004.

——. " 'My Dearest Sonne': Letters from the Countess of Rochester." *University of Rochester Library Bulletin* 25.1, (1974). 9 May 2011 <*http://www.lib.rochester.edu/index.cfm?page=3501*>

Lamb, Jeremy. *So Idle a Rogue: The Life and Death of Lord Rochester.* London: Wilson and Day, 1993.

Love, Harold. "Rochester and the Traditions of Satire." In *Restoration Literature: Critical Approaches.* Ed. Harold Love. London: Methuen, 1972. 145–175.

"Mallett Family History, Malet/Mallet/Mallett: 1066-present day." 1 June 2011 <*http://www.mallettfamilyhistory.org/index.php*>

Mitchell, Alan. *A Field Guide to the Trees of Britain and Northern Europe.* Glasgow: William Collins & Sons, 1974.

Parker, Rowland. *The Common Stream: Portrait of an English Village through 2000 Years.* NY: Holt, Rinehart, and Winston, 1975.

Patridge, Eric. *A Dictionary of Catch Phrases.* NY: Stein and Day, 1977.

Pepys, Samuel. *The Diary of Samuel Pepys.* 11 vols. Ed. R.C. Latham and W. Matthews. Berkeley, University of California Press; London: G. Bell and Sons. 1970-1983. Now online. <*http://www.pepysdiary.com/ archive/*>

Pinto, Vivian de Sola. *Enthusiast in Wit: A Portrait of John Wilmot, Earl of Rochester, 1647–1680.* Lincoln: University of Nebraska Press, 1972.

——. *Sir Charles Sedley, 1639–1701: A Study in the Life and Literature of the Restoration.* New York: Boni and Liveright; London, Constable and Company, 1927.

Price, Rebecca. *The Compleat Cook; or, Secrets of a Seventeenth-Century Housewife.* Comp. Madeleine Masson. London: Routledge and Kegan Paul, 1974.

Sedley, Sir Charles. *The Poetical and Dramatical Works of Sir Charles Sedley.* 2 vols. Ed. Vivian de Sola Pinto, 1969.

"Seventeenth-Century English Recipes." 16 June 2011 <*http:// www.godecookery.com/engrec/engrec.html*>

Sprange, Jasper. *The Tunbridge Wells Guide.* London: J Sprange, 1801. 22 June 22 2011 <*http://www.archive.org/details/tunbridgewellsg00spra goog*>

Stannard, David. *The Puritan Way of Death: A Study in Religion, Culture, and Social Change.* NY: Oxford University Press, 1977.

Survey of London. Ed. Montague H. Cox and Philip Norman. 22 June, 2011 <*http://www.english-heritage.org.uk/professional/research/buildings/ survey-of-london/survey-of-london-online/*>

Thompson, Roger, sel. and ed. *Samuel Pepys' Penny Amusements.* NY: Columbia UP, 1977.

Vieth, David. *Attribution in Restoration Poetry: A Study of Rochester's Poems of 1680.* New Haven and London: Yale UP, 1963.

Wilmot, John. *Complete Poems of John Wilmot, Earl of Rochester.* Ed. David Vieth. New Haven and London: Yale UP, 1968.

Wilson, John Harold. *The Court Wits of the Restoration: An Introduction.* NY: Octagon, 1967.

Yarwood, Doreen. *The Encyclopedia of World Costume.* 1978. NY: Crown, 1986.